Rogue Wave

Part One

By

Melissa Good

Paperback ISBN 978-1-61929-574-2
Hardcover ISBN 978-1-61929-576-6
Cover Design by AcornGraphics

Publisher's Note:

Books by Melissa Good

Dar and Kerry Series

Tropical Storm
Hurricane Watch
Eye of the Storm
Red Sky At Morning
Thicker Than Water
Terrors of the High Seas
Tropical Convergence
Storm Surge (Books 1 & 2)
Stormy Waters
Moving Target
Winds of Change (Book 1 & 2)
Southern Stars
Fair Winds and Following Seas
(Part 1 & 2)

Jess and Dev Series

Partners (Book 1 & 2)
Of Sea and Stars
Rogue Wave (Book 1)

Chapter One

Rain fell in sheets over the edge of a granite promontory, dark gray rock against a dark gray sky. Gray blue waves of a wide and endless sea frothed at its base, framing a monochromatic vison that was grim and unfriendly to life.

Natural and stark stone walls towered, broken unexpectedly along one side by huge and weather-stained metal doors, which, along with chiseled golden backlit slot windows spaced along the cliff face around it and the reinforced stone shelf within reach of the waves that thundered against it, signaled the presence of humanity.

Seabirds coasted close to the waves in hopes of a last meal for the day, feathers ruffled as they fought to hold position over the rough water.

The scene was dark and growing darker behind a dense layer of clouds. Diffused light dimmed in an unseen sunset that brought the end of day to Interforce Base 10.

Behind the doors, inside the service cavern lit with overhead halon lights, it was loud. The sound of pneumatic wrenches keening, and the low thub- thub of jets at marking idle made it difficult to communicate in words, most resorting to nods, gestures, and rapid hand signals, ears protected by plugs that blocked out most of the mechanical clamor.

One side of the cavern held a dozen large, blocky, ungraceful looking crafts, each on its own metal grid landing pad. Umbilical lines were draped over them and bodies in coveralls weaved among them, all busy with something, anything, everything. No one stood around in idle repose.

Around the perimeter, cleaning staff in gray drifted into view. They started to sweep the ground and empty the service bins, all of them silent, all with the metallic gleam of faintly lit bands around the base of their necks. That, and the repeated stamp of likeness marking them as biological alternatives assigned custodial duties.

On the pad closest to the wall, one of the vehicles had its hatch open. Seated on its deck, with both booted feet pulled up crossed underneath her, was a short, blond-haired woman in a dark green jumpsuit. Cables and tools poked out of her pockets and a small square box rested on her knee.

Unique on the service platform, the figure was slight, almost delicate in appearance, in contrast to the other figures who moved around the vehicles. Most of them were tall and broad, and visibly muscled. These were also in green, with a few in black, and some in the blues and vivid orange of technical services and maintenance.

Above her, the vehicle, a Bantam class carrier loomed, all darkly patinaed steel and blunt angles. Large engine pods were prominent, designed to overcome its almost complete lack of aerodynamics. On its side, as on all the vehicles sides, names were stenciled in matte black against dappled gray. This one said: Drake, J, and underneath that, NM-Dev-1.

The woman worked with visible satisfaction on the control module. She used probes attached to a sensor pack around her neck. She ignored the cacophony of sound around her as she nodded her head a little as though listening to some internal tune.

"Hey, Dev."

The figure looked up. "Hello, Doug. How are you?" Dev returned the greeting cordially.

One of the taller men in green came over and crouched next to the carrier. "I just heard you were back. Did you have a good trip out to Quebec?"

"I think so," Dev responded. "Jess seemed to think it was acceptable. We got the two men from the other side to follow us through the docks and then Jess got them to fight with each other. They ended up being taken to jail."

"Why?"

"I have no idea," Dev said, placidly. "But Jess found that very amusing. I think she thought the mission was optimal. We got to have a meal at Jonton's, so I thought so too."

Doug nodded and took a seat on the metal deck next to the carrier. "April told me she heard Jason's due back tonight from that big meeting out west," he said, in a confiding tone. "She figures some changes are coming."

"Really? Like what?" Dev went back to working on her module, but kept her ears cocked to listen.

"Shake ups," Doug said, darkly. "Finally nail everyone for all the stuff that went on."

Dev eyed him briefly. "Nail them to what?" She asked. "And are they going to shake them first? That all sounds very suboptimal, not to mention causing discomfort."

Doug looked at her meaningfully, but Dev merely waited

for enlightenment, her pale head tilted to one side. "It's just a saying," he finally said. "Like we'd get in trouble for the Westies we killed."

Dev nodded. "Jess said something when we were in Quebec about the other foot dropping?" She paused. "No, the other shoe dropping. Is that what you mean?" She watched him nod back. "Jess said she thought they might want to, but they won't. There aren't enough of us left to do our jobs. They can't lose more."

"That's what I think too. But you know April. She's kinda dark."

Dev looked up at him again, one eyebrow lifted. "Is that a new change? We were only gone for two days."

"Are you ever going to not take things literally?" Doug asked. "Doesn't that wear off at some point?"

"I don't think being a bio alt wears off," Dev said. "I can't really go back and not be hatched from an egg in space as an experimental prototype and grow up speaking in strange idioms instead." She eyed him. "And really, there isn't enough time for me to have to look up everything everyone says all the time."

"I guess."

Two figures walked by and looked at them. "Hey," the nearer one said. "You tell us which way the mess is?"

They were in black jumpsuits, sleek and body hugging, with dark blue piping and agent's insignia. "We just landed," the second one said, as the silence lengthened, and they were studied by the two seated techs. "We're from Rainier Island," he added. "We're assigned here."

"Hello," Dev finally said, since Doug was apparently content to let her do the talking. "The operations mess is level six, down the blue hall, third turn on the left," she said. "Are you the transfers that were expected?"

The nearer man looked at her, then glanced behind her at the carrier crouching balefully behind them and read the stencil. "Are you..." He paused and looked at her jumpsuit collar tabs, where the twinkle of senior tech insignia was visible. "The... um..."

"Biological Alternative, set 0202-164812, instance NM- Dev-1," Dev supplied readily. "Yes I am. You can call me Dev," she added. "This is Doug." She indicated her companion. "I would proceed to the mess if you are hungry. It's almost dinner. Everyone will be going soon, and it gets quite crowded."

"Uh... Thanks." The man lifted his hand and then they walked off without looking back.

"Just what we need. Goons." Doug sighed. "At least they

weren't mean to you."

"Why would they be?" Dev regarded him in some surprise. "I haven't done anything for them to be mean about, and if they have heard of my name, I expect they also have heard of Jess and would not want to upset her." She made a final adjustment to the module, stood up, walked into the carrier and to the pilot's station. She dropped into the pilot's chair to insert the module into the console. "Upsetting Jess seldom has good results."

"Where is Jess anyway?" Doug asked. "I haven't seen her around yet,"

"She is in the cavern, surfing." Dev stood up and dusted off her hands. "And now I will go there and join her." She exited the carrier, triggered the hatch, then watched it close and seal. "And then we will go for a meal during the late ops shift."

Doug got up and dusted himself off. "You like that surfing? I nearly broke my leg the last time I tried it."

Dev settled her sensor pack on her neck again. "I like doing things that make Jess happy," she demurred, "and it's not too bad now that I have obtained nose plugs and a helmet."

Doug grimaced. "Sounds like… fun?"

"Some of the time, yes." Dev waved and headed for the back passage out of the cavern that angled downward and brought from its depths a moist, briny scent. "Some of the time not really," she added to herself. "Hopefully today will not be one of those times."

****

The vast cavern under the base was mostly natural stone, with sections of crudely shaped openings and tunnels that provided space for the machinery that allowed the facility to create the power it needed to run itself.

The outer wall of the cavern was rooted and thick. Drilled out under its edge were huge intake holes that let the power of the seawater surge in and turn massive turbines. They allowed the water to move through the length of the facility and exit out further down the coastline.

When the tides were out, the lower edge of the outer wall was exposed, and waves that normally would break outside, surged inside and rolled across the width of the cavern, filling it with surge and froth and occasionally human figures on boards that let the power of the water pick them up and ride the waves across the cavern.

Today, this close to dinner, only a single figure was there. She was dressed in a worn wetsuit and paddled out from the landing slope toward the edge of the cavern, as another wave came rolling in under it.

Dev paused at the edge of the ramp that led down to water level. She watched the tall figure on the board stand, pick up the wave and ride under the curling top of it as it approached the back wall.

Just when it seemed it would slam the board and it's rider into the rocks, they popped out of the end of the wave, jumped clear and grabbed the edge of the board as they sailed over the seawall and reached the landing beach, the froth of the water drenching them.

The figure shook herself, then spotted Dev and waved.

Dev smiled and continued down the ramp. She was met halfway back to the storage area where her board was.

"Hello, Jess," Dev greeted her agent partner, who towered over her in both height and overall size. The stretchy wetsuit outlined Jess's broad shoulders and powerful body, her dark wet hair slicked back accentuating the strong, angular shape of her face.

"Devvvie!" Jess returned the greeting. "Ya finish up your wrenching?"

"I did," Dev said. "Doug came in to say hello. He said Jason is coming back tonight. April thinks there will be some difficulties. And two of the new agents from the West have arrived."

Jess nodded. "Sounds about right." Her glance sharpened. "They give you any trouble? The Westies?"

"Me? No." Dev said. "They just asked for directions to the mess hall. Why would they want to make trouble? They just got here."

"Good. You know what they think about us out here in the boonies. Glad they kept their traps shut." Jess draped a damp arm over her shoulders. "C'mon over here. I made something for ya."

Dev readily moved with her, a smile appearing on her face. She had no idea what Jess had made but presents from her partner were always optimal though sometimes surprising and occasionally perplexing. Now, a year into her assignment, she had adapted to many of the oddities of the natural born but often found herself still required to perform research to gain understanding.

Born on a space station, Dev had spent most of her life in the enclosed world of the bio alts, being prepared for scientific work in the genetics laboratories. She was a developmental new model designed by Doctor Dan Kurok as a proposed next generation of bio alt mentation.

Then one day she'd been pulled out of routine and given a surprising new assignment. She was to be trained to perform technical tasks for Interforce, the organization that existed to battle other groups that tried to steal the few and far between resources on their side of the sea. The first of her kind ever asked to do so.

A radical change. But here she was.

They arrived at the storage niche, where a crude metal bar was driven into the stone. Lines of wetsuits hung on it, bearing the marks of long, hard use. Dev wasn't fond of them, as they were all somewhat too large for her. Even the one Jess had cut down for her use didn't provide a lot of protection against the cold water and dangerous rocks.

She usually ended up scraped and bruised and had to spend a good amount of time in a hot shower afterward to return her body to a normal temperature. It was uncomfortable, and often dangerous. Only the fact that her partner dearly loved the activity caused her to stolidly keep trying it.

"I found some info buried in the back of some archive," Jess said. She set her board to one side and opened a box. "And I figured out..." She pulled a bit of black substance into view. "How to force the fabricator to make one of these in your size." She straightened up and held up a surfing suit. "See?"

"Oh." Dev reached out and took the suit. "It's different. More like one of our flight suits."

"Yep," Jess agreed. "Put it on."

Dev obediently stripped out of her tech work suit and hung it on the bar, then pulled on the new garment that covered her completely, including booties over her feet. It fit like a glove, and as she fastened it, she felt a lot warmer. "Oh," she said, in surprise. "It's warm."

Jess nodded in satisfaction. "It's got a lining in it. Between the outer and inner fabric. It's metal mesh. It holds in your body heat. It'll keep the rocks from scraping ya."

Dev opened the throat covering of the suit and inspected it, then looked at Jess. "That's amazing." She closed the fastening again and savored the comforting warmth. "Thank you, Jess."

Jess leaned against the rocks and folded her arms casually. "Figured it might make your suffering through this insanity easier. You're such a damn good sport about it."

Dev turned and went over to the small, protected pool on the side of the raceway and, without hesitation, stepped off the rocks and into the water. Expectedly she went under the surface, but unexpectedly, she popped upward. A moment later her head emerged into clear air. "Interesting."

Jess sat on the side of the rocks, hands on the surface of them, ready to jump in. "Interesting?" She asked in an interrogative tone. "In a good way, or a bad way?"

"I do not sink in this." Dev kept her arms and legs still and felt the water buoy her up, a comforting cradling sensation that also lacked the uncomfortable chill the frothy water usually brought with it. "I'm not cold." She folded her hands on her stomach and relaxed. "Except my head."

"Doesn't cover your head," Jess said. "I figured you doing this with your head in a bag would bum you out." She slipped into the water and swam over to Dev. "Really works?" She sounded surprised. "Really?"

"Really." Dev looked up at the cavern ceiling, its details lost in the dim light. Then she rolled over in the water and swam for the edge. "Let me try surfing with it now."

Halfway to the side, she abruptly got caught up from behind and they reached the edge of the pool in a surge as she was boosted easily up and out onto the rock surface. Jess leaped out after her, and they went to grab their boards and head for the front of the cave.

****

"You did great." Jess toweled off her wet head as they   changed back into their black and green service jumpsuits. "You stayed on all the way through that whole last couple we did!"

"Jess, that was amazing." Dev fastened up her suit and pulled her damp hair out from the collar. "I really liked it. It was so much more fun." She felt more than a little exhilarated. It was the first time she'd surfed with Jess without chattering teeth and bruises. "Really excellent."

Jess smiled. "Good." She put the wet towel into a small bin nearby. "Now maybe I won't feel like such a jackass for asking you to meet me down here," she said. "Let's go get some chow." She led the way up the rough-cut ramp, and they left the roar of the raceway behind as the air slowly lost its moist, briny chill.

The halls were quieter now. It was late watch, and most of the day shift regulars were in quarters or relaxing somewhere.

The few people they passed were either maintenance or bio alts, busy at their tasks.

Most of the latter exchanged nods or a small wave with Dev, as she walked briskly along at Jess's side. They made their way up through the lower levels past the maintenance bays that were now quiet and dark, and past the turnoff that would go to med, also dark at this time of night.

Ahead was the operations mess, and as Jess pushed the door open and held it for her to enter, Dev heard her partner grunt in contentment at the mostly empty room. She followed Jess over to one of the tables in the back, raised area, and they sat down.

A bio alt server came over. "Hello, Agent Jess," he said in a mild tone. "Hello, NM-Dev-1."

"Hello, AyeBee 56." Dev returned the greeting. 'How are you?"

Jess settled back in her seat and lifted a hand as the door to the room opened and April and Doug came in. She waved them over. "Gonna be two more," she told the AyeBee. "Beers all around."

"Yes," the AyeBee said. "We have fish stew and creamed seaweed tonight. Would you also like some sea grape tea?"

"That's fine," Jess responded. "Beer first."

"Yes." The AyeBee went off to the service line to assemble their trays.

April Anston arrived first and took the seat across from Jess. She was woman of middling height, with curly, dark copper hair and intense, no nonsense hazel eyes. She carried herself with a sense of confident strength, her body compact and muscular. A long, sheathed blade was strapped to her hip. "Evening."

Doug came around her and sat across from Dev. He gave her a tiny wink. "Hey, Dev. How'd the surfing go?" He was a tall, gangly limbed man with red hair and gray eyes. A sprinkling of freckles across his face gave him an air of perpetual youth that matched his jokester personality.

"Excellent," Dev said. "Jess invented a new surfing suit for me, and it's completely amazing."

Both April and Doug's eyes shifted to Jess at once, a remarkably similar expression of intrigued surprise.

The AyeBee returned and put down their mugs of beer. Jess picked up hers and sat back. "What?" She finally said as they continued to eye her. "I can't make something?" She extended her long legs out across the floor and crossed her ankles. "Maybe the wrencher queen here's rubbing off on me."

April cleared her throat and took a sip of her own beer.

Made from fermented seaweed, it was dark green and had a pungent, spicy tang to it. "Hey, if it's better than those ratty old sealskins, bring it," she said, crisply. "Get the fabs to make us all some."

"I might," Jess said. She paused as the AyeBee brought back a tray and put it down and handed them all plates full of steaming material, bringing with them the smell of fish and more seaweed. After the server left, she glanced around the room and then back at them. "Jason's back."

"Heard that," April said, and took a spoonful of her stew and chewed it. "You talked to him?"

"He's calling a meeting tomorrow morning," Jess said. "Give us all the scoop. But he didn't look happy."

April glanced up at her. "Heard that too. Brent flew him out and back and I bumped into him near Centops when they got back," she said. "Doesn't know what's up, he just hopes he's not going to get tagged with one of those new Westies."

Jess scooped up some of her stew and raised her brows, then gave a slight, sideways shake of her head. "Not like he's got much of a choice. But I guess we'll find out."

"Guess we will."

****

The operations planning room was a large, oval space with a plas table in the center and chairs around the perimeter of it. The walls were dotted with screens that could be used to display information or vids.

Right now, the screen at the front of the room showed the view out over the sea from the east facing escarpment of the base, where the weather was just heavy clouds over white- capped dark green sea. The pale gray light from the hidden sun brought out hints of color in the water.

The corridor doors slid open and tall figures entered and took seats around the table. Jason Anders came in with Elaine Cruz at his heels. Brent and Tucker trailed behind them as they took seats at the top of the table's oval shape.

It was early, before the start of first watch. The agents and techs sat there waiting for everyone to show up, faces wary and a little sleep blurred. The tension in the room was palpable.

The door opened again, and April and Jess entered and took their customary seats, roughly across from Jason and Elaine. Dev and Doug settled next to them. All the agents wore black duty suits, but there were senior ranking bars at Jess's collar that most of the others lacked.

She was the tallest person in the room and had a sense of effortless, raw presence. Even in this collection of peers she stood out.

Jess leaned back in her seat and folded her arms, as the last agents entered. Mike Arias lead the two new West Coast transfers and pointed them to empty seats on the long side of the table.

Jason pressed a button on the arm of the chair he sat in, and they all heard the doors seal, compressing the air in the room as he hitched himself forward and leaned his elbows on the table. "Okay."

Jess spoke up. "What's the bad news? Let's not waste any time."

Jason gave her a brief grin. "I wasn't planning on it," he said. "I'm just trying to find a way to phrase what I do know so it makes some kind of sense." He paused, then continued. "So, what they told us was that with all the craziness over the last year, they realized something has to change."

"Tolja," April muttered. "You mean they copped to screwing up with that dipshit raid."

Jason pretended he hadn't heard. "We can't keep doing this until we all just croak. I think we all agree that's probably true. So, what they're doing is working with the other side to set up a …" He paused. "A working group, I guess you'd call it, to see how we can stop the fighting."

"That again?" Mike said. "Isn't that the tune they played when they pulled that scientist scam?"

"Cooperation again?" April chimed in. "C'mon. We've been down that road a thousand times before. It's all just a game."

Jason nodded. "You're not saying anything I didn't," he said, bluntly. "But what they asked us to do, us, I mean us, Interforce, is to just stop." He held his hand up. "No missions, no insertions, just hold off, stay in base, let them talk."

Jess eyed him but remained silent.

"For how long?" Elaine asked. "Long enough to let them get a few over on us?"

Jason shrugged his broad shoulders. He had straight brown hair and brown eyes and wore the rank insignia of field director, as the ops admin of the Base. "My plan is, we take the downtime to get everything sorted back out, get our repairs done, get our new members settled. I'm with you. I don't think this is going to last more than a month in real-time but for right now, everyone stays within our local range here. Keep your heads down." "Gotta be more to it than that," April said in an undertone to Jess. "No way it's just a parlay."

Jess shrugged. "I'll get some surfing in," she said. "Rocket'll invent a dozen new tech modules and maybe we can take the skiff out and get some shrimp. When was the last time any of us got a vacation?"

Dev leaned close to her. "What is a vacation?" She whispered.

"It's a break from work," Doug, seated to her left, murmured. "So, you don't have to work, and you get to do stuff like... um... "He paused. "Sit on the beach?"

Dev frowned. "Why would you want to do that?"

Doug scratched his nose. "Tell ya later."

"So, is that clear to everyone?" Jason asked. "We keep our standard patrol routing for our territories, and standard internal operations, but all external ops on hold. Got it?"

One of the new West Coasters nodded. "Gives us time to get settled," he said. "That's not bad." He glanced around. "Charlie Boone, in case we haven't met yet." He had black hair, gray eyes, and a scar that went across his face from his left ear to his nose. "Hi."

"Welcome," Jason said. "And, Dave Carter, there to your right. Welcome to Base 10."

Carter had tightly curled brown hair and dark skin, and he merely nodded.

"Which one talked to you?" Jess asked Dev.

"The one on the left," Dev said. "With the scar. He is the one that Brent does not wish to be connected to."

Jess studied the room, the chairs only half filled, just like the base itself was barely half filled. So many of them lost in battles upon battles, the last of which had essentially been a battle against themselves.

"Has to be more than that," April stated, flatly. "Something's in play."

Jess nodded slightly but then stood up. "Is what it is," she said. "I vote we make the most of the downtime. Build some things back up."

Jason's eyes met hers, and he nodded appreciatively at her. "Thanks, Jessie," he said. "That's how I'm reading it too. Give us some time to get crap sorted out here after everything that went on." He also stood up. "All right people. That's all I got." He unsealed the door. "Let you know if I hear anything else."

Everyone filed out of the room, but Jess waited by her chair until Jason came around to where she stood. They exchanged glances, then she held up her fist and he bumped it with his own. "Crazy," Jess said.

"Crazy," Jason confirmed. "Thanks for backing me up."

Jess smiled briefly. "What the hell else can we do? All fly out and start bombing random crap? It's a scam. We all know it."

They were the last in the room, save Dev, who stood near the doorway and waited for Jess to finish talking before they both went off to rad.

"Don't you think it is?" Jess asked, after a brief pause.

He let out a breath and scrubbed the fingers of one hand through his short, cropped hair. "I think it's coming from them," he finally said. "But I also think maybe we went over the top, this last year. Y'know?"

"Do I know?" Jess eyed him. "Came right through my homestead didn't it?" She said. "We both said then, there has to be a better way than this." She paused. "I just don't know a bunch of bean heads in a room talking is it. We'll end up getting screwed."

Jason sighed. "Could be true, Jessie. I literally felt the bullshit in the room." He shrugged. "But, like you said, what are we going to do? I say we do what you suggested, use the time to get our crap back together and see what comes out of it. Maybe something will."

"Maybe nothing will."

"Maybe nothing will, but at least we'll have our crap together," Jason said, pragmatically. "We could all use a break. Get North back running, get numbers back up... that I didn't argue with." He exhaled. "They were hiding their cards. Those two Westies are probably sending reports back on anything they see."

Jess smiled. "Probably. They seem like lumps."

Jason folded his arms. "Yeah. Brent doesn't want to hook up with either of them." He frowned.

"Don't make him," Jess said, bluntly.

"We're out of teams, Jess," Jason said. "We lost over fifty in that fight between us and the west."

"Not just the west." Jess's pale blue eyes twinkled with something like amusement. "They chose a bad time to pick on my fam."

"Yeah, well I can tell you that got a dozen brass expunged," Jason said. "They said it was bad intel, but no one bought that." He glanced past Jess out the door. "Anyway, I get it, but he's the only unpaired tech here right now."

Jess shrugged. "Brent's a good guy. Let him stick with you."

"Do I need a tech?"

Jess merely looked at him with an expressionless face. "Yeah, I know," Jason said. "He doesn't deserve some

lump. Let me think about it." He sighed. "Okay, off to some other bullshit meeting. You know when you said no way to this? I thought you were nuts." He patted her shoulder. "You weren't." He eased past her and gave Dev a brief wave, as he left the room, the door shutting swiftly behind him.

"That was excellent of you, Jess."

Jess studied Dev. "What was?" She looked around in some perplexity. "What did I do?"

"You told Jason to keep Brent as his partner," Dev said. "It was excellent that you said it."

"Was it?" Jess put her hand on Dev's back. "C'mon, let's go get some rad, and go to the gym. I just want Brent to shut up. He's been bitching about being reassigned since Jason got booted up. Anyway, it just makes sense. Always good to have a wrencher you trust at your back." She nudged the door open. "Besides, if we're confined to base, who cares? Can't do anything anyway."

Dev smiled as they went out the door. "He's going to be really pleased."

"Then tell him to stop whining."

****

Dev twitched her jumpsuit collar straight as she walked along the corridor, a good session of rad and a tough circuit in the gym behind her and an afternoon of circuit design ahead of her to look forward to. Unlike most of her colleagues, and Jess, she found the idea of being able to spend time inside the Citadel working on her technical projects pleasurable.

Jess had detoured to the materials fabrication workshop to drop off her new swimming suit to be duplicated, and they'd planned to then meet up in the mess where she was headed now. Halfway there she crossed through an intersection and was hailed.

"Dev!"

Dev halted. "Hello, CeeBee." She stood still as the bio alt caught up to her. "How are you?" She smiled in reflex at the short, slimly built youngster, with his curly red hair and very blue eyes. He was dressed in a gray jumpsuit, the squared off neckline exposing his golden inset collar.

"Doing really well," he said. "I passed the mech test! They're going to assign me to the machine bay."

"Excellent!" Dev said. "That's good to hear. It's optimal that we can do this work."

"It is," CeeBee said. "We know it's because so many people got made dead." He sobered. "That's not excellent."

"No," Dev agreed. "That was hard, and sad."

"But we will have a chance to do good work, like you do," he said, confidently. "Maybe I'll get to work on your carrier." He glanced behind him. "Let me go tell my setmates. We saved some cakes from dinner last night in case I made it, and we could have them together."

Dev moved over and gave him a hug. "Congratulations," she said. "I hope you enjoy the work as much as I enjoy mine."

He grinned and hugged her back. "Thanks, Dev. See you around the lab." He trotted off down the hallway, heading for the lower levels where the bio alts assigned to Base 10 lived, on strict work schedules, but still with more freedom than they'd had in the creche up on station.

More than she'd had. Until she came to Interforce and took the place of a natural born field tech to become the first of her kind to do what she did and live like she did.

First of her kind to have her synaptic collar removed, and was now, to most anyone's eyes, no different than all the natural born she worked alongside.

So, in her field tech greens, she turned and walked through a gateway that CeeBee couldn't enter, that separated the operations secure areas from the rest of the base. She headed for the operations mess, where only field agents and technicians, along with the ops crews were allowed.

Inside it was busy. Dev quickly glanced around and identified a few free tables, so she went to the dispensing line and picked up two trays and slid them along the line to where the AyeBees were standing behind the machinery. "Hello, AyeBee."

"Hello, NM-Dev-1," AyeBee greeted her. "Would you like some fish and mushrooms? They brought in a boat load this morning, it's very fresh."

"I would. Could I get two portions please? I'm going to bring one to Jess." Dev waited, as the AyeBee dished up some of the baked, flaky white fish, and added scoops of mushrooms next to them, then put a plate down on each tray. "Thank you."

Dev took the trays down the line and added a cup of the fizzy, slightly sweet beverage they all drank, then weaved her way through the crowded room to a small table at the back of one of the raised areas. She sat at the side of the table so that Jess could take the chair with her back to the wall and took a sip of her drink.

Cliff leaned over from the next table. "Hey, Dev."

"Hello." Dev sorted out her plate. "How are you, Cliff?"

Cliff had a senior mech rating bar on his collar and wore the dark blue of operations mechanical. "Not too bad. I hear we're going to have plenty of time to patch up the rigs. True?"

"It seems so." Dev took another sip of her drink and kept a watch in her peripheral vision on the door. "I have heard we will not be going on missions for some time."

Cliff nodded. "Good," he said. "We need some regen time. Too much crap went on here."

Dev considered that. "It was suboptimal," she agreed, making a little grimace of agreement.

The door to the mess opened and Jess entered. Dev took in a scan of the room, noting the looks and attention her partner got as she crossed the floor and caught the range of expressions and reactions. "Hello, Jess."

"Hey, Devvie." Jess took a seat and pulled her tray over. "Thanks for getting me some grub."

Dev smiled. "You are welcome." She cut through the firm white filet on her plate with her fork. "Are they going to replicate your suit?"

"Yup." Jess took a bite of her fish. "That's not bad." She studied it. "Haven't seen that kind here in a while... wonder where it came from." She forked up some mushrooms and popped them in her mouth. "Maybe a boat didn't feel like making the run to the processors."

"It's good," Dev agreed. "It is more appealing than many of the meals here recently. I am glad we got a chance to go to Quebec City as the edible items here have been..." She paused and frowned.

"Lemme guess, suboptimal?"

"Less than optimal," Dev concluded, going back to her plate. "Not offensive, just..."

"Meh."

Dev briefly grinned. "Yes."

Jess tapped her fork against her tray, her brows contracting a bit as she pondered. "Hey, I got an idea. Jason said we had to stay inside our local range. How about we see if we can take a ride over to the

Bay? See your buddy the Doc?"

Dev looked up at her in surprise and visible delight. "That would be excellent. From the messages I have gotten from the sets there, it seems they are doing well, but I would enjoy seeing them, and of course, Doctor Dan."

"Lemme see if we can do that." Jess went back to her meal. "Make sure they're all not still pissed off at me for nearly trashing the place." She glanced up as the mess door opened again. The two new agents entered together, went to the tray line together, then took a seat together at one of the tables against the back wall.

They looked over at the table where Jess and Dev sat, their eyes holding on them with a long, arrogant touch before they turned their heads and started to eat.

"That was interesting," Dev said. "In a possibly suboptimal way."

"Couple of dipshits," Jess said. "Bet they won't be here long." She reached over and stole a mushroom from Dev's plate. "Gonna wrench later? I'm going to spend some time in the pit. Maybe those guys'll show up there and make my day."

"Yes, I have a mod to our vehicle I'm working on," Dev said. "Do you think we can surf this evening?" She added casually. "I would like to try my suit again."

Jess stopped mid chew, and her pale blue eyes opened wide. "You serious?"

"Yes. I really enjoyed it," Dev said. "It was nice as well, to have a late meal when it's quieter here." She smiled, delighted to see the happy look on Jess's face that came so very seldom. "Or we can get a box and have it in our quarters if you'd like that."

Jess took a breath to answer, then paused and just looked at Dev for a long moment. "Yeah, I'd like that," she finally said, quietly. "You're definitely on."

Dev went back to consuming the rest of her mushrooms, pleased with the reaction to her plan. It might, she thought, even end up with them practicing sex, which was nearly always optimal.

As long as they were not interrupted by unforeseen alarms that might ruin the act of course, or the occasional unexpected tumble out of bed onto the stone floor.

****

Jess paused at the doorway to the pit, flexing her hands a

little as she surveyed the other occupants there ahead of her, still feeling a sense of buoyancy over Dev's unexpected request to surf with her.

Dev would do whatever it was Jess wanted to do, whenever she wanted to do it, a legacy of her birth and early life as a biological alternative, programmed to please and assist natural born humans without any resentment of whatever odd thing they did, and of course Jess knew that.

But she seldom went out of her way to ask for dangerous experiences that weren't work related. Jess grinned. She'd make it a short session though. She wanted to make sure Dev's new interest in the craziness really was due to the new suit.

She gave her body a shake and turned her attention back to the room.

April was there, and Mike Arias, who was sparring with her. And to one side, one of the new Westies leaned against the wall and watched them fight.

Jess went inside and moved to the left, going over to the changing area. She traded her black jumpsuit for a pair of the workout shirts and pants. They were worn and dry feeling against her skin, but a little stretchy and a completely neutral dun color with the exception, on hers, of a darker brown left sleeve.

Designed not to trigger anyone. The feel was utterly different than a duty suit, and the color was designed to be mild and unlike what anyone usually wore so it didn't invoke a reaction based on a peripherally recognized outline. Jess felt the usual sense of calm she got from wearing them, and she appreciated the expectation that she could spend some time working off twitchy energy without ending up killing someone.

The brown sleeve was a visible warning that she was a field agent, active, and had the physical reflexes and triggers that entailed. Sparring partners be warned. Don't be stupid.

She went to the warmup room, found it empty and felt a moment of melancholy knowing that even though she'd disliked a lot of the other agents, it was unsettling for it to be so quiet, as though everyone were out on insertions she knew didn't exist.

Thoughtfully, she approached the target dummies and paused to take a breath, then release it. She dismissed the grim thoughts and focused on the target, dense vaguely human forms with electronic sensors that recorded hits and allowed the targets to evade or return them. "Control, dummy twelve."

"Ident?"

"Drake, J."

"Acknowledged." The room system issued two sedate, low

beeping sounds to warn her, then triggered the warmup program.

It knew who she was, so the target moved immediately and within 10 or so seconds Jess was engaged with it, moving and dodging along with it as it came at her with robotic calm, unable to be affected by fear or impressed by her skills.

That was nice about the robots. Jess slid under the robot's arm swinging across to strike her. She caught the arm in the curve of her elbow, braced a hand on its back and pulled the limb out of position until it cracked.

The robot paused, and after a moment, the limb popped back into place, and they went back to their engagement. It was all hand to hand, all grappling and shoving, the mechanical target larger and far heavier than she was, and hard to knock off balance due to its stubby, round, thick legs.

Jess enjoyed the warmup. She liked facing off against the robot because it never took offense, never got mad at her, never mocked her in the war of words the agents often used to provoke a misstep. It was just a robot, doing what it was designed to do, content to be kicked and slammed around by Drake, J. all day long with a complete lack of resentment.

Its hands were thick sealskin covered circles but if they hit you hard enough, they'd leave a bruise, and a point of pride was to come out of the warmup without any. Jess always did. Or at least she made sure they were on parts of her body covered by cloth that didn't show.

She kept at it for a half hour, aware in her peripheral vision when the newbie came to the entrance to the warmup room and watched her for the last few of the minutes. Because of this she showed off a little, vaulting over the robot as it tried to intercept her and turning in midair to kick the back of its head, sending its body violently rocking forward to smack it's face on the ground.

The watcher was the shorter and darker of the two. The one who hadn't spoken to Dev. She caught him jerk in reaction to her antics, and grinned, bouncing around the robot as it straightened up.

Jess finished up her routine by ducking under the robot's long arms and coming face to face with it. Then she slid her arms around its cylindrical metal body and lifted it up off the ground.

It's legs wiggled back and forth in surprise as an alarm went off and it made her laugh. "Finish," she called out, releasing her hold and stepping back. The robot caught its balance and straightened up into quiescence. Her body felt warm and ready for action, and she playfully swung and tapped the target's hand before she turned and started for the door.

The dark-skinned agent was still in the doorway, his head cocked faintly to one side as he watched her approach. Jess was wagering with herself about what he was going to do. She hoped it was a plan to be a jerk to her so she could get in a satisfying ass kicking to round out the pleasures of the day.

"Did you just pick up that robot?" The agent asked when she was almost within reach.

Jess paused. "Yeah," she said and turned to look back at the robot, then at him. "Want a match?" She added invitingly, her eyebrows hiking a little as she brought up her hands to waist level, wiggling her fingers.

"Hell, no," he responded at once. "I don't want to get in the pit with someone who can pick up a whole ass metal sparring robot, thanks. I have me some crazy, but not that much." He stepped back to get out of her way. "What the hell do you mix it up with, one of the carriers?"

Jess wasn't sure if she should be amused or disappointed. She half shrugged. "Nah. They mostly just point me at the bad guys." The lack of pretentious jackassery was a pleasant surprise in the newcomer and Jess briefly wondered if he was one of the kids who'd gotten sold in, not so much tested in. At her first close review, he didn't seem to have that, to her, easy to recognize edge.

He nodded. "I know. I saw the vids. I got no intention of crossing you, Drake," he said. "Call me Dave. Since my big mouth got me sent out here, I'm gonna try to keep it shut for a while." He exhaled. "But I gotta say, it's different."

"Yeah, it's different." She shrugged again and indicated the door. "C'mon. Let's go have some fun."

"Speak for yourself." Dave followed her outside though and trailed along as she slid through the gate leading into the pit, scan running briefly over both, comp registering their presence in the space alert for sudden violent action.

Agents often came out of the pit and went to med. Not usually with lethal injuries, but there weren't many pulled punches and occasionally mixups went into crazytown and there were stunners on the wall, high up, just in case.

But today it was quiet, almost empty. April and Mike broke apart as she approached and turned. April lifted a hand and made a slight, grabbing gesture with her fingers. "Us against you?" She said, invitingly.

Jess grinned, dismissing the trailing newbie at her back. "You're on."

****

Dev liked the electronics lab a lot. There was a small desk surface in a little angle of it near the back and she usually stored her projects in progress there. The area had a lot of little drawers and bins to store things, a worn, padded stool to sit on and was out of the general traffic that was usually busy in the afternoons.

She entered from the operations corridor and took a breath of the air filled with the smell of metal and epoxy spray, mixed with the distinct scent of electronics off gassing she was very familiar with. There were four other techs there, all working at benches around the room in contented silence.

Chester, Tucker, and Doug were there, absorbed in their work and the fourth... ah. The fourth was Brent.

Brent saw her enter and left his bench and came over to hers as she reached it. "Hey, Dev."

Dev seated herself behind her little desk. "Hello, Brent. How are you?"

He leaned on the desk with both hands, his bull necked muscularity evident under his tech jumpsuit. "I'm good. You hear I've been reassigned to Jason?"

"Have you? That's excellent," Dev said. "No, I had not heard that yet. That's really good."

Brent smiled. "Yeah, with all the traveling he figures he's in for, he said he wants someone who knows what they're doing at his back. Doesn't want to go headfirst into a cliff."

"It seems you will get to see more of things than we will right now," Dev said. "But having you do that is optimal. I know Jess will be really pleased to hear it. Would you like to see some of the mods I am working on? Maybe you will want them for your carrier."

"Sure," he said. "I was just tuning the gyro, but I'd like to see what Rocket's up to." He grinned again and winked at her. "Feels good to be back in my old place."

"Yes." Dev smiled back at him. "It is good to have a place that you know you belong in." She settled her feet on the rungs of the stool. "I'll get things set up here if you want to bring your gyro over. We can look at it."

He patted the surface of the steel table and then went off back to where he'd been leaning over a cabinet. Dev paused in her assembly of parts to look after him and nod a little to herself. Yes, she thought, Jess was going to be pleased to hear about that and she looked forward to telling her.

She touched the cabinet to her left and felt the tickle as it read the chip embedded in her hand and opened, keyed to her identity. Inside there were boards in various states of progress and she removed the one in the bottom slot and carefully sat it on a pad made of dried sea sponge.

She smelled the musty, salty scent of it. The rough texture against her fingers left a faint feeling of the sea, but it provided a sturdy cushion to lay the board on that wouldn't damage its delicate metal traced underside. She clipped the diagnostic leads to the edges, and before touching it further, wrapped a strap around her right wrist that attached a ground line that would discharge the dry air's static.

She pulled her scanner from another cabinet at her right knee and set it up on the table, attaching devices and turning it on.

The door opened and she glanced up to see one of the new agents enter and look around. He was the one with the scar who had spoken to her. The other techs also looked up but went back to their work and ignored the newcomer.

Clint entered from the maintenance office adjoining and casually took a seat behind the big console there. He pulled an input pad over and accessed it, his body poised so he could keep the rest of the room in view.

Interesting. Dev wondered if there was something behind Clint's activity and the new transfer's presence, or if it was all just a coincidence. Clint kept his eyes on the tablet as the agent moved around the room, apparently just taking in what there was to be seen.

It looked very normal and casual, except that Dev knew that Clint being there at the console wasn't normal or usual since she herself was usually here at this desk at this time when she was here in the Base. Part of her core programming was to review things to determine the unusual and evaluate what they might mean.

But the new agent just roamed around, and Clint just tapped into his tablet surface and so Dev merely marked it down as something out of norm and put her concentration back on the card. She wanted to get the new metrics in place before Brent returned so she could show them to him.

The new mod was designed to improve the energy transfer from the carrier's battery systems to its motive drive, and she'd worked out a little routine to precache some of the power to enhance the responsiveness of the hydraulic steering.

She set up a tablet and reviewed the card's programming. She focused on the section of the enhancement and made a slight change, observing the results as they flashed across the tablet's screen.

"Hi."

Dev looked up to find the new agent standing next to her desk. "Hello," she responded, then waited, watching him.

He had a square, blocky face, and his nose was crooked. The scar that bisected his cheek had the shiny edges that a blaster caused, and he had his hands in the front pockets of his agent's duty suit, a little different version of the one Jess wore. "Wanted to say thanks for the directions yesterday."

"You're welcome," Dev promptly responded, seeing from the corner of her eye both Brent and now Doug watched them. "I'm glad they were useful," she added, after a moment's pause since the agent seemed to be expecting something other than that.

"I've never actually spoken to a bio alt before as a grown up," the man said, in a thoughtful tone. "So, if I say something out of line, sorry."

"I'm sure you won't. I'm used to hearing all kinds of things spoken to me," Dev said. "Is there something else you would like to know?"

Doug wandered over to where Clint was and leaned against the console. Dev wondered if they expected the newcomer to do something incorrect.

That would be non-optimal. It might disrupt her plans to join Jess for surfing, and if Jess heard about it things could get incorrect very quickly. She casually glanced past the agent and met Doug's gaze for just a second.

Doug slid over toward her. "Hey Rocket," he greeted her casually, then glanced at the newcomer. "You're Charlie, right?"

"I am." The agent seemed a bit relieved at the interruption. "And you're Doug Sars, right? You're another Rainier boy."

"That I am," Doug admitted cheerfully. "I like the weather better here in the east. So, what's up, Rocket?" He leaned on the desk. "You inventing some new controller?"

"Hello, Doug." Dev amiably played along with this little game, since Doug knew perfectly well what she was working on. "How are you?"

"Doing great, thanks. April went over to the pit," Doug confided, as though they were alone.

Dev nodded. "Jess as well. I'm sure they're enjoying themselves."

"Beating the crap out of each other?" He grinned. "Yeah that's a total party time for them. Glad our hobbies are less painful."

"I as well."

Doug returned his attention to the agent. "So, Charlie. You like the tech side? You came to the right desk. Rocket's the bomb." He gave Charlie a genial nod. "Want to talk about the gen mods in that carrier they assigned you? Used to be mine."

Brent slid past Charlie to come around the side of the desk. He dragged a second stool with him and settled it next to Dev. "All right… let's see that new mod," he said, brusquely, sliding his gyro onto the desk.

Charlie looked at them with an almost amused look, then smiled at Doug. "Nope, just getting to know the place. Have fun." He took a step backwards. "No point in my looking at the rig until they assign me someone who can drive it." He nodded at them then turned and sauntered out of the room.

Dev looked from Brent to Doug. "That was interesting."

"Yeah, cause we busted up whatever that was," Doug said. "If he's got something on his mind, we'll hear it eventually. Typical Westie."

Brent lifted a faintly sardonic eyebrow. "Ain't you from there?"

"That's how I know," Doug said with a grin. "April kicked the typical Westie crap right out of me our first month together. She was like, I'm a nomad. You all suck. C'mere and let me break your kneecap."

Brent chuckled under his breath. "Yeah. Guys' a goon. Makes my neck itch." He exhaled. "S'why I really was glad Jason hooked me back up with him, not with either of those two. Just don't like them."

Dev studied her two apparent guardians. "Do you think they're incorrect?" She asked. "They mean harm?" She clarified. "They were sent here to do incorrect things to us?"

Clint came out from behind the console and joined them. "Good job, kids," he told Brent and Doug. "Guy's trouble or I'm a sea lion. Pair of bad eggs."

Dev pondered all of that, her brow in a knot. "They have barely arrived," she said, and evaded the urge to ask about the eggs. "Have they done something incorrect already?"

"Guy has a rep as a troublemaker and dog," Clint said bluntly. "He likes the ladies."

Dev stared at him in patent incomprehension. She felt like she understood what a troublemaker was since she lived alongside Jess, and she'd looked up what a dog was in the past, but neither seemed to apply to the scarred newcomer. "I... see." She said doubtfully.

"Thinks he's hot, Dev," Brent said. "Figures he'd start poking around."

Dev reached up and pinched the bridge of her nose. "I'm sorry I have no idea what you are all saying," she admitted. "What is so sub optimal about this person? Or these people? We have barely spoken a few words to them, and this one was at least nominally pleasant?"

The three of them looked away in some chagrin and embarrassment.

"Would you rather I ask Jess?" Dev suggested.

Clint rubbed his jaw. "That could solve the problem." He said. "Jess'd take care of that in a snap." He snapped his fingers.

"Could," Brent agreed. "She'd just break his neck. End that right there."

"Guys," Doug said. "Dev has no clue what you're going on about." He leaned closer to Dev and lowered his voice. "I think we all don't like them because they came from the West, and those guys didn't treat us so good not too long ago. I mean, I know there were a bunch of them who came out and said they took over, but there were a lot of them that were on the other side, you know?"

Dev nodded. "Yes. That I understand."

"So," Doug said, we don't know what side these guys were on. We know what they say. Now for the other thing," he paused, choosing his words. "Maybe he wants to get to know you, you know?"

Dev's right eyebrow lifted in question. "Do I know?"

"Like real friendly," Brent added.

"Spend time alone with you in your crib, kinda way," Clint muttered.

Dev's left eyebrow lifted to join its mate, and she looked from one to the other for a long moment before speaking. "Are you saying this person, who just arrived, would like to practice sex with me?" She asked, in a disbelieving tone. "Just because he came over to say hello?"

"He has that rep," Clint explained, blushing a little. "I

know some mech guys out west, and I got a read on him, and the other guy. Other guy's kinda a null, never really made a show for anything. But this guy, this Charlie, got a couple of marks in the ledger for screwing up on missions cause he was off in someone's bunk."

"Got a tech killed," Brent said. "Wasn't there when the shooting started. Jason told me, last night."

Dev looked at him. "Ah," she murmured in understanding. "Now I see."

"Hadn't heard that," Clint muttered.

"That's… very incorrect," Dev said, slowly. "The issue now is more comprehensible."

Clint patted her arm. "Anyway, you stay clear of him, Dev. Maybe he just got some bad breaks and made some bad choices, but we had enough crap happen here. Don't need more."

"Right," Brent agreed. "So, what's up with the mod?" He pointedly changed the subject.

Dev thought about all that for a moment, as Doug and Clint moved off a little, talking in a low tone to each other. They were all her friends, she concluded, considering the word carefully. It mattered to them what happened to her, and she thought that was nice. A little odd sometimes, but nice.

She moved over a little so Brent could see better. "It's an interface mod for the power systems," she said. "I wanted to see if I could make the control systems respond faster. It always seems a bit—"

"Laggy," Brent interjected. "Got it, yeah, so you turn and it's just a beat, like, before it goes."

"Yes."

"Been like that forever." Brent eyed her. "You fix it?"

"Possibly," Dev said. "I am going to make some more adjustments to it and then we can go try it in the carrier and see if it works."

"Can't go far," Brent said. "But we don't need to."

"Not far at all."

****

Jess stepped off the mat, her bare feet moving from the rough, flexible surface to the stone floor as she felt the chill of it against her soles. She felt relaxed, and pleasantly well stretched out from the fight, that had left Mike and April flat on their backs across from her.

She enjoyed two on one, especially when the two she was

facing off against weren't total assholes. Then it was a challenge, and fun, a friendly competition where you could concentrate on form and skills and not on what bullshit was going to come flying at you to entertain your opponent's cronies.

No real cronies here, now. She flexed her hands and glanced around. The Westie was just getting up from being dumped on his ass by Elaine and he was laughing a little and so was she.

It felt a little strange. She felt a little disconnected, almost. The echoes were too loud, and too infrequent and she briefly wished the techs would come in to watch as they sometimes did, to fill the space a little.

She felt like she'd have liked to see Dev there, hands behind her back, brow creased as she pondered the strangeness of natural born who beat on each other for fun.

April climbed to her feet and dusted her hands off. Mike rolled over and then spent a minute stretching his body out as they all sort of took a pause, the pit quieting down as echoes of punches and kicks faded.

"Wish you'd come back to the caravanseri with me and do that neck kick to my Mater," April said and glanced over at Jess. "Ouch."

"You could do it yourself now," Mike said and got up. "You were a little punk when you left there, you been back?"

"Nah," April said. "You leave, you leave. Once they know you aren't going to bring anything back to them, you ain't family anymore." She rocked her head to either side, cracking her neck. "Anyway, what do I have in common with them now?"

"Yeah." Mike paused, reflectively. "I went back a few times, but it was weird," he admitted. "You can't talk about your life with them, can you? They want to talk about the price of salt extractors, and what do I say to that? Do you know how it feels to kill a penguin, ma? They squeak when you crush em."

April chuckled, a little. "They do," she said. "Stinking little bastards."

They both sat down on the edge of the pit, and after a moment, Jess came over and sat next to them.

"Good fight." Jess said. "I like it when no one has to be carried to med."

Mike gave her a sideways glance. "Ever you?"

"Sure," Jess said. "You go full out sometimes. Forget where you are." She hiked up one knee and circled it with both arms, as they watched Elaine and Dave go at it, circling each other with sparring gloves on. "Cracked my head a few times."

"What do you think about this shutdown?" April asked, abruptly. "Scam?"

"I think it's the usual political power that be bull," Mike said. "They'll arrange a meet and yak, then someone'll kill someone, and we'll be right back to it."

Jess jerked her chin toward Dave. "He said he was one of the guys that rebelled out there. Said they ended up sending him here."

April snorted. "That was all bullshit. You're either in or you're out. We're all supposed to be on the same side. Isn't that what they teach you at school?" She smiled briefly. "You believe it, right? Until you're about ten." She snorted a little in disdain. "Same side my ass."

"There were always tiers," Mike said, stifling a yawn. "We all knew it. I was different because my family were miners. You were different because you were nomad. Different perks, different crowds... different assignments. You didn't catch any of priv dorks being sent out here."

"Nah they all went to Juneau, or Picchu, or stayed at Canyon City in cush jobs," April said. "Different world, out west. I remember us going out to the Plateau, seeing those big hydros and all those dug ins. Everyone had enough to eat, decent clothes." She exhaled. "I felt like a nomad there, for sure."

Jess listened in silence and nodded. She'd been there, gone through school just like they had. She knew.

Well, sort of knew. She had, without a doubt, been considered different. From the first time she'd sat in a bridge class, and they'd heard about things her family members had done. The whole class turned and stared at her. She'd been marked out but she'd always worn that mark of difference with pride.

Of course she was different. She was a Drake.

"I went back home all the time," she finally said. "That was never weird for me."

April chuckled her low, dry way. "Course it wasn't," she said. "Everyone there gets it. They knew what it's about. I saw those guys patting you on the back for ripping people's heads off."

"Yeah, that's true," Jess said. Then she casually looked around and lowered her voice. "Listen, I don't know what this whole thing's about." She looked from Mike to April and back. "But I'm going to take advantage of the downtime and take a ride to the Bay." She eyed them. "Wanna go?" She added, after a brief hesitation.

"Absolutely," April answered instantly.

"Sure," Mike chimed in. "When?"

Jess stood up, towering over them. "Tomorrow. I cleared it with Jason. He just said keep a low profile." Her pale eyes twinkled just a little. "I said I'd try." She winked, and sauntered out, heading for the changing room.

****

Dev triggered the hatch on their carrier and waited for it to lift then scooted inside. She removed her overnight pack from her back and stowed it inside the small compartment that had her name on its door.

Or, well, not quite her name. She regarded the chiseled metal plate, bearing the word "Rocket," on it with a bemused expression. Impossible for her to either refuse or protest, since Jess had made it with her blaster and affixed it there herself.

She finally just smiled and reached out to touch it. The metal had come from station, scrounged from the shuttle she'd flown down from it and had that odd reflectivity she remembered well.

Then she started the process of ensuring the carrier was ready to go. They would take passengers with them this time, so she pulled down the back shelf that she and Jess sometimes took rest on and made sure the restraints were in place on them and went to the frame that held Jess's drop pack that had a small ledge just large enough to sit on as well.

The fourth extra seat was the jump seat up near her pilot's station. She went forward into the nose of the carrier and sat down. She then reached forward to pick up an ear bud and settle it into her right ear as she started up the carrier's systems.

Soon, she knew, she would hear Jess and the others approach, but it was some minutes before the time they'd arranged to meet, and she spent them activating the boards and modules she'd worked on the previous days, carefully observing their responses.

She even had the new module with its engineering code in place, since the trip to the Bay was a short and easy one, and perfect for her to test its functionality. She set the startup diagnostics to run and got up, going over to make sure supply had stocked the extra things she'd asked for, short trip or not.

The carrier was designed to, long term, support two people. One agent, one pilot. Its standard operation stocked things like water and energy bars, seaweed crackers and sanitary supplies for that number. Dev peered inside the storage lockers and nodded in satisfaction.

Extra containers of all those things were packed neatly inside, where they might, in an insertion, carry spare weapons, munitions, electronics or exposure suits.

It was a short trip. Jess said they would come back the next day, but you never knew, and it always paid to be prepared just in case.

Dev went back to her seat and observed the results of the diagnostics, her fingers tapping over the control surfaces in now automatic motions, needing no thought to make the carrier ready for flight, her actions confident and assured and without the faint hesitation of a bio alt under programming.

She triggered the front shield, and it slid up. This allowed her a view of the inside of the docking cavern. There were three other carriers nearby getting worked on, one, she saw, was Doug and April's. An engine was being replaced.

Above her head, sealed now, was the huge metal ceiling that had once been used to enter and exit the docking area, certainly allowing a comprehensive view surroundings immediate on exit, but extremely inconvenient when it was pouring down rain and opening it drenched everything inside.

The doors now mounted in the east facing escarpment made a lot more sense.

Dev spotted motion in the entry from the ops corridor and a moment later Jess appeared, with April striding next to her. Mike, his partner, Chester and Doug trailed behind them, all of them carrying overnight packs on their backs.

Excellent. They were right on time. Dev felt the carrier start up around her, shifting a tiny bit on its pad as the hydraulics tightened up and the engines went through their prestart routine. "Pad ops, standby to retract our umbilical lines," she spoke into local comms and watched the bio alt mech react and step back away off the steel grating out of range.

She monitored the readout from the new module, but it seemed stable, and she nodded in satisfaction as she hit the undock and the power and diagnostic lines retracted into body of the carrier with a metallic, slithering sound and the solid thunks of covers seating.

She had done this now many times. And yet still, there was a feeling inside her of the responsibility of what she was doing, and that every time she was expected to do this work with excellence, as she had from even the very first time.

She never wanted to disappoint Jess. She always wanted it

to be perfect.

Boots sounded on the pad ramp and then Jess vaulted inside. "Hey, Devvie."

Dev glanced in the reflective mirror above her station and smiled as her eyes met Jess's in it. "Hello."

April climbed into the carrier and glanced around, then went to the jump rig and stowed her pack underneath it, leaving the longer seats in the back for Mike and Chester, who were just walking up the ramp outside.

April was the shortest of the agents, not much taller than Dev, but heavier and more muscular, with an elastic way of moving that advertised strength regardless of size. Of all of them she was the only one who could even use the ledge as anything more than a leaning spot.

The jump rig wasn't really intended to be comfortable, with its truncated platform. "How do you even use this?" April asked Jess as she got settled into the cramped niche, her back against the pack that an agent could wear to drop into a situation through a hatch below her boots.

"Try not to." Jess put her pack into the other compartment next to Dev's and went to her weapons station and sat in her chair. "Smack my head every damn time I go near it." She stretched out her long legs and wriggled her shoulders into the padding of the seat.

April glanced at the bulkhead over her. "I bet."

Doug entered and scooted past Jess to the front of the carrier and pulled down the jump seat next to Dev, "Hey Rocket."

"Hello." Dev had finished her preparatory work and now sat and waited for everyone to take their place. "Jess, I have pre-clearance from ops. They're waiting to open the doors for us."

"Anyone asking any stupid questions?"

Dev pondered that. "I don't think so," she said. "Just the usual things, routing and egress plan."

"Good." Jess pulled her restraints over her head and buckled them. "Let's go."

Dev settled her ear bud more firmly. "Centops, this is BR270006, requesting permission to lift," she spoke into comms. She studied her surroundings through the front shield to make sure no one was ignorant of the flashing lights on the engine pods of her carrier and wandering too close to her impending movement.

She spotted the new agents then, across the cavern next to one of the carriers. They were talking to Clint, apparently about the carrier she recognized as Doug and April's old one. "I think you're glad to have switched vehicles," she said to Doug. "I see they are replacing an engine for your new one."

"Sure, am and yep, they finally are." Doug leaned forward and peered out the shield. "Hahahah. Lookie there."

"What?" April asked, from her spot near the back of the carrier.

"Westies checking out our old rig," Doug said. "Good riddance."

"BR270006, you are cleared to lift. Stand by for egress," Centops finally answered her. "Bring up sideband 12, in ops."

"Yes." Dev tuned the comms. "Sideband 12 open." She moved her seat forward a little and settled her boots on the thruster pedals. "Stand by to lift."

The sound of restraints being tightened echoed through the carrier as Dev eased power into the landing jets, boosting the carrier up swiftly toward the cavern's ceiling, rising over the other vehicles and the work being done to them.

Heads turned to watch them. Dev boosted quickly and left them behind as she reached launch level and paused to wait for the doors to retract ahead of her. They rumbled open, audible through the skin of the craft. She could now see outside where the weather, for once, seemed to be mild.

"Rain stopped," Doug commented, confirming her opinion. "Nice."

"Yes." Dev spooled up the engines and as they took on power, she cut the jets, transitioning from vertical to horizontal flight in a smooth surge that took them out of the cavern in a blur, the craft turning on its side to clear the still opening doors, leaving behind a slight boom of air displacement.

Jess, in her gunner's seat with her hands folded over her stomach, snickered. "Bet we hear about that."

Once outside Dev boosted up quickly and came up over the escarpment and turned in a perfect spiral that took the carrier upside down and back upright in a powerful, elegant loop. She let her sensors get a sweep of the area before she leveled out and headed south. She wasted no time in coming up to speed as they left the base behind.

It was quiet, and though the sky was covered in thick, dark clouds, there was only a light wind and no rain for a change, as the carrier made its way through the air with a light tailwind.

Chapter Two

Dan Kurok walked into the large, high-ceilinged kitchen in the stakeholder's complex at Drake's Bay. It was early, and still mostly dark outside but he was an early riser by nature and enjoyed the quiet before the usual chaos of the day.

He went over to the heating unit and requested a cup of sea grape tea. He took the cup with him to the window that took up most of the room's outer wall. It gave him a view of the Bay that formed the front of the stakehold, a massive circular shallow length of water that extended to the craggy rock walls that protected the waters from the stormy rough deep sea.

Pre-dawn dark, yes, but he could see the froth of whitecaps past the curve of the Bay cliff. Down below in the harbor there were white halon lights on, outlining a half dozen rough and ready ships tied up at dock, taking shelter from the previous night's massive storms.

It wasn't quite time to move from mids watch to first watch, but behind him, past the doors, he heard early morning stirring, boots on the stone floor, the far off thunk of something being unloaded. To the left the noise that was the main mess readying breakfast, the thub thub of the air exchangers, the clang of metal service ware and the sound of the kitchen doors opening and closing as service was readied.

All the stirrings known and expected. Not very different than the Interforce bases north of them. Communal and insular, with the bounds of tradition firmly set, unchanged for generations here at this stakehold he now called home.

In the outer corridor, and beyond the huge main hall, the watch was changing. In operations, the mids ops were sitting with the incoming day ops, going over everything, anything and nothing that had gone on before going off to have their breakfast, and then go off shift.

It had, to him, a comforting structure and despite his history with this place he'd become accustomed to being here and realized some small time ago to his surprise that he'd come to like it.

Impossibly different than the space station he'd come from, yet there were things about the Bay that had come to fit him better, were a constant source of entertainment and provided a sense of surprising satisfaction at finding ways to move things along.

He looked around the kitchen, which was quiet and spare. It had its heating element, and the storage cabinet that would provide drinks and snacks, but he seldom had more than tea here. He spent his mealtimes in the mess with all the rest of the Bay, sharing whatever it provided without any fuss.

The stakeholder's family could choose to forgo that. There were times in the past when there'd been enough close family to fill up the compound of chambers and this room would have been active by now. A cook or two or an auntie there taking care of the family, and kids.

But there weren't any close kin of the stakeholder here now. Jess was one of the last of her immediate family, aside from Max, her uncle who stayed out on his boat and young Tayler, her nephew, who was off at the Interforce school. His mother and sister now lived in Quebec City.

The seniors had died in the fight. Almost an entire generation went with them. What they had most of right now were unskilled kids and scrubs, and many of the emptied slots had been filled by the bio alts he'd brought with him from station.

The irony of that was ethereally crunchy. Kurok smiled. He could have had his pick of housings, but he stayed here in one of the stakeholder's family residences because he knew it was expected of him as Jess's proxy and because, of course, the deepest of his connections to Drake's Bay had belonged here.

He'd selected one of the set of rooms on the far side of the kitchen from the stakeholder's quarters, three comfortably sized chambers chiseled with precision from the stone with broad, wide windows that showed the sea. He'd converted one into a   study. There was a comfortable bedroom and a large bathing room, and he felt himself very well housed indeed.

He heard boots behind him, and a tap. "Good morning." He remained looking out at the harbor as the door swung open and Mike, the head of security entered. "Have some tea." He pointed an elbow at the dispenser. "Rains stopped."

"Not bad, for o dark of the dark." Mike went to the dispenser and requested a cup. He was a towering figure, with heavy, broad shoulders and long muscular arms. He wore a Bay coverall of thick rugged fabric in a mix of steel blues and grays over a woven hoodie. The fabric bunched around his neck below his dark, short, cropped hair. "Good day for scraping the shore."

It was. Kurok sipped from his cup, enjoying the almost astringent taste of the tea, pungent and tannic. It was chilly, as it always was, and he was glad of the thick bay overshirt he wore that kept out the cold damp. "Goodness only knows what'll be washed up after that weather." He peered out. "Seems like we've got more company coming in. Two more hulls on the horizon there."

"Saw that." Mike came over with his tea and looked out. "More boats in."

"Two on a run down from Quebec," Kurok said. "We're becoming a popular stop."

Mike chuckled deep in his throat. "Gotta say," he remarked. "I thought that whole rig was a load of bs nothing. All that cavern and those plants." He glanced at Kurok. "One more thing I was crap ass wrong about. Whole thing turned out damn good."

Whole thing, Kurok knew, included him and the bio alt sets who'd shown up with him. "I think we're doing all right," he agreed mildly. "Seems like things worked out better than expected all round, hm?"

Mike chuckled again. Then he gave Kurok a quick side glance. "They got a pad ready in the number two docking bay," he said. "About polished the floor in there."

Kurok smiled his gentle smile. "I'm glad Jess is stopping by. We have a lot to show her." He sipped his tea. "Last time she came here, you know, she was pretty well convinced she was going to get shot by you all."

Mike didn't refute the mild accusation. "Nah. Too damn dangerous to try it," he said, straightforwardly. "We all knew it. All of ops saw her rip that dumb grunt apart with her bare hands. You'd get one shot, and you'd have to be dead on, or she'd pop your noggin off. She's the real deal, yeah? Drake both ways."

"Well, that is true."

"And we didn't want to," Mike went on, unexpectedly. "We wanted her here. We knew it would screw up everything probably, but we didn't care." He glanced at Kurok again. "We didn't want no more scams. But she did good, bringing you in, cause her walking out on the oath would have been a crap thing too."

Kurok nodded. "She certainly understood the challenges. She has that strategic mind, you know. Comes with the," he paused, "the territory."

Mike smiled. "Comes with the crazy. You ain't got to play word games here, Doc. We know about the crazy."

Kurok went to the cleanser and put his cup inside. "I know you do." He put his hands in the front pocket of his harbor shirt, with its embroidered Drake's Bay insignia on it. "But you know, living with Justin as long as I did, and spending the time I did at Canyon City, I can't think of it as crazy really, because it isn't."

Mike put his cup down. "Well, it ain't normal."

Dan Kurok looked at him, head cocked slightly to one side. "Isn't it?" He said. "How different is it, really?"

"C'mon doc. You seen what goes on. You seen what they do," Mike said. "You were in that. You know."

"Mm." Kurok gave a little half shrug. "Yes it's true that its brutal and dangerous, but I don't think it's crazy, I never have... it's a different mentation, yes." He took one hand out of his pouch pocket and tapped the side of his head. "Different pathways in the brain."

Mike shrugged as well. "You're the doc." He amiably pointed to the door. "Mess?"

"Mess," Kurok said and followed him out the door and down the short hallway, solid and dark carved into the stone of the mountain that held Drake's Bay. He deferred the discussion, understanding it would take a long time to budge Mike's view of it, seeing it as he did, from the inside.

Because, of course, he had it himself, the crazy. Just not quite enough to get taken for it.

Ah well. Kurok drew in a breath and released it, focusing on the day as they made their way between the thick rock walls. There were doors on either side leading to other suites of rooms, and then the large door at the end.

Mike pushed the door open, and they emerged into the central hall of the Bay, a huge cavern that went from rock floor to the ceiling far overhead, narrowing into a point that was capped by a roughly round transparent prismed block, battered by weather and impacts that nevertheless let in the light of dawn outside.

The cavern itself was enormous, with passageways leading off in many directions, some precision cut and exact, others carved out more haphazardly. On the left-hand side of the edge of the cavern was a massive wrought iron spiral staircase that went all the way up to the roof, landings splitting off to levels at regular intervals all along the perimeter.

It was vast, and impressive, and had a stark, eerie beauty that came from the unfinished slate stone walls and the mixture of evenly placed light fixtures and the pale upper glow. Raw and grand, never beautified, starkly overwhelming in its scale.

A hum of voices, echoed softly off the rock walls, and the patter of boots on the stairs as bio alts came down from their level five quarters.

He still smiled every time he saw them, now after six months an accepted part of the life of the Bay, mixing with the rough and towering locals, on their way to their daily work in utter content, blissfully happy to have good, needed jobs to do and people to do things for.

Never, in a million years had he ever expected to see that. A bizarre miracle of chance and circumstance, and in the end, a win win result. Unbelievable.

"Good morning, Doctor Dan," A KayTee, Kevin, was just pulling the sleeve of his pullover straight, ready to get some breakfast before he went to take a shift in Bay ops. "I heard NM-Dev-1 is going to visit today."

"That's right," Kurok said, aware of the bio alt heads turning at his voice all around him. "She's even bringing Jess Drake with her. So, I'm sure we're going to have a wonderful time today."

Mike chuckled under his breath.

Kevin, tall and dark haired, and trained for tech ops, smiled. "I think I will be on duty when they will arrive," he proudly told Doctor Dan. "It will be an excellent shift."

Kurok patted him on the shoulder as they entered the mess, getting into the flow of people sorting themselves out and finding a table. "Ah," he said, observing the trays being brought out. "Scrambled gulls' eggs and cockles. It is in fact going to be an excellent day."

****

It was, in fact, excellent flying weather. Dev planned a course that paralleled the coastline, and they were treated to clear air, and a view of the rolling foam touched breakers as they crashed against the towering rock walls.

Birds were awing, flying just over the water's surface to hunt, circling the precipices that held their nests. Despite their traveling speed they caught sight of a breaching whale offshore that made Dev want to slow down to watch.

She didn't though. She kept along the long, curving joining of sea and land that past the shore tumbled into bare and craggy cliffs and steep valleys where once forested land and humanity had been.

Jess had told her, in an offhand way, that once, while swimming near the coastline of the Bay she'd found a sunken city, really rubble, and Dev made a note to remind her of that, and see if they could, maybe on the way back, take the carrier down to the surface to look for it.

She glanced in the reflective panel over her station and watched Jess in it, enjoying the warm in-flight lights showing the clear twinkle of her eyes as she talked to April and outlined the distinctive shape of her face.

Dev smiled, then went back to her screens, making a slight adjustment to the course, flying by hand rather than using the automation for the sheer enjoyment of it. She boosted the engines a bit as she caught sight of the curving headland of the Bay in the distance.

She tweaked comms a little as they came within range of the Drake's Bay control ops. Right on time, she saw the return from the sensors, and waited expectantly, her head cocked slightly to one side. "Jess, we have contact."

"Drake's Bay control to incoming flight," a clear, confident, young sounding voice echoed in the bud in her ear. "Please identify."

Totally unnecessary, Dev knew. They were broadcasting their ident, and Drake's Bay absolutely knew who they were. She opened the channel. "Drake's Bay control, this is incoming Interforce flight BR270006 inbound to your location."

The voice came back at once. "Yes. You are expected BR270006. Bay 2 pad 1 is prepared for you." A pause. "Welcome, NM-Dev-1."

Dev smiled. "Thank you, Kevin," she responded. "I am accompanied by senior agent Jess Drake, agents April Anston and Mike Arias, and technicians Doug Sars and Chester Garcia."

"We have noted that, NM-Dev-1, welcome to all," Kevin responded. "Safe landing."

"Sounds calm," Jess said, relaxed in her chair. "Any action around the old rock pile, Dev?"

Dev studied the returns from her sensors. "There are eight vessels in the water docking area," she said. "And there are work crews out on shore, as well as on the front part of the cliff."

Jess unbuckled her restraints and stood up, moving forward to stand behind Dev's seat. She put her hands on the back of it and leaning forward to look out the open transparent shield. "Huh. There's Uncle Max," she said, after a brief pause. "Hey, Devvie, isn't that our old buddy Siggurd near the curve? Isn't that the old crate we stole?"

"Yes, I believe so," Dev said, checking her sensor return. "It will be interesting to see him."

"Probably all sheltering from that storm." Jess went back and dropped into her seat. "It was heading north when it came past the base. Hit here first."

"They cleaned up that harbor," April said, as Dev dropped altitude and banked to turn toward the flight bays. "Got the piers rebuilt too. Nice setup there."

"Put Interforce cred to good use." Jess smiled without much humor. "But yeah they extended the docking facility. They can fit in a few more boats along the north wall."

The bay of Drake's Bay was a huge promontory headland shaped in a rough circle of tall rock walls that extended down into the sea, providing a narrow entrance between the edges that allowed ships to pass into a sheltered open space of calm water.

At ground level, there were cavern openings, natural, that allowed smaller ships to sail all the way in to offload, while a ring of docks served the larger vessels along a steel rampway extending outward from a towering main cliff face that featured rows of carved windows and large metal hatches near the top.

One hatch was open, and as they drifted past the flash of arc welding was seen inside, along with the nose of the plasma battery gun that was hidden inside.

Dev came level with their assigned bay, the second from the top of the cliff and saw the metal doors open waiting for them. She slowed her forward speed and aimed for the pad, the Bay mechs well clear of the oncoming craft, umbilical power lines slung over their shoulders.

She cut the engines as she crossed into the docking cavern. She let her forward motion take the carrier in and over the pad, its extended skids touching down in the exact center without even a puff of the landing jets.

"Nice," Jess complimented.

"Thank you." The carrier settled into place, and Dev shunted power from the engines, turning on the secure lamps on the outside of the craft as the mechs came forward, waiting for her to unlock the power port on the outside. With a light touch, she did, then looked around the docking bay.

There were light flyers parked at the rear of it, two of them painted in Bay colors. The space was squared away and tidy, as neatly appointed as any back at the base. All signs of the previous damage she'd seen erased.

Dev shut down the carrier and released the lock on the hatch, as her passengers stood up and gathered up their things.

She waited for Doug to move out of the way then went to her cabinet and removed her pack. She set it on the ledge while she shrugged into her jacket.

Jess opened the hatch and stuck her head out. "Hey, scrub."

"Hey, cuz," the mech outside greeted her with a grin. "Sup?" He wore the typical Bay coverall, with a mech patch on the shoulder, but below it was a second emblem, a five-pointed star with an elliptical circle around it. He had shaggy brown hair and cinnamon hazel eyes, and the half grown look of a recently vacated adolescence about him.

Jess walked down the ramp and shrugged her pack onto her back. "Just taking a day of vaycay. What's the scoop here, Dusty?" She came over to stand next to the youngster, a cousin in truth to her, Dustin Drake, whose father had been her uncle.

"Hoo." Dustin shook his head. "Plenty of what the what, cuz. They got a lot for you to put your eyeballs on."

"Great." Jess hopped off the ramp and cleared the way for Mike, April, Doug, Chester, and last, Dev to exit. "Dusty I think you remember this bunch." She waved vaguely in their direction.

"Oh yeah, we rode a rocket together." April nodded. "Hey."

"Yo," Dustin said solemnly. "See ya." He finished locking down the umbilicals as they walked past him, toward the inner entry.

"He's one of the kids that went to station?" Mike said. "I think I remember seeing him when we got here."

"Yeah, he was the little scrub." Jess chuckled and led the way down the sloping ramp out of the docking bay and headed for the spiral stairs. "Let's go find the doc."

She looked around as they started down the steps, appreciating the impression of calm and order she saw all around them. They passed the storage levels and saw Bay residents and bios working at sorting and stocking bales and supplies, one battered lift plate covered in stacks of dried seaweed.

Jess smelled the tang of it on the air and nodded. "Shoreline must be full of that stuff from the storm. Make for good fish rolls." She gave Dev a wink.

Dev licked her lips in silence, looking forward to them. Several more levels down they passed the spacer's quarters, where all the bio alts lived. A glance sideways showed the whole area had been spruced up. There was now a large section, with comfortable chairs, just off the landing with worktables and a warming stove tucked to one side.

Two figures sat there poring over a screen, the light from it outlining their profiles as they talked softly to each other.

"That's where we stayed that last time," April said. "Those guys took it over? Good."

Dev was right behind her. "They did. The sets were very happy about it. They have sent me pictures of what they did to the insides of their spaces. It's nice. Really different than the creche on station was."

"I bet," April murmured. "I didn't see much of it up there but all of it was weird."

They continued downward and as they reached the second level they spotted several figures emerge from one of the lower corridors. They stopped and waved when they caught sight of them. "There's Doctor Dan," Dev said.

"And Mike," Jess added as they got to the bottom of the stairs and started across the huge cavern. "Everyone looks happy. So far so good."

"A hell of a lot happier than the last time we were here," April said. "Maybe we won't even have to sleep in a storage room or get weird looks in the mess."

****

April regarded the quarters she and Doug had been provided, which were large and high ceilinged, with windows cut into the rock walls that showed a nice view of the Bay. There were comfortable beds, sanitary units, and a dispenser area already stocked with bottled water and snacks. "Definitely better than a storage room."

"As nice as at the base," Doug said. "Probably was someone's crib who croaked in that last shootfest."

"Probably," April said. "Let's go on the tour. From that look on Kurok's face, something's up here." She glanced around the room one last time and then joined him in the hallway that connected the two. "This was the family area. I think they parked Jess down that hall there." She pointed to the right. "Def better."

"Def," Doug said. "And windows outside. Haven't seen that since I left home."

April laughed her low, ironic laugh. "Try living in a caravanserai. I'm fine with no windows thanks."

They made their way into the gathering area behind the kitchen, which had a large warming unit, and the huge, stone wall that bore name plaques on either side of element. Mike and Chester were already there, looking around.

"Nice," Mike said. "Did we see this last time? I don't think so."

"Memorial markers," April said. "Right side's just family. Left sides died in service. The red outline means they got the Star."

Mike looked up the length of the wall on the left, his eyes visibly moving back and forth. "Wow," he said. "I mean, we all went through school, and you heard about the Drakes but…" He studied the names. "It's different to see this like that."

April tipped her head back to look all the way up the hearthstone. "The Pater always argued with the Mater about coming here," she said. "He said there was no way to bargain with the Bay. Most of the time they didn't even have much to bargain with, but the Mater always said she liked the people." Her lips twitched into a brief grin. "My sibs said it was a shitfest when I got taken in here."

"Interesting point of view," Doug said. "Peeps are rough here."

"That's why she liked them." April glanced around as the inside door opened and Jess appeared, with Dev and Kurok in tow. "Ah, here we go."

"Digs okay?" Jess asked them.

"Sweet." April responded with a nod. "A lot nicer than the last time we showed up with you."

Kurok glanced at Jess in question. "Did we do something inappropriate?"

Jess chuckled. "No. When I came the first time, Jimmy decided to piss me off by housing us in the unwanted guest quarters."

Kurok's pale eyebrows shot up. "No chance of that now. The whole section's been repurposed," he said. "But anyway, shall we take a little tour? I think we've got time for that before lunch. We've got a lot of things you might be interested in."

His eyes twinkled, and Jess suspected she might be in for some pleasant surprises that she was more than willing to be distracted by. "Lead on," she said. Can't wait to see whatever the hell it is."

She could already see things were good. The inside of the homestead had been cleaned up and repaired from the attacks. The walls were patched, and the floor had been re-leveled and new stone laid over it.

She spotted the grins on faces as she was seen and recognized. She relaxed a little and returned some waves. "No guns this time," she muttered to Dev, who walked at her side, hands clasped behind her back.

"Seems optimal," Dev said and nodded in recognition as two bio alts paused in mid stride and made eye contact with her, giving her a thumbs up gesture that she stolidly returned.

They walked through the big cavern, which was full of the sounds of people and movement. Jess looked casually around as they went through and saw a relaxed mix of Bay residents and bio alts. She shook her head in wonder at how that synthesis had happened.

"No," Dan Kurok said. He walked on her other side, apparently reading her mind. "I still can't believe it either." He indicated one of the hallways. "Let's take a look at the thousand-ton whale first." He led the way down through a long, crooked passage, with newly chiseled walls and the smell of fresh caulk. "We decided to put in an inside entry, and close up the external one with that pointless hatchway."

"Smart," April said.

"Very," Jess said. "That was a mess."

"It was," Kurok agreed, as they passed a scan portal that brought the usual tickle to all of them, making Jess flex her hand a little. "I had your bioscan credentialed," he said. "It's not a lethal stop, but it would set off alarms and no one wanted that bit of embarrassment this morning." He gave Jess a droll, sideways glance.

Jess snickered.

He went to a newly mounted steel door at the end of the newly cut hallway and put his hand on a plate, which turned teal and opened in front of them. "So, now this cavern."

The door hissed a little with air displacement, then they breathed in a heady mix of air that carried the scent of plants and dirt and life, almost overwhelming in its richness.

Dev smiled. "Ah. I remember that smell from station."

"Me too," Kurok said. He led the way inside and they paused to look around. "We've extended it a bit," he added, clasping his hands behind his back.

Jess stared around the space, turning in a complete circle as she took in the stacked levels now building up toward the cavern ceiling with its embedded, steadily glowing golden crystal, where once a single platform had been. "Whoa."

"Yes," Kurok acknowledged the tone. "You know the sets I brought down here had biological training. They've done quite a job taking what was here originally and building it out," he said. "The crystalline structure of the roof, it seems, is a geological oddity, but one that is chemical and persistent."

Jess found it hard to take in. The cavern had been a simple workspace when she'd last seen it, an inner and outer ring of extruded tables full of trays with synth dirt in them, and some small variety of plants growing. Now, the levels of terraced platforms stretched all the way up to the ceiling in every direction, with a wide range of different types of things on them.

She looked at Kurok. "It's going to keep glowing?" She asked. "Is that what that means?"

"It is," Kurok said. "Originally that crystal was found here, and people thought it might be good for rad. It's not really. So, then it was just used for conveniently lit dry storage until someone," he paused and made a small shrug. "Someone thought, hey why not try growing a plant in here."

Jess regarded him. "Someone? Jimmy? No. He was dumb as a flatfish." She dismissed the idea. "Between them my two brothers couldn't have come up with that idea."

"Well, I certainly can't say as I never got to know either of them. I think it was someone who'd been either to Quebec, or the other side," Kurok said. "Who saw product from station and knew what it's value was." He regarded the terraces. "It doesn't really matter at this point, does it? It's here, and it does provide the radiation required for photosynthesis."

"Sure does," Doug said. He walked over to one of the platforms and studied it. "This one doesn't even have dirt."

They went over to examine it. It was a leafy plant with pleasant green leaves and some creamy white buds. It's roots were hanging down into a trough of liquid that was being visibly circulated.

"No, that's hydroponics," Dr. Dan said. "Station tech. But really, this hydroculture over here is something I'm prouder of." He drew their attention over to another platform that was full of thick bushes with small round objects growing on them, yet, dark green and tiny. "This is a clay-based particulate, hard fired that is found in abundance in the lower strata here at the Bay." He reached into the bins they were in and drew out a handful of roundish reddish-brown items and offered it to them. "It's volcanic in origin."

Jess took one. "It's light." She inspected it in surprise.

"It's in a way, a lightweight ceramic," Kurok said. "It works wonderfully as growing medium because it aerates the roots and it's porous. A lot better than the synth dirt." He turned and gestured around the chamber. "As you can see."

Dev looked at the rock. "This is interesting," she said. "It reminds me of the external shield tiling on station."

Doctor Dan nodded. "Yes. It's where I got the idea. I was working on seeing what could be done about protecting some of the fishing ships. They need saltwater protection but light- weight… anyway." He folded his arms. "So, this is what we ended up trying with it, and it's done quite well."

Doug fingered one of the small roundish buds on the tree. "What are these?" He leaned over and smelled it. "It's… spicy smelling?"

"Oranges," Doctor Dan replied. "They should be ripe in… oh… maybe a month, and then you can have a glass of orange juice from it. At any rate, we delivered a few things to some interested folks a couple of months ago and it was pretty well received."

Jess gazed around the cavern that was filling with quietly working bio alts, and several Bay residents. They moved amongst the plants with rough collecting sacks over their shoulders. She looked over at Doctor Dan. "A few things? That why we have eight hulls in the harbor?"

"It is," he said. "Once word got out, we started having trading ships show up here, offering catch for plants. Then they took the plants up the coast and made double what they would have for the fish."

"Oh, boy," Doug said.

Kurok now let the grin he'd been holding back appear. "Which was lovely, since the people here prefer eating fish to plants. Win win all round, as they say. It's somewhat of a cash crop. And it's a way to get the stock delivered with no effort on our part, though I suspect quite soon the Drake's Bay fleet is going to expand." He cleared his throat a little. "As we've already filled the coffers back up from what we spent repairing everything."

Jess slid the small rock into her pocket. "That's why Uncle Max is here. We haven't heard anything about this at base. Jason would have said something."

April came back from inspecting the plant with its roots in the water. "Not a damn thing. Not even whispers in ops."

"No," Kurok said. "The general sense was, after that last round of shenanigans, best not advertise. However, you obviously have a right to know about it. I wouldn't, if I were you, tell anyone else," he told Jess somberly. "No one really wants to go through that all again, so this has all been done in complicit silence." He gestured around vaguely at the cavern.

"Smart," April echoed her early comment. "Nomads are going to find out though. Surprised they're not sniffing around.

they knew about that first set of plants." She eyed Kurok appraisingly. "Then everyone on the planet will know."

Doctor Dan exhaled. "That's why I'm very glad you stopped by. I think we probably better discuss some kind of plan," he said. "I was about to ask you to visit when I got your note that you were on your way here."

Doug pointed into the distance. "What's that over there? Those colored things."

"Those are flowers," Doctor Dan said and waved them on. "Come smell them. Dev knows what they are." He started toward the far side of the space. "And if you see over there, they've opened a little entranceway. There's another cavern beyond that wall with more of that crystal. Smaller, but useful." We found it when they were drilling for a water supply."

"Oh, boy," Doug said again. "This is gonna be a thing."

"Oh, yeah," Chester said, his eyes wide as they walked along. "A gigantic, huge thing."

****

They ended up back in the stakeholder's compound, taking seats in the gathering room Jess had last been in during her mother's processing out.

Jess settled into one of the chairs just to the side of the hearthstone. She hiked one knee up over the other as a bio alt came in with a tray of grape tea.

"Thank you, Billy," Kurok said. "How are your classes going?"

The bio alt set the tray down. "I like them, Doctor Dan. I think it will take some time to understand, but my instructor seems to think I have done well."

"Great." Doctor Dan waited for the bio alt to leave, then he turned to them and sighed. "He's in training to work in the kitchens, if they'll let me put him in there."

Dev went over and retrieved two cups of the steaming tea and brought one to Jess. "The sets seem very happy, Doctor Dan."

He nodded. "They certainly are. Much to my absolute surprise."

Doug came over behind her and picked up the tray, moving around to offer cups to the rest of them. "This place really seems a lot more... uh..."

"Normal?" April suggested dryly. "Like less shoot filled nuts and more, hey we're just living here now?"

Doctor Dan put his hands behind his head. "Well, that's all likely true. You know we all really didn't have much expectation of… I at least had no idea what was going to happen after we got here. We just took it one day at a time."

"Us too, back at 10," April said. "I think we all got scratch pads with who was on what side still."

"Right," Doctor Dan said. "I mean, we all went through quite a bit of chaos here," he said. "It started very quietly, with the plants. We, or at least I, wasn't sure how to go about making it into a real trading offering, you know? There wasn't that much of any of it."

"Just a tree or whatever of things. I remember," Jess said, her hands clasped around the mug. "No volume."

"Right," Kurok said, drawing the word out. "At first it was just ... well, sort of a novelty? One of the boats asked me for some veg, you know, to stretch out the fish stew at sea. We handed over some squash, okra, a box of bell peppers and potatoes because that's what was ready. I didn't think much of it. I figured if it made things better for individuals here, well, that's what they'd hoped for at first, wasn't it?"

"All those people hammering on the doors here, figured it would be all ready for em?" Doug asked. "I mean, there weren't that many of those things then, and it takes time doesn't it?"

"It does, and that's what I told Dee, and Jean and the rest of them. Yes, we'd deal with them, but we needed to sort ourselves out first," Kurok said. "And that it would take time for that."

Dev settled on the arm of the large chair Jess was in and sipped her tea, just listening.

"What's a potato?" Jess whispered.

"It's a starchy root vegetable. You have consumed some," Dev told her. "It was in those frozen meals we had at North Pole."

Jess stared at her, eyes narrowed for a moment. "The white stuff?" She asked, her dark eyebrows hiking.

"Yes."

"Huh."

"Now, about the boat," Kurok said. "Your Uncle Max's boat in fact. They pulled in someplace a little up the coast and ran into some shore collectors from Hawkstown. They hadn't had a chance to use any of the veg, but the collectors had limpets and crab, and Max had a half load of net fish. So, they traded and sat down to make a stew and ended up reinventing some- thing called jambalaya.

"What is that?" April asked.

"Spicy seafood and vegetables," Kurok said, "mostly with some of that water grain they used for the fish rolls. At any rate, they ended up selling it at Little Quebec dock and made more than they would have wholesaling catch. Very popular."

"I see where this is going," Jess said. "Gulls don't poop on Max," she said. "He spilled to the other captains."

"Next thing I knew, two more boats showed up, full of catch, looking to trade," Kurok said. "So of course, we did. I mean, we had to do something with the produce anyway at that point since the photosynthesis turned out more efficient than I'd expected, and things were moving right along in the cavern."

"Aside from just eat it?" April asked. "I mean, you could have."

"We could. Some of it. Some of the root veg, and onions and the like were in that stew you had for lunch in fact. Homely veg, but they like it here," Kurok said. "But the fancy stuff, everyone stood up and said, hell no, sell it. Trade it. Let's get cred going. That's what we did."

Jess watched him intently. "Then you started to think, what else can we make?"

Kurok nodded at her. "Yes, we started to think about how to branch out. What would people really like? What would be sturdy enough to take a boat trip?" He ticked off his fingers. "What could we dry, what could we make into jams, for long storage, and so forth."

Jess nodded. "What did they have on the other side? But you'd need to get more seeds, right? There weren't that many different things here."

"Certainly, but seeds don't... well, they do grow on trees," Kurok said, drolly, "but there aren't any trees. I couldn't just make a call up to the bio station now, could I? So, what I did was order science gear." He smiled gently at her. "That cost some cred. But with that, I could make more seeds, because, after all, that's the business I was in." He paused, eyes twinkling. "Carrots are considerably easier than Dev was."

There was a moment of pensive silence. "I like carrots," Dev finally said. "They're crunchy."

Jess blinked a few times. "Does anyone around here realize that's what you're doing?" Her voice sounded slightly incredulous.

He shrugged. "They know we've got new crops. One would also assume they remember I'm a geneticist. It's not a far leap to put those together and get a conclusion. Cathy, my assistant, knows. The lab workers and the sets of course take it for granted." He extended his legs and crossed them at the ankle. "As long as we keep everything in small batches, like they were boutique things, I think we're okay." He exhaled. "For now."

"For now," April said. "But once everyone knows you can make what they want, that's a whole other thing."

"Absolutely," Mike echoed. "If it was any place but here, holy crap, you'd have people crawling all over you."

"We would have a lot more intense, and possibly dangerous interest. True," Kurok said, calmly. "Anywhere but here. Everyone knows, especially after that last go round, that this place is not the place to knock down doors if you want to keep your head on your shoulders."

"Just like Interforce found out," Jess said, "but eventually everyone's going to want a piece of this." She swirled sea grape tea in her cup and took a sip of it. "That why they were shining up the plasma gun?" She asked. "We saw them in there on the way in."

"That's what Security Mike wants to talk to you about after dinner," Kurok said. "About what we're going to need to protect what's here, both the plants and the people." He sighed. "As it turns out it's a lucky thing you decided to drop by." He glanced at the rest of them. "All of you at base? Must be a slow week."

"Oh, that's right we haven't told you yet." Jess leaned back in her chair, kicking out a booted foot in an oddly adolescent motion. "We're grounded."

"Excuse me, what?"

"All of us, told to stay around base," April said. "Some scam with the politicos. Some talks or something, trying to work out how to make a truce or whatever."

"Again?" Kurok said. "C'mon now people, really? Do they not remember how that ended the last time?" He looked at the ceiling in some exasperation. Then looked over at them. "I'm guessing this place is considered—around base—then?"

Jess grinned a little. "I figure Jason knows the fewer of us around the less trouble we'll get into."

"Not that many of us anyway," Mike said, after a brief pause. "It was kinda ghoulish in the pit yesterday." He glanced aside, then back across at Jess. "Glad we came out here. It's a lot more…uh… lively."

"Well, I'm glad, too, if it ended up with you lot visiting," Kurok said. "I really wasn't comfortable with you not knowing, Jess. I just didn't want to put it on comms, after that last go round." He pushed himself to his feet. "Anyway, now that you've been brought up to speed, lets show you the rest of what's been done here."

"More surprises?" Jess asked. "Not sure I can take more like that."

Kurok chuckled. "No, just fixing and improvement. Hopefully I've stood up to your trust in leaving me here to run the   place."

****

Jess sat on the bed in the quarters she'd been given and looked out the thick, plas window that curved along the wall that was the outer edge of the space.

It felt strange. She had so few real memories of living here at the Bay, but the ones she had were of being inside stone, the lower corridors, running around in the storage rooms. Swimming, first in the protected inside waters of the Bay, and then on the small beach she'd taken Dev to the last time they were here.

She knew she'd been in this room, it had belonged to her parents after all, but it struck no real chord with her and there was nothing in the décor of it, clean and neatly kept, that triggered any images. Nothing of them were here. All of her father's things were at Base 10, and they'd emptied out her mother's things after she died.

It was a large space, this wide bedroom with its long, curved window and an alcove where there were chairs and a warming stone, two smaller rooms, one of which she thought maybe had been her father's study, and a small utility space with a drink dispenser and a big sanitary room almost a dead ringer for the one in her own quarters, at the base.

But it was nice to see the birds floating in the air outside and the clouds on the horizon, the sky already darkening with the oncoming night. She got up and went over to the window and rested her hands on the curved edge of the rock outline over her head. She watched a patrol flyer drift past.

There was a faint knock at the door, and she turned. "C'mon in."

The door opened and Dev came inside, her hair disheveled, a smudge of dirt on her nose. "Hello."

"Hey, Devvie. Where were ya?" Jess came over to her and paused when Dev moved one of her hands from behind her back and extended it toward her. She held a deep red object in her fingers. "What's that?"

"It's a flower," Dev said. "It's for you."

Jess stared at the thing for a second, then in reflex she took it, surprised at what it felt like. "Oh, it's weird," she said and squeezed it very gently between her fingertips. "It's... bunchy."

Dev's eyes twinkled.

Jess looked at her. "What am I supposed to do with it?"

"I have no idea." Dev said. "I just remembered that you told me that natural born people, a long time ago, gave people flowers when they liked them. I saw a bush full of them in the cavern and Doctor Dan said I could have one to give to you."

Jess felt herself blush. "Ah." She lifted the thing up and sniffed it. The scent was sweet and a little spicy, the flower layers and layers of smooth, curved petals with ends that reminded her of fish fins. "Can you eat them?"

"I definitely never tried," Dev said, "I just thought it was pretty, like you are. Doctor Dan said it was a rose. He said it had to be picked since it was finished growing, and he already harvested the pollen. It would have fallen off and expired in any case so he said I could take it."

Jess took a step back and sat down again on the bed. She studied the round bloom in the palm of her hand. Around them the lights came in, warm and golden, reacting to the growing darkness outside. One of them caught the flower in her hand, clearly showing its natural structure. "It's nice."

Dev came over and sat next to Jess. "It's really amazing all the good work they've done here isn't it?" she said. "I found out about the patch your relative was wearing where we parked the carrier, the one with the star on it. It means they went to the bio station."

"Yeah?" Jess looked up from the flower. "The kids, you mean."

Dev nodded. "The sets made them for the ones who went there. Because they helped bring them here, and that was an excellent thing. The sets really like it here. They were very happy when they were told the patches were excellent and everyone wore them."

Jess gave her a sideways look, a bit of her dark hair falling to obscure one eye. "Did you say I was pretty?"

"Yes," Dev confirmed in a mild tone. "Is that suboptimal?"

"No." Jess's lips twitched, then she smiled. "Just unusual." She admired the rose quietly. "I'm glad those kids are having a good life here. It would have stunk if we'd gone through all that to get them down then they'd hated it."

"Me as well," Dev said, "It's excellent that we came here. I like seeing the sets so happy very much."

Jess thought about that as they sat quietly together. It had turned out pretty good that they'd come, she felt. She'd found out about all the new plants and seen how the homestead had fixed things up since she'd almost caused it to self-implode. It made her feel better about things and figured the rest of the residents were glad she'd done what she'd done in the end. "Yeah, it's pretty good," she said.

"They're doing an excellent job fixing up that place in the area outside," Dev said. "Doctor Dan said it would make good housings."

"People'll start showing up wanting them," Jess predicted. "Like they do up in Quebec. They'll hang around the edges until they stick." She shifted, extending her long legs out and regarding them. "They see a chance to make some cred."

"Oh, Jess." Dev half turned to face her. "Speaking of that. Kevin told me something today. He said the sets were getting... they had cards, and ops said they could use them to get things."

Jess eyed her. "Yeah. Cred chits. They're getting paid," she said. "They work, they get paid. That's how that goes here." She looked at Dev. "Like you do, back at Base."

Dev blinked at her in silence, one pale eyebrow hiking up.

"You did know you were getting paid, right?" Jess said. "You have citizen credentials, Dev. Interforce can't have a citizen out there flying loop de loops and risking their skin and not pay them."

"I don't really have those, Jess. That's just for our work," Dev said, in a serious tone. "I'm a bio alt. I'm contracted. I know I use my ident at the base, but I'm not really a citizen."

Jess leaned back on her hands on the bed. "Oh," she said, suddenly. "You thought the fact you can go into the base store and get things was just tied to being a tech?"

"Isn't it?" Dev asked. "At the creche, if you did something with excellence, proctor might give you a chit, and you could take that and get an extra ration, or some sweet puffs. It's the same, isn't it?"

Jess shook her head. "That ident you have is tied to the cred system. I'm sure you don't get paid what you're worth, but you get paid. We can look when we get back." She smiled. "See how much you stocked up in there. Most of the techs just save a lot of it until they retire. Some spend it. Tucker bought a light flyer. He keeps it in one of the unused storage caves."

"That sounds so strange," Dev said, in a tentative tone. "We're given everything we need there. Why should they give us something else? That's what the sets asked me here. They don't understand."

Jess let herself down flat on the bed and spread her arms out. "Why should they pay you," she mused. "How it works here at the Bay is like this, Devvie. Kids get old enough to take the battery. The junior maniacs they send to Interforce, to Canyon City."

Dev studied her seriously, nodding as she spoke.

"The rest of the kids get sorted into proficiencies. Here at the Bay, they get apprenticed," Jess continued. "When they get old enough, if they're good, they qualify for a workload, a basic rating that gets you a bunk and mess, but no pay. And then, if you got skills, and there's a position we need, a slot, you get that slot and an allotment. You get paid cred, just like we do at Base, for what you do."

Dev blinked.

"If you can't do anything useful, you get booted out into the back beyond to scrape algae," Jess said. "Scavengers. You saw em."

Dev frowned. "You make them leave?" She ventured hesitantly. "Like the people we saw at that admin place?" She had a brief internal flash memory of the ragged, hungry looking figures ducking behind crates and boxes, looking for scraps. "And the ones that..."

"The ones I blew up in the cave? Yeah," Jess said. "Same ones I broke my stupid brother's neck for screwing over. Equal opportunity homicidal maniac here." She held up a hand and then let it drop to her stomach. "Most of them croak anyway. If they weren't good enough to even get a custodial workload that's not a bad thing, y'know?"

Dev regarded her noncommittally.

"No, huh?" Jess wrinkled her nose a bit.

Dev remained silent for a minute, her eyes moving slightly. "We're all purpose made," she finally said. "But I remember one of the proctors talking about a set that didn't work out, and they were put down." She paused. "Is it like that?"

"Kinda," Jess said. "Except without all the white lab coats and cool space bounce rooms. You just die and get eaten by seagulls and crabs."

"Nonoptimal."

"Yeah," Jess said, "it's better to be a rock star. If you test in for Interforce, your family gets a bonus and a chunk of cred for ya, because they know they lost you for a slot. So, a big chunk of the cred that kept this place intermittently going all these years was our little family insanity problem."

She watched Dev reach up and pinch the bridge of her nose,

a motion she'd come to understand was Dev's way of trying to reconcile her native intelligence, and given knowledge, with an alien concept. "If the Bay's giving your buds an allotment, it really means they like them and want them here," Jess said. She reached over and patted Dev's leg. "It's all good."

A scant allotment, Jess figured. Spending money, so the kids could, if nomads visited with their trading train, get some little things for themselves. She could see it. "Weird for them huh?"

"Weird for me as well," Dev finally said. She gave her head a rapid little shake. "They really don't know what's going on with that because we never own anything, Jess." Dev lay down on her side and looked solemnly at Jess. "We're not allowed to. I had to get a special permit from Doctor Dan just to keep my book. If anyone gave one of us anything we had to give it up to our proctor."

Jess shrugged and made a face. "Different place, different rules," she said. "Bay ain't changing any time soon. Tell em to suck it up. It's a good thing."

Dev laughed faintly. "Of course, it's super optimal, Jess. I wouldn't want to change any of it. I'll try to explain to them tomorrow before we leave. I know they'll be happy about it."

Jess still had the rose in her hand and now she extended her hand with it cupped in her palm. "Thanks for the flower, Devvie. I like it." She gave the thing a sideways glance. "First time anyone's given me anything like it." She smiled briefly. "Or anything, really. You're the only one who does that."

Dev reached across and laid her fingers on Jess's wrist, above where the rose was. "Thank you for being so wonderful, Jess. I think I'm so lucky I met you."

Jess's pale eyes twinkled in wry appreciation. "Even if we're probably going to get killed together?"

"Even if," Dev said firmly. "If I have to be made dead, I want it to be with you, and I will try to do it with excellence."

Jess started laughing, her low melodic laugh that was just a little sound, and a lot of vibration. "Ah, Devvie. Let's put our Bay rags on and go see what they got for dinner. Nobody's getting made dead tonight."

Chapter Three

Dev looked around the big room, as they waited for the large bins and trays of food to be brought out. There were lots of people, both natural born and bio alts there, seated around the oval tables and the room was full of the hum of conversation all around them.

The smell of spice, and the tang of beer, was in the air. She saw runners passing out pitchers and the round, iron soup pots and bowls that went with them.

Jess sat next to her, and on their side of the oval table were Mike, April, Chester and Doug. Across from them Doctor Dan sat, along with his assistant, Cathy, Jess's Uncle Max, and their nautical friend Captain Siggurd, who kept winking at her for some unknown reason.

She and Jess wore the sea colored overshirts from the Bay, and she was glad to have the warmth of that around her as she sat quietly and listened to the talk. The people around her were in much better spirits since the last time they'd visited, and she could see the frequent glances towards their table.

Their soup arrived and Jess stood up and served around the bowls of it. She set a bowl in front of Dev with a little nudge against her leg.

Dev picked up her spoon and inspected the contents of the bowl, a medium thick liquid full of fish bits, with chunks of the tubular seaweed she particularly liked. She tasted it and nodded in pleasure, enjoying the crunch of the tubes and the chewiness of the fish.

"Storm was a kick ass," Siggurd said. "Glad we held off leaving. Woulda rolled your keel over, Maxie."

"Woulda," Uncle Max agreed. "We can chase it up the coast. Quebec'll be glad to see us." He chuckled, and so did Siggurd. "Hey, Jessie, what's this I hear about the Base being shut down?" He focused on her. "People there losing their minds again?"

Jess sat down with her own bowl and drank directly from it, sipping from the edge. She shrugged. "Political crap."

Mike cleared his throat. "They told us yesterday we were confined to base while they have some talks going on with the other side," he said. "I guess so many corpses on both sides got some attention."

Siggurd snorted and rolled his eyes. "Been that for a long time, they just never saw it out west."

Max nodded. "Truth. I saw their faces when they got blowed up here. You saw em."

"I saw them," Kurok said. "In fact, I ran into some of them as they were on their way out the back door. You're right. They weren't expecting what they got."

Sig shook his head. "Ain't gonna do nothing with that talking. Tried that a thousand times. All comes back to the same thing—you want what I got."

"Or keep them from getting more than we got," Jess said thoughtfully.

"That too," Max said. "Every couple years some jelly head puts out the idea of working together instead, and they talk around in a circle for a month."

"Then everyone gets bored and starts shooting," April said solemnly. "That's what my Mater always said, and since we're the ones who do the shooting, I guess if they keep us away from each other for a while at least they get tank capacity back."

A tray arrived with mounds of fish portions and thick leafy seaweed piled together, along with a scattering of steamed clams. The tall Bay server set the platter down and nudged it forward with his hip, then took out a stack of plas plates from the bag on his back and dropped them next to it. "Yo." He gave them all a nod and jogged off for another load.

Sig helped himself to some of the tray's contents. "They rebuilt Highland Market. That's where I'm heading next." He gave Jess a brief grin. "Gonna see if they want some of this stuff you made here."

"Highland Market," Kurok mused. "My gosh I haven't been there in a long while. Didn't I hear that volcano let loose again?"

"While we were there," Jess said, motioning to Dev. "With his boat." She jerked her head towards Sig. "Glad they got rolling again. That place is twisted fun said. You liked it, didn'tcha Dev?"

Dev considered her memories of the island, with its lines of stalls and exotic merchandise. And the spa where they'd hid out and gotten haircuts. "I did." She said. "Did all the people come back there?" She asked Sig. "That's where those black rocks came from."

"Figured," Sig said. "Charles got out and his crew, so they're back. Who's back from the sellers? I'll tell ya when I get back." He turned his head. "Wanna go with, Maxie?"

"Might do that." Max leaned against the low back of his chair. "See if we get a better trade than we did at Quebec Main the last time." He nodded at Jess. "Bay's been looking for a trade angle since it spun up. Damned if it didn't take almost blowing it up to find one."

Jess looked at him sharply, but his expression was mild. "Wasn't really the plan."

"All's well that ends to our advantage, Jessie. You squared it." Max waved his hand expansively. "Best fishing's after a storm."

Sig nodded solemnly. "Truth. You should come with me again, kids." He squinted at Jess. "Since you ain't got nothing to do right now."

Doug leaned over and whispered to April. "You think being space sick is bad?"

April snorted.

Jess just smiled. "Not this time. I want to see how this all settles out." She took a sip out of the mug she'd been served with. "But thanks for the offer."

Dev took a sip from her own mug, finding a light, effervescent beverage with a spicy tang that washed down the fish and seaweed nicely. She was glad Jess turned down the unexpected offer, though she'd learned a lot on the trip and enjoyed driving the boat.

Too much right now was changing. Better to do as Jess said, and let things settle down.

Kurok cleared his throat. "Speaking of sticking around though," he said to Jess. "We have two trading caravans arriving tomorrow, and apparently that means we've declared a market day. I suspect it won't be as exciting as Highland but maybe you want to stay over another night and enjoy?"

"Market day?" Max eyed him with interest. "Haven't heard of us having one of those in years. And two in at once?"

"Word's spreading," Sig said. "Tolja."

Kurok swirled his cup, his eyes twinkling. "Well, we have things to trade now. Who knows what will show up?"

****

Dev walked across the huge hall toward the spiral staircase, where ahead of her she saw a small crowd of bio alts climbing up to their level, their soft chatter audible to her as a buzzing echo in the tall chamber.

She'd arranged to meet with the sets after dinner, since it now appeared that the following day would be more interesting than expected, and they would be spending a second night at the Bay.

She was glad. The thought of spending a second day with the opportunity to shop and bargain was very appealing. She expected the sets would enjoy it as well. Jess was happy they'd been asked and sent a message back to Base 10 that their return would be delayed.

The other agents and techs were also happy about it, once April clarified that it wasn't her own nomad family who was arriving. Everyone looked forward to the closest thing they would likely see to a party any time soon.

All good. Jess went to talk to some of the Bay ops team, and so she was left to her own plans for a while. She reached the stairs and started up to fulfill them.

"Dev!"

Dev paused on the third level, as she saw a young woman coming toward her. "Hello."

Cathy, Doctor Dan's young assistant came to the stairs and put her hands on the metal rail that edged the floor boundary. "Are you going up to five?"

Cathy had been one of her proctors when she'd taken some of her advanced studies. Dev had always liked her. "I am. I wanted to have a chat with the sets and learn about all the things they've been doing," she said. "How are you?"

Cathy smiled at her. "Really, much better now. It's so much better here, you know? When we first arrived, it was so scary."

Dev nodded. "Yes, very suboptimal, however, more optimal than remaining on station. But things worked out better than anyone thought they might I think."

Cathy nodded back. "They did. I want to say I miss station and all the people and things there, but you know, I don't. It's better here. The sets are happy, they're treated well, they all have great work to do, and best of all, Doctor Dan gets to make things however he wants to. No politics."

Most bio alts looked past the politics. But Dev nodded, because she knew that Cathy knew she understood them better than most. "It was very good that Jess put him in charge here. He's doing amazing things." Dev paused. "Have you heard anything about what happened up on station?"

Officially, they had. A crisp, impersonal short report of an attack by the other side on the bio station, and a commendation to various Interforce personnel, namely herself and Jess, and April, Doug, Mike, and Chester for responding and repelling it. Details about the enemy shuttle latching on, and pictures of dead enemy agents exposed to the vacuum of space.

When Jess read it she literally rolled off her chair laughing.

Dev hadn't really thought it was amusing but at least they hadn't gotten in terrible trouble over it, so she supposed it was all right. There was no mention of them stealing a space shuttle, and not a peep about all the chaos, or that Doctor Dan had left with all the sets.

Cathy leaned on the railing. "Sort of," she said. "One of the lab techs there sent me a note. It was terrible after, of course."

"Yes," Dev said. "Jess knew it would be."

"It was all mixed up. But somehow, I'm not sure how it happened…" She looked in either direction. "Everything got blamed on Doctor Doss." She lowered her voice. "The sets and everything. All the things Doctor Dan did… there's no record of them."

"No," Dev said, "Doctor Dan made sure of that. I saw the routines he was running. It would have looked like damage to the main storage from all the power flux."

Cathy nodded. "So, the sets ended up okay."

Dev let out a held breath. "That's excellent." There'd been no word at all about the sets in any of the official reports. Almost as if they weren't important enough to mention, but Jess told her it was better not to ask and draw attention to them.

"I mean," Cathy said, "some of them got hurt and so did some of the citizens, you know, when the dock blew. But they put Doctor Michaels in charge, and so far it's—they're just trying to get things back together."

"That's moderately optimal," Dev concluded.

Cathy took a breath. "But then what I heard was, the report said that Doctor Doss made a deal with the other side, and then they came and damaged station when he broke it."

"That's actually what did happen," Dev remarked placidly.

"Really?" Cathy said. "I didn't want to ask Doctor Dan about it, because I think he feels bad. I mean, about leaving and the sets and all. I told him the sets were okay, and he liked that."

It occurred to Dev in that instant that while Cathy was very loyal, and friendly, and a good lab technician, she wasn't really that smart. "Yes. He was concerned. But I am glad it all worked out," she said, and I am also glad you are happy as well. I know Doctor Dan values your presence."

Cathy's face broke into to a large smile. "Oh, thank you, Dev!" She reached out and touched Dev's arm. "I really appreciate you saying that. Anyway, don't let me hold you up. Are you staying for the market tomorrow? Everyone seems to be really excited about it, like the gatherings we used to do on station."

"We are, yes," Dev said. "I think we are all looking forward to it as well." She lifted her hand in farewell, and then continued up the spiral stairs, moving to one side as Jess's cousin, the young man from the dock, came down the steps. "Hello."

"Yo, Rocket," Dustin greeted her casually. "Sup?"

He kept on going, and exited on the third level, where apparently Cathy was waiting for him. They both disappeared under the next floor level out of her sight. Dev concluded his brief utterance had not been so much of a question but some sort of greeting that didn't necessarily need to be answered.

Natural born. She shook her head as she reached the fifth level and stepped onto the rock floor, the walls here the same chiseled uniformity as the ones downstairs. The floors here were covered in sea wrack weave throws, as had been in the quarters she'd been issued, and there were decorations on the walls.

Kevin spotted her. "NM-Dev-1, we were waiting for you. Come over here to our gathering area."

Dev felt a sense of almost relief in joining the assembled sets. There was a commonality between her, and the other bio alts. They shared a lot of things she often struggled with in dealing with natural born.

Like suboptimal linguistic utterances. "Hello!" She greeted them, as they came into the space, where there was a heating stone and comfortable seats extending around it. The sets filed in, and they all took seats around the area.

The sets were all dressed somewhat differently. Most wore the Bay coverall, but all had some coloring or marking that indicated where they worked. Dev noticed that even the same birth year sets all looked a little different.

A different way of combing their hair or wearing their boots. The uniformity of the creche was greatly diminished. Dev thought that was excellent. She remembered her own urge to show off her differences when she'd come back to station. "This space is really nice."

"Isn't it?" An Ayebee called Alvin came and sat next to her. "We can't all fit in here at once, but we work different times so that is all right. It's so nice to have someplace to just sit and have a talk, with some hot beverage where it's warm."

Dev nodded and looked around. "You have made this very attractive. She studied some square items on the wall. Are those seashells?"

"Yes," Alvin said. "We get them from the area outside near the water. They have colors, and they look attractive when put in a pattern, don't they?" He looked at the nearest of them, with a nod of satisfaction. "We made those, and we made some for the natural born as well."

Kevin came over to join them and offered Dev a cup of sea grape tea. "We even found a way to use remainders of fishing wire and shells to make bracelets. See?" He rolled up his sleeve and showed Dev his wrist."

Dev looked closely at it. "That's very attractive! Really nice!"

Kevin sat down, visibly pleased. "I never thought having an assignment was going to be like this," he said. "I wanted to do good work, even hard work, but I always thought I would be treated like we were in the creche."

Dev, who had seen bio alts treated far worse in other places, remained silent.

"They're happy when we help," Alvin said. "Like they don't expect us to."

The sets pondered that and then looked at Dev in question.

Dev understood the question. She was a bit unsure of how to answer it. "They were not used to bio alts here at all." she finally said. "I think... I think they are used to people fighting them. And they expect other natural born to be mean and take things."

Kevin nodded. "Yes, they speak about that in operations. They watch for incorrect people coming here. And they talk a lot about Agent Jess. They really like her... and they like that she made a lot of other natural born dead." He paused. "Which is confusing." He made a little face.

"It's confusing," Dev agreed without trying to explain. "So, because they think that way, I think it surprised them that all we wanted to do was help them and make them happy. That's very special to them and very new."

"Yes," Alvin said. "And because we make them happy and help them, they want to take care of us and ensure we are well. It's awesome."

"It's awesome," the rest of the sets echoed a soft murmur of sound that tickled Dev's ears.

"I'm so glad we got picked to come down here from station," a female bio alt said. "Really glad, you know?" She wore a patch on her shoulder that matched the one that Dustin had.

"Me too, Tina," Dev called up her name, and her designation, TeeBee, from memory. "We are here, and we have natural born to take care of, and Doctor Dan is here making things with excellence. It's really optimal." She glanced around at the sets, and all the now slightly different faces looking back at her and felt happy. "The market tomorrow should be interesting."

A lot of voices murmured, and heads nodded.

"I have found out about those cards Kevin told me about," Dev said. "Here is the meaning of that."

The sets clustered closer, some took out the cards, glancing down as Dev started into her explanation. She hoped it would make more sense to them, than it had to her.

****

Jess settled into one of the large, comfortable chairs in front of the hearthstone in the family compound. Dan Kurok and Mike sat across from her, all three of them sipping from steaming mugs of some rich, spicy beverage of Bay concoction that scented the air with fragrance.

There was alcohol in it. Jess couldn't tell from the taste what else was, but it reminded her of the grog they served at the base during celebrations, and she figured now she knew the source of that.

Surprising to her, when she thought about it, how much of what Base 10 day to day was, had apparently come from here from the sanitary spaces to the hydro to the soap and now apparently the grog.

Even knowing how many of her family had been taken didn't really account for it. It wasn't as if they'd been the majority anywhere.

It was good, though, and she leaned back in her chair and waited for Mike to make his pitch.

"Got that whole area in the back beyond cleaned out," he started, extending his big, booted feet across the stone floor. "Figure we can set those two vans up in that pair of caverns in the west side." He studied Jess over the rim of his cup. "East side's good for shelter."

"Nice space," Jess finally said. "Lot of people going to want to park their asses there. They know there might be cred and leavings here now."

Mike nodded. "Not worried about the scroungers. Worried about all the other stakeholds ganging up and deciding to come in here."

"They're not that stupid," Kurok said. "I've spoken to Dee; she knows most of them." He held up a hand when Mike went to protest. "Yes, they would like what we have here, they're jealous of us having it, everyone knows that. But everyone around here also knows what this place is."

"That'll keep em back for a while," Mike said. "But not

forever, and not everyone's from round here, doc. More word gets out, more folks'll come by. You know it. I know it." He looked over at Jess. "And you know it better than anyone does. Used to be we had Interforce to back us up."

Jess nodded.

"Now?" Mike shrugged. "After what they did? Yeah they paid us off, and that put a patch on but no way no how I trust them. No way." He stared at Jess, as though expecting her to protest.

"No, me either," Jess said, mildly. "But at least if I'm inside, that puts a cramp on them."

"Doubt it."

"What's your idea then?" Jess asked, crossing her ankles, the collar of the woven Bay shirt brushing against the lobes of her ears. "We can only break open the armory so many times, and most of that stuff is so old it'll do us more damage than them."

"Make our own Interforce," Mike responded, and then stopped talking.

There was a long silence. "Well," Doctor Kurok finally said. "That's ambitious." He took a sip from his mug. "I'm not sure I was expecting that."

"What the hell does that mean?" Jess asked him, equally surprised. "Make our own Interforce? What the hell would we do with one?"

Mike paused to take a sip from his mug. "You know damn well, Drake, what gives them the edge." He poked a thumb at his chest. "We do. Drakes do. What if we stopped going there and just kept all of us here."

Kurok's eyebrows lifted. "Ignore the battery?"

"Just don't take it," Mike said. "Make our own, to classify the kids, but take the ones that would have gone to Canyon City and teach em ourselves. Only reason they do it there is to keep a lid on them. We got enough brawn here to do it."

Jess put her mug on the slate table at her elbow and folded her long arms over her chest. "Are you serious?"

Mike nodded. "Been thinking about it. What you said when you were here the last time, about us sending the best and brightest out there. Kinda stinks for us who didn't go, but it's sorta true, I seen it. Justin was an asshole, but he was sharp."

Kurok shifted a little, brows quirking. "He really wasn't an asshole." His eyes narrowed slightly. "He just didn't suffer fools gladly. Something we shared."

"We all share it," Jess said, hackles raising. "So, we train kids to be what I am," she said. "Then what? What do you do with them? Attack Quebec? We get bored easily and like to kill people." She watched him think. "That was the whole point of Canyon City. Take all of us and point us at the bad guys to keep us from randomly knifing the good guys."

Mike half shrugged. "Justin was all right when he lived here. He wasn't that crazy."

Kurok shook his head. "Oh, my friend, you didn't know him well enough then."

Mike shrugged again. "I can just tell you what it was like when he was here. He never broke anyone's neck in the mess for no reason."

"Neither have I," Jess said. "Yet."

"Scared the hell out of people that showed up here to make trouble, tell you that." Mike went on. "Jokers start fights out on the dock, all he'd have to do is show up there and that stopped right that second."

"Well, that's true," Kurok said. "I can imagine that."

"You didn't answer my question," Jess said. "What are we going to do with a bunch of us? Or do you mean we'd run this place like a base?"

Mike nodded. "That's what. People like you to lead the troops. Troops we got plenty of, you know? Everyone here's a fighter. We make enough cred, we can buy new guns, get rid of that stuff in the armory. We get that, and a force, and nobody's gonna think about taking nothing from us no how."

"Well, there's one obvious problem with that," Kurok said. "In the fifteen years it'll take any candidates here to grow up and become dangerous, whatever's going to happen is going to be long over."

"Wouldn't do no good anyway. We need all growed up ones here to do the teaching," Mike said. "Or someone who's been through most of it." He looked at Kurok. "Like you."

Jess snorted.

"Oh no no no," Kurok said. "I have no damned idea how to get five-year-old moppets to where Justin was when I met him." He waved his finger in the air. "He was already psychologically integrated, past puberty, on the cusp of adulthood. You think doing what they do is easy? Let me tell you it's not. It would be easier for me just to design an archetype like that from scratch."

Silence fell.

"You could," Jess said, in a musing tone. "But that'd take even longer." She rested her elbow on the chair arm.

Kurok shook his head. "What we can do is study what it

would take to harden this place and make it very hard to do what they did the last time. We started that." He glanced from one to the other. "We can make good partnerships with the nearest homesteads."

"Won't help if someone wants in bad enough," Mike said. "We need to scare the hell out of people, not make friends with them." He jerked his head toward Jess. "That's the whole point of them, ain't it? Half the half doesn't happen because they're afraid of the likes of her."

"Well..."

"No, that's true," Jess said, in a mild tone. "We're wildcards. You see it in the vids when you get to see them. Other sides there with armor and guns and they see one of us, and you can see the—oh shit—bubble over their heads. They know pointing a gun at me won't stop me. They know they have to shoot with perfect aim and hit just the right spot between my eyes and blow my head off or else they're going to die because I'll rip them apart."

"No second chances," Mike said.

Kurok sighed. "Look I agree we need to be able to defend ourselves. I'm just not convinced we need to duplicate that model to do it."

Mike pondered that briefly. "They grabbed Tayler," he said. "They done that."

"After his moron father sold him up there," Jess said. She swirled her cup in a circle, her pale eyes sharp and vivid. "Don't forget that part."

Mike regarded her mildly. "You fixed that. Good job doin it." He winked at her. "That's when we knew we had ya."

Jess' shoulders shook in a laugh. "Had me a big old beer after that."

Kurok sighed. "Yes, they certainly did all that. Madness. All madness. They were going to pay the station to deliberately create copies of him," his voice lifted in outrage. "Idiots!"

Jess just chuckled and shook her head.

"Would you have?" Mike asked, in an interested tone. He watched Kurok's face.

Kurok's eyes widened into a look of almost comical horror. "Me?" He pointed at his own chest. "Are you out of your mind, or do you think I am? Of course not," he said. "Station had no concept at all what they were being asked to do. They had no idea what that genetic structure is."

Jess's eyes twinkled. "They do now."

"Idiots," Kurok muttered again.

"I'm actually surprised they didn't try that before," Jess said. "You told me they have a bio alt program."

"Frankenstein's monster complex," Kurok said. "They're terrified something they deliberately do, deliberately create, will be the end of them. Their biological alternatives are just clones, really. They find a type they like and make copies."

"Not what you did," Mike said.

"No," Kurok answered. "My goal, if you can say it was a goal, was to take everything I did and try to move the species ahead with it. Try to make things better." He drained his mug and set it on the small table near his chair. "And because of Justin, I studied the genetic underpinnings of the Bay. If the other side had asked me, which of course they didn't, I wouldn't have told them anything, I would have just blown their heads off."

"Which is what you did," Jess said. "But what about more like Dev? Could you do that here?"

Mike looked pleased at the question, as though he'd been working on how to ask it himself.

Kurok didn't answer immediately. He thought about the question in silence for a few minutes and they just waited. Finally, he looked up at Jess and their eyes met. "Could I?" He cocked his head. "I brought the entirety of my research database with me on that shuttle. Given the equipment needed, sure."

He got up and took his mug over to the dispenser in the corner, trading the contents for a hot serving of sea grape tea. "Would I?" He turned to face them. "Why would you ask me to? Another cash crop?" He stood in the half shadows and watched them both.

Mike shrugged; his rugged, square face unoffended. "I just like em," he responded simply. "They're nice and they do what they're fucking told without needing to punch the crap out of them. If we're gonna build an Interforce here, we'll have plenty of the other kind and that one's got mad skills."

Kurok came back over and sat on the arm of the chair. "I don't know that I want to build a creche here. It's a huge amount of resources, and frankly, it'd be easier to market carrots." He eyed them. "But I could enable the sets here to reproduce."

Jess blinked, and Mike's eyebrows hiked up.

Kurok watched them with some slight amusement. "I mean, they are human beings. I'd still need some equipment, but a lot less, and cheaper to do it. Most of the sets here are relatively compatible." He held up a hand. "But I'd want their children to be registered citizens."

Jess set her mug down and leaned forward, drawing up her knees and resting her elbows on them, ankles crossed. "What happens if they breed to us? What does that look like?" She watched his brow furrow. "Just more us?"

It was over Mike's head, so he listened in silence, his hazel eyes going from one to the other.

"Good question," Kurok finally said. "They have persistent patterning, but then, so do you. I don't know. I could run some tests, but again, that's going to require some gear, and more sophisticated than what I'm using for the plants."

"Might be cool. Might be creepy," Jess mused. "Kinda like space."

"Well, we're not going to solve that question tonight," Kurok said. "But it's certainly something we should discuss again." He lifted his mug, toasted them with it, then retreated along the far side hallway that led to his quarters.

Mike also stood up. "That's two things we need cred for then," he said, pragmatically. "Guns and kids." He lifted a hand. "Night, Drake." He headed for the main hallway out and left Jess sitting there in the quiet of the family space alone.

Jess waited until she heard the outer door close behind him and then sat back in the chair and slowly looked around the room. She vaguely remembered being on the floor near the heating element playing with a horse conch.

The chair was comfortable, and she regarded it, realizing it was because the arms and the seat were long enough to match her long arms and legs, and the back was wide enough to support the width of her broad shoulders.

Because of course, it had been made for Drakes, and a Drake she undoubtably was. She sat back and folded her hands over her stomach and enjoyed the quiet, the dim light, the hint of grog still on the air, and the faintly salt infused scent of the Bay shirt she was wearing.

There was a metal sculpture on one wall of the room. Just random welded bits of something she'd probably been told about but forgotten.

After a minute she got up and took her mug into the short hall in the back that led into the kitchen space. She paused as the lights reacted to her presence and came on showing the food preparation area against the back wall.

She set the mug down in the washer and tried to remember what it had been like to live here, only calling up the smallest, vaguest glimpses of the feel of the bare stone against her feet as she ran through it, and the smell of something an old auntie was cooking.

She heard the outer door open and close, and then the soft footfalls of someone in off duty boots with a particular rhythmic stride. She smiled. "Hey, Devvie," she called out. "In here."

Dev entered the kitchen. "Hello," she said. "Is there something out there suboptimal?"

Jess shook her head. "No. I was just putting my cup away." She turned, then perched a hip on the table. "How's your buddies?"

"Absolutely excellent," Dev said. "I explained about the card, and it made them very happy to hear about that. Now they are really looking forward to the market tomorrow."

Jess unexpectedly reached out and touched Dev's cheek. The contact made Dev smile, and the muscles of her face shifted under Den's fingers. "What do you think about this place, Dev?" she asked. "You like it?"

Dev cocked her head a trifle to one side. "Your birthplace?" She asked, in a somewhat surprised tone. "I like it very much." She glanced past Jess. "I think the way you can see out from some of the spaces is very attractive, and the place with the round stairs is my favorite. It's very pretty." She paused. "I'm glad we came here."

"Yeah, it's not bad for a rockpile," Jess said. "I really don't remember living here that much. I remember school a lot more, but that was a different kind of rockpile."

"It's a lot more optimal than the last time we were here," Dev said. "I was going to go down level and see if they fixed all the damage I did that time." She looked faintly abashed. "I was glad no one was harmed."

Dev had flown their carrier into the ship docking cavern, a space in no way sized to accommodate that craft. Both the dock and the cargo ships that had been inside it had suffered impact damage.

"Turned out okay." Jess tweaked her ear, then let her hand drop. "I'm glad. I felt kind of crappy about trashing the place."

"I as well," Dev said. "However, I have discovered those that saw it happen seemed to like it?" Her voice lifted in puzzled question. "And to be honest I'm not sure what that's all about, Jess. I don't understand why that was a good thing."

Jess laughed. "It was a rock star piece of flying," she said, and then glanced across the kitchen. "Want to go relax?" She indicated the southernmost hallway that led to their quarters. "Probably going to be a long ass day tomorrow."

"Yes, that would be excellent," Dev agreed.

They keyed through the door in the hallway and walked

down along the inside passage. At the end of it were the two entrances to their rooms, and Dev walked past the one that Jess stopped at and went to her own.

She paused at it, with her hand on the access plate and looked back. "Would you like to share a drink?"

Jess grinned. "Meet you after a shower," she, then disappeared into her space.

Dev smiled, entered her own room and paused to regard the interior. It was not made on two levels, as hers at the base was, but it was not too different. There was a sleeping space, with a comfortable looking bed, a small area where there was a warming stone and some chairs to relax in. In the back, against the window on the very edge of the space, was a desk and access point.

She'd left her backpack on the bed and now went over to it and retrieved her sleeping clothes and sanitary kit. She took them into the sanitary space and went over to turn on the shower with a pleasurable expectation.

The shower space was instantly filled with water, and she shed her clothing and got under it, finding the pressure more intense than at base, and the water with a slightly different scent to it she decided she liked. She scrubbed her skin with the bit of sea sponge she'd brought with her but used the dispenser of soap attached to the shower wall.

It felt excellent. She washed her pale hair and then turned off the water and stepped out, wrapping one of the provided pieces of cloth around her as she faced the reflective surface and used a second cloth to ruffle her head dry.

She glanced at the reflection, and, as always, paused to study the spot on her neck that had, until very recently, held a metallic golden collar, along with its interspinal programming probes that had extended up into her brain. Now not even a trace remained, the repetition of rad evening out the skin tone and leaving only the tiniest of scars at the back of her neck.

The sets had talked to her about programming, since Doctor Dan only had some rudimentary systems here and couldn't really give them information that way. They'd been learning things the way she now had to, and everyone, even her, had agreed it was a lot easier to be given it.

But they were learning how to learn, and no one thought they would like to trade back, just as she felt herself. Dev nodded to herself in the mirror, then ran a comb through her hair and put on her sleep clothes, already looking forward to the hot tea she knew Jess would be scrounging, along with whatever snacks that might be found.

It would be nice. It was their usual thing to do, and then, possibly, they would practice sex, and that would be excellent as well. A comforting routine in this different place that somehow wasn't that different.

Dev went out and folded her clothes neatly, setting the heavy shirt aside for the next day, and folding the rest inside her backpack. Then she regarded the stone floor and slipped back into the off-duty boots in deference to the chilly floor of the hall and left the room.

****

Jess studied the small table near the window for a long moment, nodded in satisfaction and took a seat on one side of it. She then stretched her legs out and rested her elbows on the chair's stolid, square topped arms.

There was nothing fancy here, but everything was well built and functional. She relaxed, ears cocked to listen for the sound of the door down the hall close and the almost soundless footsteps coming over to share the small carafe of tea she'd filched from the mess kitchen.

Well, not really filched. The night cook seemed happy to see her, and gave her not only the tea, but a small plas container of just finished fish rolls. She eyed them contentedly, knowing Dev would as well.

It was her favorite part of the day, this late evening meet up, after she'd finished whatever tasks had fallen her way and Dev had finished whatever wrenching she had on her schedule.

It was time to just sit back, have a cup of something warm and talk about the day, or about some project Dev was dreaming up, or about the gossip from the lower levels, where the bio alts at base lived.

Life wasn't bad for them there. They had reasonable assignments. Interforce treated them as valued objects, as valued as the weapons and other operational items at the base were. So, they were well fed and adequately housed.

No complaints, Dev had told her. They'd been scared, during the fighting, but of course they would be. Seeing so many people from the base killed had shocked and dismayed the whole lot of them, but the comms they'd been given during the emergencies had stayed with them and there was a sense that somehow, oddly, they'd gotten some status out of it all.

Ah. Jess smiled when she heard the far-off sound of a door

close, and then only moments later, a light knock at hers. "C'mon in, Devvie."

The door opened and Dev slipped inside, dressed in her sleeveless top and shorts that matched what Jess herself wore. "Hello," she greeted Dev warmly. "The showers here are very nice."

Jess grinned. "Better than bases. Better water pressure here. Bigger tunnels."

Dev went around her over to the sanitary unit. She picked up the small kit on the counter and removed a comb and then returned to Jess and casually ran the comb through her wet, unruly hair. "I know you dislike tangles."

Jess resisted the urge to turn around to look at Dev. "Won't matter. It's just a mop anyway."

Dev paused, then continued her motion. "It doesn't even remotely resemble a mop, Jess. You have beautiful hair." She brushed the strands back from her temples, where they came back over her ears in a gentle wave. "I don't understand why you always say that."

Why did she always say that? Jess tipped her head back a little. "Maybe I just want you to tell me I'm wrong." She smiled with a hint of mischief. "Those kinds of compliments are in short supply in our line of work." She felt Dev's fingers riffle through her hair. "Or maybe I just like someone doing that."

Dev dropped her hand to Jess's shoulder and gently squeezed. "That's optimal, as I enjoy doing it." She took the comb back to the kit and slid it inside, then went back around and settled herself into the other chair. "I think this has been an excellent day."

Jess's eyes twinkled. "Sure is, now."

Dev's hair was still damp from her shower, and she hitched herself back in the chair and pulled her legs up crossed under her in a flurry of unconscious cuteness. In her brief clothes, she displayed her compact, yet well-made form, her smooth skin showing the surprisingly sturdy muscularity just under it.

On her left arm, the fading scar of a recent burn mark was evident. Jess pointed at it. "Almost healed. Near as dark as mine is." She glanced at her right arm, where a similar burn showed on the skin just above her elbow.

The two burns were close, but not entirely alike. Jess's had different dots and bars, and Dev's had a striking blue colored stripe in it and a small many pointed star that was meant to show her part in the escape from station.

Dev inspected her arm. "Yes, it doesn't hurt at all anymore.

I showed it to the sets, when they told me about the patch they made for the people here who went to station," she said. "They liked the star very much, because it was like the one they put on their patches."

"They should have given you one too," Jess said. "Since you flew their asses down from there and saved all of us. That was an especially rockety gig, Rocket."

Dev grinned. "I think everyone did excellent work on that mission. We all participated, and the sets did as well." She indicated the carafe. "Would you like some tea?" She reached over and poured out the tea into the two stoneware cups.

Jess took her cup, then nudged the container of fish rolls in Dev's direction. "They just finished these. Grab em before they get clammy." Jess settled back into her chair before continuing. "I think it all ended up all right, but damn I wish some things hadn't happened." She shook her head. "So much bullshit."

Dev took a fish roll and nudged the container back toward Jess. "I was talking to Doctor Dan about that," she said. "He told me sometimes things just have to happen." She took a bite of the fish roll and chewed, delighted with the still warm krill and stringy seaweed inside. "He thinks if it had not happened at that time, it would have still happened."

"Once they took Tayler? Yeah." Jess took a roll and bit it in half. "There was no real way out of that, once it was in work. I keep trying to go back bit by bit to see if there was a point where it could have gone another way but.." She shrugged. "Start to finish shitshow."

"We could not have stopped it," Dev said. "The persons who made it happen would have had to not do what they did."

Jess nodded. "Yeah, we just reacted," she said. "Just like anyone with half a brain would have guessed we would."

Dev nodded and took a sip of the sea grape tea. "This tea is excellent here." She regarded the cup. "Is there something they do to it? It doesn't taste like the kind at base at all. It seems a little thicker and has a rich, spicy taste to it."

Jess took a sip, and swirled it inside her mouth, considering the question. "No idea," she finally said. "I'll take you in the mess kitchen to meet Petar and his gang tomorrow and you can ask them how they make it." Dev looked at her, with an open, interested look. "Most of the grub at base they machine process. No one really does anything but serve it. Not here."

"Really?" Dev looked at the tea.

"Really," Jess said. "Bunch of allotments in the mess here. People take whatever we get and make something out of it.

Same as at places like Jontons. Like they did on Sig's boat. Never wanted to spend cred to put in the new kind of processors."

"It's excellent then, because the meals here have been better than anywhere else." Dev said in a serious tone. "If that is the reason, it's too bad they do not do that at our base. I am sure everyone would enjoy it."

"Yeah," Jess said. "This old rockpile has it's good points."

"There is a lot of opportunity for good work here." Dev nodded thoughtfully. "You know, Jess, I was thinking, about the updrafts in that circular area." She indicated the now dark view past the window. "It would be interesting to think about building something you could use to fly over the water." She finished her fish roll and dusted her fingers off.

"Like… a flyer? Like a carrier?" Jess asked, in a puzzled tone.

"No, something you could wear on your back. Like your drop device, but not for going down," Dev said. "So, you could just fly over the water, and help find things like…I think Doctor Dan called them limpets?"

Dev's dark eyebrows contracted, and she tilted her head to one side. "You want to strap a rocket to your ass, Rocket?"

"A small one. Maybe." Dev took one of the remaining rolls, while Jess still held half of hers. "It's just an idea. I was working out the aerodynamic envelope earlier before it got so dark outside."

Jess tried to imagine it, flying without the enclosure of a craft around her and then she gave Dev a wide-eyed look. "You scare the crap out of me sometimes."

Dev blinked mildly. "Is that good or bad?"

Jess started laughing. "Where do you come up with ideas like that?"

Dev took the question at face value. "Well, I've been programmed to problem solve. I think about what a problem might be then I think about what could be done to solve it." She responded. "For this… really I am not sure it's a problem, but I thought being able to fly would be fun."

"Wouldn't be much fun if it crapped out with you up there."

"That's true," Dev agreed. "But a lot of things we do have danger."

Jess leaned back and hiked up one knee to rest against the edge of the table. Her leg was bare, and the joint was large and somewhat stark under her skin, crossed with scars. She idly rubbed her thumb over one of them. "Yeah, that's a fact."

"It's like the surfing thing," Dev concluded. "It can be quite uncomfortable, but also fun."

"Now that you aren't frozen and sliced up its more fun for you at least," Jess said. "Y'know, now that I think about it, I came up with that suit because I wanted it to be fun for you and not have to stick you in rad for an hour afterward and patch you up all the time just because you humor my weird obsessions."

"Yes, it's much more enjoyable now," Dev said. "Maybe I can make a thing so it will be fun for you to fly."

A small revelation occurred to Jess. "You like making things."

Dev nodded. "I do. Dr Dan said he made me that way."

"Just like he does," Jess said. "I think he's getting a kick out of having to invent all this stuff. Like when he said he was trying to figure out how to put shields on the boats." She shifted and gestured vaguely toward the inner hall. "Like everyone here says, how do we make this happen? And he whips out a screw- driver and starts wrenching."

Dev's pale eyebrows lifted a little. "Jess, I really think that's true. I think it was a really good thing for him that he came here."

"Yeah," Jess said. "He's better off. And for sure, the Bay is." She grinned. "They must've realized what a bullet they dodged wanting to force me to stay here."

"I am confident we'd have done excellent work here," Dev demurred. "But I am also pleased that Doctor Dan is happy to be here and doing good and interesting things."

"True that." Jess lifted her cup up and toasted her with it. "All's well that doesn't end at the business end of a blaster."

Dev sipped her tea and looked to her left, out the big plas window, where the faint reflection from the dock lights threw shadows against the far wall of the rock escarpments that surrounded the Bay. She leaned closer to look out and down.

"Jess."

"Yes?" Jess leaned forward and looked out. "Something attacking us? Give me a chance to get some exercise before bed? Maybe have to take a second shower to get the blood off?"

"The marking on the flag, what is that?" Dev ignored her partner's ghoulish humor. "I saw it on the wall inside as well."

"Oh." Jess chuckled and leaned back. "It's a dragon." She wrapped her hands around her still upraised knee. "Way back in the day when they found this place, the fam decided to make a banner for it. Like they used to in the military."

"I see," Dev said. "My book had something about a dragon in it, Jess. They didn't seem very optimal though. They ate a lot of people and burned down houses."

"Yeah, they weren't nice, but then neither were we," Dev acknowledged. "Now why a dragon? Because a drake, as in our name, was a male duck." Jess chuckled under her breath, as she watched Dev turn to look at her. "They're about as scary as a puffin. So, they decided to use a dragon, which was a big scary thing that flew, and breathed fire and they were also sometimes called drakes."

"Were they a real animal?" Dev asked.

Jess shook her head. "No. Well," she relented. "Maybe back in the beginning of the world they were. They found dinosaur fossils that were sort of like that, with wings and claws. No idea if they breathed fire. Anyway, it made a better banner than a duck, so there ya go."

"That's very interesting," Dev said. "I will have to take a vid of that large one in the hall tomorrow. Will there be other activities tomorrow besides the market? Someone said something about a game."

"Game." Jess rumbled almost under her breath. "Dunno, Dev. Might be. They could do things like we do at the parties. Dunking, that kind of stuff."

Dev looked noncommittal. "Will this include eyeballs?"

"Maybe." Jess broke into a grin. "Maybe it'll be knife throwing. April'll like that." She set her cup down and pushed it back from the edge a little. "Ready to go sack out?" She inclined her head toward the bed.

"That would be pleasant," Dev said. She got up and nudged the chair back into place. "It will be interesting to see natural light in the morning."

Jess stood and backed away toward the bed.

"Uh huh."

"It never mattered on station," Dev added.

Jess pulled the woven cover back and sat down, gesturing to the other side of the bed. "Not with all that going around and around with the sun and stuff. How could you tell what time it was?"

Dev slid under the cover and stretched out. She looked past the edge of the bed out the window. "Well, that's why they put us in sleep pods, to block the sun out." she said, as Jess got under the covers with her.

Jess reached out and took Dev's hand and they interlaced fingers. Her eyes closed almost in reflex as Dev gently rubbed the edge of her thumb on her palm.

The touch took her to another place. Jess moved closer and in reaction to their presence in the bed the lights dimmed, now only the faint light from the outside was present and easy to ignore.

The heavy rock walls and the distance to the outer hall made it mostly silent. As Dev squirmed closer and their bodies touched, even the sub aural rumble of the water tunnels below them faded out and she was able to focus on the near-term immediate touch of Dev's hand coming to rest on her ribcage.

She often felt abstracted when they pleasured each other on base. There was always some faint edge sound, some echo of announcements, even in the relative safety of their quarters that made her senses twitch. But here she found a surprising true quiet she felt willing to trust.

Why trust here? The last time she'd slept in this bed her brother had tried to kill her in it, a thundering cascade of stupidity that justified his being taken out by the staff before he could make any decisions on their behalf.

But she did trust it, and it was so easy to relax into the enjoyment of the slowly intensifying sensation and focus on it.

Dev's lips touched hers and she tasted the slight tang of the seaweed on them as their bodies came into full contact, Dev's knee moved hers aside with an always startling internal strength you somehow didn't expect.

Jess thought it was sexy. The confidence in that made her enjoy the pleasure, and she knew Dev enjoyed it too.

Probably, suit or not, a lot more than she did surfing.

****

They woke early, as they always did. It was still pre-dawn dark outside when Jess and Dev settled in the big kitchen dining space at the center of the stakeholder's compound with big cups of tea and bowls of leftover fish soup from the night before, along with a handful of crispy crackers to start their day at their usual time.

The dining space window was central, and they had a good view of the gap in the half circle walls out to the horizon. Everything outside was still quiet and the air over the bay was clear of rain for now. The shadow of a seabird glided past, silent, and graceful.

Dev regarded her platter of soup and seaweed crackers with pleasure, and consumed a spoonful of the soup, her eyebrows lifted at the taste. "This is excellent," she said, after swallowing. "I don't think I've had soup for breakfast before."

"Gets better the next day." Jess propped one booted foot up against the bottom of the wide windowsill and leaned back in her seat with her cup of tea, her bowl of soup cradled in her other hand as she drank from it. "Gets thicker." She sucked in a bit of clam and chewed it. "Tastes different."

Jess glanced at Dev after the silence had gone on a minute, eyebrow lifting a little. "Penny for your thoughts."

"What's a penny?" Dev responded. "You don't have to give me anything, Jess." She didn't wait for Jess to answer. "I was just thinking about how attractive you are."

Jess's nose wrinkled. "Really?"

"Really. I think that way you have your hair pulled back in a knot at the base of your neck is very nice. You can really see your face."

Jess sighed. "Wish I was cute like you," she said. "I always feel like a gargoyle."

Dev paused and regarded her, one pale eyebrow raised in eloquent question.

"It's a weird thing with horns, wings and a forked tongue they used to make statues of," Jess said. "To scare people."

"Jess you have none of those things," Dev said, after a brief pause. "Why would you need them to scare people?" She went back to her soup, shaking her head slightly.

"Nah, you're right," Jess agreed. "I scare people just by breathing."

"Do you think I'm cute?" Dev asked, pausing with her spoon half raised to her mouth, head tilted a little to one side.

Jess blinked at her. "Hell, yeah. You're like a dozen of those bear cubs in a basket level cute." She put her bowl down, its contents emptied and pushed her seaweed crackers over to Dev's side of the table. "Here. I know you like these things."

Dev smiled. "I do. But I think I like that you like how I look more." Her eyes twinkled gently.

Jess felt a little odd, a little short of breath, but she rested her head against her fist and toasted Dev with her tea. "Glad I could make ya happy, Rocket," she said, then changed the subject. "Today's gonna be fun. We'll get to shop and not have to worry about me shooting someone." She paused. "Probably."

Dev picked up one of her donated crackers. "I am looking forward to it. But I hope they don't have expired bears at this one. That was suboptimal." She frowned. "With its head looking at you. Why would anyone want that on the floor, Jess?"

"Nah. These are land-based traders. Those skins come in from ships. From the white." Jess leaned back in her chair again and focused on the window where the sky ahead of them to the east was going from black to dark gray. "Maybe they'll have stuff from out west. That'd be fun. We can trade some of our stuff for some treats."

Our. Jess paused and thought about that. We. What was we right now to her? Interforce? Her and Dev? She glanced around the room. Drake's Bay?

Was she still holding that over from the last fight? That us and them that suddenly turned on her, and made her, and the rest of the Bay, them. She remembered Security Mike asking her, in an almost puzzled tone. "You us now?"

She took a sip of her tea, the temperature now more easily drinkable, though without the pungent steam that could clear your head in an instant. She swallowed, and imagined for a moment, putting that imagining in a carefully constrained box, to have this be normal.

When she'd tossed herself out of the force, that spur of the moment ego insanity, it wasn't to come to this. She'd had no place here to come to, far as she'd known. She'd have come to fighting for a position, starting at the bottom, collecting at the shore like many of her younger cousins.

Maybe she'd have come into security, with the background, and then be dealing with her asshole family all the time, them struggling to deal with this younger version of her contentious father, resenting her presence and yet having no option but to accept it because once upon a time Justin had signed the paperwork allowing it.

This was none of that now. No family, no shore collecting, no fighting up the pecking order. She'd come, all unknowing at the time, into an ownership no one had ever expected.

That twenty minutes of being a civ, between walking out the back door and walking up that shuttle gangway and meeting Bain had changed her future forever, and she hadn't any clue at all at the time. Hadn't even cared at the time because so much else was changing.

Hadn't cared, because the Bay hadn't been home to her really since she'd left at age six. Especially not since her father died, because he was at least someone she could talk to who needed nothing at all explained. Who, on her infrequent trips home from school would exchange looks with her without any words needed when jackassery was happening.

Most of her schoolmates didn't have that kind of understanding to go home to, and many didn't. She'd always assumed it was their choice and hadn't found out until later it was nothing of the kind. That the homestead they'd been born to had to sign a liability release to let them come there, and a second to permit them residence in those rare breaks from service.

Many refused.

Of course, that had never been a question at the Bay with her father in charge. Jess smiled a little. Justin had found it hilarious when the waiver had come to him to sign for her, and she suspected she would find it just as hilarious when Tayler came to her in his turn.

She did feel a sense of responsibility for this place now though. She wanted good things to happen here, and for the place to do well, and in one corner of that she could just... just kind of imagine what it would like to have these quarters, and this view be what she woke up to every day.

Then she shook her head and smiled. For about a week. Then she'd be looking for other places to be, things to be doing, enemies to kill. Not the place for her, making deals with the neighbors and counting fish loads.

Not yet, and maybe never. Jess dismissed the thought and glanced across the table at her companion and watched the pearlescent light outline her face as she slowly blinked into it, a thoughtful, interested look there, one side of her lips moving into a faint smile.

Dev had finished, and stacked her plates neatly, and rested her elbow on the table as she propped her head on her fist.

"Penny for your thoughts?" Jess asked again and watched Dev's eyes move as she looked out, the light outside now calling out the glints of color. "Not me again?" She added, in a hopeful tone.

"Celestial mechanics, actually." Dev looked at her, with a sheepish grin. "Should we go see what's going on? Perhaps we can take our dishes, and you can introduce me to those people you mentioned last night." She stood up and pulled Jess's dishes over to her. "And I think I hear someone approaching."

Jess belatedly realized she did as well. "Yup." She got up and stuck her hands inside the front pocket of the Bay shirt. "Let's get us another mug of this stuff and see what's up." She led the way down the corridor and called, "Morning," to April and Doug who exited their hallway just ahead of her.

****

The market started up at mid-morning. Dev strolled along at Jess's side as they exited the back entrance to the Bay, a heavily armored door that today was pushed open fully. It was huge and steel, with big round rivets in it. "They stole that from a big ass building vault," Jess commented as they went through. "From some government gig or other that fell down."

Dev observed the door. "It seems quite sturdy."

A ramp led down from the door to the valley floor behind the cliffs that held the main homestead, worn with the weather, and the marks of pallets and pullers from the delivery caverns across the short flat space in between.

It was bare rock, the ramp long and wide, lined with large stones on either side to keep the traffic contained.

The flats were filled with trading caravans, lined up neatly, separated into three groups, each set of caravans marked or painted with distinctive markings that indicated to whom they belonged.

April walked on Jess's other side. She made a low, almost contemptuous grunting sound. "Watch that one." She indicated the caravans on the far side of the flats. "Skank."

Doug patted her shoulder. "Tell me which they are when we get inside, "Boss," so I don't buy fake black diamonds from them."

Mike and Chester were behind them. Both looked around with interest. All the Interforce contingent were dressed, as were Dev and Jess, in off duty civ clothes, which allowed them to blend in with the crowd.

Even Jess, who usually stood out with her striking looks and height, blended in with the Bay residents enough to be taken for one. None of them drew a second glance.

The vendors took up the whole space, it's main entrance huge and wide and open to the elements, but narrow enough so that once inside, the large rock interior was dry and suited for their foldable stands laid out in long rows.

It already smelled like a range of things being cooked, and Dev sniffed that with interest. She noticed her fellow bio alts looking everywhere with wide eyes.

On the far side of the cavern, five or six of the Bay logistics managers stood with the same number of traders, everyone with clipboards in hand.

Jess nudged Dev's shoulder and nodded in their direction. "Bartering. The big stuff."

Dev had no idea what that meant, but she nodded back. The trader tables held a large amount of all sorts of things, as they had on Market Island. The crowd started to disperse among them, strolling through the rows to see what there was to be had.

"Jess, what's that?" Dev asked, as they detoured down a row near the entrance.

"Huh?" Jess looked up. "Oh. Music." She patted Dev's back. "You should like that, Devvie if those guys are any good."

The sound in the room picked up, voices and murmurs, and the occasional laugh began to echo up to the high ceiling.

"Ah, there you are."

Jess looked up to find Kurok heading their way with one of the traders. "That a bad guy?" She whispered to April.

April glanced up from inspecting a woven piece of fabric. "He's okay," she said, after a moment. "Josten family. They're square." She edged away. "But I don't really want to talk to him."

"He probably wants to meet the head of house," Doug suggested. "But hey… look, knives!" He pointed at a vendor nearby, who had a small anvil inside his little tarp booth. After a moment, April made an approving noise, and they headed in that direction.

Dev suppressed a smile and stayed at Jess's side as Doctor Dan arrived with the other man, and Mike and Chester wandered off toward a table with glass containers on it, adroitly disengaging from the social niceties.

Doctor Dan came to a stop. "Ah, Jesslyn. This is Trader Josten. He wanted a word with you since you happen to be here on this happy occasion," he said. "Trader, this is Jesslyn Drake, senior stakeholder here at Drake's Bay, and her partner, Dev, who are visiting us from Base 10."

"Hi," Jess responded in a mild tone.

"Hello," Dev added.

Josten was a middle-aged man, with a thick, full but neatly trimmed beard that was mostly rust red with streaks of gray in it. He was burly and had the muscular body of someone who came up through the ranks doing the work.

"Greetings, stakeholder," the man addressed Jess briskly. "We're glad to be here, and it's good to meet you here, where we can do a little business together." He'd stopped at a distance that let her meet his eyes without him having to tip his head all the way back. He regarded her in a forthright manner. "Your name is known to us."

Jess's right eyebrow lifted. "Yeah, it's nice to meet ya." she agreed. "What's on your mind?" She glanced over and past him to where a vendor was serving something from a steaming pot.

"How about a cup to talk over?"

The man half turned. "That would be welcome." He smiled at her. "By all means."

"Well, I'll leave you to it." Doctor Dan said. "I have to go finish up a chat with those fellows over there." He indicated the group near the door. "Catch up later." He went off at an angle from their path and disappeared into the crowd.

They walked over to the booth, where several Bay residents were accepting cups of the rich, pungent smelling beverage. Jess took advantage of her height and met the eyes of the stall owner. She held up three fingers to him.

With a grin, the man complied, and she handed him a chit for it. They took the cups and stepped a pace back into a small opening between the stalls. This gave them at least an illusion of privacy.

It was an illusion, they all understood that.

"Good to see trade here." Jess sipped the hot drink from her mug. Then she paused and looked at the cup. "What the hell?" She licked her lips. "What is this?"

The trader chuckled. "It's sea grape wine, lady." He took a sip. "Bredon, the vintner, is in my train. Does it suit you?"

Dev cautiously took a mouthful, wary of her partners reaction. The spicy heat was at first surprising, and then delightful as the flavor manifested on the back of her tongue. It reminded her a little bit of the spicy shrimp at Jonton's, but sweeter. As she took a breath in it infused her senses. "Ah."

Jess glanced at her. "Like it?" She guessed, seeing Dev's pale brows lift in pleasure. "You do."

Dev nodded. "I do. I don't think I've ever had anything like it."

"Nor will you," Josten said. "His family's been at it for generations. His brother runs a shop in Quebec City. He wanted to come with us down here when he heard we were coming, wants to talk to someone about herbs."

"Herbs," Jess repeated slowly.

"To use for this?" Dev asked. "For infusions? That would be excellent." She took another sip of the wine. "They used them on station, Jess. To make special things to drink. Every once in a while we got to taste them."

The trader studied Dev. "You know this?" he asked. "Top- side."

Dev nodded. "Yes."

"Sure, she does. She was born there. In space." Jess leaned her elbow on Dev's shoulder and gazed at him. She kept the words, *so be nice* inside her head, but her eyes narrowed as she silently projected them.

But he grinned broadly at Dev, expressing a kind of delight. "Ah, you're then the Rocket that I have also heard of?"

Dev shrugged modestly. "I do get called that," she said, and then turned to Jess. "The persons you introduced me to this morning are also interested in herbs, Jess. They said Doctor Dan was going to talk to them about it."

Jess took another sip of the drink, getting used to the spicy taste that left a lingering fragrance in the back of her throat. "Does he sell this by the bottle?" She asked Josten, lifting her eyebrows meaningfully. "Maybe we can make a deal."

Josten smiled now at her, a broad, unfeigned mercantile smile. "That's why we're here," he said, simply. "It's been many a year, all the years of my majority, since we've had something new under the clouds in this part of the world," he said. "I do not wait. I want to see what advantage this brings."

"Introduce us." She indicated the vendor stall, who had collected quite a big crowd by now. "Let's see what else he's got."

****

Dev had a problem. The market was progressing very well for her, and she had inspected and obtained all kinds of things and now she was out of pocket space to put them. She paused and stepped aside out of the foot traffic and looked around, pondering if she should detour up to the carrier to pick up one of her gear packs.

Jess was a few aisles down, looking at some shirts. They'd left their new nomad leader friend behind a short while ago, with promises to meet up later, and perhaps give him and his winemaker a tour of the plant cavern.

Everyone seemed happy. Dev saw Bay residents and bio alts browsing the shops. Everyone seemed to have at least one thing they were carrying.

That seemed excellent. She had spent some moments earlier showing the sets how to review what their cards had on them, a simple enough process, and they all had, delighted with the amounts that had been credited. Dev then did a scan on her own in the cred system and her eyebrows hiked in patent surprise.

It seemed that obtaining gifts for Jess, at least, was not going to be an issue.

Her eyes roamed over the nearby stalls, then she made a

small sound of approval. "Ah." She walked across the aisle to a small booth where two women sat, one of them on a stool behind a piece of plastic board set across two steel supports, the other behind her on a shorter stool working on something.

On the plas were handmade bags, woven out of a thin, worn type of cording in a tight mesh. They had a piece of equally worn rope tied to them to make sort of a strap. "Hello." Dev picked one up. "These are attractive." She glanced up as the woman on the stool stood and came over. "What are they made from?"

"Took it from the water," the woman said. "Came on the tide, from the boats. It's fisherfolk nets and suchlike."

Ah, yes. Dev nodded. "I saw things like this when I was on a fishing boat." She recognized now the slightly waxy feel of the strands. Around the top, which had a draw opening, were small bits of drilled glass in many different, faded, sea washed colors, and the weave was dense, yet flexible.

And large enough to carry all the things she'd stashed so far in her jumpsuit pockets and had tucked under one arm. "Excellent. How much credit would you like for them?"

The woman looked pleased, pulled the stool up behind her to sit down and they started to bargain. Occasionally, the second woman looked up from her work, smiled a little, and then looked back down. They were both weather-beaten, their skin wind roughened, the backs of their hands covered in tiny white scars.

All which Dev noticed and cataloged, as she traded offers back and forth with the woman, eventually settling on a mid-point that satisfied them both. "That's optimal." She removed the ident skin from one of her pockets, slid the dark, blank square chit card from it and handed it over.

The woman regarded it for a moment before she took it and applied it to a small batt device that sat beside her, which accepted it without complaint and flashed blue before she handed it back. "Didn't know you were one of them."

Dev stood for a moment and tried to sort out which— them— that them was. "I'm assigned to Interforce," she said. "Is that what you mean?" She put the card away and the ident back into her pocket. She reasoned there was no visible way the woman could know her birth origin.

The woman shrugged and pushed the bag over to her. "Cred's cred. Not for me to say, specially not here." She looked around the cavern. "Specially not here."

Dev felt it might be sub optimal, but she took the bag and

smiled. "Thank you. I'm sure everyone will like these and want to purchase them." She unloaded her pockets of her purchases and put them into the bag, then slung it over one shoulder and moved on.

The reaction to Interforce was like that sometimes. It ranged from wary respect to outright fear, with occasional forays into either enthusiasm or utter hatred. This seemed more like fright, from hearing stories rather than anything more personal.

She shrugged a little and kept going. There was half a row left to walk down, and by stretching up onto her toes, Dev could see the top of Jess's head on the next one down. With a nod she proceeded to move along the line of tables. She moved her head back and forth to see what was on offer as she did, plotting a path to intersect Jess's.

"Dev!"

Dev paused as Kevin caught up to her. "Hello," she said with a smile. "How are you doing?"

He had on a sweater with a high collar, in a gray green sea foam kind of color that Dev recalled from one of their missions. "That's very attractive. Did you find it here?"

Kevin nodded vigorously. "I did. They make them for the natural born who go out on the sea in the boats. They have them on the last row there in several colors. Isn't it nice and warm?" He touched the sleeve. "And so soft. Oh." He looked at Dev's shoulder. "That's a nice bag."

"It's a very nice garment," Dev said. "I was given one of these to wear when I was out on a mission where we were on a fishing boat. It was very warm, even outside." She swung open her bag. "I got this a short way back on this row. I ran out of pockets," she admitted. "I obtained several things for Jess."

"That is very considerate." Kevin peered into the bag. "Oh, those soaps smelled really good. Alvin got some as well."

"Yes, that and some other items I thought she might enjoy," Dev said. "It's fun. They had some spicy drops on the second row and foot coverings, which seemed useful."

"It's good to get things for other people." Kevin nodded solemnly. "Remember when they would have the little market in the creche? We all worked extra to get chits for it. Everyone wanted to get something for their favorite proctor."

"Or Doctor Dan." Dev smiled in remembrance. "We all knew his favorite treats."

Kevin looked over his shoulder. "I must go see if I can get one of these bags. I could put shells I find in it when I'm done shopping. It's a small enough weave." He inspected it. "What is it?" He ran a finger along the surface. "It's... is it rope?"

"Fishing net," Dev said. "They put it in the water and fish swim into it, and they bring them into the boat and take them to a processing station. I think it's an excellent use of it, when they can't use it to catch fish anymore."

"Optimal," Kevin said immediately. "They taught us in the creche, don't waste things." He observed. "This is fun, isn't it?" He looked around at the cavern, and his ears perked up as the men on the platform started to make sounds. "Oh!"

They were playing metal devices that had a soft, shimmering sound. Dev and Kevin stood there listening, while streams of people moved past them.

"That's very nice." Dev said, after a minute of silence. "I wonder how they do that? I remember hearing music when we were on station, but never saw it being done."

Kevin nodded, enchanted by the sound. "The natural born here make a sound sometimes," he said. "At dinner, sometimes or after. A lot louder than this."

Dev swung her bag over her shoulder again. "I hope we get to hear that," she said. "The one time I heard natural born make a sound wasn't optimal. This would be better I think."

They eased back into the crowd and strolled along, slowing now and then to look at the tables they moved past. Some of the things were incomprehensible objects, and Dev made a note of a few to ask Jess about, but some were easily recognizable, and they paused in front of a small table with a case of glittering objects.

There was a man behind it, short and gnarled, with knotted fingers and thick, bushy gray eyebrows that extended out over his eyes. "Whatcha kids looking for?" He asked. "You, boy." He nudged the tray forward. "Buy your girl a pretty."

Both Dev and Kevin stared at him for a long moment, then looked at each other. "What does that mean?" Kevin asked Dev, in a bewildered tone.

"I have no idea," Dev said, then focused on the tray. "These are attractive." She studied them. "What do you do with them?" She looked at the man, hoping he wouldn't repeat his odd language. "Do you wear them?"

One of his very bushy brows lifted sharply. "Where the hell you from, kid, you don't know what jewelry is? You from the flats?"

Kevin shifted a little, moving back from the table, clearly willing to leave this odd natural born to Dev.

"We're from Bio Station 2," Dev responded. "That's a space station in orbit around the planet." She picked up one of the objects on the tray, which was a piece of shiny metal worked and twisted into a pattern, the bottom part cradling a small, glittering stone. "This is jewelry you said?"'

Kevin eased closer to her and peered over her shoulder. "It's pretty. I like that color."

"I do as well," Dev said. "It reminds me, in fact, of Jess's eyes."

"C'mere." The man came around the table. "Gimme that." He took the object from her and reached up. "Hold still, kid." He grabbed Dev's ear and twisted the piece of metal around it, ignoring her abruptly widened eyed stare. "Ah, I won't hurcha."

It didn't, in fact hurt, it just felt strange, and when he was done and stepped back, it still felt strange. For a moment, Dev was sharply reminded of what it felt like taking a deep breath when you were wearing a metal collar. She twitched her ear.

"See?" The man stepped back. "Looks good, right?" He nudged Kevin. "Tell her how good it looks."

Bewildered, but as always ready to please, Kevin took a step closer to Dev and inspected the object. It was curled around her ear and the sparkling stone rested just below her earlobe. "It is very attractive," he told Dev. "It's wrapped around your ear."

"Here." The man picked up a flat piece of shiny metal and held it up so Dev could see her own reflection. "Space huh? More like some scraper cave," he muttered. "Don't know much of nothing."

Dev let the words go past her, as she regarded the silver mesh now folded around her ear, quickly warming to her skin temperature. She turned her head a little and it caught the light. She grinned and nodded in approval. "It is nice." She turned to regard the still muttering vendor. "What is the price of this object?"

"Whatta ya got?" The man shot back. "That piece is a lotta work, took me weeks to make it."

"That's not how it works," Dev said calmly. "I would like to buy this, and I would like to discuss it with you, but you have to have a price in mind."

"How do I know you even have a cred to your name?" The man said. "Worth my time to talk about it?"

"You put it on her," Kevin said. "Did you not think she would like it and want to purchase it?"

"Shut up, kid."

A calm, friendly voice spoke up behind them. "Well now."

Doctor Dan put a hand on both Dev and Kevin's backs. "What have we found here?" He said. "Dev, that looks really nice on you," he added when he saw her new adornment. "Look at that, very pretty."

Dev was glad to see him. The vendor was unpleasant, and she was about to take the item off and leave it behind. "Thank you, Doctor Dan," she said. "I was interested in obtaining it, but this person does not seem interested in discussing that."

Doctor Dan eyed the man. "Tell you what, Dev. You and Kevin go off and see what's on offer down on the end there. I can see Jess near the wall. I'll take care of this for you." He squeezed her shoulder almost imperceptibly. "Go on."

Kevin backed off, obeying without question. Dev paused and regarded her mentor for a long moment and then grinned briefly. "Okay, Doctor Dan. Will you come over there when you're done? I think Jess wanted to meet up for lunch."

"You bet." Doctor Dan shooed them off, then turned to face the vendor.

****

"Now for you," Kurok said. He shifted his balance a bit and put his hands into his pockets. He regarded the vendor with a stern look.

"What's your plug?" The man said. "That your kid? Looks like you. Or is she your bed warmer?"

Kurok moved closer. "Listen, you muppet," he said, in a low, but intent voice. "We're all here to make some cred and have a little bad sargasso beer. Don't end up a red blot on the rocks I have to get cleaned up." He lifted his brows. "In a manner of speaking, yes, she's one of my kids, but more importantly, she's an Interforce tech, and the partner of an easily irritated Interforce agent who wouldn't hesitate to pull your arm off and beat you to death with it if you mess with her."

His expression changed. "That one?" He blurted. "That kid?"

"That one, that kid," Kurok said. "So, knock it the hell off. Now." He pulled out a cred chit. "How much is that damn thing? Be nice, because once she shows it around, you'll probably have lots more customers."

The vendor looked upset and a little unhappy. "Don't they wear uniforms? How should I know? You could get kilt here."

"You easily could." Kurok nudged the tray. "Now come on, name your price. I've got things to do." He looked down at the jewelry. "Not even going to ask you where that silver came from."

The vendor snorted. "Wouldn't tell the likes of you even if you did."

****

"That man was strange," Kevin said, as they walked down to the end of the row. They passed a table full of large shells with iridescent insides and one of small carved pieces of rock. Neither of them really caught Dev's eye as she tried to rid herself of the jewelry maker's unpleasantness.

It hadn't really been dangerous. She'd been in enough insertions by now to be able to judge the difference in natural born between those who were suboptimal for their own entertainment, and those who truly meant her harm.

This was the first kind. But she wasn't sure why, since driving away customers would seem not to be in the man's best interest.

"He was sub optimal," she concluded, as they came around the corner to see a small area set up with battered plas tables and equally battered square low stools. A tall, weathered female huckster stood behind a high metal bench covered in baskets.

And past her? "Ah." Dev's face creased into a smile.

Jess sat at one of the tables, her long legs sprawled out. As they came into sight she smiled, raised a hand up and curled her fingers at them in a come ahead gesture.

"Dev," Kevin said. "I will come to have a meal with you, but I must first go find a bag like yours." He pointed behind them. "Is that acceptable?"

Dev nodded. "Of course. Go ahead."

Kevin turned and trotted off back down the lane they'd just come up, and Dev continued toward the small meal area that had collected a handful of others. But Jess was alone in her corner, arms spread across the crate barrier behind her that defined the space.

Their eyes met and Dev's grin broadened. She threaded her way through the tables until she reached the one in back and sat on the stool nearest Jess. "Hello."

"Devvieeeeee," Jess warbled. "What do you have there?" She leaned forward to look at the side of Dev's head. "What's that?"

Dev scooted closer. "It's a... I think the person with them called it a jewelry?"

"Ohh." Jess slid nearer and gently touched the lacy metal work clipped around Dev's well shaped ear. "I like that!"

Dev watched from a sidelong glance, as Jess's fingers explored the new adornment, a look of pleased interest on her face. "Yes, I thought you might," she said. "It seemed especially optimal to me since the piece of colored rock in it reminded me of the color of your eyes."

Jess looked up, brows hiking a little in pleased surprise. "Does it?"

Dev nodded, able to confirm the comparison at this close distance, the halon lights overhead reflecting into those pale depths. She was about to relate the disagreeableness of the vendor, then paused, and remained silent, content to just watch Jess react.

"Nice," Jess said. "They have more? I think one of those might actually look good on me."

"Yes," Dev answered after a brief pause. "I can show you if you want?" Perhaps Doctor Dan would have made the vendor more agreeable by now and it would not end up suboptimal.

Jess leaned back, satisfied. "I want, but chow first." She looked over at the woman behind the counter and gave her a nod, then indicated both. "Basket of bits," she said. "Bet you like it."

Dev settled back on her stool and tucked her booted feet under. She swung her bag off her shoulder and set it on the ground, which immediately attracted her partner's attention again.

Jess reached over and touched the bag. "Fishing line?" She asked, in a surprised tone. "That what this is?"

"It is," Dev said, as she watched the woman behind the counter take two plas baskets and fill them with something from a large pot that rested on a heating surface against the wall of the cavern. "I needed something to carry the items I purchased. I ran out of pockets."

Jess lifted the bag experimentally. "Ahhh." She grinned. "Me too, but I ended up with something scrungier." She reached to her other side and lifted a salt and weather-stained rough bag, with several patches sealed onto the side of it. "Scavengers pouch I grabbed from one of the storage rooms around the corner."

The woman came from behind the counter and put down two baskets, then went back and got two mugs and dropped them next to them. "Two," she said, brusquely, then walked back to her station and waited for the next order.

Dev picked up the mug first and took a sip from it. She found the beverage cold and fizzy, and it tasted... well, she wasn't sure what it tasted like, but it was mild and refreshing. She set the mug down and inspected the basket. "Hm."

"Bits," Jess said and squirmed closer. "Don't worry, Dev-vie. I made sure it was all dead before they put it in front of ya." She picked up a thin, plas stick that came in the basket and used it to point at various things. "That's octopus, that's sea cucumber, conch, and ray."

"I see." Dev used the stick that came with her portion and poked the sharpened end into a pale piece of something and put it into her mouth. It was moderately chewy and had a very pleasant tangy spicy flavor. "Mm." She made a sound of approval.

"Thought you'd like it." Jess speared up a bit of something and ate it. "Bycatch," she said. "What's in the nets they can't sell the processor."

"It's good." Dev eyed the jelly like sea cucumber and picked it up with her fingers instead, barely tasting it as it dissolved in her mouth. She moved on to the conch, and that seemed a lot more familiar. "Kind of like a clam?"

"Kinda." Jess took a sip of the beverage. "This is pretty fun, right?" She looked up and waved her stick at the internal space. "Haven't had one of these this big since I can remember. Usually it's just one train, and maybe one row. Two."

Dev now speared up her sea bits more confidently. "The sets are enjoying it. And I saw April with some large items she seemed pleased about." She glanced around. The rest of the tables were now filled, and everyone seemed to also be enjoying their meal. "Yes, it's fun."

She watched Jess nod and look around, a faint smile on her lips. After a moment their eyes met. Dev took a bit of the ray, a dark, thin slice of meat, and reached out to offer it. She expected Jess to take it with her hands.

Instead, Jess, with a little grin, and a twinkle in her eyes, leaned over and took it with her lips, gently nibbling Dev's fingertips as she did.

The sound of the room faded, and Dev's mind went blank, her focus on nothing but Jess's face as she winked at her.

Such an amazing feeling. Dev took in a breath and then winked back, listening to the chuckle as it was only partially successful. They both looked up as they were being hailed and saw Doug and April coming over.

For a moment, Dev sort of wished they wouldn't.

Then she shook herself, and held up a hand in greeting, as their comrades took a seat across from them. Doug unloaded a pack half the size of his body off onto the floor with a grunt.

It seemed like everyone was going home with presents.

Chapter Four

Dev sealed the hatch on the carrier and dusted her hands off as she moved away from the vehicle and back across the stone floor of the landing cavern. Her acquisitions from the market were now stowed away in her storage compartment. She would wait for a correct moment to present them to Jess once they were back at the base.

The market itself was over, and now everyone gathered for what Jess called a potluck meal. Dev resisted the urge to use the carrier's systems to look that up and instead decided to just be surprised.

She had her Bay overshirt on, as the light was fading outside and the chill of the wind invaded the hallways. She was glad of its warmth around her as she walked through the quiet spaces, the other residents all still outside in the outer caverns.

Dev spotted Kevin as he went along the hallway to the operations center. He still wore his new sweater, with a bag like hers slung over his shoulder.

Dev smiled, as she reached the bottom of the stairs and walked along the wide hallway that led to the back entrance. She could already hear the music drifting from the spaces beyond that open door.

It was more… she considered. The music had more energy. It was faster, and louder, and she heard clapping. She assumed the crowd was enjoying it actively, rather than casually listen to the softer sounds she'd heard earlier.

As she walked down the ramp and across the flats she saw some of the vendors pack away their things. Their wagons showing as faint lights in the gloom of dusk.

After the potluck, she was reliably informed, there would be games. Dev was not at all sure what that would be like, but she reasoned it couldn't be worse, or stranger, than the thing with the eyeballs, and the ball throwing dunk she'd seen at Interforce, so she resolved to enjoy that too.

Whatever that ended up being.

"Hey Dev!"

Dev paused as Doug jogged up from behind. "Hello." She greeted him with a smile. "Did you get more things at the market? The bag you had at day meal was big."

"I did," Doug admitted as they walked together. "I just stashed the lot of it in my room. They had more stuff here than I thought they would. I got some sealskin boots that're gonna be great for walking around at Base." He looked around as they neared the cavern entrance. "You got some stuff too, I saw."

"Yes." Dev smiled briefly. "I just put some things in our vehicle."

Doug looked sharply at her. "You think they'd riffle through them here?" His voice lifted. "For real?"

Dev sorted that out in a moment of puzzled silence. "Oh," she said. "You mean people would take them? Oh no. That's not what I thought at all, but I know Jess would peek at what I purchased otherwise as she suspects some of it will be given to her."

"Will it?"

"Yes, of course."

Doug eyed her. "What do you get an agent?" He asked. "I mean, what do you get that won't get you laughed at, or get tossed in the processor?"

They entered the cavern, and paused, as the big space was now full of people, mingling together, traders and Bay residents, and bio alts, with some others interspersed from the sur- rounding areas. A space had been cleared near the little raised platform that now had half a dozen people on it playing...

Playing all kinds of things she had no reference for. The sound was relatively pleasant, however. "What do you get an agent? You mean, what did I get for Jess?" She looked at Doug. "I got things I thought she would enjoy. I'm not sure it... I didn't think about it being for an agent."

"Like what?" Doug persisted. "C'mon, Dev, help me out here. I want to get something nice for April. I like her. You know, like you like Jess."

Dev folded her arms as they edged to one side to get out of the stream of people milling around. The tables that had held things to purchase earlier, were now pushed against the walls of the cavern and had dishes and containers and bowls of things sitting on them that people were taking items from seemingly at random.

"Oh," she said, after a brief pause. "I did not know that."

"C'mon." Doug g r i n n e d at her. "Occupational h a z a r d, right? That's what they told me when I was matched with her. It's cool."

Did she consider Jess a hazard? Dev pondered the question. Jess certainly was hazardous to anyone who was not being correct to her. "I just thought about things I know Jess enjoys," she said. "A cup for tea, some ties for her hair." She paused. "A bracelet."

"April would punch me if I gave her any of those," Doug said, mournfully. "And man, that hurts."

Dev tried to imagine any situation where giving a gift would produce a physical attack from Jess. She came up utterly blank. "How about some gloves for our missions in the carrier?" She suggested warily. "Or some sweet treats."

Doug made a thoughtful sound. "She's always bitching about how cold those triggers are in our bus. Maybe half gloves so she can be comfortable while she's blowing things up. Yeah." He nodded. "That's a great idea, Dev. Maybe I can find someone who has those… what were they that they had in the shuttle?"

"Ginger drops," Dev supplied promptly. "They had them on the fishing boat also. Perhaps they would trade you for some."

"Yep, that's what they were." He patted Dev on the shoulder. "Thanks, Dev. Great idea." He pointed across the room. "Looks like our gang is gathering over there. Wanna go join them?"

Dev had already spotted Jess's tall, distinctive figure, near a scattering of chairs on the far side of the cavern, to one side of a large, open space that had a sand covered floor. It had been blocked off earlier in the day and now seemed to have boxes and equipment scattered around, with the center left wide open. "Yes." She agreed, and they started to make their way through the crowd.

****

The containers on the tables were full of whatever was left from the market, along with some items that were provided by Drake's Bay's mess hall kitchen.

Dev was relatively content with the round plas full of things Jess brought back, as none of them seemed either alive, or trick foods such as eyeballs, though one was round enough to make her pause.

Jess set her own plate down on the small table between their seats, while other visitors milled around just within eye- sight. All watched Jess but pretended they weren't.

Doctor Dan was seated across from her, with a mug clasped in one hand. His eyes slowly moved around to watch the people who pretended not to watch.

Dev found it all interesting. There was an undercurrent of wary tension in the air and after a moment, April looked over and met her eyes, her own shifting around. There was a trader and his mate sitting next to her, making small talk.

Dev inspected her plate and picked up the round thing that wasn't an eyeball, sniffed it and detected the briny smell of sea- food, along with an earthy scent she recognized as mushrooms. She took a bite and was pleasantly surprised at the result.

Chester sat down on the other side of her with a plate. "Those are good," he said, "and these." He pointed at the clams covered in creamy seaweed. "This is all right."

The music, along with the level of conversation was loud enough to obscure most of the speech around them, and Dev wished she'd brought her scanner along with her. "What do you think is going on over there?" She indicated the cleared space.

"Games," Chester said. "Fight games. Heard a bunch of them talking about it when I was coming back down here." He put one of the round things in his mouth and chewed.

"Like what they do in the exercise area?" Dev asked. "At the base?"

Chester nodded, still chewing. "And some shooting, for prizes and stuff." He swallowed. "For the kids mostly. Some of the trader's youngers, some of the kids here."

"Ah, I see."

Doug arrived with two pieces of plas and deposited them down on the table next to April. He gave Dev a wink, miming a hand gesture toward his partner and gave her a thumbs up.

Dev had no idea what that meant and focused her attention on Jess, who leaned toward her, providing a more interesting focal point. "Hello," she said and pointed at the round objects. "Have you tried these? They're excellent."

"Stuffed mushrooms?" Jess reached over, took one off Dev's plate, and took bite. "That's pretty damn good," she said. "You find enough chow?"

"Yes." Dev scooped up some of the clam and seaweed, which she found she liked as well. "Chester was telling me about the activities that will go on over there." She indicated the space. "Are we expected to participate?"

Jess stopped in mid chew, her blue eyes widening. She swallowed hastily. "The games?" She asked in a surprised tone. Her eyes tracked over to the sandy floor at the far end of the cavern.

"Yes." Dev studied her, a little bemused at her reaction.

Jess was briefly silent, then shook her head. "Nah, not that… not this stuff," she said. She picked up her mug on the table and took a swallow. "Base is different. Not good to mix us with civs, Devvie. We don't react well to competition."

"We don't?" Dev said, her expression thoughtful. "Hm." Jess waved the mug to encompass herself, April, and Mike. "Us," she said, with a tone of faint regret. "One of those kids'll do something stupid, get their neck broken, and it'll ruin every- one's day."

April, who'd been listening, nodded. "People come at you in our world. It's not a game," she said, succinctly. "Reflexes don't know it's just a gag. Even in the pit they've got stunners, y'know?"

Jess shifted on her hard, metal seat, with its thin, hammered arms she couldn't quite balance anything on that was useful. "Right. We can just watch and bet."

Mike laughed. "They're not going to take our chits. They'll figure it's rigged."

"Truth," April assented. "It'll be fun to watch the kiddies though." She leaned back on her stool with her back to the wall, one booted foot hiked up on her opposite knee. "Hope they kick nomad ass."

"Or we could go dance," Doug suggested, in a mild tone. "That group's pretty good."

Jess looked sideways at Dev, who had on her most noncommittal expression, and started laughing. "What did you say it looked like, Devvie? People getting electrocuted?" She turned her attention to Dan Kurok, who merely sat there with his ankles crossed. "You forgot the dancing lessons, Doc."

Kurok lifted one pale eyebrow. "I had a week to pull together what we sent Dev with. No. Dancing wasn't on the programming list." He made a low, snorting noise. "Along with ukulele, hopscotch and poetry, or the colloquial language constructs of the Atlantia east coast." He took a sip from his mug. "Which I'm sure Dev regrets occasionally."

"Yeeees," Dev said on a long exhale. "That has been a somewhat steep learning curve."

Everyone chuckled.

Dev studied the dancers. This wasn't something she'd expected to do since the people doing it looked so ridiculous. She glanced at Jess. "It will be entertainment for us."

"It will." Jess half turned to look across the sand. "Look, they're kicking it off with wrestling," she said. "Whoever pins the other person three times, wins."

Dev watched the two figures whirling their arms around in circles with interest. "What do they win?"

"No idea," Jess responded. "Once you go in, you don't participate in any of this, so I usually ducked out and went swimming when I had breaks from school."

Kurok spoke up. "The nomads donated prizes from their stock, the Bay donated prizes from here. The winners get things from wherever they don't come from." He looked up as a slim figure appeared at his elbow. "Hello, Billy."

"Hello, Doctor Dan. I brought you a plate. I saw you hadn't gotten anything." Billy, the BeeAye, set a piece of plas down. "Some things are already consumed," he said, "and these are excellent."

Kurok smiled at him. "Did you make them?" He guessed, his eyes twinkling.

"Yes, I did," Billy answered in a straightforward, unironic way. "Let me know if you like them." He gave the rest of them a little wave and disappeared back into the crowd.

"I saw him going in the kitchen today," Jess said.

"Yes," Kurok said. He sampled one of the items on the platter. "He's just started working in there, under Petar. It was quite an accomplishment to get that to happen." He chewed thoughtfully. "Anyway, that was one of the bastions of suspicion here, because as you likely know, allocations in the kitchen are dear and very much in demand."

Jess merely nodded. "What'd you trade Petar for? He's a hard head."

Kurok smiled. "Herbs. He gets his own little patch of them in the garden. It helps that Billy learns fast, has clever hands, and does what he's told."

The two opponents started their battle at that moment, and everyone turned to watch. Dev understood at once what they were doing. It was a technique for fighting she'd seen some of the agents, and many of the techs use in the exercise area.

The two men were well matched in size, and they went at each other with enthusiasm, both bare to the waist, with half legged work pants that came to just below their knees and bare feet.

The Bay resident had the typical wide shouldered, broad boned physique common to the stakehold, and he used his long reach to good advantage, keeping his opponent away from him as he sought to grapple.

"Jess?"

Jess turned her head from facing the wrestlers. "Yes, oh wrencher queen?" She studied the ear clasp on Dev's ear, twinkling gently in the overhead lighting. "Are you going to ask me why we do these silly things?"

Dev shook her head. "No. I understand that part. We had competitions sometimes too, at the creche on station. We did labs, and worked in the gym and went against each other, for points."

"You win?"

"Sometimes," Dev said. "What I was wondering though was why it was so interesting that Billy was working in the food place. At Base, and at station, we always were assigned that kind of duty."

A loud cheer went up, and Jess looked over to see the Bay wrestler dart in and get a hold on his opponent, lifting him up and taking him backwards onto the sand. A spray of it went in all directions, and then the two of them scrambled to hold each other down.

"Kitchen's always prime slots." Jess said. She kept her eyes on the fight. "You never go hungry." She stopped speaking when the Bay wrestler hooked his leg around his opponent then twisted hard, his body arching as he flipped the other man over onto his back and then leaned forward to pin his shoulders. "Nice."

Dev waited for further explanation as the two men stood up, laughed, and dusted the sand off their bodies. They were replaced with two others, and she recognized Jess's cousin Dustin as the Bay representative.

"Smart of the doc to offer spices to old Petar," Jess said. "He's been bitching about the thieves at Quebec getting them from station for as long as I've been breathing." Jess put her fingers between her teeth and let out a whistle, raising a hand in a fist pump when Dustin looked around for the sound.

He spotted her and lifted a fist in return, and the Bay residents around the arena made a low, but loud hooting noise.

"I see."

Jess leaned close to speak above the roaring noise. "Know what's going to be real fun soon?" She asked. "They're going to play a scrum of rugger." She wiggled her eyebrows. "That'll be a show."

Dev leaned on her elbow. "That sounds excellent, I think."

"Any idea what that is?" Jess asked.

"Not in the least."

Jess chuckled. "You think this stuff is nuts? Wait for that. Half the contestants end up in med." She picked up her plate and put it down on the chair arm, holding it in place so she could share the contents. "That we should get a bet on."

"Want me to get one in the bag?" April offered. "That

wagon driver's dumb enough to do it."

Jess's eyes glinted. "Yeah."

April got up and handed her plate to Doug, then dodged past him and vanished into the crowd.

****

They ended up in the mess, all of them who lasted the distance on the game, either as watchers or players and the victorious Bay youngsters were sprawled across two of the tables covered in sand and a quantity of blood.

The mess had trays of fish rolls out and mugs of cold sea- weed beer and a snack bowl of tiny fried and sea salted fish that were being grabbed up as fast as they arrived.

"Those games seemed very ..." Dev paused.

Jess turned to listen. "What's that, Devvie?"

"The games were interesting." Dev concluded. "It seemed like mostly a fight."

Jess nodded. "Sure." She said. "It's all competition and everyone likes a scrapper." She explained. "All the kids want to be kickass. You get a good rep; nobody screws around with you."

Dev tilted her head and considered that.

"Like being Interforce," Jess continued. "People know that they don't mess with you."

Dev took advantage of the fish rolls, a cup of hot tea in her other hand. She listened to the mostly incomprehensible discussion around her of feints and dodges and body bridges as she regarded the bruised and battered players, enjoying their beer, and the engaged watchers, all chattering.

Jess put her arm around Dev and leaned close. "Rugger's weird, huh?" "But it's fun."

Dev chewed her fish roll and swallowed. "I think I like this part of the game better," she said. "It seems like there are fewer people in constant discomfort and less yelling. And there are snacks."

Jess chuckled, a relaxed and happy sound almost out of place coming from her. "Did you try the fries with eyes?" She indicated the empty bowl, now being refilled by one of the mess workers. "You only get them at parties." She scooped up a handful a fraction of a second before others dove in and offered one to Dev.

Dev inspected the object that had a spicy, salty smell, but was also definitely fish. She took a bite and chewed, ready to take a swallow of the tea to rapidly wash it down, but to her surprise it was crunchy and chewy and tasted nice. "Oh."

It was a whole tiny fish, and it did in fact have its eyes intact. But they were very small and the bones inside were very soft. She had no difficulty in eating the entire object. "That's excellent," she said after swallowing.

"Usually, they grind them up and they go into fishcakes." Jess kicked her boots out a little and leaned back. "But when there's games they save em up and make us a treat." She regarded the crowd. "Good game. We only won by one goal, so the traders didn't think we skunked em."

Dev took another fry with eyes from the rapidly depleting bowl and relaxed against Jess. She noticed how happy the players were, no matter how bruised, and how much enjoyment the rest had gotten watching them battle ferociously with the other team.

They were all brawny, most of them with brown to dark hair like Jess's, a few lighter brown to almost red, none of them pale haired like she or Doctor Dan. They had broad shoulders and long, muscular arms and legs. Their bodies were sturdy and elastic in motion and visibly strong, both the male and female players.

They seemed to enjoy the mayhem of the game wholeheartedly, pleased with having spent hours essentially fighting with other people over the possession of a small gray bag.

Jess grinned as Dustin got up with two others and started mocking out the final goal. Everyone scrambled to get out of their way and drag benches aside.

A wadded-up shirt was the ball, and they grappled and wrangled and tumbled across the room. Everyone yelled out encouragement until Dustin jumped and twisted and unexpectedly got released by the others. He spun out of control right into the table and into Jess's lap.

She tossed her cup away to grab him, and they ended up flat on the floor, gripping each other.

His eyes grew to the size of gull's eggs when he realized what had happened. He froze in place on top of Jess's tall form, his hands going up in that automatic gesture of surrender. In that moment everything went silent, and everyone stopped moving.

The wadded-up shirt dropped from his fingers in anticlimactic counterpoint.

Everyone stared at them as the danger became present and immediate when Jess tensed up and her grip tightened. She lifted him up and off her as she sat up.

Dustin grimaced. "Please don't kill me, cuz." He gave her a beseeching look, squinting at her in hope. "C'mon. I won the game!"

There was a moment when no one really knew what was going to happen. Then she released Dustin, and shifted him away with little effort, but grabbed him by the back of the neck as they stood and bumped their foreheads roughly together.

She came away with a smudge of his blood on her skin, and winked, and shoved him away from the table. "You did, ya scrub. Good job."

He hopped a few times to catch his balance, surprised and relieved when he realized he was in fact safe.

The room unfroze and everyone started moving again and the noise level bumped up, as Dustin went back to his seat and sat down, a faint glisten of sweat on his bare skin visible in the overhead light as he took a deep breath and let it out, and a mess worker came over and handed him a mug of beer.

The rest of the players looked at Jess hopefully. They watched intently as she dusted herself off.

"You all kicked ass," she told them. "Just what you'd expect from one of us," she added. A bit of tingly magic, carried on her words, made an audible pause in the room as she paused. "Hai," she ended, in a louder tone.

"Hai!" They all yelled back at her in a short wall of sound that echoed across the mess cavern. It made the workers in the night watch stick their heads out to see what was going on.

The danger was past, and it was going to be okay. Jess went back and sat down, reaching over for one of the few remaining fries with eyes, waiting for the voices to raise again, and for everyone to look pointedly away from her.

Dev slid back over from where Jess had gently tossed her for safety and handed her a new mug from one of the trays going by. She didn't comment on the event, merely sat with her shoulder brushing Jess's as she sipped from one of the mugs of spicy, pungent beer.

"That's why we're not allowed to play the game," Jess said, after a little silence. "It's fun to watch, but it's too easy to trigger us," she added in a calm, relaxed tone. "Ruins the mood, y'know?"

Invited to comment, Dev leaned over and kissed her on the shoulder instead, then leaned her head on the spot and remained like that, her hands cradled around her mug.

"I wasn't going to hurt him though," Jess went on. "I wasn't triggered."

"No," Dev said. "I didn't think so."

Jess half turned her head and regarded Dev, who looked calm and thoughtful and happy to be there, just leaning against her. "Can you tell?" She asked, in a low tone. "When I am?"

"Yes," Dev said, placidly. "Of course."

"Scare you?" Jess watched her profile intently.

Dev laughed softly, almost under her breath. "No." She looked up at Jess and smiled. "Not at all."

Jess grinned. "I think I'd kinda like it if you jumped on top of me, so ya got a point there I guess."

Dev returned the grin.

A bench scraped nearby, and they looked up to find April settling across from them, with a small bag in her hand. She dropped it on the table with a smirk. "They figured they were just kids," she said. "That was the most fun I had all day, collecting on that bet."

"Ahh." Jess upended the bag, and a cascade of small chits spilled over the table, slithering everywhere. "Nice."

Doug settled next to April. "This was a blast, Jess. Thanks for inviting us."

"Truth," Mike Arias added. "Thanks, Drake."

"Share it out." Jess indicated the pile. "I'll give mine to the kids. Their blood. They deserve a little cred." She stretched out her legs and crossed them. "Probably never have the chance to be here for one these again." She lifted her mug in their direction. "Was a good day."

They returned the small salute. "A good day," Doug agreed. "And we get to see the windows one more time."

April gave him a look and rolled her eyes.

****

Dev walked down the circular stairs and absorbed the quiet of early morning at the Bay. Below her an irregular stream of people headed for the mess, but the crowd was light yet.

The light was marginal, the clouds overhead dark and the plas surface overhead was bombarded by a heavy rain that started falling before dawn. The cavern was mostly lit by the amber tinted halons, with faint shadows of silver. The air itself vibrated with the thunder outside.

Dev was now well used to that sound, the low vibration of the rain rumbling softly in her inner ear as she considered its force and duration, and what that might mean for their trip back to Base 10.

She was dressed in her tech greens, with her flying boots on, her insignia winking in the overhead lights on the stairs. As she reached the fifth level, she waved at the bio alts who had started to make their way down.

Alvin joined her. "Hello, Dev. Are you leaving?" He asked. "You're wearing your uniform."

"Yes," Dev said. "I was just preparing our vehicle for flight and storing my pack. Jess is outside swimming in the sea."

"Really?" Alvin looked over his shoulder. "It's raining and cold outside."

Dev nodded. "Jess enjoys the cold water. There is a small beach outside she finds appealing."

"Natural born are difficult to comprehend sometimes," he offered, hesitantly. "Aren't they?"

Dev nodded. "They are weird. I have learned to just observe and accept things that often have no logic structure."

"Yes."

"Did you enjoy the games yesterday?" Dev changed the subject. "I thought they were interesting."

Bert, a BeeAye, caught up with them. "We were not sure if those were games or fights," he said. He had curly red hair and freckles and attractive dark green eyes. "The natural born seemed to enjoy them. I'd like to try it, to see why the natural born find it enjoyable."

"I as well," Dev said as they reached the bottom level and joined the stream of residents. "However, there is likely not much opportunity for me to do that at the Base as Jess has told me they don't engage in that activity at Interforce." She stopped and drew aside. "I have to finish getting ready to leave."

Alvin just waved and kept going, and Dev turned and went along the wall to the hallway that led to their assigned quarters.

She palmed through the outer door and went along the inner hall to the kitchen space whose windows overlooked the Bay. She collected a cup of tea from the dispenser and sat down at the table to enjoy it.

In the peripheral of her hearing, she picked up the sounds of her fellow techs and the agents in their nearby rooms and briefly turned her thoughts to her decision not to join Jess for a morning swim.

After all, it was raining outside. When she went to the landing bay she'd felt the wet and the coldness of the air as it blew in the opening, dusting her skin with chilly dampness. She had been glad to get inside the carrier to get away from it.

She thought perhaps Jess was disappointed when she'd

turned down the offer to join her though, and now sitting here looking out at the lashing rain and dim light she had second thoughts.

She could have managed it, even without the new suit Jess had designed. It would have been very cold and very uncomfortable, but she felt that it would have pleased Jess to have her there, instead of going out by herself into the gray green sea.

She resolved that the next opportunity that was offered, she would accept and find a way to bear it. That decided, she leaned back and sipped at her hot tea. Through the plas she saw a sea bird flying almost sideways through the rain, wind gusting it almost into the cliff.

Birds needed side thrusters. She watched the struggling creature and willed it mentally to drop down out of the updrafts before it got smashed against the plas and made them both suboptimally unhappy.

She heard the outer door open then. She set her cup down as the sound of wet, bare feet traveled down the passage and then Jess arrived, dripping wet, in one of the brief under suits she wore with her uniform.

Jess's skin was blue with cold and the fabric of the under suit clung to her body.

They regarded each other for a moment in silence. "Yeah, I'm an idiot," Jess said. "Can I have a cup of hot tea?"

"Of course." Dev got up and went to the dispenser. "Was it a nice swim?"

"No." Jess came over and sat down, dripping seawater on the floor. "You're a lot smarter than I am, Devvie. It's stupid cold out there and I went headfirst into a barracuda," she said. "Talk me out of that next time, willya?"

Dev brought the biggest cup she could find full of hot tea over and put it down. Then went back into the quarters she'd been assigned and retrieved a towel, unfolding it as she came back to the table.

Jess had both hands cupped around the mug and sipped from it. She paused as the towel touched her head and glanced over her shoulder, as Dev industriously dried her off. "But I found something for ya," she said and indicated an object on the table.

Dev peeked over her shoulder to see an oval shaped shell. She picked it up, gingerly turning it over in case there was an animal inside. There wasn't, but instead there was a beautiful multicolored polished surface. "Oh!"

"It's abalone." Jess sipped her tea, seeming pleased with

the response.

"Jess, that's very attractive." Dev put the shell down and went back to her drying activities. "Thank you!" She got all the water off Jess's shoulders and ruffled her hair. "The carrier is ready whenever you wish to depart."

"Do I want to depart?" Jess turned and regarded Dev with thoughtful pale eyes. "Yeah, we should get out of here," she answered herself without much pause. "Let's go find out what's going on back at Base. Maybe their powwow scams over and we've got plans to make." She stood up and took her cup with her. "Let me go take a shower and get my ghoul garb on."

Dev watched Jess retreat to her space and then folded the towel, putting it down on one of the weathered surfaces before she exchanged her cup for a fresh, hot one and resumed her seat near the window.

The outer door opened again, and footsteps came briskly toward the kitchen. Dev kept her seat and sipped at her cup, as two Ayebees entered, carrying trays. "Hello, good morning," she greeted them.

"Hello, NM-Dev-1," the nearer Ayebee said. "We have brought you a meal, as they said you were getting ready to leave today. We thought you would like something before you went."

The trays held bowls and cups of various things and the standard battered plates she recognized from the mess. "Thank you very much," Dev said. "Jess is just having a shower, and I know she will appreciate this as well."

"We brought enough for everyone," the Ayebee said. "Please enjoy it!"

They waved and left, and Dev investigated the contents of the trays. She glanced up when there were sounds nearby to find April and Doug come in with Mike and Chester behind them. "We have been brought a meal," Dev said.

They were all dressed in their Interforce uniforms, with light packs slung over their shoulders that were much the same as the one she'd stored in the carrier earlier. April had her dagger on, but the rest of them had left weapons behind as a courtesy, though Mike Arias now also had a knife with a beautifully carved hilt strapped to his calf.

Dev sorted out the trays and put some of the edibles on two of the plates and set them aside.

Jess appeared in her blacks and tossed her pack against the wall. "What do we have here?" She had her damp hair pulled back into a tail and tied with a piece of cord with tiny shells threaded on it. "Who ordered room service?"

"Hey, you're the big kahuna," Doug said and slid some of the hard-boiled plover eggs down to April. "Wouldn't it have had to be you?"

Jess sat next to Dev and pulled one of the two plates over. She picked up an egg and popped it into her mouth and chewed with evident enjoyment. "I didn't ask for it. Devvie?"

Dev swallowed her mouthful. "I did not request it. Some Ayebees from House ops brought it. They said they thought it would be nice for us to get a meal before we left."

"No argument here," Chester said and sat down across from Dev. "Nice to be treated like welcome guests. Most places don't."

"Unless you pay a high ticket," April remarked. "Then they don't care if you're Interforce."

Dev remembered their visit to Market Island, and the spa, and how Jonton had treated them in Quebec. "I don't think anyone here minds that," she said thoughtfully. "Our being from Interforce."

"Here? No." April chuckled. "At least not our bit of Interforce. Long as we have Drake with us, we're honored guests. Right?" She shifted her eyes to Jess, who was munching on chunks of a meaty fish. "They like you now. I heard it from everyone."

"Truth," Doug agreed. "You're the local rockstar."

"Well," Jess said, "half the people who didn't like me got splatted." She chewed thoughtfully on another egg. "Including most of my annoying family. The stakehold ended up getting a crap ton of cred, and now we got a cash crop. They don't have to deal with me on the daily. Why not like me now?" Her tone was reasonable, her expression mildly interested. "I cleaned up my mess."

April nodded. "Like in a big way."

There was one small dish left on the tray and Dev looked inside the cover of it "Oh." She removed a round, slightly fuzzy object. "A peach." She paused, then handed it to Jess. "I think you said you liked these."

Jess didn't take it. "I do," she said. "Cut it up and give everyone a piece. They ain't got many."

They finished up their ad hoc breakfast with a peach split six ways, the fruit's stone removed and left behind in the dish it had come in.

Mike licked his fingers clean of the juice. "That's nice," he said, in a sincere tone. "No idea what it is. Peach you said?" He glanced at Dev. "You could bring a crate of those with you to

Quebec and pay for a three-day party there with em I bet."
"They don't travel well, according to Doctor Dan. They're
soft. So, they wouldn't do well on a ship." Dev said in a regretful
tone.

"They'd be fine in a carrier," April mused, and licked her
lips. "Mike's right. Those shirts up there would give you the earth
for a bucket of these." She regarded the pit left behind thoughtfully.

"Maybe." Jess stood up. "Speaking of carriers, let's go get
in ours." She gave the room a last look around before they
retreated up the hallway to the large, locked door.

****

Dev settled into her pilots' seat and started her pre-checks
as everyone else filed in behind her and took their stations. She
slid her ear cups in place and clipped on her comms gear. She glanced
out the forward hatch at the Bay tech team who came forward to
disconnect her umbilicals.

It was a BeeAye, Ben, who disconnected her, his Bay coverall
with its sleeves rolled up so they didn't come down over his
hands. He waved at her through the plas, and she waved back.
She waited for him to step back before she retracted the cables.

On its own power, the carrier shifted and settled, and the engines
let out their low whine of startup as she fed them energy and
activated all her systems for flight.

She glanced up at the mirror and watched Jess settle into
her gunner's seat, extending her legs, and folding her hands
together. Did Jess want her boards active? After a moment's
indecision, she balanced the engines and retracted her own
restraints. "BR270006 to Drake's Bay Ops, preparing to
depart," she spoke into the comms. "Standing by for clearance."

Then she activated the boards to her right and left, as Doug
settled into the jump seat, and selected the sequence to bring
Jess's controls live and shunt power from the engines to the
guns. She watched Jess's reflection as she caught the change in
status lights and saw the quick smile, as she reached out to
acknowledge them with a press of her hand on the auth pad.

"Drakes Bay Ops to BR270006, you are clear to depart.
There is no other traffic in the area." Kevin's voice responded in her
ear. "Please have a good flight and come back soon!"

"Thank you, Kevin," Dev answered. She flipped on the lights
on the engine cowlings to warn anyone in the cavern that the
carrier was about to lift. "Please be aware, we are about to

depart," she warned her passengers, then shifted power to the landing jets and put the carrier in motion.

Unlike when they landed, she negotiated her way out of the landing cavern with gentle touches on the side thrusters and the landing jets until they emerged into the rain. The carrier moved from relative silence to a heavy thunder overhead.

"Glad we're not outside today," April said from the drop seat.

"Let's get back to base, Dev." Jess hiked up one knee and put her hand on the surface of her uniform boot. "See what we missed."

"Bet they missed more," Doug told Dev. "Bet it was way more fun here than back there."

Dev drifted out across the Bay and waited until she heard the bell below them, smiling, as she turned the carrier and then boosted quickly up and out of the surrounding cliffs and transitioned from thrusters to the powerful engines, rolling up into the sky and accelerating up through the speed of sound, leaving behind a solid boom to answer the tone.

****

Torrential rain obscured almost everything outside, as Dan Kurok stood quietly watching the surface of the Bay from the wide window on the northernmost curve of the wall. To his right was a large former storage area he'd taken over as a workshop, and to his left the long newly chiseled hallway that led to the plant cavern.

He saw the bare outline of a craft gently easing from the landing bay and smiled as it gracefully drifted out away from the wall and turned, then converted to forward motion and took off like what was described in the old days as a bat out of hell.

A breath later a double concussive boom sounded through the walls and rattled some of the equipment on a nearby table.

"Wow, what was that."

Kurok turned to find several young men behind him staring out the window. "Hello, lads. That was a large flying vehicle breaking the speed of sound. You remember that from class, don't you?"

The nearest one nodded. "Oh yes. From flight class, yes I do. It's loud."

"It's loud, but you don't hear it when you're inside the vehicle," Kurok told them. "But you certainly do when you're left behind." He turned his back on the Bay below. "Now, are we ready for our work today? Let's see if we can set up those tables in the lab and get that all arranged."

"Sure, Doctor Dan." They turned and went into the newly opened area and started to work, leaving him in the alcove to ponder the past few days. He was still there when Security Mike came over, a clipboard in one hand.

"Hey," he said, "that was all right."

Kurok looked at him with some puzzlement for a moment. "You mean our little market, or our visitors from Interforce?"

"Drake being here," Mike said. "It was good."

Kurok smiled. "Right up until you all thought young Dustin was going to get his gawky neck broken. That was a moment."

"Nah, he was fine. I could tell," Mike said. "It was all right because she liked the rugger. Didn't figure that. Justin never did. That was a huh." He made a huffing sound. "You heard she gave the kids the cred she won off those traders for the game? Little idiots'll probably wear it like a necklace."

Kurok leaned back against the stone wall, as he once had commonly leaned against the transparent side of a space station. "Did she? She's more social than Justin was, that's for certain. He'd have never invited other agents here or hung around with them."

"Kids, those others."

"Jess isn't much more than a kid. I realized that last night," Kurok said. "They're not a bad bunch. Glad they seemed to enjoy the visit."

Mike nodded. "They'd be all right here," he said, after a pause. "Too bad they're probably gonna croak having to do some pointless crap for people who don't give a shit about them." He shook his head and moved off along the line of the corridor toward the cross walk that would take him to security ops.

Kurok sighed. "It is too bad. Those kids could be a lot more useful to the world if they could focus on something other than violence. Except that's what they'd been bred and trained for, wasn't it?" He watched a flood of bio alts head down toward the plant cavern, the sound of their voices drifting back to him. Certainly, that was what Justin had been born for.

Justin would have killed that kid. Kurok knew that without a doubt. But, from his corner of the mess hall, just watching he'd barely started to get up when he'd taken in Jess's body posture and sat back down, knowing, as Mike had known, that Dustin was in no danger.

In no danger, and in fact, he'd gotten out of it with a head butt from his head of household and a pocket of cred. Amazing really. Or was it? Suddenly he found himself a little curious about Jess, and what her psych profile was, going through Canyon City.

Putting thought to action he pushed away from the wall and went into the large cavern that was in the midst of becoming a lab and workroom for his various projects on behalf of the Bay. There were bio alts, and several Bay residents, setting up tables and surfaces everywhere.

He walked over to where two Kaytees were wrestling a cabinet into place. "Hello there. That's just the right place I wanted that."

One of them looked over and grinned at him "Is it, Doctor Dan? That's excellent." His bay overshirt shifted a little as he took a step back and briefly, a wink of metal showed as his col- lar was exposed. "This is going to be a nice big lab for you, isn't it? Bigger than the one on station."

"Lots bigger," Kurok said. "Kelson, have you finished the work on that light flyer you were talking to Dev about?"

He nodded. "Yes. She helped me adjust the gyro for it, and it's optimal now. It was so nice of her to take some of her time and work with me," he said. "Would you like to see it?"

"I would," Kurok said, briskly. "In fact, would you like to take a ride in it with me? I need to stop by some of our neighbors, and a few other errands."

Kelson's eyes lit up. "Absolutely, Doctor Dan!" He said. "Now?"

"No time like the present, lad." Kurok clapped him on the shoulder, catching the envious look on the other bio alt's face he'd been working with. "Kurt, would you like to come as well? We can go over some flight dynamics and make it a lesson."

"Yes, Doctor Dan, I would really like that."

"Let's go then." He gestured toward the central hall. "I'll just let central ops know we're taking a little trip. You go on and I'll meet you in the landing bay."

He waited for them to scoot ahead of him, then he paused to regard the room, making a picture in his head of what it was going to look like when he was done with it. He nodded a few times, then turned and headed back to his quarters for a jacket.

And a blaster.

****

It was a quiet flight back, the heavy rain drumming on the

roof of the carrier as Dev once again skirted the coastline, finding the changing sight of the ocean's surface and the moving water more interesting than the cragged rocky landscape inland.

Below her, the waves thundered and crashed against the rock walls of the escarpment that ran along their line of flight, some ejecting up almost high enough to dust the bottom of the craft.

Dev glanced in the reflective surface, the only sound the calm whisper of the carrier's systems in her ear as it reported placidly on their technical status, the weather outside, their distance to destination. She reached over and flicked a setting, and in the other bud she could hear the weather and sea outside, and the wind that pushed against the carrier's stolid forward motion. Her new module was performing well, but she was reluctant to break the silence to discuss it, and Doug seated at her left-hand side seemed content to just look out the front screen, his boot up against the curve of the forward wall and his elbow resting on his knee.

Behind her, Jess was relaxed in her seat, her guns deactivated and pushed to one side, though Dev had power in ready reserve for them. She had her head tipped back against the seat and her hands rested on the arms of the chair, eyes half closed.

April studied something she'd taken from her pack, and Mike and Chester were side by side on the back shelf, seemingly content to just ride. Chester kicked his boots idly out a little, the heels thumping rhythmically against the steel supports.

It was hard for Dev to imagine doing that, really. She'd almost always been in the driver's seat in vehicles they were using, the exception being the shuttle on its way down that first time and the boat. After all, that was part of her function, what she'd been programmed for, and what she was very good at.

Because she was. From her very first mission, to this quiet, common flight today, Dev knew and understood that she was the best pilot in the area. She had no idea if there were better in the other areas of Interforce's purview but in this one, there were not.

She tried not to talk about it. She didn't want the natural born to get angry or resentful for something neither they, nor she could change. And performing with less than excellence to prevent that she would not do. The fact that she was the youngest field tech with a senior rating, and a bio alt on top of it, was more than enough.

She adjusted the pitch of their flight a little, as they started around the curve that would take them into Base 10's range, and glanced expectantly at the comms board, waiting for the hail from Base 10 Centops when they came into scan.

For several minutes it was very quiet. Dev reached out and tuned the comms, checking to make sure the channels were set and hadn't gotten turned off during their visit.

Then she heard a soft crackle in her ear, and she leaned back, lifting one hand to adjust the bud and signal to Jess they had incoming comms.

"Interforce Base 10 to incoming flight, please identify." Centops sounded crisply normal.

Dev gave a little nod. "Base 10, this is BR270006 inbound from Drake's Bay homestead. Requesting permission to approach and land." Ahead of her, she saw the tall promontory that was the base, and even from this distance she could see the dark shadow that was the open landing bay.

"Roger that, BR270006, pad 7 is reserved for you, come ahead and land when ready."

All as expected. "Thank you, Base 10, we are ten minutes from final approach." Dev closed the channel and turned on the carrier's landing lights.

"Home sweet home." Jess said in a reflective tone. "Least we don't have to land in the rain anymore. How idiotic was that? Taking us that long to figure out we should put the landing door on the side of the mountain instead of the top?"

"Tradition," April remarked. "Sticks like plas glue."

Dev brought them around into the landing zone and slowed as they came to the level of the bay. The inside work lights were on full blast, and the ring of inset guidance lights, a deep vivid blue, guiding them in.

The rain thundered down over them until they crossed the verge, and then it was almost shocking in its absence, until the sounds of the ongoing work flooded in, the bongs of the over- head cranes and steel being cut and someone hammering metal.

The central lane ingress was clear, and Dev drifted down it, passing carriers being worked on either side as she went to the pad in the back, the one they'd left from.

It was a large pad, with just a little extra space, and two extra work bays near the back wall of the cavern and she neatly turned the carrier as she arrived above it and settled down in one smooth motion to the skids.

Around her she heard and felt the motion as the agents and techs unclipped restraints, got up, collected their gear, while she went through the motions of shutting things down and securing systems.

"Hey, Drake," Mike Arias said. "That was a nice break."

"Yeah," April agreed. "Big props."

Jess shrugged into her pack, that had bags and other things strapped to it. "Yeah it was fun," she said. "Glad it was better than last time." She fastened the pack belt around her waist with a soft clicking sound. "Can't have things go to crap every time I guess."

Dev reached over and released the hatch, and it retracted, then swung open to let them out, the exit ramp extending and locking in place. She pushed back her seat and released her harness, going through her procedures with smooth automatic motions.

Everyone trooped out save Jess, who stood quietly by her seat, waiting for Dev to finish her tasks. "Whatcha think, Dev?" She asked, idly.

"About our visit to your birthplace?" Dev unhooked her ear buds and shut down power to the grid and stood and moved behind her station. "I had an excellent time." She went to the storage cabinets to retrieve her things. "Didn't you?"

Jess leaned against the carrier wall. "Yeah, I did," she admitted. "Most fun I've had there probably since I left the first time." She waited for Dev to finish getting her things and then they left the carrier.

"Home sweet home," Jess repeated, in a musing tone. "Let's put our stuff away and see what's been going on."

Chapter Five

Dev was behind her worktable in the tech lab, examining a circuit layout under the intense focus light when Brent found her there late that afternoon.

"Here you are."

Dev glanced around then up at him and smiled. "Yes, here in fact, I am. How are you?"

"Heard you guys had a party."

Dev sat up and swung the light aside a bit so her eyes could adjust to the lower light of the lab. "At Jess's home place? Yes, it was nice," she said. "There was a market, and they did some..." She paused. "There were some activities and music. It was very enjoyable."

Brent nodded the whole time she was talking. "Chester won't shut up about it," he said. "Can you get us on the list next time? Me and Jase?" He grinned at her. "I know Jess'll do it if you ask her."

Dev considered that. "I think Jess would do it if you asked," she replied. "I know she likes both of you and would be glad if you wanted to visit her home place. But yes, I will mention it. I think you would have had a good time."

"I saw the knife Arias brought back. It's sweet," Brent said. "Didn't figure there was much to go to on the south side. Thought we'd have to go to Quebec, and that's off limits."

"Is it?" Dev leaned on the counter. "That is the same, then?"

Brent nodded. "We can go west if we have to, and up to North, down past where Jess's place is, but that's it. Ain't nobody wants to go to North."

No. Dev herself had no desire to go there. "I remember what it looked like after it got attacked," she said. "I can't forget that."

"Everyone there's sour anyway," Brent said. "Anyhow least you got to do something. It's dead as a doornail here. Not nothing coming in. Just some word they got some big conference going on over in Juneau." He leaned closer to her and lowered his voice. "Jase thinks it's a scam. You know, to suck them in over there and keep it quiet here for a while."

Dev regarded him somberly. "That could be true," she said. "Or they do not wish to have a fight like the last one for a while."

Brent grinned briefly. "Yeah, that's bingo." He put the tip of his finger on his nose. "But hey we got time to get stuff all rigged up good, and get some newbies in. Heard a class is coming out."

The last class had produced April and Doug, and Mike and Chester, so Dev viewed this in a positive light if more people like them came to the base and ended up on their team.

Jess liked them. Jess had not liked the agents that had been there before, most of which now were gone, made dead. So perhaps the new agents, whoever they were, would be as excellent.

"Whatcha working on?" Brent asked, pointing at the card. His whole attitude seemed to have shifted 180 degrees his reassignment, to the point where he seemed like a different person.

Dev found that interesting. "So, this is an autonomic systems control module." She pushed the card forward and toward him. "It interfaces with all the flight systems and lets you program them remotely."

Brent blinked. "You kidding? Remote like, from here? Like anyone could make it do stuff?"

Dev shook her head. "No, it's biometric pattern keyed to the authorized pilot," she explained. "Because you don't want someone else doing that while you are in the middle of a mission."

"So, you could fly your rig from sitting in bed?" Brent whispered. "Is that what you mean?"

Dev sat up and frowned at him. "Why would I want to do that?"

"No," he said, "you could be on a drop, and you could make the bus come and like, distract people, or get it to where you need to be?"

"Yes, exactly." Dev glanced around the tech room. "It's very quiet in here today," she said. "I was going to see if anyone wanted to help install this."

"Count me in," Brent said, "and lemme give Doug a buzz. They got a scrounge party goin on in storage. That's where everyone is. Most of us can't build from scratch like you can."

He tapped the desk. "Be right back," he said and trotted off before Dev could answer him. She sat there for a long moment and thought about what he'd just said.

"Hey, Dev."

Dev looked over her left shoulder. "Hello, Clint. How are you?" She greeted the mech supervisor.

"Doin all right." Clint nodded, "Have a nice visit? Heard from Doug it was a good time."

Dev was a bit taken aback at how quickly word seemed to have spread about such a non-operational event. "It was excellent, thanks," she said. "Clint, may I ask a question?" She diverted the conversation, since Clint would have the answer to her pondering, she was confident.

He looked pleased and walked over to lean against her cabinet. "Shoot."

Dev paused. "During the training for the technical position I am currently filling, do they include training in systems fabrication?"

Clint laced his fingers together and leaning back against the wall. "Like what you do, you mean?" He indicated the board at her elbow. "Making stuff? New stuff? Designing and all that?"

Dev nodded. "I received programming for building components," she said, then paused. "I thought others would receive that in their preparation classes to come here."

"I came in through trade, not the tech route," Clint said, after a long pause for thought. "You know, I apprenticed to my uncle, learned how to fix stuff, that kinda thing. I can't say really about what the kids learned at school, but I'd say no, they didn't get that."

Dev wasn't sure exactly what his tone indicated. "It's useful," she said, in a diffident tone.

He laughed at that. "Yeah, but those kids... listen, Dev, you're not.... Most of those kids are book learners who want excitement. They don't want to build stuff. They want to make cred and it's a way out of their stakehold."

"I see," Dev said, but really didn't.

"If you'd have come in the regular way, you'd have ended up working over in Juneau, or Picchu. That's where they design our stuff and develop new things like what you do." Clint pointed at the card again. "That's why you stand out so bad here. No one does that who's in service, in the field. They wouldn't have sent you out here."

"Ah," Dev murmured. "That's very interesting."

Clint smiled. "Anyway, don't let it stop ya. Just don't let them talk you into going off and working out there. We need you here." He winked and patted the console, then went back to his three-cornered workstation in the very back of the tech lab.

Dev folded her arms. "Interesting," she repeated. "But weird and possibly suboptimal." Her comms buzzed and she tapped it. "Dev."

"We're in the work bay, c'mon!" Brent's voice buzzed through in her ear. "Got an engine misfiring we can't figure out."

Dev picked up her new card and slipped it into a static repellent folder, then put it under her arm and started for the door.

****

The meeting room seemed undersized for the people who were in it. Agents tended to be tall, and the space was filled with them. Jason, at the head of the rectangular table, faced Jess at the far end, with eight others crammed in on either side.

This was room was smaller than the one they used for ops briefings. This one was at the back of Centops, restricted entry, around the corner from Jason's office as the director. It was usually used for small groups. There was just enough space for all the agents they currently had, so Jason had called them there.

"So." Elaine leaned back. "Any news?"

Jason shrugged his broad shoulders. "Same as the scuttle-butt everyone's heard. Everyone is to stay put, keep your mouths shut and your guns off," he said. "So that's the rules of the road right now."

"We should at least put some scouts on the ground in Quebec," Elaine said. "They're going to take the opportunity to get in there."

"They're supposed to be staying put too."

Elaine rolled her eyes. "C'mon, Jase. "

Charlie Boone spoke up. "She's right. They bring over all the talking heads on that side, while the pointy end starts showing up on this side. They want Quebec."

Jason glanced across the table. "You're both probably right. But that's all I heard. If there's more to it, I'm not on the party list. There are folks out there who probably haven't forgotten I shoved my boot in their ass when they showed up here last time."

Jess smiled at him but kept silent.

"Anyway," Jason said. "They're graduating a class in a week and a half. We're slated to get a half dozen teams out here."

"With all that stay put stuff?" April asked. "They send a dozen more of us? What does that say?"

"They gotta do something with em," Dave Carter said. "It's rotation time out there. Gotta move all the levels up."

"We're getting space ready for them," Jason said, "and we'll have to go through the dog and pony show. Let's see what we can do to start tuning things. We're getting six pairs, North's getting three. So maybe the message that sends is, we'll stay quiet, but not for long."

Elaine nodded. "That's better," she grudgingly noted. "I just don't want them to get the idea they can wander in here."

"Everyone agrees, El," Jason said. "And even if we can't get to Quebec, maybe we can put feelers out to people who can. So that's all for now."

No one was satisfied. Jess felt it as they stood and moved toward the door. She stayed seated, because Jason stayed seated, and he was looking right at her.

No need to tell her to stay. No need to work hard to feel the jealousy and resentment of some of the others who hesitated before leaving. They hoped to be told to stay behind as well, sensing privileged communication they wanted to be a part of.

But at last, the door closed behind Elaine, who was of all of them the closest to Jason and had been paired with him in the field before his promotion. Friends from field school, and casual lovers the rumors said.

Jess assumed that Elaine expected to be in Jason's confidence. She'd made a point of shooing the others ahead of her and pulled the door closed as though she was part of the game, and maybe, Jess thought, she was.

Jess had no expectations of the kind but there was something there that had brought him down on her side when logic dictated otherwise, and she wasn't about to turn down intel regardless of the reason. Aside from the fact that she liked both Jason and Elaine and always had.

"So," Jason said, after the door was closed and sealed. "How's the old place?"

Jess relaxed and propped her knee against the table, her posture sending a friendly message. "They're doing good. Had a caravan by when we were there. Ended up watching a rugger match and almost killed a cousin." she said, casually. "Usual Bay visit. Had some clam stew, got some nick knacks."

Jason smiled. "Brent heard it from Chester and Doug. They said it was cool, and your fam didn't shiv you this time."

"Come with me next time," Jess offered as though it had just occurred to her and hadn't been suggested to her by Dev. "Not sure when next time'll be but when it is…"

Jason also relaxed, twiddling his input stylus between his fingers. "I don't think this pow wow's gonna last long. I think E's right, it's just a decoy." He looked back at her. "What I don't get is that's so obvious to us, why isn't it to anyone on the other coast?"

"Maybe it is," Jess said, then stopped.

"Part of the scam?" Jason asked.

"Maybe."

He shook his head in frustration. "Doesn't really make sense, Jess. I just don't trust anything right now. Every time I talk to those people I feel like I'm inserted. You know what I mean? Every word has double meanings."

Jess nodded in understanding. "I get it. I totally get it. Who's the enemy?" She pointed east. "Them?" She pointed west "Them? Us?"

"Who's the enemy," he repeated back to her. "I keep hoping this all ends up better than I think it will, but man, Jess, my tongue itches."

"Got it," Jess said. "All we can do is do what we do. We'll end up somewhere."

"Fish food." He smiled without humor, field school joke.

"Maybe." Jess met his eyes with calm. Death to either of them was a bland void. She didn't fear it. She knew he didn't either.

They looked at each there for a minute, in silence. "Glad you got to go home, Jess. For sure the next time I'll tack on," he said, with a faint smile. "I'd like to see the place without any guns blazing," he added. "Bet that big hall looks nice without blood and bodies all over it."

"Yeah, cleans up nice. Next time you're on the invite list." Jess pushed herself to her feet. "Now we prep for some kids," she said. "Let's see what that's gonna be like."

"Let's see."

****

"Now, when it's raining like this, you have to be careful how you take off, lads." Kurok sat in the passenger seat of the light flyer; arms folded as they lifted off from the small plateau outside Cooper's Rock stake hold. "Remember all that water offsets lift."

"Yes, Doctor Dan." Kelson was seated in the pilot's station, and Kurt was in the copilot's seat, busy with navigation. "It feels much different!"

Strapped behind his seat was a crate full of minerals, very recently traded for a crate full of plant matter, the ostensible initial focus of this little journey. Coopers was a mining stake hold and had always had warily good relations with the Bay, but now were proving to be a nice little trading partner much to everyone's surprise and delight.

Well mostly.

Kurok regarded the landscape outside the forward screen. "Now, Kurt, let's see how the flyer operates on a longer journey. I'm going to give you some coordinates and you put them in."

"Yes!" He swiveled around confidently to the navigation panel. "Go ahead, Doctor Dan."

Kurok recited them and watched as they were entered. "That's it, lad," he said, encouragingly. "Go ahead and plot that, and it's going to ask you, are you sure?"

Kurt nodded. "Yes, it says unknown destination," he reported. "It wants me to confirm commit."

"That's right. It's fine. Just tell it to commit."

The bio alt obediently did as he was told, and the flyer lifted over the cliffs and turned to the west. "Now go ahead and put some speed on, Kelson," Kurok said, placidly. "It's a couple of hours trip, but let's see how fast we can go there, and come back."

With a brisk nod, Kelson adjusted his controls and then fed the engines power. The flyer boosted up and cleared the cliffs. "Doctor Dan, should we go above the clouds? Then it wouldn't be raining," he asked, after a moment of adjusting the pitch of the wings. "Would it?"

"Excellent question, Kelson. Here's some thoughts behind that possibility. You see, there's a tradeoff in the ability of the air to lift our wings and the lack of density of the air the higher we go. But let's give that a try, shall we? Proceed to, let me see, yes, you go up another five thousand and see what that gets us."

Kurt looked over his shoulder. "Doctor Dan, this is fun. Thank you for letting us do this."

"Yes, thank you!" Kelson chimed in, as he finished adjusting the ailerons.

Kurok smiled at him. "My pleasure, lads." He glanced over to his left, where there was another small box lashed to the flyer wall. "It's great for me to get a chance to do some practical labs with you. Everyone wins, right?"

"Yes," Kurt said, in a satisfied tone. "This is excellent."

The flyer punched through the lower layer of clouds and then was in clear air, with another layer above them. "Oh," Kelson said, in surprise. "There's more clouds."

"But less rain," Kurt observed. "Interesting."

"Above that second layer, if we went there, we'd see space," Kurok said. "But there's not enough air to support the plane. That's where rockets need to be used."

Kelson nodded. "Like the shuttle. Yes, I remember the vehicle had both types of power plants. I spoke to NM-Dev-1 about what it was like to fly like that. She said it was very interesting."

Interesting. "Ah, Dev's learning the nuances of understatement. That's great. But we don't have rockets on this plane, so we'll stay here," Kurok said. "But you see, there is less rain, but we also have less lift. Watch the flaps there."

Kelson watched the control surface intently. "Yes, it feels different," he said.

The flyer was a lightweight passenger vehicle, made for six people, plus two pilots or fewer with cargo. Right now, only two passenger seats were installed, the back of the vehicle had skids on the metal composite floor with tie downs for small crates.

"Where are we going, Doctor Dan?" Kelson asked, after they'd flown in silence for a while. "Is it really unknown?"

Kurok smiled at him. "It's not unknown to me, lad," he said. "It's a place where natural born go to be taught things, like I'm teaching you now. I just have an errand to run there, and you're helping me do that." He glanced at the box. "We're going to bring a little gift to young Tayler. Do you remember Tayler from station? He came to visit us."

"Oh yes!" Kurt looked around in surprise. "We were playing with him in the lab before, when we all had to go on the shuttle." He paused. "He is from our place. He is related to Agent Jess."

"Yes, he's from Drake's Bay. He's Jess's nephew. I'm going to bring him something from there that I think he will enjoy."

"That's excellent, Doctor Dan." Kelson nodded in satisfaction. "This is very good work."

Kurok settled back in his seat and extended his legs out, crossing them at the ankles. "Oh, I think so." He smiled, his eyes twinkling just a little. "We always want to do good things for other people, don't we?"

"Yes," Kurt said, with a nod. "We certainly do."

****

It was well after noon before they came into the vicinity of Canyon City. Kurok watched through the forward screen as the once familiar landscape came into focus ahead of them, a never-ending stretch of craggy flatlands and rubble, with mountains rising behind it.

Past the nearest range they would fly over the plateau that held the gates of the Interforce training facility, which he never in the privacy of his own mind called a school.

He knew better than that.

Oh, for the youngers, the children they took in from families, some willing and some not, there was learning. The education they gave those kids was the equal of any anywhere, in math and technology, in learning skills, in science. It was where he, after all, had first realized he had the aptitude for genetics.

In those classrooms, surrounded by just post adolescents like he was, who were already so dangerous they had protocols around them.

Where he, without effort, academically excelled and achieved respect for doing so. It was here he encountered the mountain he had to climb in other areas these kids had been being trained on for half a decade already before he'd arrived.

"We are almost at our destination, Doctor Dan," Kurt said. "There seems to be something ahead of us."

Kurok smiled, without much humor. "Yes, lads, there is. That's the Interforce School there, just on the horizon. That's where we're going."

Kelson studied the readouts. "Comp doesn't recognize it," he said. "That seems unusual for such a large facility."

"No, you only know where it is if you know where it is," Kurok said. "It's a special place, and there are many youngers there, so they want it to be hard to find."

Kurt nodded. "Like the nursery rooms at our place where we protected the children, during the fight. They are behind a lot of hallways."

"Exactly, Kurt," Kurok said. "And so, here we are." He leaned over and keyed the comms panel at his right shoulder. "When they hail us, I'll answer, if that's all right with you. I know what to ask them."

Both pilots nodded. "Yes, Doctor Dan."

He had his pitch ready in his head when the hail came, and he waited the correct number of breaths before he keyed the mic and responded, as anyone else who was in a civ vehicle might. "Hello, Canyon City, this is stakeholder proxy for Drake's Bay coming to bring a bit of home to Tayler Drake."

He enjoyed the bit of silence that followed, easily imagining the comm ops tech trying to puzzle out the combination of civilian cheer and normalcy with the use of the facilities nonpublic name.

What would they do? If they'd been in Jess's carrier, it would be a nonevent. Dev would be landing it right next to the ops center, an accepted part of their world, and likely the administrator or a high-level lackey would be hurrying out to greet them.

This light flyer with a newly stenciled dragon guardant on the tail? Anyone's guess. "Now lads, don't be surprised at anything that happens here," Kurok warned. "There are a lot of regulations around this place. Just stay calm and let me handle everything."

Both bio alts looked around at him with slightly puzzled expressions, as though to indicate they never had any intent to do anything but that, a little surprised he found the need to say it.

Which of course they hadn't. They were bio alts, and he was the ultimately trusted and supremely authoritative Doctor Dan.

"Interforce Operations to incoming Drake's Bay," a voice finally answered. "Please land at the visitor facility, forward pad, and remain with your vehicle."

Kurok nodded in approval. Reasonable response, really. "Will do, IO," he said. "ETA five minutes." He responded casually, giving them a few more bits of curiosity to chew over. "Now, Kelson, when we pass that escarpment there, you will see a clear space, in front of some gates. Please land the flyer there."

"Yes, Doctor Dan." Kelson shifted a little and took a firmer grip on the controls. "Is everything okay?"

"Oh yes," he reassured him. "As okay as it could be, lad." He leaned back in his chair and folded his hands over his waist, jiggling his knees a little, a faint twinkle of anticipation in his eyes. "They haven't shot at us yet, so I'm confident it'll be fine."

Kurt looked around at him, eyes wide.

"Just fine," Kurok repeated. "Perhaps five minutes will give them time to figure out who in the hell they were just talking to." He twiddled his fingers. "Though I hope they don't remember me too well."

"Doctor Dan?"

"Never mind, lads. Why don't you just set down. I can show you something interesting on our way back to the Bay."

****

The door to the vehicle cavern was open. It let in a flood of dim, gray outdoor light, and a wash of wet, cold air from the storm lashing the walls outside. A cascade of water flowed off the top of the promontory, forming a small waterfall that ran past the opening, and a rumbling thunder faintly vibrated the walls.

Dev was flat on her back, her head inside the carrier's control console, legs stretched out and crossed at the ankles as she worked with probes to test the intake leads traced on the surface of the system over her.

So far, the testing was going along well. She felt like the board was going to be successful.

"Hey, Dev?"

She glanced toward the open hatch of the carrier. "Hello?"

Clint stuck his head in. "We can't link to your boards in here for updates."

"Yes," Dev said. "I'm testing a new component. I will revert the system when I am finished."

"No problem." Clint half waved at her. "Wanted to make sure everything was okay."

Dev looked thoughtfully at the new board. "Interesting." She probed a different area. "Unexpected, but interesting."

Sometimes modules were like that. She had intent when she programmed them, and yet sometimes when they were integrated, side logic appeared that she hadn't expected. In this case the code she'd used to allow the remote programming interface had, quite rightly, assumed she didn't want anyone but her doing the programming and wanted her auth.

Probably it was disturbing the master control systems, who also, quite rightly, expected to be able to mesh and sync programming across the fleet of carriers for consistent results.

So, interesting, but she would have to adjust it for standard ops.

Footsteps sounded, but these were not Clint returning and she paused again. She reached over and picked up her ear bud and inserted it into her ear. It chimed softly and synced with comms, and she waited as the steps came closer and someone entered, whose walking pattern she didn't recognize.

"Ah, excuse me."

Ah. The new agent, Charlie Boone, the one no one seemed to like. "Hello." She issued her standard greeting.

He stayed near the hatch and put up both hands, palms out. "Okay to talk to you for a minute?"

Interesting approach. It was almost as if he was treating her as most people treated Jess when they were unsure of her temper. "It depends on what you want to talk about," Dev answered in a straightforward kind of way. "And also, for how long as I have a task here I need to complete."

He lowered his hands and sat down on the entrance edge, so that his feet were outside the carrier and just leaned inside a little bit. "I don't really want any trouble."

Even more interesting. "That's excellent?" Dev remained where she was and let the probe rest on her stomach. "I seldom want trouble either, in fact," she added. "Did you expect me to?"

He relaxed just a bit. "The way every person in this rock pile warns me off you, I wasn't sure what the hell to expect," he answered. Despite the scar, he was not unattractive, and he had interesting, intense eyes. "You have a lot of buddies in this place."

Dev considered that for a moment. "Yes," she agreed. "And there is also my partner, Jess."

He nodded. "And also, Jess Drake. The ultimate threat, as in, look sideways at you, and I get my neck broken. You think that's likely?"

"Yes," she answered placidly.

"Really?"

"Yes," Dev repeated, with a slight smile. "Jess does not care for people who are incorrect in that regards," she said. "But you are not being incorrect, so it should not be an issue."

"Okay. Here's my question." He leaned one elbow on his knee and regarded her.

Dev waited, to see if this was going to be a pleasant surprise, like the questions the mech leader at Jess's homestead had been, or an unpleasant one that would involve personal details, or just neither and about being a bio alt or what space was like or something boring.

She was used to the last two and always looked forward to getting the first.

"What does it feel like to just know things," he asked, and then waited.

That was a little interesting. "Do you mean, what does it feel like when you've been given instruction?" she clarified. "Been programmed?"

He nodded.

Dev thought about that for a few minutes in silence, as he just sat there. What did it feel like? How could she really compare it to anything? "If you know what you are getting, then it's like reading a book," she finally said. "Except you don't have to read it."

"Its... just there?"

She nodded. "If they tell you that you are going to do this task, we're going to give you the knowledge. And when you come up, you know how to do it. It's nice. Most sets enjoy it. It means you're being made more valuable, and you will get a better assignment."

Boone remained thoughtfully silent, then took a breath. "Did you get a lot of programming to do this?" He made a vague gesture around him.

"Of course, I did," she said. "When I first came here and drove this vehicle, I would look at a board, and as I looked at each instrument, I understood what it did, and what it was for, and how to use it. That was very useful. I had to do several assignments very quickly."

"Huh, yeah I saw the vids."

Dev watched him in silence, waiting.

"My family had bio alts," he said. "I had a minder; her name was Nelly."

Dev nodded. "An EnEll set," she said. "They are excellent with children. They work in the creche in that function as well." She remembered them, a little, with their cheerful yellow jumpers and straight, dark hair, and how they would come to collect all of them for day meal and sleep.

"Coo Coo" They would call, and clap twice, and the memory made Dev smile, amidst an image of plas, translucent walls and a flash of stars. "I knew some of them." She turned her attention back to Boone.

He cleared his throat. "Well, I wanted to ask her that question, about what it was like. I decided I was going to, one day, after I went to go take some test," Boone said. "Except they took me, and I never saw her again and I couldn't." He stood up outside the carrier and gave her a little wave. "Thanks for satisfying that bit of curiosity."

He walked away down the ramp and Dev studied the now empty spot in the carrier's entry for a moment, considering the interaction. "That was interesting. Though quite unexpected," she said and shifted back and moved her head inside the console again to study her module. "But not really suboptimal."

She made another adjustment and studied the readings, her fingers moving almost automatically as she thought about what else she wanted the module to do.

Then the overhead bong'd and that echoed inside her ear

bud. She paused to listen, a little surprised when an all call requested field teams to ops conf sounded. "Also unexpected." She looked up and made a last adjustment to the module and then slid out from the console and closed it. "But maybe not suboptimal."

She dusted herself off and left the carrier to see other techs disengaging themselves from tasks as she was. She walked down the ramp and joined that movement of green, easily spotted among the brown and blue suits of automation and mech.

They all joined together on the central walkway as they approached the ramp into the main part of the facility. They made the turn up the hallway that was coded for ops and passed without hindrance the scan ring that bisected it and would brusquely push back anyone else.

"They can't have given up that parlay so fast," Doug said, a smudge of dark green grease over one eyebrow. "Something must have happened."

"Coulda," Brent said.

"One of two things," Chester predicted. "Either they gave up on the yak yak and we gotta get back to grind, or what they did was a trap, and we gotta go rescue someone's ass."

"Or take vengeance," Doug said. "I know which one April'd rather."

Dev had nothing to contribute, and no additional information to provide, so she merely walked along between them. Ahead of them she saw movement in black, as agents also headed into the briefing center.

Waiting her turn to enter the briefing center door, she looked inside and spotted Jess already there and slipped through the crowd to get to her partner's side. "Hello."

"Yo, Devvie." Jess was in one of the seats at the back, and she patted the empty one next to her. "Saved ya a place," she said with a wry smile, as there had really been no effort on her part since the rest of the operations teams assumed her presence there automatically.

"Thank you." Dev sat down and looked around to detect an uneasy air and guarded expressions on the faces of the people in the room. "Is there an issue?" She looked up at Jess, who casually looked around.

Jess leaned over and spoke quietly. "Couple of suits came in about an hour ago. Something's up."

"Is this an excellent thing, or not so much?" Dev asked.

Jess looked off into the distance for a long moment, then looked at Dev and shrugged. " I only have a gut feeling. I didn't recognize the suits. They weren't any of the ones who'd come out the last time. But I do know Jason and my read of his body language is trouble."

"Now, whether it's good trouble or bad trouble, or trouble for someone else, we'll soon find out. At least it's something, which is better than hanging around doing nothing," she admitted. "I don't like being grounded."

Dev settled back in her seat, her hands resting on her knees, waiting to see what the something would be.

****

"The decision's been made that we're just spread too thin," the suit said. He stood at the head of the table, his fingertips resting on its surface. "No reflection on anyone here, it is what it is. What happened… well, it happened," he said, with some emphasis.

The woman who'd come with him nodded in silent agreement.

They were both admin types. Dressed in almost civs, expensive looking jackets and leggings, with flashes of glitz on her ears and his fingers. A senior director and project manager none of them had ever heard of.

Jess leaned back in her seat and laced her fingers together, aware of Dev giving her a sideways glance. "It happened," she remarked mildly.

The man looked at her, then looked away, unable to return her intent stare, a slight flaring of the nostrils she recognized as someone who feared the crazy and was working hard to hide it.

Jess smiled.

He cleared his throat. "We're going to shut down these eastern stations and pull everyone back to the west and regroup. It puts a buffer between us and them, and lets things cool down while we build ourselves back up," the man concluded. "Anyone got any questions?"

April managed to speak first, ahead of the indrawn breaths around the room. "What happens to the people who live out here?" She asked in a flat tone. "The ones who depend on us being here to not get whiffed."

The suit looked at her. "They'll survive, just like they always have. There's not much to squabble over." He shrugged one shoulder. "Without us here, I doubt there'll be much interest."

"What about Quebec City?" Elaine spoke up. "They've got

something to fight over."

"They know how to make deals," the suit answered, bluntly. "You've been there. You know they play the game. They'll be fine."

The woman stepped up next to him. "We've got berths for all of you, and you'll retain all your status and rankings," she said, briskly. "I think some of you came from out there. It'll be nice to go home, won't it?" She looked at Doug, who stared back at her with a blank expression. "No? Well, you'll get used to it. More civilized than anywhere around here in case you've forgotten."

"I remember," Doug said. "Why I was so glad to get sent here."

The woman glanced at him and frowned.

"So, we'll get started on shutting things down. You all can help by getting your things packed up and getting ready to head out. We want to be out of here by tomorrow before dark," the man said. "Dark here, which means we'll get back to the coast by dark there."

He paused, as though waiting for more commentary. He seemed surprised and a little discomfited by the utter silence facing him. "Okay, so that's that. C'mon people, tomorrow's another day. We'll take the fight somewhere else." He picked up the packet of plas he'd been carrying and tucked it under his arm. "Briana?" He indicated the door behind them, which lead into the ops corridor. "Anders? Your office."

The door closed behind the three of them.

There was a moment of silence, then Doug drew breath to speak again, but stopped when April put her hand on his wrist and squeezed it. "Don't waste your breath," she said, in a flat tone. "This is a done deal."

Then she turned her head deliberately and looked at Jess.

Jess reached up and ran her fingers through her hair. "Might as well go get a last round of surfing in I guess," she said, in a casual tone. "You up for that, Devvie?" She glanced sideways at her.

Dev had her most noncommittal expression on. "That would be excellent," she said and stood up as Jess did and followed her toward the door. "I don't think I really have that much to pack anyway."

"Not a bad idea." April stood in place and dusted herself off. "You?" She looked at Doug.

"Sure." Doug got up, and Mike and Chester followed suit as they all made their way to the door and the outer hallway beyond.

There was a long pause, and then Brent stood up and went out.

That left Elaine there, with the two new agents. "Wasn't how I was looking for today to go." She said, bluntly. "With us running."

"That how you see this?" Charlie said. "Running?"

"What'd you call it, strategic rear advance?" Dave Carter spoke up, earning a surprised sideways look from Elaine. "Dude, they're scarpering their little asses out of here and running home to the Juneau hills. They're gonna go hide."

"Other side's going to come in and take this whole section over." Elaine said, with a faint shake of her head. "Doesn't even matter if it has anything but oysters to offer them. It's territory." She paused. "And they lost a lot of it over the years."

"Ah, they don't care." Boone half shrugged. "They're going to cut a deal, so we become one big happy planet again." He stood up. "Until we just start stabbing each other in the streets." He shook his head. "Glad I didn't bother unpacking."

He left, and that left Dave and Elaine regarding each other across the table. "You been here a while?" He asked her.

"All my career." Elaine responded straightforwardly. "I take it as a point of pride to be able to say that and still be around and breathing. There's no tougher station then this one." She got up. "Maybe I'll go surfing." She said. "Damned if I want to go play footsie with that pair of wankers." She lifted her voice and tilted her head at the ceiling. "Record that, assholes."

Dave sat in the empty briefing room for few minutes, regarding the walls and the empty chairs around him. Then he smiled, and pushed himself to his feet, carefully moving his chair into place against the table before he turned and walked out.

****

Dev detoured past her quarters to pick up her portable scanner in its weatherproof case. She slung it over her shoulder as she let the door close behind her and went back up the operations hall. She shook her head as she went over the meeting they'd just had.

"Dev."

Dev paused as a KayTee caught up to her. "Hello."

"We heard the natural born are going to close this facility down." The KayTee's eyes were wide. "Is it true?"

"That is what they told us." Dev saw no point in not confirming the news that had surely spread through the halls as fast as she herself could run them. "We will go to a different place, on the other side of the landmass."

"Have you been there?"

Dev shook her head. "No, I have only been to the Interforce school." She studied his face. "It could be an opportunity for good work. There will be things for us to do there."

The KayTee studied her for a long moment. "I don't think we're going," he finally said, in a low, almost breathless voice. "I don't think they want us to go."

Would that be true? Dev pondered the thought. "We are all valuable assets," she answered, slowly. "It would be suboptimal for them to just leave us behind." She paused. "Did you hear something about that?"

He shook his head. "I just think it's going to be that way," he admitted. "Just the way they looked at us."

The halls were empty, and yet Dev felt an urge to look carefully around where they were standing, or to take out her scanner and see what was in the air, what was maybe listening to them. "Well, we have to wait to see what happens," she finally said. "I'm going to go down to the caverns. Jess wishes to have a last time to surf in that place she likes."

"We have to see what's going to happen," the KayTee said, in a mournful tone. "Maybe it will be good, and you are right, Dev. It could be excellent work."

Dev gave him a little wave, then started off down the hall-way again. She felt troubled. What she'd said was true. The bio alts at the facility were all well trained, skilled workers, valuable to Interforce. It would make no sense to just leave them behind.

Why would they?

Dev turned the corner to move down the long rampway to the lower levels when the man who'd given them the news stepped out from a door and held his hand up to her.

Dev casually slid her hand under the shoulder strap of her scanner and paused. "Hello," she said.

"Hello, is it…Dev?" The man asked and smiled at her.

"Yes," she said. "NM-Dev-1, but please call me Dev."

The woman came up behind him, from the small room beyond. "Oh, it's senior tech Dev," she said. "I really hoped to get to meet you. We've all heard so much about all the things you've done here."

The man nodded. "Yes, we're looking forward to talking to you once we get back to the West, Dev. I think there's a lot of opportunity there for you. I hope you're looking forward to it." "You know…" The woman came closer to her. "I really don't know if they've talked to you about your status, have they?"

Dev's nape hairs prickled. "I am not sure who they are," she temporized. "But I am content with my status."

"Yes, of course," the man said. "You are a bio alt, after all."

"I am," Dev agreed. "I have enjoyed my assignment so far and would like to continue to do so."

The two exchanged glances. "Hang on." The woman ducked into the room and then came out with a plas envelope in her hand. "Might as well give this to you now… here." She offered it. "It's your citizen validation and credentials. I know you've been… well… acting in that regard for a while, but here it is officially."

Dev reached out and took the envelope.

"We wanted you to know, that is, Interforce did, that you're a really valuable technician," the man said, in an earnest tone. "And you're going to have a lot of opportunity in our technical centers. You can decide what you want to do there, you understand?"

"You don't have to go along with anything that might… well, with any plans that get made or with anyone here," the woman said, with emphasis on the words. "Do you understand, Dev?" She stared at Dev intently. "You can make your own choice to do what's best for you. Do you get it?"

Dev tucked the envelope under her arm. "Yes, I do under-stand," she said evenly. "Thank you very much, that's very interesting information." She paused. "Now please excuse me, I have a task I have to carry out."

"No problem, thanks for the chat." The man lifted his hand in a little wave. "I know you've got lots of things to do before we leave tomorrow."

Dev turned and continued down the rampway away from them.

"Think she gets it, Briana?" The man asked, in a musing tone.

"Oh yes, I think so." The human resources executive said.

"I've seen the files on her, Alan. She's smart, and you've seen the advances she's registered in what, a half a year? What an absolute waste having her tied up out here."

"Mm." He nodded. "One good thing that's come out of this place." He jerked his head toward the inner hallway. "Want to see what we can scare up for dinner?"

"Scare's the word."

Chapter Six

April sat on a rock, dressed in her surfing suit newly retrieved from fab. "This is bullshit," she said. "Fuck if I want to go out there."

"Fuck if I want to go, and I'm from there," Doug said, kicking his heels against the rock next to her. "Damned if I know why I'm so mad though. It's not bad out west. They got a lot more places like Quebec."

"Maybe because they came here to kill us?" April suggested. "Not looking forward to bumping into guys I had to tie up and beat senseless in battle."

"Well, there's that," Doug agreed. "But some of those guys ended up okay."

Jess stood near the edge of the flow with her hand on her board. She wore her worn old covering.

"I just don't like how they're abandoning the area," Mike said. "It just seems sketch."

"Sketch," Chester repeated. "Like it's a big scam."

April nodded. "That's what I said. Scam." She looked over at Jess. "Scam?"

Jess turned and leaned against the rock and folded her long arms as she faced them. "Does it matter?" She said. "I mean, what are the scenarios." She crossed her ankles. "One, they're doing a deal with the other side that involves taking us out of here and leaving it open to them."

"Would they do that?" Mike Arias asked. "Why?"

"If they thought there was nothing of value here? Sure. Why not? Maybe they're trading it for something on that side. Maybe Market Island. Who knows?" Jess responded. "Two, they decided being out here leads people inservice to become rebels." She grinned briefly. "Since we shot at them, and Jason told them to kiss his ass."

"We did," April conceded, with a return smile. "I guess there's a grudge coming for that."

"Like ours for what they did," Mike said.

"Three…" Jess paused, as she spotted motion near the entry and stretched up to her full height as Dev came into view. "Three, it's just true. This place is like a tomb, and it makes no sense to keep it open until there's more people to put here."

Brent was in the pool, up to his neck in water as it swirled around him. "S'what Jason said," he admitted. "Just makes sense."

Doug sighed. "Yeah. Walking these empty halls is depressing." He walked over and jumped into the pool, disappeared into the swirling waters then emerged, to swim over to where Brent was propped against the rock wall. "Least we got to try out our new togs. Dev was right. These are ace."

"These rigs are good," Brent agreed. He plucked at his sleeve. "You can sit here and get a backrub and not freeze your ass off."

"Yeah, nice job, Jess." Mike went over and sorted through the boards propped into the niche to select one. "We can take these with us, right? They got waves on that coast." He looked over at Doug, his dark brows lifted in question.

"Sure," Doug said. "Not much like this though. The water here's... I don't know... rougher?"

"Wilder," Jess said. "More cliffs to smack up against."

Dev had disappeared into the suiting area. Now she reappeared in her surfing suit, sealing the neck up as she walked across the wet rocks to where they were clustered, her booties soundless. "I have surveyed the area," she said, as she arrived next to Jess. "It seems clear here. I did not detect any surveillance, and there is no electronic signature."

She picked a spot next to Jess and leaned against the stone, a thoughtful look on her face.

"Were you expecting to find something listening?" Doug asked. "In here?" He indicated the cavern, in all its huge and rough-cut splendor. "Those suits didn't look like spooks. More like bean counters."

Dev considered. "I don't think I had any expectation," she said. "It just seemed prudent to observe if anything had." She fell silent, a faint crease between her brows. "Because things are a bit odd, aren't they?" She added, belatedly. "Suboptimal."

"How do you feel about this whole thing, Dev?" Brent asked, after they'd all been silent for a minute. "Make sense to you? Closing the place down?"

Jess watched her and after a moment spoke up. "She doesn't like it."

Dev eyed her with the faintest of smiles.

"How can you tell?" Doug spread his arms out along the rim of the pool. "You can tell."

"I can tell." Jess's eyes, colorless in the ochre overheads nevertheless twinkled a little. "That's the same look I get when I'm trying to get her to try octopus tentacles."

"Something is making me feel cautious," Dev said, as she folded her arms over her chest. "I think those people who came here and talked to us are incorrect."

Jess straightened up and looked at her more seriously. "Incorrect how?" She asked, and both April and Mike came over.

"They didn't say two words to you." Jess paused. "Did they?"

"They did," Dev said. "Before I came down here, they spoke with me and offered me citizen credentials." She looked around at them. "They think I should go with them, and there is much good work there I could do where they are taking everyone."

There was a brief period of silence. "Well, duh," Doug said. "Sure, they do. That doesn't make them sideways, it just gets them points for having a clue, Rocket. You're a star."

"Truth." April half shrugged. "I'da been surprised if they hadn't pitched you."

"It was what they said," Dev demurred. "That since I had the citizen card, I didn't have to do… what other people might choose to do here," she stated said. "It seemed like they expected some people not to go with them or agree with them." She turned and regarded Jess. "Are you going to go with them, Jess?"

It was so quiet, the thundering sounds of the water became crystal clear around them, the rush and boom seemed like the cavern itself was breathing in and out, waiting. Brent and Doug came over to the edge of the pool and leaned close, their wet hands flat on the rock floor.

Jess finally broke the silence. "They didn't ask us. They told us. We're all inservice. It's in the regs. They can tell us to go anywhere." She looked from one to the other, then back to Dev, who stood quietly, just waiting.

"But nah. I ain't going," Jess said calmly. "For what it's worth, I think you're right. I think they're incorrect, the way Bain was incorrect. The way Joshua was incorrect." She took a breath. "Abandoning everyone out here is wrong. Full stop."

Dev nodded. "Yes, that's how I feel. They mean us harm." She looked relieved. "Since they have given me citizen status I will take advantage of that and go wherever it is that you are going." She gave a little, sharp nod. "And that seems excellent to me."

Jess regarded her with a smile. "They could end up shooting us. I'm pretty sure they're not going to just let me walk out of here, even if they expect it."

"You think they do?" April looked, if anything, intrigued.

"If all of us are troublemakers, you're the biggest."

"I am," Jess quietly agreed. "Or I don't know, maybe they'll just let me walk out the door and down the coast. Maybe it's part of their game." She half shrugged. "They know I have a stake here."

"Bet Dev can hotwire that bus," Brent said, his arms folded on the stone, his chin resting on his wrists. "You ain't gonna end up walking nowhere."

Dev cleared her throat and glanced around with a brief smile.

"Let's get a few rounds of surfing in, shall we?" Mike picked up a board. "Since that's what we said we would do. No sense…" He smiled and looked back over his shoulder. "Stirring up any suspicions, right?"

Everyone went to grab their boards, leaving Dev and Jess to stand alone for a moment. Dev released a contented sigh. "I'm glad."

"Wait to be glad until we get away with it," Jess said dryly.

"I'm still glad even if we don't. I feel like it's correct." Dev unexpectedly reached out, took Jess's hand, lifted it up and kissed it, then moved to the rack to retrieve her own board, as they all jumped into the pool, crossing it toward the intake.

Jess went last to pick hers up, then took a breath and savored that inward feeling of release at the inception of commitment to a course of action. It was like finding a path through the waves and seeing a landing clear on the other side of them.

She took a loping start and ran to the edge of the rocks, throwing herself forward and into the water, welcoming the chill and the smell of brine as it rushed over her.

****

Doctor Dan gently pushed the door to the flyer open and walked down the short steps. He felt the wind against his skin as he paused to watch the small greeting party come across the stone grounds toward the landing pad.

The two pilots had emerged behind him. Kurt held the wrapped package tucked under one arm. They looked around curiously.

Kurok put his hands in his pockets and waited, relaxed, as the group came up and climbed the short ramp to the landing pad and approached them. "Hello, there," he greeted them amiably.

"Hello." The man in the lead had gray hair, and kind,

brown eyes. He wore a pullover with an Interforce logo on it. "Kenneth Crow," he said and eyed Kurok. "And you are…"

"Daniel Kurok. Stakeholder proxy of Drake's Bay."

The two behind him, one man, one woman, exchanged looks and nods, and they all sort of relaxed a little bit. "Of course," Crow said. "I remember now, there was a…" He paused. "Well, a…"

"Kerfuffle," Kurok supplied dryly. "Yes, there was, but fortunately I was around and in need of a job, so it all worked out." He half turned. "My pilots, Kurt and Kelson, who are contracted to Drake's Bay."

Both KayTees smiled, nodded, and stood tall in their Bay coveralls and pullovers they were so proud of wearing.

The three from Interforce looked at them. "Boy, that must be a story," Crow said, in a mild tone. "But c'mon inside, let's have a cup of tea, and chat about your visit request." He gestured toward the admin building, with its tall doors. "Had no idea you all were heading out."

Kurok walked alongside him. "Last minute whim, really. Jess was at the Bay just recently and we had a market. Thought the boy would appreciate a little bit of home."

The woman walking at his side smiled in a more genuine way. "He certainly does remember it," she said. "I'm sure he'll like whatever it is."

"Let's go to my office," Crow said. "Cindy, could you ask them to send a tea in? That's a cold wind."

"Of course."

Kurok watched them from the corner of his eyes. Something was up. He kept up a stream of random casual chatter, about the weather and the market, the most normal of conversations as they entered Admin and walked along the quiet sand- stone halls.

Colors were neutral and calming, and reminded him vaguely of station, the rooms on either side of the hall held various offices, and Interforce staff, all in the warm light orange color one piece work suits, not that different than the off-duty suits worn on base, or the gray cadet uniforms of the students.

"Here we are." Crow palmed open a door and stood aside to let them enter. "I think we can probably use the consultation room off to the left there for your visit."

The office was neutral and calm, the furniture carved from the sandstone that surrounded the facility and fitted with a piece of volcanic glass that was truly stunning as its top. "That's gorgeous," Kurok said, gazing at it. "My goodness."

Crow smiled a little more fully. He walked over to touch it with his fingertips. "Why, thank you," he said. "My hobby is climbing, and I found a bubble out there about a year back. I was able to get a piece brought back here and I do love looking at it. Makes it a pleasure to be at work."

"What is it, Doctor Dan?" Kelson asked, in a soft tone. "It's pretty."

"Why not sit down a minute? It'll take us some time to bring Tayler up from basic school." Crow sat down behind his desk. "You said these youngsters were pilots?"

Kurok gestured for them to sit on a bench near the desk, and he took the chair opposite Crow. "They are and shaping up to be fine ones," he said, briskly. "KT-9923 series. They both know Tayler. They were on station when he... ah... visited there."

Crow nodded. "He told us." He said briefly, then checked his watch. "Where's that tea? Let me go see if there's some hang-up with the brewer. I'll be right back."

He left using an inner door different from the one they entered. As he did, Kurok relaxed into the chair and pulled out a data tablet, casually thumbing through it. "It's nice in here isn't it, lads?"

"It is, Doctor Dan," Kurt said. "It's nice colors. I like them." He looked around the room, as Doctor Dan got up from his chair and roamed around the edges of the space.

"Are there many natural born here?" Kurt asked.

"Oh, it varies." Kurok perched on a small ledge near a set of comp, then casually leaned over and placed his hand on the access pad.

It hummed, then gently lit, and the screen unlocked. He set his data pad down next to it and crossed his legs at the ankle. "Let me see, I would guess the last time I was here, there were maybe three hundred students. Classes of different ages, you know, not that different from the creche.

Kelson nodded. "Age groups," he said. "Youngers and olders."

"Yes. Every year, some students are selected to come here to the school, and they're tested to see what level they should be at. So, they can be in classes with other students who are like them."

Both bio alts nodded. "Optimal," Kurt concluded.

Doctor Dan picked up his data pad and resumed flipping through the contents, casually glancing outside the window.

You could see the inner quad from there, the central open space between the sectors. A group of jumpsuit clad students crossed the space, six dark gray, and six a pale, mint green that marked agent and tech pairs very near to their graduation.

The screen to his left quietly shut off, and the pad's light faded. He got up off the shelf and walked over to the window to study the youngsters outside.

The door opened and Crow re-entered. "Here we go." He carried a tray and put it down on the small table to the right of his desk. "There's some of our near graduates."

"I recognize the colors." Kurok turned and came over, accepting a cup. "Lads, would you like some of this? It's a kind of tea they drink here."

Kelson put down the package and came over, and Kurt quickly joined him. Kurok set aside his cup for a moment and poured two for them. He waited for everyone to settle in with their tea. "Thanks for taking the time to humor this last-minute request. I know it must be a busy time if you've got egress and assign going on."

Crow studied him. "You do seem to know our ways," he said. "There's nothing in the records with your name though, so we're a little curious."

"Long story." Kurok sipped his tea. "But yes, I spent some time here, before I got my degree and went into science."

The outer door now opened, and the woman, Cindy, returned with a dark-haired figure in light blue, his hand tucked into hers. "Tayler, there are some people here who want to say hello to you."

Tayler stopped and regarded him, eyes widening in surprise. "Space people!" He released his hold on the woman and came toward them, with an expression of open pleasure. "S'cool!"

He seemed in good spirits, his hair cut short as all the students would have been, the plain blue one-piece suit outlining his already sturdy physique.

"Hello there, Tayler." Kurok put his tea down and came over. He knelt down and extended a hand to him. "We thought we would come and say hello to you and bring you something from home." He motioned to Kelson.

Tayler took his hand with confidence. "You're Aunt Jessie's friend," he said. "I remember you from space too."

"Yes, I am." Kurok said. "Kelson, could you bring over what you have there?"

Kelson brought the package over. "We played float ball with you in null." He offered the package out. "I remember that. It was fun."

"It was," Kurt said. "You were very good in null." He added. "Proctors said you were naturally excellent."

Tayler looked up at him with a grin. "That was fun."

"What is null?" Crow asked, from where he stood near his desk.

"Zero gravity." Kurok guided Tayler over to the bench and they sat down. "You know, we had a market at the Bay the past few days and there were lots of people there. Go ahead and open that, see if you like it."

Tayler swiftly divested the item of its covering and turned it around. "Oh, wow that's cool," he said, after a brief pause. He turned it around to show Crow and Cindy. "It's my family's place!" He said. "Look!"

A striking angle, a photo taken coming head on to the sea- wall entry to the Bay, coming through the waves with a view of the curving promontory wall behind it, the colors awash with the lighter blues of the bay, the darker of the sea, and the froth of the waves a deep cream.

Crow came over. "Why, that's very nice," he said, in a mildly surprised tone. "That's a beautiful picture of the front of it and look at those waves." He glanced at Kurok. "Who took that shot?"

Kurok smiled. "A very skilled carrier pilot. And the frame is made from rocks and shells from the beach there. Tayler, do you like it?"

Tayler turned it around and studied it, totally absorbed. "So cool." He ran a fingertip over the hammered frame, with its inset decorations. Then he looked up at Kurok. "Yeah."

"Good, I'm glad." Kurok patted him gently on the shoulder. "Maybe you could put it up in your room and look at it sometimes."

Tayler grinned and nodded. "Yeah."

"Why don't we do that right now?" Cindy suggested. "You could tell me where you would like it, Tayler, and we can get it set up for you." She held out a hand. "Ready?"

Tayler turned and looked at Kurok. "Thanks," he said. "Is Aunt Jessie comin?"

"Soon as she's able to," He replied. "I know she promised to, didn't she? She will."

He smiled again, then he took Cindy's hand and let himself be led out, the picture tucked firmly under his other arm with his fingertips curled around the edge of it.

The door closed, and then it was silent for a moment. "Well, thank you for giving us that opportunity," Kurok said.

"We'll be on our way now and let you get on with your day." He gestured to the two waiting bio alts. "Come on, lads, time for another flying lesson on the way home."

Crow was studying him. "Well, glad you stopped by," he said. "Most of the int... children who come here...they don't have a big attachment to home."

"Drakes are different," Kurok said, with a brief smile.

"Drakes are different." Crow nodded. "He's adjusting, but he misses home. So, it was a kind thing you did there, bringing that. He has some small things he brought with him, but nothing like that image. It's very striking."

Kurok lifted his hand in a genial wave, then followed Crow out of the office and out the entryway, into the cold wind.

****

Jess sat on the chair in her quarters, dressed in an off-duty suit, her still damp hair drawn back off her forehead. She pondered her gear and the large duffel on the floor just past her bare feet.

Now that she'd decided she was going to run out on Interforce, and stupidly told a bunch of people about it, the question of how she was going to achieve that without getting either shot or put in restraints swirled in her head.

Resigning as she had the last time had resulted in immediate lockdown. She wasn't sure if that was what would happen this time, but the chance was there. She would be locked in her quarters, and then... and then what? Would they fly off and leave her locked down?

They might.

And what would that mean for Dev? What if Dev also told them she was leaving? How far would that offer of citizenship really go with this bunch? Would it be valid only if Dev decided in their favor? And if not, then... oh, wait, there's a catch.

Free of her quarters, Jess would have the chance to do something about that. Something being, probably, getting both of them killed, but still. The thought of being locked up in here while they put Dev in restraints and tossed her on the transport....

Jess's nostrils flared hard. She felt the galvanic skin response that was her internal triggers firing. Her mouth went dry. She closed her eyes, took a few breaths, and released the energy that started to build, having no use for it at the moment.

The inner door in her quarters chimed gently, and then opened, and Dev entered. She came over, sat on the edge of the bed and put down a thick package she was carrying. "Hello, Jess."

"Hi." Jess rolled her head to one side and regarded her partner.

Dev put down her scanner and tuned a few settings. She paused to regard the results before she glanced over at Jess. "It's quite all right now," she said. "I am intercepting scan and returning a vocal loop of our conversation."

"You're damn handy, Dev." Jess propped her elbow on the chair arm. "You're so much smarter than everyone else is. What are they hearing?"

"Us discussing how much gear to pack," Dev said. "How many suits, and what mechanical bits I am going to bring, and asking if I could take my toolkit."

Jess smiled. "Do I tell them ahead of time, or just not get on the transport. Whatcha think?" She asked. "Go along with the plan right up until we don't? Take off at the last minute?"

"They might expect us to do that," Dev said, after a brief pause to think about the question.

"They might be expecting *me* to do that," Jess corrected her.

Dev considered that for a moment more. "That's true. They would not expect me to decide to go against their orders because they know I'm a biological alternative," she said. "And going with them to gain an opportunity to perform good work and advancement is a logical bio alt decision."

"Is it?"

"It is. The sets downstairs are very worried they're not going to be taken along, because they know that, and they want the opportunity." Dev said. "Clint told me there are places in the west where work can be done to make new things, like what I was doing here. The sets were very interested to hear that and want a chance to excel."

"The research centers. That's true," Jess noted. She looked toward the outer door, then back at Dev. "Sure you don't want to go?"

"Absolutely sure." Dev didn't hesitate even a second, as though she'd been waiting to be asked. "Unless you go. Then I will do the best I can to accommodate that decision," she added, almost as an afterthought. "But I do not feel like going with them is an excellent course of action for us to take."

Us. Jess considered how that made her feel, that little odd warm spot inside her that surrounded everything that Dev was in her life. "I'm glad," she said, quietly. "I don't know where this is going to take us, Devvie, but if I had to go anywhere, I'd like you to be there with me."

Dev smiled wholeheartedly. "I really hope it takes us back to your birthplace," she concluded. "That would be excellent."

"That would be suicidal." Jess extended her legs with a sigh. Then she frowned. "I don't know. I was just thinking me being there would make the Bay the first target, but then I realized..."

"It is anyway," Dev said. "Yes. Because of the plants and the cave. They said that when we were there, and that they would need to get more things to defend them." She paused and regarded Jess. "I think they would consider it optimal if you were there to help."

"Do they want me there?" Jess looked up at the ceiling. "I scare them," she added, with a faint shrug. "Do they want to risk having me around?"

Dev thought about their recent visit, then reached over and put her hand on Jess's hand, resting on her thigh. "I really think they do, Jess."

Jess eyed her. "Until I break someone else's neck?"

Dev's nose wrinkled a little. "I don't really think that bothers them," she admitted. "I think they think it's an optimal positive."

They looked quietly at each other, only the scanner making its soft, burbling sounds. Then Jess sighed again. "No, you're right. But... you muster out and you don't get a free pass for that anymore." She paused and frowned as her thoughts moderated. "But then again, if they pull out, who's going to be the law out here anyway?"

They were quiet again for a minute. "I have packed all of the things that were given to me here in the big bag," Dev said, at last. "And then I have my pack, where I put all the things I got, or that you gave me," she added. "I thought it might be good to just bring the pack."

Jess looked at her. "Put out the big bags for them to pick up in the morning and load into the personnel carrier," she said. "Don't take anything that's Interforce with us. But that means I'm gonna have to walk to the Bay in my underwear."

With a brief grin, Dev picked up the package and handed it to her. "Maybe you could use this."

Glad for the distraction, Jess sat up and took it. She opened the bag and peered inside. "What have we here?" She pulled out a pair of rugged work pants, with side pockets and ankle ties, along with a hooded pullover, both in the dark blues and greens of the Bay colors.

She studied them, then looked over at Dev. "Did you know all this was going to happen?" She asked seriously. "That we'd need something like this?"

Dev grinned, almost mischievously. "No, of course not," she said. "I just like giving you things and this seemed like something you would enjoy." She pointed at the front of the pullover. "Did you see? There is an animal on the front that reminded me of the creature at your birthplace."

Jess turned the fabric around to look. "Oh yeah, there is!" She touched the stitching. "Market?"

"Yes."

Jess grinned. "I love it. Thanks, Devvie."

"I also considered the sensors here would not have anything to track on it as items given us by Interforce might," Dev said. "I think that would be useful."

Jess leaned on her fist. "I think I'm lucky you're with me. You're better at planning than I am," she said, simply. "Okay, we go over to the mess for dinner and just talk smack." She carefully set the shirt and trousers on her workspace surface and stood up. "C'mon, superstar. Let's get this party started."

Dev picked up her scanner. "Switching off," she warned, then did. "Dinner sounds excellent. I will join you in the hall."

"Sounds like a plan." Jess stood, picked up the big duffel and tossed it on the bed. "Always good to have one."

****

"I think the present was considered excellent, Doctor Dan," Kurt said, as they lifted away from the plateau and started east. "It was very nice."

"Yes, I think so too." Kurok sat in his passenger seat, hands clasped over his stomach, legs extended with ankles crossed. "Always take the opportunity to do something nice for someone, lads."

Both bio alts smiled, and glanced at him, then went back to their piloting.

Kurok thought about what his opportunity had provided him. A kind thought for Tayler, certainly. Some interesting, possibly irrelevant intel about the school itself. That it had a graduating class in process, that there was a sense of normality there, that he himself had only raised a mild curiosity.

And yet, he felt, there was something else going on. Some- thing in the brief looks between the staff, and a sense, almost an extra sense of tension that the cadet graduation could not really account for.

"Doctor Dan? It seems a vehicle has followed us." "Really?"

Kurok kept his tone lightly interested. "What makes you think they're following us, Kelson? They could just be going in the same direction."

Kelson glanced in the reflective surface at him. "The vehicle adjusted course when we just did, Doctor Dan, and it is just past the range where most vehicles would not be detected."

"Isn't that interesting. But we can see it because we have excellent scanners, right?"

"That is correct," Kurt said. "They do not know that we can see them."

"Well, that seems silly, doesn't it?" Kurok mused. "We're on a direct track back to Drake's Bay, aren't we?"

Kelson nodded. "Just as you directed. I thought it was interesting as well, as they adjusted speed when I did."

Clever lad. Kurok smiled a little to himself. "It is interesting, Kelson, and a very good thing you noticed that. We always want to be aware of things around us, especially when we are flying between places where there are not many other populated areas around."

"It is very empty here," Kurt said.

It was just miles and miles of shallow inland water with the occasional rocky surface, lifting to a ridge of folded earth in the far distance. Then the stark promontory that held the Bay in a fold of what had once been called the Appalachians.

An inland mountain range that had become waterfront property, as it were, when the seas had risen and covered the coastal plains.

There was life to be found here, in the inland seas. Fish and amphibians and insects lived there, on each other, and the lichen and algae that had evolved a way to grow. There were no stakeholds though. There wasn't enough protein to support that.

"Keep an eye on them, lads. Let me know if anything changes." Kurok hiked up the knee of his pants and pulled out his data pad and activated it. "Hopefully it's all just a coincidence, and they're going to take the same route as we are and then head up to Quebec."

It was quiet for another ten minutes or so, and he was able to set up some searches, then Kurt cleared his throat. "Doctor Dan?"

"Yes?"

"They are increasing speed and coming closer."

Kurok sniffed reflectively. "Excellent." He put his data pad in the large pocket on the thigh of his pants. "Kelson, my lad, switch places with me here, would you?" He unbelted his restraints and stood up. "Let me get some practice in on this plane."

Kelson hurriedly complied, easing around the console as he traded places. "Are you sure, Doctor Dan? Maybe they are going elsewhere, like you said."

Kurok sat down in the pilot's seat and snapped the restraints around him with casual familiarity. "They could be. Put your belt on, lad." He scanned the plane's controls. "But I think we should find out. Now hold on and stay calm."

He adjusted the seat and then eased the throttles forward. The plane surged ahead and then up as he went for the cloud layer in a steep climb. "Let me know if they stick with us."

They punched through the clouds, and he arced the plane to the left, running the engines up to top speed and skimmed the tops, wisps of vapor lashing the wings as he checked his altitude. "With us?"

Kurt studied the scan. "Yes."

"Muppets."

"Doctor Dan?"

"Hold on, lads," Kurok said. "We're going for a ride." He pulled the restraints a bit tighter and slid open a small, newer looking panel on the side of the console. Angling to the right just a little, he reached in and tapped two controls and was rewarded with a rumbling roar and a kick in the back.

"Doctor Dan! What is that?"

"Afterburners," Doctor Dan replied. "Why don't we see if they've got any appetite to follow us into the white."

Kurt watched the edges of the clouds whipping by with wide eyes. "Will we see a bear?"

"We well might."

****

Dinner was odd and discordant, strange, and full of those dissonant overtones that reminded Jess of the old days, when there'd been a lot of agents around, most of them at the best of times frenemies.

She was sprawled at her usual table in the back, in the ops mess, with Dev seated next to her. Dev was stolidly chewing her way through a somewhat random mixture of foodstuffs, apparently being cleaned out of the processors in preparation to closing the place down.

The suits were in the far corner, with Jason and Elaine, at a table for four.

The room itself was half full, because the Base was barely a quarter staffed. Most of the conversation was just light commentary on what was being brought, and what was being looked forward to when they got to the west.

April entered, with Mike Arias, and went to the mess line to pick up a tray. They brought them over to the table Jess was seated at. "Mind?" April asked, looking at one of the empty seats.

"Nah." Jess waved at it. "You packed?"

"I'm packed," April said, with a tone of finality and satisfaction.

"Me too," Arias said, taking the seat next to her. There were two other chairs at the table. "What is this?" He indicated the tray.

"Protein cakes," Dev said. "It appears they had a surplus."

Edible, and what was usually packed in carriers for long duration insertions, to keep bodies alive and energized.

Arias sampled his. "They don't taste like much. But I guess it is what it is."

"It is." Jess picked up her tray. "I'm going to get more. Be right back."

Dev took a sip from her glass, swallowing the bland bar. "I was in the landing bay. The transport has arrived," she said. "They are loading it."

April grunted. "Doug said he was grabbing some personal stuff out of the carrier while he could still get in it."

"Chester too," Mike said. "I asked him to grab my pack while he was in there."

Jess returned with several slabs on her tray and sat back down. "What model transport is it, Dev?" She asked in an apparently random question.

Dev glanced at her. "I believe it's a G8 series. Maybe a 1700."

Jess nodded and forked up one of the slabs. "Comfortable ride," she said. All utterly common and conventual. Jess was aware though, that people were watching them. That the suits watched them and tried not to be seen to be watching them. They had seated themselves to be able to watch them. Jason and Elaine's backs were to the room.

Never something she'd have done. Jess smiled. From where she was, in the back, on the slightly raised platform that held three tables, two of them empty, with her back to the wall she could see everyone and everything and she saw clearly that they were being watched.

She was being watched? Jess pondered. What did they expect her to do? She was unarmed, more so even than April who had her dalknife at her hip and Mike, with his new blade on his calf. Were they expecting her to stand up and make a scene? Make a protest? Tell them they were all dirtbags for abandoning the east? She considered sincerely thanking them at the end of dinner. Walking over and saying it was great they'd decided to leave the east alone, that maybe now that Interforce was gone from the coast, the other side would abandon it too.

It might even be true, were it not for the Bay. Jess rather expected they wanted the other side to take care of that little problem for them.

She smiled again, and nudged her tray toward Dev. "Want some?"

"Certainly." Dev took one of the slabs and transferred it to her plate. "It's always good to consume edibles before a journey."

The door slid open, and Doug and Chester entered, filled their trays, and joined the table. They had the scent of electronics off gassing lingering about them, and a brief smell of hydraulic oil, and Doug had a smudge of grease on his nose.

"You get everything?" April asked.

Doug nodded. "All tidied up," he said. "Tomorrow can't come too soon."

Across the room, the suits got up and walked out without a backwards glance.

The room perceptibly relaxed once they were gone. People leaned back in their seats, and the vocal levels lifted. Brent came in and picked up a tray, hesitated, then went over and sat down next to Jason, who patted him on the shoulder.

Jess watched it all and could almost feel the pieces of a puzzle start to assemble themselves for her inspection. She moved the pieces around in her head when the inner door to the food preparation area opened and two of the bio alts came out carrying trays.

"Oh, Jess, look." Dev poked her in the ribs. "Those things you like."

Brownies. The first of the two bio alts brough his tray around to the rest of the room, starting with Jason but the second came right over to Jess's table. "Agent Jess, we heard these were something you enjoyed." He put the tray down. "We found some ingredients."

"You heard." Jess glanced at Dev, who had one of her blander expressions on. "I wonder where you heard that from."

A brief grin appeared on Dev's face.

"Thanks." Jess picked up two of the brownies and put one on Dev's tray. "I do like em."

A buzz was lifting in the room, a tone of surprise and delight as everyone dug in and consumed the unexpected treats. Across the room, Jason turned around in his seat and caught Jess's eye. He lifted his brownie up and toasted her with it.

Jess just pointed at Dev and then took a bite of the treat.

****

They punched down out of the clouds and dove, heading for the shallow waters that rapidly turned from frothed gray to icy, and into a curtain of rain. Kurt had his eyes glued to the scanner, and behind him, Kelson strained forward in his restraints to see what he could.

"They are behind us," Kurt said, after a moment.

Kurok concentrated on driving. He felt the push of the weather against the skin of the light flyer, and briefly wished they were in a much different vehicle. He got down to water level and spotted ahead of him the start of the white, the long line of glacier that extended now deep across the continent, creeping further every year.

It was a landscape of dips and crags and ice canyons, and he set the flyer toward the forward edge of them, watching the wire map as it scanned ahead and gave him some idea of the topology they were heading for. "All right," he said, quietly. "Now let's see what they've got between their legs."

Kelson frowned. "Doctor Dan? What does that mean?"

Despite the uncomfortable speed, and the uncertainty,

Kurok couldn't quite hold back a chuckle. "Tell you later, Kelson. Sit back now."

The ice cliffs were coming up fast and he plotted a course right into the face of them, at this distance looking like a suicidal track and he increased speed a little, aware from the corner of his eye the pursuing vehicle behind them.

It was a light class recon, Interforce, armed. He recognized the outline. "Maybe we're the graduation test," Kurok mused. He adjusted the throttles a touch and skewed the flaps on the flyer, as the seconds counted down to reaching the glacier's edge. "Well, if we are, good luck kids."

At the last moment, the crack in the ice he'd been aiming for appeared and then they passed into it, the edges of the ice a mere body length on either side as they were suddenly out of the wind, and he moved the rudders to handle the lack of resistance. The crack was narrow and twisting and he had to concentrate on taking the centerline of it, old memories surfacing with fingertip instincts he hadn't had to use in a very long while.

"They have turned off," Karl said. "They are taking a course back along the way we have come."

Maybe they were kids. "Well, that's great isn't it? Are you enjoying this ride?" Kurok took the speed down so he could handle the steering without worrying too much about plowing the flyer into the ice. "This is a glacier. It's made from rain."

Kelson looked out the window. "It's amazing, Doctor Dan." "Isn't it?"

"It is." Karl stared at the ice walls they were flying through. The gray light brought out deep blue highlights and it all had a fantastic, eerie beauty to it. "It's amazing."

Kurok smiled. "Well, now that we're not being chased around, let me show you a little more." He gently eased the flyer up and out of the trench, and they were above the glacier. "We'll see if we can find a bear and keep along the edge of the ice so we can dodge again if we have to."

A light flashed on the console. "Kelson, can you answer that please?" Kurok said. "I've got my hands a bit full here on manual."

"Of course." Kelson keyed the panel next to him. "Calling station, this is Bay Recon. Please repeat?" He spoke crisply and confidently into the comms.

"Bay Recon, this is Bay ops," A voice answered, one he recognized. "It's Operations, Doctor Dan," he said, and then listened again. "Go ahead Bay ops."

"What is your ETA to this location? There is a secured comms for Doctor Dan, marked urgent."

Kelson repeated the words aloud.

"Hm." Kurok adjusted his course. "Could I have caused that much trouble already? Tell them two hours, Kelson. I'll try to hurry." He kicked in the afterburners again and headed east. "The bears will have to wait for another time."

****

Jess packed her duffel, puled the zippers closed and secured the tie down. She was dressed in her sleep clothing, and before she lifted the bag, she scanned the room to make sure she hadn't left anything.

All her uniforms, check. The gear packs she'd taken on insertions, check. All the data pads and catalogs she'd used to plan. All in the bag.

The only thing left out was her clothing for the next day.

She wished the next day was over. With a sigh she lifted the bag and went to the door, touched the pad next to it and waited for it to slide open. She emerged into the hallway and dropped the bag next to the wall.

She glanced to one side, and saw a smaller duffel, Dev's, neatly tucked against the wall outside her quarters, and as she looked in the other direction, she saw a few others.

Very few.

She ducked back inside and closed the door, then went over to her workspace and sat down behind it, just looking around the place.

It was bland and lacked personality, but then, it always had. She'd been in the other agent's quarters, and it was the same there, no one kept random things around. No keepsakes, no random art. It was all dark gray stone walls, gray steel bedframes and cabinets, colorless light.

It had never been hers, really. Just her assigned space, which could be moved at ops whim, or due to maintenance, you were expected to pick up and go where you were told without bitching about it and, sometimes she'd had to. It never bothered her. After all, that was the point of what they were wasn't it?

No attachments. She had no attachment at all to this space, it was just a comfortable place to come back to most times.

The soft chime sounded on the inner door, and then it opened. Dev came in, also dressed in her sleep clothes, her ever- present scanner draped over one shoulder.

"Hey, Devvie," Jess greeted her.

"Hello," Dev responded. She walked over and sat in the chair in front of the workspace. She set down the scanner and turned it on, tuning it for a moment before she nodded. "Did you hear the announcement, Jess? They moved up the departure."

Jess nodded. "To sunrise. That actually made more sense to me than waiting until lunch." She leaned back in her chair. "They must have finished loading early." She put her hands behind her head. "Wish they'd leave now. I'm done with waiting."

They looked at each other. "Should we wait for late watch,

then take off?" Jess asked.

"Yes," Dev said, simply. "I feel like incorrect things are going to happen."

"They disabled all the hand weapons," Jess said. "I put them all in the bag and put it outside. No point in trying to take them."

They heard a hand transport moving outside and the faint sounds of the duffels being picked. As they paused outside hers, Jess felt a sudden sense of warning deep in her guts. She couldn't really put her finger on what the wrongness was, but she knew it was there.

She felt it, just like she realized Dev felt it.

The lights dimmed a little, and outside they heard the ops watch changing. The shift announcements echoed softly, steadily, with no sense that it was for the very last time, and yet it was, and she knew it. Jess took a breath and then exhaled. "They closed the landing bay hatch. I just heard it."

"Suboptimal," Dev said. "We will have to wait for it to open to leave. It might be good to get into our vehicle."

"If they scan, they'll find us there."

A faint smile appeared on Dev's face. "Possibly not. I have been considering what would need to be done to reflect the scan, as I am doing with this vocal listener." She indicated the device. "I don't know if I could do that, but there are possibilities."

Jess smiled back at her. "You really are a rockstar. I was just going to start killing everyone and figured that kind of distraction might either get us out or splatted." She winked. "I like that plan better and we might live through it. All right, Devvie. After the bell, we go."

"Excellent," Dev said, and looked relieved. "I will then go back and change and then return." She got up and turned the scanner off. "Good night, Jess."

"Night, Rocket," Jess responded. "See ya in the morning." Dev went back to the door and slipped into her own quarters. Jess nodded a few times to herself and then got up and changed out of the sleep clothes and into what Dev had gifted her. She found them to be comfortable and well fitting.

She sat down behind her work surface and pulled a pair of sealskin boots over. She'd picked them up on that last visit to Market Island with Joshua, before it all went to hell. Now they'd come in handy, and the karma in that made her smile.

What would karma bring her for this insanity? She finished securing the boots and leaned back and hiked her boot up and propped it against the desk. And what, she wondered, was the

Bay going to say about all this?

Well, with any luck, she'd get to find out.

****

Dev finished fastening the blue green colored jumpsuit and glanced at her reflection in the mirror. It was a simple garment, a tough fabric with pockets in the thighs and arms and chest. It had a gear patch on both shoulders indicating its wearer was assigned to technology in a Bio station creche. The hooks and D rings were designed for tie downs in null that no one here would even understand.

It felt strange. She'd last worn it the first day she'd arrived here at Interforce. She'd walked warily in Doctor Dan's shadow through this very strange, very dark, very violent space. It was full of aggressive agents, and wary techs and being made dead had seemed a routine activity.

Now, that life seemed so vastly far away. She could barely remember what it felt like to be so brand new. She ran her fingers through her hair and neatly folded her sleep clothes and left them in the clothing cabinet that was otherwise bare.

Her boots were waiting near her workspace, and she pulled them on and laced them, glad at least these were downside boots and not the light spacer footwear she'd originally come in. She picked up her sharkskin jacket and her scanner and slid it over her shoulder.

She had discussed the scanner with Jess. There was no doubt she'd used a scanner in her work as an Interforce technician, but this one, this scanner, she'd built and programmed herself, her regular assigned one packed in her large gear bag that had been taken away already.

Fair game, Jess had said. So, she'd kept it.

Dev stood up and looked around one last time before she went to the inner door that separated her quarters from Jess's and touched the annunciator out of polite habit.

The door slid open, and Jess looked up from where she was seated behind her workspace. As their eyes met, all the lights went out.

It made Dev inhale sharply, her skin reacting with a prickle as she moved instinctively forward to clear the door and then stopped. The door remained open behind her though, and it was very dark, and very silent.

"Crap!" Jess said. "Now what?"

Dev took that as the commentary it was, and not possibly a

cause of the lack of power. "Nonoptimal." She provided her own equivalent. She remained still, then sensed motion ahead of her and a moment later Jess's hand was on her shoulder. "What should we do?"

"Good question," Jess said in a calm tone. "I vote we wait a minute to see if the emergencies come on or if the mains come back. Could be a maintenance glitch, with them prepping to shut down."

"Yeeess." Dev extended the word slowly.

"Nah, I don't think so either, but let's give it a minute." Jess chuckled. "Maybe they'll tell us it's ten minutes and we can just stand here and kiss each other."

That seemed like a reasonable plan. Dev took a breath and then exhaled. She could smell a little bit of the sea on the clothing Jess wore, and she heard the faint sounds as Jess turned her head from side to side and her hair brushed against fabric.

"What's that you have on?" Jess asked after a moments silence. "Have I seen it before?"

Dev glanced down at herself, a useless reflex since she could see literally nothing. "I think you have," she said. "Once. It's the clothing I was wearing when I arrived with Doctor Dan on the shuttle."

"Oh, yeah," Jess mused. "I sort of remember that."

Dev's eyebrows creased. "Can you see me?"

"Yes."

"Really?" Dev was able to forget the strangeness of the situation for a moment in her amazement. "Jess it's perfectly dark in here."

Jess chuckled silently. "Not a lot," she said. "Mostly shadows but I didn't recognize the outline of your duds." She shifted. "I can see enough not to crash into things." She paused. "Should have switched to the emergency lights by now."

She put her arms around Dev's shoulders and started toward the outer door. "Let's see if we can hear anything." She moved slowly but surely and when they reached the door she put her hand on it and felt the chill of the metal against her fingertips. "Get your sniffer going."

Dev put her jacket over her shoulder and lifted the scanner, turning it on and waiting for it to come up. In the dim light from the display, she could now see Jess's form in the clothing she'd gifted her. It made her smile. "What would you like to know about?"

"Power?"

Dev tuned the scanner. "Nothing in the vicinity." She tuned

further. "I see other hand scanners in operation, and heat signatures of moving persons."

"Coming this way?" Jess asked, in a calm tone.

"Not particularly." Dev scanned further. "I can see the quiescent heat signatures of the vehicles in the landing bay, and some of the loading machinery, but they are dormant. I think everything is off. I am not seeing any active power sources."

"Huh."

"That seems suboptimal," Dev said.

"Definitely not normal," Jess agreed. "But I'm gonna go get this door open, because it might provide you and I with a good path down to the landing bay without getting shot." She turned to study the door. "Where's the controller?"

Dev went to work with the scanner, tracing out the circuitry that kept the portal shut. It was large and metal, and thick enough to be a successful deterrent to physical force, even by Jess. She found the mechanism and reviewed it, calling up the schema in the scanner's internal memory.

"Can you talk to the main system?" Jess watched her alertly.

Dev paused, and looked at her, the faint screen light outlining Jess's sharp profile. "No. Nothing seems powered, Jess," she said. "Which seems nonoptimal as operations should have emergency residual battery power."

"Doesn't make sense," Jess muttered. "I can feel the turbine intakes through the ground. The vibrations' normal."

Dev felt it too, the subliminal rumble coming through the soles of her boots that was the water intake that powered the base. "Yes. Something cut off the transfer."

Jess nodded. "Door open." She jerked her head toward the ingress. "We ain't gonna find out standing here."

Dev went back to work, focusing on the schematics as Jess waited in silence, not fidgeting as she sometimes did. She just stood next to her, hands at her sides. Nevertheless, she felt the tension build as the darkness continued and she became aware of just how enclosed they were.

Dev found the control circuit and moved closer to the wall. She studied the surface and detected the faint outline of the panel. "The hydraulic interlock is here, Jess." She looked up as Jess came up against her back to peer over her shoulder. "You can see the indents."

Jess regarded the square, then took Dev by the shoulders and pulled her. "Hang out here for a second."

Dev reversed the screen on her scanner and outlined the

panel. "I now wish I had retained my toolkit," she said mournfully. "I think I have a device that could get under that edge."

"Yeah." Jess took a step back, then balled her hand into a fist and lunged forward, slamming her knuckles against the steel surface with enough power to lift her up off her feet. The sound of her fist hitting the wall was sharp and loud and echoed.

Jess pulled her hand back and regarded the results of her effort. "One more," she said, throwing her body toward the wall and hitting the same location with the same fist. She grunted contentedly and moved forward and put her fingertips around the edge of the panel that now was sticking out.

A twisting wrench, and she yanked the panel door off the wall, exposing the mechanics underneath. "Anything you can do with that, Devvie?"

Dev moved closer and inspected the internal arrangement. "I did not expect it to be that easy." She paused to pick up the hand Jess had hit the wall with and inspect it. She found the knuckles intact. "Interesting."

"Yeah, I come with a whole bag of party tricks. Magic eyeballs, gills, steel knuckles, you name it," she muttered. "Don't look so impressed. They teach us at school construction engineering and how to find weak spots."

Dev shook her head but moved in and looked at the controls. She reached in to manipulate some of the pipes and fittings. "I think I can get this to open," she finally said. "But it could cause a mess."

Jess turned around and indicated the inside of the room. "Devvie, who cares?"

"Please go stand by the door then." Dev moved to press her own back against the wall. "And out of the range of this panel."

Jess obediently did as she was told, bouncing a little on the balls of her feet. "G'wan."

Dev slid her scanner around to her right side and let it rest against her hip, then she reached inside the panel with her left hand and gripped the hydraulic lines, giving them a hefty yank and twist, her face tightening into a grimace of effort as the pipes came loose.

The result was direly spectacular, as hydraulic fluid under pressure exploded from the wall. It shot across the room and drenched the bed and workspace in a flood of dark liquid.

"Wow." Jess's eyebrows lifted. "You weren't kidding."

While it was still arching across the space, the door to the outside suddenly slid open, slamming against the jamb with a crunch.

The sound of the fluid hitting everything was loud, and it echoed, as Jess slipped outside, motioning Dev to follow her. "Move, before that gets all over us," she said, as they moved across to the far side of the hall. There, she paused. "Put your jacket on."

Dev slid into the garment and left her scanner on underneath. "Okay."

"Hold on to the back of my shirt," Jess said. "Need to keep my hands free."

Dev took hold. "Yes."

****

"That was pretty slick." Jess said.

"The pressure was holding the door closed," Dev said, and walked along behind Jess in complete darkness. "I thought if we released the pressure, it would open them. I think it's a safety feature."

Jess considered that as they made their way along the residential hallway of operations. Would they make the doors close by default or open by default, given who the rooms were holding?

Interesting question. What was more dangerous, having your most potent weapon locked up in case of disaster or having them free?

Jess dismissed that for later consideration and focused on the direction they were traveling. She knew the internal structure of the citadel well, of course, but she didn't really know what was going on. At a crossroads, she paused to listen.

Jess touched Dev's shoulder in a warning gesture. "Don't turn the scanner on."

Dev hadn't reached for it. "I assumed not," she said in a mild tone. "It's visible to anyone scanning us."

"Not that. It makes us eyeball visible," Jess said. "Leave it off for now." She hesitated, then moved to the right, along the service hallway that led from ops to maintenance. Far off, she could hear boots on the ground, but they were moving away from them, toward Centops.

That made sense to her. If Centops was offline, they'd want to get that fixed first and she knew they had a very limited time to get under cover before all the systems came back and they would know where they were because scanner or no, light or no, base systems knew what her and what Dev's genetiscan was.

No way to hide it. Especially hers.

The outline of the hall was clear to her, grays and shadows and the faintest reflections and she felt her eyes widen in response to the lack of light, almost feeling her pupils dilating to bring in all the detail they could, which wasn't much.

But, as she'd told Dev, she could see enough for her to walk in this hallway and not crash into the wall, and to see anything moving ahead of them, potentially armed, potentially dangerous.

"Jess," Dev whispered.

Jess stopped and pressed against the wall. "Hm?"

"Behind us."

Jess put her back flat to the wall and looked over Dev's head and saw a brief, almost imagined glimpse of pre-aim splashing along the floor, flashing past them and then it disappeared. "Blaster," she said and turned her head to look ahead of them.

She took a breath, and released it, then took another. Then she saw it, two corridors ahead, another splash.

Hunters. Their side? The other side? Jess felt her pulse speed up. What did that even mean right now?

Dev tugged on her sleeve. "There's a door near here."

Jess looked around in puzzlement. "No there is... oh hang on." She pointed at a hatchway two body lengths away from them. "That?"

"Is it a door?" Dev whispered. "A small one, with a handle?"

"Yes." Jess looked doubtfully at it, then moved over and opened the simple latch. She pushed the door open and peered inside. It was a very ordinary looking mechanical space. "It's got a bunch of pipes in it."

Dev gently urged her inside and kept her hand on Jess's back to follow her inside. They stood in utter silence for a long minute, then the soft rasp of muffled footsteps came closer, just a whisper of fabric against stone.

Jess pulled Dev around behind her and got her back to the stack of pipes. She moved into a balanced stance with her hand clasped around the piece of bent metal she'd taken from the wall and faced toward the door.

But the footsteps went past, moving along the hall away from them. Jess listened intently, but it was impossible from just the sound to tell if the hunters were friends or enemies.

When the sound had faded, she turned. "Nice catch, Dev-vie." She looked around. "What the hell is this?"

Dev exhaled audibly. "It's very suboptimal not being able

to see anything," she said. "This is a service bay. If I remember correctly, there should be an inner door, and past that is the delivery hatchway. It leads down to the lower level."

Jess considered that. "Down to where the bios live?"

"Yes."

"Lead on," Jess said. "No wait. You can't. Tell me where to go now?" She slid the bent piece of metal into the back of her waistband and grasped Dev's arm firmly. "Out that door?"

"Yes," Dev whispered. "We can get to the service corridors."

Service corridors, where the ordinary people, natural born and bio alt, went about the daily work of keeping things running. In the darkness, the workers would be huddled in their sleeping chambers. They knew better than to venture out.

"Move." Jess found the door and cautiously opened it. She paused to listen inside. There were faint pops and crackles in the distance, and just a brief echo of someone yelling. Then silence.

Jess moved silently inside, aware of Dev latched on to the back of her shirt again and she released her arm so she could turn and look down a long, narrow space with a turn midway. It smelled dusty, and the floor held a hint of rock scrub they used to keep the algae down.

She walked to the midway entry and peered around it, seeing nothing but emptier hallway, dim and gray, a cleaning cart parked against the wall a little way up. With more confidence she continued. She leaned forward a little, ears straining, aware of the downward slant of the floor.

The air brought her the scent of rock dust, the chemicals from the cleaning cart, and a hint of the sea that settled on the back of her tongue and with every step she felt the rightness of the path. She reached back and gave Dev a little pat on the side and felt a brief press of fingers along her elbow.

They heard muffled movement in the corridor on the other side of the rock wall from where they were, steps and curses, and the clang of metal against metal.

"Mech," Dev whispered.

Jess nodded. "Heading to Centops."

They reached the end of the hallway and Jess paused. "Which way?"

"Right."

Obediently Jess turned right and walked along a smaller, narrower corridor that also sloped downward. As she drew in a breath, she caught a hint of dampness. "Vents," she muttered. "Must be near the outer skin." She reached out and touched the wall and felt a clammy dampness and chill. Not quite wet, not quite dry.

The hall bent around to the left, and Jess imagined in her head where they were, curving along the outer edge of the facility, and on the edge of her hearing she detected water motion far off, on the other side of the right-hand wall.

"End of this walkway, there is a door," Dev said.

"You spend a lot of time down here?"

"No. They showed me once," Dev said. "The sets did."

Jess chuckled under her breath. They reached the end, and there was in fact a door, with a handle. "Locked probably."

"Probably, but from the other side," Dev said. "I had to auth through, that time. The sets couldn't."

Jess paused and turned around to look at her. Dev stood there, her hand still gripped around the back of Jess's shirt, her head tilted a little to one side, just waiting. "They can't get into this hall from their quarters?"

"No, but they can get into their quarters from the hall," Dev said. "Now that they know, after I opened it."

"Interesting." Jess turned the handle and gave the door a push. "Hope we don't scare them to death." She peered through the door where the hallway extended another few body lengths and then turned. "Smells like people."

And then they heard voices, low and urgent, and fearful.

Chapter Seven

Jess listened to the chaos for a moment then drew in a breath. "Hey!" She barked out loudly. Her voice carried over the anxiety and caused an abrupt silence to fall after the echoes of it faded.

Dev cleared her throat. "Be calm," she said, into all that quiet. "What is the situation here please?" she asked. "It's NM- Dev-1 speaking."

The inside of the housing space was as pitch black as the rest of the halls but the difference here was there were a hundred lightly traced rings sparkling with internal light that were the biometric collars of a hundred bio alts scattered across the room.

It didn't cast much light, the faint traces powered by the life energy of the bio alts themselves, transferred down the probes inserted up into their brain stems but it was enough to locate them and provide the barest of up shadows over their heads.

The rings all moved and shifted as they all turned in surprise when they heard her.

"NM-Dev-1." Someone said, nearby. "You are here."

"I am," Dev said. "And Jess is here as well."

A murmur traveled across the room. "Agent Jess," one of the nearby sets said. "And NM-Dev-1. This is optimal. They can tell us what is happening."

"Possibly," Dev said. "What is the situation here please? Are you all safe?"

"There is no power. We heard loud noises," the one who had spoken to Dev said. "I am KayTee-512," he added. "We were all sent here after the night meal and told to stay in our assigned quarters and not to go out."

"Yes," Dev said. "We were told the same."

That got a murmuring response. "But you are here," the KayTee observed. "You did not obey the request."

"We often do not," Dev said.

Jess poked Dev in the back. "Time," she muttered. "If they're looking for us and find us here that's just going to be a whole crowd of parts flying in all directions."

"Yes. KayTee," Dev said. "We are not sure of the status of what is going on inside the facility. We will need to go to the main egress and investigate so please give us a path to the door."

"It is locked closed," The KayTee told her. "We cannot open it. There is no power to any systems."

Jess impatiently started forward, steering Dev with her as she moved. "Move away from my voice," she said. "Lemme through, kids. We got trouble to get into."

"It is locked," the KayTee observed again. "However, it would be excellent if you could open the doors so that we, too, can help investigate."

"Jess has a process to open the doors," Dev assured him, as she reached out to take hold of the back of Jess's shirt. "Our doors were closed as well in our quarters and now they are not."

"You helped with that," Jess said. "That mess probably flooded the whole level by now."

"Yes," Dev agreed. "There will be a lot of damage if that is true."

The bio alts moved a little bit to give them space to get through. Jess strode through with confidence, the crowd dark but clear in her vision, multiple shades of gray and anxious faces with eyes opened very wide trying to see.

"What are you intending to do?" The KayTee called after them. "May we help?"

"Dunno," Jess answered him. "How about we get the door open, and we'll go from there." She reached the entrance to the bio alts chambers and put her hand against the metal surface and felt the rumble of the tunnels under her touch and against the soles of her feet.

Where the hell was the power? Jess wondered. "What the hell did they do to this thing? They try to pack the batteries in that crate?" She studied the wall. "Stand back everyone." She took a step back herself and prepared to throw herself at the panel, when Dev gave one of her small, peculiar, throat clearings.

Jess paused. "What?" She looked at Dev, clearly seeing the faint, wry grin on her face. "Rrrrocket? What do you have up your sleeve?"

"May I investigate an idea?"

"Not if it involves you bashing any part of your body against that damn door. That's my job," Jess said. "Okay?"

"Absolutely." Dev walked forward and put her hands against the door, then pushed sideways. The panel slid aside grudgingly, then stuck, her palms sliding on the surface. "Jess, can you assist? I think we can move this sideways without further violent action."

Jess stood behind her with her arms folded. "Well hot

damn, Devvie. You just saved my ass some bruises." She went over to the door and grabbed the now visible edge and hauled it along. Halfway done, she got around the door itself and switched to shoving it, her back pressed against the jamb. "Get out of the way, I got this."

Dev stepped back, as the door slid past her into its pocket with a grinding, complaining screech. "It seems that your comment on the reduction in pressure in the hydraulic infrastructure could be accurate," she said, as a flow of cold, salt-tinged air flooded inward. "In a rather excellent sort of way actually."

"The door is open?" KayTee said, in a tone of true surprise. "What did you do?"

"It is a long story, KayTee," Dev said. "I can explain later. We have a task to do now."

It was still pitch black, but the chill air was a welcome reminder of the outside. "That's coming from the landing bay," Jess said. "C'mon."

The rest of the corridors around them were mostly silent, far-off sounds of bangs and thumps, and inarticulate voices floated on the peripherals. Dev turned on her scanner briefly, then shut it down before anything could pick up the signal. "It is clear," she said. "We can proceed."

"Grab on," Jess said, briskly. "Don't want to lose ya."

Dev fastened her hand to the back of Jess's overshirt, and they started forward again.

"What should we do?" The KayTee called after them. "Can we help you?"

"Stay there," Jess called back. "It's too dark to run around and bang into walls. Wait for the lights."

"Yes." The KayTee sounded a bit forlorn. "Okay."

"But if they don't, at least you can get out," Jess added. She paused at a cross corridor and looked back over her shoulder to see the doorway full of glowing collars, that seemed vivid in her eyesight. "Go to the emergency exit at the end of this hallway, down to ground side." She pointed, though there was no way they could see her. "You guys'll be fine."

Then Jess turned and started along the cross corridor and moved quickly as Dev latched on to the back of her shirt again. She was aware of time passing, minutes passing that they might need to get under cover before the lights, and systems were fixed, and they found them.

She felt like someone was looking. The pre-aim had been unmistakable. But pre-aim was uniform, theirs looked just like the other sides and right now there was no telling who was at the trigger of it. No real telling for her, personally, even which side was more dangerous now.

They got to the maintenance bay entrance, winding through a scattering of boxes and crates and evidence of rapid packing, but no other living thing was in the area. There was no sound of movement, or the smell of humanity that Jess could detect.

This was the level under the floor of the landing cavern. It went the entire length and breadth of it, with access portals to the floor level for supplies and mechanical gear to be brought up to service the aircraft the base used.

It was usually full of carts and testers and pieces of gear being repaired. Now Jess looked around and saw nothing but boxes and debris. Perversely, despite the circumstances, it ticked her off and she let out a low, irritated growl.

"Jess?"

"Sorry." Jess started forward, between two service stations.

"Figures our pad's the last one in the back," she "C'mon, c'mon." She shoved a crate out of the way and s q u e e z e d b e t w e e n t w o others. "Why not just rape the place while you're at it? Bastards made us eat rat bars to save supply for themselves."

"Jess."

"Yes."

"What will happen to the sets if they leave them here?"

"They can get out." Jess was busy finding a path through all the chaos. "Huh. Oh." She paused, at the edge of long cargo ramp, where all the boxes she'd been shoving her way through were lined up. "This way." She led the way up the ramp and up to the floor of the landing bay. "Why would they leave them? They're all trained for Interforce. It'd be stupid."

The massive door was, as she suspected, closed, but the vents on either side were open and a cold wind came in, bringing the strong smell of both rain and the sea inside the cavern.

Here she could see mostly huge shadows and outlines of carriers, everything dark and silent. It was eerie. She'd been in here a thousand times, but even in off-hours, there were always lights and always people, mechs doing work, bio alts doing work, even in the midwatch something was always going on.

Jess angled her way across the floor toward the pad their carrier was assigned to. She slowed down to search the area and avoid leading them both into the end of a blaster. "That would ruin my damn day."

"Jess?"

"Never mind."

Jess saw no one, and heard no one moving in the vicinity, no matter how hard she strained her ears.

But the sound of the wind coming in could be blocking that. She found it hard to believe she could bust out of her quarters, leave a gusher of fluid in the halls, break through the bio alts quarters and end up where she was without getting challenged no matter what the distraction was.

Security should have… Jess paused, thinking. Where the hell was security? "Probably hauling down the ops ramp yelling about flood alerts."

"Excuse me, Jess?"

"Just talking to myself." She sped up, hauling Dev along with her as she dodged between the staged carriers, all of them tied down, all of them secured for storage. "Huh." They would be traveling in the personnel transport, they'd said, everyone together, leaving all the rigs behind.

Why?

The transport was in the center of the floor, huge and hulking, it's boosters and engines prepared for flight in the morning. The vents provided flashes of lightning from the outside, brief hints of silver that flashed over the vehicle, painting stripes across its dark gray skin.

"There we go." Jess turned to the left, heading between a massive crane loader and the carrier platforms.

There was their carrier, equally secured, somnolent on its pad, shut down and dark and as they scrambled up onto the pad and approached it, Jess knew a moment of apprehension. What if someone already was ahead of her?

What if…

Dev had her scanner out and the screen briefly came to life, long enough for her agile fingers to rapidly dance across it, the screen's light reflecting on her eyes and flashing a silver sheen on her hair. "It's clear," she said, as though reading Jess's mind. "I have set the manual unlock," She shut the scanner down and slid it around to her side. "Should I start up the internal systems?"

"No, not yet. Don't want to alert anyone." Jess sidled up to the carrier, sitting there dark and silent. She hesitantly put her hand on it and felt through her fingertips the soundless sensation of motion, then the hatch undocked and lifted without any protest as it recognized her touch.

She stepped up inside without extending the ramp and paused, listening, and sniffing intently. Then she heard noises echoing from the outer hallway and pulled Dev inside and sealed the hatch.

It was quiet, with all the carriers' systems shut down and they both stood there for several minutes in utter stillness, as the sound of shouting nearby resolved into the cursing of ops techs, heading past them.

"Why the hell they want to fly outta here now?"

"Fricken suits."

"Have to leave all that shit we packed behind.. all that work for nothin!"

"What's happening?" Dev whispered. "Are they preparing to go?"

Jess nodded in the darkness. "Running." She exhaled. "They're running. Whatever's going on has them spooked."

Dev moved around the gunner station in the carrier, finding her way by touch in this more familiar environment. The blast shield was down on the carrier nose, and she slid into her pilot's seat but left all the controls off, glad to be seated inside the protection the carrier afforded.

Jess had her head cocked to one side, listening. "Getting the transport ready" She concluded, from the thunks and clangs. "Must have hand lights," she said. "Why didn't we think about having hand lights, Devvie?"

"First storage cabinet, near the drop apparatus," Dev said. "I did not expect to need them in our quarters."

Jess chuckled and then settled into her seat. The inside of the carrier smelled and looked right, the only oddity the gear bags that held all their personal possessions that were tucked inside the two big bins on the opposite side.

She heard the cargo handlers, battery powered, start up. "Loading."

"That was a large quantity of cargo," Dev said. "If they load it all, they will not have room for the sets."

There was a long silence. "Yeah," Jess agreed. "Maybe they figured they needed supplies more than Base techs, if they're closing down bases."

"That is non optimal, Jess." Dev's voice, faced away from her in the darkness, changed pitch in a way that made Jess know she was frowning, and she pictured Dev's face, with her brows creased. "What are they supposed to do?"

"Hold on that until we figure out what we're going to do ourselves first," Jess said. "Wonder when they're going to realize without power they can't open that outer door. It closes automatically if power goes out."

Dev considered that. "Oh, that's an interesting problem. I

don't think our process would work on that mechanism. It's too heavy."

Jess chuckled, a softly unexpected sound there in the darkness. "Let someone else solve that problem for us, Devvie." She put her hands behind her head and leaned back. "I can see how this is going. Those bastards are going to get who's important to them, aka, them, onboard and if anyone doesn't make it—too bad."

"Hm." Dev made a low noise in her throat. "Yes, that seems like a possible result of the situation."

Jess's eyes twinkled a little. "Works out for us," she said. "Better than having to shoot our way out with guns that might blow up in my hands."

"That is true." Dev picked up her scanner and turned it on. She tuned it as she turned in her seat. She studied the screen intently, the scanner's sensors on input only. "Yes, there are hand tools and battery powered devices active in the area, and the aircraft has started up internal systems."

"Yup."

"Oh." Dev made a hasty adjustment. "They are scanning from that vehicle the inside of the cavern," she said. "I have configured this to return a null spectrum."

"They can't see us?"

"They cannot." Dev flipped through another few screens. "Or, more specifically, they see what they expect to see, an empty carrier."

"Rockstar," Jess said. "You totally outclass them, those westie bimbos."

Dev smiled briefly. "I can see people approaching the transport." She watched groups, in ones or twos, approaching the vehicle, and the wire map showed the steady stream of boxes being loaded from the rear hatch.

Then a huge barrage of explosions echoed, and she quickly turned down the sound.

Jess hauled ass out of her chair and was at the hatch in a breath but paused just before touching it. "Can you see what that was?" She asked, in a tense, low voice.

Dev was already busy tapping. "Energy discharge," she reported. "Signature matches heavy long blaster fire."

Jess paused with her hands halfway between her thighs and the door. "What direction are they shooting?" She asked. "At us?"

Dev checked the readings then rescanned. She shook her head. "No. It appears they are firing at the cavern bay door. The rebounds are, however, non-optimal as they are being reflected all over the cavern," she added. "They are doing damage to objects inside the facility, and two of the cargo handlers have now gone offline."

"Bunch of damn brainless morons!"

Dev tuned the scanner. "More individuals are progressing toward the transport from main ops hall," she said. "The heavy fire has stopped. Now it has started again, from a different vector."

Jess backed up and sat back down in her seat. "That's what happens when you get paper pushers running operations, Dev. Maybe we can grab whatever they can't load and take it." She put her hands behind her head again. "Depends what it is. I ain't bringing those rat bars."

The carrier rocked back and forth a little, unexpectedly. "We have just been hit by a rebound," Dev said. "There is no damage to this vehicle."

"Not to these bricks. You picked the right place to hide."

"Two persons have just been made dead," Dev said, quietly. "I can see the energy dispersion. They took a direct hit."

"Stupid." Jess sighed. "Why can't someone be as smart as you are, and figure out how to release the locks?" She looked over at Dev. "Anyone we knew?"

Dev studied the information. "I would have to run a genetiscan. It could be detectable." She answered, regretfully. "It seems quite suboptimal on the floor right now. Many persons are running around everywhere." She watched two pinpoints move along the outside rim of the cavern.

"We'll figure it out once those idiots leave." Jess wiggled one booted foot in mild contentment. "These togs are comfort-able. Good pick," she said. "Can't believe someone did these pants long enough for my ass."

"There are several people using a hand lift at elevation near the doors," Dev said. "And I am glad you like the clothing. I think it's quite attractive on you."

"How can you tell? I could be wearing a sheet of seaweed in here and you wouldn't know."

"I think I would smell that. But I was looking at you when the power went out." Dev went back to the screen. "They are attempting to use the hand lift to pry open the doors."

"Finally, someone with a brain arrived. Hope they don't shoot them."

Dev put the scanner down on her panel and turned toward her controls. "I think it's safe to release the umbilical, Jess.

With all the noise outside, and the shooting, it will not be noticed."

"Yeah, makes sense," Jess said. "Stupid gunners could be shooting bits off half the half out there."

Dev released the clamps and ejected the connections to the carrier. With power down it wouldn't show on any one's board. But even with power it wouldn't have, since she'd taken care to isolate the carrier's control systems the previous day. The boards were dark, and she left them as they were.

Jess came over and sat on the jump seat next to Dev and watched the screen as the wire map showed what was going on outside. She clearly heard someone shout commands outside, telling people to board.

It felt good to know she wasn't going to obey that command. She'd started out without a plan and ended up exactly where she'd wanted to be. So, from Jess's perspective, things were going great. "If they have to work so hard to get that thing open," she said, "they'll leave it open. C'mon sea cucumber brains make it easy for us."

"They have just cut through the retaining track to better position the lift, so that would seem true," Dev said and watched the screen. "They won't be able to close it even if they want to."

"They really are running," Jess said, after a moment's silence. "They're n o t c o m i n g b a c k. They d o n ' t c a r e what they're leaving here."

"No," Dev said, quietly. "It appears not."

Jess heard running feet, and the wire map showed figures dashing across the floor toward the transport. "Any comms going on?"

Dev flipped over to a second screen and reviewed the returns. "Just hand comms," she said. "Local." She tuned a channel and then opened it.

"Get to the transport!" A male voice bellowed. "Move! They'll have that open in ten minutes. Anyone not on is staying behind!"

"That's the security chief, Barona," Dev said. "He seems upset."

"What about ops?" A yell came back to him.

"That's Centops control, mobile," Jess said. "Burton, the ops mids chief. They must have evac'd from there."

"Screw it! Not worth the trouble. C'mon, Jax, get over here," Barona responded. "Everyone on sec-chan board now!"

"We can't get to residential! It's hip deep in fluid!" Someone answered. "We gotta vent!"

"Leave it!" Barona yelled. "Just move. Whoever stayed in bed'll die there."

"The f'ing doors are locked!" The voice responded. "They can't get out!"

"Too f'ing bad for them. More space for us," Barona responded. "Move!"

Jess sniffed reflectively. "Bye, assholes."

Dev glanced at her.

Jess reached over and picked up Dev's hand kissed it. "We're home free, Dev. They don't care who they leave. Just who they take. Sometimes fate just goes your way, you know?"

"Yes." Dev leaned over and kissed Jess on the lips. "It seems so."

Jess kissed her back. The transport engines revved up, and a last scattering of moving figures approached it. Jess lifted her free hand and waggled her fingers at them, as a wash of water vapor showed the doors opened.

An air horn, the oldest of the old tech they had, sounded, a raw warning that echoed through the cavern, followed by the transport's engines spooling up, the rumble of their jet release shaking the platform the carrier as perched on.

It made their ear tickle, and Jess rubbed hers, then it receded into the distance, replaced by thunder from the outside, and the drum of rain wash flowing down the wall.

****

At last, it was quiet.

Dev and Jess sat there for several minutes, just listening to the sound of the rain outside the cavern, a booming thunder rolling in that was loud enough to make their ears itch and Jess grimaced. "Idiots," she muttered.

"To leave in the storm?" Dev asked, her booted feet extended and crossed at the ankles. She pressed her shoulders against the back of her pilot's seat, content to relax here in this one place she considered to be truly hers.

More than her quarters, though she had enjoyed the space there. This carrier had come to define her role and had brought her both notice and notoriety in equal measure, along with her unlikely nickname. She was glad they'd be taking the craft with them.

"Yeah." Jess shifted on the jump seat, which was uncomfortable and too small for her tall frame. "Whatcha say, we go out and see what the sitch is out there, then take off? I know some caves we can shelter in if it gets too hairy."

"It would allow the weather to reduce," Dev said. "This vehicle can cope with the precipitation, but I would just as soon not deal with lightning induced power fluctuations if we can avoid them. Since we will not have the option to return here for repair."

Jess patted her on the back. "I'm gonna stick my head out. Start getting this crate ready to go."

Dev activated her panels, and the interior lights on the carrier came on at their dimmest setting, enough after the utter darkness to bring everything into sharp relief around them.

Jess still sat there, watching her, head leaning against the side of the carrier, a faint smile on her face.

They looked silently at each other.

"Just you and me now, Devvie," Jess said, after a moment.

Dev grinned. "Excellent," she said. "I think we could not have asked for a better outcome."

That made Jess grin wider. "Just wait until we have to fish for breakfast, then you'll wish we went west." She pushed herself to her feet and ducked slightly to avoid hitting her head on the console above Dev's seat. "Let me make sure we're clear to leave."

Dev turned to her controls and triggered the protective screen over her station. The shield slid back to expose the darkness of the cavern beyond, briefly lit with lightning from the open bay door.

Well, half open. Enough to allow the transport to exit. More than enough to allow the carrier, so she nodded and started to bring things live.

Jess went to the hatch, put her hand against the panel inside, and waited the heartbeat it took for the door to unlatch and move silently aside. As it got halfway open, it all changed.

Pops, thunks, and light flared all around her and she slammed the hatch controls and dove to one side in pure instinct. She landed across her own console as the blare of light came in the front nose windows Dev had just revealed. "Dev! Get down!"

"Yes," Dev responded. "I see power has returned." She sounded mildly bemused. "Interesting."

"Get your damn head down!" Jess flipped herself over her chair and came around the back of Dev's seat to lean next to her. The halon lights were now on over the cavern, and she heard the hum of energy all around them. "Damn it."

Blaster shots creased the sides of carriers and consoles all around them, and not far away Jess saw two bodies, blood pooled on the floor around them. It looked like they'd been under attack.

Maybe they had been? Jess's eyes narrowed. Double scam?

"That seems like a big coincidence, Devvie," she said, grimly. "Power coming back right after those bimbos leave." She looked around the carrier. "And all I've got is a folded piece of metal to defend us with. If I touch those triggers this thing's gonna come apart with us in it."

Dev leaned to one side and looked past the front of the carrier. "Interesting."

Jess frowned. "Maybe I have something in those lockers. Damn it! Did I think I was going to throw rocks at the bad guys? What the hell is wrong with me!"

"Jess." Dev gently put her hand on Jess's cheek and pushed her head around to look to the carrier's left-hand side. "I am confident, as well, it was not a coincidence, but I think it's all right."

A figure appeared and looked at them through the open shield. It lifted its hand and made a thumbs up hand signal, and grinned.

"April?" Jess said, after a moments surprised silence.

"And Doug," Dev said, as a second figure appeared. "It seems some others stayed behind."

Jess pushed off and went back to the hatch and opened it again. She emerged from the carrier and moved out onto the landing pad to face the small crowd gathering.

"What the hell?" Jess asked April, who swaggered up. She looked extremely pleased with herself. "You guys pull the plug on this place?"

"He did." April jerked a thumb at Doug. "Finally did something right."

"That was really excellent," Dev said. She had emerged behind Jess and now came to the side of the pad. "It was very good work."

"We just decided we weren't going," Mike Arias said. He leaned on the edge of the platform, dressed in a civilian jacket and rugged overalls. "We figured if we could panic those suits, they'd take off. Make 'em think we were being targeted." He nodded in satisfaction. "I just didn't like them. Gave me chicken skin."

Dev regarded him with contracted brows.

"Worked," April said, succinctly. "No idea what the hell they thought was happening, but they couldn't get out of here fast enough."

"My dad oversaw the hydro works back on the Island," Doug said. "I know a few things about interlacing interconnects and how to decouple them. So that's what I did. I figured at night, in the dark, they'd flip out."

"A bypass," Chester mused. "Well, they flipped," he agreed. "Seriously."

Doug nodded. "Wasn't hard. The transfer switch here's in front of the batts. Cuts off everything when you take it out," he explained. "They figured that out after the last cluster, and it was on a list of stuff they were supposed to fix they never did."

"Whatever works," Jess said, and glanced at the rest of the people who had strolled over. Not a big crowd, but Clint was there, and Jerad from Medical, along with the two agents and two techs. In the back, near the wall she saw the sets gather and peer out with anxious apprehension. "So. Now what do we do?"

"Now what do we do?" April returned the question. "We figured you maybe had a plan."

"Me?" Jess folded her arms. "I had a plan for me and Rocket, sure," she said. "She rigged our bus so we could duck into it, then wait for them to give up on us and take off."

"Rocket fixed us up so we could take a hike, too," Doug said. "We did our wrenching last night when we were ah.. cleaning out the carriers."

Jess remembered them arriving at dinner with grease stains, and she turned to regard Dev. "She did, huh?"

Dev had her noncommittal expression on, and her hands were clasped behind her back "I offered to duplicate the functionality of the new module I have been testing," she demurred. "It seemed retaining local control over these vehicles could be useful."

"Ya think?" Jess swung back around to the rest of them. "We were going to duck out after the transport left. Figured we could outrun it if nothing else."

Chester chuckled. "They wouldn't have chased ya," he said. "Nobody's gonna stick with Rocket."

"We had the same idea," April said. "We were just hanging out locked in our cribs, waiting for Doug to put the juice back on after they left, when the whole damn residential level flooded out with pneumatic fluid and the doors slammed open. What a mess. I think that's what really wigged em."

Dev cleared her throat.

"Nearly screwed up the plan," Doug said. "The big hatch slammed shut." He pointed at the half open bay. "I heard em yelling through the access tubes. Then someone showed up and told em to use the hand jacks."

Clint held his hand up. "That'd be me," he said, with a twinkle in his eye. "I was fixin to just hide out in the maintenance shaft, while all the hubbub was going on and then see what my options were." He leaned against the pad. "I saw the pneumatic systems all go offline. That's what the flood was?"

"Sorry about that," Dev said. "We had to get the doors open in our quarters. I disrupted the pneumatic lines. That reduced system pressure." She paused. "Somewhat catastrophically, it seems."

"So, that's what happened." April started laughing. "I was cursing Doug because he trapped us all in our bunks while he was down in the raceway. Suddenly I heard a bam and the door whipped open, and we were all out in the hall trying to get ahead of it. My boots are purple."

Doug blushed a little. "Didn't think about that. But hey, it worked out, didn't it?"

"Apparently so," Dev said. "Even without a plan."

Jess put her hands on her hips. "Well, they're gone." She studied the opening. "But they'll be back to salvage all that crap they left behind." She looked at the crowd. "Probably a good idea to figure out what to do next to get clear of here."

Clint came over and leaned against one of the consoles that serviced the pad. "What are you doing, Drake?" He said. "You weren't never going to go, were ya?"

Jess relaxed. "Nah." She put her hands in her pockets. "I'm going to the Bay. I figure they'll find me useful for something." She glanced aside at Dev. "You still up for that?"

Dev looked at her with a slightly bewildered expression. "Of course. If by that you mean do I wish to go with you to your birthplace."

Jess nodded and gave her a brief grin.

"I would go wherever it is you were going," Dev continued in a mild tone. "It doesn't really matter to me where that is, but I am glad it's your birthplace because I am quite fond of it."

A little silence fell. Jess glanced furtively around and reached up to rub her cheek, aware of the blush coloring her skin and the grins of the others watching her. "Aww. Thanks, Devvie."

"C'mon, Drake." April climbed up onto the platform and came over to stand next to her, with a stern, almost arrogant jerk of her jaw. "We could be useful, too. Take us with you." She hooked her thumbs in her belt, her hand resting against the hilt of the dalknife in its hilt. "We got skills."

Jess regarded her thoughtfully. "That's true," she finally said. "I could probably do that."

"Well, now," Clint said, "you can't just show up at a homestead, you know—"

"She can." April cut him off. "Shut it down. You can stay here if you want to."

"Didn't say I wanted to," Clint said. "Just said it isn't that easy sometimes."

"I hear Drake's got some leverage there," Jerad said. "That true, Drake? That place needs a half-baked quack like me? Otherwise, I was going to hike up to Quebec. I figure someone up there could use first aid."

"Kurok could probably use another pair of doc hands," Jess allowed. "The two other medics got splatted in the last fight."

Dev came over and tugged on Jess's sleeve. "And we can take the sets, right Jess?" She whispered. "They are all trained in many systems. They could do good work."

Jess looked around at all of them. Then she exhaled. "Gonna take a lot of trips," she said. "Maybe we should head over first and make sure it's not going to be a crap show." She wondered if the Bay would be up for it. Were they still okay with bringing in outsiders? "Worked out the last time, but that was the last time."

"Yes, we can only take a handful in each of our vehicles," Dev agreed. "Let me go explain to them what we would like to do." She turned and went off down the steps to the carrier's platform and onto the floor, heading off toward the edge of the cavern where the sets were milling.

April watched her go. "Wasn't really in the plan, huh?"

Jess's lips twitched. "Wasn't really a plan," she admitted. "Yours was better. Get rid of all the bastards. Less chance of getting our heads blown off that way." She studied the doors to the landing cavern. "I figure we got about ten hours before they get back there, realize it was a scam, and send an armored gun platform back."

"About," April said and nodded at Mike who'd joined them on the platform. "We figured if we had our own rigs we could grab whatever's around and take it with us. Didn't figure on them leaving the bios."

"Bastards," Jess said. "They could have squeezed them in if they'd left all the cargo behind."

"Don't get that," Mike said. "Those guys are valuable."

"To run a base." Jess looked thoughtfully at the group.

"And they got bases in the West, don't they?"

"Maybe they're going to send the transport back," Doug suggested. "Cause Mike's right. Those guys would be worth a pretty penny back there. And even if they didn't have base slots, they could farm em out for a good price."

"Maybe they won't want to go," Jess said. "Maybe they want to stay here and wait for a pickup."

"I say we take them and all the gear we can haul out of here with em," April said. "We're wasting time."

Jess nodded. "Yeah. We're wasting time. Get those boxes on the edge there and see what's salvageable."

"Want a tank?" Jerad asked, "Figure you need one over there."

"Can Dev hotwire more of these buses?" Clint asked. "I got my license. I can drive one, long as it's mostly in a straight path."

Jess cocked her head. "Somethings coming," she said crisply. "Engines, heading this way." She turned. "Hey, Dev! Need your scanner!" She motioned to the opening. "We got trouble!"

Dev turned and ran back over.

"Talking's over," April said. "Get these rigs ready." She motioned Doug toward theirs.

"I'll help you pack the tank," Clint told Jerad. "C'mon, best get out of the way."

"Lead on."

Dev dove without any questioning into the carrier and instead of picking up her scanner, threw herself into her pilot's seat and hit the rapid startup sequence with her fingertips almost a blur. She pulled her comm and control headset on with one hand, as she started getting returns from the carrier's more powerful systems.

Jess was right behind her. "Hope it's just a recon," she muttered. "One of them sniffing around to see what the sitch is. They probably heard we're shutting down."

Dev moved her scan pad into position on her right-hand. "The weather is obstructing," she said after a moment. "There is a lot of disruption."

Jess leaned over the back of Dev's chair and watched the screen intently. "Not sure what in the hell we can do about it if it's them. Maybe have Doug shut the place down again. Make them think it's dead."

"It's a single craft," Dev said, after a moment's silence. "Inbound, standard heading, from the south." She studied the scan. "No ident."

"Bring up a sideband to the kids and let them know."

"It's already up," Dev responded. "Tac 1, to Tac 2, Tac 3, single inbound, dual commercial engine." She scanned the results. "No weapons return."

Jess's brow creased, "Civ?"

"Unknown," Dev said. "They're scanning us."

"That civ?" Doug's voice came through the comms. "Profile's not theirs."

"Scanner is on our frequencies," Dev concluded. "It appears to be a small flyer, with enhanced diagnostic systems." She studied the wireframe that formed in front of her. "Heading directly for the landing bay."

"We need a visual," Jess said. She leaped out of the carrier with a sense of relief as she released her pent-up energy in a speed run for the side of the cavern, dodging bits of debris, broken crates and the odd body part.

The wall was coming fast, but she didn't slacken speed. She got to a point on the ground her sense of spatial dynamics told her was the right angle. She was at the right point in space to turn her run into a leap and let her forward motion take her to the rock face.

She reached out and grabbed a handhold, then rapidly pulled herself upward as she heard yells behind her that she ignored. The doors were in a slot, and she reached the slot and ran along it until she got to the edge that was open and hauled herself around it.

She reflected with a curse at her own stupidity in not bringing an infrared scope with her, since it was dark turning slightly   less dark outside, and full of clouds and rain. Whatever was coming was invisible.

Mostly invisible. She climbed out onto the landing ledge and stood as the wind whipped against her. She then cupped her hands over her eyes and stared into the gloom.

Exposed, and vulnerable, she knew, but trusted her reflexes to throw herself out of range if she sensed inbound fire as she patiently separated the clouds and rain from the oncoming craft.

"You are out of your blasted mind," April's out of breath voice came from behind her. "What are you going to do, grab it barehand?"

Ah. Jess's eyes focused as she found her target. "Trying to see what kind of bad news this is."

April was behind the edge of the door, only her head poking out. "What do you think you can see in this mess? I can't see crap."

Jess allowed the focus to tighten and felt the tickle of a scan. "It's civ," she said. The craft abruptly turned to the left that showed its long profile to Jess. Then, surprisingly, it's flight lights came on and illuminated its chassis, and the tail that was now within her sight.

"What the…" April squinted. "It turned its lights on? Civ and insane? Better get your ass inside before they crash into you."

"Yeah." Jess leaned back against the wall. "Get back. It's gonna land." She made a long, exaggerated signal with her arms, and then pointed inside the cavern. "It's friendly."

"You think?"

Jess climbed back inside the cavern, glad to be out of the wind. "Got the Bay mark on its tail." She got back along the ledge in time to see Dev come out along the ledge. "Hey, Devvie."

"It's Doctor Dan!" Dev called out in a relieved tone. "I was able to contact him from the carrier. He's very…" She paused. "I think he's upset."

Jess dusted her hands off, as April backed away from her. "Even if he's got bad news," Jess said, "he's at least not gonna shoot at us. C'mon, let's find out what his problem is."

"Like we need more of them."

****

The flyer landed in the spot the transport had been, set down neatly before discharging its passengers.

Mike from Bay Security was there, along with Kurok in his Drake's Bay pullover, and a KayTee pilot in a flight jumpsuit with a turtleneck sweater over it.

Kurok stood with his hands on his hips and stared around the cavern with a look best described as disgusted disbelief. His silvered blond hair was almost standing on end, as though he'd run his fingers through it.

"I was trying to get here to see if I could talk some sense into those administrative idiots," Kurok said. "I got the message from West ops and then had to deal with a barrage of our neighbors who showed up in a panic, or I'd have been here sooner."

To one side, Clint and Jerad stacked gear to be moved, and a dozen of the bio alts from the base helped them.

All of them were glad to see Dan Kurok. Their stress level seemed to come right down at his appearance, and everyone enjoyed being treated to a remarkable demonstration of his righteous indignation.

"They sent a message out to the homesteads saying they were pulling out?" Jess asked, in a tone of disbelief. "What the what?"

"What the bloody what!" Kurok repeated. "Absolute idiotic muppets. He opened his pad and read the message to them.

Thank you for your patience as we work out our operational strategies. We will be closing the east coast bases until staffing levels recover. We are confident this will not affect you in any way.

Kurok shook his head. "My jaw nearly hit the desk when I read it." He looked around. "What happened here, or should I not ask?" He looked up at Jess. "Never mind, I can wait. My assumption is you lot are heading our way?"

Jess tilted her head. "That all right?" She asked.

Security Mike laughed, a rough and almost harsh sound that echoed across the cavern. "F'kn yo."

"My second reason for coming here was to provide an escape vehicle for you," Kurok said with more civilized verbiage. "Of course, it is. Mike was going to bring a squad with him, but I figured the space in the flyer was better saved for passengers."

"Jackasses," Mike growled. "They effen picked up and ran like skinks." He seemed unable to absorb that. "Left the whole effen coast to be scraped by the bastards. Surprised they ain't here by now. If we heard it, they did."

Jess nodded.

"Can we save the stories for later?" April asked. "Back of my neck's itching. We need to get out of here."

Dev rejoined them just then, returning a tool to the toolkit now strapped at her waist. "We have eight vehicles now operational, aside from the carriers," she said. "And there are six KayTees who can pilot six of them."

"Cargo craft, but we can squeeze a lot of bodies in there," Mike said. "Good job, Rocket. Gonna be nice to have you around."

Dev smiled briefly. "Thank you. The other carriers are sealed. I might be able to reverse the seal with some effort, but it would take a significant amount of time."

"I can fly one of the cargo planes," Kurok said. "And I think I heard that tech mech manager say he can fly. So that's that." He regarded Dev. "You'll have to show me that module, Dev."

"Of course." Dev looked satisfied. "But I also think it's

wise for us to leave. It's light outside, and the weather has moderated. Scan is clear, but it's limited distance."

"Get loaded up," Jess said. "Get that last batch in and lets move."

They all split up and headed for the waiting flyers, save Kurok and Jess, who stood for a moment together in the center of the cavern. "I could be an outlaw," Jess said to him. "Maybe you don't want me to stay at the Bay. That could be the wrong kind of trouble."

Kurok, surprisingly, patted her arm. "Ah, Jesslyn," he said. "It's more complicated than that."

"More complicated than this?" Jess's eyebrows shot up and her voice lifted with them. She spread her long arms and indicated the interior of the cavern. "Really?"

"Really. You see, someone made you civ," Kurok said, with his gentle smile. "That came through right before I left to come out here, in a flailing blare of change of authority. You have to come to the Bay." He looked wryly at her. "And truly, the Bay wants you. Why don't we get back there and we can talk about all the problems we just took on."

Jess stared at him, stunned. "Oh crap," she managed to say. "How the hell did that happen?"

"Mm." Kurok clasped his hands together and cracked his knuckles. "Going to be interesting times."

****

Jess felt a distinct sense of it being surreal as they got to altitude and came around to southern heading as she crossed back in front of the craggy wall of Base 10 before heading off.

She was seated in her gunner's chair, all the boards and readouts dark. It was just her and Dev in the carrier. They'd squeezed everything they could into the fliers and took off, not at all what she'd figured the day was going to go like.

Not at all.

Dev was up in the pilot's station, her comms rig on her head, exchanging quiet commentary with the other two carriers. The cargo fleet was just behind the three of them, everyone lined up and spaced evenly as they settled into flight. The sets were all squeezed into the cargo space, both thrilled and relieved.

Surreal. "What in the hell just happened here, Dev?" Jess asked aloud. "I mean, what the hell?"

Dev glanced into the reflective surface over her station, her brow faintly furrowed for a minute. "Do you mean the events of last night?" She asked. "You are not asking about this functional flight, are you?"

Jess got up and moved to the jump seat and squeezed herself in next to Dev's console. "Yeah."

"I think events are going along quite well?" She said. "We intended to leave the base, in our vehicle, and in fact, we are. This seems relatively optimal. Isn't it?"

"Yeah but... I was thinking… it happened too easy," Jess said. "And…" She paused. "I think it's a rig. Doc told me before we left someone pushed the button on me." She watched Dev's profile, outlined in the glow from the controls.

Dev's brow puckered further. She adjusted the engine output and checked the scan. "You have a button?" She asked. "Where?"

Jess grinned. "They changed my status to civilian. They booted me. Who had the time in that mess, Devvie? Had to be a rig."

"I see," Dev said. "Is that optimal or not? I don't understand what the purpose of that would be."

Jess was quiet for a long moment as they flew, glad of the distraction from their destination. "I don't know." She finally said. "I'm civ. I have to go by civ law. Had time to read about that the last time it was me that gave them a kick. They warn ya that offing people will get you in trouble, that kind of thing."

"I see," Dev said. "To get you in trouble?"

"Maybe." Jess shrugged then put her hands back down. "Make my life tough? Make them not responsible for me? Who the hell knows? Cause a problem at the Bay?"

"Will it make a problem? Does that mean you're in charge of your birthplace again?"

Jess remained in silent thought briefly. "No, I don't think so. Not like that. I… my status there is what it is. I signed over admin control to the doc." She seemed relieved, and her expression brightened. "But.. yeah, I don't know what that does on the day to day. Maybe nothing."

Dev nodded. "Excellent." She exhaled in satisfaction. "If this was intentional or not, I am glad it ended with us leaving that location and going back to Drake's Bay," she said. "The sets are glad as well."

"Instead of them being left behind in that drafty tomb with no supply? Yeah, I bet." Jess extended her legs along the deck. "I still think it's a rig. There's some game in play." She shrugged. "We'll figure it out."

****

They rode along quietly together for about twenty minutes. Jess was half turned in the jump seat to look out the front screen at the sheets of rain and the mixture of cliff, beach, and sea they were flying over.

Dev watched her in her peripheral vision, her head framed by the hood of the overshirt she wore, her dark hair in disarray from their recent adventures. There was a faint reflection from the control panels on her pale eyes, and her expression was thoughtful.

A bit worried.

Dev didn't feel worried at all about the results of the day. Now that the power outage had been satisfactorily explained to her, she thought the consequences had worked in their favor. They had obtained supplies and gear to take with them along with two other carriers, and the sets were not left behind.

All excellent things. She studied her controls, and regarded the transponder, deciding to leave it set to show their comp identity as she expected to pick up Bay ops scan relatively soon. It would be best if they knew who it was given everything that had gone on.

That made her think a moment, about her own status.

What was she now? They had left Interforce, and apparently Jess had been removed. What did that mean for her? She had brought along the packet they gave her, but in the back of her mind, Dev really doubted it was genuine.

What was it that Jess called it? A rig. Something they had put in place as part of a bigger plan. Dev nodded quietly to herself. Yes. Maybe so. Something could be behind it. Likely was, else they would not have taken the pains to give the packet to her and make sure she knew.

But was she still obligated to them? Contracted to them in some way? Contracted to anyone? Or was she in some in between state that gave her neither obligations nor protection?

Doctor Dan would probably know. She had been contracted to him, once. Was she still? After he removed her synaptics she hadn't thought to ask. Now she would probably have to.

Now she would have to know.

But anyway, now she was here in the carrier, and she was with Jess, and they were heading for a place of sanctuary. She nodded to herself, then a memory surfaced. "Oh, Jess."

Jess straightened and looked intently around. "What?"

"No, I just remembered." Dev put a hand on her wrist. "I was able to get this new module to integrate with the rest of the carrier systems. I think it should respond normally if any are needed."

Jess's head tilted to one side. "What do you mean?"

The comms crackled inside her ear bud. "A moment." Dev returned her attention to the controls. "We are being hailed."

"Clowns have arrived, circus is starting," Jess announced. "Where's the popcorn."

"Incoming flight, this is Drake's Bay control. Please identify," a voice asked briskly. There was an expectant tone to the voice, almost a lilt Dev could hear.

She took a breath, then held it a moment in some consideration. "It's Dev," she finally said. "I am with Jess, and we have some vehicles here we would like to land with."

Jess chuckled. "Nice."

"We acknowledge that, NM-Dev-1." The voice answered, now with a definite note of excitement in it. "We have you on scan, and landing is being arranged. Please stand by, stay on course."

"They know," Jess murmured. "No surprises."

"Well, it's not unreasonable that Doctor Dan advised them of what our plans were," Dev said. "I am sure he told them how many vehicles to expect."

"Yeah, probably." Jess got up and went back to her seat and folded her hands over her stomach. "You're not going to do any funny stuff on the way in are ya?"

"Excuse me, what?"

"I can leave my seat belt off?"

Dev chuckled. "I will remain at level flight," she confirmed. "There are a lot of vehicles around us, and I do not wish an incident."

She saw the promontory that held Drake's Bay now on the horizon, the half circle line of cliffs extending out into the sea. As they started to descend to land, the rain stopped.

The air cleared of mist and the gray light brought out the green in the sea. The range of grays and greens and blues of the slate cliffs brought out their eerie beauty.

"NM-Dev-1, this is Bay Ops, please use the landing location reserved for you the last arrival, and the two Bantam craft with you please use the two on either side. Please instruct the cargo vehicles to use Bay 5, 6 and 7. They are large and have been cleared."

"Yes," Dev responded and passed along the request into the

sideband. "We are on track."

"Bay Flight A, please return the vehicle you are in to Bay 1," Ops concluded. "Personnel are standing by to receive."

Jess took a deep breath. "Here we go," she muttered. "Let's hope this doesn't end up a total shit show."

Dev glanced in the reflective surface. "The landing?" She asked, her voice raising in question. "Jess, I think it will be fine. I have landed here before. Are you expecting a problem? This vehicle is responding normally."

Jess chuckled wanly. "No. The last thing I'm worried about is you landing this bucket."

"Oh." Dev adjusted her speed and aimed for the landing bay. "Well, if it's helpful, I feel confident it will be excellent for us to be here," she said. "Please stand by for descent."

They cleared the outer rim of cliffs and made the steep turn into the Bay itself, where the landing caverns on the north side were standing open.

Below them, sensors indicated sound, and Dev opened the speakers. The tolling of the sea bell, ringing repeatedly erupted into the carrier, and behind it, the sound of the smaller bells and horns on the fishing vessels echoed.

Dev looked behind her and caught the look of surprise on Jess's face. "It seems like we are being welcomed."

Jess produced a small, charmed smile. "Huh," she grunted softly. "Damned if we aren't."

Dev slowed her speed and came level with the landing spot she'd been directed to. The figures on either side of the opening stood and watched them. She was now close enough to see the smiles on their faces, and as she watched they started hopping up and down throwing their hands in the air. "Jess, look."

"I am," Jess said. "No clue what the hell I'm looking at but it's something."

Dev focused on nailing her landing. She appreciated the solemnity of the moment and didn't want to mess that up in any way. She cut her mains as she crossed the rock threshold and let the carrier's forward momentum take them inside to the pad, landing neatly on extended skids.

Exact center, neatly positioned, no bounces. Dev shut down power to the engines and turned on the safe lights, as the two other carriers came in behind her, landing with a bit less grace and a bit less precision.

Ahead of her, she saw Dustin bouncing a little on his feet as he pumped his fists in the air. She lifted a hand and waved at him, then unlocked the external hatches. "Should I open the egress, Jess?"

Jess stood up and straightened her shoulders. "I guess." She sounded more confident, however. "No time like the time it is."

Dev smiled and unlocked the hatch.

Sound flooded in—the off gassing of the carriers, the sound of the bells coming in the open bay door, and yells of excitement and running boots. Hoots, whistles, and cheers erupted as Jess stepped to the open hatch.

Then a deep, repetitive, "Drake! Drake!" A chant that echoed and echoed as Jess, a little hesitantly, waved in acknowledgement.

Dev turned her chair around as she let the shutdown processes run and enjoyed the moment as she watched Jess put her hands on the edge of the doorway and lean out as the landing bay became flooded with bodies and noise.

Doctor Dan, she was sure, had communicated ahead of them. She was confident he would arrive soon, after landing the cargo craft he'd piloted, causing no end of pleasure and excitement for the sets who had been chosen to ride with him.

She unhooked her restraints and walked over to the hatch to stand at Jess's side as they both walked down the ramp to the pad deck.

Mechs were bustling around the carriers to hook them up to power. Dev caught Dustin patting the nose of their carrier with a big, delighted, kidl i k e grin. She gave him a grin back and he came over to her.

"Rocket!" He said. "Sup?"

A tall man Dev remembered as one of the Bay domestic operations staff was talking to Jess. April and Mike joined them, and Dev judged they were discussing assignment of quarters. She decided that Jess would ensure she was adequately housed and turned back to Dustin.

"It seems we have returned in a shorter time than perhaps expected," Dev answered. "Hello again."

"Awesome sauce," Dustin responded. "This is sweet." He patted the carrier nose again. "Force took off? Just cranked out? Truth?"

Dev sorted through the language. "It appears so. We did not think that was the right thing, so we decided to stay behind and come here instead."

"Pfffft." Dustin made a strange sound. "Drake leave? No f'n way," he said. "You all are homies now, yah?" He turned and looked around. "Sweet."

"Hey, Dev."

Dev gave up trying to translate and found Doug there next to her. "Hello."

"These guys all know the score," Doug said. He waved vaguely around. "I guess it's cool, huh? That's what all the noise is?"

"F'n yah," Dustin said. "Been buzzing here since half the half busted in last night. Doc went zooming out there to eyeball." He raised one hand and waggled it with his thumb and little finger extended. "We got what we wanted." He winked at them, then hopped up onto the platform and started attaching leads, whistling under his breath.

Chester came up on the other side. "Wow." He looked around. "I guess we're okay."

"All right everyone!" Kurok arrived at the platform their carrier was on and raised his hands. "Let's settle down, and get everyone sorted out, shall we? There must be a better place to explain what's going on than the landing bay."

"Mess!" Dustin yelled out. "Chow time anyhow."

Cheers.

"Excellent idea," Kurok said. "Everyone lets head down for lunch. Abe, can you go down to the other bays and help some new arrivals get settled? They're several sets from Base 10."

"Yes." Abe, an AyeBee from House ops had appeared at the edge of the crowd. "We will help," he said. "I think we will need additional spaces. May we use level six, Doctor Dan?"

"Yes you may," Kurok said, and Abe ducked past some of the watchers and headed for the inner entrance to the Bay. "And we have some new staff arrivals as well," he said to the tall man. "I see you're already at it, Pete."

"That I am," Pete agreed. "I was just telling the Drake here, before everyone starts running around, we should get her quarters settled."

"Ah, yes." Kurok's eyes twinkled. "Yes, we should."

"Something wrong with the ones we stayed in the other night?" Jess asked. "You're not going to put us up in hammocks again, are ya?"

Dev remembered that first visit and edged closer. "That was a pleasant location we were in the last time. I enjoyed the windows."

Pete and Kurok exchanged glances. "Well, yeah those are nice, but now that your reg civ profile's open in the Bay, you got some other options," Pete said. "You can check em out, and if it's not scratch we can move ya."

Jess looked between them. "Other options," she mused.

"You mean, my citizen profile? You know about that already?"

Kurok and Pete exchanged another look. "Oh yeah." Pete nodded. "We knew. That was a thing."

Kurok just chuckled. "Go grab your kit, and get that settled, and then go get some lunch so the whole place can hear the scoop."

"We didn't bring much with us," Jess said. "Not much to get stored." She regarded Pete for a moment. "We might need some supplies."

Kurok patted her on the elbow. "I'm sure we can get you all what you need," he said. "You have duffles up in the carrier?"

Jess shrugged. "Okay." She turned and stepped back up onto the platform and went into the carrier. "I'll grab yours, Devvie."

Dev remained where she was, as the two men chuckled and shook their heads.

"Been a long day, hmm, Dev?" Kurok asked, in a kind tone.

"Yes," Dev admitted. "But I am glad we are here."

"We are too." Kurok said. "And we've got a lot to discuss." "For sure," Pete agreed. "But first things first," he said, "And maybe a cup of something second."

"That'd be great," April said. "It's been a weird twenty- four. Can stop now for a while before that all starts up again."

Pete grinned. "We'll see what we can do. At least, for that cup."

Chapter Eight

Doug and April, Mike and Chester, Clint, and Jerad were, in fact, settled in spaces in the Drake family compound. The two agents and their techs were in a large segment of rooms on one side, and the rest were in individual chambers on the other side of the hallway from them.

It was a little awkward, and nobody said that much, but everyone seemed pleased with the space they'd ended up with. Clint especially happy with the windows to the outside.

They took their gear bags and disappeared behind the doors, leaving Pete, Kurok, Jess and Dev outside the main entrance to that section.

"Okay, so now for you," Pete said. There's a little section that's residential for just the Drake, but it takes a reg cred."

Jess stood there, her duffel slung over her shoulder. "Let's get this over with," she said. "I was fine in the other spot. We could just go back there."

Pete nodded. "I know. Won't take long." He turned and went to an inset alcove to the left of the main entrance to where the others had disappeared into. "Needs your print." He indicated a worn, square panel in the shadows next to what was now visible as a doorway.

Jess studied it. "This always been here? I don't remember seeing it."

Pete pointed. "Print. You were the one who was in a hurry," he added, after Jess gave him a sharp look.

With a twitch of her lips, Jess stepped forward and put her hand on the panel and felt a prickle, then a second one. "Double scan," she said. "The hell?"

"Oh. Yeah. Looks for ident, then validates to civ status," Pete said. "Cause here, y'know—"

"Yeah, I know." Jess rubbed her fingertips together. She felt the residual tickle of the scan as the panel clicked and the lock cycled, apparently accepting her. "So."

The door slid open to reveal a set of stone steps. Jess gave them all a look then started up them, climbing up as it curved to the right. She judged the climb to be one whole level. "This must be fun getting supplies to."

Pete chuckled. "There's an internal lift."

"Can I ride in it?"

"Please don't."

At the top of the stairs was another door, with another panel. Jess put her hand on it without prompting.

The door opened and she walked inside, clearing the way for the rest of them to enter and then looked around in silence.

"Ah," she finally said, softly. "Yeah."

Dev came up next to her. "This is quite attractive," she said.

"You two explore, and we're going to get the paperwork done," Kurok said. "And answer some of the hundreds of questions I'm confident people are waiting to pounce on us with. We'll meet you in the mess." He patted Dev on the back. "Take your time though."

He and Pete backed out and went down the stairs and left the two of them standing in silence.

It was a tall room, at least two standard levels tall. In the center of the front wall was a large plas window, a panorama that showed the whole front of the Bay.

The whole structure was carved into an irregular outcropping, so the windows curved up and down, and the section extended out a little over the water.

There were alcoves cut in the rock, that seemed to be meant to store things on. But the room was empty otherwise. Off the room were carved hallways leading off into different areas, some of them inner spaces, some of them curving around to the sea wall side.

Dev turned and regarded Jess, who just stood there, gazing back and forth, absorbing it. "You seem discomfited," Dev said tentatively. "Is something suboptimal?"

"No. I." Jess exhaled. "Just haven't seen any of this place since I was five years old." She did a full circle turn, then looked back at her companion. "This was home, Dev. It's where we... where I lived before I got taken in."

Dev drew in a quick breath of surprise. "Oh!"

"Yeah." Jess started to walk along the edge of the big room. The walls were all stone cut and regular, the inner rooms she investigated empty and bare. "I don't remember much of it," she said. "A birthday party, maybe," she mused. "Might have been my last one here."

She got to the left side, and the hall that led along the wall, with doors opening to the inside. Four of them. At the last one she stood in the opening and regarded the interior. "I think this was my bedroom," she said, with mild fascination. "No wonder that other room drew a blank."

Dev was right at her heels, and she peered inside at a bare, modest space but with the awesome view out the thick plas window.

"I think I remember looking out that window to watch storms," Jess said. Then she backed out and went to the end of hallway, where there was a T junction. She turned left and went along it. It curved around again to a door at the end, and that was open. "Wonder what else we got."

There were lights on inside, sunk into the ceiling as the rest of the Bay had, and this door led into a much larger room with natural light in it. They paused inside the entrance and looked up, where, as in the main entry hall, a plas panel was set in the roof of the cavern to allow the overcast sky to be seen. They could also hear, off to the side, the sound of water.

They walked in silence around the empty space to a hall into a sanitary unit with a shower that was literally the size of their sleeping space back at Base 10. It had stone benches carved right into it.

"Nice," Jess said. She scuffed the toe of her boot against the stone floor. "Rough surface. Ya won't slip around on it with wet feet."

Dev looked down at the ground, which had an inlaid pattern in it, many shades of gray painstakingly arranged. "And it's pretty." She looked up at Jess. "This is an amazing place, Jess."

Jess looked around and grinned briefly. "Wish I remembered more of it," she said. "C'mon." She led the way along the hallway further on.

To the left of the sanitary space, they found a room carved out of another promontory that again had plas ceiling panel set in it, and a long, sweeping curve that gave you a three-quarter round view and a full sight of all the Bay, since this compound was in the far southern edge of the wall.

Inside the room was a platform and, on the platform, there was a bed frame and mattress that seemed both plush and new. Dev went over and pushed on the surface experimentally, finding it plush but firm.

Jess walked around the bed and went to the far side of the room, from which the sound of water was coming. "Someone left the plumbing on," she said "Let me go turn it off before we end up li…" She stopped speaking.

"Like the pneumatic fluid?" Dev said, with a good, humored grin. "I don't think they'd have…" She paused as she came up behind Jess and saw past her elbow. "Oh!" She blinked into the unexpectedly cold, brisk air tinged with salt.

It was outside, and not. It was a stone verge that led onto a carefully chiseled and notched platform that extended a good distance to a jagged, irregular edge.

It was a crack in the mountain wall, where the ground they were on stopped, and they were looking across at a solid surface of opposing rock, covered in a wash of water cascading down.

The sound of water was from a waterfall coming from the top of the crest, down the side of the crack, falling in a tumbling irregularity down to the sea two levels below and even from where they stood if she breathed in hard, Dev could taste the rainwater on the back of her tongue.

It was amazing.

There was a nice sized space carved out here, with a wrought iron railing like the stairs in the hall, with room near the wall to sit and watch the water, and if you walked to the end of the ledge, you had a good view of the entire curve of the Bay.

The light came down from the cloudy sky and reflected through the water and they both went to the rail and looked down, to see the froth and churn of the sea in this cut off curve in the wall. "This is a very interesting place," Dev finally said.

Jess leaned on the railing. "Yeah," she said. "It's cool. Nice spot to just chill out for a minute."

"Yes."

"Pretty sure my parents never let me out here," Jess said, in a reflective tone. "I'da jumped right over this rail."

Dev eyed her. "That might have ended suboptimally."

Jess chuckled suddenly, her face creasing into a grin. "Depends who you ask." She leaned over the railing and studied the two-story drop. "Maybe I'll try it."

"Right now?"

Jess chuckled again. "Nah, I'm just messing with you, Devvie." She straightened and looked around at the space. "But this is all right. I like it."

Reluctantly they walked back inside and finished the tour, which uncovered, along with more general use rooms and two sanitary units, a wide space with a stone-built work surface all along the plas window, and row after row of stone carved shelves along the other three walls.

Dev walked inside and turned in a circle as she observed the many shelves, and under them, steel cabinets. "Jess. Look at this."

"Workroom," Jess said, briefly, sticking her head inside it.

"Yes," Dev agreed. "This would be excellent to use for many things."

They returned to the huge entry hall, with its window, and

its wide floor, and its silence.

Jess put her hands in her pockets. "What do you think, Devvie? You like this place?"

"Do you like it?" Dev asked. "I think that matters more to me because I remember sleeping curled up in an egg. So, whatever is my situation here, it will be better than that was."

That made Jess smile. She looked around, and felt a sense of quiet, and privacy. After a moment, she nodded. "I like it," she said. "I'm glad there's no stuff in here. I don't really remember what it looked like way back when, so it can just end up being cool. I can make it what I want."

"Yes." Dev smiled at her. "It would be excellent."

Jess glanced at the floor, then to the side, then back at Dev, her dark hair falling down a little, obscuring her eyes. She cleared her throat a little diffidently. "You... ah... want to live here with me, Dev? Share this crazy place? You could set up a workroom back in there. There are power outlets all along that wall. Plenty of space for all your mods and stuff."

Dev considered that in thoughtful silence. "This is your place, Jess," she said. "You don't have to share it."

Jess was silent for a long time. Then she released a breath, as though it had been held. "I want to," she said, simply. "I don't want to be alone in here."

"I would like that very much," Dev said, quietly. "I'm really glad that you would like me to be here with you."

"Great," Jess said. "I got no idea where this is going or where we'll end up with it, but let's enjoy this place as much as we can, huh?"

"Yes," Dev agreed. "Let's put our duffle bags down in that room with the bed, since that is the only available furniture, and perhaps we can get a meal."

Jess started laughing. "We did miss breakfast."

She put her arm around Dev's shoulders and steered her back toward the bedroom. "Hope they have some places to store snacks in here."

"I thought I saw a food preparation area, in fact."

"Figures you noticed."

****

Dev hoped the plans and discussion everyone warned was coming would wait just a short while, to give everyone a chance to at least finish their meal.

The last food at Base 10 had been uninspiring and long ago. She was hungry, and she had a nice portion of the Bay's tasty fish stew in front of her and a plate of fish rolls. She looked forward to finishing them both. They hadn't gotten any sleep, but she often found a good meal made up for that.

They were seated on the side of the table with their backs to the wall, and on this occasion Jess took advantage of that to lean back and cradle her plate in one hand, scooping from it with her fork as she listened to Security Mike go through a litany of dangers he'd cataloged.

It sounded intimidating. They would be very busy, she was sure.

She glanced across the room where two very long tables were filled with the sets from the Base. They looked a little uncertain, and a little surprised, at being included. They seemed happy, and a touch overwhelmed. It was a lot of change, for them, Dev felt. They would need time to adjust.

They would all need a little time to adjust. She made a mental note to check with Kevin and Alvin later to see how it was going.

Dev plowed steadily through the fish stew, which had, she noted, a few bits of carrot in it. They were sweet and made a nice addition to the meal. She took a fish roll and dipped it into the stew liquid, chewing it and enjoying the taste.

"How's your digs?" Doug asked Dev. "Cool?"

"Empty, actually," Dev responded. "But I think they're going to be nice once we put some chairs and things in them to sit on." She thought about her new workspace. "And I have some room for my mods," she added. "It's a pleasant space. Are you all right with yours?"

Doug nodded. "Heck, yeah. We all are. I said when we were here the other day I could get used to that space easy, and here we are."

"Here we are." April gave him a sideways, wry look. "I got no complaints. I can put a sheet over that damn window if it gets too annoying for me," she said. "It's good, with that little food prep place, and plenty of space to spread out in there and set stuff up." She nodded decisively. "Have to go get a look around the area later see what else I can find."

Dev nodded and went back to her fish roll. she glanced to the side as Jess's elbow came to rest on her shoulder in a casual gesture as she set her plate down and picked up her cup of grog instead. Dev considered putting a kiss on the wrist now just to one side of her face, but decided it might distract Jess, while everyone watched her.

Suboptimal. Jess would get flustered sometimes, as though she never expected the action, and Dev judged this was likely an inappropriate location for it.

"Anyhow, we gotta start puttin up defensive walls out in the back," Security Mike said. "Not leave them holes like the last time."

"I think we probably do," Kurok said. "Our neighbors who stopped in last night are considering the place as something of a fortress and I didn't have the heart or the energy to burst their bubble." He leaned back in his seat and sipped his tea. "Bit of good luck we picked up a dozen weapons specialists from the base. I took a moment to collect their previous assignments from them."

Mike's ears perked up. "Bios? They gun jockeys? Nice. What else?"

"Pilots, and heavy machinery mechs," Kurok said. "I haven't looked at all the skill records, but all seem quite useful."

"Life's good." Mike nodded in satisfaction. "Drake, you brought us luck again."

"Ya think?" Jess eyed him drolly. "Wait and see if I brought us a thousand punks with guns on top of us trying to shoot my ass first."

"Nah, they'll stay clear of here," Mike said. "They'll go to Quebec City first, with all their cred. That's why Jacques pranced his ass in here last night. He knows."

"They are in fact conscious of their vulnerability," Kurok said. "They'll be back tomorrow. At least that will give you all a chance to settle in a bit."

"We going to go back and pick up more stuff at the base?" Doug asked. "They left a lot of stuff there. Parts and stuff. And Dev could take a crack at unzipping those other buses."

Jess was chewing on a fish roll, her long legs extended under the worn table. "I don't think we can get back there before they get back after they figured out what happened," she said. "Not sure heading into a firefight so fast is a good idea."

"Yeah, but it's now or never maybe," April said, but looked thoughtful. "Or maybe they already figured it out and don't care."

"What are they gonna say to West HQ if they do figure it out?" Mike Arias asked. "Yo, it got dark, and we ran away, but we were punked?"

Everyone chuckled. "Well, it's true," Doug said. "Maybe

it's on them to keep their mouths shut and not say anything. Just say we retrieved everyone we could and that's it?"

"Doctor Dan."

They looked up as a tall, young bio alt paused near the table, hovering a little.

"Hello, KayTee," Dev said. "Is something suboptimal?" She recognized one of the sets from the base, the KayTee-512 who had spoken to them in the dark.

"I have a task." The bio alt came closer. "Doctor Dan, someone said you were thinking of going back to get some things at the Base, is that true?"

Kurok eyed him in silence for a moment. "We were considering that… is it Keko?" He responded. "Why do you ask? Did you leave something behind?"

The bio alt smiled. "Keko, yes," he said. "It will take some time to get used to that name again. I have not used it since I left the crèche," he admitted. "I did not leave anything, but we were talking, and the sets who live at this place said there aren't any programming stations here."

"That's true, lad," Kurok said. "We have to do things the hard way, I'm afraid." He leaned his elbows on the table and laced his fingers together. "Does that bother you? I don't think you've seen a programming station since you were assigned, isn't that right?"

"There are some there," Keko said. "At the Base. In a secret place behind where we were quartered on the lower level."

Dev leaned forward. "Programming stations?" Her pale eyebrows hiked up.

Dan Kurok stiffened in his seat, his face going wary. "Really." He kept his voice even. "What kind of consoles, Keko?" He asked. "Little ones?"

"Like on Station," Keko said, his hands behind his back, but visibly pleased with the attention. "We weren't supposed to tell anyone about them, but it's different now," he said. "We're assigned here now, aren't we?"

"Really," Kurok murmured. "Well, well." He paused. "Yes, Keko, you are assigned here now, and I'm very glad you told me about the stations. That could be very valuable information for us."

Keko smiled in satisfaction. "I thought that might be the case."

"Not good?" Jess guessed as she watched Kurok's body language. "Ya look like someone kicked you in the kidney.

Kurok glanced at her. "They weren't licensed to do that,"

he muttered back. "Anywhere in Interforce. That wasn't in the contract. They all had to be brought to station for that. It's in the regs." He then turned to Jess and raised his voice. "Having that gear would be damn useful. There's a lot of tech programming we could give the sets, for the hardware that's here."

Dev caught the tension at the table. "Yes," she said. "But also, we should go get it so no one else does," she added softly. "It must be in the sub level three secure area near the set barracks, Doctor Dan. I never saw it."

Keko looked from one to the other of them, alertly. "If you go, Doctor Dan, may I fly one of the planes? I know them well and can take you right to the programming systems."

Kurok took a breath and released it. "You most certainly can, lad. Why don't you make sure you get a good lunch, and then we'll go get the planes ready. Sound like a plan?"

Keko nodded. "Yes," he said. "Thank you, Doctor Dan!" He turned and went back to the table full of his companions two rows over, and they gathered close to him, obviously excited.

"That's interesting," Kurok said. "Possibly not in a good way." He drummed his fingertips on the tabletop. "I should have predicted that though. Bricker was an absolute stubborn ass. Convinced anything we could do he could do better."

Everyone at table, listened closely to his low tones, paused and looked over at Dev, then back at him. "Never met him," April said. "Now I'm glad. He was too stupid to be left breathing."

Dev was relatively sure she and Doctor Dan had just been somehow complimented, but she merely took a sip of her drink and swallowed, remaining silent.

"We should make a run over there then. Pick up that stuff, and whatever else we can," Jess said. "Devvie, you up for that?"

"Yes," Dev said. "It will also be good to make sure we didn't accidentally leave anyone behind." She quickly mopped up the remainder of her stew. "Optimal plan."

"Let's get our explanations over with then, shall we." Kurok stood up and waved his arms, his standard way of getting attention. "All right, good people. We have a busy afternoon, so let's just get through what happened yesterday, shall we?"

Jess leaned close to Dev. "What do ya think, Devvie?" She asked softly. "Doc looks ticked."

"Extremely suboptimal," Dev answered instantly. "I would not have expected anything like that in our old place, Jess. There were no programmers that I was aware of there." She also had her voice very low. "Doctor Dan must see what's in the system if they left it. He will want to know what they did."

"To the kids?" Jess jerked her head.

"Yes," Dev said, after a brief pause.

"Glad you had those things taken out now?"

"I was glad before," Dev said. "But that's what you always are concerned about. What happens when you go down." She looked at the table full of bio alts nearby. "And what's different when you come back up."

Jess looked vaguely amused. "No rest for the weary," she said in a more normal tone. "Guess our snazzy new bunk'll have to wait." She glanced aside as she felt a tap on the shoulder. "My turn?"

"You were the witness, Jess," Kurok said. "Tell us what they said."

Jess stood up and waited a beat as everyone focused on her and quiet fell. Everyone put down spoons and cups and she felt the attention, ready to hear what her story was though she suspected most already knew. Knew, and were pleased, she could feel that undercurrent of energy again, those grins and knowing nods across the room.

Jess smiled and put her hands in her pockets, pressing her back against the cold stone wall. "Here's the deal," she said, into the quiet attention. "We're on our own."

"Always were," Security Mike muttered. "Proved that the last time."

"They decided to cut their losses and move out," Jess said. "Clear out all three bases around here and go back to the west. Their story was, they lost too much."

"Bullshit," a voice nearby said.

"It was pretty empty in those halls," April spoke up. "And a lot of them croaked right here, y'know. That was a thing."

Security Mike leaned back, with a smirk. "That's a truth." He smiled at April. "But that was all their damn fault."

"So last night, they thought they were under attack," Jess continued, matter-of-factly. "We lost power just around midnight, systems were all down. They boarded everyone they could get ahold of and took off." She lifted one hand and made a flying gesture with it. "Just left."

The silence that followed was profound. "They just ran off?" Pete asked, from a nearby table. "For real? When they were under combat sitch?"

Jess nodded. "Yup."

"Daaaamn," several voices chorused nearby.

"We weren't going," Jess added, casually, with a brief

gesture at the table. "So that worked for me. I decided I wasn't going to be a part of that retreat. Dev rigged our bus to bypass ops control." She glanced at her pilot, who regarded the room with one of her blandest expressions. "Ours and a few others. We were going to let them evac, then head off on our own."

Security Mike nodded. "Screw the oath?" He asked, looking directly at Jess.

Jess stared right back at him. "Screw the suits telling me my homestead wasn't worth fighting for." Then she relaxed again. "I didn't want any part of it, and it seems the feeling was mutual because they released me after they left. I'm civ."

Most had already heard that, too, and there were knowing grins around the room and a lot of nodding.

"You're stuck with me now," Jess concluded. "Suck it up." She sat down, and after a brief pause voice erupted in conversation again.

Kurok patted Jess on the shoulder. "Nicely done," he said. "Well, it'll do for now, at any rate."

"Yeah," Jess said. "I want to grab all that other cargo those bastards left behind." She paused and glanced at Security Mike. "Got a squad ready?"

Mike laughed, a rough, unrestrained sound. "F'ckn yeah," he said. "Looking forward to it!"

An AyeBee from the Bay was at Dev's elbow. "May I get you some more of the meal, NM-Dev-1? I think you will be very busy soon and you might miss night meal here," he said.

Dev handed over her plate and Jess's. "That would be excellent, Alex. Thank you. Yes we will be busy soon."

April winked at her. Security Mike had as much visible glee on his face he could show. At the younger Bay member's tables, there was hopeful alertness, as they watched Jess, wanting to be included.

Yes, it would be a very busy day.

****

"Bay Recon flight, you are clear," Kevin's voice crackled into comms. "Please exit at the requested intervals."

Dev was back in her pilots' seat as she finished final checks. "Please be seated and apply restraints," she said to the group of people inside the carrier. "We are cleared to leave."

"That's no joke," Jess warned. "Find a spot and strap in. We don't have time for broken necks and blood all over the place."

Across from them were the other two carriers, all three vehicles loaded down with Bay residents along with their pilot and usual passenger.

Security Mike had taken a seat on the back ledge of Jess's carrier. He had five large members of Bay security with him, four men and one woman. All with old style guns and knives strapped to them, all grinning. They all found seats where they could, two of them settling on the floor with their backs braced along the storage area.

"This is some good stuff," Elsa, the woman security guard said in satisfaction. She was seated in the space that would usually hold the drop rig but was now empty. "Nice day for a scrapping."

"Stand by for lift, please." Dev finished her prep. "We are clear of connections, Jess, ready to depart."

"Let's go." Jess was in her seat, her restraints pulled tight over her shoulders. "The Doc ready?"

"Yes." Dev applied some lift to the jets and neatly turned the carrier on its axis, so they were facing the landing bay entrance, the doors pushed open wide, and the cavern filled with many watching them depart. "Bay operations, please advise everyone to clear the flight path here in the cavern."

"I got this." Jess picked up her comms and activated the external speakers. "Move it ya scrubs!" She let out a yell into it. "Get out of the damn way!"

The words were clearly echoed through the cavern and the crowd scattered. Jess rolled her eyes and closed comms. "Lesson one. Don't stand in front of large moving rigs."

Security Mike chuckled behind her. "Hold on," he warned the squad. "I seen Rocket fly this thing. Get tight or she'll leave your butt behind ya."

The path cleared and Dev started the carrier forward. She knew that Doug and Chester would follow them out into cloudy but pleasantly rain free air.

She waited for all the cargo craft and the other two carriers to emerge, then boosted up above the Bay on her jets and waited for clear airspace. Then she coded in the coordinates of Base 10, and they were underway, the powerful surge of the engines pushing them back against restraints.

It was a short flight, just under an hour, and this time she had the carrier's sensors on full blast as they were inbound, scanning at the limits of their power in search ahead of them. Dev kept a close eye on the returns, finding nothing more interesting than flocks of birds in the air.

Dev moved her seat up a little, getting her boots on the side thrusters just in case. "Winds have reduced to twenty knots," she said. "This should be an optimal flight."

"With you flying, it always is," Jess casually complimented her. "Even if we were flying through a tornado upside down."

Dev caught her eye in the reflective surface over her position. "That is not accurate," she protested mildly. "It would be, in fact, extremely uncomfortable and possibly cause damage to   both this vehicle and all of us."

Jess chuckled.

"They teach you all that stuff upstairs, Rocket?" Mike asked. "The Doc? I know he can fly."

She got asked that question a lot, so she had a prepared answer. "I received technical programming on these vehicles before I arrived," Dev said. "In that regard, yes. I flew sims before I came down from station, as there is no opportunity to fly atmosphere planes in space."

"They gave her the manual," Jess said. "Everything else is natural talent." She looked fondly at her pilot. "Devvie just doesn't like to brag on herself, so I have to do it." She sighed. "Takes up most of my time."

"We are within range of Base systems," Dev said. "I am detecting robotic relay only." She added, after a moment. "From the beacon on the cliff summit. We are emitting our standard ident, as I did not really have time to construct something different, but there is no challenge."

"Good," Jess said. "At least we can get to the front door."

They were in the lead, and Dev started a descent into Base 10 airspace, coming in a very familiar glide path toward the large cliff side. She kept expecting a hail, an echo in her head of familiar ops watch standers confirming her approach, giving her a landing slot.

But there were just the scans, a robotic beacon returning the base's coordinates, and a warning to stay clear unless you had Interforce permission to fly.

Which they clearly did not, but there were no systems return at all from comp, nothing indicating the base was reacting to their presence, or objecting to their incursion, just the beacon. Which, Dev felt, was strange.

"Take a spin around the perimeter before we go in, Dev," Jess said, as though in response to her thoughts. "Want to be sure we don't see any visitors."

Dev quietly spoke into her comms, and then the carrier tilted a bit to the right as they peeled off, the other two carriers moving in different directions as they split up to scout the area, while the cargo flyers and Bay A continued forward at a slower speed.

Dev's hands were steady on the controls, and her senses were alert. She focused on the scan returns, ready to send the carrier skyward at any hint of trouble. "There is no biologic return, Jess," she said. "Aside from small animals I think are possibly crabs."

"We should stop and get some on the way back," Mike said. "Probably nice and steamy. We could snack on em low as you were over the rocks."

Jess chuckled. "Yeah, looks pretty clean," she said. "Go back around and clear the landing."

The Bay residents all shifted and stirred, settling their hands on their weapons, and watched through the front window as Dev brought the carrier around in a tighter curve, building up speed as she came around the front of the Base and went to landing level.

It looked just as they had left it earlier that day, the cavern doors half open, waves crashing at the base of the cliff. "We will proceed inside," Dev advised on comms. "Please stand by."

The carrier slowed, and Dev paid close attention to the returns as she crossed into the landing cavern, checking for any sign of motion. "There are no further vehicles inside. Status is the same as we left it."

Jess nodded. "So far so good."

Mike sighed. "Bummer. I wanted to shoot something."

"You might get to." Jess released her restraints but stayed seated as Dev maneuvered over the lines of crates and scattered debris they'd left and put the carrier down on what, until that morning, had been their assigned pad. "Or maybe not. Auto systems haven't been touched. It'd be alarming by now."

Dev set down on their skids, and kept the external sensors on full, opening the microphones and putting the output to Jess's screen. "I took a snapshot before we left," she said. "Everything appears on wireframe to be in the same location."

Jess got up and walked over to push the door open. She stood clear of the door until it swung all the way out and she could see the interior of the space. "Now I'm glad we had this back spot. Tell the Doc to c'mon in."

"Yes," Dev was still strapped into her seat, her comms on. "They are approaching. Doug and Chester have landed. All is so far, secure."

"Let's keep it that way." Jess reached back inside the carrier and unhooked a belt with a battered hand blaster and strapped it on. "Not reg, but it'll shoot something." She hopped out, with the security force right behind her.

Dev finished securing the carrier and released her restraints. She stood up and went to the hatch and peered out. Security Mike was directing the security guards to the perimeter, while the cargo planes were carefully setting down on the cavern floor.

Doctor Dan, piloting Bay A, came in last. He got out, with Kurt and Kelson at his heels and climbed down the ramp to the pad to join Jess at the center of the landing cavern.

"Spread out!" Security Mike yelled. "Watch ya backs! Comms if somethin twitches!"

The security patrol hustled off in every direction, all on comms, immensely excited. Jess watched them go, her hands resting on her hips. "Don't shoot anything important!" She yelled after them. "And if you see any dark red rings, stay clear of em!"

Dev had her hand scanner out and moved it right and left as she came up to Jess. "I am not detecting any signs of activity. The power is at the same level as when we left, Centops is still offline, lower doors are still sealed."

"Pneumatic fluid still gushing?"

Dev cleared her throat. "No," she said. "That has expired, apparently. It ran out." She looked up at the big door in the wall, then turned and continued to scan, as Doug and Chester came over. "Hello."

"That was uneventful," Doug said. "Here I was figuring it would be crawling with some kind of scavengers by now. Maybe everyone around here thought they'd leave it locked up."

"Don't curse us," April said, an old-style blaster rifle cradled in her arms. "I'm going to go check the area around ops. If there's anything lingering, it'll be there."

"Right behind ya," Mike Arias chimed in. "We'll comm if we find anything."

Kurok came over, with Keko. "We're going to head down to where Keko saw that gear." He had the other bio alt pilots with him. "These lads are going to start loading cargo into the flyers." He pointed at the staged crates. "Everything there first, I figure if someone thought it was valuable, we probably will too."

"We'll stick with you," Jess said. "C'mon, we know the way." She motioned Security Mike, who was hovering nearby. "Grab one of those crate lifters. We might need it."

They started off toward the ramp leading down to the lower levels that Dev and Jess had come up during their blackout tour, their bootsteps ringing on the metal grating as they descended into the halon lit hallways.

"Easy peasy," Security Mike said. "What the what, Drake?"

"We get jumped now. I'm whacking you," Jess said. "Shut the F up wouldja?"

Dev just kept scanning. There was nothing there that was alarming, everything was still. Nothing her scanner was tuned for alerting. It did, in fact, seem easy. She glanced at Jess.

Too easy.

"Stay close, Dev." Jess said in a quiet undertone. "Some- thing's not reg here. I don't like it."

Dev looked around and wondered if anything at all was, in fact, reg. She adjusted the scan, looking for something.

Anything. Regular or non-regular, anything unusual. But the halls were as they'd left them, scattered possessions on the ground, overturned carts, and all.

The halls, this time at least, were well lit as they made their way back along the route she and Jess had taken the night before. They spotted the main entrance to the bio alt barracks, propped wide open ahead of them.

"Doors open for us," Kurok said.

Dev cleared her throat. "The pneumatic system is drained, Doctor Dan. I suspect most of the doors are passable."

"Is it now?" Doctor Dan gave her a sideways look. "On purpose?"

"Sort of."

"Well, conveniently done, Dev. Excellent work."

****

Jess stood up on the carrier platform, hands planted on her hips, her head turning back and forth as she watched the large cavern in front of her. Security and the pilots were busy securing boxes, and to her right, Doug and Chester were maneuvering a cargo lifter down the ramp piled with crates and gear.

Behind them Dev and Dan Kurok appeared, with Security Mike right behind them.

Jess kept up her watchful scanning, but the interior of the landing cavern looked as quiet as it had when they'd landed, though hours had passed, and it was now dark outside the half open door.

April climbed up onto the platform and approached Jess, her old-style gun slung over her shoulder. "This is garbage weird, Drake," she said.

"It is," Jess readily agreed. "No comms, no one poking around here, no one on the grounds, not seeing anything on scan. What the what?"

"What the what," April echoed. "Glad we're almost done. Mike's still in Centops trying to see what the hell is going on with those systems. Looks like they rebooted into a loop."

Jess shrugged. "Maybe we should turn them off," she said. "Have your boy unplug em."

"Not a bad idea," April said. "If they come back and find them powered down, not much to recover huh?" She hopped off the platform and headed over to where Doug watched the Bay security detail move crates around to make space in the last of the cargo planes.

Security Mike came over and sat down. "Lotta loot." He regarded the cargo flyers with some satisfaction. "Good huntin."

"Not bad," Jess said. "Still think something's off."

He nodded. "Yeah, there's a rig in play here, Drake. It stinks of it." He kicked his boots out a bit. "Kept looking over my shoulder expecting a blast to come over it the whole time I was down in those tunnels."

"Yep." Jess leaned back against the wall of their carrier, her shoulder just a handspan away from the block lettered names stenciled on the side of it. "But we didn't find it, so what the hell."

"What the hell," Mike agreed. "I'm up to go back and get some chow. Been a long day."

Jess folded her arms, and her mind drifted to the image of returning to the Bay, and that ridiculous, empty set of rooms with it's one single piece of furniture waiting for them. She imagined herself getting into the new smelling bed, with Dev, and looking up through the plas. "Yeah." She returned her attention to the landing cavern. "We'll find a fight some other day."

"S'allright," Mike said. "My peeps got some swag, and bragging rights. And we found whatever the hell it was the doc was looking for. All good."

They had. Jess watched them lift the large cabinet and the folded long table into the hold of the last plane and then smiled as Dev turned and started making her way over.

She had a smudge of dust on her nose, and her pale hair was in disarray. Jess thought she was unspeakably adorable. "Hey," she greeted her. "All done?"

"Hello." Dev climbed up onto the platform. "I think that is it," she said. "Doctor Dan said he has all the parts and things he needs from that equipment space."

"He's ticked."

Dev regarded her a moment. "He's upset about the programming," she said. "Yes."

"Messing with his kids." Jess lifted a hand and put her fingers between her teeth, letting out a long, loud whistle. Then she pumped her fist in the air and slapped the side of the carrier, and the Bay detail started to swarm and headed for the carriers they'd come with. "Get hustling, Rocket."

Dev triggered the door to the carrier and ducked inside, very glad to see her seat ahead of her. She wound her way around the stacked boxes and crates that were now tucked inside the craft, and the security detail had to squeeze around all of them to find a space to sit.

Jess paused at her chair, then waved Mike into it. "Siddown." She edged past the clutter and pulled down the jump seat next to Dev and settled onto it as Dev got prepared to fly.

Mike gave her a grin, then sat down on the gunner's seat. He tipped his head back and looked at the trigger rigs, then back at Jess. "Always wanted to do this," he said. "I think I just missed the battery. That's what my old man said, anyway. Always bitched I shoulda gone."

Jess stared at him, and he stared right back, meeting her eyes for as long as she was minded to hold them. "He might have been right." She grinned briefly. "Thin line, at the Bay."

"True that."

"Please prepare for lift," Dev said, shutting the hatch, and the sound outside went dull and muffled as the air compressed inside the carrier. "The weather has degraded, and winds have increased, so it will be suboptimal travel."

"Oh boy." Jess braced her feet against the bulwark as the carrier shifted off the pad and boosted, moving into the center of the cavern over the flyers and pausing as Doug and Chester lifted and joined them. She reached behind her and pulled the single shoulder restraint down and buckled it.

She watched out the window as Dev used her side jets to slide over to the opening, and she could then see the rain coming down hard outside. "Hope those kids can handle this," she muttered. "Those are fifty knot winds if anything."

Dev eyed her, but turned her attention then to the weather and sent the carrier outside in a smooth move, adjusting the lower jets as the rain hit the top of the vehicle and thundered over them.

"Whoa." Mike looked up at the ceiling.

Rotating on its axis, the carrier backed away from the opening, moving across the front of the Base and the other two carriers emerged after her, taking up positions equally spaced from where Dev had stopped as they waited for the cargo flight.

Bay A came out first, but was unbothered by the weather, and flew past their line of sight to review the heavy rollers coming in across the sea.

Dev watched as the rest of the cargo planes came out, with a little more hesitance, but once in the rain and adjusted they moved off in good order. She boosted again and rotated, getting ready to lead the way south, when a blip on her scan caught her eye. "Jess."

Jess was already up, her body half across Dev's seat to review the board. "That a… what is that?" She said. "Go over there, Dev. Get a look at it."

Obligingly, Dev arced the carrier in a half circle and dropped rapidly to the surface, making boxes and people shift with startled oaths behind her. "Please hold on."

Jess was still suspended, and now she pulled herself back to the other side and leaned closer to the front window. It was ink dark outside, but in a moment, Dev lit the surface with the floodlights on the bottom of the carrier, and they moved over a ceaseless white churn.

"What's up?" Mike asked.

"Something in the water," Jess answered, in a clipped tone. "Transmitting a signal."

Mike leaned back and cracked his knuckles. "Might end up a good night after all."

"It's a beacon, Jess." Dev sorted the signals with one hand and directed the light with her other, the carrier on a slow- motion sweep as the waves lunged up and slapped them. "T2C emergency pod."

"What the what?" Jess shoved herself back up onto her feet. "Watch out." She moved around the gunner console and went to the hatch. "Open."

Without hesitation Dev did, and the carrier was filled suddenly with a howling briny fog as Jess sat down on the deck and leaned forward. "Take us over there Devvie so I can see!"

The carrier changed direction and flew sideways, and then the sea was lit with two other floods as Doug and Chester caught up with them.

Dev concentrated on flying now by wire map, studying her

grid as she flew toward the beacon, the hatch thrumming in the wind. "Tac 1, Tac 2 Tac 3." She spoke into comms. "T2C pod spotted."

"We got it," April answered. "You're almost over it but what the hell are you going to do, land on its ass?"

Well. Dev paused in thought. Now that was a good question. "Stand by," she responded.

"I'm going in, Dev!" Jess stuck her head back in the carrier. "Keep an eye out and drop the line." Then she turned and pushed off the deck, going boots first into the water and plunging under the waves.

"What the absolute fuck is she doing," Mike yelled. "Now's not the damn time to show the crazy, Drake!"

Dev rotated around to forward and went nose down, nearly rolling him out of his seat and sending the rest of the security squad tumbling. She found the pod and went to station keeping, the carrier wavering and rolling the air as it fought against the wind and the lashing rain, and the dousing of the sea while it's searchlight pinned the yellow, small, leaking object that was disappearing and reappearing through the wash of the waves in its glare.

There was no sign of Jess. She had disappeared under the waves and hadn't reappeared.

"Where is she?" Mike was now behind Dev, gripping the back of her seat. "She under?"

"Yes, of course," Dev responded calmly. "It would be easier to swim under the surface, with all of the wave motion." She got a glimpse of Mike's face. "Please sit down. It will be fine."

"You're crazy as she is!"

"Thank you." Dev smiled and tipped the carrier forward, directing the lights into the depths and settling in to await results. "Tac 1, Tac 2 Tac 3, hold, inops."

"Ack."

"Ack."

****

Jess felt the cold water cover her head and she went with the motion, bending her knees slightly and letting her body sink, gladly trading the wild rush of the waves for the calm of the underwater realm, allowing air to escape from her chest in a long trail of upward trickling bubbles.

She blinked her eyes open and felt the slight pressure as transparent lenses slid into place, allowing her to focus on the yellow pod overhead and the spears of light bisecting the water around it, noting in passing the precision of the outline and just how damn good Dev was with that clunky bus.

She waited for her downward motion to stop, then wrapped her arms around her chest and bent over, compressing the last of the air out of her lungs, until she ended with a little, grunting cough.

The next inhale was water, a cold rush of fluid into her body that came a little harder than air, but in moments had released oxygen into her bloodstream and relieved the sensation of being suffocated, making her completely neutrally buoyant.

Jess paused a moment to make sure everything was functioning as she expected it to and turned in the water. Then she unbent and moved into a dolphin like swimming movement, wishing she'd had fins handy as she found the bright spot in the ocean that was the carrier's searchlight piercing the waves over- head.

She saw the pod and moved toward it, but as she did it started to sink in the water, dipping down and then heading rapidly downward, wrapped around a twitching figure enclosed by the yellow casing.

Ah, crap.

Kicking hard, she followed it, swallowing as the pressure tightened against her ears, the light above her fracturing and fading as the darkness loomed under her, full of things and creatures she really couldn't see that well, but she was sure were there looking for dinner.

She swam faster and caught the fluttering back end of the thing just as it started to disappear into the gloom.

Reversing in the water, she took a tight grip on it and started for the surface, dragging it behind her. It felt like a dead weight, and she figured dourly that it probably was.

The signal had shown life signs, but that ended fast in the sea and anyone who grew up on or near it knew that.

Jess turned as she neared the surface and tread water, yanking the pod up to her and stripping it off the body inside. The fabric resisted her, but then gave way to a powerful yank and she saw a dark form come free of it.

She grabbed the arm of it and pulled it over her shoulder then kicked for the surface, undulating powerfully and at the same time, consciously compressing her chest to rid it of water before her head broke the surface.

Always tricky, that exchange. Do it halfway either way, you risked drowning your ass as biological signals got mixed and things went the wrong path.

Jess felt the surface coming and lunged for it, emerging half out of the water with the body over her shoulder and sucking in a lungful of salty air as the roar of the carrier came over- head. A lift line hit the water in front of her eyes. Beautiful shot. Jess grabbed it with her free hand, her other hand gripping the body over her shoulder, positioning it head down with her left arm clamped over its legs to keep it in place.

She got a quick wrap of the line around her fingers and braced herself as she was lifted clear of the sea and into pouring rain.

There was only the line, and the strength of her shoulders and body to rely on as she was pulled upward to the carrier deck, her arm curled around the drowning victim, the glare of the other carrier's spotlights blasting right into her face.

She closed her eyes against both light and rain until the line stopped reeling and she felt the carrier very close, her knuckles just brushing the bottom of it and the thrum of its engines vibrating through her body and making her ears itch.

Then the weight came off her shoulders and a moment later, she was grabbed by strong hands and hauled bodily up into the carrier and laid down on the deck, a grip fastened on her ankle and pulled her out of the way of the door as it closed.

"Thank you," Dev said in her usual calm tone. "Please hold on as this vehicle will be moving."

Jess rolled over and blinked. "That sure woke me up." She cleared her throat of the rasp from the sea. "Nice line shot, Devvie."

"Thank you." Dev turned on the inside lights to mid-level. "It was excellent you did that quickly, Jess. There were large animals approaching," she said. "I was preparing this vehicle to submerge to inspect them."

Jess chuckled. "Probably a waste of my time. The bastard was sinking by the time I got there." She got up on her knees and rolled the body over, water dribbling out of its mouth. "Let's see what we got."

She was momentarily silent as the lights steadied. "Oh crap. It's Brent," she said, in a surprised tone. "Damn. What the hell is he doing here?"

She heard Dev's slight gasp. She got her fingers into his throat, which felt cold and clammy, and after a moment, she nodded slightly. "He's still with us. Get me the med kit would ja?"

Dev had her hands full with the carrier. "In the yellow

marked cabinet, second shelf." She directed the nearest Bay security guard, who, round eyed, scrambled to do her bidding. "You will need the oxygen compressor, and the water extraction mask, and it would be excellent to turn him on his left side."

There was a blur of awkward motion, but then one guard was down on his knees across from Jess and hauled Brent over onto his side. Another had the kit out and was pulling out the oxygen. "I got med," the second said. "Basic."

"Do you wish me to land, Jess?" Dev asked. "It would be easier to help… and call Doctor Dan?"

Jess stared at the deck for a long silent moment. "No," she said. "Make for the Bay, top speed you can. We don't know why he was here. We still don't know what the game is. Go."

Dev rapidly relayed the word and then strapped in. "Please secure as best you can." She took a breath and released it as she heard scrambling behind her and then settled her hands on the controls and kicked the engines into high power as they sped away.

****

Jess sat on the jump seat, her pullover removed and the dimmed interior lights barely showing the outlines of her service burns as she pressed an antibiotic dispenser to her face. She had one knee pulled up resting against the side console.

They had far outstripped the rest of their makeshift fleet, the two other carriers staying behind to escort the cargo flyers and Bay A, while they moved at the top speed the carrier could manage, the engine vibration rumbling around them.

It was awkwardly quiet. Dev's soft voice sounded intermittently, as she returned comms from the rest of the flight, and the Bay security detail just looked around the interior of the carrier, trying not to stare at Jess.

There was a soft hum from the right side of Jess's head, the drier extracting the water from her shirt enough to allow her to resume it. She'd left her pants on, and boots, and her chest was visibly moving as she sucked in the antibiotic in a regular rhythm.

Even Security Mike was silent, until the awkwardness got to him. "What's up with the mask?" He asked Jess.

Jess looked at him over the top of it, one eyebrow lifting. "Didn't they publish my whack job resume in the mess?" She asked, in a muffled voice. "How'd they miss that detail?"

He looked at her in puzzlement. "Huh? What detail?"

Dev glanced into the reflective surface over her head at him. "Jess has a physiological structure in her body that allows her to process oxygen from inhaling water," she explained. "The medicine prevents any microscopic animals from bothering her when she does so."

Everyone's head immediately swiveled to look at Jess. Jess gave them all a silent thumbs up, her eyebrows wiggling.

Mike stared at Jess. "Hold on. What the what? You saying you can breathe water? Like in the Bay? You went down in there and just started sucking in? For real real?" He looked around at the guards then back at her. "No jack?"

"Whoa," one of the guards muttered.

Jess nodded mutely, inhaling her antiseptic gas.

The security chief grunted. "That's some crazy stuff." He studied Jess in fascination.

Jess found it funny. She lifted her free hand and made a little wiggling gesture near her head, like a fin. "I go down to the bottom and talk to turtles sometimes."

The nearest of the guard, the woman Elsa, stared at her, wide eyed. "What the hell do they say?" She asked, with a little inhale. "Wait you talk turtle?"

Jess chuckled. "They bitch about their shells being too tight."

Mike finally laughed. "No wonder Rocket was so chill about you diving in. She knew you weren't gonna drown your ass."

"Sure." Jess smiled behind the mask. "Only got to surprise her the first time." She glanced sideways at Dev. "Right, Devvie?"

"We were on a mission to retrieve Doctor Dan from a facility where he had been taken prisoner," Dev said. "Our egress from that location was underwater, but we were one breathing apparatus short." She checked a setting. "Jess removed hers to give it to someone else."

"Which flipped you all out," Jess said.

"It seemed severely non optimal," Dev agreed. "Until we all realized Jess could breathe water. That was very, very surprising."

"Yeah. Pretty cool party trick, huh?" She eyed the rest of them, and then removed the mask and closed the valve, wrapping the straps around it and putting it into one of the cabinets. "How much longer?"

"About five minutes to outer scan," Dev said. "I sent a message ahead to have assistance on landing."

Jess pulled her knees up and let her elbows rest on them, the interior lights of the carrier outlining the powerful muscles in her upper body, and the scars. "Hope they can keep him ticking. I think we need to know why he was in an escape pod in the water. They would have taken off and headed due west."

"So," Mike was still on the previous subject. "They do that to you, in service, the water breathing stuff?"

"Nope." Jess cleared her throat of residual hoarseness. "Born with it."

It was a little funny, Dev thought, as she caught the reflection of everyone's jaws dropping in unison behind her.

"No shit." Mike exhaled in wonder. "How the hell do you know if your ass is born with that?"

"Drown," Jess said. "Then get surprised when you don't." She winked at him.

"Shhhiiiiiit."

"Bay operations, this is Bay Flight TAC 1, stand by for approach." Dev spoke into her comms. "I have you on scan."

"Roger that, Dev. We're waiting," Ops answered. "Sounds like you had one of them days."

Weren't all the days one of the days? Dev saw the Bay basin ahead, awash with floodlights, a beacon in the darkness around it. "Yes," she finally answered. "It will be excellent to be at the end of this particular day."

"We'll hold a mug a beer for ya."

Non reg. Dev brought her speed down below the sound barrier, hearing the double thumps of a sonic boom that would echo over the waves behind her as she aimed for the landing bay. But possibly excellent. "Thank you."

Jess patted her on the shoulder. "Good job." She pulled her shirt out of the dryer and slipped it over her head. "I hope it was worth the effort." She studied Brent, his chest somewhat unsteadily moving. "Cause that's a story we really need to hear."

"Yeah, that's trouble," Mike said. "Ain't no doubt."

"Nope, no doubt."

****

Dev was glad to finally climb the short flight of steps up from the main level of the Bay to the new space they'd been allotted. The pad below accepted her handprint, and now the door at the top did as well. She passed into the big open space and found it as large and as empty as it had been earlier.

Expected.

They'd taken Brent to med, a somewhat scrabbled together area on the far side of the main cavern. There, Jerad took over, with the two medic trained Bay residents and they'd been chased off with Jerad's usual brusqueness, except of course for Doctor Dan.

When all the flyers returned the mess doors opened to invite them in for a snack, and so everyone could hear what had gone on. The air of excitement and interest almost visible as a swirling mist through the great Hall.

Jess had then gone to take care of some formalities, she said, and promised to meet Dev in their space. And so here she was, hoping that would happen very soon because she was looking forward to getting some rest.

She could still taste the spicy tang of seaweed beer on the back of her tongue, and she licked her lips as she crossed the space to the back part of their new quarters. She paused when she detected a flash of color in the food preparation area that hadn't been there before.

Curious, she stuck her head in, then entered to find that various things had been stocked inside. The drink dispenser had been activated, with cups stacked right next to it. There were small containers on the other side, and she found those to contain sea grape tea, and honey.

"Jess will approve of that," Dev commented to the room. She opened the chilled compartment and was very pleased to find fish rolls inside, and two plates of fishcakes. "This is excellent," she murmured. "That is even more optimal than seaweed crackers."

She left the space and went to the room with the bed in it, pausing to note that the bed was now covered with a plain, but soft fabric covering and had an equally plain, but equally soft quilted blanket on top of it.

There were also pillows. Dev touched them all, and approved, glad at least there was a simple, acceptably comfortable place for them to rest on, though she was tired enough that even the stone floor would have sufficed.

She went across the room to the sanitary space and the small room next to it where they had left their duffels laying on a long workspace that went along the length of the room. It was a narrow space but had shelves on the other side of it and the shelves had containers for storage.

Pausing, she took hold of the scanner she was wearing across her shoulder and swung it around, turning it on and turning herself, sweeping the inside of their new space. She reviewed the results, then walked back out and over to the food distribution area, tuning the scan to organic to review what had been left for them.

That was programming. Pragmatic and basic, no matter that this was Jess's birthplace, and she had detected nothing threatening here toward them. A niggling itch in the back of her head until she'd performed it and been satisfied with the results.

And now she was satisfied. The new items held nothing dangerous, and she detected, on a deeper scan, no technology that might be watching them. There were the wall plates, and the wiring for house system access pads, but they hadn't yet been installed and there were no cameras and scan relays detected.

Very basic. Far simpler than the base. Dev nodded to herself and did another full sweep, looking for anomalies and voids and finding nothing very interesting save a lot of rock, a lot of plas, and chemical indications the space had been recently cleaned.

A soft chime sounded just as she finished, and she turned to see a soft light on over an inner door not far from where she stood. There was an ident pad to the right side of it, and she walked over, pausing to scan the other side of the door before she put her hand on it.

Ah, an AyeBee. She watched the door slide open. "Hello."

"Hello, NM-Dev-1." The AyeBee greeted her. "May I enter? I have brought some comforts for you since we were told you did not bring a large quantity," he said. "I am Adrian. House ops have assigned me, and JayCee Jack to this space."

"Of course." Dev had enough time during his speech to retrieve his set details and skim them. "I noticed some things have been added already." She indicated the food prep area. "Very much appreciated."

Adrian nodded. "Yes. When you and…" He paused. "How should we refer to Jesslyn Drake?"

"She prefers to be called by her name, so just Jess, though many here call her by her family name," she said. "It appears to be an honorific."

Adrian nodded. "Yes, they were saying the Drake, which seemed to indicate some level of privilege."

Dev nodded. "Yes. I at first thought it was somewhat sub-optimal, but Jess does not seem offended by it." She paused. "What tasks are you and JayCee Jack assigned?"

"Household support," Adrian promptly supplied. "We make

sure, it is clean, and systems are stocked with items you require. Also, that mechanical devices are functioning as designed."

"That seems optimal," Dev said. "It will be pleasant to know who is assigned the tasks, as it was never identified at the Base."

"Yes," Adrian said. "We were pleased to be assigned here. When you are inside this space, we cannot enter. You have to admit us inside, like you did. When you are not inside, we can enter to provide service," he explained. "House operations explained that is reg."

"Yes, that seems correct," Dev agreed. "You want to avoid doing unexpected things around Jess, because she reacts very quickly, and the results could be suboptimal." She stood back to let him enter. "She is not here at this time."

Adrian pulled a cart inside, and behind him, Dev saw a square utility lift, it's door open. "Is that from stores?"

"Yes," Adrian said, as he moved forward. "There is a section of stores set aside for this portion of the facility, for here, and the section below this where you were staying the last time." He pushed the cart into the hallway. "I have some soaps and towels; I will put them in the sanitary unit."

"Jess will appreciate that very much. She was in the ocean earlier and a shower is always excellent after that." Dev stored the results of her scan.

"Yes, we heard all about that," Adrian said from the sanitary unit. "She saved the person in med from drowning."

"She did," Dev acknowledged. "I am hoping he improves his condition. He is known to us, a tech from the base."

"Yes." Adrian emerged and then picked up a battered plas bin. "I have some shirts and leggings from stores here, until you can select ones you prefer. We thought you would just like to have something to change to after the day."

Dev smiled. "Thank you, Adrian. We can put them in that small room there for now." She pointed. "There is a lot to sort out yet."

Adrian put the bin, and a second one into the storage room and came back out. "Yes, we were told this has not been in use for some time. You will have to come to see if there are some chairs and things you can use tomorrow."

"Yes," Dev said, and they regarded each other in silence for a moment. "Are the sets from the base doing all right?" She asked. "It's been a suboptimal day for them as well."

Adrian pondered, then nodded. "It's a lot. I remember when we came here, and it was so strange. At least they are used to being downside," he said. "They were surprised about things." He paused. "About how it is for us."

"Bio Alts are treated differently here," Dev said. "They were not treated this way at the Base. They were not treated badly, but this will be a new experience as it was for all of us."

"Yes," Adrian said. "As station was also different, for you and for us."

"Yes," Dev said. "They will get used to it."

Now Adrian grinned. "Yes." He gave her a little wave. "Have a good rest, NM-Dev-1. We will get everything sorted out here tomorrow."

"Just Dev," she said, before he could turn and leave. "Natural born all just call me that, like your creche names."

Adrian blushed a little. "I apologize, Dev. Of course. Goodnight!"

Dev watched him go through the service door, and stood for a moment, arms crossed as the door slid closed, and the panel over it went from green to a mild dun yellow color. "That was interesting," she said, out loud. "Also, it is good to know where the new things came from."

She settled her scanner on her shoulder and went to the food dispensing room, picked up a cup and opened the container of sea grape tea shards with confidence.

Chapter Nine

Jess sat on one of the heavy plas countertops, her hands braced on the top of the surface, aware of the damp discomfort of her sea and rain-soaked pants. "We done here?"

"Two more minutes." Doctor Dan was behind a keyboard with Pete and two other household ops staff with him. "I just want to get everything coded before something gets forgotten." He glanced up at Jess. "Quite a lot tied to that profile of yours."

"How much could there be? I was five the last time I used it," Jess said wryly.

Kurok sat back. "That's true, but it brings a lot of entitlements with it because of what Justin did when he made you the share inheritor." He studied the screen. "Okay, think we have everything here, Pete. All the security coding's in."

Pete had been taking notes, and now he nodded. "We assigned a couple of your boys to help out up there," he said. "Like you asked."

Jess looked at Doctor Dan with an inquiring expression. "Help out with what?"

"Well really, Jess, we don't expect you to do your own housekeeping up there, any more than you did at Base 10." Kurok regarded her mildly. "But I thought having some consistent folks there would make you more comfortable."

Jess considered, then nodded.

"When they transferred you to civilian, someone—whoever did it—was thoughtful." Kurok said. "They basically granted you retirement, and so, Jess, you have in your logon account your retirement package, including your accrued service fund."

Jess grunted softly. "Hadn't even thought about that," she said. "I guess I can go buy a couple of new shirts someplace huh?"

Kurok chuckled dryly. "For Dev, they released her technical contract." He studied the screen. "Her civ profile has what she'd earned until yesterday, and I've coded it to domicile her here to Drake's Bay."

"She's really civ?"

Kurok nodded. "Oh, yes. She had a civ profile, as you know, but within the last two weeks, someone went and converted it to a real citizen profile." He glanced at Jess. "Not that she was ever in any real danger, of course. Her bio alt registration was, and still is, coded to me, and I set it up so that if anything untoward happened to me, it would transfer to Drake's Bay until your profile converted."

"Assuming I ever did."

Kurok folded his hands together. "Well, given all of the possible alternatives I had, this seemed the best of them," he said. "One can only do so much. And after all, here you are."

"Here I am," Jess wryly agreed. "Not sure she really cares, but that was the legit thing to do, after you took her stuff out."

"It is," Kurok said. "All right, now that you're sorted out, I'm going to spend the day tomorrow going through what those muppets did in that programming schema. They didn't leave any notes, but you can't wipe the process. At least, not from me."

"Told you fast enough about it," Jess said. "The bios I mean."

"Oh absolutely." Kurok shook his head. "They couldn't prevent that no matter what muppety thing they did. I did all their primary coding. I have all their low-level triggers. Every one of them knows me so of course they'd tell me at once." He leaned on his elbows. "I'm not sure what they were up to, but I'm damned well going to find out. Maybe it ties into this inane plan of theirs."

"Make em into plants?" Jess suggested.

"Possible," Kurok said. "Idiotic, but possible. These are all a very basic service model profile and design."

"They're not Dev."

Kurok smiled. "Certainly not." He leaned over and put two metal ident disks on the table. "And there you are. You and Dev are registered to Drake's Bay. So, anyone who knows where to look, now knows where you are."

"Going to do the rest of them?" Jess got up and came over, picking up the disks. "They all get a pass? April and the rest of them?"

"April and Mike are listed as status voluntary out-process," Kurok said. "Chester and Doug had their contracts released because, as you know, techs are contractors. They can leave at any time." He consulted the screen. "They all got what was in their service accounts, but that's about it."

Jess nodded.

"But assuming they agree, I think we should issue them idents," Kurok concluded. "Soon as I clear the sets, I'll do the same for them and then code their registrations to the Bay like I did the ones I brought from Station." He sat back. "We're going to slot April and Mike as security, and of course Doug, Chester, and Clint as mech. Jerad was a timely add for med.

"Crusty bastard, but yeah."

"He'll fit right in here," Kurok said. "Brents in good hands." He looked at Jess. "Now the question is, what was he doing in an escape pod in the waters off the Base. That one of the ones that would have come with the transport, that pod?"

Jess shook her head. "Dev said it was from the Base. It's an older model of what we put on the carriers," she said. "Probably have one stuffed in mine. He could have been caught up in the chaos and went down by the tubes."

"Mm."

Jess smiled briefly. "Yeah, I don't think so either. With any luck he'll be able to tell us." She juggled the two disks. "Check in on him in the morning." She gave them all a brief hand gesture. "Later on."

Kurok watched the door slide shut after her. "What a day." He leaned back in his chair and put his hands behind his head.

"Lotta stuff going to come down tomorrow," Pete said. He finished taking notes and closed his data entry pad. "But we'll get it all square."

"No doubt," Kurok agreed. "No doubt, but we have a lot of these kind of days ahead of us. We'll use the big meeting room tomorrow for when our guests show up, I think."

Pete nodded. "Big enough," he said. "Think I got something that'll spunk up that back wall in there." His face creased into a grin. "Remind them all we got a legit Drake here now."

Kurok looked at the screen and shook his head. "Oh, that we do." He laughed faintly. "That indeed we do."

****

Dev had just finished putting away the new things Adrian had left when she heard the outer door chime and then open. She stuck her head out into the hallway, and spotted Jess enter. "Hello."

"Hey, Dev." Jess came over and handed her a metal token. "Here's your reg chit," she said. "It's what's got your cred priv and ident on it, for the Bay."

Dev regarded the item with interest. "I see," she said. "Do you have one as well?"

"I do." Jess held up hers. "They got our profiles all hooked up. Once we get crap settled here, we'll take a run up to Quebec and do some civ shopping. Deal?"

Dev studied the chit. "That sounds excellent, actually." She looked up at Jess and smiled. "Is that what it says I am?"

"Civ? Yup." Jess grinned at her. "Doc checked it out. Legit civ."

"Hm." Dev made a small, somewhat surprised, but pleased noise in her throat. "They brought up some spare things we can put on until we get that all arranged," Dev said. "Along with some supplies for the shower, and towels."

"Hot damn," Jess said. "That's gonna feel good. C'mon." She steered Dev toward the shower. "Hopefully the water works after it being shut up so long."

"It does," Dev said. "I turned it on. I was investigating if it was warm or not."

Jess chuckled deep in her throat.

They shed their clothes in the small storage room and Jess slung her pants over a bar installed above the shelves and set the shirt on a nearby shelf. "Survived its first encounter with Drake insanity, Devvie. Good choice."

"Pete asked me to describe the vendor I got it from," Dev said. "And where in the cavern they were so he could locate them and acquire more garments."

They walked into the sanitary area and Jess went to the shower and activated it, charmed when the entire roof of the enclosure produced a curtain of water, with a deep pressure behind it. "I like this." She got inside and spread her arms out.

Dev got in as well. The shower had more than enough space to accommodate both at once, even with Jess moving around in a circle with her arms extended. The water was nice and warm, and she relaxed as it thrummed against her skin. "This is very pleasant."

There were fresh pieces of sea sponge on a stone ledge against the back wall, and a pottery jar full of the typical liquid soap of the Bay. Dev dipped a piece of sponge into it and scrubbed her skin, pleased with the scent as the hot water filled the space with its steam.

Jess washed her hair and tipped her head back. "This is awesome," she said. "Better than that place on Market Island."

"It is," Dev agreed. "Please do not make it cold though."

"Not tonight." Jess leaned against the wall and closed her eyes. "Tonight, I just want to lay down and get a nap in this ridiculous empty cave we're in." She exhaled. "Hard to take in the whole thing, Dev. Can you believe what happened to us today?"

"Yes." Dev came over to stand next to her, their shoulders brushing. "It seems difficult to comprehend all that has occurred over the past 24 hours." She folded her arms over her chest. "It reminds me of the day I came down from station, actually."

"That was a weird day too," Jess said. "Let's dry off and get in bed before we fall asleep in here and make it even weirder."

They dried off and put on their sleep clothes, then walked into the room with the bed in it and sat down with twin sighs.

"This is nice," Jess said. She leaned over and sniffed the pillow, then straightened back up. "I sort of kind of think I remember that smell."

Obligingly, Dev sniffed the fabric. "It is nice." She studied it. "The clothing they brought up for us smelled like that too. Is it a different kind of soap? It's not the same as the shower."

"No idea." Jess stretched out on the bed, pleased it fit her length. "I just have such vague memories of the place, Dev. I was just a kid." She folded her hands on her stomach, and regarded the long, curving windows and the plas covered opening overhead. "Most of my memories are from Canyon City."

"As most of mine, as a younger, are from station," Dev said. "The plas here—the open view to the outside reminds me a little of that," she mused. "Except you don't see stars here."

"And you can go outside without croaking." Jess smiled faintly. "Most of the time."

It was still raining, and the lightning lit up the sky at irregular intervals. The plas was thick enough to make the sound of it soft and diffused, and the slightly slanted pitch of the overhead opening made the water run-off and down the outer walls.

"There's voice control in here, Pete said, but we have to set it up," Jess said, after a moment of silence. "Hey, you think I freaked those guys out today, Dev?"

Dev, who had been on the cusp of getting out of bed to shut the lights off, just sat up instead. "When you rescued Brent?"

"Yeah, with the gills and all that stuff."

Dev considered. "They were surprised, but so was I the first time you did that. Even Doctor Dan was startled."

"You don't think they thought it was bad?"

It seemed such a strange question. "Why would they? I think it's unusual, but certainly it's a very useful mod," Dev said. "Is it considered a bad thing here?"

Jess put her hands behind her head and nibbled the inside of her lip thoughtfully. "No, not if it's useful. You're right, it is. The shore collectors would probably croak to have it. Not have to screw around with tanks and all that."

"I heard them all talking about it in the mess when we got back. No one seemed to dislike it," Dev reassured her. "They just thought you were amazing." She paused. "And of course, I agreed."

Jess looked at her with a droll expression.

"Well, I did." Dev had to smile, a brief and charming grin that made her pale eyes twinkle. "Let me shut the lights off, so we can get some rest." She got up and went to the wall plate and put her hand on it and then selecting the controls.

The inbuilt lighting dimmed, but lightning was still overhead, and it allowed enough light for her to see her way back to bed easily.

It would be interesting to see the daylight come in the morning. Dev watched the lightning trace across the clouds and heard the thunder, a soft, far off rumbling vibrating through the stone.

Jess reached over and took her hand, clasping it.

Dev looked to the side, but Jess had her eyes closed, and there was just the faintest of smiles on her face. She just wanted the contact. That made Dev smile, and she relaxed, feeling her breathing slow as the long day caught up to her, and she surrendered to sleep.

****

Dev watched the irregular roundel over the bed slowly lighten. It changed from pitch black to the faintest of dark gray, to the normal deep gray of the daylight cloud cover. It cast a dim internal light over the bed, and Dev felt it was quite pleasant to wake up to.

Not that different from the internal light shifts of the base, but this was not mechanical, it was natural. She lay there for a bit and watched the dark clouds shift and pass overhead as they became distinct.

Across from the bed, the plas windows had also lightened. She could now see the curve of the bay and the ruffled surface of the sea just past it. She found that pleasant as well.

Waking up in bed with this view, with Jess there beside her seemed to be an excellent way to start off the day.

Dev glanced at Jess, c u r l e d up next to her, and her eyes drifted open.

Jess grinned at Dev. "Cool, huh?" She motioned toward the plas. "Better than just rock walls."

"Yes. Though these walls are also rock," Dev said. "I like being able to see out."

Jess chuckled. "Me too. I like it a lot." She swung her legs out of bed and stood up, stretching out her long body as she walked over to the plas that covered the front of the room. She put her hands on the transparent surface to look out over the Bay. "Gonna be a decent day."

Dev, somewhat reluctantly, got out from under the warm cover and came over to join her. She could slightly see her breath in the chill air. Sleeping had been comfortable, the blanket and Jess's body heat more than enough to keep her warm but she pondered if she would now have to acquire warmer garments to sleep in than the light tank top and brief shorts that were fine in the temperature-controlled Base.

The Bay was active, she noted, as she leaned closer and observed the harbor. "There are more boats now aren't there?"

Jess nodded. "Yup. Three of the Bay fleet are in, and six others. Real busy. They're out of slips."

"How many boats belong to this location?" Dev looked along the pier, and at the myriads of smaller boats that were scattered inside the sea wall already busy with something.

"Half dozen long haul deep sea. About two dozen inshore, and the clam and oyster barges." Jess glanced at her. "Hey, you're turning blue."

"I am not." Dev looked down at herself and then back up. "However, I am going to obtain a cup of tea. Would you like some?"

"I was gonna suggest a bearskin rug for the place." Jess gave her a nudge. "But I figure you'd hate it. C'mon. Let's get the day going." She followed Dev into the food prep station that had the benefit of being slightly warmer.

"An animal skin on the floor would seem to be suboptimal to me, yes." Dev pulled two cups out and put some sea grape tea leaves in them, before adding the dispenser's steaming hot water over them. "I would rather just wear boots." She pondered the cups while the tea steeped. "Or perhaps there is a way to heat the floors."

Jess went to the cabinet and removed the tray of fish rolls. "Too bad we don't have a volcano here like Market Island. They got plenty of heat there." She sidled over to one of the counters and set the tray down then picked one and inspected it. "Mm. Kelp wrapped."

"The hot pools were nice, but the explosions were unfortunate." Dev added honey to the tea and brought the cups over to the counter where Jess was. "And eventually, non-optimal." She picked up a fish roll and they stood there in companionable silence, munching their snack.

"Think we'll need some stools for in here," Jess commented. "Unless you want one of those other dozen spaces to be a dining room."

Dev chewed thoughtfully. "I have no idea what that is," she said. "Is that like the mess?"

"Like the place downstairs where we had breakfast when we were here," Jess said. "Where we can do something crazy, like sit down to eat our fish rolls, not just stand around."

"Oh! Yes, that would be very pleasant," Dev said. "That one space in the corner through the hall there might be appropriate."

"With that curved view? Sure, Devvie. Wherever ya want it." Jess finished her fish roll. "C'mon, we'll go use our primo shower and head up to the storage graveyard and get ourselves a few chairs." She licked her thumb. "Maybe a bench for the wall over there."

"Yes." Dev amiably drained her tea and put the cups in the cleaner, then followed Jess, ready to see what this new day would bring them.

And to put on some boots against the cold stone floor.

****

The storage caverns were a long climb up the spiral stair against the stream of traffic going down. They were in the upper levels of the homestead, just one level under the landing bays. As they walked along the narrow passages between stacks of objects there was a general sense of dust and disuse around them.

"When we had the last mixup, lot of stuff got whacked out." Craig, the storage master promptly arrived when they had, meeting them at the stair landing as though he'd been expecting them. He was a man of middling height, and dark rust colored hair, and his left hand was missing the two last fingers. He had a plas clipboard under that arm, with plas sheets on it, and a grease pencil behind his ear. "Swap outs, y'know."

Dev didn't know. She briefly glanced at Jess, hoping for some enlightenment.

"Emptied out the rooms of everyone who got killed?" Jess asked, after a brief pause.

Craig nodded. "Sure, you know how it is. Everyone's stuff got brought up, then everyone else came and swapped out their old stuff for any of the good stuff they left. Usual gig." He sniffed reflectively. "Just more than usual."

"Makes sense," Jess said. "What else ya gonna do with it?"

"Yes," Dev added, because it did. If you were made dead, you no longer needed things, and therefore, it made sense to allow anyone else who did want them, to get them.

"Sure," Craig said. "Back here's the big stuff. You can start there if you want." He stepped aside to let them go past. "Not much to choose from but you ain't got nothin in there now." He paused. "Figure you'd get some stuff made?" His voice lifted slightly in question.

Jess looked around the space. "Yeah. But I'd rather not sit on the floor till then"

"True that," Craig agreed. "Bed platform's custom up there, we got lucky they had a topper that fit it from storage way back when. "Had them drag that up yesterday once we got the blast."

"Blast?"

He paused. "Y'know? The news?" He said. "Bout you coming?"

"Ah, yeah." Jess nodded. "I didn't know until the Doc landed," she said. "Kind of a crap mess at the base."

Craig nodded. "Saw the change of auth come through, we all did. Everybody was buzzin, then all the stuff with Interforce. Was kind of crazy here too."

"We definitely appreciated the bed." Jess grinned and moved past him. "Right, Devvie? C'mon."

"Yes," Dev agreed, as she looked around. She was aware that Craig was watching her out of the corner of his eye as she ducked past him to follow Jess along the piles of material. "It was excellent."

It was mostly battered old counters and chairs, some broken, some with pieces missing. Nothing was in good condition, but Dev walked over to a dented set of storage, with a lot of small drawers in it. She studied it and opened a few of the drawers, which seemed to be functional. "This would be useful."

Jess regarded it. "For your wrenching space?"

"Yes," Dev said. "It would be excellent for parts." She observed the piece of furniture with approval. "Really excellent."

"Parts of?" Craig asked, raising his eyebrows.

"Electronic and mechanical integrated circuits and mods," Dev answered politely. "I enjoy working with them."

"Oh." Craig seemed a bit surprised. "Like the Doc." He nodded. "Had another thing like this here and he had them put it down in his work area."

"We'll take that." Jess pointed at it, then went over to a long, low-slung chair, with a many times patched seat. She regarded it, then gave it a sudden, powerful kick. It lifted up then dropped to the ground again. It shuddered and bounced but stayed intact. "Take that." She moved on.

Craig nodded and made notes on his plas. "Got another one like that, back in the back," he said. "Want it?"

"Sure." Jess went over and lifted a table upside down onto its three of four legs. "Got a block I can use for this?"

"Might." Craig seemed visibly more relaxed. "Got a couple stools over there, and those little square storage."

"Yeah, all that's good." Jess paused. "And that." She pointed at a slab of slate leaning haphazardly in a corner, as long as she was tall. "Bring that up and those two narrow shelf things there I can put it on for a desk."

"Like your style, Drake." Craig cheerfully scribbled. "Loaders will be up after they finish with the boats. They'll haul it down for ya, no problem."

"AyeBee Adrian has been assigned to the space," Dev said. "He can coordinate access as I think we will be occupied elsewhere today." She stood next to Jess, with her hands clasped behind her back, observing the response.

Craig looked up at her. "Uh." He paused.

Jess leaned an elbow on Dev's shoulder and stared at him. "That pose a problem for you?"

"No, no." He held up the hand with the pencil in it up, palm forward, in an almost automatic gesture. "They weren't just real clear about…" He shot a look at Dev. "You co-hab?" He asked. "Wasn't really sure…"

Jess chuckled shortly. "Treat Dev same as you'd treat me," she said. "We're partners."

"Okay, sure." Craig nodded, scribbling. "Sure, Drake. I got it."

"Good." Jess nodded. "C'mon, Dev. We'll find more trouble to get into." She headed for the spiral stairs. "That'll be enough to mess with for now."

Dev gave Craig a small wave, then followed Jess out of the cavern. "That seemed a bit suboptimal."

"Nah," Jess said. "They're just trying to figure out who's what. Don't worry about it. It's all about slots and allotments. If I tell him that, he knows you're Drake family and its cool."

"Ah." Dev pondered all that, then set it aside to review later since it didn't quite make sense. She turned to consider more immediate things instead, such as the cases of circuits awaiting her attention.

She was already deciding how to sort out the myriads of parts she'd thrown into their carrier as they reached the spiral steps, and then she had to pause because Jess had or else plow right into her.

Jess had stopped at the stair landing with her hands on the wrought iron banister. She looked out over the vast hall, with its hazy gray filtered illumination coming in from above. The light washed over her and mingled with the ochre halon wall sconces in an odd mixture of silver and gold as she gazed downward at the inside of the Bay.

"Is something suboptimal, Jess?" Dev asked, after a minute had passed.

Jess started a little. "Um… no." She stepped back and then started for the steps downward. "Just trying to absorb every- thing." She waved vaguely at the space they were descending through.

They walked past more active storage levels, then reached the sixth level where the sets from the Base were being housed. Already the space nearest the steps was filled with crates and piles of supplies, and there was a stack of blankets neatly folded waiting to be used.

"This will be a good location," Dev said. "The quarters are a little different, but the sets like them. They were surprised they were allocated single accommodations."

"Always dorms for them," Jess said. "I noticed that. At Interforce, they were always careful to make sure we had our own spaces."

"Yes. That was a surprise for me as well. I had no idea what to do with all the area I was assigned when I arrived. Was that for a purpose?"

Jess was silent for a minute, as they moved past the level where the station sets lived, and then on downward to staff quarters before reaching the bottom of the stairs. "Has to do with the aggro level," she finally said. "You saw how it was. We're assholes."

Dev gave her one of those cute, sideways looks.

Jess smiled briefly. "We are, c'mon. They always gave us space to be chill in, from earliest school. Kept everyone from killing each other." She paused. "Mostly. Had to do with the crazy too, I guess. When they're teaching you how to put a wrap on that, you can't have people up next to you."

They reached the bottom level and paused. "I see," Dev said. "That's interesting."

Jess gazed around the hall. "Yeah," she said. "You were the first person I didn't mind having up next to me. You never made me aggro." She glanced at Dev. "I wondered once if that was on purpose. If the Doc did that."

Dev looked at her with a deep, interested expression. "Gave me programming on you?" She asked. "No, he didn't. I asked him, because when I saw you for the first time, you were very interesting to me and that sometimes can be programming. But he said he didn't." She paused briefly. "And I have a copy of all the programming they gave me for my assignment, so I am pretty sure that's true."

"Do ya?"

Dev's eyes twinkled. "I took copies of it when we were on station. I was curious," she said, with a tiny grin. "I wanted to see it because I wanted to see the framework. What parts were programming and what..." She paused. "What developed after that."

"Sneaky little Rocket." Jess laughed, then clapped a hand on Dev's shoulder, and they headed for the meeting room at the back of the cavern. "You wanted to see how you got to be so Rockety."

"Something like that, yes."

"Hell, I'd want to see too if it were me," Jess said cheerfully. "I'd like to see what the script was, for what they taught us in school. The mental stuff." She made a vague gesture as they walked across the wide space. "How they got so many of us to get through it."

Dev thought about that as she walked along at Jess's side. She noticed how they were watched as they passed. Many paused to look before going back to what they were doing. It seemed to be open interest, she thought. No one seemed upset to see them there.

But was it? It would take some time to really tell.

****

The conference room was full of people, and Jess paused before she entered to study the figures already in the room.

Dan Kurok was there. Cathy stood next to him with a recording pad. Next to her were Security Mike, with his senior captain, Scott, their neighbors from Cooper's Rock and Rag- land's township, two representatives from Quebec, three people she didn't know, and a pair of AyeBees in Bay coveralls with plates of tidbits.

Spread across the back wall of the room, a draping of cloth that was new. Someone had dredged up an old dragon banner and installed it. The splash of sea colors against the granite wall made Jess smile.

Dev was off behind her with Doug. April and Mike stood nearby, dressed in their civs. They looked ready to be entertained. Both wore knives at their hips and looked at each of the visitors with casual interest.

"Any word on Brent?" Mike Arias asked Jess. "Didn't see Jerad in the mess at breakfast."

"Still out," Jess responded. "Jerad said he was keeping him down so he could regulate something or other with his chemicals." She half shrugged. "Med crap."

"Med crap," April echoed. "Hey, maybe you should go sing to him."

Jess gave her a narrow-eyed look, but April just grinned back at her. "You two get all registered?" Jess changed the subject. "Get your chits?"

Mike nodded. April also nodded, but she also smirked a little. "You weren't bullshitting me," she said. "Didn't realize they'd full scan us as part of that. Some of my guts did come from here."

"Yeah, what was that about, anyway?" Mike asked. "That for security?"

"Jess, let's get started." Kurok was at the door and motioned them in. "We're ready."

"C'mon," Jess said. "We can talk about that later." She walked into the conference room and around to the head of table. She took the seat at it as she'd done the last time she'd been in the room. This time, however, she was in a Bay overshirt and work pants like everyone else and Interforce no longer.

Dev settled at her right hand. She put her scanner on the table as the AyeBees brought in trays full of some steaming drink and offered her one. "Thank you." She took one and sat back.

Dee, from Cooper's Rock sat down roughly across from Dev, and she accepted the cup with a smile. "Boy, it's nice to get something other than cold water from an outdoor hose from here." She lifted the cup toward a short, curly haired man who sat down at her side. "Right, Glides?"

Glides Montechort from Ragland's Township nodded briefly. He seemed wary, but he also took a mug and sipped from it. "Oh. That is good," he said, in a tone of surprise. "Very nice."

"All right." Kurok closed the door to the room and came over to sit on Jess's left-hand side. Mike took the chair next to him. Cathy and Scott sat behind them with their pads and input devices. "Shall we get down to business? I'm sure everyone has a lot to do today," Kurok said, briskly. "Let me see, does everyone have some hot cider? We're experimenting with some extracts I thought you all might enjoy."

The three unknown men sat down at the far end of the table, and between them, the representatives from Quebec took seats past Glides and Dee. The drinks were sampled, though, with murmurs of surprised approval.

Most of them looked uncomfortable anyway, save Dee. Most of them watched Jess from the corner of their eyes, and glanced briefly at both April and Mike, who sat down with Doug and Chester on Security Mike's far side.

Dev took a sip of the drink. It was very warm and had a tang to it a bit like sea grape, but different, with a taste on the back end that she thought she might have had once while on station.

It was good. She nudged Jess's elbow and indicated the cup. "This is excellent," she said. "I think you'll like it."

Jess broke off her intent staring at everyone and picked up the cup to take a sip. She swallowed and blinked in surprise. "What the hell is that?" She whispered. "It's great."

"Let's just make sure everyone knows each other," Kurok said, smoothly, distracting them. "I'm assuming you all know who I am, and you've met Mike, our head of security." He cleared. his throat and half turned. "Some of you have met Jesslyn Drake, our senior stakeholder. "He glanced at Jess. "And her partner, Dev, who until lately were members of Interforce."

"It's true?" Glides interrupted him. "Now they aren't?"

"Jess was discharged from service, yes," Kurok said. "She is now a fully registered civilian, and her profile is active as the stakeholder of record for Drake's Bay, so no longer the stakeholder presumptive," he concluded. "And Dev also transitioned to citizen status and has redomiciled here along with a number of colleagues."

Silence fell, and Jess let it continue a moment before she tapped her thumbs together. "Hi." She broke the tension. "Yes, it's true." She spoke directly to Glides. "Problem?"

Jacques, from Quebec City cleared his throat. "We all have a problem," he said quietly. "Because we have been abandoned by Interforce. They promised to protect us, and to manage our defense. Now they're gone, taking their promises with them."

"Not all of us," April said. "Some of us decided that was bogus." She indicated herself, and Mike, and the two techs next to her.

"And if I disagree with you, will you then shoot me?" Jacques asked. "Interforce also protected us against having people like yourselves among us. You are, none of you, of the age they considered safe to be retired into a homestead," he added dourly. "Or so they told us. No saying if even that was the truth, or if it was not."

Jess tilted her head at him in some amusement. "Aren't we safer than a squad of the other side coming in here with blasters?" She asked, in a quizzical tone.

"That's what I said." Dee sat back in her chair. "I think you all are dipshits coming in here worried if Drake's going to break your neck. I'm worried about having my stakehold wiped off the map and my stock and people taken off to work the mines on the other side."

Glides nodded. "I am with Dee on that," he said bluntly. "This place is all we got left between us and them. You don't get that?" He turned to Jess. "My concern was that you were still in service, like the last time. There's no way I was making any deals with someone still attached. But you're reg civ now?"

Jess nodded. "We all are." She made a general circling motion with her hand.

"I figure they cut their losses," Dee said. "Didn't work out for them sending orders out here last time."

Jess decided she liked Glides. She'd already known she liked Dee. She focused on Jacques, and the squad of nervous looking bimbos with him. "So why are you here?"

"Hold on." One of the stocky, wary looking men stood up. "I'm Andrew," he said. "We're from the processors." He indicated the two men with him. "What we're here for is to find out what it'll take to keep the fishing fleet safe, and our business on track," he said. "Drake, I could care less if you're a maniac. What I care about is can you provide us protection. It's great you all took off from Interforce, no skin off my nose, not having to pay off those bastards and give them free product all the time. Ya know?"

"Well then," Kurok said. "Nothing like a frank conversation, is there."

"But you've got like six people here," Andrew stated flatly. "What difference would that make if those bastards come rolling over?"

"Those six people are actually what turned them all back

the last time," Kurok said. "So probably a lot more than you could do on your own."

"Hey, they had some help," Security Mike said. "Even you were in there shootin."

"And they, and a bunch of the kids from the Bay, took out Science Station two," Kurok continued in the same mild tone. "The other side knows all that," he added. "And we also want to protect what we have here, as we now have quite a considerable thing to protect as well." He cocked his pale head to one side. "It's not Jess you're inviting into your defense, it's Drake's Bay. It's more than six people. It's just an additional six people who know this business far better than any of you do."

April smirked a little and folded her arms over her chest. "F'kn right."

Andrew sat down and nodded. "All right," he said. "So now you got my cards on the table. I want to know what you got, and how that helps me, and what it'll cost," he said. "Most important, can we do business with you without screwing up all the other deals I got." He gave them a meaning look. "Y'know what I mean?"

Everyone's eyes shifted to Jacques, who chewed the inside of his lip. He was a thin man with salt and pepper gray hair and a highly creased forehead. He looked at Jess. "I did not care for your father," he said, shortly. "He was violent and not as you say, safe to be in charge here, I say."

Jess regarded him with a raised eyebrow. Then she looked down at herself, then back up at him. "I'm not my father," she said. "So that's not really a problem?"

"But you are the same kind. You killed your own brother. Did he annoy you?" Jacques persisted. "How can you expect to deal in good faith when you can be killed with no more thought than gutting a fish."

Kurok took a breath but halted when Jess nudged him with her elbow. "I killed Jimmy because he contracted a deal on behalf of the Bay, then reneged on it," she said. "He endangered the stake hold's ability to survive as a trading partner." She paused. "It was only afterward I found out the rest of his stupidity. And yeah, if I hadn't killed him already, I would have for that."

Security Mike nodded along as she spoke. "That's how we do it," he said. "In or out. That's the way here. We know what to do, we do the right thing, no bs."

There was a bit of an uncomfortable silence.

Jess smiled briefly. "I'm not sure how much you really

know about Interforce agents. But we're not wild animals. Even when we're in the zone, there's always a reason behind it." She held his gaze until he was forced to look away. "And I couldn't care less if you liked my father or not." She spread out her hands in a casual shrug. "Not my issue."

"I could," Kurok said. "And now I will hold that against you, Jacques. But not enough to prevent us from doing business together. Are you in for that? If not, then I must ask you to leave so the rest of us can discuss our plans." He folded his hands on the table and tilted his head in an inquiring attitude toward Jacques.

"Nice," April said. "We got stuff to do. Get the talking over."

Jacques exchanged looks with the others who had come with him, and they merely folded their arms and stared back at him. "So noted," he said, simply "We will do business. Hopefully it will end up well for all of us."

"Excellent. Let's discuss then, what you all have in mind when we talk about protection," Kurok said. "Just high level, we'll have to nail down specifics in a few days." He twitched his sleeves straight. "Please notate for us, will you, Cathy?"

"Absolutely, Doctor Dan."

                                    ****

"We'll have to nail down specifics when we know what the hell they are," April said. She extended her legs and crossed them at the ankles "What goons."

They were in the lower level gathering space, around the heating element, under the wall that held names and dates of Drakes who had died since the place was built. Jess was sprawled in the big chair to one side of the mantel, her head propped up on one fist, a sardonic look on her face. "Half shell clams."

"We kinda got nothing," Security Mike said. "They don't know it's a scam? They gotta know. We only kept this place from being trashed last time with string and duct tape." He seemed almost amused. "Cooper knows. For sure. Her ass was here!"

Dev was seated at one of the small tables on the far side of the room, working with her scanner and an input tablet.

Doctor Dan sat with his elbows resting on his knees. "I wanted to see what they were going to say. What they were going to ask for. Honestly, Mike's right. There's no way we can replace Interforce or do half the things they want." He paused. "Regardless of what they're willing to pay. It's just ridiculous."

"They want a rapid response force," Jess said. "On patrol, who can be called up when they get nervous to come chase off jellyfish or whatever." Her lips twitched. "They should just call up their own guard."

"Don't want to risk their peeps getting splatted," April said. "Jackass heads just like everywhere. Want everyone else to pay that price."

"Anyhow we gotta secure this place first," Security Mike said. "Gotta close up that rear approach, put in guard positions, put in guns… gotta get some guns that're younger than the old uncles that torched it in the last one…" He counted on his fingers and then threw both hands in the air. "WTF?"

"Not sure we can obtain those kinds of weapons," Kurok said. "Even if we wanted to provide that service. Which I'm not sure we do."

April eyed him. "We can't fight those goons with rocks. Other side goons, or goons that just want those… whatever those were we had, or stuff they have here. You got things, people want them," she said. "Nomads know. Caravansaries are armed."

Jess spoke up. "April's right. This place has to be defensible first, and with more than just my bullshit stories." There was a bit of a twinkle in her pale eyes. "That lie'll only last so long."

Security Mike nodded. So did April and Mike Arias.

"That's true," Kurok acknowledged. "But the fact is, we may have to create weapons or alter the ones we have in the armory to make that happen. We can't just buy them. That's going to take foundry work. I think we might have to trade with Dee for ore supplies and metalworkers."

"She knows that." Jess said. "She's got capital to trade with us. You could see the smirk."

"Agreed," Kurok said. "And that's making Jacques nervous, because he needs ore too. And the processors do as well, and they can pay better rates than he can. Dee's in a good spot." He smiled briefly. "She absolutely knows it. Had a chat with her about that just the other day before the whole world changed on us."

Chester came in and went over to where Dev was seated with his own scanner that he set up on the table. They stood there and compared the readings.

Mike Arias had his head thrown back and his arm over his eyes in concentration. "Would the doors to the landing bay at

10 fit in that rear approach to close it off?" He lifted his head and looked at them. "If we could cut the framework and airlift it out? We could maybe do it with all three carriers."

There was a moment of silence. "Be a hell of a lot easier than building a new one from scratch," Security Mike said. "For sure. And fast." He gave Mike an approving look. "I like that idea."

"Assuming they really have totally abandoned the facility," Kurok said. "We have plasma cutters in the armory they used to cut all these lovely rooms in here. If we recommission them, we could cut out that framework."

"That'd add a lot of space to the back," Security Mike said. "We put it in that back pass, and that brings all that inside." He nodded. "Makes me feel better with that and sealing up that whole side area near the shuttle pad like we done."

"Shuttle pad," Jess mused. "Speaking of... what happens if we get a call from stations who want to deal?" She looked over at Kurok. "They'll hear from the processors. They got a new source for bio stuff now."

A small silence fell. "Think they will?" April asked. "I'm thinking they'd rather take a walk on the creep side of space up there than ring his comms." She nodded at Kurok. "No offense, Doc."

Kurok chuckled. "None taken April, as you're probably correct. I can't see—well, certainly Bio Station 2 won't be reaching out to me any time soon. But there are other stations up there." He studied them thoughtfully. "There was always a bit of contention topside over territory."

April regarded him. "Y'know, maybe it's like that processor guy said, business is what matters to them. Someone else... was it you, Drake? Who said the us and them was mostly just us and them and everyone else was after the best deal?" She asked, pragmatically. "Sounds like the nomad way."

"Or Market Island," Jess said, in a thoughtful tone. "We all knew that was neutral because we all wanted access to stuff."

"You ain't saying we're trading with them," Security Mike said, in a flat tone.

Jess chuckled softly. "No. They won't. Not with me," she said. "Or me with them." She looked over at Kurok. "But things we trade with others will get to them."

Kurok nodded. "Has already I'm sure," he said. "They don't want to pay the lifting fee for station goods any more than anyone else does. As April said, it's business."

Security Mike frowned. "Don't know if that's gonna fly

round here.”

Jess waved a hand. “One thing at a time,” she said. “Get the wrenchers to do the math on if those rigs can lift that door.” She thought a moment. “And we should at least start scheduling a patrol routing around the perimeter of the Bay. We can use those cargos for now as eyes.”

“Excellent idea,” Kurok said with his gentle smile. “We can pair up the pilots from the Base with some of our lads here, get some cross training in.”

Security Mike drummed his booted heels on the counter he was sitting on. “Got a crap ton of peeps signing up for security,” he said. “Or whatever we’re gonna end up calling it.”

“Betcha.” Mike Arias chuckled. “Don’t want to miss a fight.” He glanced at April, who nodded, a smile on her face. “Us either,” he admitted cheerfully. “Wrenchers can do a lot of stuff. Interforce agents really do one thing well.”

“Yeeees,” April agreed. “Though I gotta say I’d like to learn how to make one of those old-style power blasters. They got a kick.” She wiggled her fingers. “What’s the go forward, Drake? You gonna lay it out for us?”

It occurred to Jess, at that moment, that the plan of whatever insanity they were going to do totally rested with her. This was not really a surprise. Though they were out of service, she was the senior agent, and she was the Drake, but what had started out to be an idea of protest against a skank suit move was now solid and real and right in her lap.

Everyone expected her to do this. They were ready to accept her direction, had accepted what she’d said should happen, and now there were Bay residents who were not only willing but excited to become named security so they could go out and maybe get their heads blown off.

Hadn’t she told Jason she was not inclined to be in charge of anything but herself? Now here she was, in charge.

Well, crap. Jess sighed silently.

“Jess.” Dev came over and brought her pad with her. “We did an analysis.”

She knelt at Jess’s side, a bit surprised when Jess threw her arm around her shoulders and pulled her closer. “Didja? Good job, Devvie.” Jess. “Whatcha got?” She added, glad for the distraction from being asked for her nonexistent plan.

“Rocket did it, we just agreed with her,” Doug called out.

“Thank you.” Dev cleared her throat and turned to her pad. “We extracted diagrams of the systems here, and we think, if we can build interlacing here, and here, and put in boosters, we can extend a protective grid all along this ridge here, and through the underground tunnels here."

Security Mike hopped up and scrambled around to look at the pad. "You got grid maps from ops?" He eyed her in question. "I didn't see no ask."

Dev eyed him calmly. "Yes, we obtained them. I am unsure if ops knows we obtained them," she clarified. "We possibly should discuss putting in a stronger security framework."

Security Mike stared at Dev, his eyes wide. "You broke in? For shit real?"

"Yes," Dev said.

"That is what we do, y'know," Doug called over. He pointed at himself, and Chester, and Dev. "Not just drive busses." He hiked one boot up onto the rung of the stool he was sitting on and leaned his elbow on his knee.

Jess chortled under her breath. "Good job, wrencher queen." She bumped Dev with her head. "Start securing that when ya get a chance, Devvie. Last thing we need is them to target ops. There's gear in there a lot older than I am."

"Yes," Dev repeated. "Regarding the analysis, we were curious about the geological readings we got back and discovered the material this location is created from has interesting properties that conduct current."

"What the hell does that do for us?" Security Mike asked.

"If we can extend the distribution to where you would like that ingress installed, we can reflect power through it." Dev paused, as everyone looked at her, Kurok's pale eyebrows lifting. "And it would forcefully return any attempt at penetrating it."

"Like…" Jess said. "Anything they threw at it; it would throw back?" She ventured. "At them?"

"Yes," Dev said. "It seems useful… as you mentioned to me once, Jess, there is a surplus of power generated from this facility. We should use it as a defensive mechanism." She paused, but everyone still stared at her. "Shouldn't we?"

"Huh," Security Mike finally said. "Y'know, Doc, we're gonna have to make a new slot for her. Not sure *tech* cuts it." He stood up. "Holy crap."

Dev gave Jess a sideways look of question.

"Rockstar," Jess said, succinctly. "Long as we're plundering, bet there's some rigs we can scarf outta 10 to help with that."

"Yup," April said. "See what else we can scrounge. I got the feeling we're gonna need as much as we can lift out of there." She chortled softly under her breath. "Now what were ya saying about new recruits?"

"We got ' em," Security Mike said. "I'll tell the whole bunch of 'em that we can meet up tonight in the market hall after late chow." He straightened up to his full, imposing height. "Hope you got some idea on what to do with 'em by then." He winked at Jess, then left, with the faintest of chuckles.

Kurok gazed at Dev, his chin resting on his fist. "Good work, Dev. That's a very clever idea. Much simpler than trying to fortify every inch of the place, because with all the tunnels and underground tubes, that would take forever."

Dev smiled in response.

"Best thing we took out of Interforce was Rocket," Doug said, a moment later. "They got no idea."

"Oh," Kurok said. "They might have had a glimmering." He stood up, and chuckled. "Let me go see what story I can craft to delay our answer to our neighbors." He picked up his data pad and headed for the door. "Dev, can you forward me that analysis?"

"Yes," Dev said. "In work."

April settled back in her seat. "So much for that. Now, Drake, remember the chits? What was all the scanning about? You said you'd tell us later," she said. "We got a few minutes before Rocket invents something else, right?"

"Maybe," Jess said, "but telling ya won't take that long." Jess leaned back in her seat. "They know about spirals here. They keep track of who breeds with who, so we don't breed too close."

"Oh," April said. "Oh, crap sure that makes sense. Nomads keep family books, same reason. They foster kids out to other families for that." She nodded. "Okay, got it."

"Oooh," Doug drew out the word. "When they said I had a zero match, that's what that was? Like mine are all different?" He asked. "Seemed to be a good thing?"

"Ours too." Chester indicated Mike Arias and himself.

"Right. If you register to cohabitate, they check that," Jess continued. "They want kids that are fully functional. Inbreeding makes some funky stuff," she added, in a somewhat diffident tone. "They won't stop you, but they keep track, and you get scanned a lot." She stopped and regarded them in silence.

Dev, predictably, immediately got it. "Is that the kind of scan they used when they found your excellent saltwater oxygen exchange facility?" She asked.

Jess nodded, then looked around at them. "I'm pretty sure

you've heard someone say, *Drake both sides* about me at some point?" She queried. "That's what that means. I have Drake bloodlines from both parents."

"Heard someone say there's no end to the jackassery in that," April said, in a droll tone. "Wasn't sure if that was good or bad."

Jess shrugged, lifted both hands up and then put them down. "They flipped out when they saw the gills, but then Dad held me under and showed them how functional it was."

She watched their jaws drop, and their eyes widen.

"Interesting," Dev said. "But possibly non optimal," she added, with a frown.

"He knew they worked," Jess clarified belatedly. "He didn't just randomly drown me in the grog bowl in the mess one night."

"Wow," Mike Arias said, after a pause. "Would they have offed you otherwise?"

"Depends how functional you are. If you can fill a slot, it's fine, but they torch you so you can't pass it," Jess said. "But general consensus was that was a pretty damn sweet adaptation." Her eyes twinkled a little. "Then I tested in, so it was kinda moot. Chances were I'd never pass it anyway."

"But you could," Doug said.

She shrugged. "That? No clue. Ask the Doc. He might know since he took pictures of my insides up on station when I was there, and that's his sweet spot."

"Yeah, it is. From what I heard in the mess." April eyed Jess. "Folks round here would like to get a piece of that. They think it's cool." She paused thoughtfully. "Hell, I think it's cool. I want f'n gills. I don't even like swimming, and I want them."

Doug stood up. "On that note, I'm gonna go see if I can find lifting chain. We're gonna need a lot of it cause Chestie and I can't navigate as slick as the Rocket." He hitched up his work pants. "Maybe I'll use a piece of it as a belt. Not used to not having a jumper on."

"I'll go too," April said. "Haven't looked around half this place so far. I keep bumping into corners where I'm saying where the hell am I?" She got up and stretched. "But I like that. C'mon Mike. We were going to find a spot we could scrap in."

Mike grinned. "Or find out where everyone else scraps, cause I know they do."

Jess stayed where she was, as the rest of the group dispersed, except for Dev, who remained kneeling at her side.

"You think people really want gills, Devvie?" she asked, when they were alone, and it was quiet in the gathering room.

"Certainly," Dev said, at once. "They spend a lot of time in or around the water, Jess. It would be convenient to be able to breathe it and not have to worry about mechanical aides. They require charging and replenishment. And yes I have also heard others speaking about it in the mess. I would not mind being able to do that in fact."

Jess pondered that. "Hm." She grunted softly. "Just always made me feel so weird. I never told anyone about it if I didn't have to."

"Do you really go talk to turtles?" Dev asked suddenly. "I would really enjoy seeing that."

Jess started laughing. "C'mon, Dev. Turtles don't talk. I was messing with those guys."

"But they look like they should," Dev said. "When we saw that one on the beach that time, and you said how old they got? They must have some amazing things to talk about." She leaned on the chair arm. "I thought that bear was trying to talk to us, that time on the boat."

"I thought that bear was trying to eat you for lunch, that time on the boat." Jess bumped her with her head again. "Let's go see if Brent's awake. He likes you. Maybe if he hears your voice, he'll come out of it," she said. "And don't tell me to sing."

Dev grinned charmingly. "I was going to," she admitted. "Because I like to hear you make that sound as well."

Jess got up. "You all are so weird. You want gills and my croaking." She sighed. "C'mon."

****

"Do you want this here, Doctor Dan?"

Kurok looked up from his worktop. "Right there against the wall, yes, thank you." He said. "And if you wouldn't mind, there are two big crates that were next to that on the plane. I need those here too."

The bio alts both nodded. "Yes. We know which ones they are. Is this going to be where the programming table goes?"

Kurok nodded. "Right there, yes."

"This will be excellent." The nearer of the two said. "It will be good to have programming again." They both trooped out to retrieve more boxes, and he paused to watch them, a speculative look on his face. "Hm."

"Doctor Dan." His assistant Cathy entered, with an input pad.

He closed his own pad. "Hello, there. Are the test results complete yet?"

She came over and sat next to him. "Another ten minutes or so I think." She indicated the programming machinery. "I didn't think they'd miss it that much."

Kurok folded his hands on the desk. "Well, we'll certainly make better use of it than Interforce did. Based on the code I've reviewed so far, even if all we do is digitize the old mech manuals and give it to them."

Cathy nodded. "I saw the schemas they were using. What on earth?"

"What on earth puts it nicely." Kurok gave his pale head a little shake. "What a mess. I want to get this rig up today so I can take a few of them down and see what I'll need to adjust out of the nonsense attempted by those ignorant muppets."

"Thank goodness you're here," Cathy said, simply. "I think that's why they're so excited, you know? They want to know they're okay, and they know that you'll know for sure."

"Don't we all want to know we're okay?" Kurok smiled his gentle smile.

Cathy smiled back. "Doctor, what is a... a co hab?" She asked. "I tried to research it, but there's nothing in general operations about it."

"Ah, well, yes, I think that terminology is rather specific to Drakes Bay." Kurok sat back. "It's when two residents here decide they're going to live together, usually because they really enjoy each other's company, or because they want to create a family."

Cathy looked interested. "Really?"

"Really." Kurok eyed her. "When you qualify for duties here, they say you have a slot. You know that it's what we classified the sets for. They all qualified for a competency slot in one area or other because, well, that's what we made them for wasn't it?"

Cathy nodded as he spoke. "Oh yes."

"A slot gets you a place to sleep and meals," he continued. "There are a lot of people here at the Bay. That's what they have and that's what they're satisfied with because it lets them survive."

"Like the sets, everywhere but here," Cathy said, with surprising shrewdness. "Isn't it?"

He slowly nodded. "Yes. Everywhere but here." His lips twitched into a brief grin. "And, when you're assigned an official position, that's called an allotment because it means you get paid, and you get entitlements. Every homestead has different ways of doing that."

"Okay, that's really interesting."

Kurok went on. "Everyone who came from station got an allocation, including the sets, because the work they do is important and valuable. Drake's Bay doesn't have a different classification for bio alts because it never occurred to them they would ever need one."

"Dustin told me. He said they'd never had any of them here before," Cathy said. "It's all about being excellent at what you do? The allotments?"

"Stupendously egalitarian, given the history of this place, but essentially, yes." Kurok smiled. "Was there a reason Dustin was having this conversation with you?"

Cathy shook her head. "I don't think so. He was just saying he was going to have to talk to his head of house about an allotment, so he could get a crib and a co hab. I had no idea what he was talking about," she confided. "But I knew you would know."

"I see." Kurok suppressed a smile. "Well, you be sure to let me know if he says anything else about that, if you need any more explanation said. It should be an interesting conversation for him."

"Of course. Let me go get those reports, Doctor. I think they're done by now." Cathy got up and trotted out, leaving him to tap his fingertips on the desktop surface for a minute in thought.

Then he got up and went to the programming console and looped a toolkit around his waist. "One thing at a time, DJ." He took out a probe and opened the top of the console. "One thing at a time."

****

The med area was a bit rough. There were two portable exam tables on one side. Past that in a second alcove the parts of the tank they'd brought from Base 10. Brent was on one of the tables with diagnostic leads connected to him. Jerad stood nearby and regarded the settings on a battered read out screen the leads were attached to.

He looked up as he heard boots enter. "Ah. Good," he

greeted Jess and Dev. "I was about to comms you. I think he's ready to come up." He adjusted a dial. "You did a damn good job draining him, Drake."

Jess dismissed the compliment. "Just hung him upside down over my shoulder. No real choice since I was hanging on the end of a drop line. But he wasn't under that long."

"Lucky it was you that went after him." Jerad made a last adjustment, then walked over to the table. "Hey, bucko. Wake up." He patted Brent's face. "No idea if you want to be here, but you are."

After a long moment, Brent's face twitched, then his eyes fluttered open and blinked. He shifted his head and looked up at Jerad, blinking a few more times to focus.

Then with a convulsive motion he lunged off the table and grabbed Jerad, sending the mobile table slamming into the diagnostic rig.

He was about to rip himself loose of the leads when Jess caught up with him and yanked him backwards, holding him still. "Hey!" She let out a bellow. "Knock that off! You're in med!"

Brent jerked to a halt on hearing her voice. He twisted to look at her, then went limp and dropped back onto the table. "Oh. Damn it's you," he gasped. "Where'm I?"

Dev ducked around to the other side of the diagnostic table. "Brent, it's Dev. Please be calm." She held up a hand. "You are at Jess's birthplace."

His eyes focused on her. "Rocket," he said. "Oh. Man. Sorry." He lay back flat on the table as Jess released him. "Sorry... didn't know what was going on." He seemed relieved. "Didn't know where I was."

"Not surprising given you probably haven't been in here before," Jerad said as he sorted out the tangled leads. "Or knew I joined team pirate. Bunch of us deliberately missed the bus."

Brent blinked at him, then turned and looked at Jess. "Your place, huh?"

Jess looked around and then back at him. "It's Drake's Bay," she responded. "So yeah."

He nodded and licked his lips, still a little disoriented. "When the base blacked out I stayed put for a while." He paused. "No choice," he added. "Then Jase got my door open and pulled me through some suit hallway or something. We got to the transport. I think we were like last. I don't know. Hard to know what was going on."

"It was dark," Jerad said." I don't think anyone really knew what was going on."

"We got inside then…" Brent's brow furrowed. "I'm not sure what the sitch was. I heard a lot of yelling and noise like fighting," he said. "Someone was yelling about a scam." He shook his head a little. "Jase was yelling, and then we lifted." He vaguely waved his hand. "No restraints or nothing."

Jerad got him reattached to the monitor. "We just sat on our behinds on a box in the dark." he observed the results. "Waiting for the transport to leave."

Brent's lips twitched into the faintest of smiles. "Yeah, you did it right," he said. "Then I got hit on the head. Not sure if it was on purpose or just got in someone's way. Next thing I remember is being ejected and hitting the water." He grimaced. "Crap that hurt. Think I went out again."

"They threw you out of the transport?" Jess asked, sharply.

Brent nodded. "In the pod. I remember smelling it, the plas and stuff. I floated around, couldn't see crap. Didn't know what to do. There wasn't no paddle or nothing in the pod. Just a tube of water and a rat bar." He blinked. "Then the storm came on, then… he shook his head. "Then I got no idea what happened." He looked at Dev. "But man, I'm glad you guys got out of there. Something wasn't right. Jase was roaring mad about somethin."

"Scam," Jerad said, succinctly.

"Scam," Jess agreed in a quiet tone. "Well, you're here now." She regarded him. "Sack out for a while and don't screw with Jerad. We had to pump ya out."

Brent absorbed that, then nodded. "Feel like I been dragged over the ground for a week," he said, then looked up at Jess. "You know what happened?"

"To them?" Jess shook her head. "No comms after they left. Just know what happened here. We picked up everyone they left and came over to the Bay."

"Jase figured. He knew you weren't goin," Brent said. "They were doin some scam. He was mad as hell." He closed his eyes, and exhaled, relaxing on the table as Jerad finished adjusting the leads. "Mad as hell."

Then Jerad looked up and met Jess's eyes. Jess had both hands on the table, her face quiet and still. After a moment they both nodded.

"We'll be back later," Jess said, finally. "Always something, huh?"

Jerad's face tensed into a sardonic grin. "Always."

****

The huge, old armory stretched back into a dim vastness, the wide doors on either end of it stood open and the scent of gun oil and hydraulics drifted through the lower level and into the outer air.

Along one wall was a huge work desk that stretched out to either side of a central console long enough to house two dozen people working shoulder to shoulder. Clint was behind the console, studying a large plas enclosed tablet with three Bay mechs clustered around him.

"This is some good stuff here," Clint said after a long silence. "Biggest issue is parts."

"Parts." The mech to his left nodded emphatically. "S'what I said. The iron's good, but the tracking mods, and that stuff, it's fallin apart."

The second Bay mech, an older woman with scarred hands, pulled over a stack of printed documentation, much folded and faded. She shook her head. "No way we can get boards for that stuff anywhere. Don't exist nowhere but here."

The three mechs had the typical Bay working togs on, but on the shoulder, there was a relatively newer patch in the shape of a gear surrounding a spear tip. "Been trying to work on this stuff since they cracked the vault open." The third mech shook his head.

Clint nodded. "Yah, we're gonna have to fab our own," he said. "Biggest pain in the ass is going to be the press for that size board and the tracing. The etcher we can pull from the sea." All three mechs focused intently on him.

"Make our own?" The woman asked, with a great deal of interest. "Even the proms?"

Clint nodded again. "Yeah. Had to do that at the base. All they sent us there was old crap. I learned how to fab mods from scratch to keep em going." He sniffed reflectively. "We can do it, and anyway, we got Rocket here if we need a bootstrap."

"Sweet," one of the mechs intoned. "What's a rocket?"

Clint chuckled. "Rocket is Dev. That's what ops called her after she flew that old crate BR around the whole planet in circles," he said. "She's a modder. I saw she hauled back a crap ton of assembly parts last time to mess with," he added. "She invented stuff right and left over there. She rigged the BR's so they could bring em with."

"Yeah?" The woman mech folded her arms. "She's a bio? I heard that."

Clint thought about the question for a minute, and they all

just stood there patiently waiting for his answer. "Yeah," he finally said. "She came from station. She talks like them, but I dunno now. She had her collar out, but I don't know if she was ever really like the rest of those guys. She's really, really, sharp. Interforce went and made her civ before we took off out of there."

"They're making a special code for her," the taller male mech said. "I heard it. Not just mech or tech or something. Get her a diff allotment maybe."

"S' good she's got all the skills, not just hangin out co-hab with the Drake." The woman said. "It's reg."

"Reg," the other two agreed. "Hey, she give us some tips on the mods?"

Clint felt like he'd lost a bit in translation, but he understood the last ask. "Yeah, sure. Dev's always up to talk bits." He assured them. "She's a real gear head."

The three mechs looked satisfied. "Good bring," the woman concluded. "So far Drake's done good with that." She looked approvingly at Client. "Real good."

Clint assumed he was being complimented, so he grinned and lifted a hand. "Let's get started, huh?" He pointed at the console. "Where you all want to start? Them big guns up top, or the mobile blasters?" He asked. "We can sort em out in workin, sorta workin, and don't touch your ass with that. Okay?"

The Bay weapons mechs all burst into grins of appreciation. "Hella." The woman gave him a thumbs up. "Grab some tags and start huntin."

Chapter Ten

Dev picked up another box of parts and brought it over to the long workbench. She opened it and removed circuit cards, bits of cards, tracings, and solder downs. At the very bottom of the box, she found a carefully wrapped package. "Ah."

She was alone in the space, content to be setting up her space, since the large set of drawers was now there against the wall.

There was one of the plas stools there, but she had it tucked under the worksurface since it was high enough for her to stand comfortably behind it. This seemed to be something common at the Bay, she'd noticed. The residents, like Jess, were mostly tall and long limbed, and the areas they lived in were built to accommodate them.

So, this work surface, which had enough space for Jess to sit behind it without banging her knees on everything, was also perfect for her to stand and work, which was her preferred method. It seemed optimal.

"Excellent," she said out loud, as she opened a narrow drawer and transferred a selection of card blanks into it.

Jess was outside inspecting the space they hoped to enclose. Dev had already completed the calculations on lift for the carriers, and now she was here waiting for Bay ops tech to arrive to connect their local data access.

Or thought they would be doing that. Dev had other intentions. She wanted to identify and make the connections herself and hoped that would not make for a non-optimal situation.

She finished with the box of parts, and then decided a drink would be appropriate. She retreated through the space to the food prep area and obtained a cold cup of the slightly effervescent drink common to the Bay.

It was rainwater filtered through slightly fermented kelp, she'd learned. It had a natural sweetness that was vaguely like sea grape, and a crisp taste she liked a lot, preferring it to the kack that had been served at the Base.

The Bay residents carried battered metal tubes of it around, and she had resolved to obtain one so that she could do the same.

She took the cup with her and walked out into the big main space that now had chairs and various items inside it. They were randomly arranged, but the room seemed like random was a good strategy, so she sat down on one of them and looked around while she enjoyed her drink.

One of the tables, the one with the broken leg now propped up with a box, was in the middle of the space, with two chairs on either side of it. The walls behind her had warming plates and she felt that against her shoulder blades.

It felt nice. She finished her drink, stood, and walked over to the wall where the piece of stone Jess had asked for leaned. Dev pondered it. Had Jess mentioned where she wanted her workspace to be?

Two narrow shelf crates stood next to the stone. Dev set down her cup on the three-legged table and picked up the crates, one in each hand, and walked through the space, pausing when she got to the last room on the outer corridor.

She entered, and regarded it, then set the crates against the plas, where the view was now of one large ship just entering the Bay. She then went back to the main space and over to the huge slab.

Two loaders had brought it, on a cargo lifter. Dev fit her hands on either side of the narrow part, her arms just long enough to reach. She took in a breath, got her center of balance over the balls of her feet, and tightened her hold. She then moved from a crouch to a stand and lifted the slab.

It came up against her body, the stone cold and solid, the chill penetrating her work suit. She paused to judge its weight. After a moment she nodded and walked slowly through the main room, carefully maneuvering through the hallway and into the room she'd chosen.

It was difficult because of the awkward size and the weight, but Dev edged forward and lowered it on top of the shelves in a single smooth move, keeping hold of the slab as it came to rest in case the supports weren't up to the task.

But they were. She released it and stepped back, pleased with the position and distance to the old-style connection panel that would work for Jess's access pad. "Excellent." She dusted her hands off and returned to the main space just as a chime sounded at the service door.

She picked up the cup on her way through and went over to the scanner that rested next to the touch pad. She glanced at it, before she put her hand on it.

The door slid back to reveal JayCee Jack, along with a dented slightly wobbly cart with access panels on it, and two techs behind it. "Hello." Dev stepped back to allow them entry.

"Hello, N... Dev," Jack corrected himself with a slight flush. He was unusually tall for a bio alt, as tall as the two Bay techs with him. He had very curly dark hair and brown eyes common to his set. "We have tech for this location."

"Yes, I was expecting it," Dev said. "Please proceed."

"Yo," The Bay tech in front greeted her as they pushed the cart past. "Inputs?" He cocked his head to one side, waiting for her answer. Both the techs were good looking and had the usual Bay build, with dark hair and light eyes.

They wore work pants and light long sleeved shirts, but over them were vests that had pockets full of various things and Dev eyed them with intrigued interest as she pondered her answer.

Jack moved along the corridor. "I will put this away." He held up a plas container. "It's from the mess kitchen. Some edibles arranged for between meals."

"Excellent." Dev then addressed the techs. "Could you please leave a work interface in the last space on the right-hand side corridor. There is a worksurface prepared for it. Then a second down this hallway in the second space."

"No prob." The techs moved along their way. "Won't take a mo." The nearer one winked at Dev as he passed. "Which way ya like the cables, Rocket lady?" He asked. "Got a pref?"

Dev drew a breath then paused as she and Jack exchanged looks. "On a bell curve, please," she said. "With clips every four inches, and a service loop."

The two techs stopped in mid motion and turned to look at her. "Say what?" The nearer one said. "You say a what?"

"A bell curve. Would you like me to demonstrate?" Dev asked in a mild tone. "That device there should go in Jess's workspace." She pointed at the larger of the two input devices.

The two techs looked at each other. "Uh, sure." The tech pushed the cart in the direction indicated. "Never saw nothing like that. That how they do it in service?"

"Not particularly. I just like it that way." Dev paused a moment to grab the toolkit she'd left on the table and clip the belt around her. She followed them inside. "Yes, that's the space there, on the stone counter."

They put the input on the slab, one of the techs nudging it a little. "Hooo. Glad we don't have to move that."

Dev scooted under the table, crossed her legs under her, and out her kit. "Yes its quite heavy and somewhat awkward to shift." She opened the connection panel and asked, "can you feed those back down that gap?" She laid out her connection kit near her knee and placed the clips with a sense of contentment.

The ends of the cables came down along the wall and a moment later the techs were on the floor next to her, resting on their bellies, propped on their elbows, with a hand light shining on the panel. "G'wan, Rocket lady," the nearer one said. "Let's see your rig."

There was really no challenge in their attitude, more an absorbed focus on a common interest, a prospect of learning something new from a discipline they both respected. Dev found that rather delightful.

She clipped a set of four cables, using spacers that lined them up in a precise curve. She paused and swung her scanner around and reviewed its screen, then inspected the inside of the patch panel. "Hm."

The nearer tech squirmed closer and craned his neck around. "Lemme vac that." He unclipped a tube from his side and extended a long arm, sucking the dust and accumulated grit from the opening. "Gar, toldja those dip heads didn't fix it up in here."

Gar shook his head. "Always forget the cable pans. Close it up, man, no eyeballs."

At that, Jack also knelt and observed the panel over their shoulders, making a small, introspective sound in the back of his throat.

Dev removed a brush from her kit and gently swiped the connections clear then she twisted the cables around and along a graceful bend and seated the first one, then paused to examine the readout.

"You're reg tech for sure," the one with the vacuum said. "That's sweet." He nodded. "You should come down and mess around with us in the build shop."

"Hella yea," Gar agreed and pushed his hair out of his eyes. "That's nice." He touched the bend. "For sig?"

"Yes." Dev glanced at him. "It provides an optimal path."

"Bell," Gar said. "Sweet."

Dev finished her connections, then spent a moment meticulously inspecting each link to be sure the connections from the inputs were going where they were supposed to, and that nothing was suboptimal. She scanned the devices in silence to make sure nothing had been inserted that would intercept signal and found no irregularities in the line.

"Thank you. Jess will be pleased she can work on things here."

Jack stood and backed up to let Dev scramble out from

under the worktop. "I will add that portal to the cleaning list," he said. "It is suboptimal there was dirt inside."

Dev stood up and regarded the input. She reached out and put her hand on it, and after a second, it glowed teal green. "Excellent."

"Next," the nearer tech got to his feet. "Hey, this is Gar, I'm Dugan," he said. "No joke, Rocket lady, you should come down after night mess. All we do is screw around with stuff and talk bits." He extended a hand, and after a moment, Dev took it and returned the grip. "You'd fit in."

Dev grinned briefly. "Thank you." She indicated the door. "I will consider that." She followed them out and down past the central space to the hallway beyond, and into the room she'd claimed for her stuff.

"Oh, yeah." Dougan looked around. "Reg tech the max," he said. "Your crib, yo?"

"Yes," Dev responded, after a moment, drawing out the word. "This is my workspace."

"Pssh." Gar made a noise like a sneeze. "Somebody said you cracked into ops." He turned a bright eye Dev's way. "They flipped out!"

Dev pointed at the corner of the workbench. "That would be excellent right there," she said. "I didn't mean to make it suboptimal for anyone." She stepped back and let them get to work. "Jess just asked me to evaluate, and it was the most efficient way to do it."

"It was a gag. We were rolling," Dougan said. "Seniors were runnin around, but the Doc was just LOL."

"Doctor Dan was an instructor of mine," Dev said. "He would not have been surprised at the activity."

"Yeah, right? LOL." Dugan chortled under his breath.

Jack stood by with a tiny little smile of amusement on his face. He edged over next to Dev. "After night mess, we often gather in spacer quarters," he said. "You would be welcome there as well, so we can share information."

"That would be optimal," Dev answered promptly. "It's always good to have information."

Jack nodded. "Yes. It is always good." He lowered his voice. "That term LOL means laugh out loud."

"Excellent," Dev responded. "That is a good piece of information that I do not now have to use these panels to research."

"Done!" Gar rolled out from under the counter and came to his feet in a smooth motion. "Check it out?"

Dev went down on one knee and examined the patch panel,

then nodded. "Excellent."

Dugan got up and slid his hand light into his pocket. "That it? Don't want no more? We got extra." He pointed at the cart. "Bunch freed up after the big bango."

"That's sufficient," Dev said. "Thank you."

"No prob, Rocket lady." The two techs retreated. "C'mon down after mess, yo? We got a rave on tonight," Gar said, and then he and Dugan started moving around in a peculiar manner, bumping each other with their hips. "Hella fun. You too, Jackie."

Dev looked at this display in bewilderment. "Thank you," she managed to respond, as the two kept up their weird motions until they went through the door and dragged the cart behind them. There was a long moment of silence after they left, and then Dev and Jack just looked at each other.

"I have been to one of those raves," Jack said. "It's very strange. But also, somewhat enjoyable. It involves bodily machinations but also pleasant sounds, and fermented beverages."

Dev pondered. "I think I was present at some events at Base that sort of activity took place," she said. "That was very strange as well, though parts were relatively optimal. Natural born customs require a learning curve."

"Yes," Jack agreed at once. "But they are also interesting." His eyes twinkled a little.

Dev smiled. "Yes, they are." She got down on the floor and slid under the counter to inspect the panel.

"Did they perform that sub optimally?" Jack inquired, observing her expression.

Dev leaned on her elbow and looked over her shoulder. "It was optimal for their instruction," she said. "I will use a different process that will be more optimal for Jess's requirements." She watched Jack nod in understanding. "And also, one of the connections was upside down."

Jack laughed silently, then gave her a little wave. "I will continue to research items that might be of use to you, Dev."

"Yes," Dev said. "Any you can find." She studied the ground around her. "Also, if there are any static pads."

Jack rocked on his heels a moment and pondered the request. "There are woven sea grass mats that are created in the fishing caverns," he responded after a minute. "I will requisition some for the space."

"That would be optimal," Dev said. "I have a spool of wire. I can create a ground, there is a post in this panel."

Jack studied the panel soberly. "This will be such an excellent assignment," he said. "I can see I will be learning many new things."

Dev grinned at him, then went back to her work.

****

Jess climbed down the last section of rock and leaped off the lowest ledge to the ground, landing with a hop. April stood at the edge of the passage, her hands planted on her hips.

A strong wind gusted through the gap, and the clouds were clustering overhead, but the air was only damp and not full of rain. The wind brought its own whistling howl but there was no edge of thunder on it and on this side of the cliffs, smelled more of the dank wetness of granite than saltwater.

Jess had removed her overshirt and was just in a light tank and work pants, her service burns showing vividly against her pale skin as she walked back to where April waited.

"So?" April said, tossing her the overshirt as she approached.

"It'll fit." Jess slung the shirt over her shoulder. "Right behind that ridge there." She pointed. "Frame'll butt up against that edge."

April studied it "Almost like it was made for it," she mused. "Might have to slag some rock in behind it to square it up."

"Might," Jess agreed. "Enough metallics in that stuff to harden it."

A dozen or so loaders worked in the pass, using cargo handlers to move all the loose rocks and any crates out of the way. Teams of stockers moved back and forth from the storage caverns to the entry, steering carts full of supply.

Storage caverns on one side extended into the second set of cliffs that were the back side of the Bay. A wall of rock faced landward, like the one facing seaward. The pitch slanted inland with a wide paved incline that led out to the remains of a high- way the traders used to move from homestead to homestead.

The other side of the ingress were lower, more irregular rock walls and shallow caves that were also irregular and scattered, sometime refuge for the shore scavengers who worked the fringes and brought in bags full of anything they found to trade for a meal.

Shells, sometimes. Limpets scoured from the rocks on the outer ring of the bay, mossy algae scraped off flat surfaces. Nets pulled in from the shore, cut loose by accident from the fishing vessels. Eggs from the legions of seabirds.

All had value to the Bay, all worth a bowlful of whatever the mess had, or a bagful of the worn beyond use fabrics and clothes that were specially treasured.

The small caves were, at least, out of the rain and the wind. They had worn hammocks slung inside and catch basins for the freshwater rain. There was also a shared sanitary space with rough reclaimed water showers.

At that, Drake's Bay was better than most. The shore was broad, the findings were enough to survive on, the scavengers were not shot on sight as they were elsewhere.

"Y'know," April said, her head tipped back. "Speaking of grabbing big metal from 10, we could put a top cover on this thing." She measured the distance with her eyes. "Bet... yeah, hey, Doug!" She let out a yell. "Measure the opening, will ya! From the gap to the wall?"

Doug was not far away, and he lifted a hand and waved.

"We could grab that cap they had to throw onto the top of that carrier bay," April continued. "Bet it'd fit."

Jess gave her a look. "You figuring to lift that whole damn mountain over here? They gotta come reclaim it sooner or later."

"I figure it ain't sooner," April said. "Put a roof up over that, metal, so Rocket's brainwave'll work and this whole area gets way more secure." She rocked up and down on the heels of her boots, her hands in the front pocket of her thick hooded pullover. "Too much open to deal with, otherwise."

Jess looked at the loading dock area, windswept and weatherworn. Always a mess to use for unload, due to the storms, always ruining stock and making the Bay an ill-favored place to trade. "From the back caverns all over to main door?" She gestured with one hand. "Might cover it."

"Yeah." April studied the space. "Way more secure, and useful. Only place you can approach then is by sea, and that's where the launch bays are."

"And the big energy guns," Jess said. "Assuming we can get them working." The wind picked up again and blew against them, ruffling Aprils curls and tangling Jess's dark locks. "Yeah," Jess said. "It's a good idea if we can pull it off. I figured we'd just shut the back entry, but that loses us everything back here if we get hit."

The outside caverns weren't used that much, since they were outside the perimeter. Aside from temporary storage, or the games, or the market, they didn't get much action. But they could, Jess mused. It could almost be a second big hall out here.

Then they could use the caverns on either side of the ingress. "Could make workshops out here," she said. "For that damn mech."

"Yeah," April agreed. "Hey."

Jess glanced at her companion, eyebrows lifting.

"That gill thing also make you not feel the cold?" April asked, her head cocked to one side as Jess stood there in her light covering.

Jess looked down at herself, then extended one arm and poked it with a finger on her opposite hand. "Got an insulating layer under the skin. Common here." She said offhandedly. "Bay's been working in the weather and crap for so long it developed."

April stared at her with interest. "No shit?"

"I get cold," Jess answered a little defensively. "It just doesn't bother me that much. "And yeah, that's useful as hell underwater but it didn't come with it." She held up one hand and spread her fingers out wide. "Like this."

April edged closer and studied her fingers which had small, but distinct webbing between them. "That's really not part of that whole thing?" She asked in a surprised tone.

Jess shook her head and closed her hand into a ball. "Ask anyone from here," she said. "Ask my uncle Max. Most everyone has it. We swim from birth pretty much. Everyone's in or on the water."

"Doc must be pissed off he's so damn busy," April said. "He'd have a picnic with this place. Makes sense then why everyone wants your gillies." She put her hands behind her back and rocked up and down on her bootheels. "You sure no one else has em?"

Jess eyed her, one dark eyebrow hiking up. "That was supposed to be a janky ass custom job on me."

"What if it wasn't?" April asked.

The loaders paused as they approached and watched them with some curiosity as they halted to wait for the techs and Mike Arias to catch up with them. "You find the scrapping spot?" Jess asked suddenly, changing the subject as she removed the shirt from her shoulder and pulled it on over her head.

"Did." April produced a satisfied grin. "It's that place they were playing rugger in. They clear out that whole area and just whale on each other."

"Yeah? That sounds kinda fun."

"They asked if you were going to come down and mess with them." April gave her a sideways glance. "Not sure if they wanted me to say yes, or no," she admitted. "But they were good with me and Mike joining in." She crackled her knuckles. "Gonna be fun. We had to promise not to off anyone."

"Can we promise that?"

April paused and looked off into the distance, her attention going inward. Then she looked up. "You ever did?"

"At Interforce?"

"Yeah."

"Besides Bain, and Stephen and the yonks who trashed the Bay?" Jess's eyes twinkled a little. "I got Joshua, my tech who turned, and anyone who got in my way when they attacked here," she answered, in a more serious tone. "But you mean like in a scrap?" She said. "Not intentioned?"

April nodded.

"No." Jess shook her head. "I never offed anyone by accident. Like I told Jacques, always been a reason. I went to the edge plenty of times in the pit but never went over the line. You?"

April stared past her. "No, never lost it in the zone," she said quietly. "Plenty of times I wanted to. Shit I went through Canyon City with such assholes." She sighed and shook her head. "But that training works. I capped it."

"Broke my instructor's neck in final." Jess smiled briefly. "But that was on purpose too."

"And they let you graduate?"

"Conscious choice. Guy was a dick, and I didn't want to take that out on a defenseless animal."

April started slightly. "Oh, crap. That was you?" She said, in a startled tone. "You know they stopped that stupid seal kill drill afterward. We didn't get it, but we heard about it."

"That was me," Jess admitted. "I told em offing a noncom just to prove I could was lame. You wanted to know I could kill something on command? Okay. I did. Graduate my ass." She put her hands behind her back and clasped them as she spotted the approaching techs. "Commandant brought an armed backup to the point with him."

"Whoa," April finally said. "I ain't never heard of that happening."

Jess smiled briefly. "It does happen. Most cadets don't know, but I did," she said. "Probably was me telling the brass he had brains for doing it that let him pass me in."

April looked at her for a long moment. "You really are

outside the box," she said, in an approving tone. "I like that."

Jess chuckled. "Yeah. So sure, I'll come play. With you two if no one else'll mix it up with me." She pulled a comms set out of her pocket and slid it over her ear. "Tac tac, Dev."

"Dev here." Dev's warm, burring voice answered and Jess half turned to listen, as Mike Arias and the techs arrived. "I have completed setting up our location. I think you will be pleased," Dev continued. "Everything is operational."

"Meet us in the mess and tell me about it," Jess said. "We're done out here, but April came up with something else now to go swipe and lift."

"I see."

"You might have to go steal one of those shuttles for this one," Jess continued.

"Oh," Dev responded. "Interesting."

"Maybe two."

"Suboptimal," Dev said. "I cannot pilot two of those vehicles at once, Jess. And it would be difficult to deliver that skillset to others, except possibly to Doctor Dan."

"I'm sure you'll work it out. See ya in a few minutes." Jess closed the channel and took one last look around. "Let's go." She turned and led the way back to the ramp up to the back entrance.

"Rocket really gonna steal another shuttle?" Doug asked April. "Boy we're zooming right on down the pirate path huh?"

"Shut up."

****

The mess hall was busy by the time they arrived, but the table along the far end had space for them, and they made their way over to it. Kurok was there, with Cathy and Security Mike and they all made casual small talk as they plowed through lunch.

It was strange, Dev thought, at how at home it felt to be there already. So completely different than the base, this huge room that could hold thousands of people all sitting together in noisy conversation. Everyone in the roughhewn Bay clothing or well-worn pullovers.

"Dev's going to write a routine to keep the carriers in sync when we lift that panel," Doug said. "Cause otherwise the most dangerous thing in the skies is going to be us trying to move that honking ass thing all the way here independently."

"Met's good for tomorrow," April noted. "If we leave early

and get back early. Front's due through round night meal."

Chester looked up from his plate. "Hey, when's Brent coming out of med? He going with us? Maybe Dev can unlock his bus, and it'll give us four," he said. "He can watch our backs while we hoist."

"Not sure," Jess said, after a pause. "He was still groggy this morning. Not sure he should be driving a bus by tomorrow."

"Still, it's an excellent idea," Kurok said in his mild tone. "Those are turning out to be quite useful vehicles." He glanced up at them. "If Dev can break the codes for a few more, I suspect we can get someone who can pilot them."

April eyed him. "Like you," she said. "I saw you doing zoomies with that light flit the other day."

Kurok chuckled. "Yes, certainly I can drive a Bantam, but likely a few of the more senior KayTee's from the base could as well, as long as they only had to get them from point A to point B," he said. "They were programmed to fly the cargo vessels and recon. The Bantam is not that different in basic operations."

"Screw it, we should take em all," Doug said. "Interforce doesn't want the old things anyway. They mothballed em, or they'd have let us fly em out west when they left."

Dev nodded in agreement. "That's true," she said. "There was no intent to retrieve these vehicles. I saw the quiescence programming for them. It was terminal." She looked up at the silence and found everyone looking at her. "I reversed it," she added, feeling as if there was some further explanation expected.

"Obviously," Kurok said. "Can you adjust the rest of the carriers there, Dev? How much time should it take?"

Dev chewed her mouthful of seaweed thoughtfully and then swallowed. "I think it would take about three hours," she said. "If everything is optimal."

"Could get that done while we're cutting steel," Jess said. "Assuming the place isn't crawling with scavengers," she added. "We'll take a bunch of your fly boys and grab as many as we can. We may not get another chance."

April swirled her grog around in her mouth with a thoughtful expression. "Unless we just take possession of the whole place," she said. "I really don't think they're coming back."

A small silence fell. "Hold on," Kurok said. "We go from we're grabbing some scrap metal to owning the base?"

April shrugged. "Why not? They left em. There's some good mech we could recover there."

"Dude." Doug looked sideways at her. "Better we make it

impossible for someone else not to be able to take them over huh? It takes like, what, two hundred people to run that place?"

Jess nodded. "Better idea. We got a lot on our plate," she said. "You can shut down the grid again, can't you? I think Dev emptying the entire supply of pneumatic fluid probably got us halfway there. None of the heavy mech'll work."

"Oh yeah," April said. "Forgot about that. Probably better to get this place planked up first. But shutting everyone else out until we're ready's ace." She paused in thought. "North never did get going again but let's leave North Pole alone. I can do without going back there. Anyone who wants that thing be my guest."

It was a long statement for April, and there was a bit of quiet as everyone absorbed it.

"No argument there," Doug said after it ended. "Never been that cold in my entire life before."

"Brr," Dev said, under her breath. "That was suboptimal."

"Yeah," Jess said. "No shielding and crap for systems. Not worth recovering. No idea why they wanted to try that after we got slammed there. "Dev had to jump start the whole thing with our bus."

Dev took a breath as if to protest, then paused. "That's actually true," she admitted. "The amount of degradation was absolutely non optimal."

"And we were skunked," Doug said. "Sold out."

"Skunked," Jess agreed. "And there's still some game in play. So, we gotta cover our backs."

"True that," Mike Arias said. "True, true that." He paused thoughtfully, "But y'know..."

"Please shut up," April growled.

"Now I wonder," Kurok mused, tapping his fork on his lower lip. "I wonder if it wasn't all just one long game." He looked up, to find the table all focused on him. "I was just thinking. We've seen so much senseless, stupid things going on. I think either they all might be pieces in the puzzle..."

"Or?" Jess asked.

"Or a good percentage of the planet is far more stupid than I thought possible," Kurok concluded, going back to his plate.

"Or both," Doug suggested.

"Or both." Kurok looked up again and winked at them. "Not sure what the odds are either way on that one."

****

Jess walked up the steps to her new abode and put her hand on the access pad. The door slid aside with no complaints. She walked inside, pausing to stand and absorb the environment. People had been there. She detected a scent, though it was dispersed by the movement of air from the external opening on the far side of the space.

That brought the scent of the sea, and the rich pungency of wet rocks, a clean crispness that Jess found she liked. Just the feel of the outside refreshing the space pleased her, though she wasn't entirely sure why.

Nothing smelled dangerous of the other presence she detected. She knew one of them was Dev, an indefinable difference she just recognized, and the rest were tinged with the cloth and salt scent of the working togs of the Bay.

Expected. The smell of plastics off gassing, expressed into air that hadn't had that in a long time, also expected from Dev's earlier report. All clear. Jess determined the space safe, and felt her body relax.

Dev could have told her that in an instant, with her scanner, but Jess had always used her own senses as a counterpoint, her hearing and sense of smell tuned and acute, and if they jibed then it meant being doubly safe.

She continued across the large open space, then turned down the hallway, pausing to glance inside the food prep area, noting the resupply of it and the neatly stacked cups. Everything was precisely aligned. It was easy for Jess to imagine their two assigned bios studiously getting things just so because that's what they did.

Just like Dev, in her own, stunningly advanced way. Not just to do something, but to do something with the best possible result. Jess thought about that a moment, standing there with her hand on the edge of the opening into the space. What was it Mike had called them? Useful.

She snorted a little under her breath. They could never have endured bios at the Bay before. There had been no slots or cred for that, for what anyone here would view as stupid coin spend, when there were bodies vying for berths all the time.

And she herself had viewed these created people, given the history of the Bay itself, with deep skepticism. Jelly Bag brains, she'd always thought, until she'd met Dev. A faint smile appeared on Jess's face. Until she'd met Dev, and seen in that very first mission, what her potential was.

Breathtakingly skilled. As capable in her realm as Jess acknowledged her own self to be in hers. And so, she'd brought

Dev to the Bay, pushing those boundaries because she was smart enough to know a good thing when she encountered it, preconceptions be damned.

So, the first bio the Bay had been exposed to close up had been the best of the best of them, in a position that they were ingrained by tradition to respect.

And then the Bay lost a thousand people in a pointless stupid fight. Slots had emptied. Knowledge had disappeared, skill sets had been bled out on the big hall floor. In the middle of all that, a couple hundred polite, skilled, eager to please people showed up, along with their creator, and the pragmatism of the Bay had pivoted because...

Well, because they hadn't had time to push back, until they could see the benefit. Like she had. Now the addition of a hundred more bios, with mechanical and military skill sets were quickly accepted, the Bay still short on slots in deep, urgent need of working bodies who could fill berths and already knew what to do with even out of date machines of war.

Fucking useful. Jess pushed away from the door and went into the large round space between it and the front hallway. The warming panel reacted to her presence and let out a soft, pleasant glow.

The furniture had been delivered and was now scattered around the space. Battered and somewhat grungy but at least they had something to sit on. Jess turned around in a circle, then walked along the front corridor. She paused at the small room that once had been hers.

She saw the desk inside and her brows lifted. She recalled Dev's comment about the access as she reviewed the neatly positioned stone surface. In here? She saw the access station, cables curled in a gentle spiral to the panel on the wall.

In here? The surface fit, and after a moment she pulled a stool from against the wall over, sat behind it, and found it a good height to accommodate her long legs.

She put her hands on the surface and looked out at the ruffled waters of the Bay, and the curve of the protective walls in the distance.

Why not in here? Dev must have guided the loaders to bring the slab into the place she knew Jess was familiar with, right? Dev would do that.

Jess nodded to herself. She could imagine Dev working through that situation and making what would seem to her to be a logical decision. The view was good, the slab fit, so why not? Jess grinned briefly and leaned on her elbows to gaze out the plas.

Busy in the Bay today. She saw a dozen small boats pulling in shallow water shellfish, and there were two limpet scrapers at work along the wall, likely bringing up urchins or maybe some sea cukes.

Along the far wall were the mussel and oyster barges, lashed to the rocks, tanks full. The long curve of the Bay nearest her window had the shallow sand flats where the clams burrowed and were picked by hand, by divers.

All would go into the live tanks in the lower caverns and be traded off to boats for deep water catch, or provisions from elsewhere. Sometimes the Bay catch would be more than the tanks could hold, and the Bay would be treated to those favorites. Just thinking about that made Jess lick her lips.

The sound of the boats drifted in from the gap to the left of the hallway and she smiled suddenly. Now that they had other things to trade, maybe the Bay catch would end up in the mess more frequently. No one would argue with that result.

Certainly, she wouldn't. The Bay clams were the only crop they kept local. They were the base of the clam stew that was not only a favorite at home but taken out on boats in frozen blocks that let the captains trade for provision anywhere they stopped on the way to delivering their deep water catch to the processor.

Jess idly watched the nearest small boat bring up its divers, the figures pulling off their breathing apparatus as they came up onto the deck and hoisted their catch bags after them. She imagined, for a moment, what it would have been like for her to have ended up in that kind of slot.

She would have been good at it. She flexed one hand and rubbed her thumb along the webbing she'd displayed for April. Would she have gone through the hassle of doing the gas exchange or just use the breather?

Jess could see the advantage. Breathers were a pain. She remembered as a young child hunting shells along that curved shoreline, happily breathing water after she'd found out she could. So okay, yeah, maybe she got what April said, about people wanting it.

But she'd been told, more than once, that it was something crazy her mother had arranged for, so no one else should.

It wasn't weird, it was just fucking useful. There was an advantage to it, and the Bay was always quick to see an advantage when there was one. Gills. Bios. Random genetic scientists. Scrap from Interforce. All fucking useful.

With a faint shake of her head, she turned her attention to

the access console and put her hand on the bio pad. It lit immediately and the screen came on. There was a brief startup, then the main command set, with a small icon on the top corner.

Jess looked curiously at it, then laughed she realized it was a tiny wire map raccoon face. Dev's sign, apparently, that she'd run the checks and all was secure. "Aww, Devvie. That's so damn cute."

There were messages for her, which was a surprise of a different kind. She drew a finger on the access pad and touched the blinking icon for them, her dark brows edging up again as a list of black lines appeared on the screen. "Eh?"

She'd always checked what was in comms at base because they would send out notifies from ops for all kinds of things you were expected to know about. Drills and alarms, and schedules when sections would be closed, who had watch… but she'd never gotten many notes that were personally for her.

Occasionally, an invite to dinner, usually from Jason or Elaine, or something from Med.

But nothing much personal, or casual because she hadn't had that relationship with anyone there. Anything casual was usually exchanged in person, over a cup or lunch in the ops mess.

Now there was a long list of messages direct to her. She started to poke through them and found they were mostly words of welcome. Just casual words, a reminder here and there from someone who went to station with them, a note from Petar telling her to stop by the kitchen and let him know what he could add to rotation for her.

It was a strange feeling and Jess sat there for quite some time just working through them, trying to decide if the feeling was good, or bad, or just…

Different.

A note from Uncle Max, about upgrades for his boat.

A list of pending trades and incoming stores.

Scattered in there were the expected notes from ops, mech and tech, confirmation of accesses. Lists of what would be offered in the mess for the week.

It was strange, and not. Like what she was used to and very different at the same time because so many of the messages were personal.

She looked at one from Dustin and read it three or four times before she figured out what the hell he was talking about. Then she paused and reread his addressing her as head of house.

Head of House? Capital letters. Was she that? Jess frowned. Wouldn't it be Max, who was the eldest of the remaining immediate family, being Justin's brother? Or had he abandoned that responsibility when he took on the ship's captaincy instead?

If he was smart, he had. Jess studied the screen. Justin was Head of House when he was alive, she recalled vaguely. Some administrative thing he hadn't talked much about. What the hell was she supposed to do if she was?

What the hell was the Drake supposed to do on the daily? Jess wondered if Dev could find her some kind of manual in the regs, some checklist of crap she had to pay attention to, something she never had to deal with before.

Being an agent, she knew what she had to do. She'd been trained extensively for it. This?

A little disconcerted, Jess selected Dustin's note and answered it. Fastest way to find out what was expected was to find out, wasn't it?

She heard the outer door start to open and instinct brought her up and heading that way without any thought, her hand dropped to her hip where no weapon rested.

The door slid all the way open as she cleared the corridor and saw it was Dev, her arms full of cloth. "Ah, it's you," Jess said and relaxed. "Whatcha got there?"

"Hello," Dev responded. "I was able to obtain some additional supplies from the storage level." She went past Jess into the hall beyond and into the small room. "Some additional work garments, and items to wear at night."

Jess trailed her into the storage area and watched her as she sorted out her burdens. "Yeah, it's colder in here than it was back at base," she said. "Forgot about that."

Dev glanced over her shoulder. "It is," she said, "but I like it. It smells like the sea in here and I find that pleasant."

"Me too." Jess picked up a long-sleeved garment in the faded green blue typical of the Bay. It was worn, but was whole, and it smelled of the cleaning soap everything else did. "They have a lot of this stuff up there?" Jess asked.

"They do," Dev said. "I was told it was because of all the people who got made dead in the fight. The sets told me that's how they got most of their clothing when they arrived as well."

Jess nodded. "I thought I'd have to have some stuff custom done, because I'm such a gargoyle, but here I'm..." She paused. "Not really that different," she said thoughtfully. "More people my size."

"Yes. I saw a lot of garments that would fit you. Would you

like me to return there and pick some out?" Dev held up a warmly lined vest, with pockets on the front. "I especially liked this." She slipped it on and fastened it. "Excellent for working in."

It came to her thighs and fit well. It was a faded teal color with a strong knit. Jess studied it. "That's really cute," she said. "And it leaves your arms free."

"Yes."

Jess glanced around the storage room and then back at her. "Would you pick some stuff for me? You got a knack for it," she asked. "I usually get stuff that doesn't match. Used to having a choice of black and black."

Dev looked pleased. "Of course," she said. "I thought I should get some things because it seems we won't get a chance to shop immediately. It would be excellent to do that for you as well."

"While we're taking over half the planet? Yeah." Jess relaxed into a smile. "Hey, want to go sit in our big empty room and have a cup of grog? Then you can tell me what I should do with all the stupid mail I have in my... oh yeah, did you set up that desk?"

"Yes, sure... yes." Dev answered in sequence. "Is it all right? I thought that room might be appropriate, and the view is nice."

Jess grinned. "It's perfect. Thanks, Dev." She put her arms around Dev pulled her in for a hug. "You really are a rockstar."

Dev knew a moment of utter contentment. She returned the hug, already looking forward to a return visit to the cloth storage to see what nice things she could find that would please Jess, confident now that they would.

****

Jess ducked under the engine pod of their carrier and walked around the craft in what she knew was a pointless inspection she nevertheless did anyway. The craft was meticulously prepared, every inch of it rubbed clean of any char by its mech crew, its systems prepped by Dev for tomorrow's excursion.

She knew that, but like April and Mike a short while before, she also knew this walk of the deck was expected and so she did it. She studied the side of the hulking machine, noting the Interforce designation had been sanded off the skin.

Her name and Dev's hadn't. There it was, Drake, J and

underneath, just Dev, in block letters. She regarded that for a minute. Someone had taken the time to reink the names, so they stood out clean and sharp against the carrier's metal skin.

"Yo, cuz."

Jess turned, to find Dustin climbing onto the pad. "Yo," she returned the Bay greeting. "Sup?"

"You gonna name it?" Dustin asked. "We can put the stencil on, ya?"

"Why the hell would I name it?"

Dustin shrugged. "Gotta call it something, yah? For the callsign, for ops?"

Oh. Jess pondered that. "Lemme ask Dev," she finally said. "It's really her bus." She regarded her cousin. "You get my note?"

Dustin looked surprised and stood all the way up. He looked around as though it might be floating in midair somewhere. "Crap, no," he said. "Wasn't near a rig. Been gettin stuff done in here." He looked a little embarrassed. "Just a Q, yo?"

Jess nodded. "You got a co hab in mind?" She put her hands into the middle pocket of her Bay pullover, a relaxed posture to signal she wasn't pissed off.

"Maybe." Dustin hunched his shoulders a little. "Can't tell if I can't ask, can't ask if I don't get a bunko, yo?"

"You just got a slot," Jess said. "You got mech. You any good?"

Dustin looked guardedly at her. "I ain't broke nothing recent."

No, Dustin probably wasn't much good. He was a simple mind, a good fit for the important but unskilled tasks around the mech, taking care of things, keeping things up. "You paint that?" Jess asked, indicating the letters with a shrug of her shoulder.

He grinned. "Yo."

The letters were, as she'd noted, crisp and precise, so there was some attention to detail. "You take good care of these old crates; I'll see what I can do."

Dustin's face lit up. "These? He indicated the carriers. "They're awesome! First time I saw one up close I was whacked!"

Jess eyed him wryly. "I remember. Devvie gave you a tour."

He nodded solemnly. "Take good care of em, cuz. I swear. "Specially this one." He patted their carrier. "Lemme know what to call it, I'll paint it on."

"Okay," Jess said. "Make sure Dev's got what she needs too, yah? Maybe she'll teach ya some stuff."

Dustin's eyes widened. "Ok! You goin down to the mixup, cuz?" He asked. "Everybody's lookin for ya."

Jess nodded. "Soon as I finish here. Lookin forward to it." She leaned over and touched the hatch and felt it slide aside. "So let me finish up."

He nodded, then backed up and hopped off the pad, jogging quickly out of sight toward the back of the cavern.

Jess ducked inside the carrier and chuckled to herself as she dropped into her seat and rotated it around to inspect the spool of steel wire that was now installed along the back wall, extending down thorough the superstructure to an egress hook below the deck.

On top of the spool a row of basic, simple metal seats had been affixed and the same on the side where the drop rig had been to provide enough space for passengers. The seats were plain and hard, but they had webbing restraints over them. On the floor, there were now tie downs for any cargo they had to carry. Totally unneeded in the craft before.

Jess looked around, satisfied that all was well, and they were prepared for their raid in the early morning. She looked overhead at her own controls, then reached up to the triggers and slid her hand into the custom fitted glove.

The carrier recognized her presence and activated. Her boards and the targeting systems were live, though there was no power since the engines were inactive. "Damn." Jess moved the triggers with a wiggle of her fingers and watched them respond. "Wouldja look at that."

Dev had told her, matter-of-factly, that she'd disabled the kill switch on the weapons comp, but hearing it and seeing systems respond, that she knew damn well shouldn't, almost took her breath away.

Stunning. And Dev did it on her own, calculating they might need it. "Maybe we should call this thing Rockstar," she mused and wiggled her fingers again. "Cause damn she is."

Jess heard steps nearby and yanked her hand out of the glove. She started to come to her feet when she looked through the hatch and saw one of the KayTee's approach. He had on an Interforce maintenance jumper, with a hoodie over it.

"Hello." He paused at the hatchway. "We saw the activity and came to observe."

"Yeah, just me," Jess said, and leaned back in her seat. "Keko right?"

"Yes," Keko said. "We considered it was likely you, Agent Jess. I remember you always check your vehicle prior to egress." He straightened a little. "I am to go with you tomorrow, to transport additional vehicles."

"Excited?" Jess folded her hands over her stomach. "To fly one of these things?"

Keko took a step closer and leaned against the hatch opening. "Yes, I am," he said. "We were never permitted to fly Bantams. Doctor Dan worked up a basic sim for us and we just finished it. It's a complex craft, but I think we can manage."

"He's the one to teach ya," Jess said. "Let's hope we get in and out with no problem and give ya a chance to fly."

Keko nodded. "Yes, sorry to bother you, Agent Jess. I will inform flight operations all is well here." He gave her a little wave, then turned and made his way off the platform and disappeared back into the shadows of the landing cavern.

Jess sat there quietly considering for a few minutes. Then she stood up and left the carrier and headed off herself.

Chapter Eleven

"This is wild." April stood to one side and watched the melee going on.

"It's wild," Mike Arias agreed. "But I like it. Can't wait to get into the mix." He was dressed in a sleeveless brown shirt and his arms were exposed, his service burns visible on his shoulder. "We next?"

"We're next." April stretched and shook her arms out. "These guys are really bruisers."

There was a large crowd gathered in the sand covered cavern. In the tiers around the rugger area were maybe two hundred people, a mixture of men and women, of all ages, all dressed in shirts and leggings, with work boots, some with gloves.

"They are," Mike said.

The Bay residents were by and large built on the same framework. They were all tall and long limbed, with broad shoulders and a strong, visible bone structure. Some were more lightly built, some were brawnier, but they all looked like they could handle themselves in a fight.

The fights were no rules, no holds barred. It was literally a brawl, all hand to hand, no weapons in evidence. Boxing, grappling, wrestling, kicking. April let out a small laugh. "Ain't seen anything like this since I left home." She sounded a touch wistful.

"Ain't seen anything like this." Mike hopped up and down a few times and tapped April on the shoulder. "C'mon they're changing groups." They started toward the center of the open space, which was now being cleared by the last group of fighters.

April noted the high spirits, despite the bruises and limps. She smiled in a feral sort of way as they joined the next group gathering, aware of rising energy around her.

"Reg ass kickers are here," one of the older men said and indicated them. "See if they hold up."

"Lookin forward to it," April shot back at him.

"Careful we don't trip over ya," the man said with a grin. He held one hand down to show her height.

"Just the right level to bite your nuts off," April responded with an equal grin. "C'mon, buddy. Put your cred where your mouth is."

A roar of appreciative laughter rose, and they started to

close in, waiting for the signal to start fighting.

Mike Arias sighed happily. "This is gonna be fun," he said. "Not like the damn assholes at Base." He let out a yell, and brought his hands up, rocking back and forth from foot to foot.

Then the signal came, a whistle from the teeth of Security Mike, and it was on.

With a lunge they all came together. A moment later there were a dozen fights going on, as opponents clashed and separated and then split out to battle. April was pitted against a man taller than her, with long, muscular arms. She barely evaded him as she slid past and got a leg tangled in his, knocking him off- balance.

Then they grappled, and she relied on her lower center of gravity to make him work for his holds. She kept herself in motion, understanding if he got those paws on her she would probably get tossed on her ass.

Rockin chaos. April dove gleefully back into it. Luckily it was a sand floor, and she was glad she had long sleeves and pants on as she skidded on her knees twisting out of the way and just barely evaded someone else's head kick.

She went from knees to her feet in a crouch then dove between her opponent's legs, her size alone her advantage as he awkwardly tried to reach down and grab her. She got a hold on him as she bounced up onto his back.

"Raagh!" He reached back but was caught in a headlock. "Ooof!'
April chuckled joyfully. Rockin chaos.

****

Jess exited the back door to the storing area and went out into the chill damp wind and the halon lit open space between the main cliff and the storage cavern promontory across from it.

She stuck her hands into the overshirt's middle pocket and headed for the opening she could see in the side of the rock, a pair of lights mounted over it spilling a reasonable guideline out across the rough ground.

She stepped over the runoff channel dug to let rain drain and her body begin to perk up, as she looked forward to the scrapping she knew was on the immediate horizon. April and Mike were already there, and she increased her pace, then broke into an easy lope to warm up.

She was genuinely looking forward to the mixup. She had that slightly antsy feeling she'd get when it had been too long between scrapping and she wanted it, wanted to feel the tickle down her spine and the energy of the fight.

It excited her because it would be so different from either the pit at the base or a real trip into the zone in the field. Going up against this random gang of the Bay, who wanted to become... security? Jess thought about that. Become soldiers? Fighters?

Become what she was? That they couldn't do, and she was pretty sure they didn't really want to, but she was also pretty sure she had no real idea what to do with them either. They saw a path, she figured, to a dream of a better slot, a better allotment. She had no argument with that.

Well, maybe big Mike had something in his head to use them, and at least in the meantime, there'd be the scrap.

The entrance was open, and she slowed up as she crossed it. She moved quickly across the front section that had held the market to the rear area where she heard yells and the sounds of fighting.

The market section was dark, the lights overhead turned off and the sorting tables they used to sort out supplies folded against the walls out of the way. Jess's boots scuffed lightly against the sand strewn floor. Her pulse picked up as she climbed up the short incline to the rugger pitch, where she could now see a knot of battling figures.

A ring of spectators was on the tiered rocks on either side, watching the fight with enjoyment.

Jess vaulted up onto the top level and found a spot to watch, enough in the shadows so she was not immediately recognized.

It was a rumble. Jess had to grin. A dozen people all whaling on each other, including April and Mike, fists and knees flying everywhere as pairs went down in wrestling holds while others dodged powerful punches and kicks.

Nearby, several Bay residents, who had been in a prior fight, stood waiting their turn again, some holding cold packs against knots in heads and bruises.

She looked around, glad to see the numbers. Then she turned her attention to the fight and watched April get an arm around the leg of her opponent, then haul backwards surprising the hell of him with her strength as he ended up ass over head on the ground.

A yell went up at that, and then Mike whistled. The opponents broke apart, laughing and talking smack, one of them grabbing his opponent by the head and rubbing his knuckles into his hair.

Then Security Mike spotted her. "Drake!" He lifted one long, muscular arm and gestured her over.

Jess walked down the tiers, past the watchers, feeling the attention focus on her as she arrived at the sand level. She crossed over to where Mike stood. "That'd be me." She turned to take in the watchers, then looked back at him. "We ready for some fun?"

Mike studied her. "You sure ya wanna mix it up?"

"Yeah." Jess turned and walked out onto the sand. She stripped off her overshirt and tossed it aside onto one of the levels as she turned and faced him, hands lifted, fingers curled into a come-ahead gesture. "Let's rumble."

Still in her tank, she spread her arms out, hopping lightly up and down on the sand.

Mike grinned. "How many?" He gestured around the rugger pitch.

"How many ya got?" Jess grinned at him. "Loser buys the first tank of beer."

April chortled softly under her breath, while Mike Arias wiped the blood from a hit to his nose. "This is going to be a mess," April said. "Too many of those damn ogres for even her to handle."

"She doesn't care," Mike said. "She wins, she wins, she loses, against that many, she still wins. Good plan."

"They want it," April said, looking quickly around, as the floor began to fill with half eager, half scared people. "You can smell it."

Jess stood in the center of the pitch waiting, the overhead halons caught brief hints of the burned color going down the length of one arm, and part of the other. She reached up and pulled her hair back into a knot as she waited for them to gather in a rough circle around her.

A cold wind blew in from the open doors and fluttered the light tank top against her body. She took a breath in and released it. Then she spread her arms out a little wider. "Well?" She stared around at all of them. "C'mon? There's beer waiting!"

That broke the tension and, with a shake of his head, and a laugh, Security Mike whistled, and it was on.

And it was on. April and Mike went over to where Security Mike stood, as the crowd closed into a chaotic scrum of circling figures, trying to get an angle on Jess, who was easily moving through them. She took on one, or two, and dodged two or three more, ducking and swerving with fluid grace.

"You holding out?" Security Mike asked.

"We've been in the pit with her," April said. "It's more fun to watch."

"Truth," Arias agreed. "Just watch."

He did. "She can move," Security Mike said, after a minute of it. "F'n crazy."

"You can't get a hand on her," Mike Arias said as he watched Jess dive for the ground, hitting it with both hands and pushing herself off in a different direction. She twisted in mid- air and then kicked out with both feet to take out two big men, who were just not fast enough to follow her motion.

Two more jumped on top of her, and then with a roar the rest followed, scrambling as the pile surged and shifted. Then Jess rolled out from under it and got to her feet. She reached out and slapped the topmost fighter on the behind.

"Too many of us!" One of the longshoremen yelled. "Back off, you all, back off, let them get in there!'

A group of six got to their feet and came at her, big and long limbed, and powerful the way Jess was powerful, but they just couldn't match her speed. Nothing could, it was fluid and unceasing motion that came in, targeted, hit, then moved past leaving doubled over bodies and gasping behind her.

"How the fuck does she do that?" Security Mike asked. "That how they train ya?"

"They train us," April said. "But you can't train what she does."

"No." Mike Arias shook his head, his brawny arms folded over his chest. "It's like fighting the ocean. Waves just come over you and knock you on your ass," he said. "None of the other agents wanted to be in the pit with her. They made out like it was the crazy, you know?" He glanced at Security Mike. "Like, Drake, you know? They got the crazy of the crazy and it was this big risk and stuff."

Big Mike snorted under his breath.

Arias smiled without much humor. "Wasn't. They just didn't want to look bad."

"Huh." Security Mike eyed him thoughtfully. "You did though."

"We did," April said. "We're newbies. No rep. Didn't matter, and sucks to be them cause you learn shit from someone who can do that." She jerked her chin in Jess's direction. "Learned moves from her I never even saw in school."

"That one, there." Mike Arias pointed. "See the way she

blocked that kick? No way she could have seen it."

Jess now bounced all over like a ball, leapfrogging over people and past hands that reached out to grab her. Then she body slammed into them in a reverse move that had so much power behind it she picked them up and threw them backwards.

It was like she had eyes in the back of her head. She evaded grabs and blows and ducked punches she couldn't possibly have seen.

She flipped in midair and came down on her feet. The breeze in the cavern at her back chilled her skin from the sweat. She looked around at the group, who'd gone still, just watching her. "More?" She asked, hopefully.

"Oh yeah," the tall man who'd challenged April said. "I gotta get you on the ground now, c'mon." He shifted into a stance. "All them jumps and tricks… let me get my hands on ya and none of that squiggling round."

He lunged for her with both hands and Jess stood still and let him come. She caught his hands in midair, bracing herself and stopping him cold in his forward motion.

His feet dropped to the ground, and he grunted in surprise, his hands held by hers. Jess stood there as he shoved against her, her body not budging an inch despite the fact he out- weighed her by at least half. He twisted and tried to pull his hands free, but her fingers clamped down and tightened and he struggled in vain.

Jess smiled.

Then she abruptly released him and ducked under his arms. She leaped forward, getting her shoulder into his gut and an arm between his legs. She then threw him up onto her shoulders and stood, lifting his weight.

"Shiiiiit!" He let out a squawk.

Jess pondered pressing him over her head, then just turned and threw him off, onto his back on the ground, a body length from her, with an offhand shrug. He fell hard, and his head slammed against the sand, sending a spurt of it across the ground.

"That's fucking sweet," Security Mike commented mildly to April.

"He your top guy?" April had her arms folded. "Or thinks he is?"

"Thinks he is."

April chuckled.

Jess waited to see if the guy was going to come at her again, but his fall had stunned him, and he was blinking up at her. She stepped forward and extended a hand to him. "Sorry about that."

He reached up and gripped her hand and was hauled up to his feet in a smooth motion, then released as Jess stepped back out of range and came to a balanced stance, knees slightly bent, eyes moved steadily in either direction.

April and Mike Arias moved out onto the floor and came to a halt just behind her, standing quietly.

Just in case it got weird.

The man wiped his hands on his trousers. "That something you can teach, Drake?" He eyed her, surprisingly unresentful. "How to fight like that?"

She studied him, then turned and regarded the lot of them, all intent eyes and shifting stances, less afraid than intrigued by her display. The mix it up was a joy to them, she realized. There was a hunger there, an interest and desire that caught her by surprise.

"Maybe," she finally said. "Some of it just comes naturally." She looked thoughtfully at them, aware suddenly of being among a lot of people who were more like her than not. The height, the broad frames, that focused stare she recognized from the mirror.

It was a strange feeling, a culmination of the intense, sometimes discordant echo she had here of a past that might have been yet never was. She looked around and saw a reflection of the glee she felt herself, and it struck her. The obvious realization that this was her kin.

Blood of her blood, to many varying degrees. She wasn't the outsider here, not by a long shot. Just one of many, in this collection of the crazy.

Her house, matter of fact. A thought occurred to her, and she motioned her cousin over. "Dustin, c'mere. Lemme try something."

He happily came forward, one of the youngers there, but one she knew might prove out the thought she'd just had, because of all the people there, he was blood closest to her.

"Yo, cuz," he greeted her. "Slick moves, ya?"

Jess nodded. "Turn around," she said, and he did. "Close your eyes."

"You going to kick my ass?" He asked, in a somewhat dismayed tone. "I didn't do nothing yet, didn't even get a chance at ya,"

"Only if you don't do what I ask," Jess said. "Close your eyes and keep em closed."

Dustin closed his eyes. "Okay."

There was a clear space behind him. Jess silently moved to the side, consciously making no sound as she slid across the opening, then paused. She took a step forward, crossing that certain point, and felt her senses recognize it.

That faint sense of constriction, a push against her senses, this impending nearness of another living thing.

Dustin flinched and ducked his head and hunched his shoulders in pure physical automatic reaction, his hands coming up, fingers spread.

I'll be damned. Jess stopped still, the words echoed inside her mind. "Why did you do that?" She asked, in a mild tone. "Why'd you move?"

His shoulders relaxed, and he tilted his head in thought. "Dunno," he said, after an awkward pause. "Felt like I…" He paused. "Felt ya comin over. Thought you were gonna whack me?"

Jess took a step backwards, just that bit of a distance, her skin relaxing. "Don't turn around. You felt me come closer. Now I'm not."

Dustin was silent, his eyes closed, head half tilted to one side, his hands at his sides.

Jess took a silent step forward, her senses prickling. And at that moment, saw his hands curl in reaction and lift, palms forward. "You feel it."

He turned his head around and looked over his shoulder at her, eyes wide. "Yo," he said on a released breath. "I do!"

"Huh." Jess exhaled. "Interesting," she said. "That's the comes natural part." She turned to look at the watching group. "I have a space around me. I just know when something's in it. The training part's how to know what to do about it."

"Huh." Security Mike grunted, and almost absently, lifted his hand and touched the back of his neck.

Dustin turned all the way around and faced her with an amazed expression. "Whoa." He said. "For real?" He said. "That was real, cuz?"

Jess relaxed a little. "Yeah," she said. "Maybe it comes from being from here."

The crowd now all looked around at each other in somewhat bewildered silence. "Like the crazy?" One of the longshoremen asked, hesitantly. "That kinda thing?"

Jess eyed him. "We call it the crazy," she admitted. "But it's not crazy. It's just a thing."

"Drake." One of the reg ops stood there, covered in sand

burns. "I was standing ops when you opened the vault up, yeah? What you did to that guy, that was crazy."

She shook her head. "No, it was goal oriented. My goal was to make sure he couldn't use that console to blow up my partner." Her eyes narrowed a bit. "It looks crazy, because we... I don't let anything stop me from achieving my goal."

"Huh." Security Mike had his hands on his hips. "You teach us all with this thing?"

"Maybe." Jess frowned thoughtfully. "With that you can be really kickass," she said. "And it scares the crap out of your targets."

She had everyone's attention now and the obvious idea was forming in her head. "So maybe that's what security's going to be here. A big ass bunch of ass kickers, who know what to do, when to do it, and who to do it to. "

"Nice," April said, with a nod.

They clustered closer in to listen, in a sudden presence of salt-tinged sweat and sand burn, studying her and the two younger agents on either side, evaluating them with that subconscious energy so much a part of the Bay.

Edgy and real, as natural for them, as it was for her, and Jess felt amazingly dense for not having realized it before.

"You in?" Jess asked, after a moment of silence. "Give it a shot?"

The silence lasted again for another moment, then suddenly, loudly, "HAI!" came back at her so forcefully it made Jess's skin react in galvanic response and her body tensed just long enough for her to recognize the sound and relax.

She nodded. Maybe she could teach a little of it. Maybe here. Maybe to these slightly mad eyed hulksters, who to some degree shared something with her. Something they'd been born with.

Something they'd probably cursed.

"Wild," Mike Arias whispered to April, whose gaze had gone inward, and who was staring past the edge of the crowd. "Right?"

April exhaled, and suddenly, grinned. "Wild," she said. "But totally, totally ace." She folded her arms over her chest. "Totally ace."

****

Dev bopped her way through the big main hall, and moved across to the mess hall, which at this late hour was quiet, only a few people passing in and out of the big metal doors.

She could, she knew, have asked one of their two assigned attendants to run an errand for her, but they'd gone to their quarters after the night meal, and she saw no reason to disturb them.

Jess was over at the storage cavern doing some fighting activities. Dev thought she might want a snack after she finished her exercise since she usually did, so she wanted to have that prepared and to take some things for their kits in the carrier.

She'd spent some good amount of time in the storage caverns, and there were many things now in their quarters she hoped Jess would find appropriate.

Some clothes, as she'd promised, but she also combed through the containers of household items and brought back two boxes full of things they could use along with six loads of various objects to be used as makeshift furniture.

She found the process enjoyable. The storage cavern material was very random, but the challenge of looking at it and constructing uses for the objects was appealing and she thought it had been mostly successful.

She'd also finished putting away her parts and gotten the few personal things she'd brought from the base put in place in her workspace, all ready for her to start modding when they got back from their mission the following day.

She considered that it had been a good day. It felt like excellent progress had been made.

Dev entered the mess and angled across the huge room toward the rear. In front of the doors to the kitchen was a dispensing counter, with snacks available for the overnight watch, and a pot full of soup that was gently steaming.

Jess might like some of that, she decided. She pushed open the door of the mess kitchen and peered inside. She spotted several of the cooks, including a BeeAye, who was busy cleaning and sharpening a set of knives.

The BeeAye was closest, so she approached him. "Hello."

He looked up. "Oh!" He put the knife down and wiped his hands. "Hello, Dev," he said. "How are you?"

"Hello, Billy," Dev responded. "Excellent, thank you. I was looking to see if there were any water bottles available. I searched through the old storage, but could not find any, and we did not bring any from the base."

He thought a moment. "Oh yes," he said. "We have some to provide to the boats in the prep room. Would you like one?"

"I would like two. One for me and one for Jess." Dev was

aware of the other cooks watching them. "May I go with you to get them? I am still finding my way around."

"Of course." Billy wrapped the knives up in a thick piece of cloth and tucked them under his arm. "It's this way." He led her through the big space that stretched the width of the mess room on the other side of the wall. One whole end of the space taken up by massive structures with deeply burnished tops, and doors that could be pulled down. "Those are the ovens," he said. That's where we cook the foods."

"It's very interesting," Dev said. "And it's warm in here."

Billy grinned. "Yes. I don't have to wear a coat, it's nice." He went to a set of doors set into the rock in the back of the space and opened one. "It's so different than station," he said, as he led her inside. "There, everything was just processed by mechs." He looked along the shelves. "Yes, here. Is this what you wanted?"

Dev inspected the shelf. "Yes," she said. "That would be excellent."

"Hey, what's up here?" A gruff voice interrupted them, and the door was thrust open. A burly man entered, with thick curly hair. "Whatcha doin?"

"Hello, Chef," Billy responded. "I was getting water bottles for Dev."

"Hello," Dev said, as the man turned toward her. "I think we met the other day. Jess introduced us."

She'd found that here, just as at the Base, sometimes the mention of Jess's name brought interesting results. Sometimes suboptimal, sometimes optimal, and occasionally enlightening.

In this case, it seemed optimal as the newcomer's attitude adjusted, and he got a lot less challenging and more correctly polite.

Interesting.

The man nodded. "Ohh. Yeah, she did, hi there." He took a step back. "Y'know, someone coulda gotten them for ya, and the Drake," he said. "Ya just gotta ask."

"Yes," Dev said. "But I wanted to select a snack to bring back to our housing and obtain some supplies for us to take in the carrier tomorrow. So that was a bit complicated to ask someone else to do." She took the two cannisters Billy had in his hands. "Besides, it's very pleasant to get to meet everyone."

"Yeah, okay," Petar said. "Hey, you take good care of what she asks for, Billy. Don't want the Drake pissed off."

"Of course," Billy said in a mild tone. "Was there anything you wanted to provide, Chef?" He asked. "If Dev is taking a snack, I mean?"

Petar paused then, suddenly, and surprisingly grinned, which changed his entire rather grumpy exterior. "You're a sharp one, you are," he said. "Yeah, you hang on there a minute. Lemme get you a little something."

He whisked out the door and disappeared. As his footsteps faded away, they heard the activity in the main space increase exponentially as pans and pots and the clanging of things being put away rang out loud and clear.

Billy and Dev looked at each other, then Dev chuckled. "I am sure Jess would appreciate a treat, if that's what that is."

"Yes. The Chef is excellent," Billy said. "He did not wish me to be assigned here at first, but Doctor Dan spoke with him. All of the natural born want to be assigned here, so it was very special that he allowed me to be."

"Yes." Dev tucked the bottles under her arm. "It was like how it was when I came down world."

Billy nodded his head solemnly. "I had to work very hard. I did not want to disappoint Doctor Dan in any way."

Dev smiled at him. "I as well. But it seems it turned out excellently for both of us." She stood back and let him lead the way out of the storage room, her gaze traveling over the supplies in case they had any further need.

"Yes, and the other natural born are becoming less suboptimal about it," Billy said. "Doctor Dan told me to just be calm, and it will be okay."

"Doctor Dan understands these natural born with excellence," Dev said. "He always knows what to say."

"Yes." Billy pulled the door closed and they walked across the space to the cooking area, where Petar was busy at a worktable, one of the cooks standing by to assist, and the rest finishing up their tasks.

Dev watched them watch her as they came to a stop at the side of the table Petar was working at. He was taking pieces of fish, and setting them onto small clumps of the tiny, beaded sea- weed often found in their meals, and wrapping them with a thin strip of kelp.

"That's very attractive," Dev said, after a moment of silence.

Petar looked up. "You think so?" He asked. "Is a snack. Just a little bite." He put the piece he was working on in a battered plas container and then built another one. "But it's pretty, isn't it?"

"Like a flower," Dev said. "Do you create all the meals here?"

Petar finished the last little piece and then looked up.

"Yeah." He straightened up and put his hands on his hips. "And?" He jerked his chin at her with a slightly challenging gesture.

Dev nodded. "I think you must be excellent at that then, because the meals here are the best I have had anywhere," she said. "Better than the station or at Base 10."

"Yes," Billy said and nodded his head. "Much better. And the sets from the base say the same, that they are better than it was there."

Petar looked positively charmed. "Yeah?" He looked around. "It's an old fashioned kinda place. Nothin fancy."

The other cooks approached and stood nearby, just listening.

"Jess told me, it's excellent because people do it," Dev said. "She says in most places, it's not like that."

One of the younger cooks nodded and came over to her "S'right," he said. "My pap said it, he worked in here."

"He was a good cook," Petar said. "Maybe in a thousand years you'll do half as good." He handed Dev the container. "See if the Drake likes it. Hear she's out the back mixing it up."

Dev accepted the container. "I'm sure she will, and yes, she is involved in the fighting activity. She enjoys it a lot."

"Sure." The young cook grinned briefly. "We all like scrapping." He glanced at Petar. "Off shift," he added hastily as the chef gave him a dour look.

Petar smiled at Dev. "Come in here any time, long as you tell me how good my chow is." He winked at her, then dusted his hands off. "What the hell you all standing here? Get out!" He yelled at the cooks. "You want to sleep in here? Move it!"

The cooks scattered, and he strode after them, shooing them ahead of him like a flock of puffins. Dev regarded the noisy retreat and glanced at Billy. "That was..." She paused. "Probably optimal?" Her voice lifted in question.

Billy nodded. "Optimal. He likes you. May I help you carry something across the hall? I am going to put my tools away and it's the same direction."

Dev handed him the bottles. "Yes. I have to get some soup and those cakes that will be excellent to take with us on our mission." She headed for the dispensing counter. "I should have brought along my carrying bag."

****

"That was good," April said, as she and Mike Arias walked

alongside Jess across the big hall toward their quarters.

"Yeah, not gonna have to worry about getting workouts here." Mike sighed in contentment. "We can just do this every night."

April rocked back and forth, shadowboxing as she stepped. "Felt great." She glanced up. "You kick enough ass, Drake?"

Jess nodded. "It was good," she agreed. "Way better than the gym. Real work." She scanned the inside of the hall, which was quiet, the late watch moving to station in ops, and a maint team fixing a door to one of the inner hallways.

Overhead the plas cap was pitch dark, the clouds moving over it invisible. The chill damp emerged from the lower hallways and pushed against them as they crossed.

"Got some potential there too," Arias said. "They can all whup." He glanced at Jess. "We could train em up, I think. Focus them."

"Might be able to," Jess said. "We'll see." They reached the far side of the hall and the branching ingress that would lead to their quarters, and the steps to hers. "See ya in the dark O."

"See ya." April lifted her hand, and walked with Mike to the inner hall, pressing her hand to the ingress panel and waited for it to open.

Jess watched the two of them disappear into the inner halls and then turned and went to the sealed doorway to the right and put her hand on the pad and. The door opened to reveal the wide steps up to her crazy, empty, weird housing.

Funky and strange, but the expansive space was kind of appealing to her, and she trotted up the steps, already thinking ahead to the blast of the shower. She heard the door slide shut behind her and put her hand on the inner door. She then felt the tickle against her palm as it identified her.

The panel turned a pleasing teal, and the door slid aside. Jess took a step forward, aware of some additional adornment in the hallway, and the smell of something edible. "Hey Devvie."

Dev's head popped into view from the inner hallway. "Hello Jess!"

Jess surveyed the hall and saw some blocky cabinets against the wall, and a long table. "Went shopping in storage huh?"

"I did." Dev emerged from the hallway. She had on a hoodie that was large on her but tied with a piece of harbor rope around her waist, and leggings. "I think the storage persons were pleased with my attention."

Jess entered and looked around. "They must have been if

they called up the loaders to haul this up for ya this late in the watch." She walked over and sat on the long counter and bounced up and down on it, pleased when it didn't budge. "Nice."

"Was your session optimal?" Dev asked. "I brought back some soup from the mess, as I thought you perhaps might like some after the activity. And the person in charge in the kitchen sent a small treat."

Jess got off the counter. "I would. Let me go shower all this grit off me." She headed off to the inner section of the housing and paused as she passed her office, noting a storage cabinet was now against the other wall, and a chair was inside. "Been busy, hey Dev?" She called back over her shoulder. She heard a slight chuckle echo back as she kept on going.

She went along to the sanitary space, ducked inside, and stripped out of the gear she'd fought in observing that a laundry basket was also now in evidence. She shoved the gear inside and went into the shower and let the powerful jets rinse her off.

She glanced down and found a few bruises along her ribcage and a long scratch down one forearm from the grappling. She felt good though, energized, and relaxed, pleased with having a big group of people around who enjoyed scrapping as much as she did.

Agents mostly did it because they had to. Hand to hand were skills you had to hone, and systems knew when you avoided the pit. Most of them preferred the gym to keep their bodies strong and only spent the amount of time in the fighting facility absolutely required.

Always had seemed a shame to her, because without a doubt she found fighting a lot more fun to keep in shape than working with pressure machines and so she always checked the pit when she passed, hopeful someone was there looking for a bout.

Here, two hundred big, strong, if somewhat unskilled people showed up and she could have all the scrapping she wanted. And nobody got mad about it.

Sweet. Jess scrubbed the sand out of her hair and sighed in content. Maybe she'd even be able to teach them something.

Maybe. She thought about the swirl of energy she'd felt around her, and the laughter. Maybe there was something here that couldn't exactly replace Interforce but could be a different kind of answer to some of their security questions.

And anyway, finding out would be a hell of a lot of fun.

****

Dev warmed up the soup in the food processing station and took two bowls of it into the half circular space they'd identified as a place to consume edibles. It now had a square pedestal inside with a round piece of metal on top, and two stools. She put down the dishes then went back for some drinks.

She brought them, and the container from Petar, into the space and then stood near the entrance and waited for Jess to appear.

In a minute, she did, ruffling her hair dry with a towel, a tank and shorts covering only a small amount of her body.

That was pleasant. Dev found Jess's body very attractive, and she enjoyed the precise symmetry of her form and the smooth power of the way she moved.

She regretted that it was just too cold in the space for her to dress the same. Dev pondered what could be done about that situation. "I have set up a platform here." She stepped back to allow Jess to enter. "I think it's acceptable to use for a meal."

Jess slung the towel around her neck and sat down on one of the stools. "Awesome," she said and pulled the bowl over. "What have we here? Ah. Bycatch soup."

"Yes." Dev seated herself on the other stool. "It smells appealing."

"It does. Good pick." Jess picked up the bowl and drank from it. "Just the right thing for after a mixup," she said. "It was fun. Had a big bunch of people show up. We figured we might be able to teach them a few tricks."

"Excellent." Dev used a more conventional spoon-based way of ingesting her soup. "Brent was released from med. I encountered him exiting and accompanied him to a space near Mike and Chester's location."

Jess glanced over the rim of her bowl. "Glad he's feeling better."

"He feels well," Dev said. "Chester spoke to him about our mission tomorrow and he wishes to attend." She looked up at Jess. "I could release his vehicle. It had most of the same mods as ours does."

Jess rested both elbows on the table and cradled her soup in both hands, gently biting on the edge of the bowl. "What do you think about that?" She asked. "You think he's okay?"

Dev took her time, ingesting a few more spoons of soup as she thought. "I think he's…" She paused. "Something is making him upset."

"What happened at the base?"

"I think so," Dev said. "It's like when they take you down, and you come back up, but something is different, and you don't know what it is. He doesn't know what happened and it is suboptimal for him." She looked up at Jess with a serious expression. "I do not think he's incorrect, if that is what you are asking me."

"That's what I was asking," Jess said simply. "I don't think he's screwball either, I just don't really know what side he's on."

Dev considered that thought. What side would Brent be on? "He could be his own side," she suggested. "I think Jason is his friend." She set the spoon down. "I think if it had happened to me, I would be most concerned with finding out what happened to you."

"Maybe." Jess put her empty bowl on the table and pulled over the small plas container Dev had placed on the table. She opened it and inspected the contents, then picked up one of the small snacks and looked at it. "But would I have dumped you out the back of a transport?" She mused. "Nah. What are these things?"

Dev smiled. "Those are from Petar. He thought you might like them. I scanned them and they are apparently safely edible."

One of Jess's very dark eyebrows hiked up as she looked at Dev over the small snack in her fingers. "Apparently?" She looked warily at the object. "Any reason you think they're not?"

"Not really, but there is no branching routine in that programming I received regarding the safety of consumables," Dev responded promptly. "I am always interested to see if they might have unexpected things in them."

"Like live animals?" Jess's eyes twinkled. "Let's find out." She popped the object into her mouth.

Dev sat back and took a sip of her grog and watched Jess chew thoughtfully. Her face made several curious twists, and her eyes widened. Hard to really determine what that indicated.

Jess swallowed. "That's good," she said. "I like it." She nudged the box with her knuckles. "Give it a try."

Dev obediently took one and eyed it. "All at once?"

Jess nodded. "Yeah, it's fish and crunchy seaweed, it's a

good mix." She picked up a second and put it into her mouth. "A little spicy. He put something on the fish maybe."

There was a little tang to the scent, but it was mild. Dev put the bundle into her mouth and bit down, finding the flesh of the fish firm but flaky, and the center, a wrapped coil of the stringy seaweed she liked, astringent and crisp as she chewed it.

It was good. She nodded and glanced up at Jess. "It's nice."

"It's a good snack." Jess studied the box as she took a third piece. "Good energy boost." She sat back and exhaled in contentment. "This is great, Devvie. I like this spot." She tapped the tabletop, it's rough, battered surface dented but mellow looking in the overhead recessed lights. "Good place for us to just to hang out."

Dev finished her share of the treat and smiled. "Yes, I thought it would be very functional," she said. "After our mission, I will continue researching what is in storage to see if there are other useful things."

Jess stood up. "C'mon." She held her hand out. "Let's go try out our bed again. At least it'll be warm enough there for you to take off your boots." She draped her arm over Dev's shoulders as she joined her, and they walked from the little nook down the hallway toward the bedroom.

****

Dev sat quietly in her seat, all her prechecks done, and waited for her passengers to finish boarding and settle into their seats in the carrier. She relaxed and folded her hands across her stomach as the other two carriers prepared to depart as well.

There would be no light fliers this time, just the carriers, and the gear they needed to complete their mission.

Jess was already seated in the gunner station. She wore her hoodie and work pants, with a serviceable hand blaster hanging at her hip. Behind her were Keko and Kevin, Doctor Dan, Security Mike, and one of Mike's lieutenants, who had an old school long gun cradled in his hands.

Brent was seated at Dev's side in her jump seat. He looked pale but well, his hands resting on his knees. He glanced at her. "Hurry up and wait, like always, huh?"

Dev grinned. "Yes," she said. "I think we are just waiting for Chester to reset a mod, and then we should be ready to go." She regarded him. "Did you get good rest?"

He nodded. "That's some comfortable beds they got," he said. "Better than med. Got me a good sleep in." He tapped his thumbs on his kneecaps. "Better than base," he added after a brief pause. "Less yakkin."

Ah, the overhead announcements. Dev nodded in agreement. "Yes, they don't use them here, just local comms."

"Like it," Brent concluded.

"I as well." Dev saw the status lights shift on one of the neighboring carriers. "Jess, we are now prepared to depart." She sat up and tightened her restraints and switched on the flight beacons. Their reflection blared across her landing pad.

"Siddown and strap in," Jess ordered and pulled her restraints on over her head and fastened them. "This ain't a transport." She looked around warningly at the rest of them.

The order wasn't really needed as her passengers were already getting ready to go without any hesitation. The security lieutenant propped his long gun against the sidewall and attached it's woven plas strap to one of the cargo tie-downs to keep it in place.

Then most looked up and around in bright eyed expectation, as though ready to enjoy a treat. Only Dan Kurok met Jess's eyes with a look of wry amusement. He folded his arms over his chest and leaned back.

Dev sealed the hatch and ran the engine prestart as the doors to the landing bay were shoved open and the darkness of the very early morning appeared ahead of them. The rumble of energy surrounded them, mixed with the faint rustle of the Bay chop outside.

Brent pulled on his restraints, and locked them in. "Feels kinda weird," he muttered.

Dev finished reporting her flight plan to Bay ops, then turned off her mic. "Going to the base?"

"Raidin it," he said, wryly.

Dev glanced in the reflective surface over her station, and confirmed her passengers were all secure, then she boosted up on the landing jets ready to start for the exit. "The first day or so were very strange," she admitted. "But now I think I am all right with it, as utilizing material left behind seems both useful and correct."

"Before someone else does, yeah," Brent said. "Just feels weird." He braced back against the floor as the carrier drifted forward, responding to Dev's deft touch on the controls. "Guess I'll get over it."

They emerged into the outer curve of the Bay and Dev took them out over the calm waters, the fleet nose to pier along the far wall, and the navigation floats small and lightly bobbing underneath them. It was hours until dawn, but there were already power craft moving across the water, heading for the entry to the docking caverns.

"Bay operations, this is Bay Flight, we are preparing to depart." Dev glanced to her right and left as the two other carriers drifted out and formed up with her. "We will be departing at speed."

"Bay Flight, we got cha," Bay Operations replied in their usual casual tone. "Got booms coming."

"Yes." Dev switched to the sideband. "Mark ten, depart." She spooled up the engines, boosted skyward and arched up over the top of the Bay cliffs. Then curved out to sea, leaving the night work lights and the boats behind, accelerating past the speed of sound in a smooth surge with the two other craft on either side.

It was a mostly quiet flight. Jess leaned back in her seat with her hands folded over her stomach.

Winds had come down, and it was an easy flight for Dev. "Thirty minutes to target," she said into the sideband link between her and the other two carriers.

"Ack," Chester responded.

"Ack ack," Doug echoed him. "Met's a go," he added. "Storm offshore but heading east."

Dev was glad of the wind shear dropping. She'd worked out a script to sync the three carriers in their effort to lift the massive door, but the weather was still a factor, as enough fluctuations would make it impossible to keep the giant panel steady. Things could get suboptimal quite quickly.

But so far, so good. "Vector twenty, mark," Dev said quietly, a short time later, as they cruised at speed over the ruffled surface of the sea below them.

"Ack," Doug responded.

"Ack," Chester echoed. "We crossed over a group of three fishing vessels, heading southwest," he said. "No alerts."

Jess let her head rest against the back of her chair and watched the scan return screens on her boards. So far everything was clean. There were no returns or echoes, nothing being picked up landside as they skimmed over the water toward the Base.

The ocean surface below them was empty, and ahead of them she could already see the curve of the promontory range that came right down to the sea, and the crash of waves against it that would take them along the curve of the walls to Base 10.

They were within scan range. Sensors hadn't picked up any

returns, and there were no hails. But that really meant nothing, Jess knew. Someone could be in there waiting for them, not stupid enough to advertise that, but aware of them because they were actively scanning.

Double edged sword. Jess had considered going in scanner blind, but given they were flying in the dark, the risk was deemed worth it, and so here they were, three bright beacons of signal in a coastal wasteland for anyone to see who could.

At ten minutes out, she straightened up a little in her seat. "Devvie, give me some juice." She glanced forward and caught the reflection as Dev looked up and their eyes met in the mirror over her head. Then her boards came live, and she reached up to pull down the triggers and settled her fingers.

"Trouble?" Kurok said, from his seat near the hatch.

"Maybe I want to make some," Jess responded with a brief grin. "Just pays to be ready." She turned up the targeting arrays, and watched the carrier recognize its surroundings, coding in the sounding buoys and nav markers that marked the approach to the base.

"Automatic signal received," Dev said. "It's on repeat, as it was the last time, Jess."

"See it." Jess swung her head slowly right and left, taking in all the metrics, comparing them to what she remembered from the last time they'd approached, opening her instincts up as Dev made the banking turn in toward the shore.

The Base escarpment was mostly dark. There were external halons on at the sea-level viewing platform where, a year and ten thousand lifetimes ago, she'd shown Dev the sea for the first time. As they got closer, they saw the landing bay door hanging open as it had been, the work lights left on inside reflecting out at them.

"Zero output," Dev said. "Scan shows systems still offline, no returns on energy exchange, no local signals."

"Huh." Brent watched over her shoulder. "Man, that's creepy."

"Yes," Kurok said, and leaned forward to study Jess's screens. "That it is."

"Stand by for approach," Dev told the two other carriers. "We are active armed."

"That should scare em," Jess said.

"That was sideband, Jess."

Jess snickered. "I know. I was talking about the kids. They've seen me aim."

That broke the somewhat somber silence. "All right. Let's

get a move on," Security Mike said, with a chuckle. "No sense trying to find a wave where there ain't none."

Jess chuckled softly and watched the targeting scan intently. "Max would tell ya, never turn your back on the sea. It's the rogue wave you never see coming."

Dev came flight even with the opening and then slowed their forward momentum. She focused every scanner she had on the landing cavern and its surroundings as she made her approach to the opening. The crippled door was just as they'd left it, and there were no biological returns on any level, save birds in the cliff face, and deep below, some fish.

Aware of Jess's live weapons, Dev cautiously entered the docking cavern and fed everything her intake was getting into the targeting scan for Jess's review. She took a fast full visual scan, then compared it. "There have been changes since our last entry," she said. "Tac 2, Tac 3, remain in pattern, do not enter."

"Ack," Chester and Doug answered together.

Everyone jerked a little. "What changes?" Jess asked, her fingertips twitching a little.

"Boxes that were on the ramp are missing." Dev slowed now to a standstill, and the carrier hovered in midair. Her hands remained on the controls, ready to shoot them into reverse. "There is debris near the lift station," she added. "There is energy dispersal in the surrounding underlying ground coverings."

"Scavengers," Jess said. "Someone's in here mooching."

"Yeah," Kurok murmured. "That's how I read it. Those were crates of rations we left behind, on the assumption that nothing here would be appreciated back at the Bay."

"Any life signs, Dev?"

Dev shook her head. "No. A seagull has made a nest in the corner of the instrument loft. But it is empty currently."

"Okay, so tell everyone be careful," Jess said. "If there were scavengers here, there might be more after they bring back some haul. Go ahead and land on the top platform, Dev. Keep the guns pointed down that slope to the lower entry."

"Yes." Dev passed the orders along on sideband, then slid the carrier sideways while rotating it neatly in position. "I think we should proceed with our tasks as quickly as possible."

Jess paused halfway standing, her restraints released. "Something you see?"

"No." Dev unclipped and got up. She removed her work pack from the back of her chair and slid it onto her shoulders." I just think it's a good idea." She handed a second pack to

Brent. "We will start with your vehicle."

"Rock on, Rocket." Brent took the pack and slid it over his shoulders. "Never thought I'd be so glad to see that old damn bus."

Jess undogged the hatch. "We should stay just in the cavern," she said. "Let's just get done what we need to get done."

No one argued, and Jess didn't expect them to. She followed them all out of the carrier, as the other two set down nearby, and paused to step to one side and expose her own senses to the air in the large space. She breathed in with both her nose and mouth then tilted her head to one side to listen.

Dev was already off the platform with Brent at her heels. As they passed the platform April's carrier had landed on Doug hopped out and leaped off to the ground to join them, a tool pack on his hip.

Kurok stood quietly next to Jess, his eyes scanning the inside of the bay. "The game is afoot," he said cryptically. "Though I think your guess about scavengers is right, Jess. There are three large containers missing, but they're all consumables."

"Not mech."

"No." Kurok pointed. "That cabinet there, it was too big for us to carry onboard, but it's got stacks of useful parts. Wasn't touched." He half turned. "Lads, let's get those plasma cutters put together, all right? Up there on the ledge, so we can cut through that lower track."

"Yes, Doctor Dan. We understand." Kevin waved at him, as he and Keko joined the bios and mechs from the other two carriers and began removing the sections of cutter that had been stored inside.

Kurok tipped his head back and looked at the ceiling. "Now this, on the other hand."

"Yeah. That's gonna be a bitch." Jess stood next to him with her hands on her hips. "Gonna have to go in sections."

Kurok sighed. "I'd say it's idiotic, but it's a damn good idea and I've thought of so many bloody useful things we can do in that back section now I don't want to let go of it."

"Ah. We'll figure it out." Jess dismissed the challenge, surprised when Kurok started laughing.

"What?"

Kurok let the chuckles run down. "Echo from the past." He patted her shoulder. "I'll go give Dev a hand. I want to see that routine she wrote in any case." He turned and made his way down the steps from the platform and headed toward the other side of the bay.

Jess remained in her elevated position, slowly scanning the inside of the bay from side to side as the crews dispersed, the bio alts hauling the cutter up to the opening level and Security Mike roaming a slow perimeter of the cavern with his long gun, his lieutenant going counter to him on the other side.

Chester was inside his carrier, watching scan, while Mike sat on his guns, it's landing pad provided a good view of the inside of the landing bay, all as they'd planned.

It was as safe as it was going to get, Jess considered. Maybe they would get lucky. She scanned the interior again, making note of the shadows, and echoes coming to her ears, and the scents surrounding them to make an imprint in her head.

A motion caught her eye, and she looked up to spot a seagull glide in, coming to land on the nest Dev had spotted. She watched the bird turn and settle down in the sea wrack at the corner of the shelving structure as it looked back at her.

Didn't take long. Jess looked away and suppressed a grin. Not for nature or scavengers. They saw an op, they took it.

Chapter Twelve

Dev sat on the platform cross legged, the carrier umbilical draped over her shoulder and concentrated on her handheld scanner. She tuned the signal again, then looked up thoughtfully at the carrier before she made an adjustment. "Please attach this." She shrugged the umbilical a little.

Doug lifted it off her and crawling under the front landing skid. He ducked around t pausing. "Straight in?"

"Yes." Dev shifted one of the clamps from the other end of the umbilical leading to her scanner and made another adjustment. "It's a bit tricker than yours was."

"Okay." Doug pushed the connector in, while Brent crouched at Dev's side and reviewed her screen. "Cause of that mod we did, right?" He gave the connection a twist. "It's in."

"Yes." Dev tapped quickly on her screen and recompiled the routine she'd designed. "This will require some revision."

"Have you rerouted the security probe?" Kurok knelt behind her and watched over her other shoulder. "Ah, yes you have. Very clever."

Dev smiled but kept her eyes on her screen. "I have record of the ops codes," she said. "So, I am just using one of those, and the carrier expects it."

"It sounds so easy, right?" Doug said, with a mock sigh.

"Well really, when you have the central code repository, everything is easier," Kurok said. "The clever bit is to realize you need it and capture it before you don't have access to it any longer." He patted Dev's back. "Well done, Dev."

"Thank you, Doctor Dan." Dev redirected the response she had just crafted to the carrier's control systems and paused, glancing aside at it. "However, we should wait to see if this is functional before the work is approved." After a moment, the sound of the locking mechanism for the hatch cycled. "Brent, please try to access."

"Yup. Heard that." Brent reached out and touched the side of the carrier. After a second, the hatch lifted and swung aside, revealing the inside of the vehicle. "Sweet." He got up off his knees and climbed into the carrier. "Home sweet home."

"Yes." Dev got up onto her knees. "Now is the difficult bit on the inside."

Doug lifted his kit. "Brain transplant time," he said. "Let's go."

They moved into the carrier behind Brent. "Please don't touch any controls," Dev said. "It might get suboptimal."

"It might blow up," Doug translated. "Which would be a bummer."

"It would, indeed." Kurok removed a hand light from his pocket and moved around so he could see the control panel main access. He twisted the light on and directed it at the panel Dev sat in front of. "Astonishing how they really haven't changed much in these things."

Dev took out a set of retractors and attached a probe to the panel. "I think the mods have altered." She tuned her scanner. "They have several times just in my participation time here."

"Well, yeah, you altered yours," Doug said. "So, you should know." He gave Dev a slight nudge along her shoulder blade. "Don't be so modest."

Dev cleared her throat slightly.

"I certainly hope they've changed since my time," Kurok said. "But where they put them hasn't, apparently." He edged over a bit so he could get a better look at Dev's screen. "Though really, would it make sense to move things around? If someone's in here opening panels you've got big problems to start with."

"True that," Brent said. "Anyway, guess they thought the stuff they got back west is a lot better than these are. S'what they said." He glanced at all of them. "Cause I asked, y'know? Why they'd said to just leave em."

"We all asked," Doug said, sourly. "Assholes just laughed at me."

"This was the pointy end of the spear. Why hadn't they sent the new ones out?" Kurok asked. He leaned on one elbow with his back pressed against the pilot's console. "It's been the battlefront for a damn long time. Leaving these old piles out here makes no sense."

Brent just shook his head. "Scam," he said. "S'what Jase kept saying. Some scam."

"That's what April figured," Doug said, and handed Dev a probe, as she delicately shifted the frequencies she was balancing. "After they told us, that night." He scratched the side of his nose. "Just felt like a play, you know?"

"Yes. That occurred to me too, after I had a moment to stop cursing at the stupidity of it all." Kurok said. "Ah, there you go, Dev." He saw the sine wave coalesce. "Very nice."

Dev quickly sent her instruction set into the command mod in the carrier. This released it from stasis and unlocked the retaining panel. It thunked and popped out, exposing the mod to her and she clipped the probe to it. "Excellent." She pulled up the changes she'd put in her own and the other carriers and started to reprogram the internal brain of the vehicle

Kurok nodded. "I think I've got the idea." He clipped the light to the side of the pilot's seat and got up. "Let me go get started on the next one in line." He dusted his hands off. "Or maybe go across the way, hm? In case I goof up." He winked at them and stepped around Doug on the way to the hatch of the carrier. "No sense in blowing us all up, now is there?"

"That's nuts." Doug watched him hop off the platform and disappear. "But hey if it gets us outta here sooner… g'wan up in the saddle, Brent. She's almost done. I recognize that much of it."

Brent got up and went around the pilot's seat and dropped into it. "They're jacked about Rocket," he said. "Them suits. Had some big plan or something. They wouldn't talk about it to us, but they were all hot about you going west."

Dev looked up at him. "Me?"

Brent nodded. "They told Jase they wanted to get you out of here. He told em they were idiots." He pondered. "Maybe that's what the mixup was on the transport… they were goin off to try and grab ya."

Dev's brows hiked up. "That would have been extremely non optimal." She frowned.

"Yeah, no kidding. Especially for them." Doug eyed her. "Jess would have whacked em," he said. "Just for thinking about it."

Brent nodded. "Oh yeah for sure. Dumb idea."

Dev completed her task and told the mod to recompile. It spun through its new routine with no complaints and a moment later the internal systems of the carrier lit, and the boards came online.

She regarded the results. "I'm glad they decided to just exit," she said, as Brent checked in sequencing. "However, if it was when they were preparing the transport, we were already in our carrier. They would not have located us."

"Jase told em they'd never find ya." Brent reached over and removed the commset from its attachment on the console and slid it over his head in an automatic gesture. "Wish he hadn't gone with em. Figured he could talk it down or somethin."

Doug picked up the pack. "Not people that dumb. C'mon, Rocket. Let me carry your bag to that next bag of bolts over there. Faster we get done with these, faster we can get outta here before my partner gets any more crazy ideas to take the place over or finds some other honking humongous thing to swipe."

Dev closed her scanner. "It should go through the standard routines," she told Brent. "Ops is offline, but I restricted the umbilical to power only."

"Heard that." Brent studied his readouts. "Looks reg." He glanced at her. "Course it does."

Dev grinned slightly in acknowledgement of the compliment. "I am glad you came with us. It's excellent to have another person here who understands these vehicles."

Brent looked at her for a long moment, then grinned a little. "Yeah, I'm glad you let me come out," he said. "Just wish I knew what the hell was goin on." He then admitted, making a vague gesture at the inside of the cavern around them. "Just feels weird."

"Yes, it's confusing," Dev said. "However, I am confident we will figure it out." She slung her scanner over her shoulder and got up off the floor. She glanced up as the carrier rocked a little to see Jess enter. "Hello," she said with a smile.

"Done?" Jess stuck her hands into her hoodie front pocket. "You teach the doc how to do it? Saw him heading over to that next bus."

Dev assumed a deprecating expression. "Doctor Dan watched me do this one, then went to take care of that vehicle," she said. "I don't think I taught him anything."

Brent laughed shortly.

Jess moved over to stand next to Dev and tilted her head to avoid banging it on the ceiling. "They got one side of the track off already," she said. "Figure another two hours and we'll be ready to lift." She regarded Brent. "You up to flying point while we try this insanity?"

He nodded. "I'm all right. Mike said he'd fly the back seat in case we need shootin."

Jess grunted softly in agreement. "Yeah, we all are for the rest of the crates. More people who can fly these things than work the guns without blowing someone's head off," she said. "Like usual." She paused and studied him. "Hey."

Brent looked at her, in question.

"If you'd rather take off from here, and go west, you can," Jess said, unexpectedly. "No one's gonna make you stay if you don't want to."

Dev's brows lifted a little, but she remained silent and watched her colleague with interest.

Brent looked at Jess for a very long minute, in equal

silence. "I don't want to go out there," he finally said in a somewhat thoughtful tone. "Figure if it's trouble, it'll come here. We'll find out what the scam is sooner or later." He glanced away then back up at Jess. "Anyhow, I like your place."

Jess just grinned. "Yeah, me too." She put a hand on Dev's back. "Let's go, Devvie. Your buddies are waiting on the next one." They stepped down from the carrier deck and looked down the line of craft that now showed additional lights on, returning a sense of life to the bay. Overhead, the plasma cutters were working their way across the massive opening, lending the scent of ions and hot metal to the air.

All seemed to be going well. Jess walked alongside Dev as they headed for the next carrier.

Which was, in her experience, never a good sign.

****

Dev was on her back, her head up inside a console when a soft alarm went off on her scanner. She quickly looked at it, keeping her hands in place on the component she was handling. "Doug, please communicate there is a biologic reading approaching, multiple. From the shuttle landing platform outside."

Doug was already on comms, one hand cupped over his ear. "Ack ack," he chattered into it. "We got company." He went to the door of the carrier. "Glad this is the last one." He hopped outside and waved at April, who was now racing across the cavern at top speed.

"I, as well," Dev commented in an undertone, as she continued working on the console. "It would be optimal if they all functioned as intended." She shifted position a little, and the small light at her temple moved to cover the integrated panel she was working on. "And if they did not have odd anomalies."

Behind her, she heard voices outside the carrier, and she reached over and tuned comms, to hear what was going on.

"What we got?" April said to Doug as she arrived.

"People, coming in the shuttle landing pad. That door's half open." Doug said, half to her, half to the sideband channel.

"Heading over," Brent's voice broke in. "S'all quiet round the rest of it."

"That's where they got in I figure," April said. "Let's wait for... there she is."

Jess vaulted up from the lower level to the platform they were standing on. "Trouble?"

"Visitors," April said. "Shuttle door."

"Sure," Jess said, "it's the unsecured area."

"Visitor's entry in fact," Doug said. "Brent's coming over the top to check it out. Dev said it was multiple targets."

"Let's go check it out," Jess said. "Dev still wrenching? Stay here," she instructed Doug, then waved everyone else off the grid and toward the ramp to the inner halls, as Security Mike and his lieutenant arrived to follow.

"Sure." Doug gave them a little wave. "You guys want to go play with Brent? Maybe there'll be something to shoot at?" He told Chester, as that carrier's flight beacons lit. "We're almost done here. Rocket's on the last bus."

"Ack," Chester said. "Clear pad?"

Doug looked over at it. "Clear."

"Ack."

Chester's carrier lifted on its landing jets and elevated to the level of the opening, then moved outbound, clearing the entry, and moving into a fast bank upward.

Doug watched the vehicle disappear, then regarded the work site. The doors had been fully separated from their track and were balanced on the edge of the entry somewhat precariously, with the three lift points with their solid heavy rings welded on and waiting. "Not sure repelling an attack on this old barn won't be easier than that lift."

The plasma cutters were disassembled and stored, and the newly woken carriers were being checked over by their some- what apprehensive, but eager pilots. Doug walked down the line of them, stopped at one then stuck his head in. "You hear?"

Kurok was in the pilot's seat, with a diagnostic panel open. "I did," he said. "Seems like the problem we all expected materialized. What fun. Real trouble?"

Doug shrugged. "Depends on who and how many. I'm guessing it's probably not more than our peeps can handle." He glanced up at the doors. "Worse comes to worse we can drop that on them and be done with it."

"Mm." Kurok eyed the portal. "Well, let me make sure these are all ready to take off then. Not that bad so far, but goodness these things do need some work."

Doug nodded. "Yeah, it was rough getting anything for em," he said. "But we had Rocket, so that was okay, you know? Stuff we didn't have she could make." He paused. "She and Clint put their heads together and I figure they could make whatever."

Kurok smiled his gentle smile. "Yes, Dev is a significant

asset. I'm not surprised that Interforce realized that and offered her citizenship," he said. "And of course, they wanted to remove her contracted bio alt ties so they could deal directly with her and not have all those legal ramifications around."

"Kinda scummy."

"Not really," Kurok said. "Practical. I might have done the same myself in their place." He wiped his hands of some silicon grease. "Except of course I am, or should I say, was Dev's contract holder and would have shot them if they'd really had a go at it." He turned and headed back to the line of carriers and shook his head. "Muppets."

Doug smiled and turned back to the last carrier in the row. "Thanks for the heads up, Rocket," he said as he entered it. He picked up his own scanner and sat down behind the pilot's station. "The whole gang's out there checking it out."

"Yes, I heard the comms," Dev said, her voice slightly muffled. "Whose vehicle was this?" She asked.

"This one?" Doug pondered the question. "Might have been… no, I don't really remember whose… Oh. Wait I'm an idiot. This was mine," he said. "Yeah, whatsisface was going to get it. You know, the jerk. He was bitching and bitching about what a piece of crap it was."

"Hm." Dev continued working. "I see."

"He was messing with it the day we came back that last time." Doug craned his head to look inside the panel. "Did he screw it up? Figures he would. Looked like the type. You know, thinks he knows more than he does."

Dev removed a card, somewhat irregularly shaped, and with red gold leads traced across it. "Could you place that in a static container? I would like to look more closely at it later."

Doug took the card from her and looked at it. "Looks kinda new."

"Yes." Dev inserted a mod from her vest pocket into its place. "Possibly it was brought with the new agents, since they came from locations with newer materials." She fastened the mod down and activated it.

"Maybe." Doug put the card into a carry bag and tucked it into Dev's pack. "Yeah, maybe he brought it so he could show off." He tucked his ear bud more firmly into his ear, listening to the background chatter on comms. "Guess he's back where he wanted to be now."

"Possibly." Dev finished the installation and then pulled her scanner over and recompiled a routine. "The controls are reset. I think this vehicle is now finally ready." She slid out from the console and closed the access hatch, then boosted herself up into the pilot's seat and triggered the startup sequence. "Yes."

"Great." Doug reported the work done into the comms channel. "Any luck out there?"

"Still hunting," April answered tersely. "Having to haul these doors open all the way down." Behind her voice there was a screech of protesting metal. "Brent, you see anything?"

After a moment, the comms crackled. "Just got down into the shuttle channel, holy crap," Brents voice came back. "There's a crap ton of people here, with pallets and hand carts and I... hey they saw me."

"Oh boy." Doug looked at Dev, who had paused in mid motion to listen. "That's—"

"Non optimal," Dev finished for him. "We should prepare to fly." She got up and urged him out ahead of her. "Our vehicles might be needed."

"Might be?"

****

"Knew it was too quiet." Security Mike shifted his grip on his long gun, as they shoved open the main door leading to the shuttle entrance a little further on. "I can hear em," he said. "Ain't no sneaking around here going on."

"Brent said it was a crap ton," Jess mused. "That pads big."

"Should we just go back for the rigs?" April asked. "Wide hallway out there." She evaluated the space. "We could hold here but it'd be a pain."

Jess paused as she shoved the door into its wall pocket and looked past it to the hallway beyond. "Yeah," she said. She turned and looked back the way they came. "Let's shut this back up and wedge that table against it. Lemme go up and get Dev to get me a shot in that ingress."

"We're not gonna shoot no one?" Security Mike's lieu- tenant sounded disappointed. "We go a...ho watch it!"

Everyone ducked behind the doorframe save Mike, who dropped to one knee and lifted his gun, tucked the stock under his arm and braced as he fired the powerful projectiles thumping across the hallway as a line of bodies came rushing in at them.

Jess drew bead from her spot near the edge of the door and shot the gun out of the hands of the one closest to them. The second and third going down from Mike's projectiles.

Todd, the security lieutenant, dropped to his belly and

squirmed out into the line of fire. He propped his gun up as he leaned on his elbows and let off a barrage. "Hah!" The fourth attacker went down in a crumple of shattered bone.

April got her blaster around the doorframe at Jess's knee level and focused on the hallway beyond the initial surge, sending blasts against the wall to ricochet along the angle of the wall past the entrance. They heard yells and bangs in a flurry of panicked confusion.

"Hold on! Hold on!" A man's voice yelled out. "Stop movin! Just stop! Ever'body stop! These ain't scroungers."

"Hah," April muttered. "No, we ain't, jackasses."

Jess let out a bellow. "Who's in charge there? Who's talking!" She repeated. "Identify yourself or you're all gonna end up fish food."

There were four bodies on the floor, and flickers of motion behind the corner in the hallway. They heard heavy breathing and soft cries of pain. Burnt flesh scent wafted through the hall.

Then a tall, bearded man with curly light brown hair slowly came out from around the corner. He was dressed in the common work suit of a shore collector, waxy indeterminate color, thick knee-high boots, and a heavy protective over jacket.

He had a battered, worn fish pike pole in one hand, and a long knife in the other. "Tom Weathers," he said, with an almost arrogant jerk of his chin. "Who's you? Yelling woman?" he added. "What's your business doing in here?"

Jess stepped into the hallway to face him. She held her blaster with a casual, easy grip, the muzzle just touching her ear. "Jesslyn Drake. I used to work here." She studied the cluster of figures now edging out from behind the angle of steel to stare at her. "As an enforcement agent, in case you were wondering if I know how to use this." She wiggled the weapon. "I do."

"Hold, hold," April said into comms. "Don't blast anyone yet." She came around the doorsill and stood with her hand on her gun, staring dourly past Jess. "Yet," She repeated with a humorless smile, as Security Mike and his lieutenant came to join them. "F'n civs."

The shoreman shifted his grip on his pike. "Blackies," he finally said. "Thought you all from here done left."

"Not all of us," April said. "So, what's your game here, scraper?"

Two figures, a man and a women dressed in much patched, almost colorless coverings typical of those that lived outside came warily into view. "They left it open. We look to take it for shelter," the woman said. "Got a lot of us round here," she added. "Lot of us brought stuff in here for them, so now what are we gonna do?" She asked, "Nobody else to trade with. They didn't let nobody settle near here."

Jess lowered her blaster and put it back in its sling at her hip. "You take those cases of rat bars?" She asked Tom, in a crisp tone. "We don't want them back," she said, when he hesitated. "Just want to know what the score is. We're just here scavenging ourselves."

The man who'd come around the corner looked at the ground. "They dead?" He looked up at them. "You kill them?"

"We don't shoot at no kneecaps where we come from," Security Mike said. He had gotten to his feet and come forward, cradling the long gun in one arm. "But you shoulda figured on that, busting your asses into a Interforce base and hauling on people you don't even know without askin first."

"Thought some other gang'd moved in ahead of us," Tom said, reluctantly. "Weren't gonna let that go just like that, and they said all you'd left," he added. "Weren't no one here last time we came lookin." He eyed them. "Cause we looked good around before we came on in."

More of the intruders clustered into the hallway, filling it and the doorway to the shuttle pad that was braced wide open. They all carried something that could be used in a fight, and were in heavy clothing, carrying sacks draped over their shoulders.

They all looked haggard. Their skin was chapped and roughened, most had scrapes and old bruises on their hands. And they had a close on the edge of desperate look in their eyes that was at stark contrast to the four people holding the hall against them.

Comm crackled in Jess's ear, just as she was about to answer. "Jess, It's Dev."

The voice tickled her, and she put one hand up to her ear to cup it. "Hey, Dev. What's up." She stood braced in the middle of the hall, her eyes sweeping from side to side as she listened.

"We have a meteorological alert. The front is arriving before we expected." Dev said. "I think we should perform this activity quickly." There was a pause. "Is everything optimal there?"

Jess exhaled. "No," she answered. "But I'm not sure hanging around here's going to make it any better." She closed the channel. "Weathers," she addressed the man. "How many you got out there?"

The woman was the one who answered. "Bout five hundred." She stared somewhat insolently at Jess. "All them folk who depended on this here place. Bet the likes of you didn't know nothing about that."

"Wasn't our job to know that." April shifted her grip on her gun. "So don't be an asshole about it."

Jess made up her mind. "Yeah, okay. Here's a deal," she said. "Bring em in. You all want to bunk in here, have at it. We don't want it."

They eyed her suspiciously. "Could you stop us?" The woman asked suddenly. "You ain't got so many people here. Why should we deal with ya?"

Jess grinned suddenly, and April laughed outright.

Todd shook his head. "You all are some stupid people. Don't mess with the Drake, yo?" He told the woman. "You want dead? You'll get em, yah? That's how we do it at the Bay."

That seemed to click something, bodies shifted and almost instinctively April took a pace closer to Jess and lifted her gun. Jess herself let her hand rest on her blaster and tensed, hoping they really weren't going to have to shoot their way through five hundred scrapers on the cusp of a storm.

"The Drake?" Weathers asked. "Hold on. From that Bay? Thought you were in service."

Jess shrugged. "Before I ended up at Interforce, I came from somewhere. That somewhere was Drake's Bay," she said. "That's where we're going back to. So, you want to camp here? We want mech out of here, and we'll be coming back for it. Leave it alone, the rest of the place – have at it. Deal?"

The woman came around him and already started looking around the hallway. "This real?" She asked. "You ain't fooling with us?" She stared sharply at Jess. "Ain't a game?"

The sound of boots coming from inside the facility made both April and Jess turn, but the space behind them was soon filled with bio alts holding prybars, Dev with her scanner and Dan Kurok with a long gun cradled in both hands.

"Cavalry's here," Jess said in a wryly humorous tone. "Make up your minds, cause now you're in real trouble."

"Ah, hello." Kurok strolled in and came to stand between Jess and Security Mike. "My goodness, what have we here?"

"Civ," Jess said, succinctly. "Scavengers who used this place as a drop-off."

"I see." Kurok studied the group. "That explains the missing supplies, hm?"

"I told em to camp out if they keep an eye on things for us,"

Jess said. "What's the met scoop, Devvie?"

Dev showed her the scanner screen. "It's a very large system," she said to Tom, who sidled over to glimpse at the device. "Its excellent that these people will be able to shelter here, Jess. But we need to lift now if you want to remove that door."

"Right," Jess said. "So, you in with this?" She asked Tom, and the man and woman who had confronted her. "Yes or no? We're outta time."

"Yeh," the woman said, forestalling the other two. "Ain't no real choice anyhow."

Jess nodded and made a circling gesture with one finger to the rest of her group. "If you know how to tidal trap there' s a cavern on level five down you can get catch out of," she said briskly. "I got bored with mess snacks." She took Dev by the shoulder and turned her around. "Let's go."

She guided Dev out and Mike and April quickly followed with Todd walking backwards after them, watching everyone with a skeptical eye.

"That's that, lads," Kurok told the sets. "Now let's get back to our ships, shall we?" He clapped Keko and Kevin on the shoulder. "Next time we stop by I'll bring schematics of the place," he told Tom, with a wink. "Not much is working here but the power, but it's a lot drier than shore caves."

"Ain't even got that here," Tom said. "We just use plas." He looked around. "Megan, let's get a move on," he told the woman. "Jesar, we can fix it up later on just get every'body under cover." He looked at Kurok. "This all real? You from here too?"

Kurok regarded him, the long gun still clasped in his hands. "Long story we don't have time for right now," he said. "Take it as it comes. I can tell you that was the Drake of Drake's Bay, and she'll do what she says she will." He ushered the bio alts out ahead of him. "Do yourselves a favor and don't poke her."

The three scavengers watched them head up the long sloping hallway lit with a blare of piercing halon light. "Don't like it," Jesar said. "Everybody knows that Bay place ain't nothing but trouble."

"What ain't trouble?" Tom said. "Any case we got shelter

****

"That a good idea?" April asked, as they made their way to the landing bay. "Letting those scroungers in here?" She walked along at Jess's side as they crossed between halls, moving through the security doors they'd forced open.

"I don't have time to kill all 500 of them," Jess said absently. "And it'll piss off anyone who comes back here." She led the way into the chamber and leaped up onto the nearest landing platform. "That makes me happy."

"Point," April conceded. "Could cause us a problem getting stuff out, though."

Jess glanced at her. "One of a thousand things that could cause us problems, and not the most lethal." She glanced around at the walls. "And anyway, when you really don't have a choice, it's always good to make it seem like you made one."

April pondered that as she climbed up after her, then chuckled under her breath. Then she turned her attention to comms and opened the sideband channel they'd kept open. "Scoop is, we're moving," she told the sideband that Brent and Chester were on. "Get ready to get getting. Rocket says the weather's goin skank."

"Ack," Chester responded. "I'm dropping down to let Mike off."

"Ack," April said. "Brent all good out there?"

"Ack," Brent said. "Thought they were gonna start throwin rocks at me but it's all right," he said. "Was up over the pad just watchin, but on the way back over to that side now."

"Got it. See ya." April arrived at Jess's side, next to her carrier. "Who goes where? Those bios probably can just get these things airborne?" she asked Jess. "Can't do nothing tricky with em."

The carriers around them were all lit up, lights flashing as they went through various startup tests, hydraulics pumping a little as they shifted on skids. The air of the cavern was filled with off gassing, and the scent of warming metal.

Jess put her hands on her hips and looked around the cavern. "Yeah, leave Dev, Chester and Doug alone so no one's messing with them," Jess said. "They're not going to be able to maneuver anyway." She watched Chester touch down, and Mike emerged from the carrier with his pack on his back.

"Yup."

Jess pondered. "You're the best shot. You want to go with the doc? He can fly. Might argue with ya though."

"Think he'd rather have you," April said, in a mild tone.

"Maybe, but he'll argue with me too." Jess's eyes twinkled a little bit. "He knows I like to mess with him."

"Truth," April said. "Let me sit backseat with Brent. You go with the doc, put Mike in with… what's his name. the one that came from here. One of the K's."

Jess nodded. "Keko. Yeah he's got the best shot at it. Flew light recon in Killian class scouts." The carrier she stood next to suddenly shifted on its platform and its flight beacons flashed on, the soft rumble of the engine prestart audible to them. She stuck her head inside the hatch. "You ready to go, Devvie?"

Dev was in the pilot's seat with her comms kit on, her boards lit on either side and the front windscreen slid back to give her a good view. She turned to look at Jess. "Yes," she said. "We are prepared. Doug has exited into position."

Jess stepped back and patted the hatch. "G'wan, Rockstar. We'll meet ya back at the Bay." Dev still watched her. "Be careful, huh?"

Dev smiled. "You as well," she replied. "I will miss having you here."

Jess only just prevented herself from climbing onboard. It was a weird and uncontrolled feeling that should have been profoundly uncomfortable and yet wasn't. "Awww." She finally managed to get her tongue untied. "Thanks." She ducked outside and stepped back. "Clear."

The hatch sealed, and both Jess and April retreated from the craft and then jumped off the platform to get out of the way as Dev took off, sliding sideways to clear the rest of the landing areas and then move forward through the opening in the wall.

Outside the cloudy sky was still dry, but darkening in the north, and the winds were starting to pick up, bursting fitfully through the bay and blowing debris around them.

"Let's go," Jess said, "before it gets wild."

"Ack." April headed for the highest landing pad, where Brent waited to pick her up. "Cept all our days are wild," she remarked to herself. "But I think I like that."

Jess walked along the deck to the carrier Dan Kurok stood outside of. She put a hand on the edge of it and vaulted up to its surface to join him. "Your kids ready to go?"

"As can be." Kurok gave her a wry look, as they went inside. "Now let's hope we beat this weather."

"Let's hope we beat the weather, let's hope those steel cables hold, let's hope we don't take out the loading dock drop- ping that door in…" Jess settled into the gunner seat with a sigh. "Can't possibly have a smooth ending to this day."

****

"Drakes Bay operations, this is Bay Flight." Kurok's voice echoed through comms. "We are on initial approach."

"Drake's Bay Ops acknowledges your presence," a bio alt voice promptly answered. "Welcome back, Doctor Dan. Scan registers ten vehicles and one large object."

"That is correct," Kurok said. "Seven additional Bantam class carriers that will need landing pads, and the three we started out with, who will be maneuvering over the landside access corridor. Please have everyone clear of that area."

"Yes, Doctor Dan. We understand," Ops responded. "The space is prepared." Behind the comms, there were whoops and cheers audible in the background. "Ground operations confirm all is secure."

"Landing those carriers is probably going to be what turns out to be the most dangerous part of this flight," Kurok said to Jess, who was relaxing in her seat behind him. "Tremendously noneventful travel. Quite surprising."

"Scary," Jess said. "I don't like it when everything goes smoothly. It makes me itch." She looked past the pilot's seat out the uncovered half circle windows on the front of the craft and watched the curving coastline slowly resolve into the outthrust she knew was the Bay. "But here we are."

"Here we are." Kurok glanced to his right and left. "Our new pilots seem to be doing well."

"Nothing crashed," Jess said. "Yet."

"Jesslyn."

Jess looked up to see him watch her from the reflective surface over the pilot's station. "Hey, I expect perfection after my last experience with your work." She grinned briefly. "I remember coming out of that first flight we did and flipping out."

"Ah, well. They're good lads, but they're not Dev." Kurok said, then checked his screen to see the three burdened carriers in the center of the wide sphere of the rest of them at staggered flight levels.

The three experienced pilots were flying in a triangle, with Dev at the front point, long cables descended from their structures down to the huge cavern door dangling below them. "That's a once in a lifetime result, I think," Kurok mused. "I really don't think I could duplicate Dev."

Jess grinned in reflex. "Yeah." She put her hands behind her head. "She's for sure unique. Not sure I'd want you to try."

"Dev probably feels the same." Kurok made an adjustment then sat back in the pilot seat. "Though I know it's a bit difficult when you aren't like everyone else around you, as she was when she was growing up."

"I felt like that at Canyon City," Jess said. "So, I get it."

"Did you?" Kurok half turned to look at her. "You know, there might be something in that. Before this all happened I made a trip out there as I had some questions."

Jess looked at him, head halfcocked to one side. "You went to school?"

He nodded. "I did. I brought your nephew a present from home. A picture of the Bay, actually. As an excuse to let me get at a comp console and pull your records."

Jess blinked. "You hacked Canyon?"

Kurok nodded. "Yes. Unfortunately, I haven't had a chance to look at any of it since it was on the way back from there I got told of that message from Interforce and we've been a bit busy since then. "I wanted to see what their records showed because you're not exactly the profile I expected."

"You flew out there, walked in, and hacked them?" Jess repeated.

"Mmhm." His eyes twinkled. "I've never been very conventional, I'm afraid," he said. "Gotten me into all sorts of trouble over the years. But in this case, it was relatively simple as I was hosted in the administrator's office with a cup of tea next to his console while he went to get Tayler for our chat."

Jess started laughing.

"Incoming new vessels in Bay Flight, please use landing bay one, two, and three, they are prepared for your arrival," Comms echoed suddenly. "Tech Brent, please land on pad 2, in bay eight."

"Roger that," Brent answered. "Headin over."

"Right." Kurok adjusted course again. "Here we are. Let me take this one in." He banked and set a course for the lowest of the landing bays. "Now, Keko, follow me to landing bay 1," he instructed into the sideband. "I'm going to land on pad 1, you take pad 2."

"Yes, Doctor Dan," Keko agreed. "This vehicle is handling well. I do not see any difficulty."

"Kevin, you and Karl take landing bay 2, you take pad one, Karl take pad 2."

"Yes."

"Yes."

"Bet Mike's glad he didn't have to get on the triggers," Jess said. "But I know Mike from Security was hoping he'd get the chance."

"Mm. I'm certain that's just a matter of time." Kurok made an adjustment. "Kerin, you, and Keith take bay 3, pads 1 and 2. Now take it slow into the bays, we don't want to cause any fuss. Come level, and then reduce speed until you're just drifting in. Just a touch of jets once you're inside."

"Yes, Doctor Dan." A chorus of voices, eerily the same, with just slight inflection differences answered him.

Jess felt her ears pop as they lost altitude, then the outside sensors turned on and the sea bells chimed in, echoing loudly as they came in over the wall and entered bay waters. She saw a flurry of activity around the landing caverns, stacked up the rock wall from near water level to the top of the cliffs.

In the past, only one or two were used for the working light fliers that belonged to the Bay, and they were small, nothing like the massive hangar Base 10 had kept.

Now the three upper level and three lower level had their access doors spread wide open to the Bay frontage to allow the incoming carriers to enter and land on service pads just large enough to accommodate their much larger bulk.

"Bay flight, we are going to proceed over to the landing zone," Dev said. "We are detecting wind speeds increasing."

"Confirmed," Ops answered. "Met topside agrees this is a good course of action."

Below them, Jess saw vessels heading into the inner ship docking cavern, and a quick glance showed the long slips on the large vessel piers being secured. "Docks are full again."

"Mm." Kurok slowed his forward motion further. "Either that or outrun the storm. I saw the pressure gradients on that front, it's not to be trifled with. So, let's get ourselves inside before it becomes an issue."

He leveled out and approached the lowest landing bay, its steel doors flung wide open. Two Bay workers on either side watched them approach, the winds fluttering their overshirts and sending their hair into wild disarray. They raised their arms and pumped fists as the carrier drifted gracefully past them, crossing the threshold as its landing skids extended and locked.

A moment later and they were settled on the left-hand side pad, with two bio alts and one Bay resident waiting with connections for them. Kurok shut down the engines and popped the hatch open. He turned in his seat to watch Keko coming into land on the right-hand side pad. "Easy now."

Jess was already loose of her restraints and at the open hatch and watched the other craft land in a gingerly, but relatively competent way, settling on its skids on the metal grating with an almost audible mechanical rattle. "Not bad."

"No." Kurok ran a routine on the boards and slid the pilots' seat back. "Not at all, for some basic instruction. When I get that programming rig operational, that'll be an advantage."

The door of the other carrier opened, and Mike Arias emerged, pausing to look behind him inside. "Good job, K-Man!" He called back, giving a little wave before he emerged and walked over to the edge of the platform to face Jess. "Nice ride," he said. "Everybody did good."

Kurok climbed down after Jess and came over, hoisting his pack to his back. "Yes that was exceptionally successful so far." He glanced across as Keko emerged, looking a bit drained but happy. "Keko, excellent work," he. "Really well done."

Keko produced a tired, but pleased grin. "Thank you, Doctor Dan! It was hard, but I enjoyed it very much. These craft are much more interesting to fly than the others." He looked at the carrier, as one of the mechs came over and attached a power lead, then reached out to give it a pat on the hull. "Optimal."

"Excellent. You spend some time shutting things down, and we can schedule more SIM time," Kurok said, then hastily followed Jess and Mike to the inner hall as they headed for the rear of the stake hold. "And shut that outside door!" He yelled at the bay mechs.

****

Dev inched her seat forward a bit, leaning against her restraints as she angled the carrier just a trifle, giving her a better visual look at the cliffs underneath them. She felt the tug of wind against the carrier's skin, and the engines rumbled on either side of her as the craft worked to move the heavy weight dangling beneath it.

It was hard. Dev studied all her consoles, her head moving back and forth as she kept track of their progress, the target they were aiming for, the rapidly approaching weather front, and the sync program that was running on the three carriers to keep it all in place.

So far, it had worked. Each carrier control system was taking signal from hers, using her gyros to plot course with. This insured they all moved in concert and didn't drift off course.

They had sideband up, and both Doug and Chester were making small talk, which Dev only half listened to. The most difficult part of the activity was ahead, and she checked and rechecked her plots. They slowly drifted over the tall range that held Drake's Bay and moved along the top of the ridge toward the rear escarpment and its jagged surrounding walls.

"Hey, Rocket, we got what, now ten knots aft?"

Dev glanced at her met station. "Yes," she said. "We are five minutes from mark. Ideally it will not get stronger before that time." She drew in a breath and exhaled. "Please stand by to maneuver."

"Roger that," Doug said. "I can see the tracking... looks good."

"On target," Chester chimed in. "Man, I can't believe we got this all done without that being a shitshow back at base."

"No kidding, and six... no seven other busses?" Doug practically chortled. "They may be old, but damn, that's a scoop for sure!"

"Yeah, great idea April had," Chester said. "Freakin useful crates. Nothin they had here coulda lifted that door but these big ass donks had no problem."

"True that."

Dev triggered the delivery program, and the carrier slowed and drifted downward toward the gap in the cliffs. Below her the wind whipped the ground and several alerts went off as the carrier shifted. "Wind shear rising."

"Yeah, plus two," Doug said. C'mon, Rocket, land this puppy and let's get back in the barn before we get blown over."

Dev checked the comms panel briefly. "Programming is in work," she responded, as they shifted sideways in unison. "Please be prepared to take control of the vehicles if autonomics do not perform."

"Got my hands on the rockets, Rocket," Doug said. "But man, I hope I don't have to. I'm gonna fly this crate right into that wall for sure."

"Yeah, that last gust was no joke." Chester sounded worried. "Look at that damn sky."

The clouds, always present, were thick and darkening. They moved in rapid sequence from the north and the tops of the cliffs. Dev felt the carrier shift against the pressure, and gripped her throttles, her boots against the thrusters.

Nonoptimal.

Out of parameters. Dev reached out and deactivated her program then took back manual control. She immediately felt the pressure against her hands as the wind drove against the front of the carrier and her body made automatic adjustments, trimming the control planes on all three machines.

Driving a single carrier in these conditions was a bit difficult.

Dev had all three under her control, though, and watched the two readbacks from the other two vehicles closely as she navigated over the gap and saw the space cleared below them of all obstructions.

"Got it nice and clean, hah?" Doug said. "Nice."

Dev edged them forward and tried to judge the extra movement from the wind as it pushed against them and the giant door dangling underneath them. The bottom of it cleared the cliff and then they dropped down again, moving toward the angled gap the door would fit into.

Dev swallowed and licked her lips. She felt anxious and more than a little stressed as she took all the inputs from three scan systems and tried to judge how to move their huge burden across the pass.

"Don't drop it, huh, Dev?" Chester said. "We'll have a hell of a time getting it back up."

"Yes," Dev said, shortly. "Please do not disturb the controls at this time."

There was a brief silence. "Uh oh," Doug muttered softly. "You're on manual aren't you?"

"Yes," Dev said. "Stand by wind speed is increasing."

It got a lot harder then and she had no time to discuss it. She felt the carrier shift and immediately reacted, applying side thrusters as they twisted, shunting the craft into the wind to reduce the drag as they approached the drop point.

There would be no second chance. Dev understood that at once. She added power to the carrier's engines and the three craft moved faster toward the gap, traveling rapidly over the ground just as the winds started to push them into the cliffside.

"Dev!" Doug yelped. "Yow!"

"Be calm," Dev called out sharply. "Stand by to lift and maneuver."

"Oh shit."

Dev hit the landing boosters, and all three craft shuddered and lifted in unison, bringing the huge door, now swinging in the wind, up and over the outcropping just inside the gap the door would go into. Then she hit the engine reverse hard, sending them all backwards, while the door swung forward, and then dropped, its edge slamming into the ground.

She shifted the engines into forward and they came up and over the top of the door, pulling it upright and into place. Alarms went off as the winds were too high for the carriers to handle. "Releasing load," Dev called out, and hit the cable controls, freeing them from the door.

"We can't get back over!" Doug yelled back. "It's a

hundred knots!"

Dev still had control of all three vehicles. "Please hold on." She slammed all three engines into emergency mode and drove them forward, and then up. She used the wind to force them aloft and then tumble them head over tail in the air.

"Yah!" Doug yelped.

"Oh shiiiiit," Chester responded.

"Be calm." Dev wrenched her throttles around and booted the thrusters as the outwash slammed against the rock walls and brought them upright, enough in the lee of the rock to regain full control. She directed the three craft into a landing spot near the inner wall and quickly set them down hard. The skids barely extended in time to catch them as they slammed into the earth.

The wind grabbed them and nearly tumbled them all out of her control. For a moment Dev felt things slipping out of her grip. She threw herself forward into the console and kicked the side thrusters hard, the carrier shuddered, alarms flaring all around her.

Then they were all down fully, and the storm came over-head, cutting loose with a thunderous wall of rain that rocked the carriers violently, skidding them across the ground and bumping each other until Chester's thumped against the rock wall.

That, and the solid door they'd just landed behind them, cut enough of the force to allow them to settle. Alert lights flashed in the dim gray light outside.

"Oh. Crap," Doug groaned. "What the hell was that we just did?"

"Ooof," Chester managed to cough into his mic.

Dev released her throttles and leaned back in her seat. "Hello?" She spoke tentatively into comms. "Are you all functional?"

"Thank f'n eff I was in restraints," Chester responded. "Ow," he added. "Gotta nosebleed I think."

"Pretty good here," Doug added. "I think."

Dev concluded that was a reasonable assumption that both her companions had survived her aerobatics and their hard landing. "Excellent." She exhaled and looked around at her protesting boards. "But something less than optimal."

She started a check of systems, running through the alerts that lit the inside of the carrier in an offended red color. She turned them off and acknowledged they'd kicked off far too late as she'd rotated the carriers in space in a way they'd never been designed to either perform or tolerate.

"Holy crap," Doug's voice echoed through comms. "Did you really take all of us upside down, Rocket?"

"Yes." Dev got everything quieted down, then another soft alert sounded, scan noting a bio reading. She looked out the front plas at the sheets of water and spotted something moving in their direction.

Dev coded a scan in a rapid motion, of the rain obscured blur, and then grinned. She hovered her hand over the hatch trigger as the carrier rocked in the wind. She waited until the figure got closer and became recognizable as it fought hard against the gale, the force of the wind almost impeding its forward motion.

Almost. Then it lunged for the ground and used an odd, crablike motion to duck under the wind shear in a swift and powerful move directly toward the carrier, refusing to bend to the weather.

A moment later Dev hit the release. The storm burst into the carrier with a wild howl and a blast of icy cold rain, along with a tall and extremely wet figure who slammed across the floor and hit the wall. Dev resealed the hatch and it thumped closed with a robotically outraged sound.

Jess slid sideways and landed on the jump seat, spraying Dev with a fine shower of stone scented rainwater. "Dev!" She got out in a gust. "That was freakin awesome!"

Dev regarded her with a smile. "Hello. Are you okay?"

"Everyone," Jess said, "is flipping their damn lids inside."

"I see." Dev removed a dry piece of cloth from her kit and reached over to wipe Jess's face off. "I have no idea what that is," she admitted. "Was it suboptimal? I don't think we damaged anything too badly."

Jess laughed her silent laugh.

Dev felt the chill of Jess's damp skin against her fingertips, but the sparkle of those eyes made her smile again. She laid her palm against Jess's cheek to warm it. "And you could have called me on comms, Jess. You didn't have to come out in the rain. That must have been very uncomfortable."

"I didn't want to call you." Jess took her hand and kissed the back of it. "Can't do this over comms." She smiled back. "You nailed it. Was that the program? It wasn't right?" She asked. "Wasn't the script?"

"No," Dev said. "That was written for the expected weather. Not what we experienced. I switched to manual control as we came over the top of the wall there." She pointed through the window, at the back side of Drake's Bay. "There wasn't really any time to discuss it."

Jess kissed her hand again. "What was there to discuss? You were flying." She grinned. "Whole place is in there talking about it."

Dev made a face. "I didn't do that on purpose, Jess."

"Aww, Devvie." Jess leaned her long frame back against the wall and gazed fondly at her. Then she looked down at her drenched pants. "And yeah, I coulda just raised you on comms. Whole stakehold must think I'm nuts running out here like an idiot and nearly getting my ass blown into the wall."

"Actually, I'm glad you did," Dev said, with a smile. Jess looked up at her in surprise. "I felt like I did something difficult and scary and possibly incorrect. I wanted to talk to you about it." She continued to wipe the droplets of cold rain off Jess's face. "I hope I did the right thing."

"You did the perfect thing," Jess finally said. "You kidding me? Wait till you see the vid. You landed the door, and all the buses, and nobody croaked. It was awesome!"

Dev's nose wrinkled up into a wry expression. "I don't think it was very comfortable for Chester and Doug."

"Don't worry about it. It's all good," Jess said. "Those guys know you're legit a rockstar." She paused, thoughtfully. "Hey, that's what we should call this thing." She patted the jump seat. "You like that? Dustin wants to paint it on the outside."

"Um. What?" Dev looked at her with an adorably bewildered look that made Jess grin all the wider. "Jess, what are you talking about?" She finally asked, in a plaintive tone. "He wants to paint what where?"

Jess flicked some droplets of rain off her hands and extended her long legs across the deck. "This ain't Interforce anymore," she said. "We gotta play by Bay rules."

"Yes," Dev agreed. "But what does that have to do with painting something on the outside of this craft?"

"They want to give these old crates Bay names, for comms," Jess explained. "Dustin wanted to know what I wanted to call this one, so he could put it on the outside, like our names. All the ships have em."

"Oh." Dev considered that. "Can't it just have a number, like it did there?"

"Nope. Ops likes names," Jess said. "Like the doc's flyer. It's Bay Alpha. Bay A." She bumped Dev's knee with her own. "What do you think... Rockstar?" Her eyebrows hiked up invitingly. "C'mon, it's cute." Jess paused. "Like you."

"Um. Okay. I suppose that is better than some other

possibilities," Dev said, with slightly knit brows.

Jess snickered.

"Ack ack." The comms channel opened "We got winds coming down to sixty knots, Rocket," Doug said. "We'll end up drier if we fly over to the other side."

"Yeah, got this thing to stop bitching," Chester said. We could maybe fly out in like ten?"

Dev reached over and released the sync that linked the carriers and reset her boards. "I have unlocked all the controls," she said. "I agree it will be more comfortable exiting into the landing bay." She paused and regarded her passenger. "At least, for myself."

Doug chuckled. "We saw Jess haul in," he said. "Thought she was going to get airborne there for a minute."

"I thought so too," Jess said. "You all okay?"

"Roger that," Chester answered. "Now I know what it's like going upside down. Got the blood all cleaned up. Banged my face on the console."

Dev grimaced.

"Oh, hell I knew better," Doug said. "Had every strap in this thing wrapped around my ass. Great ride, Rocket." He sounded cheerful. "Super glad it was you on the stick."

"Yeah, sweet flying," Chester agreed. "First mugs on me when we get inside."

Dev felt her face heat. "Thank you," she finally said. "It's excellent it turned out well." She gave her head a little shake, then looked over at Jess, who was watching her with a grin on her face, her wet hair in remarkable disarray. "I think I should establish that this activity is neither regular nor optimal."

"Me too," Jess said. "Otherwise, you won't get a damn thing done cause everyone's gonna want you to give them rides in this thing, repeating that little trick."

"Jess."

"Think I'm kidding?"

Chapter Thirteen

The storm was still blowing hard as they made their approach to landing, and Dev could see the mechs at their landing bay piled out onto the verge of it, literally being almost lifted by the gusts of wind coming in over the water as well as being drenched by swathes of rain blowing against the stone.

She glanced in the reflective surface. "Jess."

Jess slid sideways to meet her gaze, from her gunner's chair. "Sup?"

Dev pointed at the bay entrance. "I think they are going to be damaged. The wind gusts are not very predictable."

Jess obligingly got up and came forward. She sat on the jump seat and leaned her elbow on the arm of the pilot's chair. "Idiots," she said as she looked past Dev's shoulder. She sighed. "Their asses get blown into the bay I ain't jumping in after them."

Dev frowned. "They do realize this vehicle moves unexpectedly in the wind, correct?"

Jess snickered. "They probably think you can do a somersault in there and they don't want to miss it."

"Jess, I can't do that."

"Ya tried?"

"Of course not," Dev said. "I could seriously damage many things, including us."

"Then how do ya know?" Jess's eyes glinted with mischief. "You drove this carrier into a cavern and out with less than zero clearance. Maybe you could flip it in there. Who knows?"

Dev sighed again.

"Not today, Rocket." Jess bumped her gently with her head. "I'm just messing with ya. Those yonks can all swim if you knock em off the ledge. Relax. You get thrown in the water here before you can walk."

The carrier dropped to landing level and Dev maneuvered her way through the entrance. She shook her head as the mechs reached out to touch the sides of the craft as it moved past them, their yells of excitement audible through the metal skin.

Jess was still leaning on the arm of the pilot's seat. "Y'know, way way back in the day they used to paint pictures of women on the outside of fighter planes," she said. "Maybe…"

Dev focused on landing the carrier without hitting anyone. "Jess, I would not find having a picture on the side of this craft optimal."

Jess snickered again. "C'mon, land this thing. I want to get out of these wet clothes."

Dev set the carrier down on its assigned pad, rotating as she reached it so the nose was pointed back at the entranceway. She shut down the engines and started the process to turn things off, then turned in her seat and regarded the mischievous expression at her elbow.

Jess was absolutely in a good mood. Dev leaned over and rubbed noses with her. "We have landed," she said, meeting her eyes. "Were you going to take your clothes off now?" She asked, with interest. "That would be excellent, but I would wait for the front screen sensors to quiesce."

Jess's eyes widened, then she blushed and looked quickly toward the opening, only to find it already covered by its protective overlay. "You're trying to distract me from that picture," she said. "Sneaky, Rocket."

"Was I successful?"

Jess laughed. "Yes," she said. Let's go." She stood and offered Dev her hand. "Open the hatch." She waited for Dev to finish the close out routine and undog the exit, which popped open and let the sound of cheers and rain and thunder inside.

Dev collected her pack and settled it onto her back, checking to ensure all her tools and kit were accounted for as she stepped around the pilot's seat and followed Jess to the door.

Outside the mech crew, and lots of others were celebrating. Dev assumed that's what they were doing because they were waving their arms and cheering and performing odd gyrations and bumping into each other in a raucous and random manner.

Hesitantly, she waved at them, and the crowd obligingly chanted Rocket at her, while Jess stood there with her hands tucked into her front pouch pocket, looking amused.

Dev walked over to stand next to her. "What are they doing?" She whispered, but loud enough for Jess to hear her. "With all that jumping around?"

"Huh? Oh. Snoopy dancing," Jess said. "It's a Bay thing."

Literally incomprehensible. Dev watched as the work suit covered figures capered around, pumping their arms and legs up and down, and bouncing off each other like rubber exercise balls.

What was it that Security Mike said at times? What the what? That seemed to Dev to fit the occasion, and she mouthed it to herself silently. Yes. What the what?

"C'mon." Jess nudged her. "This'll go on for a while, until

we get called to mess." She put her hand on Dev's back and guided her forward, and like magic a path appeared through the crowd for them to walk through, despite the celebration going on.

Jess spotted Dustin nearby, coming down from an actual somersault in the air. "Dustin! Hey!"

He paused in mid wiggle and bounced over. "Yo, cuz." He pumped his fist at Dev. "That was awesomesauce, Rocket lady!"

"Thank you," Dev said.

"Hey," Jess said, "Dev okayed the name. The one I told you about."

His face lit up. "Rockstar? Yeah?" He hopped up and down. "Sweet."

"Okay, we're outta here," Jess said. "Make sure these things get taken care of." She reached out and slapped him on the shoulder. "Later."

Dev allowed herself to be steered on out of the landing bay, returning the congratulations from the mechs until they reached the inner passageway that led through to the grand hall, and the top of the spiral staircase that would let them travel down to the level their quarters were on.

As they reached the levels where the sets lived, there was a more sedate event going on. The new pilots were being congratulated by their set mates and both gathering areas were full as they listened to the experience being related, so absorbed they didn't spot the two of them descending.

"Really was good stuff," Jess said, as they reached the ground level. "I hear we're gonna get something good for dinner tonight."

"It's amazing," Dev said. "Really amazing how happy everyone is about what we did." She paused thoughtfully. "I think we did other things before, Jess, and it wasn't that exciting for everyone."

Jess nodded as they crossed to the steps up to their rooms. "We pulled off way bigger gigs for Interforce, Dev. You and me. What did you get for that first one? A comfort pack and some supplies." She looked around the cavern, full of people watching them, waving at them, happy for them.

Happy for themselves. "It's different," Jess said. "It's different, here."

"In an excellent way," Dev said, soberly. "It's optimal to have good work recognized."

"Yeah." Jess put her hand on the scan pad. "Well, today we all did a good job." She pulled her sodden shirt away from her skin as the door opened and they entered their space. "Happy my reward right now is that warm shower waiting for me and celebrating your rockstarness."

"May I share the shower with you?"

"Sure!"

"Then that's enough reward for me," Dev said, with a smile. "Though I will consider shrimps for dinner as an extra benefit. "

"Aww Devvie …."

****

Jess went down to the admin area to talk to Doctor Dan, so Dev finally had a chance to sit down in her workspace and request vid of the flight outside. She was perched on her work stool, in her lined jumpsuit, warm and with a cup of hot tea at her elbow. She settled in to watch whatever it was that was so interesting to everyone else, while outside, the storm still raged.

The carriers had been docked just in time, as another wave of high winds and squalls now lashed the Bay. Torrents of rain- water cascaded off the top of the cliffs, coming past her plas window and thundering into a waterfall in the crevice at the edge of their quarters.

"Now." Dev started the vid playback. "Let's see what this is all about."

The vid started up, a timestamp visible on its upper left corner from the security cams that captured the approach of the flight toward the Bay. She saw the carriers, moving gingerly, with Brent stationed off to one side in the point position in more confident motion.

In the middle were the experienced carriers with herself, Doug and Chester in the pilot seats, the huge door hanging from what seemed like impossibly thin metal cable attached to the bottom of their three crafts.

Then the six carriers and Brent broke out of formation and headed for the landing bays. All normal, and she nodded as she saw the three experienced carriers change direction and head up toward the top of the mountain facia.

She remembered that well, seeing the weather shift, and directing them to their destination. Yes, that all made sense.

Made sense, and there was nothing special about it.

Now the vid abruptly changed focus, going from the ocean facing cams to the loading dock cams on the back side of the cliffs. For a minute it was just the cliffs, with visibly rising winds picking up debris from the ground and causing tiny dust cones, and then the sound cut in.

Rumbles of thunder, sounds of the wind, and then the sound of carriers in flight as the massive steel panel drifted into cam range, moving in the wind, swaying back and forth.

Dev watched in fascination as the carriers moved in synchronous flight, then sped up, her mind remembering bits and pieces of it happening.

She recalled realizing the winds were going to rise past their ability to stay aloft with their heavy burden and as she remembered that the motion increased in a surge and she saw the moment she took manual control and that memory overlaid what she now watched, her heartbeat increasing.

Dev stared at the screen when it was done, now understanding a bit better the reaction of the people who had watched, while she had been working very hard to do the right thing at the time. "Ah." She exhaled. "Now I see."

She ran through the whole vid again and thought about how it must have looked to everyone else because the motion, on the vid, looked easy, as though she'd planned it out and executed it that way instead of just… Dev sat back. Instead of just being a reaction to the circumstances she'd found herself in.

Was that praiseworthy? "Hey, Dev."

Dev looked over at comms and touched the control. "Yes."

"You see the vid?" Doug asked with a knowing tone. "Yes," Dev said. "I have just observed it."

"Crazy, huh?" Doug said. "Like… I know I ask this all the time, but how did you do that?"

How had she done it. "It was not a planned activity," she finally said. "So, I can't say what the process flow was for it. "

"You just did it."

"I just did it," Dev agreed.

"Wow." Doug sighed. "That was something. Like a toss my stomach up through my nose something, but something." He cleared his throat. "So, all the other drivers asked me to ask you if you could walk us through it tomorrow."

Dev stared in silence at the comms.

"Dev?"

"What does that mean?" Dev asked. "You want me to do that maneuver again?" Her voice lifted in astonishment.

"No no no," Doug replied, "Just like… watch the vid and talk about it," he said. "Like we used to do at Base."

"Oh." Dev pondered. "Yes, I will do that," she said. "It

would be good to explain what happened." She turned off the vid and sat back on her stool. "Did the sets do well in their mission? I was occupied and couldn't watch them."

"Oh yeah. They did good, and they're super happy," Doug said. "Great, I'll tell them you'll be there. They're all chuffed at getting to drive these old busses. It's funny kinda," he said. "I mean, here we are bitching, you know?"

Dev smiled. "It's good work," she said. "It's an advanced assignment. They would value it very much since bio alts were not permitted to operate Bantams in the past."

"Oh," Doug said. "You mean you actually were the very first?"

"Yes," Dev said. "Now, possibly, Doctor Dan can give them the tech loading I was given before I came down world. That would be very helpful to them in operating these vehicles. In any case, we can discuss it tomorrow, will that be acceptable?"

"For sure, Dev. Talk to you later." Doug signed off comms with an echoing click.

Dev sat back, picked up her cup of tea and took a sip, savoring the rich, pungent taste of the sea grapes. She turned to watch the storm outside the window, the deluge still drenching the Bay and waves crashing on the outside of the seawalls.

She thought a moment of the scavengers, sheltering in the now empty Base, possibly standing in the lower hallways looking out of the gap where the door had been, watching the rain fall as she was. Glad not to be in it, dry and comfortable for probably the first time in a very long time.

She wondered how that would turn out. Would they get to stay there? Would Interforce return and chase them out? Would some other group try to replace them? Probably they had learned to appreciate the moment, as she had on insertions, and were just enjoying being in a good place for however long they could.

Bio alts lived that way. You really had no control over what happened to you so when things were excellent, you appreciated them, and held them in high regard for the times when they weren't. There would always be those times, after all, even for natural born it seemed.

Her thoughts turned to the day, and the sets in their comfortable quarters here at Drake's Bay, all clustered around the new vehicles, and their smiling new drivers, as they stepped down from the decks of the battered craft in that glow of good work well done.

The KayTees had been tremendously excited to get to pilot the carriers. Dev wondered if they would be allowed to continue doing that, or if Bay residents would be trained up for it. Perhaps both, since the KayTees would be able to get programming that the natural born couldn't.

They would have to learn the hard way, like natural born always had. Like she herself needed to.

She made a note to ask Jess about it, then turned back to her input console and reviewed the screen. "Now." She switched displays. "Let's see what this Snoopy thing is." She typed in an input, then sat back when the results returned a cartoon animal on the screen. "What the what?"

****

"It was astonishing," Dan Kurok said, seated at the conference table in the Bay's small meeting room. Jess and Security Mike sat across from him. "I literally have never seen anyone do anything like that." He made a vague gesture at the screen they'd just watched the vid on. "Incredible flying."

"You teach them all to be like that?" Security Mike asked, bluntly. "That'd be a thing."

"Certainly not," Kurok retorted, just as bluntly. "I have no idea how she did it, much less how one would teach that sort of thing. With the rig we got, I can, and will, give them the technical background on those crates. That will certainly help them operate them. But do what Dev did?" He lifted is hands and let them drop. "I couldn't even begin to solution that."

"Bummer," Mike said. "That'd be killer having a dozen Rockets around."

Jess spoke up. "That's not learned. It's instinct. Dev just does it. She doesn't have to think about it. No time to with that kind of sitch in work."

Kurok nodded. "I think that's true. There are things that all of us have that came with the package, so to speak. You can tune a subject's proclivities – you can give them a body of supportive knowledge, like we did with the technical background Dev got, but the integration of that with actual performance—"

"Turned out way more kickass than you expected," Jess finished for him.

Kurok smiled. "Well, I really wasn't sure exactly what to expect, you know. That's what the developmental new model was about, after all. I had a theory and assembled what I thought was the right design, but honestly you never really know with a developmental model until they come to a final integration of it all."

"'Cause in the end, she's a people," Jess said. "Even the prod models you did are a little different from each other."

"We like that," Mike said. "S'why we wanted names not just those weird letter things."

"They are people," Kurok said. "And they adapt to their environment, and the way they're living just like any other people, at least..." His lips twitched a little. "My version of them do at any rate. There are sets out in the world who are not quite the same mold." He paused thoughtfully. "Constant argument, on station. I encouraged their senses of individuality and many of my colleagues disagreed."

"You landed right," Mike said. "Bay's the place for being your own thing."

Kurok smiled again. "By some very odd quirk of fate, it seems so." He folded his arms. "In any case, we did manage to pull the thing off." He changed the subject. "We now have a fleet of ten mostly functional last generation heavy carriers, complete with all the work it's going to take to keep them running."

"Gotta figure what to do with those rigs," Mike said. "Least they fit in the docks. Much bigger and no idea where we'd kept em."

Jess sat relaxed in her seat, now in dry clothes and boots. "We'll figure it out," she said. "We got the things; we'll do the most we can with em." She leaned her elbows on the chair arms. "We can rig em like we did ours, with seats, and use em to fast deploy if we have to."

"Can't put that many bodies in them," Mike said. "But they can hella move. Tell ya that."

"Dev's got some tweaks in mind," Jess said, and grinned. "I heard her talking to Clint about them on the deck when we got in. They'll end up better than whatever they got out west."

"Mm." Kurok considered that. "Might have been a twist of fate in a good way, that," he mused. "Old, forgotten technology can end up biting you in the ass when you least expect it."

"Bay knows that." Mike chortled softly.

"Well," Kurok stood up, "let me get back to reassembling that programming rig. Now we really need it." He picked up the drink thermos he'd had on the table in front of him. "Since from what I saw, it's going to take all of those carriers to lift that roof section we want to bring here, and it's a bit much to expect Dev to handle all of them herself."

Jess's eyes twinkled. "Bet she could."

Kurok gave her a look. "Let's not test that. We won't cut it that close on weather the next round either. And I got a note that we're due a visit tomorrow from the buyers consortium at Quebec."

"Veg?" Mike asked.

"They want to see what we have." Kurok gave them both a wry look. "And at least now we have rapid delivery vehicles for it." He winked at them and ducked out of the room, closing the door behind him. "Whatever it ends up being," he called back.

Jess sighed. "Never-ending complications."

Mike chuckled. "F'n yeah. Good kind of crap tho. That was a blast today. Wish I'd been in one of them rigs."

"That Dev landed?" Jess eyed him. "With those ace moves?" She made a circle in the air with her finger. "All the upside down and sideways crazy?"

He nodded.

"Yeah, me too," she admitted with a grin. "First time she took us upside down I nearly lost my mind, but you get used to it. Let's you wiggle the kinks out of your back." She looked thoughtfully at him. "You looking to change slots?"

"Maybe." He watched her steadily. "Depends what that turns out to look like." He regarded Jess with a speculative eye. "After dinner should be a hoot tonight. Kids all talked it up. Few more people showing up to see what the what," he said. "Air show put a nail on it."

Jess nodded. "Yeah. Figured that."

"You got a plan?"

"Not yet." Jess put her hands behind her head and leaned back.

"Ain't got much time for it."

"Never really needed much." Jess stood up and stretched. "And most of the time plans weren't worth a cred anyway. Gotta just take what comes at you and make it work. That's field." She headed for the door to the conference room. "You just take what intel you get and go."

****

It was still raining as they walked out of the mess with a crowd of others, a low rumble of conversation around them. "Jess," Dev said, as they moved to the outside of the flow of walkers. "I would like to observe your activity tonight. Would that be all right?"

Jess glanced at her. "What? Oh, the mixup? Sure. If you want to. Come hang out with us." She glanced up at the darkened roof of the hall. "It's gonna be wet getting over there."

"Once we have the ceiling in place, that will not be an issue," Dev said. "I think I have a piece of material I can use for tonight."

"Supposed to be more people there. You got em all jazzed up," Jess said casually. "Not really sure what that's gonna mean for tonight's scrum."

Dev's brows creased. "What does that landing have to do with your activity?"

Jess didn't answer, as they strolled through the crowd. Then she laughed shortly. "Beats me. I guess we'll find out. I'm glad you'll be there."

Dev felt a sense of pleasure at that and drew in a breath, exhaling in satisfaction. They got to their space and Jess went inside first. She stopped and held a hand out to keep Dev from going any further. "Someone was here."

Dev took that at face value since Jess was always right about that sort of thing. "Should I get my scanner?"

"No, hold on." Jess turned her head slowly, drawing in a breath, her hand still extended. "Ah." She relaxed. "Resupply, I guess." She continued into the outer room, with it's odd and mismatched furniture. "I can smell the lift mech."

Jess was amazing that way. Dev went into the food preparation area, and found, in fact, that their small cooler had been replenished with snacks, and the drink dispenser was filled. "Yes," she called back. "It seems so."

She then went to her workspace and retrieved her scanner and brought it back to review the new contents, finding all to be in order. She looped the scanner over her neck and went back out through the hallways, peering inside the storage cabinets that lined the walls on the way to the lift.

All good. She paused in the hall, then swung her scanner around and moved through the hallways to the cleft at the back of the space, where the thundering sound of rain pouring down off the mountain. Dev went outside and walked along the covered area to the very back edge and knelt.

She tuned the scanner and inspected the results then looked around the area with some interest. Then she sat on the ground, cold and damp as it was, and balanced the scanner on her lap. She reviewed schematics one after the other to follow an interesting trail she'd found earlier in the day.

"Dev."

Dev looked up to see Jess peering out at her. "Hello."

"What the hell are you doing?" Jess came out into the outer area.

Dev tapped lightly on the screen. "There was this diagram I found before the night meal, and I wanted to track down where the power trace went."

Jess wandered over and sat down next to her. "Maybe drag a box out here to sit on?" She suggested. "What is it?"

"I don't know." Dev showed her the screen. "See, these are LED leads. I don't know what the point of them being here is so... wait." She tapped briefly. "Let me see what that does."

A moment later, a thin line of cool light came on at the edge of the overlook, shining up through the water pouring past it. "Oh," Dev said, in delight. "That's so pretty."

Jess sprawled next to her with her legs splayed and her weight resting back on her hands. "Huh. The hell?"

Dev typed another command in, and the light dimmed, then she reversed it, and it came back up. A few moments of experimentation and she'd found a similar line of lights on the top edge of the overlook. The combination of the two sets with its range of light made a very attractive curtain of illumination with the rain pouring through it.

"That's pretty cool," Jess said after a few minutes of silence. "Any purpose for that or is it just...?"

"I think it's just supposed to be attractive." Dev regarded her work with some satisfaction. "I like this," she said. "We could put a place to just sit here and watch it."

"We could," Jess agreed. "I could see us doing that." She looked around the platform, which now showed a slim colored light edge along its entire length. "Probably they put it in to keep people from walking off the end of it into the Bay." She waggled one booted foot. "It's nice."

Dev leaned against her shoulder. "It is. I'm glad I found it." She felt the chill of the rock under her bottom and her legs, but it was worth it to sit here and enjoy this moment with Jess. "I will program it to illuminate at night and turn off in the morning."

Jess nodded. "We gotta get some seats for out here." She hoisted herself to her feet and offered Dev a hand up. "You're turning blue again. C'mon."

Dev was pretty sure she wasn't turning any unusual color, but she stood up and dusted her heavy work pants off and followed Jess inside as the sound of the water faded, becoming a rough murmur in the background as she walked along the hall and into her workspace again.

She checked the time on her display, then set her scanner down and went over to her workbench, to stand behind it and adjust her input to include the new circuits, as the scanner synced its information over.

"Hey, Dev?"

Jess was in the doorway. "What do you think for the mixup? Should I wear this?" She held up a long-sleeved garment. "Mike figures there'll be more eyeballs there." She eyed the shirt. "That thing I was in last night was not great to rumble in. Too stiff."

Dev turned and leaned against her counter and gave the question serious thought. "I think there is something I found upstairs that might be better," she said, after a long moment. "Let me retrieve it." She went out of the door, but Jess was at her heels. "You could have remained there."

"Nah." Jess ambled along. "Save you the trip back."

They went into the closet and Dev opened the drawer that held some of the clothing she'd brought back from storage. She sorted through it and held up a handful of fabric. "See if you would find this more optimal?" She said. "It does not have sleeves."

Jess tossed the other shirt down and held up the one Dev handed her. "Oh." She put it down then stripped out of the shirt she was wearing and put the sleeveless one on instead. "It's a… what the hell is it?" She said. "It's got a hood but no sleeves?" She glanced at herself in the mirror. "Huh."

"Yes," Dev said. "I think it will be easier for you to move around in, won't it? It seems comfortable. I think the fishermen use it underneath the garments they wear as a layer." She studied the drape of the fabric. "This color seems excellent on you."

It was very light, but warm, and Jess touched the fabric on her chest with her fingertips. "Thermal," she said. "Yeah." She studied her burn marked arms, vivid and visible, her skin contrasting against the deep red color of the shirt. "Scary." She glanced at her reflection in the mirror. "But kinda cool."

"I don't think it's scary at all," Dev said. "I think it looks nice." She reached over and straightened the edge of the hooded attachment, seeing Jess's face move into a smile. "They had leggings to go with them as well. I think that would be very useful for your exercise."

"Didn't want some for yourself?"

Dev grinned ruefully. "They did not have any that would fit me," she said. "I would have liked some, yes."

Jess smoothed her hand down over her chest and nodded. "Yeah, nice," she said. "That'll work, Devvie. We'll find someone to make you some too." She leaned her elbow on Dev's shoulder. "Good job finding it in all that mess."

The garment looked as attractive on Jess as she'd hoped it would, and the color was interesting and different than either Bay colors or her customary dark shades. Dev put her arms around Jess and gave her a hug. "It's been an excellent day."

Jess gently rubbed her back. "It has. C'mon. Let's go rumble." She nudged Dev toward the door. "D'ja like your grub?"

"It was excellent."

"Y'know what dessert was?"

"Do I wish to know what dessert was?"

Jess laughed, a soft and surprisingly light sound that echoed off the stone walls.

****

Dev stood just inside the back door of the main cavern and watched the rain pour down across the ground between the main cliffside and the opposing one. Through the wash of the halons, she could see the shadow that was the new steel portal, and a scattering of scampering figures moved through the rain over to the market cavern on the other side.

"Okay, Dev." Jess came up behind her and fastened a long, canvas and plas weather cape around her. "This'll work." She wrapped her arm in one side of the cape and extended it. "Get in here."

Dev stepped up next to her and they went out into the storm and immediately felt the impact of the rain against them. Tucked against Jess's tall body, the weather cape held over her head, Dev remained dry, only her boots splashing through the ground water. Though winds were whistling overhead, the addition of the portal had reduced the tunneling effect at the level they walked through.

"Hey," Jess said and looked around. "It's not blowing sideways in here. Nice."

Dev smiled. "I thought maybe after we get the curved roof on, we could put wind turbines there," Dev said. "We could charge batteries in the caverns on this side that way. The small caves on that side don't have any power right now."

Jess looked across at the far side of the ridge. "Oh," she said. "Where the scavengers hang out sometimes."

"Yes," Dev agreed.

"Where I put a plasma bomb down."

"Yes."

"That's not a bad idea. Easier than trenching through all that damn rock to the main switchboard," Jess said. "Secondary power's never a bad thing." She bumped Dev lightly with her hip. "Another Rockety idea."

They reached the other side of the opening and crossed into the pool of light coming out of the market cavern entryway just behind a few other people. They paused as they listened to the rumble of conversation going on in the far side.

"More people," Jess said. She unhooked the cape and hung it on one of the iron hooks hammered into the rock wall. Then they crossed the quiet, darkened floor of the front of the space toward the sand covered stadium behind it.

It was a small slope upwards. They reached the top and went to the practice grounds to see the entire space packed full of people.

Jess came to a halt. From instinct, Dev did the same, as they both stared around the space with surprisingly similar looks of astonishment.

"What the what?" Jess said after a moment.

"Interesting," Dev commented. "It will be difficult to find space for this exercise to take place with all the participants here."

"Damn. No kidding."

They walked forward to the center of the stand and were spotted, the sound in the cavern rapidly falling as everyone turned to face them.

There had been two hundred the last time. Now, at least five hundred bodies were in the space. The same group of relative youngsters, but more of them. And scattered here and there older adults, men, and women, watched Jess with intent curiosity.

Dev saw everyone focus on Jess and took a step sideways. She slid her hands into her pockets and waited to see what Jess was going to do with this interesting situation. She realized that she herself didn't have much advice to offer.

Literally this was Jess's world. Dev resolved to observe closely and consider what thoughts and ideas she could contribute after the activity was concluded.

Jess hitched her thumbs into the waistband of the slate-colored light thermal pants she'd put on and waited until all the noise around them faded. The focus in the room fixed on her as she stood in the pool of light in the center of the crowd.

All those eyes watching. There was barely room in the cavern for everyone to stand, and she focused on Security Mike, who was off to one side. "Hey," Jess called out. She lifted her arms and spread them in question.

He ambled forward. "Yo?"

"What the hell are we supposed to do with so many people in here?" Jess asked, in a plaintive, but normal tone that carried over the sand.

He shrugged a little. "Everyone wanted to see what's up," he said. "So." He eyed her approvingly. "Sup, Drake?"

"Sup's that we're going to knock ourselves out hitting the damn walls," Jess said. "That's what's up."

Two men came forward, not anyone who'd been there the previous time, and Jess recognized them as head of houses, perhaps ten or so years older than she was. One ran the docking cavern, and the other oversaw Bay operations.

Both were big men, with long arms, and thick necks, and hands with roughened surfaces and calluses that showed a life spent working with them. "Drake." The first one said.

"Yes," Jess said. "John, head of house Starling," she added, glad she'd taken the time to at least run a cursory eye over the list of them as she picked her way through the bewilderment of administrivia.

The naming pleased him, and his body shifted in acknowledgment as he relaxed a little bit, his hip cocking out a touch as he faced her. "Kid was here, said you told em all something about some special thing we got. What's that about?" He asked straightforwardly. "Sup? With all this?" He lifted one hand and made a circle with his finger to indicate the cavern. "What are ya doin?"

A dozen others came forward then, evenly divided between men and women, all with that stolid assuredness that marked them as long time slot and allotment holders, comfortable, dues paid. They came in close to listen, the youngers hanging back in a thick ring behind them.

"We saw the gig you all did today," the second man said. "Sweet, and we got ten new rigs, but what's all this?" He gestured vaguely around at the group. "We looking for trouble? It's all right." He grinned a little bit. "We like trouble. But what does that get all these kids? What are we doin here?"

"Evan, head of house Roust," Jess replied. "So, here's what's up." She shifted to one side and scuffed a bit of a dip in the sand. "We got a different thing here at the Bay. No choice in it." She reached up and tapped her own chest. "I had no choice in what I got."

"Truth," John said. "Crazy's here. We know it. Them on the outside of here know it. Don't want us around most of the time. We're trouble." He shrugged his big shoulders. "Even them traders, who came in, all looking side at us. We saw it. We didn't have cred; they'd never have stopped. Can't turn it down when we do." His lips twisted into a wry, knowing smile. "But they looked side long and hard."

Jess nodded. "It's the Bay," she said with a faint, offhand shrug. "We got different stuff. Some of us get enough of it to get sold off to Interforce." She produced a brief grin. "Drakes more than most."

"Lot of us got it," one of the women spoke up. "It's the crazy. Curse of the Bay." She exhaled. "We can't get away from it. We know it."

Jess put her hands back in her pockets. "It's not really crazy, Meg." She repeated her statement from the other session. "It's something that happened a long time ago, and its inside all of us, to some degree. But it's not crazy, and it's not really always a bad thing."

"You say, sure," John smiled at her. "Cause you got sent into service."

"I say because it's true. Drakes know, and I'm Drake, both sides, so I know more than most." Jess smiled back, and then she paused. "But some of that stuff from way back, its useful if you want to kick ass."

"Like being good fighters," John said. "And liking it," he added. "S'why they don't like us. We're always ready to mix it up."

Jess nodded. "We have stronger, bigger bodies than people from other places. You can ask the doc about how we're built different. I have..." She extended her arm and touched the inside of her elbow. "I have more tendons here, and the bone's much thicker inside. My skeleton's tougher. It's not just what's in our heads." She paused for a moment. Then she said, in deliberately spaced words. "We are different."

John looked around at the silently listening crowd. "Well, that's true. I see them that come in here. Not always but most times." He looked back at Jess. "But they been saying now, long time, we just gotta keep having kids and that'll all fade."

Jess shook her head. "That's not true."

"No, we know it." Meg shook her head in echo. "Just gotta look around this room," she said. "Had six go last year with Tayler." She eyed Jess meaningfully. "Two were mine. I ain't Drake, and my co hab ain't neither."

"We breed out," Jess said. "Not in."

"Maybe you should go get them six and him back," Meg said, watching her face. "You ever think maybe that cred's worth more to us 'n them now?"

Jess regarded her in silence for a long moment, and the room just waited, heads cocked, as interested in the answer as she was herself.

Would Interforce take the findings from the battery now that they'd pulled out? Jess wondered. What would happen when that came around again? It was the local regional councils that gave the tests so they would, she assumed, continue.

But those kids classified as BD? Behaviorally Dangerous. Who got taken and sent out to the midlands to that remote wind- swept canyon school and a structured environment that would carefully shape them into tools in service to the greater good?

Jess let the emotionally echoing chamber fade out a bit, as she imagined for a minute what it would have been like for her to have been bypassed by that, and grown up here, at the Bay. After a moment she dismissed it. She was here in the end, and that's what mattered.

But.

But would Tayler be the last Drake to go to Canyon City? What would he do when he grew to understanding and came to that point they all did when he would realize what he was?

Huh.

Jess nodded at Meg. "Maybe we should. We're going to have to see how that's going to work now, I guess." She gazed thoughtfully around. "Anyway, what we got comes with stuff that makes you a good fighter. Right now, our neighbors need— want to pay for— people to help defend them. Good op for us."

John nodded. "Cred in that. K, so that makes some sense, yah?" He looked around at the wet intent faces. "Get them a slot," he said. "Cause we got a problem now, Drake. So many got offed in that last dustup we ain't got people to teach the skills for these kids. Got no way to bring all em up in a craft. They ain't' got no chance at district school, told us they're too wild for us to send em, unless they're specials."

Specials, the few kids who were exceptional in some realm. Even Bay kids, those that weren't heading to Interforce were taken for that and sent west, to completely different kinds of schools. Very few ever came back.

"Yeah I get it." Jess said. "But they got natural skills. Bunch of them went up and kicked ass in space without no training at all. Why not use them here?" She grinned. "Why only have a few of us generate cred for it? And either way, we got stuff here now we need to defend."

It was such blunt, straightforward, understandable logic it seemed surprising she'd even had to say it, but it sent a thrill of reaction around the room.

"Yeah." John smiled again, this time with a true emotion behind it. "We need it. Now we ain't got anyone around but us."

"F'n yeah. Never did," Security Mike said. "We were always here only when they needed crazy kids," he said bluntly. "Now it's different. Drake's right. We can make slots for peeps we can train up to kick ass for us and for anyone who wants to lay down cred or trade for it."

John looked at Jess. "You said you weren't crazy. We all called it that forever on back. If it's not crazy, what is it?"

"Crazy implies irrational stuff," Jess said mildly. "I'm not irrational. None of us are, in or out. We've got a quirk in heads that's different, like our bodies are different. We have no consciences. We do things that seem right to us with no regrets and no emotional attachments." She regarded them with a benign expression. "Think about it."

There was a brief, pensive silence.

Jess looked down at the sand, drawing a line in it with one toe. "It's not crazy. It's just different." She looked up with a faint smile. "We're different. It's okay."

Dev watched the watchers all react, focused and absorbed with Jess's words and that smile. She herself could feel the warm emotion in her chest that smile evoked in her.

It felt good. She thought that Jess's words were optimal, and that she had made an impression in an excellent way with the large group assembled. They had been the right words to use for the people here. She nodded and remained silent there a few paces from Jess's side.

"Anyway," Jess broke the silence and shifted the mood. "Enough talk." She lifted her hand and waved at the huge bunch of people waiting, watching. "Half you get down here, half you stay up there against the wall, so we got room," she said. "Let's get this moving or its gonna take all night."

John gave her a brief nod. "All right, Drake, we got it. It's good. We'll stick around. Maybe we'll learn something too." He winked at her and took a step back with his companions through the crowd as half the room filtered through them, scuffing sand that stuck to their damp boots.

Jess backed up, motioning them forward. "Keep coming and spread out until you're all comfortable," she directed. "First thing we do is feel the circle."

"Yo, what you mean by comfortable?" A tall, gangling youngster asked her.

"You'll know," Jess said. "Move away from everyone else until it feels right."

They looked at each other with mystified expressions and moved across the sand until they were spread out and then adjusted so that it ended with the whole floor filled, bodies standing, evenly spaced from each other to the point some had hopped onto the first tier of spectator seats.

Jess stood in the very center of them, everyone spread equally away from her. "Nice," she said, as they waited in silence. "You defined your space. That's your circle." She moved toward the nearest girl, who instinctively moved away from her, and the whole line shifted that way. "It's a space around you that you can feel other things come inside."

Then she stepped back and the girl, a little unsettled, edged back. "So, the first thing you learn is how to defend your circle. Let's you plow through a crowd of bad guys without having to look at em."

"Like you did the other time," Security Mike said. He was there, just off to her left, participating in the drill. "Was like you had eyes everywhere." He paused. "That's..." He looked suddenly enlightened. "That's it? That's this?"

Jess nodded. "No one at school had this that didn't come from here," she said. "We just didn't talk about it. Made you weird. Even there no one wants to be different." She glanced around. "You don't want to stick out or be odd out."

Mike stared at her now, eyes wide. "Thought it wasn't real," he said. "Convinced myself it wasn't. That I was just making it up."

"Me too," Jess said. "Except I couldn't not use it, and then one day my dad clued me in." she shrugged. "C'mon, there's a pile of rocks over there and some rugger balls. Let's throw em at each other and test it out."

Dev sensed the excitement in the room and stepped back out of the way and up onto the spectator level, as the mob rushed for the stacks of rocks and the rugger balls laying nearby.

"That's wild, huh, Dev?" Mike Arias said as Dev came over to him and April. "Can you do that?"

"Certainly not," Dev said at once. "However, I have seen Jess use it and it's amazing. I never really understood how she did it." She watched as Jess positioned herself in a circle of rock armed people. "I will bring my scanner the next time to see what it detects."

"What about you?" Mike said to April, who stood as though in a semi trance, her eyes focused on the sand a little in front of them. "Ap?"

April turned her eyes to them, then took three steps to the left and stopped, her expression shifting to blank amazement, her hand coming up to cover her mouth in almost comical surprise. She took a step back toward them, then moved back. "Holy shit."

"You can!" Mike said. "Wow. What does that feel like?" He looked envious.

She came back over and folded her arms over her chest. "There's no f'n way to describe that," she said. "It's just a… it's like a… crap I can't explain. Figure it's not as strong as the rest of these yonks, but I can work with it."

Mike sighed. "I'm gonna have to mix it up with Doug and Chester and Brent I guess," he said mournfully. "But wow, this bunch turns out to fight like half of what Jess does. These people round here don't' know what's gonna hit em."

Dev remembered on station, the hundreds of security guards coming up against fifty kids from the Bay, with their table legs and bats, and considered that it was likely quite true. She turned to watch Jess evading missiles being thrown at her from every direction, dodging them or easily slapping them out of the air with a sweep of her long arm.

"That's a cool outfit," April remarked casually. "You find that upstairs?"

"Yes," Dev said. "However, they did not have them in appropriate sizes for myself, or you. But I would like one."

"I think everyone's gonna want them," Mike said. "Based on what I heard in that crowd. They love seeing her marks."

"They're gonna want marks too," April predicted. "Maybe we can talk em into the pierced patterns my clan uses. I hate the smell of burning skin."

"You think they'll like being poked with a nail more?"

"Yeah. I do."

Chapter Fourteen

Jess stood in the shower, eyes closed, enjoying the warm pressure of the water as she reviewed in her mind the fights and the exercises, cautiously pleased with the results both for the Bay and for herself.

She felt pleasantly tired from it, a rare experience from a bout in the gym—the reason she usually ended up surfing at the end of the day. All that energy had to go somewhere. But to have it expended in a group rough and tumble was new, and she really enjoyed it.

Now she slowly stretched her body out and shifted from foot to foot as the warm, slightly mineral scented water thrummed against her skin, relaxing into the pressure.

She thought her, put together at the last moment, class was successful. Dev had roamed through the crowd and collected feedback that indicated the Bay was happy. The big groups had managed to get in a decent amount of action she suspected would be carried over long after they'd finished.

Dev thought it had gone well, and Jess figured if that was the case then it probably had. Tonight gave her a few more ideas about things to try with her surprisingly large group of recruits, who were surprisingly all in for the experience.

Even the weird parts of it.

Jess rinsed out her hair and reluctantly shut the water down. She shook herself violently to remove it from her skin before she went to grab a towel. She wrapped it around her and moved into the main part of the sanitary unit to find a set of sleep clothes laid out waiting for her.

It made her smile, this offhand care delivered from Dev as naturally as breathing. There was no currying for favor points, just a gentle, natural caring that was very matter of fact and not at all servile.

She expected when she emerged, there would be hot tea waiting. She smelled the tang of it on the air, and she looked forward to the taste, and sitting down for a bit to talk the day over with her tech.

With her tech. With her co hab. With her partner. What the hell was Dev now? Jess ruffled her hair dry with a second towel. With her friend, she decided. With her cute, funny, smart as hell friend who'd probably invented twelve things in her head while Jess taught rock dodging with half a thousand yonks.

Jess found Dev in the food prep station, as expected, waiting for tea to steep. She was seated on a plas stool near the wall, her sock covered feet resting on one of the supports and her hands clasped in her lap, patiently watching the timer. "Devvie."

"Hello," Dev responded with a smile. "How are you?"

"Awesome," Jess said readily. "All that work tired me out for a change." She sat down on a second stool Dev had scrounged for the place. "And it feels so damn good."

"Excellent. I think everyone else was also pleased."

"Probably not for the same reason." Jess hung the towel she'd been drying her head with around her neck. "I think that's gonna be all right."

Dev got up as the timer chimed and picked up the tea dispenser, swirling it around before she poured the contents into the two waiting, beat up plas mugs. The smell of sea grape filled the prep area. She picked up one of the cups and handed it to Jess. "Should we go to our other location?"

"Why not?" Jess got up and led the way out and down the hall to their little low-lit nook, and they settled at the table together, looking out over the night shrouded Bay. "I figure I'll start em out with practice sticks maybe tomorrow," she said. "Less blood that way."

"The rocks did produce damage," Dev said. "It was very interesting to watch, since I had never seen anyone do that before besides you." She paused thoughtfully. "Though it seems that April could have done it. She didn't seem to have known however."

Jess grinned briefly. "Never occurred to her to try. Why would it? Why would any of those guys even think about it? Once you have it pointed out to you it's obvious, but before that, Dev, it's just a weird prickly feeling." She sat back on her seat and took a sip of her tea. "I thought I was imagining it until Dad asked me about it." She made a vague gesture toward her head. "Just some weird thing I made up."

"Really?" Dev rested her cup on the low table.

"Sure. It's like a..." Jess paused. "It's like you're walking around, and you smell something weird. You don't want to turn to someone who's with you and say hey you smell that weird thing? Cause they might say, what weird thing, you know?"

"Sort of." Dev made a little face. "I guess it's like if your whole set had dark hair, and you didn't, it would be a strange and incorrect feeling, I guess?." She paused. "I never had anyone to compare with. I was always different because I was a single instance."

Jess nodded. "I just used it and kept my mouth shut. Then one visit Dad asked me— you can do this right?" She chuckled a little. "Then it was okay. I still didn't talk about it, but I knew it gave me an advantage, so it was cool."

"So interesting," Dev said. "I think the others from Base are envious."

"That's why I never talked about it. It felt like cheating." Jess hiked one ankle up on her opposing knee. "I just wanted to be like everyone else there. But it was what it was." She regarded the cup. "Different. But okay."

"That's how I feel as well," Dev said. "Different, but that's all right." She paused a moment. "But Jess, I watched you do that exercise, and wished I could also, just because it seemed so amazing," she admitted. "So, I understand if the others are envious of that too."

Jess eyed her. "Devvie, you do a thousand rockstar things we all wish we could do, y'know."

Dev smiled and glanced down. "We always want new skills," she said. "It's part of how we're made, but yes of course I know that." She took a sip of her tea. "The sets hope Doctor Dan gets the programming system rebuilt soon. They really want to get more tech loading on the carriers. I extracted the manuals for them and shared them, but it's not the same."

"Takes time," Jess said. "Doc'll sort it out. And they got you, Brent, Chester and Doug to coach em," she added casually. "We'll need em all if we use these crates for transport and the rest of it. Need multiple shifts."

Dev nodded. "Then they will continue to have that assignment?"

Jess blinked. "Sure. They're pilots," she said, in a slightly bewildered voice. "They don't want to?"

"They do. But I don't think anyone's told them."

Jess's expression shift to a puzzled one, her eyebrows contracting over the bridge of her nose.

"You don't assume things, Jess," Dev said. "They either came from barracks or from the creche. You wait for Admin to code it to you. It's like when the Director on station told me I was going to go down world, that was interesting, but I waited to see what would happen because what they tell you isn't always true. But then when I got out of the next sleep cycle and went to dress, there was a tech jumper in my locker and an assignment group change. Then I knew it was really happening."

"Um."

"The sets here," Dev continued, they don't have any proctors, so, they don't have anyone to ask what's going on. So sometimes they ask me."

"Ah." Jess's expression cleared. "Got it. We should tell em," she said. "Not assume they'll figure it out."

"Yes, exactly." Dev smiled. "That would be excellent."

"Ok. Well, we just got the rigs today," Jess reasoned. "We can let em know tomorrow, right? I mean the doc's probably in there wrenching right now with that stuff," she added. "He said he wanted to give them more tech, like what he gave you, for em."

"Of course." Dev sat back and relaxed. "That will be very optimal for them. They all did good work, but there were many things they asked about that they didn't have programming for."

"They'll be the experts," Jess said. "Right? Not as expert as you are, but they'll do okay, with the other guys helping em."

"Yes." Dev sipped her tea. "I am confident they will do good work for the people here. They all like it very much, especially the sets from the Base," she said thoughtfully. "The ones from station hadn't been assigned yet, and they only had the creche to compare it to."

"Was Interforce that bad to them?" Jess propped her elbow on the table. "I never saw them doing crappy things to those guys, but to be honest, I never really looked for it either."

Dev thought about that. "I don't think they were bad. Not in the way natural born think of how to be, to bio alts, anyway. They never did an... well, Doctor Dan is upset they tried to use a programming system on them, but they were treated as valued."

"Until they didn't want em and just left em here." Jess's dark brows drew in a little. "They were part of the operation. Like the machinery."

"Yes," Dev agreed. "They were on contract from station, and they felt they gave value and were given shelter and meals." She looked at Jess. "But it wasn't like it was for me," she admitted. "That was very different."

Jess smiled at her. "You were one of us. Even from the start. And after that first run with me, you weren't going back."

"Even before then. Doctor Dan warned me. The night before I left station, he took me to a natural born meal facility and told me I was going to be treated differently. That I wouldn't be in barracks or have proctors to instruct me." Dev tilted her head thoughtfully. "The sets are envious of that status. They want to excel."

Jess studied her in silence for a moment. "Those guys are

not you," she said. "They never will be."

"No, they aren't. I am New Model, Developmental," Dev responded with a smile. "They know that, but they also can't help wanting it, just like I can't help wanting to do that amazing thing you were doing tonight."

Jess pondered that. "Huh."

"The sets were talking about that when they saw all of us coming back," Dev said. "I think they… they want to be sure they keep their value."

Jess's eyes grew a little round, her eyebrows lifting. "Dev, no one cares if they can dodge rocks. The reason everyone here loves them is all the stuff they can do. You think anyone here coulda figured out how to drive those crates back here but them? You think anyone here could have taken up ops and mech and all that stuff with no one to teach them like they did? Bay knows they hit a gold mine."

Dev rested her chin on her fist and just looked at her.

"I know I did," Jess said, after a brief pause. "Cause I got the best of the best. "

Dev's smile became wider and charming, her eyes expressing a depth of emotion that just made Jess stop talking for a long minute, before she cleared her throat.

"Gotta be honest. I never looked at where bios lived or what they did or how they thought." She regarded Dev with a wry little grin. "I had no use for them until I met you." She paused in thought. "I look back and feel like such an idiot," she added. "Kind of a personal bummer."

Dev edged herself closer and reached out to touch Jess's hand. "I would like to tell you something."

"Uh oh." Jess's eyes widened. "You going to tell me I am an idiot?" She glanced to the left as a rumble of thunder came through the plas, and a far-off bit of lightning outlined the clouds out to sea. "I am sometimes."

"No of course not." A tiny twinkle appeared in her eyes. "Actually, in the creche, we thought most of the natural born were silly. I had no idea how excellent and amazing a natural born could be until I met you." She tilted her head slightly. "There's nothing idiotic about you, Jess. You're just awesome."

Jess tried to remember if anyone had ever said that many complimentary things about her in one little spurt of language before."

No, they hadn't. Was she awesome? Jess looked across and into Dev's clear, steadfast eyes. "I'm glad you see me that way, Devvie," she said, in a somber tone. "It's nice someone does."

Dev looked at her with a bemused expression. "Jess, I think many people here think you're amazing if the commentary I was listening to means what I think it does," she said. "Although the language here is often..." She made a brief, wry face.

"Weird." Jess started laughing.

"Nonstandard," Dev concluded. "Different. But that's okay." She stroked Jess's hand. "I think we are both fortunate."

Jess clasped her fingers around Dev's, feeling their warm strength. "Yeah, we're a pair of weirdos," she said in a wry tone. "But that's cool."

Dev chuckled softly. "I don't think it's weird really." She rubbed her thumb across the back of Jess's hand. "I just think it's wonderful."

"Well. We're here." Jess finished her tea and set her cup down. "So, it must be okay. Want to go get in bed? Been a long ass time since we were in it." She stood up and kept her grip on Dev's hand as she joined her. "I'm too whacked to keep talking right now."

"Absolutely." Dev went with her down the hall, the large space quiet, the sounds of the water outside becoming louder as they went into the bedroom. The soft rumble of thunder sounded overhead.

They climbed into the large bed and under the covers, and Dev exhaled in pleasure as she was surrounded by the warmth of both the blanket, and Jess next to her. After a moment she felt Jess shift and roll onto her side, and then one long arm slid over her.

Excellent. Despite the long day, it was always optimal to spend time at the end of it with each other, sometimes practicing sex, sometimes just being close. It filled her with reassurance, and a connection to Jess and she leaned her head over, resting it against Jess's darker one.

It was quiet for a moment, save the background sounds of their space, already becoming normal for her. Then Jess's voice came in a low mutter.

"Everyone was talking about me?"

Unseen in the dark, Dev grinned. "Yes," she said solemnly. "They were."

"Mmm." Jess rumbled softly under her breath. "Anything bad?"

This seemed very typical of Jess. "Well," Dev responded in a thoughtful tone. "From my perspective, the amount of discussion regarding your ability to practice sex was non optimal."

After a moment, Jess convulsed in silent laughter.

"But the approval of your garment was pleasant, and the approval of the exercise was excellent," Dev said, as if she couldn't feel Jess shaking next to her. "The people there were excited and very happy to be instructed by you."

Jess let her laughter wind down. "Teach me to ask dumb ass questions." She shook her head and snuggled closer to Dev. "All good, Devvie. All good. "

Dev gazed out over the night Bay view, the lightning in the distance, and had to agree. She looked forward to what the coming days would bring and all the interesting possibilities along with them.

****

Jess got a container of grog and brought it with her into her office space, regarding it a moment before she pulled the plas stool over and sat down behind the stone desk.

It was morning and the rain had stopped. The light outside was the pale grey of clear weather and the Bay was busy with activity just below them. She set down her container and then paused to study the rough tabletop, the only thing on it the access panel.

Then she got up and went back to the storage closet, going to the gear bag that she'd brought with her from the base. She opened it and felt around inside until she found something and retrieved it. With a grunt of satisfaction, she took it back and put it on the desk, routing the power input from it down and connecting it to a source.

She got up and gazed at the small acrylic underwater scene, with a bit of golden light in it, and moving shadows from the electronic signaling that Dev had designed for it.

Jess nodded in approval and resumed her seat. She put her hand on the input pad and felt the tickle of scan before the screen lit. She opened the messaging portal and reviewed the lines of new messages. Nothing exceptional was there waiting for her attention. Jess opened a new message, then paused, and closed it. She then opened one of the ones in her box that was a broadcast and reviewed how it had been sent.

She had never sent a message to more than a few people before. The Bay was a big place. She copied the method and then opened a new message again, pasting the line in and waiting to see if the program was going to give her a hard time.

She didn't much like comp. That, she had always told everyone, was what wrenchers were for. But Dev said everyone here used comp to make things official, so she sat there for some time, trying to figure out what to say.

She decided to keep it short and simple. "Okay." She then pulled up a notification from the day before, about pad assignments, and copied the carrier idents from it. "Gonna have to be good until they get some other freaking name."

Somewhat laboriously, she typed in the new acquisitions and then typed in what she wanted done with them. "Make em useful," she instructed. "Put cargo platforms down, and lift spools, and uncomfortable as hell seats for yonks with guns."

Like they had with their three carriers. The seats folded up and the floors now had lash down points. They could be used for a dozen things that Interforce would never have considered for them. They were too small to carry that much cargo, but they could carry it fast, and with the seats down they could lift ten fully armed fighters along with their pilot and gunner.

"Now." Jess studied her text. "Let's put pilot names down, and that'll make it good for the kids."

She typed in the KayTee pilot's names in next to the carriers they'd flown, and paused, then she added permanent assignment next to them, and reviewed it. Was that what Dev would think they'd want to see? She looked over the note from admin, acknowledging their new craft, and the slots that would be assigned to them.

So, the KayTees would get cred, as well as the assignment, because that was a skill slot. Jess studied the note. Should she go explain that to them? Would they get it? "Better have Dev do it," she said to herself. She completed her note, and then attached her ident to it, before sending it on its way. "There ya go, Devvie."

The KayTees, and the BeeAyes that were mechs for the hardware, would work with Clint to keep the old crates in the air. "Okay." Jess stood up and dusted her hands off. "Enough typing for today." She paused and put her hands on her hips. "What the hell do I do next?"

She looked around her space, then went out into the hallway and down to Dev's workspace. "Find a way to get this damn thing warmer," she decided. "C'mon, fish brain. You figured out how to make surfing bearable you can figure out carpets."

****

Dev was on her back, her head inside the large, battered console, her scanner resting on her stomach. "I think this module is not seated correctly, Doctor Dan." She inched around in the small space, barely enough to contain her slim form. "It seems not."

"That would make sense," he said, "based on these reading returns. Can you reseat it?" He asked. "Thank you for the help. I'd have had to take the top of that console off to get in there."

"No problem at all, Doctor Dan. Of course, I can reseat it." Dev removed a small wrench from her vest and loosened the housing on the module, carefully wiggling it loose. She inspected the tracings with a brief glance, then reached down and ran her scanner over them. "Oh."

"Oh?" Kurok stood and came over and dropped to a crouch next to her. "Oh what?"

Dev slid out from inside the console and held up the module so he could see it. "It's missing a trace." She put down her scanner and indicated the missing lead with one fingertip. "Here. Either it was missed, or it broke out possibly."

"So, it is." Kurok tipped the board toward the light. "Well, that explains a lot," he said. "The logs in the console show it's been malfunctioning for quite some time. Poor lads there had no one to call to fix it, did they? Calling up to station wouldn't have gotten them a pleasant response."

"Sub optimal," Dev said. "But they should not have been attempting it."

"No, but if they hadn't, we wouldn't have this in our hands just when we needed it. Ever heard the saying not to look a gift horse in the mouth?"

"Well, actually." Dev gave him a sideways glance. "Jess usually says not to look a gift horse in the ass. I assume that means something of the same thing?"

"Something like that, yes." He chuckled. "Not surprised it's a somewhat stupid saying and definitely unnecessary since horses no longer exist." He took the mod from Dev's hands. "Be right back. I've got a bit of what these needs in the other lab. Don't go away."

Dev remained where she was, relaxing on the floor with her boots crossed, propped up on her elbows. Hopefully the module was the last defective piece in the console and Doctor Dan could continue with his work, and she could return to a navigation adjustment that had occurred to her over breakfast.

She heard footsteps approach, and then Cathy entered, stopping short when she spotted Dev on the ground.

"Oh! Dev! There you are!"

"Yes, here I am." Dev confirmed the obvious. "How are you?"

Cathy came over. "Everyone's so excited about the note that came out. The KayTee's were looking for you."

"I don't think I have seen anything," Dev said. "I checked my access pad before I came here but there was nothing very important there at that time."

Cathy came over and took a seat on the floor next to her. "It just came out. It was a note about the planes that were brought back yesterday, you know?"

"Yes?" Dev waited for her to continue; her head inclined to one side in a listening attitude.

"Oh, well, I mean it was about what was going to happen to them, and the KayTees were told they were going to be the pilots from now on!" Cathy smiled. "They're so excited."

Dev held back a smile. "Did the note come from operations?"

"Oh no. It came right from the top. Jess sent it out," Cathy said. "She even signed it with her key, so we'd know it was official. And Dustin's happy that there are seven more of these planes to work on. He says it means his slot's more important and he's on the team that are going to take care of all of them."

Now Dev smiled. "As soon as I am finished here with Doctor Dan, I will go find them," she said. "Excellent news. They will be my colleagues, after all."

Cathy looked at Dev in mild surprise. "Oh, you mean with flying the craft."

"Yes," Dev said. "I am also a pilot." She added, somewhat unnecessarily from her view given that everyone in the complex had a demonstration of that the prior day. "Brent, and Doug and Chester and myself," she said. "We will help them." She wiggled one booted foot. "I am very glad Jess communicated that information."

Amazing Jess, who had promised it would be taken care of in the morning, and here it was, just past the early meal and it had been. She felt proud, amazed, and happy. A side part of her mind went off to think about what she could do to provide a treat in return.

"Yes, it was really good," Cathy said, then looked at Dev. "What are you doing here on the floor?"

Dev pointed at the console. "Helping Doctor Dan fix this, so he can proceed with testing it," she said. "He's adjusting a module for it."

Cathy nodded. "I'm going to go back to working on the

programming template then." She got up and dusted off her leggings. "Talk to you later, Dev."

Dev waved goodbye, then leaned back against the console, grinned. It had already been a very successful morning.

****

Jess settled her comm set in her ear and trotted down the steps to her quarters. She paused at the bottom to regard the vastness of the tall cavern at the Bay's center. Gray light poured down from the battered, but mostly clear plas roundel in the top of it and there was a good amount of activity moving across it.

She watched the flow of movement for a minute, then the image of the stone ledge in the middle of her quarters occurred to her, and she turned and headed for the spiral stairs, jogging up them to the storage level.

The visitors from Quebec weren't due until lunch. Jess had a role to play in that but for right now she was free to do as she pleased, and she pleased to find some material she could put outside to sit on with Dev to enjoy Dev's new lights.

As she reached the old storage rooms, she heard the murmur of voices. She rounded the corner and was more than a little surprised to see a reasonably large group of people in the cavern rooting around in the leftovers there.

One of the storage workers came over to her. "Yo."

"Hey." Jess put her hands in her pockets. "What's up here?"

The man shrugged. "Dunno. Everyone got a bug up their ass for junk I guess."

"Guess I do too." Jess moved past him and roamed the aisles in search of something she could use to construct a bench with. She spotted another long slab of rock like the one that made the top of her desk and sidled over to examine it.

"Oh, hey, Jess." Craig, the storage master spotted her and came over, dodging the other searchers, who looked up and around on hearing her name. "Whoof... what you all started."

"Me?" Jess touched her chest and then looked around in bewilderment. "What did I do? I've only been up here twice."

Craig chuckled. "I dunno. Something about the shirt you found up here. Everyone's trying to find one too," he said. "They saw it last night."

"Oh," Jess said. "I didn't find it, Dev did. It's just a damn fisherman's underlay. Like what they wear on long hauls." She drew her finger across her arm at the shoulder. "No sleeves, hood, you know em."

"Ahhh." Craig nodded in enlightened agreement. "Yeah, I do. Anyway, it's popular. So Jax from processing was here before to see if there's a pattern they can use to make em. He might come see ya to get a scan."

"Sure." Jess tucked that information away for her next place to visit since providing a scan would also achieve her other goal of getting one of the garments for Dev. "Right now, I'm looking for more banged up furniture. Freaking space is huge."

He chuckled. "You know, it's cool you're mixing it all up from the trash. You could have it made."

"No time for that crap." Jess started to move off. "I want this thing." She pointed at the slab of rock. "That other one worked out good." She glanced at Craig. "Thanks for having the loaders get it in there."

Craig kept at her heels, making notes on his plas clipboard. "No issue. Guys were bitching about that other top, said it was too heavy to shift so they left it against the wall. Sorry you had to wrangle it."

Jess paused and looked at him. "Huh."

"Loaders." Craig shrugged. "Least they got it there. Figured you could handle it anyway. You're stronger than any of those guys, and they know it." He winked at Jess. "So, what else ya want down there?"

"That, and that." Jess pointed and moved along. "Those pipes? What do you got there, six of em? Send em up, and that pile of chain."

Craig shook his head. "Hey, at least I'm finally gonna get this place cleaned out again," he said. "Hot damn."

"Yo, Drake!"

Jess returned the waves of the Bay residents searching around in the crates and boxes. "Hey, ya scrubs."

She then stopped next to a stack of grid squares, beaten, and battered but not much different than the constructs the carriers were resting on in their bays nearby. "What the what?" She jerked her head at it.

"Ancient brass fishing platform," Craig said. "Been here since old Uncle got blown up during the attack. He had it built down near the shore and he'd sit and fish from it." He kicked the edge of the pile of battered metal. "Tried to send it down to the caverns twice, but they said it's too small to use so they sent it back up here."

Jess studied it. "Send it down to our place," she said. "If

anyone can figure out something to make out of a bunch of brass chunks, it'll be Dev."

"You got it." Craig glanced around. "Be a while to get it all down there."

One of her students from the night before came over, a thick iron pipe in his hands. "Yo, Drake," he said. "We can haul it for ya, yeah?" He eyed her hopefully. "Loaders won't be round now till way later."

Jess was about to refuse, when she caught from the corner of her eye the group of them watching her, alert, ready to jump in and help. Then she thought about the loaders who had refused to help move something and caused Dev to have to do it.

Dev hadn't cared, she was sure. She would have done it anyway, but still. "Yeah." She nodded at him. "That'd be cool."

He grinned at her agreement and held up the pipe. "We found these. Good for mixing, yo?"

Jess took it from him, and heft it, spinning it in her grip and then flipping it. "Real good. Everyone grab one," she ordered the gang, who now clustered in the next aisle, waiting to jump to it. "That'll work good."

"Yo," the first one said. "C'mon, let's get a move on and get this stuff over to the Drake's crib." He took the pipe back and moved toward the brass plates.

"Start with those," Craig called out. "Stu, here." He handed his clipboard to one of the other storage staff. "Show em what to grab and key them down the back lift."

"Yo." Stu took the board and headed off.

"Make my life easier, don't have to call the loaders up from the dock," Craig said, with a pleased expression. "But you know they just want to get a look at your place, right?" He chuckled. "You got em all riled up."

Jess continued to wander, noting that much of the material she'd seen there a few days prior was now gone. "Just about cleaned you out up here."

"Between them wanting to set stuff up out in the caves and the spacers scrounging pipes and stuff, yeah." Craig was still at her heels. "It's good. Place has just been a junk yard for years. Now we got space. I'm gonna pull it all into the inside section and this'll be all clear for a change."

Jess nodded.

"Until we go raid 10 again." Craig winked. "Plenty of scrap there and we're gonna need it if we build out the back like I heard we were."

"Yeah, that can't go on forever," Jess said. She found a

battered metal box on a crate near the back wall and idly opened it, to peer inside. It was empty, but it had a handle on each side, so she closed it up and lifted it to carry along with her. "They can't just leave that place there."

"Why not?"

"So much stuff in there," she said. "A ton of mech and material. It's nuts."

"Maybe it's just not worth it to them to come haul it," Craig said. "They shut the door and walked out, don't want to look back. If I ran my ass away, I wouldn't."

Jess paused and considered that. "You'd have to have a conscience to do that, Craig. We don't. That's the whole point. They might decide to leave the bases to rust out here because they weren't worth recovering but they wouldn't care about their reputation around it."

"Maybe they did what they did then, and just moved on," he said.

Possible. Not probable. But Jess shrugged. "Maybe." She lifted the box to her shoulder and headed out, back to the spiral stair to descend back down in a rhythmic rambling pace.

At the base of the stairs, she spotted Dev coming from the tunnels on the land side of the cliff. She looked unspeakably cute in her tech vest and jumpsuit, her flight helmet hanging from one hand.

Jess changed her direction to intercept her and saw Dev smile and her eyes light up at her approach.

"Hey, Rocket," Jess greeted her as they met in the center of the cavern. "Sup?"

"You are the most wonderful person," Dev said, and gave her a one-armed hug, right there in the center of the hall. "Thank you for sending that note out."

Jess grinned. "Was it good?"

"It was amazing." Dev gazed up at her with a wholehearted grin. "Thank you."

How, Jess wondered, could having done something so minor feel this good? She reached out with her free hand and ruffled Dev's hair. "Anything for you, Devvie." She savored the warm appreciation in Dev's eyes. "Whatcha up to?"

"Finishing some work," Dev said. "I'm going to go install the gimbal tuning upgrade I mentioned yesterday. How are you? What is in that box?" She looked at the battered metal square on Jess's shoulder.

"Box?" Jess frowned then made a face. "Oh, this thing." She brought the item down. "Just an empty box. I was up in the tombs scrounging." She opened the box for Dev's inspection. "I figured we could use it for something. It has handles."

"It's a very good size," Dev said. "That storage facility has a good quantity of useful items."

"Not as many as there used to be. It's emptying out. I just had em send some more stuff over to mess around with," Jess said. "You going to go for a ride?" She indicated the helmet.

Dev nodded. "To validate the mod, yes. But also, Doctor Dan said he would like me to take the carrier on a test flight later on when the Quebec City merchants are here."

"He wants you to show off?" Jess gave her a knowing smirk.

"Something like that," Dev admitted. "But I wanted to be sure everything was in functional order before that, after the flight yesterday." She looked up and around and then back at Jess. "And then after the day meal the pilots are meeting to look at the vid."

Jess chuckled. "They want you to show them all the rockety bits."

"Yes." Dev looked a bit abashed. "But now, I'm sure, they also will talk about their assignment as I know that was very exciting for them. Doug is going to bring some treat to the meeting he said."

"Mm. Maybe I'll come watch if there's a treat involved."

"That would be excellent," Dev said. "I would very much like you to be there." She put a hand on Jess's hip. "It's in the mech workshop, level seven."

"Count on me," Jess responded after a brief pause. "Go fly, Rockstar." She touched Dev's nose. "Don't scare the fish."

Dev grinned. "I won't. See you in a while." She turned and jogged off toward the steps that Jess had so recently descended, heading for the upper landing bay where their carrier was parked.

Jess watched her go, then turned and headed for the steps to their quarters.

****

"All right." Kurok dusted his hands off. "Keko, are you ready to help me test this out?"

Keko got up off the stool he'd been sitting on. "Yes, Doctor Dan. I am. I am glad the test is ready as well, as we are meeting up today to see the vid from the flying yesterday and I don't want to miss it."

"I bet you don't." Kurok patted the converted table. "Go on and lie down, lad." He adjusted the overhead gimbal. "And I believe congratulations are in order. "

Keko grinned broadly. "Yes! That was very exciting! We're all very happy to have Agent Jess tell everyone that we are to be assigned to fly the Bantams."

"Yes, it was well done thing." Kurok adjusted the leads on either side of Keko's head and gently settled them over him. "We were going to just post it, but I think Jess sending it out was much nicer."

"Yes." Keko settled his hands at his side and drew in, then released a deep breath. "I am glad you got this machine to work, Doctor Dan. I felt very strange when they used it on us."

"Did you?"

"Yes. They kept saying they didn't do anything they were just… inspecting?"

"As if they'd know what they were looking at," Kurok muttered. "But you think they did something?" He rested his elbows on the table. "That's all right if it's true, Keko. I'll look and make sure everything's all sorted out for you in there. There's nothing they could do that was very horrible. I made sure of that in your design framework."

The look of relief on Keko's face was very evident. Kurok found that a bit disturbing. He settled the leads onto the slots on either side of Keko's head and adjusted them. "That all right?"

"Yes." Keko kept his head still. "It's good."

"Let me check the balance." Kurok slid back on the rolling stool and peered at the screen. "Yes, that's fine." He went back to the table and gave Keko a reassuring look as he touched his fingertips to the bio alt's forehead." Go down now, Keko. Relax for me." His voice took on an even, measured tone, a trigger he would have heard from his youngest years.

Keko responded to the trigger with utter trust. He obediently closed his eyes, and his body lost tension at once and his hands went limp.

Kurok waited a moment, then returned to the makeshift console and sat behind it. He moved closer to the screen to study the results. As the electronic signals steadied and evened out, Keko transitioned into a deep almost trance state that was not unconscious and not sleep but a twilight in between. "Good, lad," Kurok murmured under his breath. "Let's see what those idiots tried."

He started a slow, even pattern match, sliding his eyes across the screen and comparing what he saw from the base programming the KayTee's received, with what was present there today.

Of course, it was different. Just living and experiencing things made differences just like it would for anyone. So, areas that were not well developed in young bio alts were fuller built out here after living at the Base and learning about life.

All that was normal. As he continued further, he relaxed a little when he confirmed that the broad structures hadn't been altered, and he wasn't facing a real problem. One that the rudimentary systems here under his fingers wasn't designed to cope with.

He paused to think, remembering Bricker and his ego, and tried to imagine what he would do, what he would want to know from a bio alt to have something like this built. "What did you poke around with, hm?" He did a quick check of the technical underpinning, the layers of detail and information the bio alt had been given on station before he went downside.

All seemed intact. There was a decent amount of space there for the dump of detail he had prepared for the pilots, the bundle of tech loading they'd given Dev about the carriers and their systems. Then he slid over to the less technical and more instinctual sectors and paused.

"Ah." He explored further and saw an area of disturbance. "What have we here?" He muttered under his breath. "What did you try to do, you little muppet you?" He eased a digital capture into position and carefully detangled the crude and somewhat irregular code written in binary tucked along the curve of the center of Keko's brain.

With infinite care, doing work he would never have let any of his assistants do without long prep and careful planning, he untwisted the bits of data out and stored them into the probe's memory, then removed them. He eased along at a dead slow speed, pausing to reach out with one hand to hit the control that would seal the door to the workroom to prevent any intrusion that might make him react.

Then he moved further along the curve and extracted enough data to almost fill the probe's memory until he came to the bottom of the sub area, where there was only some basic instruction about protocol.

He worked his way back out again and checked all the branches and side channels, searching for any bit of detritus left behind until he was back at the main intersection. He then retracted the probe and sent its memory to storage for further study.

He was satisfied with the performance of the rig, and after a brief final check and a full scan for later review, he closed the session out and deactivated the leads then got up to retract them and draw them back from Keko's head.

Keko's eyes were still closed. He was still very relaxed. Kurok reached out gently and touched his forehead with his fingertips and pushed lightly in a second trigger. "Keko," he said in that same calm, measured tone. "Come up."

For a moment he remained still, then his eyes fluttered open. "Oh." He seemed surprised. "That seemed so fast."

"Only a half hour." Kurok smiled. "How are you?"

Keko sat up on his elbows and blinked a few times. "I... oh!" His brows elevated and his eyes widened. "Oh, Doctor Dan! You found it! You fixed it!" He said, in amazement. "It's... it's gone!"

"Yes." Kurok pulled his rolling stool over and sat down. "It wasn't very much, Keko. I don't think they had the time or skills to really do any harm."

"Yes, it wasn't... it wasn't anything..." He groped for words. "It wasn't incorrect, it was just..."

"Odd but nothing specific," Kurok said. "Yes, it was just a messy bit of something. I'm going to look further at it later, but for now I just cleaned it all up." He patted Keko's hand. "So, you'll be all ready for the bundle we're preparing for your new task."

"Oh, it feels so good," Keko said. "Doctor Dan you are so amazing." He rolled his head back and forth. "It was like having a little bit of a headache this whole time, and now I don't."

Kurok's eyes twinkled. "I'm glad," he said simply. "But if everyone else's got that in there I've got a lot of work to do." He got up and booted the stool back over to the console. "Thank you for being my tester, Keko. That was very useful to me as well as it was for you, I think. You can go on with your day now if you like."

Keko got off the table and stood. "Yes," he said. "Thank you, Doctor Dan. We're going to do awesome work here." He rubbed the back of his neck a little bit. "We're so lucky to have come. This is the best assignment ever."

Kurok went behind the console and unlocked the door, giving him a wave as Keko straightened the sleeve of his coverall and walked briskly to the door. Cathy entered. "Are you done, Doctor?"

"Yes!" Kurok leaned on the console. "Good news is it works." He glanced at the screen. "Bad news is it works." He sighed. "I need to spend some time with this later and see exactly what I found, but right now…" He checked his chron. "Right now, I expect our visitors from Quebec are about to contact ops and I have to go deal with them."

"Yes, Doctor," she said. "Are the programming frameworks all right? I'll keep setting them up for you."

"They're just fine, so please do." Kurok closed his console input out and dusted his hands off. "Tomorrow, let's start to schedule all the sets who came from Base in for a check." He headed for the inside door that would lead back around to his quarters. "Hopefully it'll end as well."

****

There were six of them, three men and three women, all of them with salt and pepper hair and caramel-colored skin. They were accompanied by two big, tough looking guards with muscular, toned bodies and visible lumps that indicated they were armed.

They got out of their flyer on the level six landing bay and a man with short, sandy blond hair advanced to meet them.

"Hello." Kurok stopped in front of them. "I'm Dan Kurok. Welcome to Drake's Bay."

"Hi," the tallest of the women said. "Stella Gateau." She looked at the rest of her group. "Steven Heuler, Jives McRae, Sally Lichton, Beniface Jas, and Jayce Bluegill." She looked past them. "Our security. That's Billton and Malagut, they stay with us."

"Sure," Kurok said. "Where would you like to start? Your guards are welcome to join our tour. I just ask you please don't start randomly shooting things because it won't have a good result for anyone."

"Your joint, you pick a route," Stella said. "First time any of us have been here."

Stella seemed to be in charge. The merchant's guild was something of a mafia, from what he'd ever seen, but their motives were straightforward and purely in their own interest, and so he felt comfortable dealing with them. "Excellent then, let's go this way." He gestured toward the hall inward. "We don't get many visitors."

"Bet not," one of the men muttered.

Stella turned on him. "Beni, shut it."

"It's all right," Kurok said amiably. "We're not sensitive, as a rule."

Level six was a good level for it, high enough to get a sense of the space, and low enough to have to take a breath as it arched away ahead of you, tall and vast and with its opening to the sky letting the light in to reflect off the angles in the stone and the faint glints of minerals in it.

It was stunning. Whatever one thought about the rest of Drake's Bay, this was a stone cathedral of monumental proportions and the route he'd taken was calculated to impress.

It had.

"Ho." Beni let out an exclamation.

They went to the railing and looked out over the space. "Bigger than I thought," Stella said. She gave Kurok a sideways glance. "I figured it was just…"

Kurok smiled. "A few caves carved in the mountain? I came in that same way the first time I saw this place. It took my breath away." He started for the steps. "It's more than meets the eye." He waved at the few bio alts who were sitting in their gathering space and they all waved back. "In many different ways."

The visitors glanced at the bio alts as they started down the steps. "So that's true," Stella said. "They have them here now."

"Yes," Kurok said, as they went past the fifth level, which was almost empty this time of the day.

"Spacer quarters," Beni read. "What does that mean?"

"The bio alt sets who live on that floor came from Bio Station 2," Kurok explained. "That's the name the residents here gave them when they came to live here. Spacers. The ones that live in the next level came from Interforce Base 10."

"They don't mind?" Stella asked. "The people here? I always heard…."

"Yes, well, people change." Kurok bypassed the question. "Here are our residential areas, and ah, there by the steps there our senior stakeholder's waiting for us to catch her up." He figured that would distract them, and it did, as everyone's eyes immediately shifted from the steps and the bio alts to the tall figure relaxing against the wall ahead of them.

Jess had her arms folded and her ankles crossed as she waited for them She remained that way until they were halfway across the floor and then she pushed off the wall and straightened up, walking toward them at an unhurried pace.

Jess had, Kurok knew, a pretty good idea of the effect she had on people. The visitors shifted nervously. The two security guards looked uncertain, unsure if they should put a hand on their guns or not. As if reading their minds, she fixed her eyes on the two of them, her head lowering a little bit until the two men let their hands fall to their sides.

"Ah, Jesslyn," Kurok greeted her fondly, noting the mischievous twinkle. "Here are our guests from the Quebec merchant's guild." He turned to them as she arrived at his side. "This is Jess Drake, our senior stakeholder."

Jess put her hands in the front pocket of her hoodie, the gift from Dev with its stylized dragon on the chest. "Hi," she said amiably.

It was deliciously awkward. Kurok enjoyed the moment quite a bit as none of their visitors seemed to know what to say to her, not even Stella who had some amount of presence herself. "Let's take a walk along the bay front first, shall we? Then we can get down to business." Kurok suggested. "To the right here."

They tried to find a way to group themselves in a way that would keep the guards and Kurok between themselves and Jess, and still be able to see everything, then they were distracted by a deeply echoing chime. "Mess," Jess said, as they jumped a bit at the sound. "That's the meal bell."

The hall erupted into motion, as Bay residents and bio alts appeared from hallways and the spiral stairs, heading across the wide floor to the large mess hall entrance on the back curve of the inner wall. It was a cavalcade of purposeful motion, and when Jess was spotted, it skewed.

"Hai!" A loud roar went up, echoing against the stone and buzzing the eardrums.

Jess removed one hand from her pouch pocket and waved casually in response, as the lines of tall figures half turned to watch her as they passed.

They were, Kurok calculated, scaring the crap out of the merchants. But not in an altogether bad way. "Shall we?" He inquired politely, gesturing to the bay side hall, that would lead them down along to the viewing balcony for a view of the Bay, then back inside to the new corridor to the growing cavern. "Jess, get the door there would you please?"

Jess put her hand on the plate and the large metal door opened, exposing the viewing corridor with its balcony. She led the way through, and the door closed behind them cutting off the echo of the hall and the rumble of voices.

Here to the right was a nice view of the wide circle of the Bay, where workboats were busy, clam barges were visible, and the long-range fishing boats were moving around the far side docks. One boat was in the metal dry dock, lifted clear of the water as its hull was scraped.

In this more usual setting, the merchants recovered and watched with wary interest. "Big operation," Stella said.

"Yes, it is," Kurok agreed. "Getting bigger too. Some of the long-range ships are bringing catch in here for a bit of trade before they go up to the processors."

"Thought I saw a few familiar hulls," Beni said. "Bet they don't like that."

"Market is market," Kurok said, reasonably. "We can't take a volume, of course, so they get the large share of the fish, but we get the first offload, because we have material now here they can't get elsewhere at the same trade value."

Stella nodded. "Always had good clams here." She noted. "So damn few flats on this coast."

"Clam stew's what's for lunch," Jess said. "Yum."

They were about to turn when motion in the air caught everyone's attention. As if on cue, because it was, two carriers appeared from the upper landing caverns and cruised across the Bay at a gentle glide, then split and headed off in opposite directions.

Everyone's eyes were glued on them. "Those are Interforce," Stella said.

"They were," Jess said. "A few came with us, then we went and got the rest they left behind."

All the merchants now focused on Jess, and the two guards settled against the back wall of the hall, their hands clasped in front of them.

"Always heard they'd blow up if anyone tried that," Stella said, but in an openly curious tone. "More lies?"

Kurok shook his head. "Oh no," he said. "But like anything else technological, surmountable by the right skill set. Which we have here. We have ten of these crafts now. We're remodeling them to serve as cargo as well as other things for us. Those two are going out to do a perimeter sweep I believe."

"Huh." Stella looked out at the cruising carriers who were about to lift and curve back in a patrol routing. "So that's what Jacques meant, you could drop material fast. Those go… what, Mach two?"

"A bit more," Kurok said, and looked casually out over the water. "Ah, now here's something to watch."

Everyone quickly looked out to see a ruffle on the waters past the breakfront that protected the Bay through the gap in the craggy rock walls. Coming dead center to them, visible and head on, a carrier was at sea level, its engines sending up a wall of water on either side as it displaced it.

Both Kurok and Jess put their hands on the balconies mist dampened edge and leaned against it as the carrier came in at a frightening speed.

"Something up here?" Stella asked sharply.

"Oh no. That's just some new capability being tested," Kurok said casually. "Don't worry."

Jess grinned, as she watched the carrier come barreling in, shooting right through the gap and elevating up just as it cleared, coming right at them so fast no one had any time to even breathe before the craft rotated in midair and then changed direction and went up the face of the cliff, rolling in a long twisting spiral as it disappeared and leaving behind the chime of the sea bell outside ringing in celebration of its passing.

Its wake washed up against the wall and almost came up over the side of the corridor, but stopped just shy of topping it, leaving them dry as the waves rocked against the stone surface.

The visitors stared out at the now empty space with similar stunned expressions. Even the guards took a few steps toward the opening in reaction, their hands coming up in helpless motion at the sudden approach and then just stuck there.

"What the hell was that?" Stella blurted.

"What was that... was that the new navigation mod, Jess?" Kurok asked, in a normal tone. "Dev told me she was working on one." He turned to the stunned merchants. "Our senior tech. Who was flying that Bantam class heavy carrier."

Jess nodded. "Yeah, she said it increased the accuracy of the gimbals." She put her hands back in her pockets. "She's gonna work on boosting the engines next." She looked at the group. "It's a trip to be inside. But yeah they can move."

One of the guards, surprisingly, spoke up. "And you just went and took em?" He turned and stared at Jess. "Just like that?"

"Uh huh," Jess said. "Better than letting them rust."

The guard straightened up and gave her a respectful look. "Damn."

Jess grinned at him, a charming expression that lightened the purposeful intent of her usual attitude.

"We all recycle scrap," Beni said dryly. "Better job'n most, that was." He glanced at Jess and nodded.

They seemed to be over the shock of being in close quarters with a former agent, so Kurok figured it was time to move along and get the cavern tour done to complete the impression in one go. "Shall we? Lead on Jesslyn."

Jess turned and started along the viewing hallway. They walked past the out-processing station with its usual churn of fish life and up the slight slope back into the main part of the Bay. They continued through hallways with workrooms on either and then up the long stretch of newly cut stone to the interior opening of the growing cavern.

"This is new," Beni said, and touched the wall. "My family are stonemasons, I know the look."

"It is." Kurok waited as Jess put her hand on the ingress panel, and the first set of doors slid open. They walked through and the doors closed behind, and then Jess was at the large main opening. She turned and looked at him, and he nodded.

"Here we go," Jess said, she put her hand down and the lock cycled. The two doors slid open ahead of them, releasing a rolling barrage of rich biological scents to wash over them like a wave, of synth dirt and plants and the fruits and vegetables and flowers that were inside.

It was like being hit in the face with a cool, wet towel full of unusual, unexpected smells and they all stopped in mid motion to stare and breath it in.

Kurok paused to let them absorb it, while Jess sauntered inside and inspected the nearby plants. "Rather stunning, isn't it?" Kurok asked, in a mild tone.

Stella turned in a circle, her eyes wide, an unfeigned expression of amazement on her face. "By all the fish in the sea," she said. "How is this possible? Jacques told me, but I never thought it would be like this."

In every direction on terraced platforms were growing things. Jess had spotted something colorful and now sauntered back with a small object in one hand. She stopped near Stella and offered it to her on her palm.

Stella stared at it, then at Jess. "What is it?"

Jess looked at Kurok.

"Something you'll never see from station," Kurok said. "It's too perishable. That's a fresh strawberry. You can eat it," he reassured her. "We don't have that limitation. We're also researching methods of preserving them to make jams and so forth, or extract the flavonoids, which is what you've tasted I'm sure."

Stella hesitantly reached out and took the object. She brought it to her nose, sniffed it, then took a bite off the end. She chewed slowly and swallowed it, then looked at Dan Kurok. "You could sell a box of these for max cred."

Kurok nodded. "We can undercut station pricing as well,

since our costs are lower. The last question we had was, can we deliver this fresh, and that was answered by our new acquisitions." He concluded with a smile. "We're ready to trade. You up for it?"

Beni gave the remains of the strawberry that Stella put in her mouth, an envious look. "We trade all over," he said, gruffly. "No bullshit around that."

"We won't," Kurok said. "But we will trade with our neighbors. Whoever they trade with otherwise."

Stella nodded and licked her lips. "Got any more of those?"

"Oh, I'm sure we can find a taste for everyone," Kurok said cheerfully. "Let's keep going shall we? I think we've also got some lunch lined up in the conference room." He gestured to the group to walk on. "We can discuss things over that. "

Jess strolled along after them, noting the merchants and even their guards were no longer staring sideways at her. She had to admit the doc's plan had worked out exactly as he'd thought it might. She caught his eye, and he winked at her. She grinned back and listened to ops acknowledge Dev's coming into land in her ear.

Stupid good day so far.

Chapter Fifteen

Dev crossed the hall and trotted up the steps quickly to the seventh level. She moved along the inner hallways to the workshops. The largest of them was here, with surfaces sufficient to allow a dozen projects to occur at once, and the room was almost full as she entered.

"There she is," Doug said. He was at the front of the space near the assignment worktop. "Rocket!"

The KayTee pilots all turned. They were dressed in the Base work suits they'd come in, with pullover hoodies over them for warmth. Keko had just entered, eyes bright with excitement. Brent sat on a worktop near the door, and Chester had just put down a box next to him.

"Hello," Dev responded. She had changed into her lined jumpsuit and had her scanner looped over her shoulder. "That was excellent news this morning wasn't it?"

"Jess's note?" Doug grinned. "Yeah that was pretty cool."

"It was excellent," Kevin said. "I did not expect to hear that!"

"No, we did not either," Kelson and Kurt chimed in. "To be called out by name!"

"What'r they gonna do for triggers?" Brent asked. "Train up some of those kids?"

"You mean gunners?" Doug said. "April figures they're going to find a few good shots, use our busses to test out a few."

Brent nodded. "Saw em in there sanding off the Interforce markings."

"Yeah," Doug said, "they were painting on Rocket's bus." He removed some small packages from a box he carried in. "We got some treats from the mess kitchen." He looked over his shoulder at Dev. "Mentioned your name and they were gonna hand me anything I wanted."

Dev took a seat "I am confident they would have provided you with sustenance in any case."

Footsteps approached, and they all looked up to the doorway in time to see a tall, dark-haired figure pause in the entry with a large woven sack. "Hey." Jess looked around. "This where the party is?"

"Hello, Jess." Dev got up, then frowned at her. "Were you outside? Is it raining?"

Jess was dressed in dry clothing, but her hair was wet and

slicked back from her forehead and the sack she carried also seemed damp. She held it away from her as she went to a washing sink and deposited it inside. It made a soft clacking noise. "It's not. I just fell off the ledge in our digs into the Bay."

Everyone reacted, and Dev's brows shot right up. "Non optimal," she said, at once. "Are you all right? How did that happen?" She immediately approached Jess and studied her in concern.

"It's a short drop. Not a problem." Jess turned and took a seat on the counter next to the sink. "I was just messing with something. Anyway, right under that ledge, in the whirlpool, there's a sand bottom. Guess what I found in it?"

The KayTee's stared at her in fascination. Dev folded her arms over her chest and pondered, chewing her lower lip. The potential answers seemed somewhat endless.

"Water?" Doug hazarded a guess. "Rocks? Something someone else dropped off the ledge?"

"Oysters," Jess said. She opened the sack and pulled out a large, roundish craggy dark gray object. "See? Not the crate grown ones, these are legit wild ones."

Dev sidled closer. "I think you have mentioned those before," she said. "As an edible item."

Jess nodded. "You eat them raw." She removed a bladed knife from a pocket in the leg of her pants and pried the object open with a powerful motion. "Just slurp em down."

It came apart, and they all leaned forward to look at it. "Huh. Sort of like a clam, right?" Chester, said. "Only... gooshier."

"Jess." Dev put a hand on her arm. "Is that alive?"

"Sorta," Jess admitted. "But that's not the cool part. C'mere." She took the tip of the knife and moved the sand-colored substance around.

"Are you stabbing it?" Dev asked. "Is that to made it dead first?"

"No." Jess held it out. "See that?"

There was something dark and round inside that surprised Dev a lot. She reached out and touched it, feeling the chill of the water against her fingers and the slimy sensation of the animal. She closed her grip on the round object and removed it. "Oh."

It was mostly round, with a glistening, almost translucent surface. "What is it?" She looked up at Jess. "You don't eat this, do you? It's hard."

"You keep it." Jess picked up the shell with its disarranged animal on it and lifted it to her lips, slurping the creature down and swallowing it. "Mm. You get the pearl; I get the oyster." She licked her lips and winked. "Since I know you're not into it."

Dev regarded the object that was now resting on her palm. "Thank you, it's very attractive," she said. "Does it have a purpose, or is it just nice to look at?"

"Depends." Jess threw the now empty shells into the bag. "So, here's the deal," she addressed the rest of them. "I figure since you got a new slot here, a new kind of slot, you should get a Bay keepsake for it." She looked at them. "Right?"

The sets looked at each other in bewilderment.

"Oh, you mean, for like a... like a marker," Doug said. "Like the star they gave those kids. Or what we got here." He pointed at his cloth covered arm. "After the big fight."

Dev nodded in comprehension. "An achievement token," she told the rest of the bio alts, who brightened in surprised delight.

"Right." Jess pointed at the round thing. "That's what happens when a bit of sand gets inside an oyster, and it makes that hard surface around it to protect itself from the pain in the ass a piece of sand is. "

"Really?" Kevin got up and walked over to Dev and looked at the item she held in her hand. "That's a very unusual process, isn't it?" He asked. "But it's really pretty," he admitted.

"I brought enough oysters in the bag for you each to get one," Jess said. "You're the first air force the Bay's had forever. Okay?" She looked around at the bio alts and the techs.

"Sure," Brent said, with a brief grin. "I'll take one of those critters, though. I like em."

"Me too," Doug said. "Haven't had one since I went home last time." He licked his lips. "Too bad we don't have any pep-per sauce here."

Dev put her pearl in her pocket. "That's an excellent idea, Jess, and really kind of you to go swimming in the water to find them for us. May I help you get them out?" She advanced over to the bag and glanced warily inside. "The outside looks like rocks."

Jess chuckled then removed another oyster from the bag and opened it. She handed it off to Brent, then one to Doug. "There ya go."

Chester extended his hand. "I'll try one."

Kelson unexpectedly rose to the occasion and came over. "I would like to try one of the animals as well."

And so, they all did. Jess shucked them and handed them

out. The sets clustered around her and took them with cautious regard.

Kevin poked his finger into the oyster and removed the pearl that was underneath. His eyes widened at the golden sheened roundel. Then he hastily put it into one of his pockets and addressed the shell. He looked up to see if anyone else was consuming one.

Doug fished out his pearl then held the oyster up. "Just put your lips to it and suck it down," he said. He swallowed the mollusk and licked his lips. "Hey! Good oyster!" He looked over at Jess. "Really sweet! Reminds me of my grandy's little patch back home."

Encouraged, Kevin put the shell to his lips and tipped his head back, letting the contents slide into his mouth. He went still, his eyes wide, then he hastily swallowed the oyster, his body reacting with a little shiver. "Oh!"

Jess smiled at him. "Good job." She had her arms folded over her chest.

He looked around with a stunned expression. "It just slid right down," he said, in an astonished tone.

Kurt straightened up and copied his motions, but with a look of pleased surprise when he'd gotten the creature down his throat. "Oh." He licked his lips. "That was more optimal than I expected."

Jess glanced in the sack and pulled out the last oyster. "Guess you get two, Devvie." She opened it and was about to fish out the pearl when Dev gently took it from her and examined it.

She nudged the animal around and found the pearl and removed it. "Oh, it's pink," she said, in surprise.

"Salmon," Jess said. "Don't see those too much."

Dev handed her the pearl. Then before Jess could really do more than close her hand, she lifted the oyster and sucked it into her mouth, swallowing it quickly.

"Whoa." Jess said, in a surprised tone. "Devvie!"

Dev put the shell down, closed her eyes and swallowed a few more times. Then she exhaled and opened her eyes again. "That was interesting." She managed to get out. "I think I prefer them in soup," she added, as Jess draped her arm over her shoulder. "But I am glad I tried it. Now we all have the same."

She turned and leaned against the counter Jess was seated on and watched as all the rest of the pilots finished up. "Jess, that was amazing." She half turned her head to address her partner. "Really great."

Jess thumped her boots against the counter, a smile appearing on her face. "Just thought it would be cool when I saw them down there," she said. "You could make a necklace or something out of them, or whatever."

Dev removed her pearl from her pocket and compared it to the one Jess had. "They're all different," she said. "So now we all have something that's part of this place, but it's unique as well." She looked up at Jess. "As unique as you are."

Jess blushed a little and grinned. "So, where's the vid?" She asked. "I came here to see Rocket Racoon do crazy flying tricks."

Doug came over and handed her a packet. "Here. I had some extra," he said. "I thought maybe a few people might stop by." He winked at her. "Let me get the screen going." He went over to the input and started typing, as the pilots shifted around and found seats on benches and counters, keeping Jess and Dev in the corner of their eyes.

Dev leaned against Jess's leg as she waited for the vid to start, savoring the excellence of the moment.

She did, however, wonder what Jess was messing with on the ledge that caused her to fall off.

****

Jess leaned back in the worn seat and took a sip of grog, the overhead halon casting a warm glow over her bare arms. "So, tonight's topic," she said, "three busses with pilots and us." She indicated April, Doug and Mike. "Now we got seven busses with seven pilots."

April nodded. "Who do we pair em with?" She asked. "Mike and I were talking about that at chow. You got enough maybe candidates here." She looked faintly amused. "Enough wannabes, anyway."

Jess nodded. "In or out's a thin line here," she said. "None of them tested in. But I bet most of them can shoot those guns and not care."

Mike stretched in his seat. "Yeah, so how do we pick who to stick in the seats? Drivers were easy, we had those bios who already had flight basics, and Brent, and our guys."

April laughed. "Yeah, and Doug went from newbie kid to old man teacher in like a month. He showed me that marble, or whatever it was, you gave em all, Jess. They were lit."

"Chester said that was gonzo," Mike said. "What gave you the idea?"

Jess drank from her mug for a long moment then held the cup in her hands. "What gave me the idea?" She shrugged. "Crap if I know. Just something Dev said last night maybe, about those guys thinking stuff like that was important."

"Doug said they spent all dinnertime talking about how to fix em up," April said. She rested her elbows on the worn chair arms and hiked one knee up against the surface of the steel table. "So, after that I heard the yonks all talking during the mixup about the gunner slot. They want it."

Jess nodded. "S'why we're here. I got no idea how to pick," she admitted. "Those things pack a lot of punch and the last thing I want is one of them to take out a boat or another bus." She pondered. "I never thought twice about it. Aim. Fire."

"Yeah, you don't really think about it," Mike said. "I mean, you train on sims and on mocks all the way through school, right? It's natural."

"Natural," April agreed. "Just get in there and do as much destruction as you can. You should know about that, Jess, you're damn good at that. I saw the vid of you blowing up Gibraltar."

"That was Dev's flying."

"Her flying was ace, but she didn't aim those plasma bombs. While going upside down sideways," April bluntly disagreed. "So, we gotta find some of these yonks who can do that. That's who sits in the gunner seat. Like us, cause I don't know that we're agents of anything anymore."

Mike nodded. "Truth. That's not the gig, right? Send us out individually to go make trouble and stuff? Like it was?"

Jess sat there for a long moment, thinking.

"You even think about that yet?" April asked. "As in, what the hell we are now? I mean, no dis, Jess, it's only been like what, four days since the whole planet started spinning the other way. Maybe we should figure that out sooner than later."

"Yeah," Jess finally said. "This isn't Interforce."

"Who wants it to be?" Mike said, straightforwardly. "Whole thing was going down the tubes."

"I kinda like the idea of…" April paused. "Maybe it's coming from being a part of a clan. I think a bunch of mad ass kickers works better than one." She seemed slightly embarrassed. "That wasn't a thing at school. You never teamed up."

Mike leaned forward and put his elbows on the table. "Y'know, that's different here. They like doing things in bunches," he said. "Meals, raves, mixups… it's only been like Ape said, four days? They already forgot we're inservice. They were crawling all over you tonight at the mixup. Nobody even flinched."

"Not for a second," April said. "Nobody backed up, put their hands up…everyone was just like we're here to rumble, let's go." She grinned a little. "Ace for me, but they did it to you too. That one big guy went after you like crazy."

Mike grinned. "Until Jess slugged him and put him to sleep. Man, I felt that in the back of my teeth."

"You know what," Jess said, "with all that throwing down I never felt…" She paused.

"Never went to the zone," April said. "Never felt like it."

Arias said, quietly. "No trigger."

"So, a big group of ass kickers pointed in the same direction," Jess concluded. "Maybe we get rigged up to find the best shooters. They get to sit in the bucket seats. Can't be the bios, they're not geared for that."

"Right." Mike nodded. "They go around saving turtles going for the Bay, I seen em. They ain't shooters."

"But everyone maybe gets to learn how," Jess said. "What that's like, for the rigs and for the portable rifles once we build em." Jess slowly felt her way through it. "We all go out in a big ass team and wipe the floor with whatever we need to bring with us."

"Kinda not what I expected, y'know," April said, but in a mild tone. "I was thinking, here's a place full of jerks, like agents at school and at base. But they're not. I guess that's why they didn't get selected in the battery. They're not psychos. They're just wild."

Jess nodded thoughtfully.

"In a cool kinda way," Mike Arias said. "I like it. I wanna be a wild boy. I never liked all the rules and regs inservice." He somewhat comically wiggled his ears. "How many times I got my ass zapped for acting out."

April regarded him with a sideways look. "You were such a punk."

"I was." He nodded. "I always thought maybe my parents were glad I got taken. I must have been an exhausting pain in the ass little kid." He tilted his head thoughtfully. "Thought maybe they just took the cred and didn't care."

April's lips twitched in reluctant humor. "S'why I liked hanging with you. So damned random and not so in your face."

Mike nodded. "You always just did what you did. No bull-shit or competing. You never gave a crap about what anyone else thought."

"No patience for the politics."

They both looked at Jess, who was smiling. "You liked us," Mike accused her. "Right off, even at that half assed party before it all went to hell. I told April, hey, Drake's kinda cool."

"Everyone else treated us like snot nose kids," April said. "Like anyone there was not hanging on by a nail."

"You were nice to Dev," Jess responded mildly. "Everyone else there was being jerky to her." She folded her hands around one knee. "Even after she kicked ass. Maybe because she kicked ass. Scared the crap out of all of them. Pissed me off."

"They told us about her," April said. "Before we left Canyon City. I didn't care. You see bios all the time when you're in and out of the big trading places. I'd been to Quebec. Thought they got treated like shit there, so I thought it was all right one was getting a break, y'know?"

"Doug came over to us after he talked to her and told us, dudes, that's some smart smarts right there." Mike nodded thoughtfully. "He said, that's not a bio."

"That's what I said too." Jess smiled again. "I said, no way. I've talked to them, had them around the Base my whole career. But they said she was." She shrugged a little. "Then I flew with her, and I didn't care if she was or wasn't. I won the lottery."

"Big time. I guess that's why those mooks from admin wanted to hoist her back with them. They knew," April said. "Doug showed me what she did to bypass all the security on our rigs." She laughed and shook her head. "Kurok gonna make more?"

"Of Dev?" Jess's brows lifted. "Nah, even if he decides that he's going to set up a rig to cook spirals here."

"Bet he does." Mike said."

"So, we get a gun rig set up tomorrow," April said. "We start teaching the yonks to shoot. When do you figure to go out and get the roof? That back deck'd be a good place to get some practice in."

Jess grabbed her cup and stood up. "Soon as the doc's done with his brain stuff. A week maybe?"

April also stood up. "Lot can happen in a week."

"Heard that," Mike said. "No telling what'll be happening by then."

****

Dev trotted up the steps to their quarters, her scanner hanging over one shoulder and the carry bag she'd gotten at the market over the other.

She opened the door and went inside, pausing as Jess often did, to examine the space and detect anything out of order. Nothing occurred to her, but she lifted her scanner and turned it on, running a sweep of the interior just to be doubly sure.

It was always good to be sure, even though she thought there was more reason for this place to be safe than any other they'd been. Satisfied she turned off the machine and continued inward, slowing down as she detected some new things.

Ah, yes, Jess had said she'd had some things brought up. Dev went across the big entryway where there was now a large square box against the wall, and three more padded stools scattered around to sit on.

She moved further into the space, seeing some pieces of flat stone leaning against the wall and she paused to study them. Then she turned and looked back at the box.

With a soft, speculative grunt she left the room behind and went to the storage area where she set her scanner down, removed the carry sack, and opened it.

Inside were several lengths of neatly folded cloth that she removed and put on the counter. Then she removed two modules wrapped in plas and set them down as well. She then exchanged her lined jumpsuit for a pair of heavy work pants, a long- sleeved shirt, and her pocket filled vest.

She glanced out the other doorway and paused, spotting something near the outer entry to the service lift.

With a slightly puzzled expression she emerged into that hall and went over to the large space just inside the entry where stores usually put things while they were making them ready to put away.

 Stacked higher than she was tall, and taking most of the space there, were squares of metal, battered and tarnished, grid like in construction like the service pads up in the landing areas. "What is this?" Dev wondered aloud.

She lifted one down and examined it, then was distracted by a soft chime at the service entry. She hoisted the piece of metal back up onto its stack and went to the entry, reviewing the pad to determine who was outside.

Two idents, unknown to her. Dev paused for a moment, regarding the readout. Then she decided to test her theory on the relative safety of the location and put her hand on the entry pad and released the door.

It opened and she got into position to prevent entry just in case. She found two youngers outside whose eyes opened wide as they spotted her. "Hello," she said. "How are you?"

They were both roughly the same height and size, with dark hair pulled back and tied into a tail at the back of their neck. They wore the standard work coverall of the Bay with scuffed, worn boots and sleeves rolled up past their elbows. "Yo," one returned the greeting, somewhat hesitantly. "Hey, Rocket."

"Hello." Dev waited a moment, but they just stared at her. "How can I help you?" She asked gently. "Did you need something here?"

"Nah we uh..." the one who'd spoken said. "We brought stuff up here before for the Drake." He eyed Dev with some apprehension. "Came to see if she wanted anything more done."

"Oh," Dev said. "Yes, I have seen a lot of new items here. That was excellent of you to help." She backed up a step and pointed at the stack. "Did you assist with this material?"

More confidently, the chatty one nodded. "Yo."

"Excellent." Dev nodded. "Please enter." She waited for them to step inside and let the door close. "Jess has not returned from her exercise, so perhaps you could give me some information about this," she said. "What are you called?"

Chatty had his hands in his hip pockets. "Gus," he said. "We were at the mixup too, yo?"

Dev had guessed that by the sand burns on their arms and hands, and the bruises that Gus had across one cheekbone. "Yes, I as well," she said. "I thought the work was very interesting."

"We saw ya," the other one said. "Call me Hank."

"Thank you, Gus and Hank," Dev said. "Did Jess mention what purpose she had for this material?" She pointed at the stacks of salt scented metal.

Hank and Gus exchanged looks. "Said you'd figure it out," Gus responded, with a little grin. "Yo?"

"Ah." Dev folded her arms over her chest and regarded the piles of beaten-up sections. "Interesting." She lifted the end of one piece and inspected it. "What was the last thing it was used for?" She looked at Gus. "Do you know?"

Hank sidled over and studied it. "Stores said they fished off it," he said. "Down by shoreside. The olders did." He scratched the back of his head. "Craig-o said nobody wanted it down the caves no more."

"I see." Dev put down the square.

"Drake said, if anybody could figure out what to do with this here stack of brass, it'd be you," Gus said. "So, we brung em."

"Oh. Brass?" Dev straightened up and scratched the edge of

the metal with her fingernail. "Interesting," she murmured. "They are made to clip together?"

Gus and Hank obligingly took down a section and held it next to the one she was looking at. On the edges there were welded clamps, and they worked their section into place, so it fit against the one Dev had her hand on. "Yo. Yeah?"

"Please remove that one." Dev said. "Would you like to assist me in using this material?"

"Yo," Gus agreed. "S'what we're here for." He worked the section loose. "Sup?"

Dev picked up the section she'd been examining and turned. "Please bring some of those." She walked along the hall- way and moved past the large bedroom to her workroom in the rear.

She put the section down in the center of the floor and waited for them to each bring in another one. "I would like to cover this room with these pieces of metal."

Gus walked over, knelt and worked the clamps into place, while Hank did the same on the other side. They both carefully banged them with the sides of their hands until they lined up. The three were now attached at right angles. "Yo?"

"Yes," Dev said. "As far as they will accommodate."

Gus put his thumb up in the air and stood up, then waved at Hank to follow him back out. "S'go bro. No problem." He paused at the door and turned. "Gonna need snips." He pointed at the corner of the cabinetry that filled the walls.

"And a welding device. Yes," Dev said. "I have those tools."
"Yo."

She was left in brief quiet to consider the floor, until the sounds of metal being shifted echoed down the hall. Then she went over to the lower set of cabinets and opened the doors and knelt to retrieve the tools and move them up onto the top of the workspace.

Then she went and retrieved her scanner and brought it back into the workspace that, in the time she'd been gone, had gained a half dozen more panels. "Excellent." She sat down on top of the workbench and opened the scanner, running it over the panels with a smile of approval. "This could be optimal for a certain purpose."

****

Jess palmed the door to the housing open and entered, then

paused at the sound of voices. She moved quickly across the main room and deeper inside but relaxed a little as she heard a third voice she recognized as Dev's.

It was calm and relaxed, and a bit at odds with the scent she picked up of carbon work going on, the clanging and noise, and the two young sounding male voices. "Dev?" She called out cautiously, ready to bolt into action regardless.

"In here, Jess," Dev called out. "The work area."

What the what? Jess moved quickly along the hallway to the big space Dev had claimed. She stopped short in the door- way at the activity inside. "The hell?"

The floor of the room was now covered in the metal panels she'd had brought down, and there were two scrubs there, staring at her in some slight alarm as they worked a section into place. "Yo, Drake," they chorused softly.

"Yo," Jess responded absently. "Sup?"

"Hello, Jess," Dev said, pushing the eye shield up on the welding shield covering her face. "It was so excellent of you to find these sections in storage." She shut off the welding torch she had in one hand. "This is Gus and Hank. They offered to assist."

Jess put her hands on her hips. "They did, huh? Hey scrubs." She regarded the two youngsters. "Whatcha doin with this stuff, Devvie? Didn't figure you needed a landing grid in your crib."

"I don't." Dev took the question at face value. "But these are conductive, and they interlock, Jess," she said. "So, I was wondering if I could pass a low-grade current through them and produce heat." She indicated the room. "I think there will be just enough to cover the space."

Jess came inside and walked across the new metal floor and sat down next to Dev on the workspace. "You came up here after the mixup and invented a heated floor?" She looked at the two Bay youngsters. "Tolja she'd think of something to do with these damn things."

"Yo." Gus had just cut one of the grid pieces in half with a pair of heavy snips. "Gonna heat up the deck, Rocket lady?" He looked around at the floor. "Huh."

"S'wrong with the floor?" Hank asked, a bit puzzled.

"The floor is cold and when you stand on it for a long time it causes discomfort. This will assist with that." She leaned over to examine the line of welding she'd just laid down. "Though I think I will have to consider what to put on top of it to disperse the heat evenly."

"Damn." Jess rested her elbows on her knees, her bare arms vivid and colorful. "That's pretty slick, Devvie."

Dev grinned. "It's not as interesting as a flying suit, but it will make it more comfortable to work."

Gus and Hank were just crouching there on the ground, eyes wide. Then Gus's expression cleared. "It's too cold in here for ya?"

"Yes," Dev said. "I am not used to living in facilities that do not regulate temperature." She swung her boots a little bit. "This location does not."

Hank slapped him on the shoulder. "Like the spacers," he said. "Bout froze when they all got here." He gave Dev a nod. "Rocket lady came from space, dude."

Dev nodded. "Yes. I was born on Bio Station 2," she said, "as were the rest of the sets here. Space is a lot colder than it is here, but you can't touch it."

"Weird ass?" Gus said. He glanced at Jess.

"Space is weird," Jess confirmed. "Thanks for giving Dev a hand." She regarded the two youngsters. "C'mon by tomorrow after your work sched, yo?"

"Finish this?" Gus asked, his eyes lighting up.

"More stuff," Jess said casually, with a faint smile. "We got a lot of crap to do in here."

"Sure yah, Drake." They both stood up hastily. "Morra, yo?"

"Yo." Jess lifted her hand, and the two disappeared, and a moment later they heard the door cycle near the lift. "Kids." She chuckled. "All hot to help out."

"They did an excellent job," Dev said. "Really good help. They got all those parts into place while I was fastening them." She regarded Jess. "Of course, they want to do good work for you, Jess. If they are useful, you might give them interesting assignments."

Jess gave her a sideways look. "Should I?"

"Of course. Would you like a beverage?" She asked. "I think I too am finished with work for the day." She looked around at the floor. "I will continue on this tomorrow."

"You been out to the ledge?" Jess asked.

"No."

Jess got up and held her hand out. "C'mon."

Dev put her scanner down and took Jess's hand, following along agreeably as they walked out through the halls toward the chill breeze that came in from the ledge outside. "The lights should be on," she said, as they turned the last bend and moved out through the crack in the mountain wall and emerged on the outside of the wall.

There was no rain today, so no cascading water, but the lights at the edge of the precipice provided a blue and green glow that backlit the ledge. Dev totally forgot about the lights when she spotted something new there. "Oh!" Her eyes widened in surprise.

Jess put her hands behind her back and rocked up and down on the balls of her feet. "What d'ya think?"

In the back curve of the ledge there was a new construction. Pipes had been hammered into the rock going lengthwise from side to side. Thick chains hung from them. The chains were wrapped around a big piece of battered, stone colored extruded plas, as long as Jess was tall, formed at a right angle providing a seat.

Dev immediately went over and sat on it. To her delight it rocked gently. "Jess this is excellent! Did you construct it?"

"Yup." Jess came over and sat next to her and used her long legs to push the seat back and forth. "Cool, huh? I was getting that chain fastened when I pitched my own ass overboard," she cheerfully confessed. "But I think it ended up worth it. At least we got someplace to sit."

"It's amazing." Dev touched the plas. "It's the perfect shape."

"Yeah, some corner of some storage crate, or something somewhere that broke. I had to sand off the edges, so they didn't draw blood." She pushed her heels against the ground and moved the seat back to reach behind her and pick something up. "Left this out here."

The plas seat was a good temperature, not at all the stinging cold metal would have been. Dev touched it in delight as she watched Jess bring a bottle into view, along with two cups that were hanging from a string around the neck of it. "This is absolutely optimal," she said. "It's perfect, Jess."

Jess filled two cups from the bottle and handed Dev one, taking the other for herself as she put the bottle on the ground. "This is some of that sea grape wine we got when we were out for the market," she said. "Didn't figure we'd end up drinking it here."

The wine was strong and just a bit effervescent, and Dev let it linger on her tongue as she watched the lights and listened to the rush and bubbling of the water two levels beneath them. She let her head rest against Jess's shoulder and felt the warmth of her skin against the side of her face.

It really was a perfect moment. The glow of the lights and the smell of the sea, fresh and rich; the taste of the wine and the feel of their bodies against each other. An awesomely comforting way to end the very busy day in this moment of quiet reflection.

Busy, but good. They were doing very different things, but Dev felt like she might be enjoying them more. She wondered if Jess was. She looked up at her profile as she watched the far-off flicker of lightning behind the clouds and saw the faint, easy grin there, but also almost an expression of wonder.

"Hey, Jess?"

"Hey, Devvie?"

Dev thought about how to ask the question. It was hard to put into words the thoughts. "I … find that it makes me…" She paused and switched to different words that seemed to fit better.. "I really like it here."

Jess's grin expanded into a wide smile, a rare one that was warm and expressive, and made her eyes twinkle. "Yeah, me too." She rested her head against Dev's. "There's something right about it. About being here," she added. "I don't know what'll end up happening but I'm glad we're going to find out together."

Dev lifted her cup up and touched it against Jess's, as she'd seen done at some of the natural born celebrations.

"Know what that tradition is from?" Jess asked, shifting the mood.

"No."

"Don't look it up. It's kinda grim." Jess turned her head, and they kissed. "And it's not the time for grim."

****

"Good morning, Dev."

Dev paused in her progress down the hallway and waited, as Kevin hurried to catch up to her. "Hello, Kevin. Good morning. How are you?" She responded agreeably. "Did you just finish with the lab?"

His hair was in some disarray from the clamps and leads and he rubbed his fingers through it. "Yes. So much information!" He said. "But it feels good to understand so much more. It makes the work so much…" He paused. "I don't feel so uncertain about everything. That's so suboptimal. But Tech Brent said that's how natural born feel all the time."

His eyes widened as he said it, his head shaking back and

forth almost unconsciously.

Dev nodded. "Yes, that's true. It can be very uncomfortable. I have had to learn to not let that bother me."

Kevin blushed. "Oh, that's right," he murmured. "I forgot… we all can't see our collars here." He touched the high- necked collar of the tightly woven sweater he wore under his coverall. "Are you optimal about that?"

"Yes. I don't think about it anymore." Dev answered mildly. "It was my choice, anyway. I could have said no, but as it turned out it was excellent that I did not since they could not put me down on station and I had actions I had to take there."

He stood there in silence for a moment, in deep consideration.

"That was not what you wanted to ask me was it?" She asked, then waited; her head tilted slightly to one side to see what else was forthcoming.

He was in his Bay coverall, a thick woven fabric that had been altered to fit, the sleeves and legs that they had at first rolled up now trimmed off neatly and hemmed. The extra fabric, Dev noted, had been fashioned into pockets to carry things, not too different from the vest she was wearing over her own lined jumpsuit.

Adjustments. They'd all made them, over the weeks since their collective world had so radically changed.

"Oh no, that was not why I called out. I was requested to ask you if you could give some advice on a project we would like to do," Kevin said, straightforwardly. "It would only take a moment."

"Of course," Dev said. "I have some time now. What kind of project?"

"It's on the other side of the large space." Kevin pointed down the hall. "This direction."

They walked on down the hallway and past the turn off to the plant cavern. Another roughed out hallway now went farther to the back of the cliff, to where new work areas had been opened on the edge of the back wall.

"We are looking for a location to construct an exercise station," Kevin said. "And we think we found an optimal place for it."

"Aside from the big location on the other side of the opening?" Dev gave him a sideways glance. "There is a good amount of space there."

Kevin remained silent for a moment as they pushed through the back door and went outside. The space beyond had changed, the surface had been leveled, and overhead there were two large metal sections in place, though the center was still open to the sky.

"Yes, that is true," he said. "But it is a different kind of exercise, for us. The machines the natural born use here, they are not scaled in a way we can use them efficiently."

"Ah." Dev nodded in understanding. "Yes. That is true. They are difficult to manipulate."

"We want to make sure we are strong and can help, so we want to make machines like we had up on station, and they had in the Base," Kevin explained earnestly. "At the base, Keko said, they could adjust them."

"Yes. They had many people there that were many different sizes," Dev said. "The machines there, they scanned you when you used them and reconfigured to adapt to the difference." She glanced up overhead as they heard a welding torch ignite, one of the Bay mechs was suspended from the metal piece sealing a seam. "I did miss the plus grav lab however."

"Faster, when you could double the G," Kevin agreed. "Abby said that yesterday." He pondered. "Could you make a grav adjustable space?"

Dev's brows hiked up. "Could I? I have no programming for that." But then she paused and remembered station. "And it was easier to do it there. You could store grav in the flywheel." She frowned thoughtfully. "But it might be interesting to try. I know Jess would really enjoy a null space."

"A project to consider."

Dev spent a moment briefly imagining Jess's delight. "Yes."

They crossed the open ground, and Kevin led her past the big set of gates that stood open to reveal a stack of huge metal pieces lying outside them.

"It was an excellent idea to have those cut in sections," Dev said. "I'm glad you suggested that to Doctor Dan."

"Yes, it seemed like it would be more optimal. This way two of the Bantams can handle the placement," Kevin said and smiled with visible pride. "Lifting it in one piece would have been extremely difficult, even with many of us attempting it."

Especially with many of them attempting it, Dev thought silently. Even with just the three experienced pilots it had been dangerous.

He went into the set of shallow shelters and caves on the right-hand side, now empty of people and full of building sup- plies. There was a caravan standing under one of the already placed metal sections, two loaders moved crates from the main area over to them.

Here it was quieter, and the passages narrower, lit by temporary halons strung along the halls. Kevin moved along the passages, counting under his breath and then took a turn and stopped in front of a narrow opening. "It's in here," he said. "Abby found it." He went through the opening, it's slender dimensions easily admitting him. Dev slipped in behind him.

It was a narrow, angled opening but then it turned again and opened into a cavern of reasonable size, but relatively low height, the surface of it just about a foot over Dev's head. Inside there were piles of metal, angle irons, poles, and scraps and a plas trestle table with stacks of parts on it.

Four larger halons were propped up on the sides of the cavern, which lit it with a warm, golden glare, their dark cables tucked neatly against the walls.

"We think this will give us enough room to set up the exercise stations," Kevin said. "We can't all use it at the same time, but we can in rotations by shift."

Dev looked around the space, which did in fact provide a large area to work. It had a somewhat irregular sandy floor and at the end, a second passage she felt air blowing in from. "It seems very pleasant," she said. "I think it would be optimal for the work."

Kevin nodded. "Yes. I know the natural born could use it for other purposes. We hoped you could ask permission for it to be assigned to us for this." He folded his arms and regarded her.

One of Dev's pale eyebrows lifted. "I think Jess would approve the use of this facility for that purpose if you asked her. You do not need my intercession. She is very reasonable."

"It is possible," Kevin said. "But it is more probable if you ask, as your input is very highly valued."

He made the statement in a very pragmatic way, and Dev took it as such, just a statement of fact they both knew was true. It was highly likely if she asked Jess to assign the space, Jess would, though it was also likely that she would if Kevin, or any of the other sets, asked because the request was logical and probably did not interfere with any plans she had in mind.

All true. However, Dev felt that she could take advantage of the facility herself, and so she also had a vested interest. "Yes, that's true," she said. "I will see if Jess can make the assignment. She will understand the request since they are building more exercise spaces into the other hall as well."

Kevin nodded. "Yes, and the new practice area for the aiming systems." He looked around the space in satisfaction. "This will be excellent. Thank you very much for helping us with this, Dev. It's really optimal of you."

They both paused and looked up instinctively, as a low, rolling sound echoed through the rock walls. A second later, the comms set in Dev's ear buzzed. "Dev," she responded instantly. "What is the situation?" She glanced at Kevin, who also had his hand to his ear.

"All call! We have communications from Cooper's Rock, a dangerous situation," Bay Ops said, succinctly. "They are reporting an attack."

"Dev to operations." Dev waited for the channel to clear. "Please call all pilots to their vehicles."

"Operations, acknowledge. Please stand by."

"Interesting." Dev turned and started quickly for the door. "It seems our morning schedule has altered." She darted through the narrow entry and then broke into a run, heading out and across the open space at her top speed with Kevin hot at her heels.

Chapter Sixteen

"What is it?" Jess said as she came out into the big hall. "What are they saying? Ah, never mind, let's go find out. Tell everyone to get to the flight bays." She clicked off and ran for the stairs that now had people dashing up them, all heading for the same place she was.

She leaped up and grabbed the iron frame of the steps and climbed up the side of them. Halfway up she hit her comms, crouched and leaped up a floor while she keyed in Ops. "Tell group one to get to the landing bays with their whackers. Ten per bus."

Then she released the comms and continued climbing up the railing, passing everyone on her way up to the top-level bay.

She swung over the rail at the top and loped down the hallway toward the flight deck, already hearing the whine of systems starting up and the distinctive rattle and shift of the carrier engines spooling. She saw April come bolting from the other direction as she came around the corner, and the hatches on all four of the carriers in the bay opened in sequence.

She hurdled onto the deck and into her carrier, spotting Dev already in her seat, flight helmet on, as she'd expected she would be. "Hey, Devvie."

"Hello," Dev said. "What is the situation?" She was adjusting and running checks, but her eyes watched Jess in the reflective surface.

"Beats the hell out of me." Jess thumped into her seat. "But we're gonna have ten yonks in here in a minute sitting on each other's laps while we get our asses over to Cooper's Rock to see what's attacking them. Dee sent out a mayday."

"I see." Dev finished her preflight checks. "Two carriers are making a delivery to the processing station. Shall I recall them?"

Jess got her restraints wrapped around her and connected. "No time," she said. "Let em know what's going on ... oh crap, the doc's with them."

"Doctor Dan?" Dev straightened in her seat and set up a comms link.

"Yeah, he's gonna be pissed he missed a scrap," Jess muttered, then turned her head. "Move it you scrubs!" She let out a loud bellow. "You got ten seconds!"

There was a sound of running boots outside and then the

bay was flooded with moving bodies. "You ten, over there!" Security Mike stood like a rock column directing traffic. "C'mon move it move it!"

"Brent is asking if he should activate weapons," Dev reported, busy with comms. "I have advised Doctor Dan. He said one of those words I generally have to look up in comp."

Jess chuckled faintly, easily imagining it. She studied the gunner console, running her mind over the week's targeting trials and grimaced.

Ten work suited bodies came rambling into the carrier in a crush of motion. "First six, take the seats, rest of you on the floor, and grab on!" Jess directed. She unhooked her own restraints and stood up.

The Bay residents were wild eyed with excitement. They each had a three-foot-long metal pipe in their hands, and they all took their places quickly, clearing the floor so that Jess could move to the hatch and lean out. Dustin was the last one in, and he hit the deck between the gunner's station and the pilot's, bracing his booted feet against the stanchions. "Awwww yeah."

Dev glanced at him and muffled a smile as he wriggled in happy motion. She looked in the reflective surface at the ten large figures crammed inside the craft, all with expectant grins on their faces.

"Mike!" Jess let out a yell to catch his attention. He looked up at her, and she pointed to the fourth carrier on the far end of the bay. "Gun for him, wouldja?"

Mike's eyes lit with surprised delight. "Hell yah!" He wasted no time in hustling over to the last carrier and vaulting up onto the platform, pulling the big projectile rifle off his back as he ducked through the hatch.

Jess ducked back inside and sealed the hatch then dropped into her seat. "Get moving Devvie." She fastened her restraints again as the carrier lifted, its flight beacons flashing through the clear front windscreen. "I'll probably regret that but hopefully he won't hit us."

"Stand by for egress," Dev said as she made rapid, light adjustments. "Flight lead to flight, we will egress over the Bay, then elevate to flight level and accelerate. Please validate the coordinates are present."

"Good here," Doug answered at once. "G'wan, Rocket, before some of those guys decide to hop on our backs." He paused and went slightly off mike. "Hey, buddy sit the hell down or April's gonna stab ya."

"Good here," Chester said, echoed a moment later by Brent,

and then a soft chorus from the four carriers in the lower bays. "Wow this is crazytown."

"Yes." Dev coasted out of the landing bay and out over the water, moving quickly out of the way to let the other carriers come out behind her. They emerged into the gusty winds over the water, dark clouds moving overhead in the as yet dry skies. "Flight is assembled, Jess, coordinates have been locked."

"I'm sure they have," Jess muttered. "All right." She focused on her boards. "Give me power, Dev, and the rest of the four of us too." She saw the guns come live. "Everyone else just stick close, and we'll see what's the story when we get there. Move."

"Stand by for acceleration," Dev said as she swung the carrier around and boosted it. "Please hold on."

Dustin wiggled his boots. "Whoop, whoop! Go Rocket!" He hooked his arm around one of the supports as the carrier went for altitude and the engines spooled up. "We're gonna kick it!" His eyes widened in surprise and excitement as they felt themselves shoved back by the acceleration. "Oh yeah!"

Dev glanced in her reflective mirror and caught Jess's wry look in response.

She got the carrier up to speed, and they arched across the barren ground behind the coastal cliffs that held the Bay. The ground was covered with rocks and debris, a mild flat stretch before it lifted into the hills on the horizon where Cooper's Rock mining camp was. Even at this distance, she could see a tiny trail of smoke rising over it.

"See if you can raise em, Dev." Jess did a quick scan of her boards and brought the targeting scans online. She reached up to pull down the triggers, aware of the eager eyes of the eight men and two women of their passenger load watching her.

"Gonna blast em, cuz?" Dustin asked, bright eyed. "Boom boom!"

"Probably," Jess responded, then pulled on her comms set and brought up the sideband between the four senior rigs. "Hey."

"Hey," April responded. "Nice way to finish up breakfast. I like it."

"So, listen. Try not to splat anyone," Jess said. "We're civs now."

"They're plugging those guys out there, Drake. You want to drop flowers on em?"

"I didn't say not to blast their gear. Just try not to blow up people," Jess said. "Could be a try out, see what we'll do."

"Meh," April grunted. "Civs."

"Ack," Mike Arias acknowledged.

"Who the hell they gonna call?" Security Mike rumbled. "Let'm see what we'll do. Better for us."

"I have Coopers Rock on comm for you Jess." Dev tightened her restraints and ensured her flight helmet was secure. 'It's a somewhat unstable signal."

"Gimme." Jess hit the transfer." Dee?"

"Jess! You get the damn message?"

"Heading your way," Jess said. "What's the sitch?"

"Someone didn't like me choosing who I sold my ore to, I guess. Came in and blasted through my damned front doors. They're taking everything they can load. My guys are pinned down inside the entry. Got a couple dozen dead."

Jess was briefly silent. "Keep your heads down," she finally said. "You should hear our engines inbound any minute."

Dee snorted. "I can't hear a dam... oh wait." She paused. "Let me get people under cover. Hurry, Jess."

Jess closed comms, then opened the sideband. "They shot first," she told April, Mike, and Mike. "So, I guess, let's do what we do."

"Muhuhuh." April chortled softly. "What's the plan?"

Jess switched to all band. "Flight, drop into the mine entrance, that's where the bad guys are. Everyone out of the carriers and kick ass as hard as you can. They'll be the ones stealing ore and firing at the doors."

The ten Bay residents let out a rumble of approval, and hands shifted on pikes as they leaned forward to watch the view out the front window as the carriers raced over the barren ground.

"Go in fast, Devvie. Don't give em a chance to figure out what's going on."

Dev glanced in the reflective surface again and then concentrated on her entrance vector, sending routing idents to the rest of the flight.

She and the rest of the veterans would come in first. She had a wire trace of the layout up in front of her, with the target drop location outlined, a tight space inside the bowl at the base of the mine.

Fortunately, the veterans knew what to do, and the new fliers just did what she told them to.

"Got it, I'll take the left, Rocket," Doug said. "Chestie, you come in right and let Brent take the back."

"Gonzo," Brent's voice sounded cheerful for a change.

"Stand by for ingress." It was a very short arc to come in, and Dev got her boots settled as they came in behind the mountain ridge of the stake hold and then abruptly lifted over the top of the cliff, then diving back down to the massive dig on the back side.

There, huge transports were landed, and past them she saw the wide-open ingress to the mine, the destroyed gates allowing powered lifters to take hold of the mining loads and crates and rush them to the transports while a line of armed figures pinned the defending miners inside the doors of the mine.

All taken in a single second's glance.

No time to really ponder. Dev aimed for the doorway that hung half off its hinges, with a line of attackers blasting at it. She drove the carrier right to the deck, getting the landing jets on and skids extended just in time to meet the ground.

"Ready!" Jess barked.

The Bay fighters were already on their feet and at the hatch as it opened before they even stopped moving and they poured out with booming yells that rattled the inside of the carrier and made ears itch as they hit the ground running.

"Go!" Jess yelled. She sealed the hatch and got her triggers in line as Dev lifted and spun the carrier to face the transports, taking fire on the underside of the carrier. "Gimme a view!"

Built to withstand the full out assault from their own class of vehicles, the hand blasters didn't even make a mark on them. Jess got her aiming in place as Dev shifted the carrier sideways so her blasts would not take out any of their colleagues.

Jess laid down a line of fire that forced the attackers to dive back behind the transports. This gave the other four carriers space to land their troops, and they did, coming to ground behind them as Dev moved forward and pushed the line of attackers back, the landing jet exhaust sending a whirl of dirt and gravel everywhere.

The carrier's forward blasters abruptly took apart one of the ore loaders, sending rock and steel flying and providing coverage as the Bay fighters dove through it, swinging poles that knocked the debris out of their way as they engaged the attackers.

Jess stopped firing, to avoid shooting her own fighters. She stood up in her station and leaned over the console. "Lemme see how those yonks are doing."

Dev obligingly tipped the nose down to give her a better view, making Jess grab hold of her boards to keep from catapulting over into the pilot's station.

Jess peered through the windscreen as Dev shifted position. "Wow," she said, after a pause. "Look at them go." She studied the line of fighters galloping across the rocky ground, zig zagging and bouncing over obstacles and climbing up onto the loaders as the drivers bailed out. "Yay us!"

Heavier firepower came in from the right suddenly and Jess sat abruptly down in her seat. "See what the hell that is!" She yelled. "Spin to the right!"

To the right was a huge gap in the rock face, the massive entrance to the mine and Dev neatly rotated the carrier, her eyes widening as she saw the giant metal gates flat down on the floor with armed and armored trucks outside, racing toward them. "That is suboptimal."

The trucks had mounted heavy blasters on their roofs, and they fired as they came in, somewhat indiscriminately it seemed. Their powerful bolts hit the transports themselves, and an engine of one blew off and went flying right at Dev's wind- screen and then over their roof as the carrier slid out of its way and it smashed into the wall of the mine. It came apart and scattered flaming metal everywhere.

"Hahaha. Morons!" Jess stitched the road in front of them with a rumbling thump of blaster fire, sending vehicles flying off in both directions. Dev pitched them down and forward, while behind and underneath them the Bay fighters landed by the other veteran carriers came bolting across with their poles and eagerly joined the fight.

The Bay fighters raced across the ground and hurdled up over the line of smoking ore carriers and went at the attackers without a second's hesitation. Yells rang out over the concussive sounds of blaster fire, audible in the speakers Dev had tuned to pick up the battle.

They were fired on, but they were fast, and agile and they ducked the blasts as though they could sense them coming. They used the metal poles to yank weapons out of hands and smash bone and skulls, scattering blood and fragments across the dusty ground as they all went full out, no holding back.

"Lotta trucks out the front there," Brent called. "Gonna go strafe em back." The fourth carrier peeled off and accelerated through the gap.

"They should..." Jess paused. "Oh crap!" she said, her eyes widening as her boards reflected the energy return blossoming. "He's shooting!"

"Plasma released," Dev said instantly. "Stand by for a blast." She added into comms while she shifted the carrier around and headed them up and away from the gap just as a set of plasma bombs emerged from either side of Brent's carrier and impacted the cliff walls. "Flight five through eight stay on the ground, do not lift. Do not lift!"

Dev got the carrier out of the wash of destructive energy, and it came back through the gap as a backflow that flipped downed vehicles and rocked the transports, fanning the flames on one of them that had been hit by blaster fire. In the scan she saw solid rock start to implode between the walls. "Brent!"

Jess saw it. "Oh crap."

Brent kicked the afterburners on, and the carrier surged away from them outbound as the walls on either side lifted then collapsed, dropping tons of rock into the gap in an explosive avalanche that sent rocks flying in every direction, a wave of them peppering the ground on either side of them.

"Booyah." Brent came up and back over the top again and dropped down into the mine chasm. "Ain't bothering nobody now," his voice echoed in comms. "Take your time."

Jess checked her scanner, as the walls collapsed and filled the gap, blocking any chance of the forces outside of coming in to help. "Nice shot," she finally said into comms. "Put our back to that, Devvie. Now that we know nothing's coming through it."

Dev obligingly brought them back around and tipped the nose forward again to give Jess a good view of the ground as she moved sideways across the still rumbling wall, rocks rattling and tumbling down behind them from the residual energy.

To one side, on the right, four carriers sat in solid formation, with their blast shields down, and hatches closed, as she'd instructed. April and Mike Arias were taking point on the far side of the mine opening and Brent had flown his machine down to Dev's left-hand side, over the destroyed mine entrance.

Jess unhooked her restraints and came up to the pilot's seat. She rested her hands on the back of it while she looked over Dev's boards at the ground, deciding where to take the battle next.

A moment's scan though had her surprised to find the fight over, the raiders all either on the ground or on their knees with their hands over their heads, surrounded by tall figures in Drake's Bay work suits.

There was no more firing. Bay fighters collected dropped weapons and shoved them into their belts. They looked around as though in deep surprise that it was all over so fast. Some of them tipped their heads back and waved their pipes cheerfully at the hovering carrier.

"Rock the wings," Jess said, almost under her breath. She gripped the back of the seat as Dev complied, and the carrier tipped in either direction. "Look at that, Devvie. The kids rocked it."

"Yes. It seems the activity is reduced," Dev said. She regarded the transport in flames. "Unfortunately, they did a lot of their own damage it seems. Should we descend?"

"Go ahead and land there near the doors," Jess said, in a somewhat bemused voice. "Cause I think we won," she said into the sideband. "We're going to put down. See what's up."

"We'll check out what's left on the other side there," April said. "Ace shot, Big Mike."

"Scared the crap out of me," Mike's rumbling voice responded. "Wow." In the background of his comms, they heard Brent chuckling. "Damn head's ringin like the Bay seabell."

Dev settled the carrier back down on its skids outside the broken door to the inner halls of the stake hold. Dozens of Cooper's Rock residents poured out the door, skidded to a stop, and stared at the Bay craft. They held guns, and mining tools. "Interesting," Dev concluded. "It seems we were not exceptionally expected."

"Ya think?" Jess unlocked her restraints. "Well, now they know what it's like when we show up."

Dev peered out the windscreen at the miners, who stared at the Bay residents with equal surprise. "Do you think they found us optimal?"

Jess laughed, as she went to the hatch and looked out, tucking her worn civ hand blaster into the small of her back. "We did what we do."

Dee Cooper was leading the way over to their carrier, a bloody gash on her shoulder seeped lurid red as a gang of her miners followed.

Jess walked down the ramp and went to the front of the bus. "That what you had in mind?" She asked Dee when she came into hearing range.

Dee looked around at the destroyed loaders, and the burning transport, at the pile of rubble where the entrance to the stake hold had been. At the line of attackers who sat on the ground watching their captors with wary eyes, as those tall figures in rough work gear roamed among them collecting booty.

She turned and looked at Jess. "Yeah, Jess," she said crisply. "That's exactly what I had in mind. Someone to come in and kick these bastards where it hurts." She leaned over a little and peered at the collapsed entry. "Can you shoot through that mess though? To get supplies in is gonna suck otherwise."

Dev had come to the hatch and heard the request. "You mean, remove the rock?" She asked. "This vehicle can do that, yes."

Dee looked up at her. "Oh, hi, Dev."

"Hello," Dev said courteously. "How are you?"

"Been a hell of a lot better, thanks for asking." Dee exhaled. "Bastards."

"Damn." One of the miners had a blaster rifle slung over his shoulder. "That's crazy." He looked at the filled gap. "What did they shoot that with?"

"Plasma bombs," Jess said. "They make a big boom."

Comms crackled. "Bunch took off down the trade road," April's voice came over the link. "Want us to stop em? They'll blab."

Jess looked around at the fighters, fifteen minutes past their first fight, all grinning despite some bumps and scratches. "Let em talk," she responded, with a slow smile. "Let em tell every- one they see. But follow em and see what direction they go."

April chuckled. "Scare the crap out of them. They had no idea what they were getting into."

"Yeah." Jess turned to Dee. "Any idea who they were? Who paid em? Those are big guns they had. Not anyone local."

"Didn't give me a chance to ask them." Dee held her injured arm against her body. "Just pulled up and started shooting." She looked at the transports. "They're not marked. Guys aren't marked. No terms. I tried to talk to em, they told me to shut up and stay out of their way." She regarded the men seated on the ground, and past them, at the bodies lying crumpled. "I didn't do either."

Jess smiled without humor. "Sucks to be them."

****

The processing station was roughly halfway between Drake's Bay and Base 10, an artificially blasted set of docks built out against the rock cliff face where fishing boats could pull up and offload their catch. It was exposed to the sea, but the docks were semi sheltered by concrete buttresses that provided a seawall enough to allow a reasonable place to pull in and get into the receiving system.

The boat's catch was sorted with rough simplicity. Basic scans went over the tanks and sorted out the biologic material inside them, and the weights as they offloaded. Then cred was issued to the ship owner. The processing station took the catch and converted it to something that could be sold in a form that let it be transported. Either they dried it, smoked it, canned it, or vacuum sealed the edible parts and then took the non-edible parts and processed them further into something useful.

Nothing was wasted. The processor took anything and everything from the sea. Some boats specialized in seaweeds, others long-range deep-water fish, some inshore small boats came in with sea cucumbers and limpets.

You had to be a certain size for the processor to bother with you. The rest of the smaller boats went stakehold to stakehold along the shore and traded or met up with inlanders, who had a more equal set of items to trade with them for what they could.

Dan Kurok leaned back against the skin of the carrier they'd flown in on, hands in his pockets, as the processor's receiver looked over the crates they'd just offloaded on the small, rough flight deck the processor station provided.

Standing on the other side of the carrier ramp was a big Bay lad, in his work boots and pocketed pants, along with a brand- new ocean colored pullover hoodie with the Drake's Bay dragon's head embroidered on the breast that matched the block painted sign on the tail section of the carrier.

He had a long metal stick slung over one shoulder from a braided strap of fishing line, his dark brown curly hair was caught in a small tail at the nape of his neck.

Inside the carrier, Keko contentedly ran some routines, keeping scan up, and in general going over the technical bundle he'd recently been programmed with. He remained quietly at the controls, just as Kelson was in the other carrier with his own Bay security guard, Emily, who sat in the hatchway casually blocking entry.

It was early morning. They'd left the Bay just after break-fast, to bring over a crate of dainties for the processor's leadership, and a full load of produce in the second carrier of more sturdy edibles the processor's kitchen staff had asked for.

"All right." The intake inspector nodded and slid his scanner around to rest against his back. "It's clean."

"I certainly hope so," Kurok responded mildly. "Would you like to tell your boss it's ready for him then? I've got things to do today."

The inspector stared at him insolently. "Maybe this ain't clean."

Kurok shrugged. "All the same to me. I'll enjoy sharing a picnic with my friends on the way back to the Bay then. Douglas, would you mind retrieving that box?" He asked the guard leaning against the carrier.

The Bay guard licked his lips and grinned, as he went over to the crate and grabbed one handle of it. He lifted it up and let it thump a little against his shoulder. "Your loss, my yum, yo," he said to the inspector. "No problem!"

The inspector looked like he wanted to mouth off at Douglas, but the Bay guard stood there hoisting the big crate easily, staring at him with that peculiar non blinking stare common at the Bay, utterly unimpressed by his attitude.

"Yeah, all right." The man finally waved at the lift, at one side of the loading dock. "Put it over there and we'll take it up."

"Doctor Dan," Keko's voice sounded quietly in his ear. "A message has come for you from Bay Operations."

"Go ahead," Kurok said just as quietly. He listened to Dev's calm, even tones, despite the impending chaos the message itself related. "Thank you, Keko. Well noted," he said briskly.

"Shall we prepare to depart?"

Kurok watched Douglas saunter across the dock to deliver their box. "No, I have every confidence Jess can handle whatever that turns out to be. Let's get the other carrier unloaded, shall we? I want our muppet friend to sign off on this transfer chit, so this isn't a complete waste of time."

"Yes, Doctor Dan," Keko said. "Relaying."

A moment later there was motion in the other carrier. Emily stood up and extended the ramp from the craft. She slid her metal stick around to her back and started to move the crates out and over to a nearby steel pallet.

Kelson joined her, and a moment later Keko emerged from his carrier to help. The pilots were in standard Bay work wear, but each had, wrapped in a thin metal wire, a pearl earring fastened through their left earlobe, softly gleaming in the overhead lights in counterpoint with the comms set wrapped around the ear on the opposite side.

Kurok watched them unload for a moment, then casually strolled toward the entry, as Douglas came back from depositing the crate into the lift and went over to join the other three with their unloading work.

The inspector and the crate disappeared as the lift, an open metal platform, moved upward with a rattling jiggle and disappeared into a square gap in the roof of the cavern.

The unloading went quickly. Emily dusted her hands off when they were done and looked around. She spotted a manual loading jack near the inside wall and headed over to it.

She reminded Kurok a lot of April, with the same rounded

gymnastic build and thick red curly hair that like Douglas, was caught at the nape of her neck. Her face was oval shaped, and she had a smattering of freckles across her cheeks and nose, and dark sea green eyes with interesting silver overtones.

Reaching the pallet mover, she worked the controls of it, turning and hauling it along after her moving back toward the waiting offload, where Douglas was standing with one hand on the boxes waiting for her to arrive.

Kelson and Keko had moved aside a pace to the engine cowling of Kelson's carrier and were examining the air intake of it, smoothing the metal surface with their hands.

Kurok just leaned back against the metal railing, arms folded, and ankles crossed affecting a bored expression, watching a sea bird drifting in off the water with his focused vision as he watched the entire scene in front of him in his peripheral.

The platform came back down empty.

The two mugs stood up and started to saunter closer.

His ears both twitched a little, and a faint smiled appeared as he moved a little farther down the rail, apparently studying the gull with deep interest.

He saw two other tough guys enter on the other side of the cavern, these with long blasters, old ones, slung casually over their shoulders and he finished his study of the bird, coming back around to face inside and sliding his hands into his Bay overshirt front pocket where he had a hand blaster resting.

"Keko and Kelson," he said quietly into comms. "Let's get ourselves ready to move on once they sign off on the delivery, shall we?"

Both pilots went into motion, leaving the pallet and going up the ramps into their respective vehicles. A moment later the access ramps retracted and the external beacons lit.

He watched Emily look up from her steering of the pallet mover and meet Douglas's watching eyes, as the two mugs headed toward her. The two Bay fighters grinned in knowing conspiracy at each other.

The first mug caught up to Emily and grabbed her shoulder. "Hey chickie."

Emily released the pallet handler and turned, pulling herself clear of his grip and then launching an attack without any hesitation. Leaving her steel rod on her back she brought a knee up into the mugs ribcage and twisted her body to the right, slam- ming her elbow into his face with a solid crunch of impact.

Douglas bounced up and down on the balls of his feet. As the second mug came flying over he let out a booming yell and leaped onto the stacked crates then over them, launching himself in the air to intercept the second attacker. He slammed into him and took them both to the ground.

Emily had things well in hand. She drove her opponent back with rapid-fire punches, taking steady, digging steps forward, her body sinuously evading his return punches at speed, her head snaking one side to the other as his fists whiffed past her.

Douglas rolled clear of his target and got up to body slam him again, driving him against the wall and then turning to let him bounce off that surface, his arms flailing in surprise as one of them were grabbed and Douglas applied a twisting motion, pulling his arm and shoulder out of place and dislocating it with a sodden wrenching pop.

The man's body arched in pure shock, and he dropped to his knees with a pained grunt.

Kurok kept it all in view, and as the other guards started to react and pulled their blasters off their shoulders he calmly removed the gun from his pocket pouch and with one careful aim, hit the closer man's rifle in the trigger, making him hastily release it as it heated, arcs flashing across its metal skin. He then turned to the second guard's raising blaster, hitting it right at midpoint shooting it out of his grip and sending it spinning across the floor.

The nearer man took a step in his direction, and he let the blaster rest casually on his shoulder turning his head fully to stare at the goon, content the kids had things under control on the other end of the platform.

The guard took in the gun and the stare and stopped, bringing both hands up. "Okay, buddy. I got the message."

Kurok smiled his gentle smile. "Good lad," he said in approval. "Now go sit down."

The two guards backed off, careful not to move toward their grounded weapons. He watched them go to the panel on the wall, hammering one of the buttons on it, and briefly considered removing the panel from function, then he shrugged and turned again toward the mixup going on.

It was over. The two guards were on the ground, the one Emily had pounded on out cold, with blood coming out of a gash on his head and bruises emerging on his face and the mug with his shoulder dislocated laying on the ground gasping in pain.

Douglas and Emily bopped over to each other and exchanged high fives.

"All right now," Kurok said. "Let's see if this is going to get extremely stupid, or if it was just a little test." He put his blaster back into his Bay shirt pocket. "Well done, either way."

"Jerks." Emily went back to the pallet loader and started it toward the pallet again.

Douglas came over, shaking his hands out, his eyes bright. "Think they were just messing?"

The elevator lift started working and it rumbled into motion.

"We'll find out in a moment," Kurok said, placidly. "Either they'll bring us some tea and those poor lads some bandages or we'll have a chance to see how you're doing on your targeting skills."

"Sweet." Emily made little motions with her hands, squeezing invisible triggers.

****

Jess paused outside her carrier, one hand resting on its mottled surface as April and Doug landed right next to it, the steam and dust from the landing jets fluttering her clothing against her body.

The engine whine cut off and the hatch opened. April emerged and come over to her, a satisfied look on her face.

Jess eyed her. "So?"

"Pretty weird," April said. "We followed them out of the hills, and like you'd figure they went east and got on the caravanseri road. I expected them to go left and head up the coast, but they split up and just went in all directions, like they met up for a party."

"Hm."

"I went north a while and Mike went south. Tracked two of them to a couple of small stake holds and then saw another two take a hairpin, head west, and kept going," April said. "You get anything out of these guys?"

"Fits what they say," Jess answered. "Said they were recruited at two of the big nearby markets, said they were paid to come in here and get ore, just pay for play. Said they were told there was a sitch going down and they needed to get ore out so Dee couldn't hold the coast hostage."

"Sounds like a scam."

"Sounds like a scam," Jess agreed. "Or it could be true. Maybe they figured she's just going to sell to us."

"Now she might." April looked around the big space, where

debris was being moved out. "You should take those transports for our payment," she said. "Easier to tote these yonks around than stuffing them all in our busses."

Jess chuckled. "Yeah, I told Dee that already. She figured I wanted to trade for a load of iron." She gestured toward the nearer transport with her jaw. "Dev's over there seeing if she can get the thing moving after they took it's damn engine off."

April nodded. "Yeah that's gonna be good." She put her hands on her hips. "Scam or not, this went all right. Yonks did good, bios did good." She exhaled. 'You send back those other four?"

Jess nodded. "Told em to drop off the yonks and take one bus back here in case we need pilots for those things. Or to fly ours while they fly the transports."

"Nice."

Dee emerged from the hastily boarded up entrance and came over to them, her bandaged arm in a sling and dressed in a fresh, unbloodied shirt. "We're betting it was the merchants," she said. "That whole, hey buddy, wanna make some fast cred? No risk routine sounds like their speed."

"You got what they want maybe," April said. "Or Doug thinks maybe it was a try on."

"See what you guys got?" Dee pursed her lips. "Maybe the council paid em off. That's an idea." She looked at Jess. "You got the invite to the meetup yet? I heard they wanted to have a chat next week."

Jess nodded. "Yesterday. Yeah, if some of those guys went off to the west it could be. If it was, hope they got what they were looking for." Her pale eyes twinkled, and she wiggled her eyebrows. "It ain't Interforce."

"It is not." Dee studied a group of the Bay fighters, passing the time by mixing it up with each other while the miners warily watched. "But it is something."

Jess nodded. "It's something." Dev emerge from the transport, a service kit fastened around her waist and her scanner hanging around her neck. Brent was at her heels, along with Kevin and they started across the open ground toward them. "Here come the wrenchers."

"Hey, you want to hear a funny?" Dee said, suddenly. "Joanie just came over here laughing her ass off. They started shifting the ton of rock your guy dumped in the passage and guess what?"

"Okay. What?" Jess went along amiably.

"Big old line of silver ore in it." Dee laughed. "Told your

guys to leave it where it fell. We'll dig it. Make a nice little extra. We can use the back entry to the road there until it's worked out." She held out a hand. "Thanks Jess."

Jess returned the clasp. "Glad it worked out."

"Glad we could be good neighbors," April said and grinned. "And you got to try out some moves."

Dee gave them both a wave, then turned and made her way back to the entrance, where two miners were busy securing an additional steel plate over the upper section.

"These guys are looking sideways at the bios," April said, as they watched the wrenchers approach. "And looking side- ways at the yonks."

"I noticed."

"Didn't see any bios here."

"Like at the Bay," Jess said. "Until now."

Dev arrived at her side. "Hey, Devvie."

"Hello," Dev said. "Lifting the damaged machine will be difficult," she reported. "It has unbalanced flight characteristics due to that missing engine, and it's not ideally designed in the first place."

"We got time for you to redesign it?" April asked. "I figure we got a couple hours till dark yet."

Dev paused and looked at her, both fair eyebrows lifting.

"Kidding." April rocked back and forth on the balls of her feet. "Chill."

"Thank you?" Dev answered after a brief pause. "I'm a comfortable temperature at the moment."

Jess draped one arm over Dev's shoulders. "That mean you need to fly it?"

"That would be optimal," Dev said. "Kevin has reviewed the controls and can fly the other craft. I would l like Kurt to fly our vehicle."

"I don't get to fly with you?"

Dev paused, slightly nonplussed. "For the flight to the Bay? It's a very short flight."

Jess merely looked at her sadly.

"Of course, you can come with me in the damaged vehicle if you want to, Jess," Dev said. "It will probably be more optimal for Kurt in any case."

"Without my maniac self sitting behind him with my fingers on the triggers? Probably." Jess relented and gave her a little squeeze. "Just messing with ya, Dev." She touched her comms set. "Okay, ya scrubs. Get in the tanks. We're heading home."

The Bay fighters broke off their tussling and started to retreat to the carriers, walking through the groups of working miners removing debris and ignoring the looks they were getting, most adjusting their metal pipes to lay across their backs as they split up and went to their berths.

"Dustin," Jess called out as her cousin ambled by. "Yo."

Surprised, he paused and turned. "Yo? Sup?"

"I'm riding with Dev in that torched transport. Take my seat in that bucket," Jess said. "Don't shoot anything." She gave him a shove toward the carrier as he stared wide eyed at her. "Move it!"

"Scrub." Jess sighed and waved the rest of the fighters on. She felt the faint motion as Dev softly chuckled.

The Bay dialect floated back to Jess, along with the bright, high energy as the fighters talked about the fight, and looking forward to mess, calling out to the carrier pilots as they waited to board. She let the last group go past, then gave Dev a nudge. "Let's get going," she said. "Add this to the patrol routing. Let's put some visible eyes in the skies and maybe they won't pull any stupid crap after this."

"Heard that," April said. "See ya back." She turned and headed for her carrier.

Jess took a breath and released it. "We have any place to put those things, Dev?" She asked, as they were left alone to walk across the mostly empty ground to the big transports. "Ain't fitting in any of our landing bays."

"We can land them in the old shuttle area," Dev said. "It has space, and Doctor Dan does not wish that area to be used for shuttle landings any longer, I believe."

"Huh. Yeah." Jess still had her arm around Dev's shoulders as they walked. "We can rig these out and fit a bunch of scrubs in there, or a ton of crap. Pretty good trade, huh?"

"I think this went excellently," Dev responded. "Your instructions were optimal. Everyone was saying so. They expressed that you nailed something, which I assume means a positive thing rather than a piece of metal used to fasten material together."

Jess smiled, as they walked up the ramp into the transport the attackers had nearly blown apart. "I think you're all biased."

"At least people do not expect you to build vehicles from scrap in three hours," Dev muttered as they climbed up into the craft. "Oh, there is some cargo still loaded in here. Let me..." She paused as Jess turned and triggered the loading hatch to close.

"Leave it." Jess watched the hatch seal and went over to bump her shoulder against it. "Dee got a silver lode out of this trash panda carnival. She can afford a few boxes of whatever the hell that is."

Dev ran her scanner over the crates. "I will adjust the trim for it." She inspected the results and went up to the cockpit, a broader console than the carrier's, with two seats for pilots. She settled into the left-hand seat and brought power up to its basic systems.

Jess checked out the inside of the craft, which was roughly twice the size of the transport they'd sent to Base 10 for the evacuation. "Can you fix that thing they shot, Devvie?" She asked, as she pictured the inside full of her scrubs. "This is the bigger of the two of them."

"Yes," Dev answered in absent confidence, as she pulled the comms set onto her ears and settled the cups into place. "But it's a relatively low power engine system. We can improve it."

"Good." Jess went into the front of the transport and found a relatively comfortable seat waiting for her on Dev's right side. She settled into it, pleased to find enough legroom, and looked around at the boards. "Can I press some buttons?"

Dev looked over at her. "Do you want to?"

"Not really." Jess folded her hands over her stomach. "I do want to kiss you though."

"Really. Right now?" Dev asked, with interest. "Because I think that would be excellent, though confusing to the rest of our colleagues." She half turned and leaned on the arm of the pilot's seat and regarded Jess. "I am not sure they would understand the delay in our departure."

Jess leaned toward her. "I'm not sure I care."

Dev looked even more interested. "A moment." She keyed in the sideband. "Kevin, please lift ahead of us, to give this vehicle additional space."

"Yes," Kevin responded instantly. "Excellent plan."

"Slick." Jess put her hands on the battered console between them and lifted herself up and over so they could kiss. It was awkward, but neither of them cared, and the rumble of Kevin's engines had faded before they paused and regarded each other. "Glad I came with you."

Dev smiled. "Absolutely. That would have been difficult in separate vehicles." She drew in a breath. "Should we depart?"

Jess had to think hard about it, but she reluctantly moved back to the other pilot's seat and dropped into it with a disgruntled pout. "G'wan."

Dev spooled power to the remaining engine and started up the landing jets that would boost the craft up and out of the giant bowl that held the main structure of the mine stake hold. A glance into the monitor board showed the ground cleared. She applied power as the craft groaned and reluctantly lifted. "Sub- optimal."

Jess reviewed the boards. "Sorry, Devvie." She looked at the controls. "Want me to get out and push?"

"Please do not attempt that. Opening the door would disrupt the lift." Dev frowned in concentration, struggling a little to keep the craft from tilting as it lifted slowly up.

Jess chuckled.

"It would be optimal if you secured your restraints."

"Any chance of you flipping this to one side and throwing me over on that side?"

"Yes."

"I'll take my chances." Jess caught the reluctant grin on Dev's face as she fought with the controls. "Only live once, Devvie. Let her rip."

Dev checked the angle they were lifting at, and the edges of the cliffs and boosted the front jets, then ignited the main engine, shoving the throttles forward and flinging the craft up and into flight, putting abrupt distance between the transport and the ground and sending the carriers, waiting to escort them off into scattered directions. "Like that?"

"Ooof."

****

Dev was glad the approach to the Bay that the shuttles had used was open and over flat grounds. The craft she was flying was difficult to steer, and it kept pulling off course to the side of its damaged engine. She drifted a little to the right and slowed down as Kevin gingerly landed ahead of her, in the big open patch of wind scoured rocky ground on the north edge of the Bay.

There was a jagged escarpment at the edge of the water, and it dropped down to the surface of the sea on the outside of the ring of stone that plunged around to make the protective walls of the Bay. Rough waves blasted up against it and a strong onshore wind buffeted them on their approach.

Dev released one hand off her controls and made a quick adjustment, then quickly grabbed the thrusters again as the flyer rocked, and they tilted.

It was a very short flight, so Jess hadn't had time to get bored. She sat back and watched out the front windscreen with interest as they drifted closer. "What a rockpile," she said, studying her homestead idly.

Dev eyed her. "Jess, may I ask for a favor?"

Jess slowly turned her head to one side and her right eyebrow lifted. "Sure. Ya want to land first?" She grinned in a particularly saucy way that made Dev understand her comments were sex related.

Which was excellent.

However, not entirely optimal now. "I could use a hand with the controls," she said. "Could you hold on to the directional thrusters and keep them stable while I lower us down?"

Jess sat up in her seat. "You want me to help you fly this thing?" Her eyes widened.

"Yes, please." Dev had both hands on the thrusters, the harsh vibrations from the working engine thrumming through her.

"Uh... sure." Jess studied the controls, then glanced quickly at Dev's hands, wrapping her own around the same set of controls in front of her. "This? Just... what... hold it in place?" She asked. "Like that?"

"Yes." Dev eased off her grip and saw the tendons on Jess's wrists suddenly stand out as she took the strain of it. "Thank you." She switched over to handle the landing systems, extending the big sets of double skids the transport used to go to ground. "It took a lot of energy to keep us on track."

Jess looked at her, then at the controls. "No kidding." It was taking a surprising percentage of her strength to keep the plane level, and she took a tighter grip on the controls. "This thing always this hard to fly?"

Dev leaned forward and watched to either side as she brought the craft in to land. "I don't think so. The damage is making the control systems difficult to manage. But it is a much larger craft than our carrier."

"Tough for you. Must mean it would have shot off into the water for anyone else." Jess concluded. "Yeah?"

"Possibly," Dev said.

With a rocking thump they touched down. It tilted a little bit to one side and then leveled again. Jess felt the strain against her forearm muscles reduce as Dev shut down power. The noise of the damaged craft slowly ebbed in a dying flood of rumbles and clangs.

There was a hissing noise. Dev checked the boards hastily,

then vented the engine cowling, aware of the steam escape just to her left-hand side.

"Suboptimal." Dev watched the pressure and heat come down slowly, then she relaxed. "There will be a lot of work required on this machine to make it function properly, but really, Jess, it was optimal that they prevented the vehicle from lifting and causing more damage to the mine."

"Ya think?" Jess cautiously regarded the console in front of her. "Big ass plane."

"And I am confident everyone will enjoy fixing it," Dev continued in a mild tone, as she finished securing things. "Kevin was talking on comms about what they could put inside these as we were flying. The Kaytees already have programming on them."

"Do you?" Jess inquired, giving her a knowing, sideways look.

Dev smiled, and after a second, returned the look. "There really wasn't time to give me general aviation schema," she said. "But flight systems have the same function. These will be useful vehicles, even if they will require some repair."

"Yeah, give the scrubs something to practice on anyway." Jess leaned back and ran her fingers through her hair, then pushed it back off her forehead. "I need a scalping." She pictured in her head exactly the expression she saw when she looked over at Dev, looking back at her. "Haircut," she clarified.

Dev studied her seriously, as she waited for the boards to settle. Jess's hair was grown out a bit, with a wave her typical trim had removed. "Does it bother you like this?"

Jess tugged on it. "Gets in my eyes," she said. "And I think it looks weird."

"I think it's quite attractive like that." Dev turned back around and started the shutdown process. "But you should do what is more comfortable. I liked the adjustment you got on the island." She glanced over at Jess, who had her head tipped back on the chair and watched her with a charming little grin on her face. "Didn't you?"

Jess stood up out of her chair and stretched. "Yeah, I did." She stepped over the seat and moved back into the rear of the craft. "C'mon, Devvie. I see the Doc waiting for us. Let's hear what his day was like." She depressed the door hatch and stood back as it creaked open grudgingly.

The smell of sharp, clean salt air rushed in, mixed with the off gassing from the craft, and the sounds of the Bay floated in behind them. Seabirds, and the movement of water and the clang of fishing gear faintly echoed from the large open door into the cliff.

Jess took in a breath of it. The other transport was parked ahead of them nearer to the cliffs with its hatch open. Kevin stood near it, talking to two other KayTees and Clint, along with a group of mechs.

Behind them, near the entryway that they'd once walked through to find piles of dead bodies, was Dan Kurok, who casually leaned against the stone, his hands in his Bay overshirt front pocket. He waved at them as Dev hopped down from the plane and started walking over.

Clint spotted them and angled over to intercept their path. "You two always have to wreck things?" He asked. "How did that other engine not fall off?" He stared at the second transport. "What the what?"

"What the what," Jess said. "Bunch of half assed pirates dumped in on Dee Cooper and were raiding her stock."

"Heard that," Clint said. "How'd we end up with these junkers?"

"We took those as payment for our services," Jess said. "Got two boxes of something in the back of that one as a bonus," she added, as Kurok came over to join them. "How'd it go at the processors?"

A grin briefly appeared on Kurok's face. "We had an interesting morning," he said. "As did you, I hear. Was that a difficult flight back, Dev?"

"The control plane is very damaged," Dev responded straightforwardly. "I had to manually manipulate the steerage without hydraulics engaged."

Both Clint and Kurok turned and stared at her.

"Jess was kind enough to help me land," Dev concluded. "I think it's going to require a platform rebuild."

"Well then." Kurok took hold of Jess's elbow. "Let's go inside and have a cup of tea, shall we? There's lots to discuss." He looked over at the other plane and shook his head. "But as a matter of fact, I think these are going to come in quite handy."

Jess suspected that had a double meaning.

"Think I might know where they came from," Clint said, unexpectedly. "Let me go see if my guess is right." He winked at them and then went over to the closer flyer.

That probably had a double meaning too. Jess sighed as she let herself be led toward the big, steel armored door leading into the Bay, suspecting the conversation might also need more than just tea.

Chapter Seventeen

"So." Kurok sat at the table in the kitchen that serviced the Drake family compound on the first level. There were bowls of leftover lunch from the mess, and mugs of grog. April, Mike Arias, Chester, Doug, Brent, Security Mike, and of course, Jess and Dev were all there. "It was a try on."

"Scam," April said, with a faint jerk of her head. "We figured."

"Too bullshit," Mike Arias agreed. "Some guys, all random, all picking up some extra cred, had to be. We figured the neighbors wanted to see what we got before they put any ask down."

Jess was seated against the window, the vast expanse of the Bay visible behind her, her face cast a bit into shadow from the pale light outside. "That's a lot of risk for a try on."

"Well, Jesslyn, how exactly do you try out a military force you want to hire otherwise?" Kurok said, in a reasonable tone. "They took two angles, it seems. One, a full out reasonably full-size attack on a neighbor, including weapons. Including killing force."

April frowned. "Idiots. That coulda been a lot of jackass."

"And a second, a more subtle play to see what we would do if they messed with us in commerce." Kurok leaned back in his chair. "I daresay they got more than they were looking for on both accounts." He took a sip of his tea.

"Idiots," April said again. "What the hell's Cooper thinking of? She buying in to that? Her people got splatted, and not even by us!"

"Cliff got blowed up too." Security Mike snickered. "Didn't figure on that neither."

"No. Turn it around," Jess said, thoughtfully. "Maybe she took the risk. Put it on the table. That could have gone ugly for her, and she agreed to do it to give us a showcase."

"Oh, they would have returned her minerals, likely," Kurok said, then paused as Jess shook her head, and then April lifted one hand and let it drop. "What do you mean ugly?"

"If we'd ended up being the homicidal maniacs they all think we are," Jess responded, with a faint smile. "We came in, shut it down, and stopped." She nodded thoughtfully. 'Was a good op."

"Yeah," April said. "That's a good read, Jess. I saw those

guys looking at our guys. They know how that coulda gone, and Dee's been here." She nodded. "She saw this place after that last mess and showed up to fight at it."

Mike Arias made a hand gesture of agreement, extending his thumb and pinkie finger and waggling his hand. "I buy it," he said. "I think Jess is right. They copped the demo."

"And the scrubs only had pipes to kick ass with." Jess glanced at Kurok, who now looked very thoughtful. "What'd you tell them at the processors?"

"Oh." Kurok took another sip from his mug and hiked up one foot onto his opposing knee. "Well, you know, after that little scrum was over their big cheese came down and loudly blustered at me. I told him I had taken the opportunity to extract his system schema and datafiles and would be glad to sell them to whomever was interested if he tried that little unpleasantness again."

There was a brief silence, as Kurok sat there smiling, a mischievous glint in his eyes.

"Interesting," Dev said. "Did they question the accuracy of that statement?"

"They did," Kurok said. "So, I tapped in a few things on my pad and shut down their power and they left us alone after that. I think we convinced them. "

Doug started laughing. "Nice!"

Jess grinned. "You're scarier than the scrubs are. But I knew that."

Kurok tilted his head in modest depreciation. "Ah well. Those muppets think they know more than they do. At any rate, they were also impressed by our little vegetative gift to them, so it ended better than I'd hoped it would." He exhaled. "I suspect the region will be making us an offer at the conclave next week."

Security Mike nodded. "We gonna get those yonks some guns?" He asked bluntly. "Or just let em whup up with pipes? Be better with some shooting stuff, once they learn to aim em. Got projectile rifles we could give em from the stash."

These old-style arms, in the armory of the Bay, now always kept open and full of ancient weapons that half functioned. Or all the way functioned for very limited periods of time. Enough to turn the tide in the last fight, but in no one's minds anything they could continue to use with a very limited amount of ammunition.

Jess pondered that. "Yeah, we gotta amp it up," she said. "We're gonna have to make them here. No one's going to sell them to us on the market."

They all sat in quiet thought for minute, no one disturbed by the silence. "Still a scam on our side," April finally said. "We just threw crap at the wall, and it stuck today."

"True," Jess said. She didn't look offended and wasn't. "But that's what field was. You just didn't get to do enough of it to know that."

Kurok chuckled. "Oh goodness that was true. We never knew what in the world was going on." He relaxed in his chair. "It was just react, react, react. Your father once said to me, no point in planning, DJ. The more you plan, the more things can go wrong with the plan. Just run it out."

Jess could almost hear Justin saying it and knew the truth of it herself. "Intel's important. Planning?" She shrugged. "So maybe we get the best shooters, like a half dozen, and take em to the conclave with us," she said. "We probably got enough long guns and slugs for that."

Security Mike nodded. "Works," he said. "Lemme see what I can haul out of stores."

Jess leaned forward and looked past Dev at him. "Yo."

"Yo, Drake," he responded, eying her warily. "Sup?"

Jess paused, then looked at April, who smirked. She turned to Mike Arias, who gave her a thumbs up. Then she looked back at Security Mike. "You like it? What we did today?"

His eyes, a pale cloudy gray color, widened just a bit. "Yeah," he responded slowly, drawing the word out. "So?"

"Wanna stick it?" Jess offered casually. "Wanna change jobs?"

"Ace shot," April added. "Sweet timing."

Security Mike sat there in silence, his face shifting expression as he realized he'd been asked to this room at this time for different reasons than he'd thought he had. "Didn't really think about it, just did it," he said, hesitatingly. "Dunno…"

"Yeah, that's the point," Jess said. "You just did it. Like I just do it. It's a thing." She met his eyes and smiled. "You know how it is with us, Mike. Thin line, in or out. C'mon and be crazy with us."

"F'n yah," Mike finally said, in a rush of words, almost stumbling over them as they tried to get out of his mouth and past his tongue. "You makin this up, Drake?"

"No." Jess seemed a bit bemused by his reaction. "Why would I? We're looking to fill those seven seats. You're the first. If you want to be."

"Hey, none of us got a choice," April said dryly. "You got

one, and never had to spend f'n ever listening to psych gonzos."

Mike Arias kept quiet, drumming his fingers lightly on the table, but he laughed silently, his shoulders shaking.

Finally, Mike smiled. "Yeah, I wanna do that," he said, with a sigh of almost relief.

Jess nodded, then glanced over at Brent and raised one eyebrow at him. "You good with that?"

Brent was already nodding as she started to speak. "Yeah, I'm good," he said. "That was a sweet run. Liked it. Liked seeing the look on those dudes faces when we came out ahead of the boom." He gave Mike a thumbs up.

"That was something," Doug said. "You squeaked out of there. Nice move."

"We're gonna have to give him a new name," April said. "Can't have two Mikes. Too bullshit on coms."

"Well, this is all very exciting," Kurok said. "I'll start the paperwork. I assume you'll move Mike into that suite across the hall from me?" He smiled at him at his look of startled pleasure. "We have plenty of room in here. Why don't you all go give him a hand."

Recognizing a dismissal when they heard one, all the agents and pilots, except for Jess and Dev, got up and hustled— used to be in Security Mike—out the door. This left the two of them across the table from Kurok in a now mostly silent space.

"I think he's very happy," Dev said. "I think Brent is too. He really liked that event earlier."

"Yeah," Jess said. "It's good."

Kurok got up and came over to the end of the table and took a seat next to them. "That group takes a hint very nicely," he said. "So today was quite the day. I have heard a lot of excitement in the halls from the folks who went with you, and from our pilots. "

"They did great," Jess said. "Did just what I asked em to do, scared the pants off everything moving. That's what clued me to it being a scam. They held ground for maybe two seconds then started running or just lay on the ground with their hands up."

"Not hardened outbackers," Kurok said. "Douglas and Emily did a fine job as well. They, on their own, put on a scrapping show while we waited for all the posturing to end that had even those hardened tough guys back up." He chuckled. "I suspect we'll have a deal to review when we get to the meet up."

Jess was briefly silent then cleared her throat. "Whatever the offer is, I want a cut to go to the scrubs," she said. "That's their slot. They're due an allotment."

Kurok smiled gently at her. "There's a lot of them hoping for that. You got a lot of kids hanging on your every eyeblink because they see a place for themselves here that doesn't involve scouring the shore or cleaning fish."

"If they bring value, then they should participate," Dev said, with a slight hesitance. "That is how it was for the sets, Doctor Dan, even if they didn't expect it." She reached out in a natural motion and put her hand on Jess's wrist. "And they enjoy the work."

"They enjoy the work," Kurok agreed wryly. "Most wouldn't, but the people here are a little special that way."

Jess chuckled softly. "But I figured out, they gotta be told what to do. None of us is really trained for that." She rested her head on her hand, leaving her other hand in Dev's grasp. "That's not what agents do. They work alone. You're the weapon. I'm the weapon," She amended. "I don't need to tell me what to do."

"That's true," Kurok said. "But I think you can figure out how to do that, Jess."

"Do I want to?" Jess sighed. "I remember telling everyone back at Base 10 that I didn't want to oversee anything. I was part of the deal they cut to give the brass to Jason."

"That was before," Kurok said, not without sympathy. "You really don't have that choice here, you know. You are the Drake. At Interforce, you were just an agent. Valuable, expendable, duplicatable... directable."

"Not always." Jess's eyes twinkled. "Anyone there'd tell you I was the biggest, most annoying pain in the ass in the corps."

"I don't think so," Dev said. "I always found you very kind and very nice to me, and not a pain in any body part, Jess. And you were very nice to many others there, like Elaine and Jason."

"I punched Jason in the face and broke his nose because he called you a jelly bag brain," Jess said, "when I barely knew you."

"You did?" Dev studied her with interest. "When was this? Oh." Her eyes opened wider. "Was that the time before you gave me this mark?" She touched her shoulder.

"Yeah."

"Hm. Interesting."

"Anyway." Jess looked over at Kurok, who was watching them with a grin. "I know I'm here now and not there. I gotta figure it out. I just don't want to look like an idiot," she said. "If stuff I do myself doesn't work, I'm just pissed at myself. "

"Jess." Dev gave her a sternly cute look. "You have never done anything that I know of that hasn't worked."

Jess looked plaintively at Kurok.

"Well, she hasn't seen you fail, Jess." He grinned ruefully at her. "Even in our recent acquaintance you have a very good success ratio, you know. You find a way to win, which is, I can say, a Drake trait that was quite well known when I was at school, as anyone who ever played your father at any game would have told you."

"I've heard that," Jess said. "But then we get back into the conversation about who's the biggest asshole again, because I heard that too." She straightened up and stood. "C'mon Devvie. I'm sure I have a thousand weird incomprehensible messages in my crib. You can help me read them."

Dev obligingly stood up to join her. "Excellent. I have a number of tasks to do in our space as well, and Kurt has contacted me to advise we have been invited to a celebration this evening about our events today."

"Ah, a party," Kurok said. "Well, no harm in that."

Jess grabbed Dev's hand and made for the door. "C'mon, Rocket. Let's get rocketing."

****

Dev heard excited chatter as she climbed up the last of the spiral stair and made her way down the passageway into the top-level landing bay, where her carrier had been landed for her earlier by Kurt. She had her carry bag slung over her shoulder and it bounced gently against her side as she emerged into the bay and a hive of activity.

Dustin spotted her. "Yo! Rocket! Sup?" He ducked under her carrier engine pod and came over.

There were three or four mechs moving between the landing pads. All four carriers there were getting attention, hooked up to support lines and already cleaned off from their earlier activity.

"Hello," Dev returned the greeting. "I am retrieving some modules. Is everything optimal here?"

Her carrier hatch was open, and the boarding ramp was extended. Dustin had cleaning rags hanging out of all the pockets of his coverall and Dev could smell the cleaning and lubrication fluid on them. It occurred to her that the vehicle probably got far better care now than when it was at the Base.

"A-1" Dustin nodded at her. "Just gettin the dust off."

"Thank you." Dev looked approvingly at the mottled gray skin of the carrier that gleamed in the halon lights, her name and Jess's sharp and clear in black lettering against it. "It looks very nice." Across the back flight surface was lettered Rockstar, where the numerical designation had once been stenciled.

Dev regarded that for a moment, then smiled and shook her head. She entered the carrier, walked past Jess's seat, and sat down in her chair.

The doors to the landing bay were propped open, and the bay itself was chilled by the outside air coming in. But inside the carrier the breeze was blocked and in her lined jumpsuit she was reasonably comfortable.

"Yo."

"Yes?" Dev glanced around.

Dustin came up onto the deck and approached her, pausing behind Jess's chair. "You coming to the rave tonight?"

"The celebration?" Dev clarified. "I think that is what we were invited to. If so, then yes, we plan to attend." She included Jess in the answer as she reasoned the question was really directed at Jess, in an indirect way.

"Yo." Dustin grinned. "S'gonna be cool. We whupped up first time!" He held up a rag. "Just gonna be swabbing. Let me know if you want something in here." He went to work rubbing down the seats.

Dev swiveled back around in her seat and slid over to the control panels to pop one open. She kept it ajar with her knee while she took a headlamp from her carry bag, placed it around her head, and directed the light into the console.

For a few peaceful moments, she worked on the mod. It was tight going inside the narrow metal cabinet, and it took some maneuvering to get to the components she wanted to work on.

"Yo, Rocket?"

"Yes?" She answered, shifting a little as a sharp edge pressed against the back of her neck.

"Drake ask you to co-hab?"

Unseen, one of Dev's pale eyebrows hiked up. "Yes," she said. "She asked me to live with her in her new space." She wasn't sure why the question was relevant to the youngster. "Is it of interest?"

"What'd she say?"

Dev now pulled herself back out of the cabinet and twisted around to look at him. "Excuse me? What did she say about what?"

He was on his knees polishing Jess's gunner console and

peered furtively at her across the top of it, his dusty brown hair coming down to cover a bruise he'd gotten in the fight. "Bout co-habbin." He eyed her. "Just wondering."

"Oh." Dev considered that for a minute. "You mean, how did she ask? What words did she use?"

Dustin nodded.

"Oh," she said again. "Well, she just asked me. She said would I like to live there with her in her new space. Just really that. So of course, I said yes, I would." She leaned back and put her head back inside the console. "It made me very happy that she asked."

"Nice crib," Dustin said.

"It is an amazing space," Dev said. "But what I found the most optimal about it was that it was Jess's space." She removed the second card and examined it, the light flickering around the inside of the console. "And she wanted to have me there with her."

There was a long period of silence, long enough for her to finish her work and stash the replaced card in her carry bag and wriggle her way out of the cabinet. Behind her she spotted Dustin still there. He worked industriously on his cleaning, a faint, almost introspective, smile on his face.

"I am finished here," Dev said, and slung her bag over her shoulder as she sat up in the pilot's seat and then stood. "Thank you for doing such an excellent job on this vehicle."

Dustin gave her a quick grin. "Yo."

Taking that as a response, Dev made her way to the hatch and walked down the ramp to the deck. She glanced up at the outside of the carrier and paused as she spotted something new. The call sign of the vehicle was stenciled on the tail fin, and she'd seen it before. But now there was a decoration surrounding it she had missed on the way into the craft.

Curious, she moved closer then hopped up onto the engine cowling and leaned against the body of the carrier to inspect it. Around the call sign was now a design pattern both intricate and precise. It reminded her of the many mod boards she worked on.

She hopped down and went to the door. "Hello," she addressed Dustin.

He eyed her, "Yo?"

Dev pointed at the outside of the carrier. "Did you make this new marking?"

His expression shifted to a mixture of apprehension and sheepishness. "Yeah, I done it." He answered after a pause. "Want me to sand it off?"

"Not at all. It's very attractive," Dev said. I like it a lot."

He straightened up and then got to his feet and came over to the hatch. He hung on to the edge and swung around to see the work. "Yeah?"

"Yes." Dev took a step back to avoid getting bumped. "It's nice. Where did you get the idea for it?"

Dustin looked at the pattern, then down at her, and shrugged. "Dunno. Just wanted to put somethin round it."

"It reminds me of a control surface mount mod," Dev said. "The micro traces look a bit like that." She opened her carry bag and removed the card she'd taken from the console and dis- played it to him. "Like this."

Dustin peered at it, then looked up at the decoration. "Yo. Check that out." He sounded surprised. "That come from inside here?"

"Yes," Dev said. "This is part of the engine control subsystem. But you see the lines here? That's what it reminds me of." She touched the card surface, tracing the thin designs in gold and silver. "I think it's really excellent."

"Huh. Wasn't tryin to copy nothin." Dustin crouched down to get a closer look. "Just thought it'd be cool like that." He seemed bemused.

"Well, it is," Dev said. "Thank you."

He stood up and grinned. "No prob, Rocket lady." He glanced again at the new design then ducked back inside, leaving Dev to stand and study it herself for a moment longer.

****

Jess pushed back from her stone desk, stood and hopped in place to get the blood flowing again after her stint at her input screen. She turned and walked over to the opposite wall of the small room and flipped herself into a handstand, her bare feet against the cold surface of the stone wall.

In a little while, she'd go find Dev from wherever she was wrenching, and they'd go off to grab some chow, then head over to the party to celebrate the successful scrap out at Coopers.

Even though she knew, and she guessed that the word had gotten out to everyone else as well, that it had been a scam. Both had been a scam, but regardless, the Bay had come out ahead and that was worth a keg of spicy sargasso beer, and maybe some fries with eyes for it.

They'd play some noise, and the kids would probably end up boxing, but it would be all right. After all, they'd all done good in the crazy mess, and no one had gotten hurt. So, no matter if it was a try on, they'd brought it, no question.

They'd shown their stuff. Jess crossed her ankles and then started doing push-ups, enjoying the feel of her spine realigning as she went over the day again, thinking about what she'd have done different if she'd had the chance to.

She'd always done that, coming off a gig. But in this case, aside from wishing she'd really had a plan she could have talked about, there wasn't much she'd have changed. Everyone had done what she'd told them, and damned if Mike hadn't made his bones blowing up a cliff.

And they'd made out with two clunky junker transports that they could fix up and use to dump a whole squad of scrubs the next time someone tried that nonsense. Jess nodded to herself, finally accepting a sense of satisfaction. She suspected she'd even enjoy the party over it.

"Jess!"

Startled, Jess flipped herself upright and dusted her hands off. "In here, Devvie." She glanced around, a little embarrassed that she hadn't paid attention to the outer door opening.

Dev appeared in the doorway, her carry sack slung over her shoulder. "It's excellent you're here."

"It is?"

"Yes." Dev entered and looked out the window to the office. "I got a message from your relative with the deep-sea fishing boat and I would like you to examine it."

"Uncle Max."

"Yes," Dev said. She pulled out her data pad and called up the message. "He says the echolocation device that was installed found a lot of fish!" She turned the pad around and displayed it to Jess. "I think that's what he said. I don't think he quite believed it would."

"Never thought it would do a damn thing," Jess said and studied the note. "Rock headed old jackass. I told him it worked. Damned Sigurd told him it worked. Sig's following him around now cause we wouldn't put it back on his tub."

"Is that good or bad?"

"Pisses Max off. Fishermen don't like other fishermen on their little secret spots." Jess handed the pad back. "But hey, he's heading for the processor with a full load. So good for him. Good job, Devvie. Maybe he'll defer his retirement now that he's hitting bullseyes."

Dev's eyes narrowed slightly, and her fingertips twitched as though she was considering typing something.

Jess reached over and ruffled her hair. "He's a cranky old sea bass. Glad ya made him happy. Hope he makes a killing over at the plant, maybe they'll give him good pricing cause they don't want to make your buddy, the doc, mad at em."

She draped her arm over Dev's shoulders and steered her back out into the big living space. They dropped down onto the makeshift seat she'd assembled out of packing crates and a tarp and settled next to each other inside the big room where the roundel overhead was already darkening into night.

"Doctor Dan did well at the processing place," Dev said in a thoughtful tone. "Keko said he was very calm."

"He had enough firepower in those busses to take out the whole center and he knew it." Jess put her feet up on a packing box, regarding her bare toes, a little dusty and scuffed from con- tact with the stone floors. "He'd have gotten out of the way and let those kids take target practice."

Dev thought about that. She remembered being on station, and seeing her mentor, gentle Doctor Dan, blow the head off the Director of station just before the force from the Bay came to the rescue. "He's not afraid in any situation," she said.

Jess smiled. "He's not. Total badass."

Dev hiked up her own boots and put them on the crate. She sat there quietly for a moment and enjoyed the gentle heat from the central warming plate in the rock wall surface.

It took the chill sting out of the air, just a little, and made it comfortable to sit nearby without her jacket, or an extra layer of clothing. She smelled the fresh air coming in the opening to the back deck and there was a mineral tang to it that she'd come to understand as rain.

Far off, she heard thunder.

She looked across at the central stone wall that held the warming plate. "Have you seen what your relative put on our vehicle?"

Jess turned her head and focused on Dev. "Which relative?" She asked warily. "Dustin? The scrub? What the hell did he do?"

"Yes," Dev said. "He put a decoration around the name of the craft. I think it's attractive." Dev dug into her carry sack that still hung off her shoulder. "It looks something like this." She indicated the metallic tracing across the system board she'd taken.

Jess took the card and examined it. "He drew a picture of a mod?" She queried, in a puzzled tone. "Why?"

Dev now wished she'd taken a picture. "It isn't this, but the decoration looks like these patterns. It's just something nice. I was thinking he could make a pattern on that wall there for us." She pointed at the central wall. "Would that be all right?"

Jess handed back the mod. "Whatever you want, Devvie," she said, her angular face moving into a relaxed grin. "Have the little scrub come up here and scribble all over the place if it makes ya happy." She leaned back on the couch. "Never had the chance to decorate anything so don't count on me for ideas on that."

"Well, us either," Dev said. "We had nothing to decorate. We were not allowed to make any changes to our environment on station. Only the natural born could." She looked around. "So, it's interesting to me to be able to do that. Was it allowed at the base?"

Jess considered. "Was it allowed? Yeah sure, you could put stuff up on the walls if you wanted to, but if they had to move ya, it was a pain in the ass to pack all that stuff up and I don't think… no, wait, a few people did. Jason did. Pictures of Rainier Island, and that sort of stuff." She wiggled her toes. "I never bothered."

Dev looked up at her profile, relaxed and unconcerned. "But this space is different, isn't it?"

Jess lifted her head to look around the large stone chamber, with its roundel showing the darkness of night, and its rough, unadorned walls.

Had it been decorated? She tried to remember all the way back then, searching for memories of what it was like in this room and really found nothing. A few of the kitchen downstairs, some brief flashes of the hall outside. There was no emotion tied to this place, but she expected none. "Well," she said. "No one's gonna tell me to move my ass out of it, so I guess it is?"

She extended her right arm across the back of the makeshift couch, her left already draped over Dev's shoulders. "Yeah, you know… we can do anything you want in here. So have at it, Devvie. I don't have an artistic bone in my body. You've got a lot better taste than I do, make it cool."

Dev absorbed the emotion that stirred in her. "Thank you," she said. "I would enjoy that a lot."

"Then we both will." Jess leaned over and gave her a kiss on the side of the head. "C'mon, let's go to our party. Should be fun. I hope."

"Aren't parties supposed to always be fun?"

Jess gave her a sideways look. "You were at the ones at base. You tell me?"

Dev made a face. "I think they'll be fun here. No one said anything about jellied eyeballs or throwing things to make someone fall in water."

Jess chuckled silently, her body vibrating with it.

"Are you going to give the people that were part of the activities today an achievement?" Dev asked. "Since it was a success?"

"It was a scam." Jess shrugged faintly, then paused in thought. "Doesn't matter, I guess. We should." She frowned. "No time to go dive for anything." She reached over and touched the pearl in its filigree hanging from Dev's ear. "Besides, that should be special for you bus drivers."

Dev folded her arms, her expression thoughtful. "Will they ask for a mark, like we have?"

"Oh crap. I hope to hell not." Jess put her arm over her eyes. "Not seventy of them. That'll take for damned ever, Dev. We can't use that for everyone. It's a mess, and we don't have the burn cream here. Think of something else before we get there, huh?"

Dev's eyes widened a little. "I have no real references for this. For us an achievement token was an extra ration at the next day meal."

"I have confidence in you."

Dev sighed. "Suboptimal."

Jess gave her another kiss on the side of the head. "You'll think of something. You've got at least twenty minutes, right?"

"Suboptimal."

****

The only space large enough for all of them to get together and have a party was the exercise area, once again cleared of its assorted gear. The sands they used for scrapping evened out and raked to somewhat disorderly evenness.

The overhead halons were on, but only half of them, giving the space a half-shadowed look that somehow made it seem more private.

On one side of the exercise grounds five or six folding tables had been set up, with some of the standard Bay bowls of edibles. On the ground next to the table was a large metal tank, with a hose and a spigot attached.

There were piles of plas mugs on the table near the metal tank, and behind the table was a bunch of sturdy metal stools. Laying around on their sides in the sand were various implements unfamiliar to Dev's eyes.

It was all very casual, very much in keeping with the style at the Bay. The room was starting to fill with the two hundred regular scrapping crew, along with quite a few others, drawn by curiosity, or perhaps just wanting a mug of beer and to be part of the celebration.

Dev, along with some of the other pilots, made her way across the sand to a spot near the tables, which were emitting a spicy, tasty smell. "I think Jess said there would be snacks," she said to Doug, who was ambling at her side.

"Sure," Doug said. "Those little fish, and some other stuff. I heard em talking about it when I headed past the mess."

"Excellent," Dev said. "We missed late meal as I was arranging for something." She was aware in her peripheral vision of Kevin and Keko catching up with them, and a cluster of the others as well. The KayTees looked proud and confident as they walked along.

Brent and his new gunner, who used to be Security Mike, came toward them from the far side of the scrapping grounds.

Dev noticed there were at least twenty other bio alts there, talking quietly near one side of the tables or scattered amongst the other Bay residents who wandered in.

One of them went over to the pile of equipment and picked up a piece of it, settling down on one of the stools and starting to do something with it.

To her delight, sound emerged, melodic and charming. "Oh! That's nice."

"That's Tunes," Doug said." They got a few buskers around the working gang, but I think he's about the best of them. I've been to a few of these." He indicated the crowd. "Not this big though."

"Hey." Brent arrived to walk along with them. Mike angled off to join April and the other Mike, while Chester jogged over to catch up with them. They reached the far set of irregular rocks and looked around for a spot to sit down.

It was kind of uncomfortable. The rocks were hard and somewhat pokey but that, Dev considered, was really what the Bay was like. Hard and uncomfortable, but there were snacks to be had and so no one really minded.

She didn't mind. She went over to the snack table and collected a plas bowl full of various items, including the fries with eyes, but also some other small crunchable things, and big seaweed crackers. She always enjoyed the crackers along with a serving of creamy looking fish dip.

Jess appeared at her elbow, nearly making her drop her plate. "Ah, there ya are," she said. "Whatcha got? Oh. Bone glue."

Dev eyed her.

Jess winked and picked up two big mugs. "I'll get the grog." She glanced casually around at the growing crowd, some of whom started to drift over to the snack tables now that she had. Aside from the scrubs, some of the olders were there as well, and two of them came over and picked up mugs as she finished filling hers.

"Drake," one greeted her casually.

"Bolan," Jess returned the greeting. "Your little squid did a good job today. Knocked the crap out of a bunch of the bean- bags we fought with."

Bolan grinned. "He told us." He stood spraddle legged near the keg and filled a mug. "Scared the pants off his ma when he heard the bell ring and took off. Left a crate in the middle of the holding he was unpacking for her."

The squid in question, with a head full of lushly curling black hair held back in a tail, stood nearby in a group that had all ridden in Jess's bus. All watched Jess out of the corner of their eyes. "We figure that was a try-on," Jess said. "We'll get pitched at the conclave next week."

Bolan nodded. "They're gonna need more than those sticks," he said, "but first things first, let's get a contract."

"First things first." Jess took her mugs and followed Dev back to where the pilots were all seated. She took a bit of rock next to the one Dev was on. It only took a moment for April, Mike, and Mike to join them, and they settled in to enjoy their snacks.

The music lifted sweetly over the sound of voices and a second person walked over and took a different piece of gear. He sat down next to the first.

So far, so good. Jess stretched her legs out and enjoyed the bowlful of random goodies Dev had selected. She took a sip of the sargasso beer, fermented from the top drifting seaweed the boats dragged in along the length of their nets and tossed to the dock for a fraction of a cred.

It was spicy tasting and kept cold in the lower caverns in the sea wash. Jess enjoyed the taste. It left a faint tingle on her tongue that was slightly effervescent. Spicy, and just a bit sweet. Literally made from sea garbage.

"This is interesting," Dev said, after tasting her drink.

Jess eyed her, evaluating if that was a good or bad thing.

"Like it?"

"Yes. It has a lot of competing flavors." Dev swallowed a mouthful of the beverage. "And I like the sounds," she added. "Not as much as your sound, but they're nice." Her head began to rock back and forth as the music changed and became more energetic. "Really nice."

"Yes, it is nice," April said from her seat on the other side of Jess. "I think I only heard you sing that once. And that was a weird ass day."

'Yeah, it was." Jess bit into a crunchy something, inspecting it to find it was filled with creamed seaweed, the soft, plush kind she liked. She munched it contentedly and watched as the room filled. The furtive glances clearly aimed at her.

"Speech first." April nudged her. "G'wan."

"Yeah, I know." Jess took a swallow of her beer. "C'mon, Devvie." She got up and set her cup down as Dev complied and followed Jess across the sand floor to a spot near the tables.

On the top level of the rock was a large bin, very battered and in some places dented. It, too, was getting some furtively curious looks.

From one of the entrances on the far side, Kurok appeared. He moved easily around the side of the sand pit, and climbed up to sit next to the pilots, who moved over to make room for him and offered him a share of their snacks.

Jess turned in a circle then put her hands on her hips. She was dressed in her scrapping shirt, her arms bare and vivid with their scars. Dev took up a spot just to one side of her and stood quietly with her hands clasped behind her.

The room got quiet, and Jess felt the attention focus on her. The fighters all stood up, and the two buskers quietly putting down their instruments and folded their hands over them.

She relaxed and stuck her hands into her front pockets. "Today we started a new thing." She said conversationally. "Someone had a problem, they called, we went and took care of it." After a brief pause, she continued. "Regardless of whether that was a test or not, they got what they asked for."

The fighters all grinned and looked around at each other. "So now we'll see what that brings next week," Jess continued. "I think it'll bring a deal. If it brings a deal, and its cred, everyone gets a piece of that action."

There was an unconscious gasp, a tiny shiver of surprise and delight, expressed with widened eyes and the beginnings of smiles.

Kurok cleared his throat. "It will be a new class of allotments," he said. "We're working on the entitlements and the rates now."

Peter Bolan spoke into all that silence, as he stood next to his son. "You going to rate a place for ass kicking?" He looked around the room. "For real?"

"There's a market for it," Jess responded with a smile. "Why not?"

"Why not," he echoed softly, then looked back at her. "Enough of a market to want some part timers in the mix?"

Jess removed her hands from her pockets and spread them out in a shrug. "We'll find out." She dropped the gesture. "Let's get this party started."

Chapter Eighteen

Dev picked up two additional mugs of beer and made her way back across the sand pit to where Jess was sprawled over the second-tier rock seats, surrounded by other revelers at a respectful distance, and with a cleared space to her right-hand side earmarked for Dev to sit in.

Her token was a huge hit, and she was happy about that. Seventy fighters who had accompanied them that day, plus the two that were with Doctor Dan, now wore long, sharp knives either at their waists, slung over a shoulder, or emerging from the top of a boot. She'd found them in the inventory of the weapons battery from days long past.

Made of a patterned and honed reinforced steel, a beautiful patina on them that had held up over the years as they'd sat wrapped in oiled paper, in storage, when no one needed to arm large groups of soldiers anymore.

The huge, battered cabinet had sat there in the back of a section of storage, the only indication of its presence an entry in a log made by one of the store master's predecessors, just waiting for Dev's heuristic search request to find it.

Please find, she'd asked, items of a durable nature, quantity over two hundred, classified as a tool, meant to be carried by hand. She'd hoped for something like her multi tool, that would be useful to them, but she supposed that the large, sharp blades also fit that bill.

An exploration of the armory uncovered the storage bin, buried under stacks of metal grid plating that she earmarked for later investigation. The powerful scent of metal and machinery oil, and layer upon layer of the knives, was revealed when the bin was opened.

She hadn't been sure at first, but one look at Jess's optimal reaction when she brought an example to her, reassured her. So, she reserved one for Jess, April, Mike, and the other Mike. She'd enjoyed passing them out to the others and was aware of the envious looks from the fighters who hadn't gotten to fight yet, glad she had enough to eventually provide them one as well when their time came.

So that was excellent. She felt that she'd done what Jess asked, and even Doctor Dan had been interested in the knives, admiring the pattern hammered into the blade. Optimal all around. The knives even came with holders and straps, ideal to prevent them from doing unintended damage.

Excellent.

The music ramped up. Now there were six people with the various instruments collaborating in a sometimes pleasant and sometimes raucous mixture of sound, but the crowd enjoyed it, letting out yells and whistles of appreciation.

Dev arrived back at Jess's side and set the mugs down, then took a seat on the rock surface pulling her legs up under her crossed.

"Thanks, Dev." Jess picked up her mug. "This is a pretty good batch." She took a sip. "Not bad for flotsam and jetsam of the sea that otherwise clogs up the intakes." She wriggled a little closer, so her knee touched Dev's.

Dev leaned her elbow on Jess's thigh and held the mug in her other hand. She took a sip as they sat and listened to the sounds, which were picking up in tempo. Some of the youngers were moved onto the sand and after a moment they started doing activities.

Activities, because Dev had no idea how to otherwise classify what they were doing. It wasn't the dancing she remembered from the base parties. It also wasn't the snoopy thing Jess told her about.

As the music got louder and faster, so did the activities. "Jess." Dev half turned and leaned against her partner. "Could you explain what this is?"

Jess braced one arm against the rock and leaned toward her, so their heads were close together. "You mean the dancing?"

"Is that dancing?" Dev asked. "It does not resemble the motions they did at the Base."

Jess chuckled. "It's breaking. Sort of more like a competition than a dance, I guess. The kids do all that moving around ... see, look at that one." She pointed. "It's like tumbling. You do all that stuff to one up, right? Like who can do the craziest stunt."

"Interesting." Dev's brow creased as she watched. "I think."

More people joined them on the sand, spreading out across the soft surface. To Dev's surprise, several of the sets joined them, more reserved and less gymnastic but obviously enjoying the activity. The natural born accepted this readily, and two of them broke off and joined two of the KayTees in a square, trading spins and drops.

So, this was the rave the mechs and techs had talked about. Dev watched in bemused amazement. She looked over at Jess, who also watched, a faint smile tugging at the edges of her mouth. "Did you perform this activity?"

"No," Jess answered softly. "I was too young when I left to come out to these kinds of things, and it wasn't something they did at Canyon City. Too close to fighting." She paused, chewing the inside of her lip. "Damn I wish I'd grown up here."

Dev reacted to the wistful tone. "And not gone to the school?" She put her hand on Jess's arm and felt the tension in the corded tendons across her wrist.

Jess sat there quietly breathing for a minute, her eyes flickering over the dancers. Her head moved a little to the music. "First time I came back here, I think I told ya, dad met me and told me how it'd be different." She half shrugged. "I didn't belong here anymore. I was different. I wasn't one of them. I told him it didn't really matter."

"Was that true?"

"It was," Jess said, in a mild tone. "I mean, what choice did I have?" She grinned wryly. "It was okay because he talked to me about it, and because he told me he went through the same thing. That made it okay. I told everyone I didn't care."

"Yes," Dev murmured. "It's like what we say, you know. Everything's optimal because it is what it is. You can't change it."

Jess nodded. "That's it. The more I see of this place, though, the more it bums me that I missed out on it all those years. Crap loads more fun than school was."

"But you're here now."

Jess paused, then smiled. "Truth. You and I are here now." She bumped her head gently against Dev's. "Right?"

"Yes, we are." Dev watched the dancers. "Would you like to learn to do that?" She asked, in a straightforward way. "I might. The KayTees seem to be enjoying it." She studied the motions. "It seems more organized than the same activity at the Base."

"Less like people being electrocuted?"

Dev smiled. "Yes."

"I'd look like an idiot," Jess said. "You'd look cute doing that though," she added, almost as an afterthought. "Can you do that?" She pointed at Kevin who was doing a backflip.

"Yes," Dev said readily. "I can do that without using my hands."

Jess focused on her. "You can?"

"Yes."

"I've never seen you."

Dev gave her a sideways look. "I've never had an occasion to have to do that downside, Jess. It wouldn't really be useful while piloting." She grinned at Jess's expression. "And counter-productive while working on mods."

"I can do that," Jess said, after a brief pause.

Dev nodded. "Yes, I have seen you do it. "So that is why I don't know why you think doing this activity would make you look suboptimal, Jess, because you look very…" She paused, considering what word to use.

"Stupid?"

"Graceful," Dev said. "I think you look very attractive when you perform motions of that kind."

"Oh. Hm." Jess watched the acrobatics on the sand floor. "I'm usually avoiding being blown apart when I'm doing that crap. Distracts people and screws their aim."

"That's very attractive," Dev said. "It's excellent when you are not damaged."

Jess started laughing. "Okay. I see that point." She leaned back on her hands. "Maybe we could try it out," she said, after a pause. "Later. Not here."

Dev nodded. "Possibly we could try it in the bed in our space."

Jess's eyes popped wide open, and she turned fully to stare at Dev. "Possibly we could what?"

"If you miss your landing, it's painful on a floor like this." Dev kicked the rocks with the edge of her boot. "I landed on a metal grating on station once and did not find that very optimal at all." She paused, then looked sideways at Jess.

"Are you messing with me?"

Dev's eyes twinkled. "Possibly. However, I thought if you didn't find the activity optimal we could practice sex instead, which you always seem to enjoy."

Jess started laughing and lay down, her boots on the next level, her eyes covered with one hand. She gained the attention of those nearby, who half turned from the dancing to see what was going on.

Dev picked up her mug and sipped from it, looking back mildly at the curious eyes that watched them. Bay parties, she decided, were to be preferred over the ones at Interforce, with a much higher ratio of interesting edibles and entertaining things to observe.

April came over with a fresh bowl of fries with eyes and sat down, she offered the bowl to Dev. "You telling jokes over here in the corner, Rocket?"

"Yes," Dev said and took a few of the small fried fish. "It seems to have been moderately successful," she added as Jess continued to laugh. "Are you enjoying this celebration?"

"Yeah, it's cool." April extended her legs out and crossed them at the ankles. "It's chill, but those kids are crazy." She indicated the spinning dance moves going on across the sand, which was now full of bodies in motion. "Someone's gonna break a leg."

"Nah." Jess finally let her laughter wind down but remained laying back on the stone. "They got tough bones here."

"Yes, Jess's are excellent," Dev said. "Doctor Dan was very impressed."

Jess rolled her head to one side and eyed her. "When did... oh right. In space." She sat up, picked up her mug and took a swallow of beer. "Feels like years ago." She kicked her boot heel on the rock. "Crap, last month seems years ago."

"It does," April said. "Place is easy to get used to though," she added, with an introspective look around. "I guess we really didn't have that much time to get used to 10. We were either out rampaging with you, or getting blown up there, or flying to f'n space or whatever."

"True." Jess took a handful of fries and changed the subject. "Tomorrow we can put the last section of roof on out there. That'll make it different as hell. All that space can be useful for once."

"These here too." April gestured to either side, vaguely encompassing the cliffs. "Got some decent room in there, was going to waste before."

That spurred Dev's memory. "Oh, Jess." She put her hand on Jess's leg. "May I show you something? It's nearby. It won't take long."

Jess's dark eyebrows lifted, and a grin appeared on her lips. "You going to drag me off to be alone, Devvie?"

"Yes." Dev considered explaining, but she enjoyed the widened eyes now focused on her, so she remained silent after that.

"Well." Jess got to her feet, brushing the sand off her work pants. "Then lead on."

Dev got up and set her cup down. "We'll be right back."

"Or not," Jess cut in, giving them all a wink.

Everyone chuckled. Dev just smiled and waited for Jess to join her and then led the way across the sand, heading for the entrance to the cavern on the far side.

It was raining, and as they emerged from the doorway the

rain was coming down in torrents through the remaining opening in the roof covering. It ran through channels cut in the rocks and drained off to the side as the slanted surface carried the rest of it off to catch basins.

The sound was a drumming rumble as Dev led the way to the left, toward the random storage caverns and makeshift shelters on that side of the cliff. The more irregular and louder vibration of thunder was a counterpoint to it, and periodic flashes of lightning blared against the dark rock surface they were walking across.

"We really going to look at something?" Jess asked, as they neared the cliff face.

Dev grinned. "Yes. Although being alone with you is never suboptimal."

"Aw." Jess shook some of the rain out of her hair as they got under the covered portion, their boots splashing slightly through the runoff. "Where are we going?"

"The sets asked me to ask you about a project." Dev pointed at the open door ahead of them. "They found a location they would like to do something with and wanted your approval."

"My approva..oh." Jess followed her inside. "Wait, it's... oh, they ran lights," she muttered under her breath. She almost crashed into Dev, who had paused at the inner hallway. "Dev, you don't need to show me anything. They can do whatever they want."

"It's this way." Dev guided her along the hallway and made the turn, then indicated the small, narrow entrance. "I think you will need to go sideways."

"I think it would be easier for me to go get my blaster." Jess warily squeezed through the opening after her, having to let out her breath and hold still to wriggle through. "Damn, Devvie."

"Well, most of the sets are quite a bit shorter than you are." Dev led the way into the chamber, still full of the table, its blue- prints, the temporary lights, and a pile of steel poles. "The sets would like to use this space for an exercise location."

Jess ducked her head a little, the ceiling coming uncomfortably close to her head. "They don't like the one in the big cave?"

"They do," Dev said. "However, as you just commented on, the mechanisms most use here are too large for us. Here we can make smaller ones." She made a complete turnaround to survey the space. "And it won't be in anyone's way."

Jess also turned and surveyed the room. It was a large,

roughly square void in the rock with a uniformly low ceiling except on the far side, where it angled up. She scooted over there and stood fully upright and put her hands on her hips. "Sure," she said, after a moment's pause. "Yeah, sure. They'd have to blow a hole in the wall to make it useful for anything else."

The room was a good size, but the walls and sandy floor were unmarked. There was no sign the Bay's rough shelving had ever been installed, so likely it hadn't been used as too tough to get into. Jess evaluated it. "Ceiling's too low in here. Drive everyone else nuts," she said. "Tell em to have at it."

Dev nodded. "That was my thought also." She walked over and put her arms around Jess. "Thank you, Jess. I know it'll make everyone happy." She gave her a squeeze, pleased when Jess returned the hug. "They want to be able to be strong and able to help when needed. This will be excellent."

"Okay," Jess agreed simply. "Not much for a mixup huh? I noticed." She rocked gently from one foot to the other. "We do a lot more of that here than we did back at base."

"We're not really programmed to fight with each other," Dev said. "And definitely not to fight with natural born."

"Unless you need to cause I've seen you whup up, Devvie." Jess bumped her gently. "And I heard about those guys going wild on those jackasses in the big Hall."

"Yes. We can do what is necessary, to prevent harm to ourselves or natural born," Dev said. "But not for exercise. I think the natural born here enjoy that activity a lot."

"Ah," Jess murmured. "Yeah, okay. We do love it. We like beating the snot out of each other. It's fun. I've always enjoyed asskicking. Not everyone inservice did." She sighed. "It'd be cool to find some place to surf around here. "I like the scrapping but I kinda miss that."

"I as well," Dev said. "But swimming in the water near where the boats go into the mountain might be pleasant. Or at the place where we had the fish the first time we came here. That was quite optimal."

"Tomorrow." Jess promised. "You're on."

An excellent end to an excellent day. Dev concluded. She was content to stand there in the lurid yellow glow of the halons, just being there with Jess, until they decided to make their way back to the celebration.

Jess ducked her head down and they kissed.

Or until they decided to bypass the celebration and go back to their space, hopefully also bypassing the whole somersault in the air idea since it was not nearly as interesting to her as kissing Jess was.

They kissed again and then parted. Jess leaned one shoulder against the wall and smiled. "Wanna get back to the party?"

"No," Dev replied at once. "I would like to go back to our space and practice sex."

"Love that honesty," Jess said. She put the palm of her hand along Dev's cheek in a gentle gesture. "Yeah, me too. We did our thing there. Let's go home."

Dev offered her a hand and Jess took it, and they walked to the side of the room where the second entrance was, the narrow, crooked channel a second challenge for Jess, who whacked her head a little on the low verge. "Oof."

"We should probably put a larger entrance in," Dev said, and folded her fingers around Jess's as they walked through the empty storage chambers, newly swept, into the smell of salt air and rain. "It would make it easier to fit the exercise machines inside."

"Yeah you're going to have to bring them in piece by piece otherwise." Jess rubbed her head. "Glad this is gonna get some use, not just be junk rooms and hideouts for scavengers."

They skirted the downpour and crossed the new hall to be, heading for the entrance to the main cavern of the Bay chased by thunder and the flashes of brilliant lightning that showed the sky stark and silver through the remaining gap.

Tomorrow, they would close it. The next time she and Jess walked this way they would be inside, sheltered from the rain, and dry shod. She wondered what else would change after that.

Maybe nothing.

Maybe everything.

****

Dev patiently waited for the grounds to be cleared. Three steel cables extended from the bottom of her carrier to solder points on the huge piece of metal sitting on the ground outside the new gates.

She checked the clearance again, shifting her flight boots a little on the thruster pedals and inching her seat forward a bit to get a better look through the forward plas.

She was alone in her vehicle, the rest of the carrier darkened and silent behind her, wanting to save all the carrier's thrust for handling the weight of the metal. Now she sat there, while everyone cleared out of the area, and listened to the ops chatter on her ear buds.

The rain had paused, spurring her to get aloft and in motion to avoid the need to deal with the weight and wind of a storm while she tried to place the last piece of covering. It was very early, the light barely turning the sky from deep black and gray to the lighter color of early day, which outlined the shape of the Bay and the cliffs in faint silver.

She felt excellent, despite the early hour and the scant sleep their evening activities had left them.

"Rockstar, Rockstar." Ops interrupted her thoughts. "Clear to go."

"Ack." Dev ran a scan anyway, just in case, but found the area clear of biologic activity. She engaged the engines and lifted straight up. She felt the weight come on the cables and then the drag as the huge slab of metal left the ground. "In motion."

"See ya," Ops said.

Dev ran a quick systems check, acceptably pleased with the response of the carrier. She came up over the curve of the new roof over the gap and moved forward once she was clear of the big gates and the top of the enclosure.

The big sheet of metal swung a little in the motion and she had to adjust quickly, side thrusters firing in brief bursts as she moved forward into position, glad, at least, she had only this one carrier to deal with, though both Doug and Chester had suggested a repeat of her sync'd flying.

She inched into position and glanced over to watch the wind indicator on her panels. There was a five-knot inshore breeze, but after a moment, the panel below her settled down and she was able to shift a little faster to fit it into the remaining open space.

Below it, she saw the ground of the gap, and on the far side of the new roof she spotted six tall figures with welding tanks on their backs, well clear, waiting.

The position indicator beeped softly in her ear, and Dev brought her forward motion to a halt. She looked right and left to ensure it visually matched what the scanner told her. With a grunt of approval, she resettled her grip on the throttles. "Ops, stand by for lowering."

"Go go go," Ops responded. "Right on target, yo?"

Dev grinned. "Yes, thank you." She started the sequence to reduce the carrier's elevation to lower the steel onto the rest of the roof, covering the remaining open space.

The forward piece, right up next to the inner cliff touched first, scraping down the rock face that had been chipped clear to allow it to a ledge that had been left. Then she lowered the back two cables to set down the heavier rear section into place. She felt it as the weight came off and she adjusted instantly so the carrier would not go shooting off into the air.

She heard cheers through the ear buds, from ops. Then she spotted the six figures climb up the curve of the roof toward the mount points, ready to release the cables so she could retract them.

"Nice work, Devvie," Jess's voice broke into the channel, her smile audible in her tone. "First shot, right on target."

Of course. Dev didn't say that audibly. "Thank you," she responded. "It was excellent we got this done while the weather cooperated."

"Rockstar, you're loose," Ops reported, relaying from the welders. "Pull em back."

Dev started the retraction, and the cables came dangling upward to seat into the lift housing in the forward nose under her feet, and at the aft of the carrier under the fighter seats they'd installed.

"Retracted and cleared," she reported to operations. "Initiating patrol routing."

"Gotcha. Have a nice ride."

Dev took advantage of the break in the weather and cruised over the top of the mountain. Below her the Bay spread out, busy with early fishing going on. Beyond the seawall, at the far end of the Bay, lay the zig zag exit to the depths of the ocean waters, crashing against them as she watched.

Dev admired the engineering of it. She circled the walls and reviewed the rolling waves, regretfully concluding that surfing them would likely result in both her and Jess either slamming into the rocks or being sucked into the tunnels. While Jess could breathe under water, neither result seemed optimal.

She turned the carrier north and began a quick inspection of the coast to see what other possibilities she could find.

****

Jess walked along the corridor, an earbud tucked into one ear as she listened to ops chatter, that included Dev's periodic check ins while she was out on patrol.

They were, sometimes unintentionally, funny and Jess enjoyed listening to them as she wandered around the stake hold, investigating some small and little used spaces.

The were oddly spaced, due to their original organic nature. Some of the hallways were irregular, all large and cut to even lines, but following whatever the original rock passages had been when the mountain that Drake's Bay was cut into was formed.

On this side of the main hall most of the spaces were turned over to working areas for everything from salvage sorting to the sorting and cleaning of fabrics. She walked through a broad mixture of smells from pungent and soapy, to solid, heavy brine.

Big sections of it had been taken over by the Doc's plant factory and the work that came out of that. Jess stuck her head into a few chambers filled with tables, and contentedly working bio alts, who had containers and bins of things they were messing with.

They looked up at her entry and paused in mild surprise. They waved at her in greeting, no one alarmed at her presence.

Jess waved back, left them alone, and moved on to other workspaces

"Drake."

Jess turned as Clint caught up to her. He wiped his hands on a piece of rough cloth. "Hey," she replied.

"Those crates," Clint said, without preamble. "I thought I recognized them, and I did. C'mere." He motioned Jess to follow him. They moved through the workshops to the big mech station nearest the back entrance they'd parked the transports in. The mech station was large and full of random pieces and parts of various machines, the smell of grease and metal pungent in the air.

They entered the space, and Clint walked confidently toward a large table at the back wall where a piece of mechanical hardware sat disassembled. "I opened this thing up to check the levels of the mods in there. Older'n dirt."

Jess considered briefly how old that would be, then went over to peer at the thing. "Yeah?"

Clint turned over one of the brackets and held it into the overhead light so she could get a look. "See that?"

It was an old card, the tracings half rubbed off, the edges dented from many insertions and removals. Jess saw lettering on one side and leaned closer to peer at it, her vision tight focusing. For a minute her expression was blank, then she straightened up a little, her eyebrows arching up.

Clint watched her face and smiled. "Know that?"

"Yeah, I do," She murmured. "Interforce." Then she

shrugged. "Old junk."

"Older'n you are," Client said. "Your dad might have seen these in the mech lab when he was in school. Thats where I saw em." He studied the part. "Those old buckets are cargo transports used to make the run back and forth from Canyon down to Picchu."

Jess considered that, faint memories surfacing. "Special service," she said, after a pause. "They took couriers for the suits, if I remember my history senior classes right."

"Good memory," Clint said. "That's right. VX 24 A's."

Jess nodded. "Okay. Anything special there? Just looked like beat up crates to me. They probably sold them as surplus back in the day, and they've been rattling around. Maybe up in Quebec."

Clint shook his head. "Uh uh. No oxidization. No salt corrosion. Never flew in coastal air. Just dry dust in everything. If they were an old junk sale, it wasn't long ago if they came here."

"Huh."

"We'll have to spray coat everything we put back in em and seal the hull metal like we did for all the stuff at Base," Clint said. "But these mods now—"

"Could have anything in them," Jess said, quietly.

"Could," he agreed. "Just weird. I'd like to know where they came from. Who's hands they went through, y'know?"

"I do," she said. "Good catch, Clint. We had to rebuild the one Dev flew in here anyhow, right?"

"For sure." Clint smiled at the brief praise. "Good thing for the kids to practice on. But I thought you'd be interested."

"I am." Her lips quirked into a brief grin. "Feels like there's scam in there somewhere, even if it's just in my suspicious old head."

He nodded in confirmation. "Feels like it. If there is, we'll find it. But we should check careful in it if we plan to put our folks inside."

Our folks. Jess had to smile. His transition had become so complete and sudden. "Especially if Dev's driving them."

Clint smiled back. "Specially that. You don't need me to tell you, but driving that thing in here was a once and only thing, right?" He said. "As in, nobody else I know coulda landed it without it rattling into pieces."

"Yup." Jess heard the faint sound of an opening voice channel in her ear bud and took a step back. "Keep at it," she said in a lower tone. "Not looking to be a second story about a Trojan horse." She slid out of the mech workshop and listened as Dev checked in.

"Will do," Clint called after her. "And I read that story, believe it."

Jess raised her hand in a wave as she disappeared, then focused on the audio feed in her ear.

"Bay operations, I have received a fragmented communication," Dev said. "It was unintelligible, but I recorded it and have squirted back."

"Gotcha, Rocket," the Ops on duty said. "Ya see anything?"

"No, nothing on scan," Dev responded. "Just this message fragment. I am at the end of the northern patrol range, returning along the western side to the south."

"Copy that."

Jess reversed her steps and headed for Bay ops.

****

Midmorning ops was busy. Jess paused just inside the main door and glanced around at the double circle of consoles that made up the facility. They were big, old, metal housings, bearing the scars of bangs and scrapes. On one side of the room, blaster melt where Interforce had tried to stop her, without any understanding of what they were trying to stop her from doing.

She'd felt the change in everything in that moment when she dove across the console. The ops watch had all grabbed hold of her and hauled her out of the hands of the corps trying to kill her. That was when she'd absolutely become—the Drake—in everyone's reckoning. She felt it every time now when she entered the space.

The ops watch glanced up from their stations and grinned a welcome to her. The watch captain sauntered over with his clipboard, the one that until very recently Mike had carried tucked under an arm.

Today, Mike was with April and Mike Arias, working with guns, watched by a hopeful bunch of scrappers nearby.

"Yo," the watch captain said. "Sup, Drake."

"You get that squirt from Dev?" Jess asked. "Lemme see it, Bobby."

"Just noise," Bobby answered. "Sure, got it up on the board there." He pointed to his left. "Don't even know how it got picked out."

"Thanks." Jess went to the board and slid onto the

uncomfortable metal stool behind it.

On the screen was a waveform, and Jess picked up on the unnatural rhythm that Dev had also seen. She tuned her ear bud to the output and played it in her ear, eyes half closed, concentrating.

The cap was cleaned of internal sounds. Dev had stripped out all the things that weren't the signal she was interested in. Jess detected the underlying repetitive variation in frequency, just at the edge of audible, as it rolled past her excellent hearing.

She ran it through again and again and tried to listen past the variations for structure in the faint, warbling sounds. She closed her eyes completely to allow herself to concentrate on them.

But no. Except for that tonal signature there was nothing else to be decoded, though there was an audible artificial structure behind the noise. She opened her eyes and studied the screen, chewing the inside of her lip.

"Anything?" Bobby asked.

Jess lifted her gaze up and looked at him. "I can't get the payload, but that's an inservice alert," she said. "Someone out there, somewhere, at some point, wanted help and sent that out. No telling how long it's been propagating."

"Yeah?" Bobby came over to look at the screen, his dark brown eyebrows hiking up. "That's in there?"

Jess traced a waveform on the screen with her forefinger. "That right there," she said. "They taught us a few things at school. Recognizing that's one of them." She straightened up on the stool and pulled her boots up under her. "But there's no data."

Everyone in ops listened, eyes on their displays, pretending they weren't. "What's it mean?" Bobby asked for them all, clasping his hands over the clipboard as he looked at her.

Anything. Nothing. Jess triangulated the location Dev had taken the cap at, northwest of Base 10, over the ridge that sloped downward to the inland sea. A flat expanse of nothingness other than rainwater washing the rocks and spawning rock mites the scavengers caught and made soup from.

Wide open. The signal could have come from anywhere, other than where it had crossed Dev's path. Jess felt it had to come from the west. "Something had a problem, sometime between yesterday and a week ago, and let out a squawk," Jess finally said. "And it has an Interforce sig."

Bobby shrugged his broad shoulders. "D'we care?"

"Depends on what they were running from," Jess said, with

a brief grin. "Put feelers out on the wire. See what the other ops are saying. If there's any chatter."

Bobby nodded in agreement. "All right." He made a mark on the clipboard with a graphite pencil and moved along. He started at the back of the console row and moved from position to position to pass the instruction along.

The ops on watch were about half and half, bay and bio alt, and the bio alts listened to Bobby with deep attention, while the bay residents just gave brief nods.

Jess watched a moment more, then got up and slipped out, continuing her prowl of the corridors.

Chapter Nineteen

Dev finished her deep scan, a high-powered sweep of the perimeter of the area they'd decided to patrol. It ranged from the Bay in the southeast, up the coast of the sea to north of Base 10, then west to the flatlands, back down south in a line that also included Cooper's Rock, and then east again back to the Bay.

It was a quiet patrol, as most of hers were. Aside from the message she'd sent back, she'd seen no activity, nothing had hit scan or alerted. She was free to just enjoy flying the carrier and took it through a schedule of aerobatics that would have greatly entertained anyone on the ground watching her.

She was within range of the visual scan at the Bay, and suspected she was possibly providing some of that entertainment for her fellow pilots and the mechs who were now attached to the flight squad. Strange at first, but now she was used to the attention, having realized there was a true appreciation from her colleagues for her flight skills and not the veiled envy and resentment she'd felt from some at the Base.

They were a natural ability, Doctor Dan had explained. There was an affinity in her construction to this function that had gone past anything they could have given her, a coordination of hand, and eye and instinct that was individually and distinctly hers.

No need to feel bad about it. So, she didn't.

Now she took the carrier around the last checkpoint and headed back east to home, abruptly sending the carrier skyward, directly up at the clouds and then through them to the top of the craft's range, where the engines struggled against the elevation.

She pushed them to their limit until the upper layer of clouds was near, and then arced over and groundward, testing a theory.

As the carrier tipped over into its parabola, Dev felt herself lifting out of her seat into the familiar sensation of microgravity, only her restraints held her in place, as things around the cabin floated free and drifted through the air.

The motion lasted for the length of the arc, and Dev knew a moment of delight as she felt grav come into play again and things settled back down. "Interesting," she said, and shifted in her seat as she returned to it. "I think Jess would enjoy that."

Was there any useful function for that? Probably not. Aside from possible entertainment for her partner. She set the thought aside and felt the g-forces as she pulled the carrier out of its dive and moved into a barrel roll before heading up toward the clouds again.

At this end of the patrol, ops scan covered a wide swath of ground and south of the Bay there were miles of rocky, mostly flat coastline.

There were no large settlements south of the Bay, only a tiny scattering of scavengers living in shallow hollows in the rock walls at the edge of the waters, barely surviving. So, Dev usually took this part of the patrol to put her craft through its paces and test the modifications she'd been doing on its control systems.

She did another parabola to judge how long she could extend the experience. Then she was at the end checkpoint and overflew the Bay, bending a gentle arc over and around it's rugged, graceful circle, merely enjoying the process of flying.

For fun, she coasted out over the deeper gray blue of the outer waters, turned and flipped the carrier a hundred and eighty degrees, and headed back through the opening that allowed the ships into the Bay. She turned the carrier onto its side and zagged through the gap before coasting across the shallow waters, with their frothy blue green chop and the busy boats moving in every direction.

Loaders were coming out of the cavern she once flew into and she curved the carrier past that entrance and then scaled up the wall, turning over as she slowed into a landing glide and lined up with their assigned bay, high up on the cliff wall.

The mechs waited for her on the ledge well clear of the opening as she slowed and came down to gracefully land on her pad. A quick glance showed her Jess's tall body leaning against the wall waiting for her.

Excellent. Dev leaned over and released the hatch as she started her shutdown checklists, killing power to the engines as the carrier rocked back and forth a little from Jess jumping inside. She glanced in the reflective surface over her position and watched Jess circle the gunners chair and come over to squeeze into the jump seat. "Hello."

"Deeevvviiiiieee," Jess warbled. "That was an SOS buoy," she added, in a more serious tone.

"Yes," Dev said. "I thought it might be." She removed her flight helmet and half turned to face Jess, leaning one elbow on her seat arm. "It triggered programming. Do you know whose it was?"

Jess shook her head. "No tags. But I think we should go out

and take a look around."

Excellent. More flying to be had. "Yes," Dev said. "It will be good flight practice for the sets. I think they would like that very much."

Jess grinned at her. "Let's go get that party started." She levered her body up out of the jump seat, just missing smacking her head on the roof. "No rest for the wicked." She ruffled Dev's hair and stepped back out of the way to allow her to exit the pilot's position.

"Are we wicked?" Dev slid into her jacket, which had been draped over the back of her seat and fastened it as she followed Jess to the hatch. "I thought wicked was suboptimal."

"Depends who you ask."

****

The rain had started again, as the doors to the landing bays were pushed open and folded flat against the rock walls. The coveralled figures moving them were instantly drenched, turning their workwear a dark almost black color.

They ignored it, used to the nearly constant downpour. They shook their heads to fling raindrops out of their eyes and pushed the wet hair back from their foreheads as they propped the doors in place and sauntered back inside.

In Rockstar, Dev was back in the pilot seat, communicating quietly to ops, and the other five carriers they'd decided to take with them on the search. Behind her, Jess was in her gunner chair, talking to April, who carried her flight kit tucked under one arm.

Behind them were six fighters, all of them new, almost bouncing in their seats with excitement, pleased and proud to be in this carrier as they waited to take off.

"Decent route," April said as she reviewed a data pad over Jess's shoulder. "There's a trench, old road base that runs along here, we can check that out. Goes around and down to the flats. Hey." She paused. "You think maybe it was some of the bing bongs the Doc told us about, who chased his ass?"

Jess shook her head. "Too recent." She paused. "All right let's get out there. Either we'll find signs of the ghost, or we just get a training run in."

"Got it." April got up from her kneeling position and stood. "Nobody shoots but us, right?"

"Nobody shoots but us," Jess confirmed. She activated her boards. "No gunners in those other four. Let Mike and Mike hold the fort here. We run into anything that needs more than us it's more than we want anyway."

"Truth." April nodded and headed out of the carrier, striding over to where her own craft waited. She vaulted onto its deck and the hatch closed behind her with an audible whomp.

"Ready, Dev?" Jess glanced outside the hatch to make sure they were clear, then reached over to seal it.

"Yes," Dev said, as she felt the air compress around her in the carrier as the seals pressurized. "I have set and transmitted the coordinates. The flight is ready."

"Let's go," Jess said and glanced around at the fighters, who watched her with bright eyes. Six kids, four male and two female, ready for whatever the adventure would bring them. Hoping that was a fight, while she hoped it wasn't the kind of fight that might cause an Interforce team to send out that squirt.

That usually meant them. Jess didn't know if her little yonks and the bio pilots were in any way ready to go head-to- head with them, a very different prospect than knocking around some bozo civs. She thought about that as Dev rolled them out into the storm, with Doug on their tail, holding outside the landing bay for the other four to join them.

It was, at least, just a steady rain, with only the usual winds to deal with.

"Please prepare to move northwest on my mark," Dev said quietly into comms. "Stay at the directed flight level and use full scans. Report anything on a return."

"Roger that," Doug replied promptly, echoed by the four KayTees. "Let's go sightseeing!"

Dev looked up in the reflective surface and saw Jess's eyes meet hers, a slight grin on her face. She returned it. "Mark," she said. "Proceed."

They flew off in an arrow pattern, with Dev front and center, leading the flight. They swept over the high mountain ridges that fell into the sea and moved inland, over the repeated lines of the range that arched away to the north.

Jess got her targeting boards set up, with the long-range scanners that fed data constantly back to Dev's station. She slid her hands into the trigger gloves and felt the contacts on the inside of them tickle her skin, and the screens react in a flicker of grids and lines.

"You blow up a mountain with this?" One of the kids said and leaned forward with interest to peer at the boards. "Heard that from someone."

"I did," Jess responded. "A pretty big mountain matter of

fact." She finished calibrating. "I needed a distraction to get something done." She glanced at the kid, a tall, well-built young woman with dark straight hair cut short. "And that sure as hell distracted everyone."

"Lotta splat," the girl said.

"Sucked to be them," Jess agreed. "Ten, twelve thousand maybe. No one counted Too much vaporized rock. Dev's first flight." She glanced around the kids, who now looked up at the back of Dev's head. "Blew everyone's mind and Gibraltar to hell."

The girl made a low sound of appreciation, echoed by the others. "Wow."

One of the kids worked down on the offloading docks, Jess recalled. "Better than hauling scales?" She asked the kid, indicating the carrier with a motion of her hand.

The girl made a snorting sound. "Damn sight better. I tried for a spot on my dad's boat but I freakin get seasick just crossing the Bay."

The other kids chuckled and relaxed a little.

"Kicked me off after the first trip," the girl concluded. "I said screw that. Hauling net gets me a bed anyway."

"The way Dev drives, you could get seasick here in this thing," Jess told her. "If it goes upside down, hold your breath." She offered solemnly. "And try not to chuck up in my direction."

"Took a pill before I got on," the girl said, with an almost cheeky grin. "Wasn't gonna lose my slot."

Jess laughed. "Good job." She leaned back in her chair and studied them, guessing she shared some spirals with the lot of them, and quite a few with that girl, because she had that look. "Kirin." Jess recalled the name. "Your dad runs Headwind."

Kirin nodded. "Bastard."

"They all are." Jess's eyes twinkled. "My uncle's the worst of em."

The girl grinned. "Truth, he is."

"Hey, Drake, what's the gig?" The boy next to her asked. He cradled his pipe in his arms, his elbows on his knees. "They just told us load on."

Jess turned a little in her chair, so she was facing them. "Dev picked up a distress call from someone at Interforce when she was on patrol."

The kids didn't look either worried or impressed. "We going to give em claps?" The boy said. "We care?"

"Depends," Jess said, after a long pause. They all shifted

uncomfortably. "Something happened. I want to know what it was."

In Jess's ear, Dev's low, melodious voice kept up comms, directing the KayTees, passing along helpful hints, and fending off Doug's attempt at humor. It was a low-grade comfort, half heard, and half just sensed through the sound waves hitting the delicate inner bones the comms were pressed against.

She pushed the sleeves on her hoodie up on her arms, exposing the burns down both. "Keep everyone's scans at max, Devvie."

"Yes," Dev said. "Thank you, Jess."

Jess realized the reminder was probably unnecessary, that Dev had a much better idea of what to do with those scanners than she ever would. She turned her attention back to the yonks. "So anyway, that's what we're gonna go find."

"So, we're like hunting," Kirin said.

"We are," Jess said. "Who was it? What were they running from? Was it someone like me? If it was, I want to know what happened, because we don't call for help easy." She leaned her elbows on the chair arms. "Something that dangerous to someone like me, can be trouble for us." She gestured around the inside of the carrier.

"Ain't gonna come at us. Found out last time what that's like," the boy said.

"Doesn't mean it's not trouble." Jess regarded him steadily. "Ten thousand of the other side I offed in that cliff blow up had no idea I was around. No idea who I was."

Not exactly true. Given what that installation was. Jess smiled inwardly. They'd know her name, if nothing else, and probably more than one of them, at least had died in a firestorm cursing it.

"Stand by," Dev's voice said quietly in her ear. "Jess, we're almost to target."

"See if you can pick up an echo," Jess said. "Spread out in a spiral pattern, you go furthest west."

"Ack." Dev relayed the instructions, and the carrier tilted slightly as she vectored off and crossed the invisible line that was their patrol limits, heading due west.

Jess set a few parameters on her own boards, then put her hands back down on her thighs. "Now we wait."

"Hey, Drake," Kirin said. "What's that one for?" She pointed at one of the burns on Jess's left arm. "That the big blow up?"

"Nah." Jess glanced at her forearm, then pushed the sleeve

up further. "That one is." She studied the mark. "My first mission with Dev." She glanced up toward the pilot's station and found Dev watching her in the reflection. "Devvie has one almost like it."

The yonks were interested. "You got one too, Rocket?" Kirin asked, leaning forward to look at Dev.

"Yes." Dev paused in her instruction and glanced at them in the reflector. "I thought it was an interesting thing to experience, and Jess agreed."

"That's cool," Kirin said. "Does it hurt?"

"Yes."

"Still cool," the boy next to Kirin said. "We gonna do that?" He eyed Jess hopefully. .

"No."

The kids looked disappointed. "We'll find something else," Jess told them. "Burning yourself on purpose is stupid. It was just something we did, in service. I ain't in service no more, and I ain't getting any more of these damn things."

"But it's cool."

"It's not. It's stupid, and it's painful and you have to let it heal, and it's a mess," Jess said. "We'll figure something else out."

"Dev even thought it was cool," Kirin said.

"That's not exactly true," Dev spoke up, in a mildly bemused tone. "I thought it was a valuable experience."

"Same thing."

Dev put her attention back to her scans, figuring she wasn't going to win that argument. The frequencies were clean, there were no reflections, nothing to parse. "Jess, I'm going to see if we have any atmospheric bounce."

"Go for it." Jess reached up and tightened her restraints in an automatic gesture. "We can argue about self-mutilation later."

Dev warned the flight, then took the controls and sent the carrier abruptly skyward, shooting up toward the cloud cover and then through it in a surge of power, opening the spectrum to see if she could catch any echos, any signals reflecting off the upper cloud layer.

"Whoa." Kirin grabbed the belt holding her in place. "Evan, hang on to that damn pipe before you hit me with it."

Evan shifted the pipe and braced his feet against the floor, as the craft leveled out and surged forward, the sound of the engines now louder in the thinner atmosphere.

Dev set the scanners to the furthest range possible, her eyes moving from one output to the other, watching for anomalies.

They flew in silence for a minute.

"Dev," Jess said, suddenly. "Go back along a line twenty-five degrees northwest."

Dev adjusted their course, restarting the sweep, taking in the wire map of the ground beneath them that was flat and rocky."

Jess watched her screens intently, and the yonks watched her, their eyes wide.

"Echo," Dev said, suddenly. "I have a repeat of the squirt, end one, capture." She hit controls. "Sending it."

Jess saw the echo appear on her input screen and studied it. "Same as last time."

"Yes. It's a loop."

"Tell the squad to spread out on our course. Slow down." Jess encapsulated the signal and sent it out to April, who would know what it was. "Tell them to do a deep search scan for particulate, metallic."

"Yes."

April's voice crackled into the sideband. "Def someone from the force, flying." She said, crisply. "Figure they got caught in weather?" She asked. "Doug saw your course change. You got some intel?"

"No. Just what's the first thing west and north of us?" Jess said.

"Yeah."

Dev did a quick comparison of their course with the history of flights they'd taken and observed the potential match. "Interesting." She changed the scan slightly and added a filter. The ground they were covering was sterile and lifeless. She picked up nothing with advanced biology at all.

Just rock, and rain. "Squirt is looping and detectable, Jess. It's an automatic, power gradient fading point two percent every cycle."

"Beacon," Jess said. "Let's go get it."

"Flight, please target source of signal, standby to shift coordinates by two degrees," Dev instructed the other pilots. "We have been directed to investigate the source of the beacon."

Jess nodded quietly to herself. She curled her legs around the base of her seat and leaned forward against the restraints to study the targeting data she extracted from the scans that Dev was running. The arms comp analyzed what it saw with an eye of finding something interesting for Jess to shoot.

She ran the signal through the filters again, but it was the same as it had been when she'd first heard it back at the Bay. Just an alert frame, set on repeat, with no detail behind it, like a seagull squalling for no reason on the rocks outside their space.

She'd nailed one with a rock only that morning, chasing its noisy ass away. This was the same sort of thing, just a squealing beacon left to transmit a loop that told them nothing.

So, either an automatic system triggered by some catastrophic event to the craft that carried it… or potentially a trap trying to draw them in.

Jess smiled in anticipation, folding her hands together as they flew towards it. "Keep an eye out for weird stuff, Devvie," she almost whispered into the comms. "Might be a scam."

Dev was briefly silent. "Someone is expecting us to investigate."

"Could be." Jess looked at the silently watching fighters. "Ready to mix it up?"

"Oh yeah," Kirin said, instantly. "You serious?"

"Yeah." Evan, seated next to her, chimed in. "Let's do it!" Jess felt the tickling sensation on the palms of her hands as, despite all evidence to the contrary, she felt a fight coming. "Take it slow, Devvie. Bring us down to ground level as we get to the spot."

"Ident," Dev said. "The signal is coming from that rock structure two nautical miles from our current position. Ground ahead of it is clear, no biologic signs."

"Drake," April broke in again. "You figure this is a trap?"

"Yeah," Jess said.

"Nice." April's tone was satisfied. "I wanted a shootfest today. Want to keep two of these guys up here with scans?"

Jess paused and considered the question. She knew she had only perhaps a minute to decide what to do, and realized it was again a situation where she had to decide for more people than she was used to. She hadn't really thought about how to approach the escarpment. She'd assumed she and Dev would land, and she would take the kids out and they'd see what they'd see.

But... was that smart?

"They're not armed. No point," Jess said. "We all land, key's gonna be how fast they come at us after we're down." She paused again. "And how fast you and I can get back to these buckets and get behind the triggers."

Logic dictated that she and April stay behind, in the carriers, and let the fighters go out and trip the trap. But these kids were raw. Jess internally cursed. Too raw, and the pilots save,

Dev and Doug would not take independent action.

Was this stupid? Should they just turn around and get more people?

"Target in range," Dev said calmly. "There is metallic residual. No electronic footprint except for the beacon."

Too late. "Okay. Land in an arc, Devvie. They can't sneak up behind us we've got nothing but dead flats on the approach but tune the alerter."

"Yes," Dev said, having already done so. "I have synced the scan consoles." She slowed the carrier's speed, extended the landing skids and put the craft down at a distance that would allow them reaction time if something burst out at them, despite the empty scans.

Sometimes scans could lie, and she could see Jess was triggered, her knees jumping in a faint rhythm and her eyes searching her boards with focused intensity.

She kept the engines powered, and the skids only lightly touched the ground, holding a point in space. "Please remove your restraints before you attempt to exit the craft," she reminded the fighters. "Standing by to open the hatch."

There was the sound of belts being released and Jess released her more extensive restraints. "Kick it open."

Dev did, and the door opened with a thunk as it popped outward, and swung out of the way, but she kept the ramp from extending, not wanting that to impede any urgent lifting.

Jess stood and picked up one of the spare poles, her hand blaster tucked into the small of her back. "Let's go." She jumped out of the carrier and the kids scrambled after her, leaving the carrier startlingly empty.

Dev tied in all the scans and started running her recently tuned situational analytics on them. She watched all the other fighters emerge and April join Jess at the front of them and then the group started toward the outcrop where the beacon was, weakly, sending.

"Is there something we can do to assist, Dev?" Kevin asked, his voice calm. "We would like to help."

Dev reflected her output screens to the other carriers. "Study these results. If anything seems suboptimal, advise everyone."

"Excellent," Keko responded. "Is this what is called an insertion, NM-Dev?"

Dev watched the gang of fighters, and their two leaders advance on the rock formation. "Yes," she said, after a brief pause. "Hopefully it will be an uneventful one."

"Are they often uneventful?"

"No."

"I see."

****

The rain drenched them quickly as they approached the escarpment, now visibly pocked with dark, uneven openings that promised an ingress and at least shelter from the weather. A quick scan of the surface indicated to Jess that this was not a habited area.

April came up next to her, curly hair plastered down to her skull, eyes flicking over the ground with a look of pleased anticipation. "Scam?"

Jess shrugged her shoulders eloquently. "Does it matter?" She studied the gaps in the rock and picked one at random, whose roof seemed least likely to smack her in the head. "Okay," she said into comms. "Break into squads, everyone takes a tunnel."

"Yo." Many variations echoed back at her. The scrubs ganged up by their carrier group and trooped off into the caves, and as they crossed out of the rain and into the shadows, she saw them slow, and blink as she herself was slowing and blinking, transitioning from the gray light of outdoors.

Inside, the cave was shades of darker gray and silver, an odd reflectivity that briefly made Jess pause, then move on, her six yonks at her back. April and her gang had split off at the first branch, and she heard them moving along through these natural twisting passages.

She took in a breath. It smelled of rock, lacking the salt on the edges she'd smell at the Bay. Just the metallic biting tang that made the back of her tongue twist.

"Been water through here," April said in her ear. "Flood. You can see the drain off."

On the ground, yes. Jess saw it, a line of sediment she felt faintly crunching under the soles of her boots. She reached out and touched the wall, its surface cold and damp against her fingertips. "Yeah. Flash from runoff. Line of cliffs west of here."

"Nothin's round here," someone said, in a low mutter.

All the scans said the same, but her skin prickled, and Jess knew there was something. "Keep going. Something made that squawk."

There was nothing alive around them, nothing she could

smell or hear, no taint on the still air in the tunnels of creatures, aside from the ones she'd brought with her, who were spread out in a loose circle around her with their ears twitching and noses searching as hers was.

Jess felt a sense of mild revelation. All her life she'd been different. Weird. An exception. Now, standing here in this drippy wet cave, she realized she wasn't. It almost made her smile but then a faint change in the air made her halt. The rest of them halted too and went still, watching her.

After a moment of silence Kirin said softly. "Sup?"

"Silicon sealant," Jess responded quietly. "Coming from that northwest facing passage, there to the right."

She started off in that direction, and they hustled to follow her as she shifted her grip on the pipe she'd picked up. She took a deeper breath. "Burned rock."

"Got it," April said. "Void ahead. We're in the next chamber, I can hear you moving." A moment later a faint tap against the rock sounded. Jess reached out and tapped back. "Watch it."

"Sup?" Kirin repeated softly.

"There's something in here that ain't natural," Jess said. She sped up the pace a little, wanting to get to the fun part. "Mech."

Ahead she saw the branch off, and then a flash as the two passages conjoined. Then she saw a shadow she identified as April coming toward them.

They joined as a group, and as the passage widened they spread out. The smell of mech was stronger now and the burned smell of components overpowered that of the shattered rock they started to pick themselves through.

Jess was the first through the crooked, crack of a gap into the void April had detected. She moved into the space, aware of no life movement in the air, just a large, looming hulk half buried in rubble and rock fragments. Behind it she saw a huge opening, and at the very end, rain and outside light.

"Someone flew their ass in here," April said, as she climbed over the rocks. "They tried a Rocket. Didn't go so well."

The vehicle was cracked almost in half, its nose battered and crushed, as though it had fallen right out of the air into the cavern. As she got closer, and the scrubs spread out to investigate the cavern, she realized the outline was somewhat familiar. "Crap."

"Training rig," April finished her thought, as she peered inside the wreck. "No bodies inside." She pulled out her blaster and turned on the pre-aim, illuminating the inside, as Jess came up behind her and looked over her head at it. "Clean."

The inside was devoid of any hint of power. The hatch was open, and the rudimentary pilots and gunner's seats were empty, just frames with old plas webbing on them that made Jess grimace in memory.

"Junkers," April said. "What do you figure, some neo off course? Make sense if that's where the screamer came from."

Possible. "They're usually a lot more careful of how they let go of these things," Jess mused. "Hey, Devvie? Could use some wrencher brains in here."

"Ack," Dev's voice answered at once. "Be right there."

"Yo," Evan grunted into the local comms. "Heard something out there."

Jess looked up quickly. "Out where?"

He pointed at the large gap. "Clank," he said. "Like this." He whacked his pipe against the rocks."

Everyone started toward the exit. "Hold up," Jess ordered sharply. "Dev, g'wan up over the ridge and see what's over on this side before we walk our asses out into it?"

"Ack," Dev said again, with the sound of the hatch closing behind her and the distinctive thrum and vibration of the restraints on her pilot's chair retracting. "Stand by. Flight two and three, please lift and do a full scan of the area. Flight six please accompany me."

"Sure," Doug responded amiably. "You always get the fun stuff."

"You think something's out there?" April said. "They didn't see anything on scan."

Jess stared at the opening. "I think something's out there. I can feel it. Move against the walls, "she ordered and moved away from the wrecked training carrier. "Don't look at the opening, keep your night eyes."

"Yo." The twelve scrubs moved back, pressing their backs against the damp rock.

"Hey, nothin round here," another of the groups reported in. "Wanna go over by you?"

"Everyone c'mon back to the entrance we used," Jess said. "The more the merrier."

April drew her blaster and cradled it in her hands.

"Jess," Dev's voice cut in, loud and urgent.

"Thought so," Jess said. "Keep your head down Dev!"

"It's a security transport, grounded." Dev said. "It's not showing on scan, but I can see it. Something is blocking scan. I am going to see if I can..." She paused. "I am taking fire," she said calmly. "I am going to take evasive action."

"Oh boy." April spun. "Let me go get in that damn bus. Doug!"

"No time," Jess said. "Hang on, Dev!" She bolted for the entrance, picking up speed as the scrubs reacted and bolted after her with loud yells.

"Doug get your ass over here and be a decoy," April said, as she took off after her. "Pick me up on the ground!"

"Roger that, boss," Doug said. "C'mon the rest of you, lemme teach you about dodge ball. Everyone get up to level and follow me!"

"Shitshow." April picked up speed as Jess emerged into the light, then abruptly whirled around, and leaped up against the rock wall of the escarpment. "What in the f…"

What in the F was Jess climbing up the side of the cliff. She moved from handhold to handhold as easily as if she was walking up the steps at the Bay. She was spotted from the ground and bolts started her way, hitting where she'd been a moment before as she moved quickly along.

****

Dev was busy. The security guards, who were part of the transport, were on the ground using the vehicle as shelter. They were firing up at her with long, powerful laser rifles that slammed against the lower armor of the carrier as she shifted and dodged in midair, keeping the hits squarely in the thickest part of her shields.

She wasn't really in much danger. The carriers were designed to survive air to air battles, so though the long rifles could blow holes in stone, they merely rocked the craft she was flying.

But there were a lot of them. "There are fifty individuals," she reported. "They are heavily armed and are wearing standard class three armor."

"Get out there and kick ass!!" Jess yelled into comms.

The entrance was suddenly a boil with scrubs and Dev quickly dove the carrier down between them and the security guards, taking the hits on the outer shell as they barreled across the wet, rocky ground.

A motion caught her eye, and she saw Jess leap up onto the rock wall and start to climb upward. Dev judged the angle of her climb and concluded what she was up to. "Suboptimal," she muttered. "Flight six…"

"On the way, Rocket," Doug called back, as the five carriers came arching over the top of the wall. "Whatcha… oh. Oh crap."

"Please assist in distracting those people and drawing fire," Dev told him. "I have a task."

The five carriers plunged down and headed right for the security transport, as though they were going to crash right into it. Dev took advantage of that distraction to move her carrier into a rolling circle, looking quickly at the wall to see where Jess was.

There. Near a point of rock and exposed to the sky, a perfect target. Dev hit her landing jets and a moment later a huge cloud of steam rushed up past her, obscuring the view. She shifted the craft forward and then slid sideways near the wall as close as she could get.

Jess crouched and leaped in perfect confidence. She turned a somersault and landed on the roof of the carrier with a solid thump as she lay down flat under a barrage of fire.

The nose came up and she almost slid backwards off the end of the craft. "Slippery up here Devvie!" She yelled into the shortwave comms.

"Stand by please." Dev shifted away from the rock wall as she lifted, getting clearance to maneuver. "I assume you wish to enter?"

"Yeah, let me try to get over onto that en… ow!" Jess yelped. "Bastard!" She drew her blaster and got her arm round the edge of the carrier and returned fire. "Someone get that… yeah! Good one!"

The sniper was piled on by three scrubs, who took him to the ground with booming yells they could hear aloft. This got the attention of the surrounding security guards who turned to go help their comrade.

That gave Dev the chance to punch the hatch opening and then without warning rolled the carrier onto its side and then tipped it aft upward. Her motion and gravity did the work as Jess was tumbled onto the side of the carrier and then into the open hatch.

"Yow!" Jess yelped into her comms. "What the what!?"

Dev had barely enough time to close the hatch before a bolt took out something inside. She completed the roll and came upright again, her hands moving in a blur to transfer power to Jess's console as she punched the armed lights on the bottom in warning as their armament came live.

"Don't you even think about doing that to me, Douglas,"

April's voice cut in abruptly. "Land your ass."

"Landing my ass," Doug said and held back a laugh. "Stand by."

"Nice!" Jess caught her breath as she pulled herself into the gunner chair, wet, bruised and bleeding from a gash on the side of her head. "Good job, Devvie!"

Dev frowned. "Non optimal. You are damaged."

"Not nearly as much as I could have been, and not nearly as much as I'm gonna damage them. Get past those kids." Jess got her hands in the triggers and pulled them down, priming the guns as she wrapped her legs around her chair support in lieu of her restraints.

Dev went to ground level, and they skimmed the rock surface as the scrubs ducked and rolled and powered forward. They evaded the blasts as they reached the transport and threw themselves at the line of guards who came out to engage them.

Caught by surprise, the guards weren't prepared. They relied on their long-range weapons to hold opponents off, they were not ready for opponents who ignored the fire and just came right at them. Opponents who ducked and dodged the energy bolts without fear.

Jess saw the security guards look up at her and realize what the profile of the vehicle was. She grinned and sent a rapid-fire set of blasts against the side of the transport as she understood that they now understood what they were facing.

She could almost hear the silent—oh shit.

"Get out of the way!" Doug yelled into the comms. "Get back! Get … just don't go that way!" Move Move! Keko, Kevin get around that rock point there!"

"Please clear this vehicles range of our motion," Dev warned. "We are actively firing."

"That means all of it. All the motions!" Doug yelled over her. "Chase those guys down there, just run on top of them! Go over there! To the right!"

The scrubs were in heaven. The guards had lined up behind the transport and were now fighting hand to hand with them, unable to use the long rifles to any good effect and their armor proving more a hindrance than help.

They weren't trained for this. They were not prepared to deal with an enemy who paid no attention to their perceived threat and just wanted to get their hands on them and tear them apart, yelling in gleeful delight.

One guard got taken right off his feet by Evan, then Kirin yanked the helmet off his head, as they battered him with their pipes.

Over their heads, Jess was laying down gunfire that rocked the transport continuously. The rest of the carriers peeled off and started flying around the escarpment in a wild confusion of dark hulls. They ducked the scattered bolts from the long rifles, or deflecting them against their lower armor, becoming more assured as the sets realized their vehicles could take the hits with no damage.

"Don't tank this one, wouldja, Jess?" April broke in. "It's in better shape than the other clunker."

Two of the carriers raced off to the north. They stayed close to the ground and sent back scan that showed detail Dev couldn't see when they were behind the escarpment to the south. She made a note to return and sample the material of it as an urgent to do item.

The entire security platoon had been hidden from them. Dev shook her head a little. Hidden from all their technology but not, she recalled, not from Jess, who sensed them. Not in specifics, but in that knowing that was a mystery to her.

No time to wonder about it now though.

"Come over the top of that damn thing, Dev," Jess said. "How are the kids doing?"

Dev did as asked and circled the transport. She tipped the carrier forward so Jess could see out the front windscreen, which nearly sent her pitching over her station.

"Ooff."

"Sorry." Dev adjusted the pitch. "You might want to put on your restraints."

"I might." Jess yanked herself back, releasing the triggers and sparing a moment to pull her belts on over her head and fasten them. "Okay." She stood up and leaned into the straps and peered at the transport. "Yonks are doing it! Look at em!"

There were enemy guards down on the ground, and guards that were now pelting across the rocky ground in the rain, headed away from the transport. They discarded their weapons, and just ran in visible terror from the large, eager eyed fighters chasing after them.

Jess chuckled. "Go, baby go," She murmured happily.

"Are we going to take that craft as well, Jess? I have to see if there are mods that can deal with the security of it."

Were they? Should they? It reminded Jess suddenly of something. "Don't touch those weapons, ya scrubs," she warned into comms. "Leave em lying. They'll blow your asses up."

"Yo. We got that," one of them answered. "They told us."

"And those," Dev muttered, writing down a note. "Many tasks."

"Land," Jess said. "Lemme get out there and see what's going on."

"Are you finished shooting?" Dev asked. "I will then safe the arms." She put a hand on the console and waited, watching Jess in the reflector.

Jess hesitated, then closed off comms and just addressed Dev. "Damn it. I can't do everything at once can I?" She said.

Dev smiled at her expression. "April is now in her carrier. Perhaps she could cover?" She suggested and watched Jess's eyes flick to the side then back to her. "I think she would perhaps enjoy that."

"Perhaps you're better at this tactical shit than I am," Jess said wryly. She opened comms again. "April, you on trigger? Need a backup."

"Right behind ya. What're we shooting? The kids are taking care of these guys fine," April said. "Got two of them chasing down some of the ones running off."

"Just cover the area and blow up anything that gets stupid," Jess said. "I'm gonna go see if there's anyone with a brain still moving and find out why these guys are here." She paused. "Find me some guys with metal on their shoulders, ya scrubs. Bring em out."

"Yo."

"Gotcha," April responded in an approving tone. "We're good."

Dev slid the carrier sideways into an open, flat area and lowered it to the ground, as a whole group of fighters surged out from behind the transport. The shoved a line of security in front of them, all with their hands up, and sans weapons.

Jess released herself and stood up. "Open." She went to the hatch and waited for it to clear enough space not to hit her head. She walked out and dropped to the ground, striding across the rubble, rain hitting her, pipe clenched in her hand.

April's carrier hovered at an angle to them, weapons active, lights flashing, baleful and at the ready.

Behind the windscreen Dev saw Doug at the controls. After a moment he looked back at her and gave her a thumbs up.

She waved back and watched Jess walk to the transport, where two of the fighters had their grip on one of the guards, this one in a set of armor and shoulder splashes she recognized as a captain.

After a moment Dev locked the controls and stood. She pulled on her jacket, slid her scanner over her shoulder and went out the hatch, turning to close the ingress behind her.

Then she started the scanner up, as she walked after Jess in the rain.

****

The security captain stared at her, his face white with shock, and covered in blood from being divested of his helmet and dragged across the ground. "You're Jess Drake."

Jess nodded. She faced him with her hands on her hips, her hoodie and work pants fully darkened with rain. "What are you doing here?" She asked crisply. "Dugger, right? "

"Yeah," Dugger blinked. "Was about to ask you the same. HQ said you were dead."

Jess looked at herself then at him, then she spread her arms out. "Wishful thinking?"

"What the hell is this?" Duggar looked around at the yonks, all in their hoodies, drenched in the rain. "What are these guys?"

Jess smiled at him with no humor. "My fam."

"Oh," he said. "We heard something about that, at Canyon. Some dust up."

"You could call it that," Jess said. "You know Interforce pulled out of here." She made a circling motion of her hand. "I was at Ten when they took off and left a bunch of us behind."

Duggar nodded. "We know. We got our own job here… we were tracking down a deserter," he explained. "From Canyon. That's our station." He looked at the hovering carriers. "You… are those from Ten?" He asked. "I thought… they told us they—"

"Never mind that," Jess cut him off. "What kind of deserter? Some kid?"

He hesitated.

Jess took a step closer and shifted her grip on her pipe. She saw his instinctive reaction, that drawing back of the shoulders and the twitch along his forearms. "What kind?"

"Cadet," he finally answered. "Had some argument with the CO there, I don't know the deets. You know they don't tell us nothin, Drake. We just got orders to search."

Jess was aware of Dev's arrival at her side. She stood just a pace or so behind her, far enough not to hinder Jess if she had to start fighting. Her pale hair was darkened with rain and pulled back from her forehead in a messy tangle, the rain rolling off the surface of her sharkskin jacket.

"Transport with fifty troops on it to look for one runner?" Jess studied his face. "He kick the CO in the crotch or something?"

Duggar grimaced. "No idea. Just did what they told me." He looked away then back at her. "I'll tell em I didn't find anything." He looked around at the scrubs, who listened with interest. "Your fam huh?"

"My fam," Jess said. "This is Drake's Bay." She indicated the scrubs, who grinned in joyful pride. "Tell them to keep the hell away from us, if anyone asks."

"Yeah, no kidding." Duggar lifted his hands now in the familiar gesture, hands facing forward at shoulder level. "I get it. They pulled out, you pulled in. Got it. I heard what happened in that fight, Drake. I don't want any mixing up with you."

Jess relaxed her stance and let the pipe rest against her shoulder. "Smart man," she said briefly. "Dev, anything about this missing kid?"

Dev glanced up from her screen, her pale green eyes fixing on the security guard in sharp inspection. "There has been nothing to indicate any presence of anyone in this vicinity, Jess," she said. "I think they are looking in the wrong location."

"That's the bio alt," Duggar said, after a pause.

"Yes," Dev responded in a mild tone. "I am also not dead," she added. "In case that was in question."

"You gonna off em, Jess?" April asked in a conversational tone, over comms. "Rocket could probably unleash that transport. We could use it," she said. "And no mouthing off to worry about."

The scrubs heard this and perked up, looking at their captives with renewed interest.

Jess considered for a long moment. Then half turned to obscure her voice. "No." She then said. "This is not a scam. Wasn't aimed at us. We just walked into it." She turned back to Duggar. "Put your arms down on the ground, all of them. Then you have ten minutes to board that thing and get out of here. Don't come back."

He closed his eyes, drew in a breath and released it. "Okay," he said. "Understood."

"Shoo." Jess waved the pipe at him.

He kept his hands up and backed slowly away from her. The scrubs let him go and stared at him until he got back to the line of beaten-up guards. "Board," he ordered. "Move it."

Evan picked up a piece of their discarded armor and casually broke it into pieces in his hands as they retreated, the sound of boots hitting the stone loud as the security guards moved quickly to get onboard.

Three dead bodies were taken with them, dragged by their comrades. The thirty-six scrubs, some with cuts and bruises, all mobile and active gathered around Jess in a cluster.

Kirin regarded Jess. "Sup? He asked. "Who were those turds?"

"Security from the Interforce school," Jess said. "Chasing a cadet who took off running." Might have been in that trainer we saw inside."

"Dja tell him about it?" April asked.

Jess grinned. "Nope. Would you have?"

"Someone running out on Canyon who stole a rig?" April said. "Nope."

The ground was littered with armor bits and dropped weapons. Dev diligently kept scanning to look for anomalies. The weapons seemed standard Interforce issue, and she didn't detect anything unusual.

However, they should have been readable from the other side of the ridge, and they had not been. It made her doubt her results, which she found profoundly uncomfortable. She continued to run the scans as they waited for the transport to load, turning in a circle to gather everything she could.

She paused with her back to the transport, and looked up at the large, irregular hole in the side of the escarpment. With a frown, she changed the scanner from biologic to geologic and started a new evaluation.

"Move it!" Jess bellowed, as some of the security guards paused to turn and watch them as they waited to board.

"Ow," April yelped. "Would you turn off your damn mike before you do that?"

Dev, having seen Jess's deep inhale had already plucked her ear bud out. Now she put it back in and studied her results. "Interesting."

"What is?" Jess leaned over and peered at her screen. "Looks like rocks."

"Yes," Dev agreed. "With an interesting metallic component. A bit like the ones at the Bay, but with an internal structure I have not seen before," she said. "It might have caused the scan block." She felt a bit better about that if there was a reason. "See? I can't scan the interior of that structure."

Jess studied the screen. "You can't see the trainer in there." "No.

I assume they could not either," Dev said. "But you found it."

Jess lifted her eyes to study the escarpment. "We found it," she said. "I could smell the mech. But no people. Not even dead people."

Behind them, the transport powered up and cautiously lifted, easing up past the hovering carriers and edging away toward the northwest.

"Whoever piloted that craft had to go somewhere," Dev said, after a long pause.

"Yeah," Jess said. "So, let's see if we can go find them."

Chapter Twenty

The rain started to come down harder, and the pilots were happy to land their carriers on the more sheltered side of the escarpment, as the fighters re-entered the tunnels to search.

"Should we exit and assist?" Keko asked. "We have infra-red lenses in these vehicles that would allow us to see in that space."

Dev pulled a dry shirt on and a sweater over it. "Jess requested we stay with these carriers and keep prepared to depart." She ran her fingers through her hair and shook herself. The rain was cold, with a tinge of ice in it, and she now investigated the holding cabinets behind her station to see if she had a spare garment for Jess packed in one for when she returned from the cave.

"April has our set," Doug said over the station-to-station comms between the carriers. "She's ticked she can't just see in the dark like Jess can."

Dev paused in her search and looked over her shoulder at the comms panel. "Is that something to be upset about?"

"That Jess, and the rest of these guys, can see in the dark and she can't? It sure is to April."

"Ah." Dev went back to her methodical search of the cargo locker. "Yes, it's amazing."

"We did excellent work earlier, didn't we?" Kevin said. "In preventing those guards from firing on us."

"That was good." Keko agreed. "That was interesting flying."

"That was interesting flying and really excellent work," Dev said. She went back to her station, took her seat and leaned back in her pilot's chair. "Kieran, is the transport still on scan?"

Kieran was hovering at altitude just under the cloud cover so his scan would see over the escarpment. "The vehicle has maintained course and is on trajectory to the coordinates you provided," he said promptly. "There is no other activity at this time."

"Thank you." Dev picked up her bottle and took a sip from it. "Can you navigate to the other side of this ridge, and perform a deep scan for biologic signs please?"

"Yes," Kieran said confidently. "I have programming for that."

"I am sending over a biograph," Dev continued. "Please filter it out of the results and revert."

"Yes."

"So, what's in this rock pile, Rocket?" Doug asked. "That's weird that it blocked all the scans. It's just a hump of stone, right?"

"I have a sample to bring back for Doctor Dan to examine," Dev said. "I sent back a geologic scan, but it was not specific enough to determine the structure." She studied the screen at her left hand. "It is almost as if there is something inside the rock that was melted into it."

"Something?"

"Some metallic substance," Dev clarified. "But it could be useful." She pondered. "There is no detectable radiation, or emittive properties. It just seems to be a particular construction and density that absorbs or blocks radio signal."

"We could coat the outside of these things in it and be invisible," Doug said in a conversational tone. "That'd be cool, right?"

Dev stared at the comms panel, both her pale eyebrows hiking up almost to her hairline. "That is a very interesting idea."

"If we put rock on the outside of these vehicles would change the flight dynamics," Keko said. "As well as increase the lifting weight."

Doug chuckled. "I was kidding. Sorta."

He had been. But it was an interesting idea. Dev took another sip of her beverage. Interesting, because plastering rock on the outside of Rockstar really wasn't a feasible idea, but what if she could extract whatever the metallic substance was and use that? Would that be useful?

Yes, she thought that might be useful. She picked up her data pad and tapped some notes onto it, to a scrolling list of possible tasks and things she wanted to investigate.

On the comms digital display, she had the sidebands that allowed Jess and the rest of the fighters to communicate through their earbuds, relayed through the carrier's comms systems. "Interesting that the comms signals penetrate that substance."

"They don't want to make Jess mad," Doug bantered. "No serious, its frequency maybe. Sidebands lower."

"That's true," Dev said.

"Dev, this is Kieran. I have applied the filter and scanned. Are you expecting a result?"

"Yes."

"Interesting," Kieran replied. "There might be a reflection. I am going to triangulate."

"Excellent." Dev propped one boot up against the console and drummed the fingers of her right hand against her thigh. Then she went to the library in the carrier's systems and reviewed the location they were perched on. She flicked back through screens of geologic history.

Jess's voice rumbled in her ear, the tones making a faint tickle against her eardrum. "Devvie."

"Here, Jess." She glanced up at comms and saw they were on a private sideband. "Is everything nominal?"

"No."

Dev focused on the comms. "Is there an issue?" She flicked her eyes over the control consoles to take in the condition of the carrier in a single sweep. "How can I assist?"

"I'm here in a hole in the ground in the dark and you're not here."

Dev stood up at once. "A moment. I will egress."

Jess chuckled. "Nah just kidding. Stay in there it's raining ice. I'm gonna give this another ten minutes then we can take off and head back to the Bay and chalk it up to a unicorn hunt."

Dev regarded the boards. "Are you certain?"

"I'm sure I don't want you turning blue." Jess's voice was warmly teasing. "I'd have to kiss ya."

Dev pondered "That's a very attractive idea."

Jess chuckled again. "Yeah, let me finish this up and we can get out of here. I'm guessing if there was someone stupid enough to be in that brick while it flew into a mountain they're a burned-up splat."

Dev remembered what North Base was like, and the sense memory made her grimace. "Unfortunate."

"Let that be a lesson to ya. Don't fly into mountains."

"I did, actually." Dev remarked in an offhand tone.

Jess smiled, and you could hear it in her voice. "Don't fly into mountains unless you're Rocket Raccoon, the best pilot on planet Earth."

Well, there was some small bit of truth in that. There, in the privacy of the carrier, Dev could glance at her own reflection and grin at herself. "Perhaps they ejected and landed in another area," she said. "And programmed the carrier to crash."

"Could be," Jess said. "Damn good thought, Devvie. We should patrol around."

"Dev," Kieran's voice broke in on the other channel. "Sending output."

"A moment, Jess." Dev sat down and slid her seat forward. She tuned in the squirt and pulled it up into her analytics module. Her pale eyes scanned it, then she slowly went over it again, leaning forward a little as the cryptic output scrolled.

"Anything cool?" Jess asked.

Dev sat back. "Possibly."

"Oh, hey, hold on to it. I think we may have found something," Jess said, then clicked off, the carrier going quiet.

Dev frowned and sat back. "Kieran, what is your position?" She listened to the crisply presented coordinates. "Please hold at that location, I will join you."

"Thought Jess said to stay put?" Doug said. "Aren't we supposed to be running a hot stick?"

Dev put her craft into flight. "It's also possible she would not mind repeating our earlier activity," she said. "But in any case, I would like to inspect this anomaly." She fastened her restraints and boosted up on her landing jets. "Please remain here."

It felt odd giving direction to a natural born. The rest of the pilots were sets, and that was no problem. Dev didn't feel strange at all directing them, she was the senior, and they knew that, and were fine with it as well.

Doug was, however, a mild natured natural born and she felt he might not be too upset. He also had become accustomed to being directed by her while they were Interforce.

"Okey dokey, Rocket," he said in a cheerful tone. "We'll hang out here, but y'know, we might be better aloft. I know Jess didn't want us out of range of the Bay, but if we were up in the air, if they come out on that side we'd be able to get to them faster."

Dev was already lifting. "It is a compromise, as if they come out on this side, it would be faster to recover them."

"Yeah, that's true. But I'm kinda bored."

Dev grinned to herself. "We could take the opportunity to practice close order motion."

"We can do drills!" Doug said. "C'mon kids, let's get some practice in."

****

Jess squeezed through a crack in the rock, the rough stone rasping against her wet hoodie. She licked a droplet of rain off her lips and eased forward, following that indefinable itch, that odd and sometimes disconnected instinct that moved her in a particular direction toward a particular goal.

"Nothin?" She heard a yonk whisper in her ear. "Don' see

nothing."

"Don't try to look," Jess whispered back. "Don't try to do anything. Just let your body move." She tried to explain it and couldn't really find the words. "Think about something else."

She was doing it, her footsteps gentle and soundless on the ground, her body tensing as she sensed there was something there. Something ahead and to the left. She felt the hair lift on the back of her neck.

"It's like hunting," she finally said, in a low mutter.

"How do you know where to go?"

They'd probably never even thought about that, and the silence that followed was oddly profound. When your daily task was to find stuff, you didn't question success, now did you? You walked along, and went where your feet took you, and there were mollusk blowholes.

There were the crannies that held sea urchins.

There were just the rocks that had limpets on them, on the back side. You just knew, you just did, you brought back your bagful. Did you think about how you knew? Was there really anything to even think about?

"Yo," a yonk said into the comms. "Here maybe."

And Jess knew where he was, to the left of her, in the direction she was already heading. It made her smile as she squeezed through another gap and found two Bay fighters in the shadows of the caves, arms distance from each other. They faced a rounded cap of rock ahead of them.

"There," Kirin said, and she turned and indicated the protrusion. "Just feels different."

"Does." Jess moved around to the far left of it and examined the surface. There was something less than authentic about it. Something shaped, rather than natural. "Back up," she told the fighters, who now gathered around her.

They did, and she picked up a rock, a heavy one with sharp edges, and hefted it. As one they all scattered and moved as far back as they could in the cavern when she lifted it over her head and threw it at the cap.

It slammed into the stone with a loud sound that wasn't much like rock, and echoed loudly, but not quite enough to muffle the faint sound that was behind it.

"Heard somethin," Kirin said. "Like a seal blowhole."

April came in behind them and crossed the cavern to Jess's side. "Heard what?" She said. "What the hell was that?"

"Me throwing a rock at that wall."

April eyed her. "Bored?"

Jess faced her, shook her head, and then made a quick hand signal. She nodded as April pulled out her blaster and gripped it two handed. Jess pulled her own gun out of the holster in the small of her back.

"Jess," Dev's voice popped unexpectedly into her ear, as the rumble of carrier engines suddenly penetrated the rock at their backs. "There is a biologic signature ahead of you." She spoke quietly, but quickly. "I was able to alter the scan properties to resolve around the metallic interference."

"Good job, Devvie," Jess muttered. "What is it?"

"A natural born. It doesn't signature match anything I have in my library," Dev said.

"So not one of us."

Dev paused. "If you mean, not a relative of yours, or from Drake's Bay or a bio alt, yes."

"Only one?"

"Yes."

"Even a baby one of us, is one of us." Jess glanced around, then replaced her blaster in its housing and walked forward toward the protrusion and laid her hands on the rough surface in gentle silence. "Stand back and let me and April handle this."

April adjusted her goggles and nodded.

Jess breathed in the scent and tasted the mineral tang of the stone, and behind it, the acid taint of metal. And behind that? What did she feel was behind that? An immature but potentially dangerous unknown?

Could well be.

She closed her eyes and breathed in through her mouth, aware of the tense silence behind her as the scrubs watched her intently. April waited, slowly lowering her gun into position, the red pre aim splashed against the surface to one side of Jess's head.

Jess ignored it and stretched her arms out and fit her fingers into angles in the stone, then tightened her grip and leaned back. She arched her body and drew in a deep breath.

"The hell are you doing?" April whispered.

"Just being Bay," Jess muttered back as she hauled against the rock surface, enduring a moment on the verge of falling back against it before it let loose with a crack. She almost fell over as the rock facade came away in her grip.

She hopped back awkwardly, dragging the piece with her. The scrubs bounded forward, and April scooted in ahead of them with a bold yell into the void behind it, the vivid splash of her pre-aim blaring across the space.

There in the dark, in the shadows, Jess caught again the soft gasp she'd heard after the rock toss repeat itself.

"I…" a small voice echoed softly. "I give up. Please don't shoot me."

The thrum of the engines of Dev's carrier rumbled again, so close Jess had to stop herself from turning to look through the tunnel they'd come through as though her partner had found a way to fit the craft inside it.

"Jess," her comms crackled. "That was a loud sound."

"So'kay, Dev," Jess said into comms. She dragged the rock facade aside and threw it against the wall again so she could muscle her way through the ring of scrubs, and bristling ex agent, to inspect her booty. "We found him."

"Excellent," Dev said. "All is well then?"

Jess snorted softly. "For us." She peered through the shadows, where April's blaster had found a target. The red splash centered on a human head and reflected off pale, very wide eyes.

Behind the ripped away place was a small depression. Inside that, huddled against the back of it, was a short, slight figure wearing a Canyon City jumpsuit, so dirty with rock dust it seemed black. Smudges of dust obscured his face.

Jess studied him. "Hi, kid," she finally said. "Sup?"

He stared blindly around, clearly unable to see them. His hair was curly, and some indeterminate darkish color. He had a snub nose and was so damn young it made her grimace.

"Uh hi…." He had his hands in the air, raised at shoulder level, palms out. "Please don't kill me. I didn't do anything to you."

"Yo," Evan said. "You ain't big enough to do anything to us, dude."

The scrubs chuckled, and turned to look at Jess in question, while April lifted her blaster and held it at her shoulder, one eyebrow lifted. "They letting juniors play around in the sims these days?" She asked, in a quizzical tone.

"Take him outside," Jess said, after a pause. "Let him see what he's gotten himself into."

Two scrubs went over and took hold of him. They lifted him up onto his feet, but his legs collapsed under him. Kirin picked him up and put him over her shoulder then headed out of the caves, into the thunder and rain.

****

Dev landed the carrier outside the cave tunnels entrances, turned the fuselage sideways, and opened the hatch when she saw tall, rain drenched, figures heading in her direction.

Jess was in the lead, and apparently undamaged, she was relieved to note. April walked next to her.

"Flights please land and prepare to board crew," she instructed the hovering carriers overhead, who immediately started to descend into the flat area that the security transport had been parked in. She felt the damp cold coming in from the open hatch and extended the ramp to the rough ground.

Jess thumped up into the craft, making it rock slightly. "Put him down over there." She pointed to the back row of seating.

Kirin obeyed and dumped the slight figure onto the seat and stepped back as he twisted himself upright. The boy appeared more than a little disoriented and rubbed his eyes, his face red and flushed from being carried head downward.

The rain had washed some of the rock dust off him and in the overhead light of the carrier his mud-colored hair resolved into a deep rusty red that matched the spattering of freckles across his face as he stared around at them with wide gray blue eyes.

Dev watched in the reflector, busy with scans.

The six scrubs they'd brought clambered in. April came in as well and pulled the night vision glasses off her head and let them hang around her neck.

Jess sat in her seat and turned it around to face their captive. She laid her forearms against the padded metal and watched the rain drip off her hands to the ground. She studied the diminutive figure as the scrubs settled themselves. "What's your name, kid?"

"Ryan," the boy answered promptly. "Ma'am."

April hastily covered her mouth and looked away, while the scrubs all snickered.

Jess ignored them. "Ryan what?"

He took a breath. "Hendler." He paused. "My family runs Beartooth Power," he added. "Out west."

Jess remembered the name, vaguely, from school. "Tech?"

He looked down at his hands, cut up and covered in scrapes. "I guess," he said. "I mean, I was." He glanced at the open hatch. "Not now. Since I run off, probably not."

"How old are you?" April asked suddenly, from her spot hunkering down on the deck, the gun held loosely in one hand.

"Fifteen," Ryan said.

"You musta just gotten in."

He nodded. "About six months, I guess." He looked around at them again. "I was just gonna get moved to advanced." He put his hands on his knees, the fabric under them slashed and worn. "Then all that stuff happened."

April and Jess exchanged glances. "What stuff?" Jess asked, still in a mild tone.

He looked surprised. "All the close down stuff. They stopped our tech classes. That stuff." He looked from one to the other. "You heard about it? They sent out comms, we heard it. My dad heard it, wanted to get me home again."

"No, we didn't hear it," Jess said. "What're they gonna do with everyone there?"

Ryan shrugged. "I dunno. I figured, only chance I'd get to fly me one of those rigs, so me and Carson... he's my buddy from there, we were hoping we'd get assigned the same, you know? So, we made it up we'd go grab one of the rigs and take a ride."

This was totally not what Jess expected. She could see by the outline of April's profile she felt the same way. "Then where is he?" Jess asked in a casual tone. "Your buddy?"

"They caught him sneaking out. Locked him down," Ryan said, glumly. "They didn't watch us so good, so I got to the hanger and got me my ride." He looked at them with a defensive expression. "Didn't do so bad, till the end there."

"Till you flew into a mountain," April said, dryly.

"They were chasing me," he shot back. "I did all right." He paused, then looked furtively at them. "Where are those guys anyhow? I know they landed round here somewhere." He hesitated. "Guess I better go give it up."

"We chased em off," Kirin told him. "Kicked their asses outta here."

"Yo," Evan agreed solemnly. "Drake told em to take on off and they done that."

"Drake," Ryan said in a hesitant voice. "Where am I?"

"Tanner's escarpment," April said. "That's where you crashed your rig at." She paused, as though for effect. "We're from Drake's Bay."

Ryan looked around at the interior of the carrier. "Oh boy," he muttered. "Went too far east."

Dev got up and came back to the gunner's station, drawing the boy's attention. She handed Jess a dry long-sleeved shirt. "This was packed in the cargo cabinet. I thought you might like to be dry." She glanced at their captive, who watched her with interested surprise. "Hello." She turned back to Jess. "Should we depart?"

Jess draped the dry garment over her console. "Thanks, Devvie," she said. "Yeah, button it all up and let's get going. I think we've had enough surprises for today."

"Hey, I can just hang out here," Ryan said, and started to get up but stopped when the hatch powered closed at a touch of Jess's fingers. "I mean, thanks for chasing those guys off but I..."

"You want to go back to school?" Jess asked. "They're gonna roast ya."

Ryan licked his lips, now visibly nervous. "Maybe some detention." He shook his head. "Won't be so bad... it's pretty cool there."

Jess stood up, towering over him and he straightened back away from her as she casually pulled her hoodie off, baring her torso. "No, it's not." She bundled the shirt in her hands and squeezed the water out of it with powerful twists. "We know."

"We know," April agreed, with a faint grin. "Some of us more than others." She jerked her head toward the service burns outlined in the overhead halons of the carrier.

Jess set the hoodie down and pulled on the dry shirt Dev had provided. She watched the kid watch her. She pushed the long sleeves up to keep her burns exposed, then put her hands on her hips and hiked her eyebrows. "Well?" She stared at him. "You really want to go back there? We'll take ya. I can visit my nephew."

"Tttttayler," Evan warbled. "Little crazy dude."

"Or you could come back to Drake's Bay with us," Dev said. She picked up Jess's hoodie. "If you enjoy technical work, it might be interesting for you." She smiled politely at him. "We always have a lot of that available."

Ryan licked his lips again and slowly sat back down on the seat. "Okay." He took a breath and released it. "But I can change my mind right?"

Jess snorted and resumed her seat then pulled her restraints on over her shoulders. "Buckle up everybody."

Dev took the shirt to the dryer, put it inside to start its cycle, and went to her seat. April shoved her blaster back into its holster, took the jump seat, and fastened the belt. "Freaking day."

"Yes," Dev said and started up the engines. "I can't quite decide if it was optimal or not."

"Me neither."

Dev pulled the comms onto her head and settled the ear

buds. "Flight, prepare to lift, and return to base."

Soft responses came back, and then, "Roger that, Rocket." Doug's voice was confident and louder. "You got April with ya?"

"Yes." Dev glanced to one side. "We have ten on board. I will try not to do anything unsettling." She powered the engines and sent the carrier skyward. "There's not enough seatbelts."

"Good," Doug said. "I ain't had lunch yet. That upside down stuff makes me upchuck on an empty stomach."

Dev grinned briefly at that, then glanced in the reflector, pleased to find Jess peering back, her hands folded over her stomach with its dry cloth covering. Jess winked at her, and she smiled back, setting course for home as the rest of the flight lifted around her and formed up.

It had been an interesting day. Interesting in a good way, she thought, and possibly in a future problem way, but she was glad they'd rescued the pilot, however reluctantly he was to be taken, and that the scrubs had their battle and would get their markers from the bin.

****

Dev only half listened to the chatter around her, focusing on flying the carrier through the rain across the dark, wet ground.

The already shadowed sky was deepening into a thicker gray, and she watched her scans carefully, checking the wind on even this short trip back to the Bay, traveling over flatlands as the elevation slowly built up into the ridges where Cooper's Rock was tucked.

Ahead of her she saw the faint lights from the mine, and turned on their running lights, casting a faint shadow along the ground ahead of them.

She tuned the scanners to sweep their path. Her eyes flicked casually to her boards then paused and changed a parameter. Then she repeated the scan. She absorbed the return, then in an instinctual motion reached over and activated shields. "Jess."

Jess was already coming forward to slam into the back of her chair. "What's up?"

"I am getting an energy return in the northeast quadrant there," Dev said, pointing. "High ion return, it's a large capacity engine."

Jess studied the screen. "Put that back to my station." She turned and went back to the gunner's seat. She slid into it and pulled her restraints on and snapped them into place. "Move in on it but watch out."

"Yes." Dev pulled her flight helmet onto her head one handed and tightened it, then opened the sideband channels to the rest of the flight they'd shut down for the short run home. "Flight flight," she stated her findings. "Sending metrics."

"Got it," Doug responded. "Bad guy?"

"Unknown."

"Got it."

Dev moved her seat up a bit and got her boots onto the side thrusters and felt her heartbeat speed up a little bit in anticipation. She expanded the scan and fed the results back to the gunner station, then kept on course as though nothing had happened.

High ion, it could be a generator. Could be something on the outskirts of Cooper's that powered working stations, or a remote mining facility.

The yonks were thrilled. They craned their necks to watch out the front screen, or in the case of those behind Jess, craned their necks to see her screens and what she was doing, eager to end the day with a little more action.

Dev spared a glance at their passenger, who looked surprisingly worried. The scan picked up the arms fire almost before it emitted, and she tightened the shields as it headed their way. "Incoming fire."

"Oh ho." Jess seemed more interested and delighted than upset. "Someone else wants to see what we got."

"Ho ho ho." Evan chortled softly.

The incoming blast hit their shields and was absorbed and gave her a chance to analyze it. "Jess, that's a class four energy beam," she said calmly. "Interforce frequencies."

"Even better." Jess pulled down her triggers. "Especially since they fired first."

April had spun in the jump seat and took possession of the secondary panels to her right. "She's right. That's a Caralon class hunter," she said, bright eyed. "They've got heavy weapons and carry a dozen tin cans."

"That was a warning shot," Jess said. "Keep on track, Dev- vie."

"Yes." Dev triangulated where the shot came from and adjusted her track to focus on that location. She changed trajectory and sent the change to the rest of the flight.

Comms crackled. Not unexpected. "Incoming vessel, acknowledge." An unfamiliar voice sounded on Interforce frequencies.

Dev glanced in the reflector and saw Jess nod.

"Hello," she responded cordially into comms. "How are you?" She added. "It's fortunate this craft is configured to repulse plus six power level energy beams, or we might not be having this conversation."

April shook her head and silently laughed.

The yonks didn't bother being silent. They all laughed and let out low hoots of approval. "Go, Rocket!" Kirin added.

"I would suggest you do not repeat the exercise," Dev added after a brief pause where there was just silence on the other end. "This is a Bantam class heavy carrier, and we are fully armed." She regarded the scan. "Jess they are lifting."

"I bet they are." Jess wiggled her fingers. "Let's see if anyone with brains is onboard, or if they're going to take us on."

"See other sigs," Doug said briefly. "Heading this way coming in west, very edge of the scan."

Jess glanced at April. "Wish you'd stayed in your bus. Anyone on there you trust to fire?"

April grimaced, her eyes sliding sideways in thought. "Didn't expect to need to on a ten-minute ride," she said. "They're all kinda wild seagulls." She pondered a moment more. "Maybe Jojo," she finally said. "He might not shoot us in the ass."

Dev flipped to sideband. "Flight two, this is Flight one, advise Jojo to take trigger."

"Roger t…" Doug started, interrupted by a howl of joy. "Would you just shut up and get in the chair! You shoot my partner I'm gonna boot you at altitude."

"Aw," April snickered. "He cares."

"Standby to maneuver, rest of flight," Dev said. "You will be performing evasive maneuvers unless otherwise instructed."

"Yes," the KayTees answered placidly. "We will try to distract vectors," Keko added.

"Excellent." Dev focused on the oncoming hunter and sped up a little, pointing their nose right at their opponent and preparing to maneuver. "Everyone please tighten restraints and hold on."

"Let's take out the one here," Jess said. "Before the rest of them show up." She got the firing systems down into position and curled her legs under her chair as she brought the carrier's armaments into targeting range.

"Hold on hold on," Ryan spoke up for the first time. "The hell you all doing? That's reg Interforce." He started to stand up but found himself grabbed and sat back down. "You going to go get killed, let me out."

"Stand by for engagement," Dev said quietly into comms.

"Siddown and hold on," Evan advised Ryan. "Don't matter who that is."

"Go for it, Dev." Jess ignored the slight tussle at her back and leaned forward a little. She flexed her hands as the carrier sped up and Dev went head on toward the rapidly closing hunter craft. It cut loose with a barrage and without warning the carrier swerved and slid sideways in the air, letting the blasts move past them as Jess's forward guns returned fire.

The hunter couldn't quite get out of the way fast enough and the blasts stitched along the side of it, shields holding but a moment later Dev brought them up and over the top of their opponent and around the other side, then turned the carrier in a tight circle and came in behind them, letting Jess hit them from three different angles.

The hunter tilted, swerved, and darted off, to bank in a circle and come back at them. Dev didn't wait for them to come head on. She went for the ground unexpectedly, the g forces slamming against everyone inside as she reached the rocky surface and pulled up to run barely a meter over it, as the hunter's blasts went right past her and shattered a pinnacle of rock into dust behind them,

She hauled up and applied power and the carrier shot briefly toward the clouds, until she cut power and hit her side thrusters, bringing them back around as Jess kept up a thumping barrage, her body shifting back and forth with the movement.

"Holy, shit," Ryan burped out, his face red from the pressure.

"Oooo, yeah." Evan was dancing in place.

"Run em down, Dev," Jess requested. "Let's see what they got for guts." She glanced forward. "See what we got for plasma, yeah?"

April was busy with the supplemental arms board. "We're good for about a half dozen," she said. "Put em right at the joint there, where the wings tack on, or if we can get under em, bottom of the nose."

"Stand by." Dev calmly plotted a course. "Bay flight, we are overshooting please stand clear," she told the sidebands.

"Rocket, we're all just hanging out here watching and

keeping an eye on that crowd coming in," Doug reported. "We're gonna go swing out to the west soon as you finish your show."

Dev took off after the hunter, who had screamed out over the hillside and was banking to come back after them. She hit the afterburners, and the carrier launched forward, moving right at the hunter, coming nose on to them and holding course.

It would only be ten seconds to impact. She focused intently on the craft, who boldly responded to this gambit and refused to yield.

Five seconds.

Dev's hands were steady on the controls, her boots firmly on the thruster pedals, her body utterly still as she counted down in her head, and the proximity alarms flared loud and insistently.

Three. Two.

And the hunter sheared off abruptly, flaring up and out, moving at the very last second out of her way.

Dev smiled, listening to the hoots and cheers from the troops behind her, then she flared her own engines and brought the carrier up and skimmed under the hunter, swerving her course, and almost slammed into them with the top of the carrier and it's blunt, ugly tail.

She got past them, then hit the retros and tipped sideways to expos the plasma vents on the bottom surface to the side of the hunter. In that second Jess fired.

"Energy disruption," April announced, in an almost pleasant tone. "Everyone grab your ass."

Dev kicked the engines in again and headed for the sky, moving out of the expanding plasma field and into clear air in an explosive arc, clearing the debris that ejected from the disintegrating hunter ship from the impact.

She did a barrel roll as she reached the top of the arc, just under the level of the clouds and came over the top. The yells of excitement turned into yelps of delight as they came into a brief null while she held them in a long parabola that would bring them back into alignment with the rest of the flight.

"Oh boy." April grimaced and held her breath. "That's not funny."

"My apologies," Dev told her. "It will just be a moment."

They took on G again and reached the flight, who was in formation near the ridge just shy of Cooper's Rock, and they arched into a turn that would bring them to intercept the oncoming targets.

Dev studied her screen. "Bantams. A newer generation."

"And?" Jess felt her body tense, her knees thumping the underside of her console as she wiggled them. "Bring it."

"We've only got two guns," April reminded her.

"We've got one Dev," Jess shot back. "That's all we need."

Dev made a face, as the yonks started chanting her name, dancing in their seats. She opened the comms panel to the Interforce channel the hunter had used. "Oncoming vessels. We were fired upon by that Caralon class hunter unprovoked. Please do not make the same mistake."

There was a moment of silence. "Ident," a stern, no nonsense female voice responded. "Who is this?"

Dev considered. "I am Biological Alternative, set 0202- 164812, instance NM-Dev-1," she said. "And this is a defense force flight from Drake's Bay."

Everyone in the carrier got a little quiet, the scrubs leaned forward to listen. Jess watched her boards, her fingers on the triggers, her forearms tense, allowing her instincts full control.

"Dev," Jess spoke quietly. "Tell the flight to turn on their weapons, and light up."

"Ack." Dev passed the request along.

"Dev, there is no one in the position," Kevin uttered back quietly.

"Pick someone and put them there," Dev responded just as quietly.

Along the line on either side of them as they flew forward Dev saw the firing lights come on, as they were already on for them, and for Doug's carrier.

"Tell them to turn around and leave. This is our territory now," Jess said.

"Ack." Dev changed the comms channel. "Oncoming flight, this area is under the protection of Drake's Bay. Please remove yourselves from this location." She paused in thought. "Do not return without communication to Drake's Bay operations control."

They flew toward each other in silence for another long minute as the comms channel just carried static. Then it cut off abruptly and became silent.

"That channel is no longer available to this comms," Dev said. "They have deauthorized the transmission."

Then the opposing flight lazily slowed, and arched to the north, turning with a casual, studied nonchalance and headed off as though they were just on a casual patrol and left the six

Drake's Bay carriers behind them.

April let out her breath. "Nice. Damn I'm glad they scampered off, the little bastards."

Jess glanced at her in surprise.

"Want to be on my guns when it happens again." April smiled at her. "Though that was an ace kill." She sighed happily. "That was fun." She looked at Dev. "Except for the floating."

"That was awesome," Evan chortled. "They ran off!"

"They'll be back," Jess said. "But not today. Devvie, get us headed back home." She leaned back in her seat and released her triggers. "Nice piece of flying, huh?" She looked casually over her shoulder at Ryan. "We don't care if they're Interforce." She indicated herself and April. "In case you haven't figured it out, we were Interforce. This carrier was."

Ryan stared at her. "I got it," he finally said. "But this is crazy."

"Heck ya." Kirin slapped him on the back. "This is crazy town, yo?" She danced a little, rocking back and forth. "We are the Bay!"

"We are the Bay!" The other yonks chorused.

Jess chuckled softly. "We are the Bay," she agreed. "Let's hope they remember that once those tin cans get back wherever they came from."

"Probably Picchu," April said. "They had that attitude. They'll be back."

"We'll be here." Jess rested her head against the high back of her chair. "Dev, reach out to Dee. Find out if they were here for a reason."

"Ack."

"That conclave's gonna be a thing." Jess put her hands behind her head. "If they wanted to know who we are, now they do." She exhaled. "Now everyone does."

"F'n yah," April assented. "F'n absolutely yah."

****

They reached home as the last light was fading. Dev was glad to cross the plane of the landing bay and have the rain stop slamming the top of the carrier as they entered the cavern and landed on their pad.

It felt good to hook up to Bay control, and transfer their logs, spooling their video of the encounter into the ops systems just as they would have at the Base. Dev was glad to see the now familiar scurry of mechs around the pad, as she opened the hatch to allow the fighters to exit.

Eager to share with the rest of them what it was like to be inside Rockstar, no doubt, while in a full-on air fight. These yonks, these six, would be the heroes on the mess, people fighting to sit next to them to hear all about it.

It was already starting; Dev could hear the yells from mechs as they hopped out.

Doug allowed them to exit then popped his head in. "Got some great vid of that mixup, Rocket!'"

Dev turned around and looked at him, an expression of mild exasperation visible.

April chortled, as she got up from the jump seat and made her way to the hatch. "Ace shot, Jess." She patted Jess's shoulder as she passed behind her and joined Doug at the hatch.

Then she turned and looked back. "What do you want to do with junior there?" She pointed at Ryan, who sat in his seat in silence as though hoping to avoid any notice.

Jess swirled her chair around and regarded him, watching him shiver in the chill wind coming in the hatch, and how he was biting his slightly blue lips. "Take him to house ops, get him something dry, then bring him with you to chow."

"Got it." April snapped her fingers. "C'mon, kid. No one's gonna kill ya," she said. "Yet."

Ryan slowly got up and moved over to where she stood, then hugged his arms across his chest. "Freezing here," he muttered, his eyes straying up to the pilot's station where Dev had just stood up, after finishing her tasks.

She'd turned and kneeled on her seat, resting her arms on the back of it. Her flight helmet was fastened to its holder on the side console. Her disordered hair from its confinement lent her a rakish appearance.

Ryan stared at her. "You really a rag doll?"

He was looking at Dev, so he didn't see Jess's expression change, but before she could even move, Doug stepped up onto the deck and punched him in the side of the head so hard he slammed against the back wall of the carrier and dropped onto the floor, blood exploding from his nose.

"Be glad a tech took you out for that, little man," April said, and let her clenched fists uncurl. "Don't talk crap here if you want to live to dinner."

Ryan wiped the back of his hand across his face, staring at his bloodstained hand.

Dev cleared her throat. "I have no actual idea what a rag

doll is, though I can assume it's a derogatory term for biological alternative," she said, in a mild tone. "Yes, I am. I was born from an egg in space, as were many of our other pilots."

"Didn't mean—" Ryan started to say.

"To be an asshole? Sure, you did," Doug said. "I know your kind." He reached across the deck, grabbed Ryan by the shirt, and yanked him onto his feet. "C'mon. Move it before you end up with a lot more than a broken snout."

He pulled him down the ramp. April winked at Jess and Dev. "Chivalry lives, huh?" She said, then whistled under her breath as she headed out toward the inner passage.

"Grr," Jess uttered. "Shoulda left him there."

"It's fine," Dev said. "I'm not offended. Really Jess."

"I am," Jess growled.

Dev got off her chair and came up to the gunner station and put her hand on Jess's shoulder. "We're programmed to ignore things like that from our first basic instruction sets," she reassured her. "It really doesn't bother me."

Jess took hold of her hand and, surprisingly, gently kissed it. "It bothers me," she rumbled under her breath. "Not you, really?"

"Really." Dev regarded her and smiled, then lifted her hand and touched Jess's cheek with her palm. "It does surprise me however that breaking someone's nasal passage seems to be a standard reaction of natural born to that."

Jess grinned briefly. "Yeah." She exhaled, then frowned. "You really wouldn't care if I said something like that to you?"

Dev reviewed that. "Yes, of course I would care," she said. "I care very much what you think and say about me." She stroked her thumb across Jess's cheekbone. "So, yes I would be very upset. But not about other people."

"Ah." Jess rested her head against the back of her seat, as they let the sounds of the landing cavern echo through the hatch around them.

"I get upset when you say things like that about you," Dev added. "So of course." She gently pushed the draggled still damp hair out of Jess's eyes. "Would you like a shower?"

"With you? Absolutely." Jess produced a charming smile. "Let's go do that." She unclipped her restraints and stood up. "And hey... can you do that space thing again?" She cleaned the boards with a swipe of her hand and stepped around behind her chair to join Dev at the ramp. "That was cool."

"Yes. But I think April did not care for it."

"Teach her not to come riding in my bus." Jess glanced

around at the still gathered crowd of fighters and mechs, all trading tales. They turned as she emerged and let out an echoing "Hai!", to which Jess lifted a hand in acknowledgement. "I wanna do that again."

Her other arm was draped over Dev's shoulders, and after a moment, Dev put her own arm around Jess's waist as they walked along toward the inner hall, bumping together as they got through the entrance and evaded the flood of wet, but happy, fighters flowing around them on their way out to the mess.

"Jess," Dev said as they reached the spiral stairs. "Cooper's Rock stated they were not aware of their presence in that area."

"Yeah?"

"I wonder what they were doing there then?"

Jess thought about that as they descended the steps, being jostled, and bumped by rambling mechs and fighters. "Good question," she finally said. "We should go find out tomorrow."

Dev nodded in satisfaction. "And, yes, we can try the parabolic arc again."

Jess snickered. "Awesome."

Chapter Twenty-one

The mess was raucous. It was packed nearly full, with Bay residents, family and bio alts. Even the head table was mostly filled, there being a half dozen administrative officers from nearby stake holds clustered around Dan Kurok's chair.

Jess was in her usual seat in the center, her back to the stone wall. Dev was at her right hand, with April and Mike Arias seated on her left side, their partners next to them.

Big Mike, which is what they had all started calling him, was on Dev's other side, with Brent. The whole side of the table was full of pilots and gunners, everyone talking about the fights.

Kurok was on the other side of the table with his guests. He interrupted right and left to ask for details on the action, clearly a little miffed he'd missed it.

The admin visitors were from Coopers, but also from three smaller fishing stakes north of them, and two shore collectors just to the south. All of them much smaller than the Bay, most of whom had been in casual trading relationship with them for years.

They would not be ones who made deals, they were too small to be of interest to anyone, but it seemed they felt they should tighten their ties with their neighbors, aware that together they were a more significant market.

Tables spread out from the head one had a thick mix of people. Grouped mostly by job, there was also now a more even mix in of bio alts, who were busy with their plates, the pilots in the afternoon's fights taking turns describing what had gone on.

Ryan was seated next to Doug, a bandage over his nose, a glum, wary, suspicious expression on this face as he examined the food someone had just put down in front of him.

"Interesting acquisition," Kurok said. He glanced at him, then at Jess. "Tomorrow I want to have a chat with the young man."

"Good idea," Jess said. "Got the feeling there's a story there."

"You think?" Kurok said, dryly.

Servers came around with the big stewpots in their worn, over the neck webbing supports, resting against a solid plas shield between the hot metal and the server's hip. "Lookout." The server waited for Jess to move aside then deposited two large ladles of fish stew in her bowl.

"Yum." Jess regarded it, as he moved on to serve Dev. "That's a lot of chunks."

The server grinned. "Good fishing. No krill today."

Dev inspected her portion, where there were quite a few of the circular, pink and white striped shrimps. She liked them better toasted and spicy, but these were good too, and she proceeded to dig into her meal with appreciation.

"A Caralon class?" Kurok said, as he listened to April's laconic report. "What the what?"

"Yeah," Jess said. "In the ridge valley just west of Cooper's. Dee said she didn't know they were there, but she wasn't really looking for them."

"We need scanners," Kurok muttered. "Damn it, how can they not see a Caralon? You picked it up." He frowned across the table. "And a carrier squad? How many?"

"Four," Doug answered, spearing out a big chunk of meaty fish. "Man, is that tuna?"

"Swordfish," Big Mike said. "Nice one."

"I think we can mount a relay on the north facing upper slope," Dev said. "There is a consistent water movement there that could power a regen battery." She consumed a shrimp, chewing contentedly. "But it appeared the vehicle was grounded, and they claimed to be looking for something."

"Besides trouble, which they found," Jess said. "What the hell was that? Just firing on us without any uptick? What kind of intel does that get you?"

"Interesting question," Kurok said. "What kind of intel did that get them? I'm sure they'd heard where their carriers had gone. We haven't been quiet about that. I'm sure they heard about the scrum at Dee's. So why were they there? No one needs to tell them what to expect from Drake's. They had ample experience with that not too long ago."

"That's what Dev was wondering. Looking for something?"

"Like those guys from Canyon," Big Mike said. "Lookin," He eyed Ryan, who was chewing on a shrimp. "What're they lookin for, kid?"

Ryan stared at him.

"You?"

The youngster snorted softly. "Nobody cares about me," he muttered. "I ain't nobody. Probably was lookin to get their rig back."

Kurok looked thoughtfully at him, then glanced at Jess. "I'd like to see this spot." He picked up a cup of Bay grog and drank from it. "Like to see why it's all of a sudden so interesting."

"Maybe they were looking to raid Dee. Get swag or ores. Figure if she starts dealing with us it'll be harder to get," Jess suggested. "Coopers has some of the best metal ore. Used to hear Base talk about it."

"Mm. It does." He drummed his fingers against the table surface. "That rings a bell. Let me go check my notes after dinner." He went back to his plate.

Dev knew his notes were all the intel he'd taken from station, from his own archives, and now, probably also from both Canyon City and the processing station. He had a massive datastore. She had permission to send queries into it. Very valuable. She'd added what she'd collected to it, a tiny percentage.

"Dev." Dev turned to find Kelson kneeling with one knee on the bench seat next to her. "I just wanted to tell you that we finished the exercise facility."

"Oh!" Dev put her spoon down. "That's excellent. So fast?"

Kelson smiled. "We had time today, so we all worked on it. I think it came out excellently. Will you come see it after the night meal?"

"Absolutely," Dev said. "I have a task after the meal, but then I will come over there."

He stood up and waved at her. "Later."

"Later."

"What's up?" Jess said and leaned closer to Dev. "What kind of trouble are ya getting into?" She offered Dev one of her shrimps, extending her hand over to have it touch Dev's lips.

Demurely, Dev took it in her teeth and then bit a piece off, removing the rest of it with her fingers. "Thank you," she said. "These are really good."

"Not as good as Jontons. We should go back there." Jess winked at her.

"I would enjoy that. But to answer your question, the exercise space is complete. I have been invited to participate this evening."

Jess nodded. "While we're beating each other senseless. Sounds like fun. You guys should make a swimming pool, like at base."

Dev stopped chewing and regarded her with deep interest. "A swimming pool?"

"Yeah, you know, like where you learned to swim." Jess half turned toward her. "They could make it warm. Remember? I bet you could do that."

"I think there isn't space in that location," Dev said, with true regret. "But I will try to find a place that could be possible." She sighed "I haven't finished making my workspace floor warm yet."

"We gotta do that." Jess was now totally focused on her and ignored the looks of the others around the table. "Have all this crap stop happening for a few days."

It was such a warm, nice feeling having that serious regard in Jess's eyes fastened on her. Dev smiled gently back, then made a wry face. "We get involved in a lot."

"We do." Jess reached over and tousled her hair. "We'll find some time."

It felt excellent. Dev suspected her face reflected that because Jess's body posture shifted, and her shoulders relaxed as she leaned against the wall. She leaned back as well, and extended her legs out under the table, crossing them at the ankles.

Meals were a fast event at the Bay. There was no time wasted in consuming the edibles, and no lingering around either. When the last round was passed out—in this case, jellied sea grapes—everyone would drain their mugs and move along to finish out their day.

Also, a difference. After dinner at base, people usually were free to spend their time as they wished. At the Bay, people usually had a nighttime event to move along to, either some organized recreation or a gathering, or in their case, to the scrapping and scrums they would shortly be heading off to join.

It wasn't their daily work, it was something other, and Dev considered that as she watched the chilled sweet be passed out. "Is that what was used in the party items at base?"

"The eyeballs?" Jess watched the items be doled out. "Yep."

"Mm."

"They don't draw veins on these though. Just ice em down." Jess picked up one of the roundish objects and popped it in her mouth. "They part thaw them, so you crunch through ice to get to the goo."

"Mm." Dev picked up one of the cold balls and inspected it, then put it in her mouth and bit down, experiencing the expected mild explosion of liquid contents, sweet and gelatinous as the flavor filled her mouth.

They weren't unpleasant. They tasted much like sea grape tea, only they were cold and rather refreshing after the hot soup and hot fish stew. She decided in this new context, she liked them. She picked up a second.

"Like em?"

"I do," Dev said, and bit into it.

April leaned over. "Hey, Jess. I hear rock climbing is on the agenda for our scrap."

Jess gave her a thumbs up.

Dev peered at her. "I would not like to attempt bringing our carrier into that exercise area if that is being contemplated as well."

"I'm sure ya could." April regarded her innocently.

"Not with its engines and tail attached and that would probably defeat the purpose."

****

Dev walked along the new inner hallways, the overhead lights tuned from a bright yellow halon of day to the half brightness of evening, the Bay's concession to adapting to the time. She was wearing her newly acquired sleeveless exercise shirt, and she rubbed her arms against the chill. She looked forward to getting to the new space where it would be warmer.

"Hey, Dev." Kevin came out of a side corridor coming from the direction of ops and joined her. "Oh, that shirt is excellent."

"Yes, though better inside the space I think." Dev rubbed her arms again as they moved into the long parallel corridor that would lead to the new exit into the back space. "I forgot I had to walk over there."

Kevin grinned. "Yes, that's true. Maybe we could have a space there to keep our exercise wear in. Like on station, a locker."

"Base had that," Dev said. "But you didn't have your own articles. They provided one for your exercise, and you put it into a cleaning bin when you were finished."

He nodded, then glanced sideways. "Oh, you have some of the marks," he said. "May I see them?"

Dev held her arm up and extended it, twisting the limb to display the burns. "Yes, for my missions with Jess," she said. "The one on top was my first mission, very soon after I came from station."

Thus invited, Kevin peered closely at the marks. "That seems like it would have been painful."

"It was," Dev said. "Painful to achieve, and also for some time after."

"Was this required?"

Dev glanced at him. "Do you mean, did I have to do this thing? No." She shook her head slightly. "Techs were not required to do it, but I wanted to."

"To achieve a positive status?" Kevin asked. As the first of us to do what you did, that was probably optimal.

They walked along in silence for a minute, and then Dev smiled. "No, not really," she said. "My performance of the work had already achieved a positive status at that time. I just wanted to do it for Jess."

"She saw value in it," Kevin suggested.

"Yes," Dev answered thoughtfully. "And I saw value in her knowing the level of my commitment went further than my assignment."

Kevin nodded. "Like when we defended the children in the fight. We did not have to."

"Yes," Dev said. "The natural born call it having skin in the game, though I have no idea what that actually means."

"Lots of suboptimal language variants," Kevin said.

"Yes," she said. "But anyway, the burn healed quickly. There is a medicine for it. But I am glad Jess has said we would do something else here."

"These were far less painful." Kevin touched his ear and nodded in agreement. "And they are visible."

"Yes. And we can change and add to this decoration with different items," Dev said. "Or add a second ring. That will both be more attractive and less painful as well."

"Excellent," Kevin said. "Do you think today's activity will require a new decoration? I think you should get one in any case, for your excellent flying."

"Hm." Dev pondered that. "Everyone did very well. They accommodated some unusual requests and performed with excellence. I will consider what we can do. "I am sure those who participated in the fighting will also want to mark their success."

Kevin nodded. "They want to learn how to jump on the outside of our vehicles now." he added wryly. "I have investigated. We do not have programming on that."

Dev sighed. "I will have to consider that the next time I contemplate that sort of activity."

"We all want to practice assisting the natural born in boarding the craft at altitude," Kevin said. "Though Keko thinks we should try with bags of sand first."

"That could be an excellent idea." Dev smiled as they went out the back entrance and into the now covered space between the main stake hold and the rock caverns on the far side.

Overhead they heard the rain come down hard, and the rush of water as the downpour was captured and funneled into the fresh water supply tanks below ground.

The Bay maintained massive osmosis tanks of course, and converted sea water at need, extracting the minerals and salt and producing water for showers and operational use, but the residents preferred to drink rainwater, and this new catchment provided a clean, frequent resupply of it.

A win win, Jess had said, since the runoff had been used, but had to run through a few cycles of purification first due to crossing the rock ground where this just ran right into newly laid and extruded pipes.

The ground was now planed flat, roughly finished and dry. There were already projects and newly laid out works in progress flanking the offloading ramp that led up into stores, and with the overhead lights just connected the previous day there were clumps of techs and mechs gathered around them.

They crossed the space, and went to the right-hand side set of cavern entrances, where there was already a small gathering of sets as well, dressed in variations of clothing they could use to exercise in.

"This should be excellent," Kevin said, as they approached and returned the waved greetings.

"Definitely," Dev agreed. "And presumably I will not be asked to fly a vehicle into the space."

Kevin gave her an alarmed, sideways glance.

"That was a joke," Dev reassured him. "I am not contemplating that."

"Was it funny?"

"It was to me."

****

Jess stretched her body out and bounced up and down a little on the balls of her feet, looking forward to the mixup.

To her left was the casement of old knives, it's top open, the scent of oil rising from it plainly detectable to her. She rubbed her fingertips together and felt the residue of it from her just completed delivery of tokens to her successful force of the day.

The space was packed. April sauntered over to stand next to Jess. She held one of the old knives in her hand.

"Hey," April said. "Did you realize this thing has a hollow space in the hilt?"

Jess turned and regarded it. "Does it?" She asked in surprise. "What the hell for?"

With a quick twist of her hands, April separated a section of the hilt. "Hold your hands out."

Jess did so, and then April dumped something from inside the hilt into her palms. "What the what?"

"Zactly what I said. Doug found it when he was messing with mine."

Jess moved a little bit into better light and examined the items. "Huh." She separated them, finding a fishhook and some line, in good condition, along with a small compass, a bundle of wax covered sticks, and a long piece of metal with a second piece attached to it.

Jess held up the fishhook. "I get what this is for. Not useful to me, but maybe to someone else." She grinned saucily. "I don't waste my time fishing above the water."

"Compass I guess might be useful," April said. "That's a flint and striker. No idea what you'd set on fire, maybe dried seaweed. My mater had one, from back in the day."

"Back in the day when there were things to burn," Jess said. "Batt pack would be more useful now. But it's sorta cool they thought of stuff like this." She unwrapped the wax paper. "Oh." A memory stirred. "Matches. My dad showed me some once."

"Yeah?"

"They took pieces of wood and put phosphorus on them for starting things on fire."

"That's wood?" April's eyes opened wide. "For real?"

"For real." Jess handed the items back. "They were fixated on setting things on fire back in the day. I guess. But there ya go. A bit of priceless history with your stabby. Go spread that around to the yonks. They'll love it."

"Heard that." April moved back toward the nearest group of fighters.

Jess chuckled softly under her breath, savoring the sense of well-being she felt as she looked around at the filled space, and thought about the day's successes.

She half turned and looked at one of the platforms they'd built near the wall of the cavern and put her hands on her hips as she studied it. Then she nodded. "Yo!" She yelled and got the attention she'd expected as everyone turned and looked at her.

"Yo!" A group of the yonks yelled back. "Drake!"

Jess chuckled. "Wall climbing," she said. "Not hard."

She dropped her arms and loped toward the wall with long, easy strides as they scattered to get out of the way.

She sped up as she reached the craggy, arched surface. At the last moment she leaped up and took hold on the uneven surface, her fingertips finding cracks and fissures with easy skill. She got a foothold on a crag and pulled herself upward continuously in a slanted path upward.

A bit more difficult due to its extreme vertical surface, than the cliffside had been earlier in the day, but Jess was up for it. She felt a sense of excitement and pleasure as she got higher on the wall.

She reached the top of the slant, fifty feet off the ground and then abruptly turned and kicked away from the wall into free fall. She spread her arms out and her body arched around toward the top of the gunner platform thirty feet below.

She tucked her arms and legs inward and got her hands and feet downward, and then landed on the platform, just as she had on the top of the carrier. She flexed her knees and elbows to absorb the impact and then pushed back up to her feet.

She walking to the edge of the platform and spread her arms out palms up. "S'easy."

Every eye was on her. Jess enjoyed the moment. She flexed her hands and swung down off the platform, hanging on the edge of it by her fingertips and then let go to drop to the ground, again letting her knees take the brunt of the drop before she stood up.

Dustin stood at the base of the platform. "Whoa, cuz, that's crazy awesome!"

Jess indicated the wall. "G'wan and try it," she said. "Go slow. Worst you can do is fall on the sand." She motioned them all forward and went toward the wall. "C'mon."

Mike Arias stood next to April. "There is no freaking way."

"We climbed in school."

He laughed. "Not like that. We climbed reg walls, ropes, stuff you were meant to climb. Not like that."

April started forward. "If those yonks can learn it, we can. We might need scaling grips though. C'mon, squid."

"Don't call me a squid, ya landie!"

****

"Okay!" Jess rolled to her feet, feeling a very pleasant sensation of a body well used. "That's it for today."

"Woot!" Kirin got up from the sand, covered in it, some of it sticking to the cut on her arm that had been broken open by the scrum. "Good one."

"Sweet," Duncan said. He was one of the older scrubs. One of the Drakes, a cousin of a cousin. He dusted his work pants off, his hair a tangle of sweat soaked dark chestnut brown. "Rockin day, rocking night. I'm gonna go take a dive in the Bay."

"Oh yeah!" A chorus went up and the word passed across the big hall.

"You up for that, Drake?" Evan asked, carefully strapping his knife to his boot. "Feel good after that scrum."

Jess drew a breath, then paused when she spotted Dev's slight figure next to April, her blond hair mussed. "Nah. You go on." She waved them out. "I got other ideas. Next time."

She shook the sand out of her clothes and headed toward the edge of the pit. She climbed the stone steps up onto the viewing platform.

Dev turned her head and smiled as she approached. "Hello."

"Hey, Devvie." Jess regarded her. "You been having fun?" She straightened out the sleeveless hoodie. "That looks good on ya."

"Thank you," Dev said. "Yes. We were trying out the new exercise space. It turned out excellent. The sets wanted me to tell you they really appreciate your support in obtaining it."

"Me and Mike are gonna get a little of that action," April said. "That okay?"

Dev blinked. "Of course. Everyone is welcome to use the constructions if they wish."

"If they fit, ya mean." Jess rested her elbow on Dev's shoulder. "That was a good idea. Not everyone here's a gargoyle. "Wanna go take a shower?"

"Absolutely," Dev said at once. "We were in discussion about how to pipe water into that location to allow rinsing off." She paused and glanced at Jess sideways. "And heat it."

Jess chortled softly. "We could just go out in the rain."

"We could do that," Dev responded in that mild, noncommittal tone that indicated unspoken lack of enthusiasm for the suggestion.

Doug appeared at April's elbow. "Hey!" He had a length of cloth around his neck. "Those guys did great on that new gym."

"You been there already?" April asked. "What the what?"

"C'mon and see!" Doug said.

"Hey, I'm up for it." Mike Arias nudged him. "Lead on, c'mon Ches. Let's see what they came up with. Can't scrap all the time."

"Why not?" April asked. "That climbing's a decent workout."

"Ha ha."

They trooped off toward the door that exited to the newly covered gap.

Suddenly, it was quiet. Jess looked around. The fighters had all headed off to the Bay, everyone else had moved on to see the new gym. She and Dev were left alone in the huge scrum pit, it's lights glaring, the sand surface utterly disarranged.

Someone would have to come through and rake it back into order. There were ridges and hummocks that would cause havoc to anyone using it, and one large depression where the last scrum had landed, everyone clawing and digging for the rugger ball, sending sand flying in every direction.

Jess had ended up with the ball and curled her body around it making a cage of her arms and legs. She'd resisted all efforts to untangle her from it and had some of that sand firmly lodged in her hair and clothing.

It felt like it was a lifetime ago when she'd worried about them playing rugger. Worried she, or April or Mike would lose it and break someone's neck, or back in a flare of the moment, the zone taking over.

Why had she been so worried? She took a deep breath and released it. "Good day."

"Yes, I think so, too," Dev said waiting at her side in stolid patience. "I was thinking about an activity token." She looked up at Jess in question. "I think they did really well."

"I think you did really well and deserve whatever token you want," Jess said. "They all did what they were told." She shook the sand out of her shirt and motioned for the exit. "They're your kids, Devvie. You can do what ya want, but I would save the sparklies for when they produce. Y'know?"

"Hm." Dev walked alongside her as they headed for the door. "I suppose I was used to getting tokens for our activities."

"You did mind blowing things on all of our activities," Jess said, placidly. "I figure it's fine to give the scrubs a knife when they see action the first time, makes sense. Don't make your sparklies too cheap."

Dev thought about that as they moved out of the exit and into the covered space. "That's very wise, Jess."

Jess chuckled.

"No, really, it is," Dev said. "We want to excel, because that's how we're made, but if we reward people for just doing what they're supposed to it's not special."

"Yeah. Like me making Mike one of us. He did something." Jess said.

They crossed what was now the wide, long loading cavern with its metal roof, the rain still pounding down on it. Most of the projects had completed work for the night, and the various platforms and areas were clear of people, quiet and still.

There were a few still active, new work surfaces and trestles being shaped, bits of metal and beaten up plas being planed into shape and fastened together. They passed one of the gangs of workers and Jess paused to look at the results.

The foreman of the group glanced aside and saw her. "Yo, Drake."

The name made all the workers look up and around, their hands with their worn, battered tools fell to their sides.

"Yo," Jess returned the greeting. "Sup?" She indicated the work.

"New cribs," the woman answered. "Back in the back, that new side." She indicated the set of cliffs to the right-hand side. "Greg figured we'd have more bunkers, ya?"

Jess regarded the tables and work surfaces. "Need more scrap."

The woman nodded. "Maybe we can go grab some from your old crib?" She gave Jess a brief grin. "Heard that's full of what the what."

Jess wiggled her eyebrows thoughtfully. "Might," she said. "Maybe we can take apart North. Lots of crap there to recycle."

"Yo." The foreman lifted her hand. "Later."

"Later." Jess moved on, and they walked up the long ramp to the big cargo doors.

"The place at the North Pole had some interesting mate-rial," Dev said, after they'd both been quiet for a while. "Those square containers might be useful."

"You really want to spend time up in the white?" They walked through the cargo corridors, that branched off on either side, to the huge storing elevators along walkways that had been chipped and beaten by loaders for generations.

The walls showed it. Even the ceiling had gouges, and the loading lifters staged along the hall were equally as banged up.

They emerged into the central hall, vast and half lit, a focus beam outlining the iron spiral stairs that curled up one wall that lead to the upper levels of the homestead. Levels four and five were still bustling, bio alts moving around and third shift preparing to go to their workstations.

Above them in the storing levels it was dark and quiet, and at the very top of the hall, the plas roundel showed brief and regular flashes of lightning that revealed the gray solid of the nighttime sky overhead.

As they crossed the wide space, a chill draft came up from docking cavern level, on it the sound of shouts and laughter, and the rich smell of the sea.

Jess detoured. "Let's see what the scrubs are up to."

Dev kept pace with her and wished that she'd remembered to pick up a jacket as the cold air hit her bare arms and ruffled her hair. "What is it that they are they doing?"

"Plunging." Jess led the way down the ramp to sea level, and the corridors that bordered the offloading docks for the smaller boats. Here the walls still showed some damage from the Interforce attack, but all the rubble had been long cleared, and they walked along a pounded smooth floor that held wet boot prints freshly laid.

It smelled strongly of the sea, seaweed, and fish. A deep briny scent you could feel entering your nose and taste on the back of your tongue. Dev felt it brush against her senses with a feeling of pleasure at its rich texture. She reached out to touch the chill rock walls and remembered that time she'd found Jess here, covered in blood.

The utter relief in that reunion. She still remembered how that embrace felt, vivid and so very intense. The smell of the docking cavern brought that all back once again.

They emerged into the cavern and Jess pointed at the sea level entrance, wide enough for a small fishing vessel, or a carrier in a hurry if the pilot was very, very good to enter. "Over there." She indicated a path along the entryway that curled around and let you go to the very edge of the Bay. The water rushed in and sloshed along the walls and past it, a curtain of rainfall in the dim halon reflection from the night lights.

It was uncomfortably cold. Dev resisted the urge to shiver and followed Jess to the edge of the entryway, and looked past her, out into the rainswept Bay, erratically lit by lightning across the wide breadth of its huge expanse.

There, to the right-hand side of the entrance was a rock platform, somewhat narrow and perilously sloped. On it were the scrubs, who leaped from the platform into the dark water, all of them completely stripped of their clothing.

The lightning showed pale skins and vigorous motion as they swam in the chop, then returned to the platform and jumped in again.

Jess had paused before exiting, just short of the rain curtain. She turned and looked at Dev, then belatedly took a step back and pulled her own shirt over her head and wrapped it around her. "Here. Keep you from becoming a popsicle. Just want to wave for a minute."

"Thank you," Dev managed to get that out without chattering, as the fabric covered her and brought warmth and the scent of Jess's body to surround her. "That seems like excellent exercise," she added politely, indicating the scrubs. "I think?"

"It's lunacy." Jess stepped out into the rain and let it hit her with ferocious intensity. "But it feels kinda good."

She walked along the ridge as the icy cold deluge pummeled her body. It did feel good. She breathed in the wet and the brine and raised a hand as she was spotted, and they yelled her name.

She opened her mouth and stuck her tongue out, the icy rain spattered onto it as she swallowed the water in its heavy drops.

"C'mon in, cuz!" Dustin had just climbed up out of the water onto the ridge, his hair plastered back. He straightened up as the lightning flared again and outlined his brawny, naked form. "S'good!" He indicated the Bay.

Jess lowered her arms and put her hands on her hips and stood there, enjoying the rinse. "Next time," she said, "Just wanted to show Devvie what the plunging was." She rubbed the rainwater down her arms and ran her fingers through her hair, appreciating the chill against her scalp as it removed the sweat. "But yeah, s'good."

Dustin turned and took two running steps and leaped out, turning a somersault before he hit the surface of the water. The area in front of the platform was full of bodies in motion, flip- ping and swirling in the choppy seas.

"Not all damn night people!" Jess waved, then made her way back over to where Dev waited. "Crazy, huh?"

"Not at all." Dev took a step back to allow her to move past. "I would like to try it in fact if I could use my suit. It seems quite calm for swimming and less likely to causes bruises from the waves," she said. She offered Jess her shirt back but was waved off. "And it appears to be fun."

"Take your fun where ya find it. Let's go find some in our shower." Jess ran her hands through her hair again, then flicked the water off her fingers. "It does feel good." She admitted. "Cool down after all that rugger and the climbing insanity."

She walked back along the path and then paused, as there was motion ahead. From instinct she stepped to her right and blocked the way. Water dripped off her tall body as her hands came up a little bit near her hips, fingers flexed.

But it was a group of bio alts, sensibly dressed in coveralls and sweaters. They carried a large metal box, and behind them, a further group with a portable drink dispenser and a folding metal table.

"Hello," the one in the lead said. "It's Agent Jess, and NM- Dev-1," he said to the group behind him. "We are at our location, please prepare."

The group paused, and in a curve of the path they set up the table. The two carrying the drink dispenser stood by waiting as the ones with the larger box set it down next to the table and moved to help unfold the big, unwieldy surface.

"Hello, Abe," Dev said cordially. "What is the task here?" She eased past Jess, who was more than willing to let her do the talking now. "Hello, Alvin."

"Hello, Dev." Alvin put the dispenser he'd helped to carry on the table. "We thought the people who are outside swimming in the water would like some towels, and a hot drink when they finish."

"That's excellent," Dev said. "I am positive they're going to enjoy that a lot." These were the AyeBees, and CeeTees. They had the domestic programming track.

"Yes," Alvin agreed. "We saw them go by when we were finishing up our shift, so we decided to bring these things down. Would you like some beverage? It's sea grape tea," he offered.

"Thank you, we have some in our housing," Dev said. "It smells very good." She lifted the cover on the larger floor box and peered inside. "This is warm."

"Yes, we thought a heated enclosure would be excellent for this," Abe said. He reached inside and picked up one of the folded pieces of fabric and offered it to Jess. "Would you like one, Agent Jess?"

Jess took the warm towel that was soft against her fingertips. "Wow." She unfolded it and instead of using it she draped it over Dev's shoulders and wrapped it around her. "Whatcha think?"

Dev smiled in delight. "I think that feels excellent," She said, immediately, as the warmth of the towel surrounded her in a really very nice way. "But I am not wet. Perhaps you should use it?"

Jess smiled at her. "I'm fine. I'm just gonna go get wet again."

A final set of CeeTees arrived. They carried a tray of fish rolls. They set them down on the table as well.

"Good job, guys," Jess said. "Probably the nicest thing anyone's ever done for those yonks." She patted Alvin on the head and moved past. "C'mon, Devvie. Hopefully we got some of those rolls up in our crib."

"Hopefully," Dev said, and gave the bio alts a wave as she hurried to catch up with her half naked partner. "That really was nice."

Jess chuckled. "Those yonks will have no idea what to do with a warm towel and a cup of tea. They'll probably pass out."

"Suboptimal?"

"Nah, it's fine. It's good for em." Jess chuckled again.

Dev felt a bit torn between wanting to remain and observe, and the urge to get out of the cold, and into their housing. Comfort won out. She made a mental note to ask Alvin in the morning what the reception had been and trotted with Jess up the steps, clutching her cooling towel around her.

****

Dev glanced up at the plas window in her workspace and regarded the fierce weather outside with some sense of appreciation. The wind was so ferocious it was blowing the rain sideways, and the flight conditions were extremely suboptimal.

That meant she was free to work on her tech projects. There would be no flying out to reconnoiter today, at least until the weather eased. Met had said possibly by the evening.

Or possibly not.

She went back to the large logic board on her table and reached up to adjust the light to beam down onto the surface of it.

Jess was in the living space, she could hear her moving around near her little office. Small bangs and thunks indicated she was doing something to alter some facet of their habitat that would surely be pleasing and useful for them.

She used her tracing tool to heat, and then remove, a section of circuitry. She paused again when she heard the soft chime of the service door behind her.

She put the tool down and moved to the delivery space and put her hand on the lock, which obediently turned teal green for her and unlocked the door. "Hello," she said, as the panel slid open and a AyeBee appeared.

"Good morning, Dev." The AyeBee had a cart with resupply on it. "How are you?"

"Very well, thank you." Dev stepped back to let him move the cart forward. His name was Alan, and he was one of the sets who had come from the base. "And you?"

"Excellent, thank you." Alan pushed the cart past her into the storage space. "A trading caravan arrived, and we just finished stocking. I brought up some things here I thought you might like."

Jess appeared without warning and leaned against the doorway. "What do we have here?" She wore her hoodie and a pair of soft fabric leggings, that neatly fit her long legs, and bright blue foot coverings. Dev thought she looked extremely cute.

"Hello," Alan greeted her.

Jess slid around the corner of the door and prowled the cart. She lifted the boxes and containers with interest. Dev walked over to the storage closet just outside and picked up her scanner. She brought it back and ran a scan on the contents.

Alan nodded on seeing that. "We checked this before we brought it up, but it's best to be sure."

"Always best to be sure," Dev agreed. "I did not know we were expecting a trading party."

"We didn't know either. It was a surprise. The cargo master thinks it was due to the weather. The trader was glad to be out of it, and under our new covering."

"Figures." Jess put the container down. "What'd they trade for? Some of the doc's stuff?"

"I do not know," Alan said. "They had a lot of material. They were offloading for a good amount of time."

"Interesting," Jess said.

"Interesting," Dev echoed. "This seems optimal." She put the scanner around her shoulder. "Excellent timing. Doctor Dan said he had some plants that were ready to harvest."

"Yes, he was summoned to the caravan," Alan said. "He seemed pleased."

"Good sign," Jess said. "I'm gonna go back to building a table. See ya." She disappeared back into the inner hallway, while Dev slid her scanner around to her back and moved forward to help Alan unload the cart.

"Were you with the group that was in the docking cavern last night?" Dev asked, as she carried a box of what smelled like sea grape tea leaves to the storage shelves.

"I was, yes. I came a bit late though. The natural born seemed very pleased with the service. Abe was very happy with the result."

Dev smiled. "I thought they would enjoy that. Jess seemed to indicate it would be a novel experience for them."

"Yes," Alan said. "It resulted in an amount of sex practice," he added in a mild tone. "Which was unexpected, but pleasant."

Dev paused and looked back over her shoulder at him. "Really. That's interesting."

He nodded. "Very." He grinned and his eyes twinkled. "It's excellent you instructed us about that."

"Well." Dev came back over and picked up another box. "Sex practice is excellent, that's a fact." She grinned back. "Not exactly expected for a towel and a drink."

He shrugged and kept grinning. "Natural born," he said. "There's no explaining them, but I think it was optimal for everyone based on what was said after the activity was complete."

"Indeed," Dev mused. "In-deed."

****

Dan Kurok was seated in his lab, a cup of steaming hot tea at his elbow as he reviewed the wide, curved screen facing him.

His back was to the wall, so he had a good view of the door to the lab, the desk positioned so that he could see past it into the hallway beyond.

To his left was the big plas window to the Bay, currently awash with rain, the downpour so thick he could hardly see past it. On one hand, it put a damper on some activities. On the other, it put a damper on other activities and let day to day chores progress.

All good. He scanned the operations report.

"Doctor Dan?"

He glanced up at the comms. "Yes?"

"This is Bay ops comms, the relay device at Cooper's Rock has been activated."

"Ah." Kurok switched screens and called up a second input. "Is that on Delta six twenty?"

"Yes, Doctor Dan."

The probe relay was a three-hundred-and-sixty-degree sensor tied into a point-to-point link between the top of the ridge of Cooper's Rock and the top of the back ridge for Drake's Bay. It extended their scanning view out further than where the fight had taken place the day before.

Having that scan made him feel better. "Excellent," he responded into comms. "Add this into the rotation please."

"Of course," the young bio alt voice said. "Thank you, Doctor Dan."

He closed the comms and reviewed the scan results again.

He saw nothing much except rain and more rain, washing down the side of the mountain and onto the flatlands beyond. The sensor picked up the sound of mining and heavy machinery in motion, weather not preventing the work going on there to continue.

He leaned over to comms again. "Kirk?"

"Yes, Doctor Dan," Kirk responded immediately.

"Please call Cooper's Rock and let them know we're getting signal."

"Yes, Doctor," Kirk said. "Jensen did that after we saw the signal come up. They were pleased to hear the device was functional."

"I'm sure they were." Kurok grinned briefly at the screen, then shut down comms again. Jensen was the natural born watch commander, young and new at his post, and accordingly conscientious. Kirk was as well, a KayTee who moved into operations when Kevin took on his new piloting role.

Movement and opportunity. Never-ending delight for the bio alts, who were given the opportunity to achieve new skill sets, and the shift of ops workers to the fighting cadre was doing the same for some of the natural born.

Win all round. He studied the screen in front of him, where one window showed the long form listing the new slots he prepared for the fighters to be submitted.

Two hundred, with board and housing and an allotment, and a small addendum for completed missions, based on the eventual value of the contracts he expected to be spun up at the conclave in a few days.

He had one, already, with Cooper's and a signed agreement with their visiting neighbors done the day before. Small, and not enough to cover the slots, but it was a start. He scrolled idly down the list. A start, and something they would need to do, regardless of contracts.

The defense would be needed, especially now that Jess had gone head-to-head with her former employers and told them to keep clear. Kurok could only imagine the reaction at Interforce HQ.

"Hi."

Kurok glanced over his screen at the doorway. "Good morning, Jerad," he said, cordially. "What can I do for you?" He waved him forward. "How are things?"

Jerad entered and came over to the two stools that served as visitor's chairs here in the lab. He sat down on one and scooted a bit closer. "You really don't need much med here," he said bluntly and without preamble. "You got midwives to handle the kid work, and most of the rest get stuff that can be handled by those two or three people you got who can apply a band aid."

"True," Kurok said. "They're a healthy lot, and I designed the sets that way. Nice really. Saves time and effort." He rested his elbows on the desk and waited, assuming there was more forthcoming.

"Right." Jerad nodded. "So, I'm kinda bored."

"Are you now." Kurok regarded him. "How can I help? I've got lots of things I could suggest for someone with a background like yours. Or we can give you a ride west if you'd like that."

Jerad shook his head. "Nah, I like it here. What I'd like is to do some work on the plant side. I did that as a credited secondary going through med training and liked it. Got some ideas for stuff to maybe try out in the hothouse." He paused and waited for a reaction, one brow lifted.

"Absolutely." Kurok sat back in some slight surprise. "Matter of fact I need someone in there to push the new things. The sets can do all the upkeep you want, but they don't have enough programming to initiate."

Jerad nodded. "Yeah, saw that. The people here too, they don't know much about any of that," he said.

"No one does, really." Kurok smiled briefly. "Except refugees from science stations," he added. "And I don't really have time to teach everyone scientific theory and problem solving. I can't give that in programming. It's a synaptic growth artifact."

"Dev's got it," Jerad said. He eyed Kurok shrewdly.

Kurok smiled. "Yes, well. Dev is quite a different story." He tilted his head to one side and thought a moment. "If you come up with a value crop, you know, you get a percentage," he said. "That's how it works on that side of the house. I like to reward clever ideas."

Jerad smiled. "I was hoping you'd say that." He leaned back on the stool, visibly relieved. "I like a useful occupation, and one that gives me spending money more the better." He exhaled. "But I'll throw in a bandage if anyone needs one."

"Then by all means," Kurok agreed readily. "I'd welcome any work you'd like to do in that area, and I'll add it to the slot you're occupying."

Jerad stood up and adjusted the sleeve on the pullover he was wearing. "S'what I was lookin for."

"Glad I could help." Kurok chuckled, then looked up past him as motion caught his attention at the door. "Yes, Cathy?"

"Hello, Doctor." His assistant entered, dressed in a work jumpsuit, a pair of gloves tucked in her belt. "Excuse me." She paused and started to back up. "I didn't realize you were speaking with someone."

"Oh no, we're done," Jerad said. "Thanks, Doc, let you know if I cook up anything useful." He sauntered out and nodded his head in respect to Cathy as he went past. "Morning."

Kurok took a sip of his tea as Cathy crossed the room and took Jerad's place on the stool. "Sometimes I don't mind a day of rain," he said. "Lets you catch up on things." He hiked one knee up. "Now, how can I help you, Cathy?"

"Thank you, Doctor." Cathy smiled at him. "It's just a question."

"Yes?"

"Can you clarify for me what a registration is, in regard to sexual activity?"

"Ah."

****

"They what?" Jess paused in mid motion, the top surface of the table held in both hands. "They jumped in the sack with them?" Her voice lifted in interested surprise. "Really?"

Dev puzzled at that statement while she watched Jess place the top on the new piece of useful furniture. "I think they probably used a sleeping surface," she said. "A sack would seem constrictive. As well as not entirely comfortable."

Jess straightened up and folded her arms. "Huh." She seemed intrigued. "Bet that was interesting."

"Well, the sets enjoyed it," Dev said, in a mild tone. "But they do enjoy sex practice, so that is not surprising."

"Sure," Jess said. "They're people." Her eyes twinkled a little. "People enjoy that."

Dev smiled. "Yes they do."

Jess paused. "But the boys can't make kids right?" She asked with a slight hesitation. "You said once that was a thing."

Dev nodded. "Yes. There is a biological block that inhibits procreation," she said, without any sign of embarrassment. "Female bio alts do not ovulate; males do not produce sperm. We do have the functional structure, but it is dormant."

"Can the doc change that?"

Dev's pale brows lifted. "I have no idea," she said. "Do you want him to?" She studied Jess's face, which had an expression of perplexed pensiveness. "Given the broad range of biologic response to gene combination it's possible the physiological differences between natural born here and bio alts might also be problematical."

Jess frowned. "Huh?"

"The sets might not be physically able to bear offspring carrying the size range of the natural born here."

"Oh. Right." Jess chewed the inside of her lip. "I thought maybe the doc could make a cooking chamber like you all had up on station."

"He could," Dev said. "It takes a lot of tech, space and mechanical structure." She eyed Jess. "Would you want him to do this?" She asked curiously.

Jess exhaled. "Well, the issue we have around here is lack of spirals." She sat down on the surface of the table she'd just finished assembling. "Bios have spirals." She cocked her head to one side. "Really nice, cute, good spirals."

"Oh." Dev sat down on a nearby plas stool. "Most of the time no one wants to have much to do with bio alts in that regard. I don't think I ever thought about it that way," she said, scratching the side of her nose. "I don't think any of us has."

"Uh huh."

Dev propped her elbow on her knee and rested her chin on her fist. "Interesting," she concluded.

"Freak you out?"

Dev considered that thoughtfully. "Not at all, because duplication of our genetic material is a given with us. We just never considered it valuable for natural born." She looked up at Jess. "Or that natural born would want to make use of the genetic material."

The new table or desk or whatever it was Jess was building was tall enough for her to swing her legs when she was seated on it and she did now, clasping her hands between her knees in an oddly adolescent posture. "They give us a choice at school. Turn that off when we get to that age or leave it alone."

"Really?"

Jess nodded. "I had em turn it off. Never figured I'd need it, just a pain in the ass."

Dev's pale brows contracted a little.

"Figured I'd get splatted before I aged out," Jess said. "Active inservice doesn't get to spawn and I'm not really into pups."

"Ah." Dev mulled that over. "I remember you did not seem to care for the nursery in the creche." She paused and glanced at Jess. "Do you want to procreate now?"

"Nope." Jess vigorously shook her head back and forth.

"Even if Doctor Dan could construct a lab for it?"

"This is a weird conversation."

"Well…"

"I started it," Jess admitted sheepishly. "Teach me to keep my yap shut."

"It's an interesting idea," Dev responded straightforwardly. "But we should really consult Doctor Dan. He knows a lot more about it, after all. I think also that some of the other residents here might have asked him about it."

"Yeah." Jess stood up. "Bet he's got it all planned out." She put her hands in her pockets. "Those guys all okay with that stuff?" She asked, after a brief hesitation. "Sacking out? That doesn't freak them?"

"Oh, no, of course not." Dev shook her head. "Once Doctor Dan said it was all right, they seemed quite happy about it," she added. "As I would expect them to be, given my experience in that area."

Jess grinned.

"Anyway." Dev stood up. "Let me finish working on my project. There was a substance on our vehicle that came from the place we were that might be useful for my floor."

"Yeah?" Jess joined her. "What did we bring back except rain?" She bumped Dev toward the door. "Show me."

"Your relative brought it up here."

"Hope it's not seagull crap."

"It's not, unless those animals exclusively consume nonorganic minerals and excrete them."

"Ya never know, with seagulls."

Chapter Twenty-two

It was evening before the storm finally moved inland and away from the Bay.

Dev could see the sky now outside. The clouds were lighter gray rather than dark. She stood at her work desk and finished up the prototype she'd constructed from the material Dustin had brought her.

It was an interesting substance. Thick and dense and some- what sticky when wet, which it had been when caked all over their landing skids, but after it was shaped out and dried, it seemed like it would be in fact very useful.

She looked at the square, ochre block that had resulted under the powerful light, and tapped it with her fingertips. It sounded solid, yet there was an echo to it, the mold around it formed it into a neat square and the top surface roughened with particulate.

It was called clay, she'd discovered, and this clay had the metallic material they'd found in the rocks of the escarpment embedded in it. She clamped on two probes to either end and set up her scanner. Her ears pricked up a little as she heard the outer door slide open.

There was no chime, so that would be Jess returning. Dev smiled in reaction as she observed the scan results, pleased with the conductivity of the material and considered it a good possibility for the covering of her workspace floor.

It would take collecting, and several trips to find enough of it to do the job, but she was pleased with the progress. It would provide a flooring over the metal grid that now covered it. This would distribute generated heat across the surface and make it very comfortable to stand on.

Which would be excellent, and meant she'd be able to wear light clothing inside to work on her projects.

"Hey, Devvie." Jess slid around the corner and came inside. "How's your gig?" She ambled over to the workspace and looked over Dev's shoulders. "Hey, that looks good." She studied the mold.

"Yes, it's a tile," Dev said. She stepped to the side so Jess could get a better look. "I think it's going to be excellent." She tapped the surface again. "I think it will look very attractive as well."

"Little scrub did good." Jess put her hand flat on the

surface. "Not slippery either," she said. "Nice."

"Yes, it has particulate in the material. It dries rough," Dev said. "And it's conductive, so I can pass current through it and produce warmth."

Jess wrapped her arms around Dev. "I can think of a dozen spots in this icebox that'd love one of these. You'll get a bonus for it," she said casually. "Bet the Doc'd like his lab done, and the place where they spend all day with the plant stuff. Kids were wearing earmuffs in there."

Dev glanced up at her. "I made this for my location. Anyone else is welcome to take advantage of it."

"Nope. You built it, my scrub cousin found the mud. Take the cred, Devvie. You earned it. C'mon, this is good stuff."

Dev turned and put her arms around Jess and gave her a hug. "Okay. Whatever that is I will share with you, in any case, so that's fine. And I am confident that your relative will enjoy whatever benefit comes from it as well."

"Yeah." Jess pondered that thoughtfully. "Somewhere in all that scrubbiness there's some Drake in him. Maybe we give him his crib, yeah? Think he'd like that?"

"Absolutely."

Jess chuckled. "Let's go get some grub." She gave her another brief hug and released her. "We have target practice tonight and my ears are already ringing thinking of it."

"I will obtain some protective devices," Dev said. "Or we could observe from inside our carrier. That would possibly be safer."

Jess kissed her. "And more private."

"That as well."

****

Dev changed out of her work coverall for a clean pullover sweater, soft and warm against her skin, tucked into a pair of the sturdy work pants and her casual boots.

She glanced at her reflection and ran a comb through her hair, sorting it into orderly waves, then folded her sleeves up one turn so they didn't cover her hands. It would be warm enough for the walk through the hall to the mess.

By the time she emerged into their larger living room the skies outside had darkened into dusk. Jess had gone around and adjusted the inside lights to a golden glow, seemingly convinced that doing so made the inside of their domicile warmer.

It didn't. But Dev appreciated the thought and walked over

to stand in the center of the living space to watch her approach; her tall figure encased in its hoodie with its pocket in the front and her hands tucked into.

She had run a brush through her hair and pulled it back into a tail, tied with a piece of string. And she was smiling to herself, which made Dev wonder what she was thinking about.

They walked down the steps and across the wide hall, joining the flood of people heading for the mess in summons to the bell sound that was ringing off the walls.

Jess casually scanned the crowds as they moved along in the flow of bodies moving into the mess hall. "I think I smell that spicy soup you like, Devvie."

Dev amiably followed Jess through the scrum, tangling her fingers in the back fabric of Jess's hoodie as her partner plowed her way through the line toward the table at the side of the hall that they usually sat at.

Three quarters of the way there they moved out of the throngs of people sorting themselves out in seats and had a clear space to walk. They joined the half dozen people already gathered there and preparing to sit down.

Kurok was there, with his assistant Cathy, and a stranger who was apparently from the trading caravan. April stood next to him in wary conversation, and as they came up, so did Doug and both Mike and Big Mike and Chester.

The big hall was filled with noise, voices and echoes off the stone floors, the rounded ceiling and the walls. A rumbling din very different from either the ops mess at Interforce, or the quiet purposefulness of the creche.

Dev had gotten used to it. She sat at Jess's side and tucked her boots under the worn mid height plas seat and accepted a battered mug from the tray being held out from one of the night servers. "Thank you."

"Yo," the server acknowledged and moved on, A big Bay resident took his place with a plas tank strapped to his back with a hose hanging over his shoulder. He extended a hand and triggered a flow of beverage into the mug, and by the smell it was fermented seaweed beer.

It was cold and refreshing. Dev took a sip and enjoyed the spicy tang on the back of her throat, as a tray of bowls were distributed with the dented metal spoons that meant Jess's prediction of soup an accurate one.

The table conversation seemed cordial. Even April seemed relaxed as she spoke with the trader sitting next to her, and Kurok interjected with introductions to the rest of their companions.

Dev looked past him and spotted the boy they'd rescued the day before. He was seated with Brent at the end of the table. He looked wary but less disgruntled, and she wondered what Doctor Dan had found out with his interview of him.

She watched him in her peripheral vision as he cautiously took a sip of the beer. She felt there was something about him that was not exactly optimal. Was it his attitude? What he'd said to her? She saw him look carefully around from behind his mug.

There was something. Dev turned her attention to her bowl that was being filled to the brim with a golden red liquid filled with edibles, emitting that enicing spice filled smell. She made a note to ask Doctor Dan after the night meal what he thought.

Because there was something.

****

After night meal was finished, the greater crowd dispersed to their evening activities. The noise of the group slowly faded into the tunnels and up the steel stairs, work boots scraping against the metal and hands sliding up the bannisters.

As mild thunder rolled overhead, Jess, Dev and the rest of their gang moved from their table into the family chamber on the first level of the hall.

The gathering room, with its tall walls, its Drake crest, and the litany of family member names up both sides of the warming stone had taken on a more cheerful cast now, with colorful banners hung around and additional casements against the walls.

Kurok wanted to show off some new tea possibilities, and so Alvin was there, expertly working with the tray, the dried leaves, and hot water, as they settled in the long, surprisingly comfortable pieces of furniture that were scattered about the room.

It was pleasant in there, and with the heating plate on, nicely warm. Dev was happy to take a seat at the end of one of the benches and lean back, as all the residents in the family area came in, talking casually.

"Busy week," Kurok said, as he dropped into the seat across from her. "And tomorrow promises our little shindig with the rest of our fellow Eastern Atlantia residents."

Jess picked up two cups of the steaming hot beverage Alvin was portioning out and walked over to where Dev was seated. She handed her one and sat next to her.

"Thank you," Dev said.

"You figure they're gonna give us a hard time?" Jess examined the cup, which had a golden colored liquid inside it with a brisk, tangy smell. "What is this?" She asked after a brief pause.

"Try it first," Kurok said, and accepted his cup from Alvin. "Then I'll tell you."

Jess eyed him over the rim of the cup, one dark eyebrow hiking up. But she picked up the drink and took a wary sip, then licked her lips. "That's…" She paused and looked at Dev, who drank hers without comment. "Different. You like it?"

"I do," Dev said. "I think it smells really nice."

Kurok chuckled. "Dev's had this," he said. "It's mint." He swirled a mouthful around and swallowed it. "I have a box of it to take with us tomorrow in case someone needs a sweetener."

Jess drank the liquid slowly. It had an almost sharp taste to it, and the smell was a little sweet and very pleasant. "It's nice," she said. "Kinda tangy."

"The herbs are doing well," Kurok said. "Even with us splitting off that whole section for the kitchens here, we've got plenty and they grow fast. I sent a small crate up to Quebec City to Jonton. Waiting to see what he thinks."

April entered and came over near the heat plate and sat on the floor cross legged. "Caravan's settled," she said. "Harrison likes that new cover, tell ya what." She extended her legs and crossed them at the ankles. "Said they'd set up a little market tomorrow before they move on, heard they had some folks here interested in some trade. I figure we'll see more of them now."

"Good," Kurok said. "I'm glad they like the shelter. That word'll get around and do us nothing but good." He cleared his throat. "Now, as to the stakeholder's conclave, that will be interesting."

"Interesting, good or bad?" Doug said from his sprawl at the other end of the bench. "What is it, afternoon tomorrow?"

"Mm," Kurok said. "From what ops said, they can see transports on the move toward the meeting place. Should be quite a crowd." He looked over at Jess. "We should probably bring a presence."

Jess smiled. "Yeah," she said. "Last time it was just me and Devvie. We'll bring a crowd. Ten busses loaded." She sipped the remainder of the cooling tea. "Might give out two of those projectile rifles to yonks in each of em."

"Long as they don't let those things loose inside the bus," April said. "Let's do a contest tonight and only give em to the winners."

Kurok nodded. "Yes, I think that's a good idea. Put on a show for anyone who still has a doubt. And in case anyone gets any funny ideas."

"If they do, everyone'll get their stickers," Big Mike said. "Finish out that big ass crate n'we can use it for stores."

"Mech's want it," Doug said. "Want to do a mech kit for each wrench bay. With spares and stuff." He glanced over at Jess. "Speaking of, we should make a trip back to the old shoe- box and grab whatever's left there."

"Spares?"

Doug nodded. "They can fab off the mods, but it's easier if they can mold blanks first."

"We should go see what's the what there," April said. "Make sure no one's making trouble." She thought a moment. "Maybe put one of Rocket's reflectors on the top of that ridge, and one on top of North."

Big Mike nodded approvingly. "Extend the watch. That'd be good. That Cooper's relay's ace."

"Ace," April repeated.

"We should put more up," Big Mike said. "Mark our patch."

Kurok swirled his tea in its cup. "Well, let's revisit that tomorrow night after the conclave. Might change what we consider our patch to be." He smiled briefly. "Or not. It's always possible our little displays scared our neighbors more than encouraged them."

Big Mike chuckled. "True that," he said wryly. "Don't take much to scare em, some of em."

"Could go either way." Jess leaned back and stretched her arm out along the support of the bench, behind Dev's head. "Guess we'll find out."

"F'ck em," April said. "Don't matter. We need the troops anyhow."

"Yes," Kurok said. "That had occurred to me as well. No matter what our neighbors do, we're on our own and we must be able to, as Big Mike said, hold our patch."

"If anyone can, it's us," Doug said confidently. "I think they'll pay to play."

Dev was content to listen and enjoy the bright taste of the mint tea as it lingered on her tongue. She extended her legs and crossed her ankles, pondering on what tasks she could get done before the conclave tomorrow.

A thought occurred to her. "Jess."

"Yeees?" Jess angled her head to one side and turned half sideways. She turned her cup in her fingers idly around in a circle. "Sup?"

"I would like to obtain more of that clay substance. Can we take the transport to that location in the morning?"

"Sure," Jess responded.

"What are you after, Rocket?" Doug asked.

Dev explained. "This substance, when dried and hardened, would make a useful floor covering. The conductive properties are excellent."

"Oh ho." Kurok listened with interest. "Dare I think a heated floor is in our future?" He asked. "That would be a prize indeed, Dev, especially if we're going to think about putting a creche in here." He drew the words out, with a twinkle in his eye and a smile. "Which it seems we are."

Everyone focused on him with sudden interest. "We are?" Doug asked, in some surprise.

Kurok cleared his throat. "Well. If we want to build a population here, there are only certain ways to accomplish that, and the fact is, I've had at least four people come talk to me today about whether the sets could participate in the process."

Jess's dark brows shot up.

Big Mike nodded. "Peeps been asking 'bout that since they got here."

"That's true," Kurok said. "There's more asking now. I was going over their charts to see what the potential would be if I were, let's say, to make some changes to allow them to."

"You could?" April asked.

"Oh yes." Kurok smiled at her. "We put the block in. I can take it out. It's not even that complicated. The issue is that many of our sets are not functionally constructed to bear children, as they were never intended to," he said. "It's not that they can't, but there are certain things you can do, genetically, to make it easier and we never did that."

"Huh."

"And actually, those born to the Bay are not really that great at that either. It's very difficult for them to get and remain pregnant," Kurok said. "My conclusion was, if it were something we would want to entertain, then the safest way for everyone would be to do it with a birth lab."

"Huh," April repeated.

"What's that going to take?" Mike Arias asked, his arms folded over his chest. "That's a lot of gear, I guess?"

"A lot of gear, most of which is restricted, stupendously expensive, and only licensed to be sold to the bio stations," Kurok said. "So, a bit difficult, yes. But not impossible." He took another sip of tea and watched them over the rim of his cup. "Especially when you have trade which interests everyone involved."

"Well," Doug said, thoughtfully. "We could steal a shuttle again and go up to that station and yank it down here for ya." He looked over at Dev, who regarded him with hiked eyebrows. "Rocket could do it."

Everyone was thoughtfully silent.

"Excuse me," Dev spoke up. "You are not actually suggesting we deorbit a space station and make it crash downside are you? I would suspect much of the gear in question would not survive that."

"Nor the people either," Doug said. "But we could do it."

"Non optimal," Dev said. "Extremely non optimal."

Kurok chuckled. "He's joking, I hope. Anyway, let's see what this conclave turns out to be. You never know, it could open some possibilities. There's not much off the table with Interforce's withdrawal."

"I was joking about pulling it down," Doug said. "But we went up there once. "I bet Rocket could rig up one of these buses to go there."

"Excuse me?" Dev said again, a bit louder this time. "I could not without space engines."

"We could find some, right? Must be a junkyard somewhere with old shuttles."

Jess chuckled. "I think the Doc means is we can find a way to get what we want by having something they want to trade us for." She looked at Dev. "Let's hold off stealing a space shuttle until we try that route."

Everyone chuckled.

"Besides," Dev said. "It was not I who initially took over a space shuttle." She looked over at Doug and April.

"Leave me out of this," April said. "I'll stay here and guard the pineapples. You can go float around up there and barf."

"But space was fuuuun," Jess whispered for Dev's ears only. "I liked it."

"You just liked the null." Dev relaxed, reassured she was not going to be asked in the short term to either fly a full grav carrier to space or participate in the theft of a space vehicle. "We were discussing in our new gym the possibility of building a gravity space."

"Really?" Jess's ears and eyebrows hiked up and her voice took on a tone of amazed delight. "That'd be awesome, Dev!"

Dev looked at her wryly. "I'll put it on my list of tasks."

Jess chuckled. "Okay, well, we've got target practice," she addressed the group. "Let's go see if we've got anyone we can trust a rifle with." She got up and shook herself. "Damn we have a lot of stuff to do."

April got up to join her. "List is getting longer every minute we're sitting here. Good stuff here, Doc." She lifted the cup. "I remember some other ground stuff my mater got hold of once." She stopped and thought. "Cimmanim?"

"Cinnamon," Kurok said. "It's a bark, so it'll take a bit longer, but it'll come." He held his cup up. "Alvin could I trouble you for refill?" He asked as the rest started to file out.

"Of course, Doctor Dan." Alvin started to work.

"And a cup for yourself as well," Kurok added, as the room quieted down. "Since I know you picked and dried those leaves."

Alvin smiled. "Yes, I did!" He poured the hot water expertly. "Getting a birth lab here is very exciting," he said. "Are you also going to produce more of our sets?"

Kurok regarded him thoughtfully. "Am I." He pondered, his eyes going to the wall on either side of the heating plate, and those lines of names carved into the rock there. "I have all your genetic profiles. I could."

Alvin nodded, and brought over the teapot, setting it on the table next to him, allowing it to steep. "The natural born here seem to want everyone to be individual," he said. "I wondered if that would be good or even expected."

"They do, that's true lad," Kurok said. "It would be easier to do it that way. But you know, I think it would be wrong. I think if we want to combine the genes of both the natural born here, and you sets, it should be very individual."

He watched Alvin smile, a real one, not the polite one they were all taught, but a big grin with some heart behind it. 'You like that idea."

"Yes."

"Me too." Kurok produced his own gentle smile. "And I'm actually arrogant enough to believe I could take that nightmare of a genome here and maybe make it into something amazing," he added in a musing tone. "But let's see if we can get even a portable bio lab first, hm?" He chuckled. "Start small."

"We are not going to go retrieve station?" Alvin asked, as he poured out two cups of the tea. "That was a joke, right?"

Kurok laughed. "Oh yes. Doug likes to tease Dev, you know, by proposing these crazy things for her to do, but he's not serious." He lifted his tea in a slight toast. "Come, let's celebrate all the good things that are getting done."

Alvin picked up his cup and lifted it in mimicry, then took a sip. "All the good things!"

****

Dev pushed the sweat soaked hair back from her forehead and took a step back. She cleared the platform and moved to the edge of the sandy floor in the gym.

She felt pleasantly tired, happy to have gotten in good work on the somewhat crude, simple machines they'd built that were sized for them, and could be adjusted to add tension and allow for more activity.

The gym was full of bio alts, and a handful of natural born, all a smaller stature than what was the norm at the Bay. All taking advantage of the new space. Aside from the machines, there were open floor spaces for wrestling, and a set of bars and beams to swing and balance on.

Tonight, she'd done a round of all of them, glad of the sleeveless garment and the light leg coverings that were made of the same material and from the same source, fisherman's underlays.

She looked around, mourning the one lacking item, a shower to clean off before changing back into her heavier clothing. It would feel good, and she spared a moment of envy for the fighters the previous night splashing in the rain and the Bay, clearing the sweat and sand off their skins.

She felt a bit sticky, even despite the light fabric and her lack of sleeves. She could almost imagine what it might be like to dive into the Bay and enjoy it, except she knew she wouldn't. The shower in their habitation was much more appealing.

However.

This side of the rock escarpment that faced the Bay had no piping or water facility supply yet. It had some roughly run power inputs, but even those were very limited. They were enough to run the halons in the corners of the exercise chamber, and the simple mech for the equipment.

The caves on that side had mostly been used for random storage of things the Bay didn't really care about, some partially exposed to the weather, or to the scavengers who would creep inside and shelter there.

Their new space, in fact, had been a shelter. They'd found debris in the sand of the floor that were left behind by the scourers, bits of shaped rock and small pieces of cloth accidentally left behind. The small bones of fish, and birds.

Meagre and bleak. Many of them had died in both the fight and before, when Jess had obliterated a group of them grown desperate enough to try to get back what they'd been promised. Now, she'd been told, many of them had traveled up the coast to Base 10.

Ironic and interesting. Dev felt that April was right, that they should pay a visit to that facility, and see what was transpiring.

A cold breeze crossed through the space from the inner entry to the outer. Dev walked along the wall to the crooked opening and squeezed out into the gap.

Near the entry and ramp to the Bay the vendor caravan was parked, and she heard faint laughter and see lights from its transports that served as both cargo and living space for the traders.

Along the other side there were dozens and dozens of Bay residents with old style projectile rifles, loaded with metal slugs firing at random pieces of metal and boxes, marked with haphazard circles.

There was laughter from there too, and the sound of the projectiles striking the targets, or in some cases flying past and slamming into the huge metal doors she'd lifted into place. It made loud and clanging noises that were random and startling,

She spotted Jess there against the opposite wall as she watched the activity. Dev leaned back to observe a moment, noting that Jess almost immediately swung her head around and looked right at her, making her smile. She lifted one hand in a little wave.

"Oh, Dev, there you are."

Dev turned to find Kevin emerge from the space, his hair disheveled and his shirt torn a little along the sleeve. "Hello."

"This new space is excellent," he said. "Everyone is very pleased about it."

"I as well," Dev said. "I was just evaluating the possibilities of bringing in a water source." She looked up at the curved metal surface. "Perhaps we can split off one of the rain catchments and bring it down into the chamber in front of that one."

"To rinse off?" Kevin nodded in agreement. "I would like that."

Dev shook out the front of her sleeveless hoodie that sent sand in all directions. "Yes, I would as well." She glanced up at him and saw him look past her over her shoulder. His eyes widened and he took a step back. She felt sure if she turned around

Jess would be coming her way.

She turned around, and a few body lengths away, there she was, walking with that little bounce to her motion that Dev found charming. Her shirt was darkened with sweat, and what Dev concluded was blood. She spread her arms wide as she approached as though she were about to fly.

There was something always just barely contained about Jess. Dev grinned. "Hello. How is the target practice going?"

"Devvvie!" Jess launched herself into a handstand as she arrived and walked the last few paces on her hands, then let her boots thump against the wall Dev was leaning against. "Not as bad as I was afraid it would."

Dev looked at her upside-down partner. "That's… optimal?" She glanced over at where Kevin had been standing, to find he'd vanished back inside the cave. Then she sat down on the ground, as Jess crossed her ankles and flexed her arms. "Is that blood on your shirt?"

"Yup," Jess said. "Kicked Big Mike in the nose."

Dev winced little. "I see. It wasn't something he said, was it?"

Jess chuckled, her happy little snicker. "Didn't do it on purpose," she said. "We were mixing it up and he got in my way. How's your gig inside?"

"Excellent." Dev said immediately. "I really like the space. I was just trying to sort out how to put a shower in."

"You don't like ours?"

"I love ours. I just would like to rinse off after I finish, like we could at the Base."

"Or go swimming," Jess mused. "Yeah, I miss that pool, and surfing. We could go dive in the Bay."

"If I could stop for my suit, I would enjoy that."

Jess turned her head, and her face creased into a faint grin. "You would not." She tipped her boots up and out and gracefully turned in midair then ended up seated next to Dev. "Got twenty-five scrubs we can hand a gun to and not worry about being shot by em."

"Excellent."

Jess sighed. "We really need to get plasma guns. This stuff's just for bs show." She leaned against the wall, her shoulder pressed against Dev's. "Everyone knows we don't have crap for ammo, and there's no point in trying to make it."

Dev pondered that. "With their sticks and those knives, I think they are quite formidable, Jess. I was observing the vid of the fight earlier. It did not seem that the guards they were fighting had any advantage due to their energy weapons."

"Hm." Jess grunted softly. "Problem with that is, they need to be in close, and there's a good chance they're gonna get mowed down if whoever they're running at gets their act together. Those guys yesterday just had no clue what to do," she said. "But they're gonna figure it out and the next time they hit our scrubs with a wide spectrum energy beam they can't just wiggle past."

"I see."

"But not today." Jess bumped her gently. "Wanna go clean off in our nice warm shower?"

"Yes." Dev laid her cheek against Jess arm. "That would be very pleasant."

"Lets' go." Jess got to her feet and offered Dev a hand up. She kept hold of it as they turned and walked across the huge open space, leaving the sound of slugs hitting metal and laughter behind them.

Dev was glad to get inside the door to their housing. She followed Jess across the living space and into the far corridors, past the food storage area to where their closets were and the shower facility.

Jess peeled off her shirt and tossed it into a utilitarian bin they used for needing to be cleaned clothes. "Never gonna get that blood out," she said. "S'allright I guess. Bloodstains scare whoever you're mixing with."

Dev stepped into the shower area and turned on the water, blinking as the blast of water filled the space, and quickly warmed it. She moved back and took off her clothing, folding it neatly and putting it down to be tossed in the bin later.

She glanced at her reflection in the mirror and grinned briefly at the utterly disheveled hair from her exercise as Jess came in behind her, likewise naked.

The smell of the shower water filled the space, and they stepped inside to be drenched by the pleasantly warm liquid. "Ah." Jess spread her arms out and tipped her head back. "Damn nice not to worry about banging my head in here."

Dev glanced upward, squinting into the wash of water that emitted from across the roof of the shower. It was, in fact, several feet over Jess's head and considerably over her own, and there were spouts from side to side and forward to back in a thick curtain. "It's a very pleasant shower."

Jess grabbed two pieces of sea sponge and doused them in the slightly spicy smelling body cleanser and handed one over to Dev. "Good day."

"I think so." Dev scrubbed herself down, glad to be rid of the sand from the workout space. Then she reached out and rubbed the breadth of Jess's shoulders, in that spot that it was difficult to do on your own, as the shower filled with the smell of the soap.

Dev remembered bringing some of it with her, up to station, a thought that now made her smile at her earlier worried self. "Jess."

"Yeees?"

"This mark on your back seems much better." Dev washed around the scar from the knife wound Jess had gotten from her former pilot in a terrible betrayal. The mark had faded, and the ridged, tense skin had eased and smoothed out under her touch. "Will it go completely away?"

Jess looked over her at Dev. "What... that scar the asshole gave me?" Her dark brows knitted together. "No." She reached around to feel the place, then grunted. "I never look at it. Feels okay. Haven't been shot at in a few months, maybe that helped."

She put a blob of soap in her hair and scrubbed it. "I realized something this morning. No rad here," she said. "I don't feel like I need it. Maybe it's the air or the clam stew or something."

"Hm." Dev washed her own hair. "I hadn't thought about it."

"See?" Jess rinsed the soap off and turned around. "There is rad here. No one uses it. I found one of the rigs when I was scarfing around for junk. Had old boxes stored in it." She let the dousing shower rinse the soap out. "What the hell? We always had it at school, and at the base." She turned and looked at Dev and spread her hands out in a shrug.

"We should ask Doctor Dan," Dev replied. "He would probably know."

"Did we need it?"

Dev thought about that, until Jess's hand touched her cheek, and they moved closer, and she set it aside to ponder some other time. It was interesting, but not as interesting as that touch, and the warmth of their bodies coming together.

She felt a pulse of passionate energy raise her breathing and a deep prickle in her guts in anticipation of a very satisfactory way to end their long and hectic day.

****

The large open plateau had a lot more people and vehicles on it than the last time they'd been there. Dev brought in a tight scan and distributed it back to Jess's screen, as she looked right and left at the flight of carriers spread out in a wedge around her.

"Someone threw a party," Jess said. "And we were invited this time. Nice."

Behind her, squeezed into every space available, were ten fighters, watching bright eyed out the wide plas screen in front of Dev.

Dustin was in the jump seat next to Dev. "Oh man," He muttered under his breath. "S'big."

"Crazy," Kirin added softly. "Lookit that."

The last time there had been perhaps a dozen flyers scattered around the big, weather-stained rock building. Now, all around the structure, and for quite a distance around it were trading caravans, overland transports from further away homesteads, and dozens of light flyers on the landing field on the far side of the space.

They had ten carriers in flight, plus Bay A. Dev studied the potential spots to land, as she slowed her forward motion. The rest of the flight did the same. There was no space on the landing field. Most of the craft that had already landed there were scattered from each other, guards around them, tiny but distinct.

Behind the building was a rugged upthrust of stone, leaving a small stretch of relatively flat surface that would take a sharp angle and rapid deceleration to land in. Dev put the path into comp and sent it to the flight. "Suboptimal," she said.

"That they didn't leave us space to land?" Jess leaned back in her chair, hands folded over her stomach. "They didn't think we'd bring a crowd," she said. "Or they didn't figure you were flying in here."

Dev glanced up into the reflector, expecting and finding Jess looking back at her, with that mischievous grin. Solemnly, she stuck the tip of her tongue out, then went back to plotting their landing.

"Jackass," Kirin said. "Should land on top of their asses."

Dev cleared her throat. "There is insufficient skid space on top of anyone's anatomy." She triggered the route. "We will land in front of that ridge," she said. "It will require a sharp turn."

Jess nodded in satisfaction. "Scare the crap out of em, Devvie. Boomerang off the damn thing and roll in on top of the ramp there." She bounced the heels of her boots on the deck of the carrier. "But that's cool if they've got some traders there. Guys at the Bay didn't have much this morning."

"Didn't expect customers," Kirin said, shortly. "Snobby screwballs. Thought nobody had cred."

"Boof. Well, we didn't, yeah?" Evan, seated next to her, snorted. "Think they gave their stuff up for those plant things," he said. "We'll get em next time. I heard the guys talking." He bounced his knees up and down. "Maybe by then we'll have a lil cred."

"That'd be sweet." Dustin sighed, from his seat up front.

Jess let her head rest against the padded back of her seat. "We'll get there," she said.

"Please hold on," Dev announced mildly. "We are going to maneuver to descend and land."

Hands went to grip the steel supports and stanchions. Dustin twisted around in the jump seat and braced his boots against the front of Jess's console, wriggling his shoulders against the thinly padded bench. "Here we go."

Dev tapped the throttles, and they surged ahead as she took the lead. The flight formed up behind her and she headed for the ridge, losing altitude in a sharp angle. Around her she heard the rumble of engines as they swept over the top of the meeting place.

Surely, they would be hearing that inside.

Dev smiled and transmitted a path code and then took the carrier down to the deck in a sweeping curve, losing speed and heading for the ground in a rush, her landing skids extending out and the jets cutting in just in time to bring the craft to a halt within its own length from the massive entry stairs.

Jess chuckled. "Hope the rest of them can do that, Devvie, or we're gonna be in a pileup."

"I developed a guidance profile and transmitted it," Dev said, in an absent tone as she secured the carrier and started shutting down systems. "I think they should be fine."

The flight landed behind her, in a respectable, if not perfect pattern as they evaded the rubble on the ground and settled on their skids, flight beacons flashing. They were a little askew, and two of them bounced a bit, but still.

"Well done," Kurok said placidly over comms. "Excellent," Dev echoed to the pilots on Bay frequencies. "Very well executed."

Bay A had come to rest next to them, and now its hatch opened to allow Kurok to climb out, along with Kelson who'd piloted the plane, and Brandon from Bay operations, Kurok's administrative right hand, with a small metal box.

A moment later Douglas, the tall Bay guard, emerged, with a much larger box in his hands. He transferred it to his shoulder as he cleared Bay A's hatch.

Jess unhooked her restraints and stood up. "Okay. Let's go." She hit the hatch release, and the carrier twitched as it lifted and folded up, and the egress ramp deployed. "Out." She gestured to the troops, who rambled out the door and thumped down the ramp to the rock ground.

Then she turned and waited, as Dev closed her station and gathered her scanner. "Are we to wait out here, Jess?" She asked.

Jess walked over and picked up the shark skin jacket draped over the seat and held it for her as Dev got into it with a smile. "Hell no. We're here to make a show, aren't we?"

"The sets will be pleased" Dev said. "They appreciate being included."

"They are part of the gig, right? Can't drop scrubs without the drivers." Jess responded in a practical tone. "Just like I can't do crap without you."

Dev didn't really think that was at all true, but she smiled at the compliment and fastened her jacket, glad of its warmth as the cold wind pushed through the open hatch and brought the scent of off gassing and stone.

Jess guided her out the hatch and down to the ground where scrubs poured out of carriers all around them. "Ready?" She asked Dan Kurok, who had joined them.

Kurok chuckled wryly. "No idea really," he said. "And yet, here we are. Let's go bring the chaos to the table and find out."

April and Mike came over. "This looks like a carnival," April said bluntly. "You want us to go topside again and put eyeballs out?" She looked around. "Got a half dozen nomad trains around, it's gonna end up with blood all over the floor."

Jess thought a moment. "Good idea," she said. "You go and take Brent and Big Mike and do a triangulated flight pass, so we don't get our asses caught on the ground."

April nodded. "Ace. Not into the yak yak anyway and that building seems full of it. I remember coming here as a kid. Never got out without a fight and someone breaking a leg."

"Sounds like fun," Jess said. "What's the problem with that?"

Kurok chuckled. "I remember hearing about your father breaking someone's leg in there, matter of fact. Hopefully they'll remember that and refrain."

"We left the vehicles on fast start," Dev said in a mild tone. "If anything requires us to leave in an expeditious manner."

"You all think these people here are dumb enough to try and jump us?" Doug asked, his voice lifting in disbelief. "Dude, C'mon." He waved an arm around to indicate the gathering scrubs. "For real?"

"They could just be a diversion," Kurok warned. "And I agree, a patrol's good insurance. Now, let's get moving. I just spotted the elected spokesperson in the doorway over there and I suspect he wants a word in advance." He jerked his head toward the steps. "Shall we?"

Jess grinned. "We shall. C'mon. Everybody up the stairs!"

Motion suddenly erupted. Jess started through the crowd with Dev on her left-hand side, and Kurok on her right. As she walked the scrubs sorted themselves and formed around her, picking up her energy as they headed for the stairs.

It was, Kurok thought to himself as he hastened to keep up, really a singular moment. The scrubs were in their work clothes, heavy salt water-stained boots that came to mid-calf, many of them adorned with their ancient blades, the coveralls bearing patches and pockets.

But they had their hoodies on over the coveralls, sleeves pushed up and providing a mottled sea color uniformity. They surged like the sea up the steps toward the small group of stakeholders who stood on the top level, their size and energy becoming apparent as they reached the platform and strode forward.

The stakeholders all stepped back in pure reflex. Kurok pursed his lips and repressed a smile, acknowledging a moment of utter personal irony that he was there amid them, in a real sense, one of them now.

Justin would have howled in absolute delight. He shook his head in silent bemusement as he walked along next to Jess and Dev and relished it all as he took a breath and greeted the tall, grizzled elder the rest of them now hid behind. "Hello, Jock."

He slowed to a stop to face the man, and the wave of the Bay came to a halt, clustered close, listening.

"Dan," Jock Somtang replied. He gave them all a quick glance. "I'm not sure we have room..."

Kurok moved forward, took him by the elbow, and urged him along inside. "They'll find or make space, Jock. Come along now, let's get this started." He paused. "Before they get hungry."

Jess snickered. "Move," she added briefly. "We're busy people."

"Yo," Kirin echoed from a pace behind her. "Scoot."

Jock stared at them, then lifted a hand and nodded. "To the hall," he said. "We can sort it out there."

They flooded inside as the stakeholders fell back and hastily got out of the way, clearing the wide stone hall that had counters long unused on either side of it, and a tall domed ceiling that was all just a breadth of time worn and stained granite surface.

It smelled of age, and minerals. Dev remembered it from their last visit when it had just been her and Jess, and they'd walked through with very little notice. This time the Bay filled the space, overfilled it, their brawny, tall bodies brushing against the walls as they moved through the outer chamber and up the second set of narrower steps to the meeting hall.

It was round, and stepped, and she was just behind Jess and Kurok as they entered the passage that would take them down into the area reserved for Drake's Bay homestead, which the last time had been dusty and empty and lacking any adornment.

The wedge of stone space was the same, but her quick glance showed that a cleaning had been done. The floor was dark and free of dust, and the back wall now had a long banner across it with the Drake's Bay dragon on it, darkly colorful and vivid.

The scrubs all saw it, and swirled over to it, reaching up to touch it as they filled the space, then moving past to take up a spot in the area, looking around at the inside with interest.

Dev moved with Jess and Kurok to the front of the section, to the stone wall that loomed over the wide-open space in the center that had desks and two battered comps. Then she looked around to see the other sections for the other stake holds also filling with people.

Everyone stared at them. Dev let her hands rest on the wall and looked back, aware of her partner's tall form moving as she levered her legs over the edge of the wall and sat down on it, relaxed, her heels thumping rhythmically against the smooth stone surface.

There had been seats the last time that were gone now. There was no place to sit, but with that lack, there was just enough space for them.

Dev turned to look at their section. It was packed full of fighters, who stood shoulder to shoulder. Interspersed between them were the pilots, in their work coveralls and high-necked pullover sweaters, their bio alt collars hidden, but their origins utterly obvious in the stamp of their identical features.

KayTees, all of them, and they were visibly a set. Kelson stood quietly at the end of the front row, his hands held behind his back, the light of the chamber picking out the spacer patch on the front of his coverall and glinting off his pearl earring. He caught Dev's eye and winked at her, and she winked back, enjoying that moment as only a bio alt really could.

She twitched the sleeves of her sharkskin jacket straight and faced forward.

"We shoulda brought snacks," Jess said, in a mock mournful tone. "This's gonna take forever."

"I have some fish rolls in my bag here," Dev said. "Would you like one?"

Jess chuckled. "Always prepared. That's my Devvie." She reached back and patted Dev's leg. "I'm good for now."

She slowly let her gaze run over the room, sensing the rising tension as the crowd absorbed what they now had in their midst, the throng of scrubs behind her watching all of them with that unblinking, intense stare of the Bay.

Jess had always had it, and had to consciously moderate it, learning how to lower her gaze, turn her head, blink her eyes - all of them laboriously gained in her interaction classes at school. But it was always naturally there, and it had hit her when she'd come home to the Bay - that unwavering regard she'd easily slipped back into.

It made people nervous. It made these people in the room, all looking up at them, seeing a hundred tall, powerfully built men and women staring back at them suddenly feel apprehension, an uneasiness rooted in the awareness of difference.

To one degree or another, it was there, and it disturbed the crowd. Jess smiled and kicked her heels against the wall.

Dev took a moment to carefully scan the faces, seeing a wide representation of types of natural born she was familiar with. There were, she realized, a handful of bio alts lingering near the edges of the space, dressed in utility coveralls, most with cleaning implements in hand, some with trays they were bringing out to the small group of stakeholders in the center of the space.

Dev could see their quick glances and knew they were focusing not so much on the Bay natural born but on the KayTees in their midst, standing with a proud stance, sure of their place, overhead light reflecting on the pearl decorations they all wore.

And of course, on herself. Dev was sure they all knew who she was, if for no other reason than that she was standing between Jess, very recognizable, and Kurok, whom every bio alt in the space knew absolutely.

"What do you think, Dev?" Kurok asked, suddenly.

"I think I would be pleased if this activity was complete," Dev responded. "The natural born here are very uncomfortable."

"Mm," Kurok said, with a swiftly hidden grin. "They certainly are. Jock!" He called out. "Everyone ready to get this show on the road?"

Jock raised a hand in his direction and then motioned for his cohorts to go to their seats. These were the elected representatives from the Eastern Atlantia stakeholders, always conspicuously drawn from the wealthier homesteads.

Humanity never changed, at some level. He had checked the records. The Bay had never been called on to send anyone, and from what Kurok had sussed out, never had interest in it. Knowing them now as he did, there wasn't really the talent for it in them.

They were too blunt for it, and looking back along his own history, he could see that bluntness surface in Justin, disrupting his ability to participate in the manipulative hierarchy of Interforce in any truly significant way.

It just wasn't in him. It was Justin's way, or no way and Kurok could well imagine that turning this crowd ass over teakettle with his unrepentantly aggressive arrogance.

Jess, on the other hand, had some subtlety to her. He glanced sideways and watched her watch the crowd, absorbing the situation with a faintly wry, knowing twist of her lips, aware of the attention in the room, and judging how to shape that to her advantage.

Justin had been a smart guy. But his daughter had a different plane of comprehension that he'd lacked. Not a greater or lesser intelligence, just a different application of it. "Well now." He pushed away from the low wall. "Douglas, lad, can you bring that box with you? Let's go deliver our presents." He pointed at the gate at the edge of the bottom row of their space, that led down a handful of steps to floor. "Come along, Brandon."

"No prob." Douglas hefted the crate to his shoulder he'd taken from Bay A and ambled along after Kurok, the others edging aside to make space for them to walk. Brandon joined them coming down the far end of the group, his little box tucked in one hand.

"Would you like to join us, Jesslyn?" Kurok called back over his shoulder as he pushed the gate open. "Chop chop."

Jess put her hands on the wall and lifted her body up an

inch or so, then ejected herself out and let her body fall through the air to land on her feet on the central ground surface. She waited for Kurok and Douglas to descend and then joined them as they walked across to the desks where the other stakeholders had gathered.

Jess stuck her hands into the pockets of her hoodie, her expression slightly amused as she looked around this smaller circle of people now staring at her.

They were all older than she was and had that look of years spent dealing with the challenges of their world, tense lines along their eyes and their lips, wary expressions on their faces. Distrust, and to some extent, distaste was evident.

"Hi, again," Jess said, having met some at the last meeting at the Bay. "We brought presents," she added in mild tone.

"We did," Kurok agreed. "Put that there, Douglas." He pointed at the dais. "Now, Jock. Before we get your assembly started, let me please hand over this." He took a comms chip out of his pocket and extended it toward the assembly tech, who was seated behind one of the beat-up comms sets.

Warily he took it, then inserted the chip and started to process the data inside it.

"What's in the box, Daniel?" Jock asked and glanced from him to Jess and back, as Douglas set the box on the top of the counter and stepped back to stand next to Jess. "I assume that's your records update on the card."

"A selection of dried fruits," Kurok said. "We just finished up with the remainder of the recent harvest and produced some of these to see if they took anyone's fancy." He went over and opened the top of the crate. It gave a tiny sound of pressure releasing, and then the scent of the treats emerged, drawing sudden, distracted interest at its surprisingly enticing fragrance.

"Apples, pears, peaches, nectarines, and a few oranges," Kurok said. "Our most successful crops so far. We've delivered fresh varieties to several of you by now."

He took a step back and gestured toward the box. "Try them. They're sweet and tasty and completely unlike the other product we brought with us." He grinned at the man. "Go on, it's safe."

Jock looked over at the two tall figures who watched him, then he moved to the box and looked inside and inspected the contents visually before reaching inside and selecting one. He sniffed it, then tentatively nibbled an edge, his brows contracting as he evaluated the taste.

Change the conversation. Kurok was well versed in reading

his audience and understood the value there.

"Nice," Jock said, finally. "Which one is this?" He held the remaining part up.

"Nectarine," Kurok supplied helpfully. "It's a fuzz less peach actually."

The rest of them just stared. No one moved.

After a moment Jess stirred and walked over to pick up the box in both hands, then started around the circle, stopping at the first of the tables.

It was an older woman, wiry and spare, with curly gray hair. She slid back in her seat as far from Jess as she could go without standing up and leaving.

Jess lowered the box to her eye level and opened the top, then waited. After a silent minute the woman looked up at her with a cold stare. "No thank you."

Jess didn't react to the tone. "If you're going to trust me to come save your ass, you probably should trust taking a treat from this box," she said. "Unless you're trying to prove the point you're a bigger asshole than I am. Are ya?"

Kurok sighed inwardly. It wasn't the route he'd have chosen, but then, he wasn't a Drake. Leanne Boost had been elected from her stake hold for years and wasn't a novice at this game.

The woman stared up steadily at Jess, who remained where she was, extending the box down at her. She finally looked down at it, then reached inside and took a piece of the dried fruit. "I'm not trying to prove a point," she said, then looked sharply up. "I'm waiting to hear what your price is, Drake."

"Fair." Jess moved on to the next stakeholder and held the box out. "We're waiting to see what it's worth to ya." She winked at the next man, whose lips twitched faintly as he readily took a piece from the box. The next one didn't wait for Jess to approach, he stood up and walked over and took two pieces.

By the time he did, the rest had gotten up and stood around Jess, waiting their turn.

"Okay." Jock finished his piece of nectarine. "Siddown." He gestured to some seats left empty on one side of the smaller circle. "You said you'd bring what ya done." He looked up over Kurok's head to the Drake's Bay section, where the scrubs waited and listened. "Now we know what we got pinched for from Interforce. Let's see if you bring a better deal."

Kurok slowly sat down on one of the chairs and hiked one knee up over the other. "Pinched," he said. "What does that mean?"

Jock regarded him dourly. "What we got charged. Every quarter, they'd show up for it. Percentage of our take. For protection."

Kurok's head tilted to one side in an almost comical look of confusion. "Beg your pardon?" He finally coughed out. "Interforce?" His voice lifted in disbelief. "Are you saying they shook you down?"

Jess paused and turned to look at Jock, then swiftly around at the other stakeholders. "Huh?"

"Of course, they'd leave you out," Leanne growled. "Bet they gave you a cut."

Both Jess and Kurok turned and looked at Brandon, who looked equally confused "Any idea what they're talking about?" Kurok asked him. "Since I'm rather new around the place?"

Brandon shook his head, with honestly bewildered wide eyes.

"You had to know," Leanne addressed Jess. "It was agents that came and got it."

Jess was briefly silent. "Not this agent," she finally replied. "I have no idea what the hell you're talking about."

"Nor has this retired field tech ever heard of it," Kurok said. "I would have seen that in the records and it's not there. Not for the Bay." He paused. "But that explains something I heard at the processors." He frowned and stared off into the distance briefly.

"Only thing the Bay ever paid was in blood," he said at last. "Maybe they figured that was enough."

"And a percentage of every generation," Jess added quietly. "At least we got a stipend for that."

It got a little quiet then.

"Well." Kurok cleared his throat and straightened up in his chair. "Seems we have a lot to discuss." He shook his head a little bit. "Goodness."

"Yeah." Jess put the box down on the counter with a sigh. "We should have brought more snacks."

Chapter Twenty-three

Jess walked outside onto the front breadth of the gathering hall building, into a cold, brisk wind coming across the hills. She paused and leaned back against the rock wall, her hands in her pants pockets, as Dev came out and joined her.

"That was interesting," Dev said.

"That was a damned cluster bomb."

"Hm." Dev made a small, thoughtful sound.

"Now I get why those small holders near us were so up to join the fight." Jess sighed. "Interforce was bleeding em." She shook her head. "I feel like such a mook."

Dev took up a spot next to her against the wall. "Because you were not informed about this?"

"How could I not know? I was in there all that time." Jess shook her head again. "I'm an idiot."

Dev folded her arms over her chest. "Actually, I think they did not tell you because they knew you would not like it," she said. "You do the right things, Jess. This was not a right thing."

Jess turned her head and stared at her, that fierce unblinking stare of the Bay. Then she smiled, and the stare moderated to one of gentle affection. She removed her left hand from her pocket and draped it over Dev's neck. "Anyway, it worked out for us," she said. "That deal'll cover all the new slots, and more."

"And will be less than what they were being charged," Dev said. "It seemed relatively optimal."

"Relatively," Jess said. "Yeah, it's a fraction of what they were being hosed for. Win win," she said. "We'll need to throw together scan points for all those areas."

Nearby on the open plateau the scrubs worked up a game of tag ball to pass the time while all the yak yak went on. They had split into two sides and were using an old flight helmet, that one of the KayTee's had found inside a carrier cabinet, for a ball. Around them a crowd of watchers gathered.

Dev touched her ear and tilted her head slightly. "Jess, Doctor Dan requires your presence inside again."

"I'd rather go play ball." Jess sighed but pushed herself off the wall and trudged back inside.

Here, one level above where the game was, Dev had a good view, and she stood there quietly watching. She glanced aside as Kelson came outside and joined her.

They exchanged looks. "Natural born," he said, simply.

"Yes." Dev chuckled faintly. "I think April always says, it's a game?"

"Or a scam," Kelson said. "They all speak in circles."

"No one wants to say yes until they feel they have more than the others," Dev said. "It's like the admin arguments about office space on station," she said. "Doctor Dan always won those."

Kelson laughed. Then he glanced around. "The sets that belong here spoke to us, to me and Keko," he said. "They are interested in our place."

"Yes." Dev watched at least ten scrubs chase the one holding the helmet, punching, and grabbing for it. "That could be suboptimal."

"It could," he agreed readily. "They are assigned here, as we are assigned to Drake's Bay." He stretched and flexed his hands. "But this activity seems to have been optimal?" His voice lifted in question. "Doctor Dan seemed pleased."

"I think so yes," Dev said. "Jess seemed cautiously pleased with the outcome as well. She thinks the others will appreciate the service we offer."

"They are afraid of the natural born from the Bay," Kelson said. "The sets here said so." He observed the game. "I am not exactly sure why."

"They are excellent at the fighting activities, and they are large," Dev said in a reasonable tone. "We know they are kind and appreciate our participation, so we do not feel like they are dangerous to us. These natural born here do not know them and view them as dangerous."

"Yes," Kelson said. "Agent Jess is very dangerous."

"Very."

"But not to you."

Dev smiled. "Not to me. From the moment I arrived from station. I always felt very safe with Jess."

"And now we do as well," Kelson said. "It's really excellent." He paused. "Is it true we are going to go back into space and retrieve one of the stations?"

"No."

"Oh."

"Not unless we absolutely have to." Dev sighed. "And only if I can obtain another space shuttle."

****

It was a much smaller room, to one side of the big hall, and there were the small group of elected stakeholders and one of the data entry techs, Dan Kurok and the recently entered Jess.

"It has to do with your records update," Jock said, when Jess had seated herself. "Look, Daniel, you can do whatever you want within the Bay's borders, that's the rules. We all go by that."

"Yes." Kurok had one elbow on the arm of the chair he was seated in "We've already made all our records whole from the Bay side."

"You can't make engineered bios full citizens of Atlantia," Jock said, bluntly. "We don't allow it."

"That what this is?" Jess gave them all a somewhat unfriendly look.

Kurok patted her hand. "There's a bit of contention about our filing for status for the sets who have slots and allotments. They've been given full status at the Bay."

"Sure." Jess eyed them all. "What's the problem?"

"They're bio alts," Jock said. "That's the problem. Having full citizen status includes the obligation to participate in our laws, and that requires self-determination, and that requires that no one is providing your thoughts for you."

Jess drew in a breath, but then paused as Kurok squeezed her hand.

"There is no real difference," Kurok said. "Between how a bio alt is programmed and how you teach your own children." He held up a finger as they started to interrupt. "Ah ah ah. You don't get an opinion on that unless you're a registered synaptic programmer. Anyone here in the room a synaptic programmer?" He asked. "Aside from me?"

He raised his hand and waited, as the men and women in the room frowned and scowled at him.

"I thought as much. So please dispense with that nonsense. Biological Alternatives have thoughts and opinions just like any of you do." He paused. "They just receive instruction that teaches them to withhold them."

"Still, it's the law," Jock said. "You can't ignore that, Daniel."

"Certainly, I can. I do it all the time." Kurok smiled his gentle smile. "I probably break more laws in fifteen minutes than anyone else here in their adult lives."

"It'll set a bad precedent," Leanne spoke up. "We all have contracts."

"There's already a precedent," Jess said. "Dev."

Everyone looked at her, except Doctor Dan.

"Dev was given cit status when she came into Interforce," Jess said. "She has cit creds. You can't put your ass on the line without them." She looked from one to the other. "It's reg," she said. "I had to arm wrestle her into believing they were real, but they are."

"Is that so," Jock murmured. "Well, but..."

"Actually, she wasn't the precedent. I was," Kurok said mildly. "Jess is right. It is reg. I was given cit status when I took the oath for just that exact reason. I wasn't qualified for it otherwise, because I was born on the edge of the North Sea and was a prisoner of war at the time."

Now everyone stared at him. Kurok looked placidly back at them. "But that's all water under the bridge. So just process the damn records and move on."

"It's dangerous," Leanne stated, not obstinately, but with a definitive firmness. "You should know that, if you're as familiar with them as you say you are."

"He is," Jess said. "Dangerous because the ones you kick around might get the idea they want to run off to the Bay?"

"We have contracts. They're property," Leanne said. "If you want to treat them as residents, that's on you. But the rest of us do not view bio alts as people." She drew in a breath as Jess stared at her. "Don't like that? Too bad."

"I feel sorry for you," Jess said, after a brief pause. "Does having a mind that small give you headaches?"

Leanne blinked. "What?"

"You're stupid," Jess said. "Don't like that? Too bad." She remained in her seat, her posture easy and relaxed, one elbow over the back of the chair and her long legs extended. "How'd you last so long in charge of anything?"

Kurok cleared his throat. "We have rules for residency at the Bay just like anyone else does. You have to have a skill set that fits an open slot. These sets were fortunate enough to arrive when there were a lot of slots available. We would not just allow anyone, including bio alts, to come there."

"What if one does? Runs off from our platforms and ends up there? You give them sanctuary?" Leanne asked. "I've got several hundred bio workers. I can't afford to lose them."

"Reasonable question, Daniel," Jock said.

"It is reasonable," Kurok answered thoughtfully. "I would say if there was a set member who showed up at the Bay, and they had a skill set we needed, and they qualified, then we'd have to pay off their contract."

There was a pensive silence after that, and even Leanne faintly nodded. "Doesn't replace them though," she said. "Hard to get now. Bio station has a long lead time."

Kurok smiled at her. "Well, we're working on that too."

"It's illegal to create bio alts outside a licensed laboratory," Jock said. "We've all heard that ten thousand times. Not that any of us could or would want to."

"Define licensed." Kurok's eyes twinkled. "To produce biological alternatives, you need specific machinery that is difficult to obtain but legal, and a certified genetic biologist with a license to practice gene manipulation and development along with a few competent synaptic programmers."

"Which we got." Jess pointed at Kurok. "Don't believe it? Ask any of your own bios. There're bunches of them peeking out from every damn doorway here hoping he'll wave at them."

Kurok chuckled. "I'm notorious."

Now the looks being traded included a dawning of potential they hadn't expected. "You got someone licensed to do programming, for real?" Leanne asked, after a long pause.

"Yes of course," Kurok said. "At least two people." He paused thoughtfully. "And I might be willing to train others to."

Jock leaned forward and propped his chin up on his fist. "You bring a lot to the table, Kurok." His tone bore a touch of admiration.

"I don't know," Leanne said.

"Jess," Kurok said. "Could you ask Dev to join us please?" He sat up in the chair. "Since she is a citizen, she has the right to advocate on behalf of her creche mates."

"Sure." Jess got up, instead of calling on comms and headed for the door. "Be right back."

Kurok watched her depart and then got up and went over to the box to retrieve a dried piece of peach, bringing it back with him. He detoured over to where Leanne was seated and leaned on the dais she was behind.

She looked up at him. "What? Being too mean to her?"

"No," Kurok said. "You don't have it in you to be too anything to Jesslyn Drake. She doesn't give a damn what you think about her," he said. "But if you want to keep your teeth in your mouth, be civil to Dev."

He stood up and went back to his seat, as the door opened again and Dev entered, with Jess at her heels. "Hello, Dev," he greeted her. "Thanks for coming to chat with us."

"Hello," Dev responded agreeably, as she walked over to the center of the circle of desks. She took a seat at Kurok's side as he waved her to it, then cocked her head and waited, casually scanning the faces watching her.

Jess turned her own chair around and settled on it, resting her elbows on the back of it as she silently watched as well.

"This is Dev," Kurok said. "Dev is our lead carrier pilot. I think you saw her fly when we arrived. She was the first one to land."

They had no idea what to ask her. But Jock gave it a try. "You think you're as good as a real person at that?"

Dev's eyes twinkled a bit. "Well, I've been told I'm better at flying that craft than anyone I have ever met as of yet either natural born or biological alternative," she replied. "I taught flight dynamics and technical integration while at the Base to my natural born colleagues."

There was another awkward silence. "Did you?" Jock muttered and glanced at Kurok.

Kurok merely nodded, with a slight smile.

"I did," Dev said. "That was before I earned a senior ranking. There was value seen in sharing my experiences with the others."

"Dev was the youngest person to ever earn senior tech bars," Kurok informed them. "She exceeded our expectations by a significant percentage."

"How come Interforce just let her walk off then?" Jock asked. "Valuable piece of property you were to em." He directed the last comment to Dev. "They wanted you to leave?"

"I was offered transport and work in another Base after operations were being shut down here," Dev said mildly. "I informed them I was not interested."

There was an awkward silence as the stakeholders all looked at each other, and Kurok remained silently amused.

Jock leaned forward. "Then what were you interested in?" He asked, "Since you seem to think you have a choice."

"I was interested in going wherever it was that Jess went," Dev said. "I felt it was likely she could find something useful for me to do." She glanced over her shoulder and then back at the stakeholders. "I think it worked out all right."

Jess chucked audibly.

"That's not a bio alt," Leanne said, flatly. "That's not real. That's made up. You're trying to fake us out," she said. "This is a regular human."

Kurok shook his head. "Sorry no. Dev's a biological alternative, born on station, with the set designation to prove that."

"I've seen her baby pictures," Jess said, a faintly amused

look on her face.

"Put your hand there, Dev." Kurok pointed at an ident square, with its worn surface and slightly cracked edges near the data input terminal.

Dev got up and went over and put her hand on it. She felt the twitch as it read the chip in her hand and scanned her genetics.

An older, cruder system than what even Drake's Bay had. She removed her hand and glanced at the data tech, who studied the screen. He looked up over the edge of it at her. "She's been made civ by contract release, and cit before that," the man said briefly. "Says it here, through Interforce, from the station. Got station origin scans."

"Coulda just been born there," Leanne scoffed.

"Of course, she was born there," Kurok said, then paused. "As all the sets are, or were, at the Lifeforce facility. In the creche, from a genetic purposeful design."

Dev nodded. "Yes," she said. "Biological Alternative, set 0202-164812, instance NM-Dev-1" She went back to her seat and sat down. "But most people just call me Dev."

"Or Rocket," Jess said.

"Or Rocket," Dev conceded. "The other pilots at Base named me that."

"Getting back to our original discussion," Kurok said. "The sets at Drake's Bay fill work slots and allotments that qualify them for residency, and from my view, also qualify them as citizens just like anyone else who domiciles there." He indicated Dev. "And as you can see, they're as sentient as you are."

There was a long silence, then Jock shrugged. "It's your cred," he said. "But I find you giving shelter to any of mine, there'll be hell to pay."

"Same," Leanne muttered. "Ridiculous."

The others lifted their hands in assent but remained silent. The data clerk, watched them, waited, then nodded, and went back to typing on the input pad, looking from one screen to the other, muttering under his breath.

"That all?" Jess said. "I got a measure of the top of this ridge being taken for a reflector. You'll all get a visit in the next day or two for the same." She stood up and stepped around the chair. "Bay op's'll set up comms."

Jock stood up to face her. "And no matter who it is, they come, you come," he said. "That's the deal. No BS."

"That's the deal." Jess walked forward toward him, her hands buried in her front pouch pocket. As she reached the chair

Dev was in, Dev rose to stand next to her. "Interforce, the other side, renegades, scavengers." She smiled without humor. "We don't care. We're happy to fight em all."

"No nonsense," Jock said. "No showing up wanting free from us, nothing extra. No special assessments'"

"No, certainly not. A deal is a deal," Kurok broke in smoothly. "Just like you don't show up on our doorstep, wanting free fruit. We're a stakehold like everyone else is, and this is one of our export products."

That seemed to be the right thing to say, and the stakeholders relaxed. "Business is business." One of them said. "I can deal with that.'

The data tech stood up and reached over the desk and offered a chip to Kurok. "All registered," he said briefly. "Everything's updated."

"Thank you." Kurok pocketed the chip. "I'm sure we're going to enjoy doing business with each other." He stood up. "I see you took the opportunity to put up a market. Now that we're done here, we can go spend a few creds there."

Jock eyed him warily. "No trouble," he said, in a warning tone. "I don't need any complaints."

"Only trouble's going to be if someone tries to scam us." Jess smiled. "Might want to spread that out there."

"Oh, come now, Jess." Kurok patted her arm. "No one would do that."

Jess gave him a skeptical look.

"I would be glad to bargain on your behalf, Jess," Dev said, her eyes twinkling. "I'm sure it will be an excellent result."

"They have no idea what they're getting into." Jess clapped her hand on Dev's back and guided her to the door. "Let's go see what they got."

****

"Not exactly enthusiastic clients," Kurok said, as they left the gathering hall and emerged onto the plateau on the opposite side of their landing site. The gray skies overhead promised rain and far off they could hear thunder in the distance but now the air was still clear.

"Deal's a deal." Jess paused to regard the ball game still going on. The KayTees had joined in and were darting in and out of their larger natural born cohorts and leaping for the tossed helmet. "Tell em now, or wait until we get back?"

They paused at the edge of the game area. Dev saw the

KayTees spot them, though they didn't stop their play. The game had gathered a large audience it seemed, people wandering up from the market and those there for the conclave.

"Oh, I think now," Kurok replied. "Not fair to make them wait, especially since the Bay knows by now since it updated with the records acceptance in that little farce back there." He folded his arms. "Give them a shout, would you Dev?"

Dev smiled. "Flight lead to flight and fight teams." She turned up the comms channel. "Please approach the location where Jess and Doctor Dan are currently standing."

The bio alts immediately complied, reaching out to get the attention of the scrubs, and point in their direction.

The game dissolved into a swirl of arrested motion. The scrubs started loping their way and the pilots only just beat them, arriving at the entryway to the hall in a throng of alert, interested attention.

A hundred fighters, and seven pilots, six of whom were about to join them in a change of circumstance, to join Dev, Doug, Chester, and Brent as citizens along with the hundreds of sets back at the Bay.

They all fell silent and focused on Jess, who lifted one hand.

"We got a gig," Jess said. "Contract's signed."

"Whoa," Dustin said. "Yo cuz!"

Kurok cleared his throat. "You're all now assigned our newly created slots, and you have allotments attached," he addressed the scrubs. "You all have a lot of things to do when we get back home."

"Oh man," Evan, the closest to him breathed audibly. "Is this for real?"

"For real." Jess settled her hands into her front pocket. "We're gonna add em all to our watch. Someone causes trouble, we fix it."

"Daaaaaaamn."

"And of course, we'll protect ourselves," Kurok said. "Along with that achievement for you folks, our sets have been granted citizen status." He smiled at the pilots, whose eyes widened in delight. "You're no longer assigned here, lads. You are contracted to Drake's Bay."

They weren't even sure what to say, it was sudden and unexpected. "Dev can talk to you later on about what that all means," Kurok added. "For right now, we'd like to spend a little time in the market, then we'll head home to get all these new changes started."

"Wow," Dustin rumbled softly. "That mean I get me a crib?"

"Yes." Brandon had caught up to them. "As the Doc said, we got to get gettin when we get back." He had a small sack on his back. "Tea was big pop, Doc," he said. "Appreciated."

Kurok smiled. "Figured it might be. We shook them up a bit, Jock did well. He deserved a treat." He looked around at both Bay born and bios and saw various shades of surprise and wonder. "Now let's go get a treat ourselves shall we?"

"C'mon," Jess said. "I'm buyin. Let's go." She made a pushing gesture with both hands. "Hai!"

A booming, resounding "Hai!" Echoed across the plateau and the wind carried it out and over the market. Heads turned as the throng of Drake's Bay residents headed their way, a large, energetic flood of bodies dressed in colors of the sea.

"Day of change," Kurok said, as he walked along between Jess and Brandon. "Good or bad, here we come."

"Here we come," Brandon echoed. "Ready or not."

"They're not."

****

Kurok strolled along the narrow aisles between the trader vans, a full sack carried over his shoulder. He kept up a casual scanning of the booths, apparently just a random glance that took specific details he was interested in.

People. Things. Idle words. Body language. He was looking for trouble. The mixing of so many Bay residents with traders, and stakeholders, who had heard the worst of them and were wired to be argumentative at the best of times.

Not to mention the sets, who becoming used to the casual equality and respect of the Bay, might be seen in fact as uppity.

Ahead of him, he spotted Keko, along with April. They stood near a table and were in discussion with its owner. He kept walking past, confident that whatever was being bartered was in good hands with April supervising, and in fact there was no indication of strain in anyone's body language.

Further down the same row, at a different caravan, he spotted Doug with three or four of the fighters trailing along, and he relaxed a little. The visiting homesteaders kept their distance. The traders were more agnostic, more used to dealing with the riff and the raff of their pattern of travel, more apt to find in newcomers' potential new customers rather than threat.

Well. Perhaps it would be a reasonably good day after all.

Something then caught his eye, and he wandered over to a small end cap, the tailgate of a travel wagon let down to show some long patterns of re-knitted fabric on a surface long beaten and dented. Its vendor looked warily at him as he strolled up, an older woman with dye-stained hands and long gray hair pulled into a gather at the nape of her neck.

"What have we here," Kurok said, looking at the items. "Gloves?"

The woman eased forward, picked one up and held it out. "Keep ya hands warm and let ya use em."

Kurok put down his sack and took the glove, inspecting it. It wasn't really a glove in the classic sense. It was made to cover the hands up to the first knuckles, leaving the fingertips free. He pulled it over his own hand and inspected the result.

The inside was lined with some soft substance and the warmth was immediately apparent. "I see." He scanned the meager stock, counting a dozen pairs of the things that had patch- work on the outside of any bit of fabric the woman could find, likely thrown off clothing too tattered to wear, and too worn to re-weave into new.

He looked up at met the woman's eyes. "I'll take them," he said. "All of them." He circled the one he had in his hand over the top of the table.

Amid taking up the other glove of the pair, the woman started in surprise and stared at him. "Alla them?" She asked, her voice raising. "How many hands ya got?"

Kurok chuckled gently. "I have some friends who could use these. They're not all for me." He pulled out his credit chit, one of the newly punched out ones that had the outline of the Drake dragon on it. "They are for sale, I assume?"

"Ya, ya, course they are." The woman hastily gathered them up. "F'shure."

He hoisted his sack up to the battered tailgate and opened the top of it. "You can put them in there." He watched her study the chit, then put it through the register nailed to the side of the gate. "I'm good for it, really."

"From that place, ya never know." The woman handed the chit back to him. "You don't look like one of em."

Kurok slid the chit back into his pocket. "Well, strictly speaking, I'm not. I wasn't born there. But I do live there and, they're a good lot once you get to know them."

The woman carefully folded the gloves into pairs and put them into the sack. "You say that." She sniffed as she finished. "Each as own." She shrugged.

"Thank you." Kurok closed his sack and hoisted it to his shoulder again. "Well, give them a chance. Maybe we'll see you at the Bay sometime."

Before she could answer, he turned and walked off, half-way already regretting spending cred with her. But the patch-work half gloves would be fine presents for the sets, for the pilots in their chilly carriers, and so he finally exhaled and dismissed the woman as he walked on.

Chapter Twenty-four

Dev sidled up to one of the bigger wagons, where a half dozen men and women browsed, looking over a display of decorative jewelry made from bright metals and sparkling stones.

They were different than most of the ones she'd seen before, and the wagon itself was a little different shape and size, a different design. There was a bit of space between it, and the next one and the vendors standing behind the letdown shelf where the merchandise was had a little different type of dress.

So, from another area, she concluded.

She thought she blended in with the other shoppers, until she saw the nearest man behind the shelf glance at her and she read the head tilt and interest in his eyes. She edged patiently through the gathered crowd and settled in front of a tray with tiny, glittering stones suspended on silver rings.

The vendor sidled over. "That's a good-looking pearl you got there, lady," he said, without preamble. "Where'd ya get it?"

Dev touched her ear and smiled at him. "Thank you," she said. "It came from Drake's Bay."

"Yeah?" Thus invited, the man leaned closer to inspect it. "Really nice," he said. "Want one of these to sit with it?" He nudged the display of sparklies. "Seems like ya got an eye for pretty things." He winked at her.

"Possibly." Dev could see the brief glances from the other shoppers, then her gaze was caught by a pendant set just behind the row of tiny dangles. "Possibly we can discuss prices?" She paused. "On several items."

"Now ya talkin." The man settled down on a stool behind the counter and spread his hands out as though to claim her. He leaned his elbows on the metal surface. "Let's talk," he said. "What'cha name?"

Dev eyed him. "Many people address me as Rocket."

"Rocket?" The man stirred a bit in surprise, then shrugged. "Okay, Rocket. I'm Charlie. Let's talk."

****

Jess was at the next stand over, in the shadows between the wagons. She stood quiet and still and listened to the boot seller talk to two well-dressed men who argued over the material being used in his display's merchandise.

Jess knew the truth of it. She recognized the sealskin for what it was, and judged the quality to be quite good, with a tight, neat stitch and a thick, flexible sole that would be good for shore climbing. They might even be waterproof, they had that sheen to them.

They were also attractive. They had a pattern sewn around the tops of them and well-made fastenings designed to bring the hide in close around the leg.

Behind her, she heard Dev bartering with the sparklie vendor, her low, even tones crisply audible to Jess, along with the gruff responses from the seller. She studied the boots thoughtfully. All the ones on display were too small for herself, or the men who were arguing with the seller.

But not too small for Dev.

Jess eased forward and picked one up off the end of the display and ran her fingertips over it, looking at the workmanship. It was a well-tanned and softened seal hide, and it was lined inside and as she put her hand inside, it felt warm.

She glanced behind her quickly, then eased forward and distracted the boot vendor from his argument. She held the selected pair out and lifting her eyebrow. "You wanna shut up long enough to sell me these?"

The stakeholders turned and gave her an offended look at the interruption, then immediately took a step back as they recognized her.

The vendor, however, didn't seem fazed, as a vendor wouldn't to someone offering cred to him. "Ain't' gonna fit ya." He indicated the boots, with a brief nod of his head. "Too small. Sold off my bigger ones already, s'what I was telling these fellers here."

"Yeah, I know," Jess said. "I've been dressing myself since I was six. I know my boot size." She handed over her cred chit. Then she turned her head and looked at the two men who edged away from her. "Relax. Just buying a gift. Not gonna shoot at ya today."

They stared at her. Jess just smiled back at them. She remembered them from the gathering hall and knew them for two smaller stakeholders on the west side of the processors. They lived off the berths there and dependent on the jobs.

As the Bay had been.

She took the bundle the vendor offered, and her credit chit back and tucked the boots under her arm. She suddenly felt Dev's warm presence at her side, her pale hair reflecting the overhead gray light as she peered at the table.

"Those are attractive," Dev said. She looked at the boots on the table with interest.

"You have a pair," Jess told her.

"I don't think that's true."

"Trust me it is." Jess hoisted the bundle under her arm a little.

"Ah I see." Dev's eyes twinkled. "Hello," she greeted the vendor, and the two stakeholders. "How are you?" She added conversationally. "Jess, would you like a cup of hot beverage? I see some down there."

"Sure," Jess said. "Anything interesting at that last crate? Guy from the North?" She half turned. "Heard ya arm twisting. I'm gonna see what they got."

"You actually already have something from there," Dev said. "I didn't touch anyone's arm, but I think it was a successful session."

"Do I?"

"Yes. I will be back in a moment." She eased from the stall and walked off down the aisle and headed for a kiosk that had a large dispenser, and stacks of cups, her carry bag tucked along her side.

Jess watched her go, a grin on her face. Then she looked back to find the two men, and the vendor looking at her with expressions that were hard to decipher. "These are seal skin from up in the white," she told the two stakeholders crisply. "Someone went crevice hunting for em. Ain't easy."

The two men looked at each other, then moved up to the counter and studied the boots. They watched her out of the corner of their eyes, wary, but now with more thoughtful expressions.

The vendor nodded. "S'why they ain't cheap," he said. "Drake knows." He glanced at Jess. "That who the boots'r for?" He jerked his head in the direction Dev had gone.

"Yeah. Pick the right size?"

The vendor now also grinned, very briefly. "Got a good eye, Drake," he said. "You been up the white?" He continued the conversation in a more casual tone. "Sure, ya have."

"Sure." Jess relaxed a little herself. "Training rounds, some gigs," she said. "Been to North Pole, whole tour. It's tough up there."

"Heard that," one of the stakeholders said. "Cousin works the boats, got stuck up in the ice for a month." He turned the boot over and looked at it. "Got here too late, stuck in that storm." He sounded regretful. "Like me a pair."

The vendor shrugged. "So did a bunch here before ya. No telling when we can get hold of them skins again. Hit or miss, ya know."

Without really thinking about it, Jess glanced at the vendor. "This work's good. You want me to hook you up with a guy who's got skins? Showed up in our docks yesterday." She saw his eyes widen and his body language shift. "Figure you gotta have material to get this stuff done."

The other stakeholders were now focused on her with more interest than wariness.

"Sure, Drake," the vendor finally spluttered. "If it's good stuff, y'know, not chewed up in the lines and that stuff. Don't want shreds."

Jess nodded. "Stop over at the Bay when you're done here. See if it's worth your time." Her peripheral vision caught Dev returning, a covered mug in either hand. "I'll tell the dock master to get you a manifest."

"Got a lotta boats coming in there now," the stakeholder closest to her said. "Shore combers said, saw em rolling down the coast headed your way."

Jess nodded thoughtfully. "Yeah, we're seeing more traffic," she said. "Good for everyone around, right?"

Three more locals paused to listen and now gathered behind the two initial stakeholders. They were two women and another man, in weatherproof cloaks with hoods.

Dev arrived with the mugs and handed her one. Jess took it and sniffed at the steam coming off the top of it. It was pungent and spicy smelling. "Grog?"

"Yes."

She took a sip, and found it fermented and warming. "Nice."

"Hey, Drake," the vendor said, after a moment of somewhat awkward silence. "What's your take on all this?"

Now a half dozen others stopped and listened.

Jess took another sip of grog. "All this what?"

The vendor gestured vaguely. "Interforce pulling out, all that, you people staying behind. good? Bad? You don't care?"

Jess felt the focus sharpen on her. "Do I care." She pondered the last question first. She shrugged slightly. "Nah. Not after what they did to the Bay. Good riddance," she said. "Whadda you think, Devvie?" She asked. "All good with being at the Bay?"

Dev looked at her in somewhat comical surprise. "I think our situation now is far more optimal," she finally said. "Absolutely!"

Jess nodded. "S'cool," she said, briefly. "Landed right."

"Yeah, well you're the Drake," the nearer stakeholder said, but in a mild tone. "Course it worked out for ya."

"Worked out for the Bay is what I hear," one of the passersby spoke up. "Maybe worked out for more'n that." The woman looked around and then back at Jess, and as she did a few of the scrubs happened past, and they too paused when they saw Jess there.

Another awkward silence fell. "Sup?" It was Douglas, the Bay guard who usually trailed Kurok. With him were Kirin and Dustin, and then Keko and Kevin emerged from behind them, bright eyed and interested.

Both KayTees had bags slung over their shoulders and with their high collared sweaters under their coveralls only their identical features advertised there was something not natural born to them. A moment later, that multiplied when Kelson arrived and squeezed in next to Dev.

All three pilots immediately spotted the boots. "Oh," Kelson whispered to Dev. "Are you obtaining some of those?"

Dev sipped her grog. "It appears Jess has obtained them on my behalf." She indicated the bundle tucked under Jess's arm. "But there are some left and these other natural born find them too small," she whispered back.

"Excellent."

"Hey, Drake." The older stakeholder looked over at Jess and pointed at the sets. "You ain't never welcomed them before, by the Bay," he said, but also in a mild tone. "Nobody there wanted them around, I remember them talking it."

She shrugged. "S'true. "But we know better now. She rested her elbow on Dev's shoulder. "Right, scrubs? We're up for the spacers, aren't we?"

"Oh yeah!" Douglas responded instantly. "You kiddin? They're awesome."

"F'kn yo." Kirin grinned and draped her arm over Keko's shoulders. She peered past Douglas at Dev. "Hey, is that grog?"

"Yes," Dev said. "There is a stand just over there." She half turned and pointed.

"Shall we obtain some?" Keko asked, then glanced at Jess. "Doctor Dan said it was appropriate for us to use our chits to obtain items for everyone until we get back to the Bay," he said. "It's been very enjoyable."

Jess grinned. "Doc's a smart guy. G'wan. It's good." She lifted her cup.

The scrubs and pilots scooted along down the roughly

created aisle, headed for the drink stand. The crowd parted to let them through and stared after them in bemusement.

"Spacers?" The vendor asked, in a questioning tone.

"That's where we all come from," Dev explained. "From space. Many of the sets who live now at the Bay came directly from Bio Station 2, as did I."

"Heard stories about that," the vendor said. "Bout Station."

Jess smiled and gave Dev a little nudge. "Stop by the Bay if you want to hear more," she said. "C'mon, Devvie. Let's see what else we can find to get each other." She gave the vendor and the watching stakeholders a wink, and they moved on.

"That was an interesting conversation," Dev said.

"Very," Jess murmured. "And y'know, Devvie, I think you do good things for my image."

"I do?"

"Yup."

"I guess that's optimal?"

"Yup."

****

The dark clouds gathered, and their shopping would soon be over, giving way to the weather and the oncoming night.

Jess considered a recall and a return to their carriers as she and Dev neared the end of a row and started up along the next back toward the grog stand. "Today went all right."

"I think so as well," Dev said, swinging their now empty mugs by their handles gripped in one hand.

"A lot better than I thought it would," Jess admitted. "I never like it when a plan goes too well." She glanced at Dev, who gave her one of those noncommittal looks. "Makes me wonder when the other boot is gonna drop."

"I see." Dev detoured over to return the cups and waited as the vendor handed her back two pieces of metal without comment. She peered at them, then returned to Jess's side. "I am not sure why a piece of footwear is involved, but I hope nothing drops and things continue to go well."

Jess shifted the bundle under her arm. "I need a backpack."

Dev was a bit surprised at this change of subject. "Would you like me to put that package in my sack?" She offered.

"No." Jess spotted a table at the end of the row they were walking down. "I got a bunch of stuff in my pockets," she said. "Lemme get something to put it all in, then we can haul out of here and get going home." She looked around and saw all the hastily averted glances. "I'm tired of being entertainment."

"Excellent." Dev hitched her carry sack over her shoulder and fell in alongside.

The stall ahead indeed had some sacks, made from patch- work cloth, of various and sometimes mismatched colors. They were oddly shaped, and non reg, and they had metal rings on the outside you could clip things too.

"Interesting," Dev said.

"Scrounger bags." Jess reached out to finger one as they came to the stall.

The man behind the counter watched them. He had on a vest made from the same oddly matched, patchwork cloth, and thick work pants with strips and patches on them as well. He had on a long-sleeved woven shirt under the vest and his hands were full of scars. "Don't dis my stuff."

Jess looked at him.

"I don't care who the f you are," the man said, flatly.

It made Jess smile.

"May I ask why you considered those words derogatory?" Dev said. "I think these are interesting and attractive." She looked at him in question and touched one of the bags that hung down from the caravan's lift gate.

The man took a breath to answer, his face twisted in dis- taste. "You that little f'ing..."

"Stop," Jess said, in a sudden, very cold, tone.

He glanced quickly at her.

"Don't dis my partner," Jess said, enunciating the words very clearly. "I don't care who the fuck you are either buddy." She stared at him with unblinking eyes, intent and expressionless.

For a long minute, there was a sense he was going to risk it. Then he let out a breath and looked away and then back. "No dis," he finally said. "We don't call it scrounging. We collect," he said in a flat voice. "They're collecting sacks."

"Thank you," Dev said, sincerely. "I don't think the word scrounge was meant to be disparaging. That's what it's called at Drakes Bay when things are repurposed and everyone there per- forms that function." She regarded the sack again. "Was this the one you were interested in Jess? I think it's very functional looking."

Jess studied it, and past it, him. The trader was at the very end of the row, almost not on the plateau itself, in a fringe area, and she saw the transport behind the man was made of spare parts, battered, and scraped together as was the man himself, and the products he had to sell from it.

A scavenger, with an attitude. Jess decoupled the internal rage that had almost, almost triggered and took a mental step back. "Yeah, that's the one, Devvie," she said, in a normal voice. "Bargain it for me, will ya?"

"Of course." Dev settled against the edge of the table.

The man behind the table glowered at her. "Don't do your own deals, Drake?"

Jess smiled at him, without humor. "She's better at it than I am," she said. "Wanna make cred, or not?"

His hands clenched a little.

Thunder rumbled overhead.

****

It started raining before Dev finished her patient bargaining with the irritated scavenger. He'd been brusque and almost rude, skirting Jess's toleration but Dev didn't respond, politely ignoring his remarks until he finally was reduced to responding to her calm, reasonable objections.

The wind turned cold and drove the rain against her and she edged to one side a little to avoid the worst of it as she pointed out this flaw, and that. She turned the bag over and inspected every inch of it. "I think this will have to be repaired." She pointed out a seam. "That is missing stitches."

"Yeah okay point two cred," he said, through gritted teeth. "Take you five minutes."

Dev looked up at him with her mildest expression. "The point would be if I am purchasing this, I should not have to immediately repair it."

Behind her, Jess's eyes twinkled.

"Would you hurry up?" The scavenger finally snapped at her. "Two cred eight. That's my last offer. I wanna close." He hunched his shoulders and looked up at the sky, lifting one arm to shade his head from the droplets. "I can't pay to be in the tent with the big shots."

Casually Jess eased up behind Dev's back and spread her arms out, blocking the worst of the wind with her body. "What's the rush? You should be used to the wet." She angled her stance, so the wind was behind her and leaned forward a little, her tall form shielding Dev with reasonable efficiency.

The man gave her a sideways glance. "C'mon. Pay up or not." He pulled his roughhewn, ragged jacket up to cover his head. "Two eight."

Dev examined the back side of the carry sack. She paused as she ran her fingertips over the slightly stretchy material that made up the surface. A sense memory flared, and she felt the fabric again, tensing it between her thumb and forefinger.

Then she went very still, and looked up at him, her eyes now sharp and intent. "This came from Interforce." She indicated the fabric.

"You can't tell that, "He said. "It's a little patch."

"Certainly, I can," Dev said, in a mild tone. "This is a piece of cloth from an agent duty suit." Her lips twitched into an almost smile. "As a former field tech, myself, I am quite familiar with them."

"So what?" He said. "I don't say what the water brings the shore." He jerked his head at the material. "I just use what it brings." But his body tensed, and he darted a quick look at Jess. "You don't ask where collections come from."

Jess leaned over to inspect the bag. "Fair," she said. "Recent?" She looked at him sharply.

He returned the look warily. "Week maybe," he said. "Last one I made." He jerked his head at the bag again.

The patch was a small, irregular ragged one that had the frayed surface one would expect of something coughed up by the sea. Jess reached over Dev's shoulder to touch it. "Coulda washed up from the Bay," she said in a casual tone. "We didn't strip em. Just chewed em up as they fell."

The scavenger grunted.

"Interesting," Dev said, and then cleared her throat. "Two cred point six," she said, briskly. "That is the most we wish to exchange for this item."

"Fine." He abruptly shoved his hand out. "Let's get it done. I want outta here." He looked around and past them, with more than a touch of nerves as Dev fished in her sack for her cred chit.

Jess unexpectedly reached over past Dev's head and extended her own hand out, with glittering metal in the palm of it. "Here," she offered. "Save the transfer hit."

He stared at the metal in some surprise and then his attitude abruptly shifted perceptibly. He took the bits from her hand and inspected them, a faint smile tugged at the corners of his thin lips as his body relaxed. "Hadn't seen none of that that in a long time," he admitted. "That's all right, Drake." He reluctantly nodded at Dev, who was neatly folding the bag up. "Use it good."

Jess took it from her hands. "Use it right now." She

unloaded her pockets and the bundle of boots into it, then unslung Dev's carry sack from her shoulder and put it in on top. She then swung the bag up and over her own shoulders, buckling the worn web strap across her chest. "There ya go."

"Excellent," Dev said. "Thank you for engaging in commerce with me," she told the scavenger. "I appreciate the courtesy," she added, with a smile.

Caught off guard, he hesitantly smiled back.

"Let's get our asses out of the rain," Jess said. "Good market." She gave the merchant a brief wave, and then briskly gathered Dev up in the curve of one arm and guided her toward the end of the plateau and the narrow path that would lead around to the other side of it.

"That was interesting," Dev said. "I think."

Jess chuckled dryly. "He was an asshole, and I would have broken his jaw if he'd continued to mouth off at you. He was smart enough to know it. Smarter than the average skank."

"So, it seems." Dev tucked her hand along the inside of Jess's elbow. "But I am not sure why he was so non optimal to me," she said. "Was it just because I'm a bio alt?"

Jess drew in a breath and exhaled, as they walked along the path, going the other direction from all the rest of the stakeholders and merchants, who were hurrying down to the bottom level of the market where there were some broad tents set up for temporary shelter.

"He sees a slot he could have had, maybe," she said after a few moments silence. "He thinks if there weren't any bios, all his kind would have bed space and not have to scrape lichen to survive."

"You mean, they could take the jobs that the sets have? The ones who are not at Drake's Bay, the custodial and service positions?"

Jess nodded. "Problem is, they're clueless assholes. Most of them," she said. "They'd never get picked for a slot no matter what. Homesteads don't need that kind of jackassery, they got enough already." She half shrugged. "And even scrubbers have some skills. These dorks weren't good enough to even be scrubs."

Dev frowned a little bit. "But they made this bag?" She glanced aside at it. "It's useful."

"Broken chron is right twice a day."

Dev eyed her.

"Okay, maybe once, if it's twenty-four-hour time," Jess said. "Anyway, he doesn't matter. What's the scoop with the rest of our gang?"

"I have recalled everyone to the carriers. They are heading there now," Dev said promptly. "But… wasn't it interesting that some of the fabric for this item came from uniforms?" She asked and glanced at the bag again.

"Yeah, interesting." Jess glanced around as she slid around and got between Dev and the wind as they turned the corner. "And I gave him a pat on the head for that piece of info. Maybe he'll remember more next time."

Dev pulled the collar of her jacket up to protect her neck from the driving rain and blinked as it dripped down through her hair. "About the fabric?" She hazarded a guess.

"About anything." Jess cocked her ears and heard carrier engines spooling up. "Too bad it started dumping. Ruined the market." She changed the subject, as they came around the back side of the gathering hall to see their landing field abuzz with activity.

"The sets were very excited about the market, but glad to be leaving." Dev went along with it. "And I know the fighters were as well. They wanted to get back and find new housing."

Jess chuckled. "Cribs. Yeah, I heard em." She guided Dev toward their carrier, where a group of the scrubs were gathered around the vehicle, huddled under its blunt wings as the weather worsened.

"Open," Dev spoke into her comms, muttering a vocal code after it that resulted in the carrier hatch unlock, and swing up, the boarding ramp extending down to the rough surface as the rain started to come down harder, it's wet sting suddenly becoming a pelting sensation as it got perceptibly colder. "Oh!"

"Nice," Jess said as they reached the ramp and strode up it, the scrubs already inside scrambling around to clear the way for them. "Hailstorm," she said as she dropped into her seat, and turned to hit the hatch close, but paused as it swung shut ahead of her touch. "Thanks, Devvie."

"Flight, please prepare to lift. Moderate the external conditions, use heat setting level three," Dev said into her comms, then transferred it to the side of her flight helmet while she slid it on over her wet hair in one fluid, graceful move.

She slipped into her pilot's seat and sent it forward into flight position, then shook the rain off her hands before she started to prep the craft to take off.

Jess wondered if there was a towel in the stores and only just stopped herself from popping back up to look for one. She watched Dev lean over and activate the carrier's systems while overhead, the hail rattled down on the roof of the carrier with sharp, staccato pings.

After a moment, Jess did push herself up and out of her seat and went to the lockers and rooted around inside.

"Standby for a met update," Dev said, burring and calm in Jess's ear. "Low pressure system coming overhead in ten minutes. We will lift and head immediately to the southeast, to divert around."

With a frown, Jess closed the locker and went to a second. "Don't go upside down without warning me," she said. "I ain't strapped down."

Dev glanced in the reflective surface. "Neither is anyone else. It would be a bit of a mess."

The scrubs all laughed, not fazed at all by the idea of being thrown ass over teakettle. "Oh yeah!" Dustin wriggled side to side. "Rockin!"

The carrier powered up around them, the engines spooling audibly and the craft going through its rumbles and thumps of startup, the faintest of whines as power transferred back and Jess's boards came live, monitors lighting up with sensor output.

Finally. Jess found several soft cloths in one tool locker and went forward to the pilot's station, hanging over the back of the seat. Dev paused in her startup and looked up inquiringly.

"Here." Jess offered the clothes. "Thought you'd like to dry off."

Dev gave her a charming smile. "Jess, you're so kind. Thank you." She took one of the clothes. "Maybe you would also like to dry your face with that other one?" She suggested, then saw the depreciating shrug shift through Jess's tall body.

She unlatched her restraints, stood, and reached up with the cloth to dry off Jess's rain spattered skin, the water dripping down off the ends of her hair as she moved it. "There."

Jess realized the scrubs were all watching them with bright eyed interest, and a blush rose to her cheeks and made her nostrils flare a little. After a brief hesitation, she took the remaining cloth in her hand and returned the gesture, drying the part of Dev's face she could reach around the edges of her flight helmet. "There," she echoed Dev's comment. "Now we can go."

Dev winked at her and then sat back down in her seat and buckled herself in, returning to her tasks. Jess, then, retreated to her gunner's station. She looked around at the scrubs. "What the hell you all looking at?" She barked.

"No sweat, cuz." Dustin sprawled his legs out along the

floor. "You co-hab, yo?"

"Yo." Jess leaned back in her seat, the inside of the carrier full of the smell of wet cloth and the faint sting of the woven bags and the mineral smell of the mud they'd brought in on their boots. With an automatic gesture she pulled her restraints on and buckled them, then sat there in reflective silence, folding, and unfolding the bit of cloth she'd dried Dev's face with.

Dev led the flight up and away from the plateau in a tight arc, the caravans below them closing and the lights fading as the clouds came down and dark encroached to douse the plateau, leaving solitary beacons scattered across the space.

Dev settled back into her seat and flexed her hands. She was wet through, but the carrier was at an acceptable temperature inside and they were not that far from the Bay. She now looked ahead to their arrival, and the celebration that would surely follow the success of the day. It made her smile.

It had been such an excellent result. She saw Dustin's profile in her peripheral vision, and the grin that seemed permanently etched on his face. He bounced up and down on his seat, wiggling his knees and his visible happiness made her feel happy.

Comms crackled in her ear, the soft bong and echo of channels opening on Bay frequencies.

"Scan shows a large cell of weather to the north of us," Kevin's voice, calm and confident came to her. "Dev, we received intel from the new beacons at Cooper's Rock homestead. They are transmitting excellently."

Dev glanced at her screens. "Yes," she said. "It is good to know this information now ahead of time. And Bay Ops also knows."

"Bay operations does acknowledge," a voice answered. "Bay flight, we have you on deep scan and see your echo from those beacons."

"Thank you, Kirk. Weather is suboptimal," Dev said. "We are trying to beat it back to your location before it's arrival."

"Ack," Kirk responded. "The landing stations have been notified of your approach and are preparing for you."

"Eta, fifteen minutes," Dev said.

"Yes," Kirk agreed. "And the mess is being held for your arrival as well, as they have prepared some special things to celebrate the day's events."

"Ah. Interesting," Dev said, as she made a slight course adjustment. "I think that sounds excellent."

"Is it true, Dev?" Kirk asked, after a brief pause. "That we are credentialed?"

Dev smiled, glancing across her screens. "It is true," she said. "Doctor Dan talked to the persons who were assembled and told them it was the correct thing to do, and they agreed that it was."

There was a momentary silent pause. Then Kirk exhaled. "So excellent."

"It was," Kevin agreed, softly.

"Absolutely it was." Dev set up their approach, running scans on the weather. "And I think it made Doctor Dan as happy as we were."

"Very excellent." Kirk said, with a smile in the tone. "We have you on initial approach, Bay flight," he added, in a more formal tone. "The landing bays are open; they advise there is freezing rain impacting the surfaces."

"Understood," Dev said. "Bay flight, this is Rockstar, please deploy ice handling surfaces to the landing skids after extension." She slid forward into the lead position. "The frozen precipitation will need care in landing on the pads."

"Yes," Keko responded. "Understood."

"Understood," Kevin echoed, and then the rest of them did as well.

"We'll hold off until you're in, Rocket," Doug added. "It'd suck if all of us collided in there." He was tucked in on Dev's right side, Chester was on the left. "Man, that's a lotta hail."

Dev saw the promontory of the Bay come into view on scan and the outline of it was blurred with the frozen rain as they crossed over the back dome and came around the craggy front of the stake hold, the Bay itself a choppy froth from the weather.

The landing bays were, as promised, wide open, their interior lights shining out invitingly to the carriers, the outside halons of the Bay also turned on with an unusual blare of illumination that caught them as they approached to land.

Below, the sea bell rang, and Dev injected the sound into the cabin of the carrier, it's rough, raucous sound loud and full, and seemingly full of its own kind of happiness.

"Yeah!" Kirin laughed. "There she goes! Ding da ding da donga!"

The rest of the scrubs caught up the rhythm, singing along with the bell and rocking back and forth to its pattern as they chanted, their voices rough but surprisingly melodious.

Jess jiggled her knee to the rhythm and smiled.

They were all turned forward, to see out the windshield as Dev brought the carrier smoothly down and into the top landing bay cavern, passing from the thunder of hail into the echoes of engines inside the rock walls as she aimed for, and settled onto the back pad with cautious precision.

There was a rough, grating feel to the landing, from the spiked extensions on the landing skids, but they touched down without incident, the sensors still pulling in outside sound as the carrier was surrounded by mechs and the chanting faded.

The sea bell still rang, and that sound amplified as Jess undogged the hatch and opened it to let in the chill air of the cavern and the rumble of Doug's engines as he followed them cautiously inside.

The scrubs gathered their sacks up and bumped each other as they got to the hatch and went down to the pad just as Doug touched down and Chester started his approach, the sounds of off gassing and boots on steel almost painfully loud.

Dev cut the external monitors to reduce the clamor and shut down the systems, opening the external ports for the umbilicals before she pushed her seat back and unlocked her restraints.

Jess came up next to her and sat on the recently vacated jump seat. She leaned one elbow on the arm of Dev's chair and just sat there and smiled at the clamor of voices, and the ring of happiness in them.

"You seem pleased," Dev said, after a moment watching her face.

Jess took a breath and exhaled. "I never figured we'd see all this so fast," she said. "It seems so crazy." She plucked Dev's damp sleeve. "C'mon."

"I think there is going to be a celebration," Dev said. "It was on comms."

Jess chuckled. "Oh yeah. They'll hand out the new chits and the creds at mess. I heard the doc tell Brandon to get it going." She let her head rest against the back of the jump seat. "Maybe we'll get brownies." She wiggled her eyebrows at Dev.

"Jess, I think they would make you brownies whenever you want them," Dev said placidly. "You are in charge of this location."

"Yeah I know." Jess's bright eyes twinkled a little bit. "But it's better when it's a surprise." She got up and offered Dev a hand up from her seat. "Let's take our swag up and get on our party duds."

Dev got up and joined her and they walked down the ramp into the landing bay. She was glad to see the outer doors were shut, so the air was just cold and not uncomfortable as it hit her damp clothing, and they joined the outflow of pilots and scrubs on their way through the halls.

****

The mess was in party mode. Dev took her seat at the head table and looked around, slightly surprised to see colorful hangings on the wall all around the huge room. They brought a pop of brightness to the granite surface.

The tables were covered with cloths. She wasn't sure what that was all about, since certainly they would get covered with drippings and crumbs, but like the hanging, it made everything seem more festive. She noted that there was a group of the rave musicians setting up on a steel platform on the far end of the hall as it started to fill up.

There was also a sort of excitement in the air, a buzz of laughter and sense of anticipation and as Dev sat there and observed, she smiled in pure reaction to it. It was a very different mood, she thought, and she turned to watch for a reaction as Jess came in from the back entrance to the mess.

Jess stopped walking and looked around the room, her dark eyebrows lifting a little in intrigued interest.

Dev waited until Jess's gaze landed on her, and she pointed at the decorations with a smile.

Jess gave her a thumb up, and grinned. Then she continued through the hall, though at a slower pace than usual as she kept looking around her. As she moved through the crowd, curled fists were extended to her, for her to bump with her own and amiably she did so as she passed through the tables.

Kurok made his way across the floor to the head table and Brandon was right behind him. He held a large plastic bin hoisted to one shoulder.

Dev extended her feet in their new boots under the table and leaned back against the wall, as she watched the tables fill, the cloth on the surface gaining a lot of attention and the buzz of conversation growing louder.

She was freshly showered and dressed in her lined jump-suit, with her work vest fastened over it, providing enough warmth for comfort. She looked forward to whatever the night meal offered, having bypassed the somewhat random offering of snacks at the market.

She reached up and ruffled her hair out from under the col- lar of the jumpsuit and ran her fingers through the thick strands at the front of her forehead to move them back out of her eyes. A trim, she felt, was probably a good idea and she made a mental note to talk to Abe and find someone who had the skillset.

Jess arrived at her side and dropped down into her seat. She had on a simple, dark red shirt on and dark work pants. Her hair was caught up in a tail at the back of her neck.

She looked around at the room in satisfaction before regarding Dev. "Place cleans up nice," she said. "Where the hell did they get those old sheets?" She looked around again with idle interest. "That's been in the back of some crate somewhere."

Dev of course had no answer to that, so she just nodded appreciatively. "It does look excellent in here," she said. She folded her hands over her stomach and absorbed the festive feeling in the room. "Everyone seems pleased."

"Should be," Jess said. "That was a big ass contract."

"The sets were very happy to hear about their citizen status," Dev said. "They had not expected that in any way."

"They can go and live somewhere else if they want now," Jess said. "They should be chuffed."

Dev gave her a sideways glance. "Why would they want to?" She asked in a puzzled tone.

Jess shrugged. "Quebec City's nice. You've been there."

"Yes. But I never had the slightest desire to change my domicile," Dev said. "Have you?"

Jess straightened a little, eyebrows lifting in consideration. "Me?"

Dev nodded.

"Never had a choice, Devvie."

"Well, neither have I. But I enjoy our space here and would not replace it unless you wished to."

Jess grinned. "Aww. Even if it's an icebox full of crazy?"

"Yes," Dev said at once.

Jess settled back with a pleased expression and exhaled in satisfaction as she looked around.

Kurok arrived at the table and patted its surface, where Brendan set down the big plas case. "Chits and creds," he said, briefly. "My goodness what a day. The creds just finished printing."

"Crazy," Brendan agreed. "But good. They started up the extruder once the comms hit." He sat down next to where Kurok still stood and looked around with bright interest. "Gonna be all night with them finding cribs."

"Do we have enough?" Kurok asked. "I know they were fitting out some net new across the way."

Brendan nodded. "More than. Between the upper lev on this

side, and the new ones, we got about three hundred done. So, all good, though the ones across still got some stuff pending. Cabinets and stuff."

Kurok nodded. "I'm going to guess the inside ones here will fill up first."

"Might," Brendan said. "Heard some of them hot for the other side though. Some of your kids want to move out there too."

Kurok looked at him in surprise. "Really?"

Brendan nodded. "Gangin up." He supplied succinctly with a one shouldered shrug and a sideways look at Kurok. "Y'know."

"Interesting." Kurok stood there, with his head cocked slightly to one side, and his hands on his hips. "All right, let's get the distribution done, so they can get service started." He looked around the room and got ready to let out a shout.

Jess forestalled him with a wave, as she stood up and then hopped up onto her seat, so she was visible to everyone in the room. The sudden motion caught attention and in a distinct wave of noise abatement the chattering fell off as the room focused on her.

She waited for a beat of silence, then let out a shout. "Hai!"

The response was immediate and loud, a blended roar of sound from everyone, scrubs and sets and residents cheerfully returned her yell.

When that echo faded, Jess put her hands in her pockets. "Doc's got something to say," she remarked in a mild tone. "All I got is a hella yah, cause today was a day."

"HAI!" The yell sounded again, with a deep, joyous enthusiasm, even echoing into the doors to the kitchen cavern, propped open, its staff standing crowded in the gap to listen.

Jess grinned and turned to Kurok. "All yours," she said.

"Oh no." Kurok smiled back at her. "They're all yours. As they should be." He reached out and slapped her on the back of her leg, then turned to the room. "Well, we have quite a lot of distribution to do, as we have four hundred recipients today, two hundred who will become registered allocated residents, and two hundred who will be granted citizen status. So, let's get on with it, shall we?"

Kurok half turned. "Dev, would you like to give me a hand with this?"

"Of course," Dev said, as she looked around the room. She recognized the ceremonial nature of the request, and stood up and moved around to the other side of the table to join Brendan next to the big box.

She was the first. But, as they said, and she agreed with them, not the last. She looked at the now open plas bin, which had two distinct other plas bins inside, one with the metallic chits that were the physical representation of a financial account at the Bay, and the other with the biologic credentials that indicated citizenship.

She lifted out the box full of the latter and set it on the table. Then she moved a few paces down to clear some space, riffling through the creds to see how they were sorted. Alphabetically by set name. She picked up the first and inspected it.

Then she looked across the room. "Abe, please come forward."

The AyeBee took a breath and moved toward her. He slid between the standing crowd, as rough hands reached out and patted him on the back, and the shoulder. One big hand ruffled his hair in teasing affection.

He had on the working coverall they all wore, with a high neck sweater. He presented himself in front of Dev and she extended the new credential to him and smiled without speaking as there was no need.

He knew. Their eyes met, and he knew, just as Dev did, what the moment was.

"All right." Kurok said, standing a little way away from her, at the front edge of the table. "Alan Brass, please come up and pickup your chit." He waited as the first of the scrubs scrambled up from his place at a far table and came rambling up to him, a tall boy, with curly brown hair and vivid hazel eyes. "Now everyone please remember, let's wait to get all of these handed out before you all start picking your locations."

A low, half snicker, half laugh rose from the avidly watching crowd.

"Thanks, doc." Alan took the chit and scampered back to the table.

"Alvin," Dev called out. "Please attend."

Jess leaned back against the wall and kept her hands in her pockets and watched the process as scrubs and bio alts came up to accept their new tokens.

"Those kids'll be too manic to eat," April said.

"More for me," Jess said equably. She chuckled, then glanced aside as an older resident approached from the other side of the table. "Yo," she greeted him as he arrived and edge into an open space facing her.

"Drake," the man said. "Got two of my kids getting put on

the reg list today." He stood there, his hands also in his pockets. "I got a stupid question."

"Sure," Jess said, then waited.

"This gonna be tested for, like the rest?" He asked. "We get a slot next time, no bs?"

Ears pricked all around and the noise abated with such suddenness, it was startling. Jess paused to look around her to find eyes fastened on her with interest, bodies turned half round at tables. Even Kurok and Dev paused in their distribution activities to wait.

Jess was caught somewhat off guard. She stood in all that silence, thinking about the question, refusing to feel the pressure of all the attention as she considered the implications. Then, at last, she took a considered breath and released it. "Huh," she said. "Not sure it'll measure at five or six."

"Not sure it won't," the man said. "Need to figure out how to catch it." He stared hard at Jess. "You'd know, yeah?" He said. "And we're gonna keep them like you now, yeah?"

Jess glanced over at Kurok, who just stood there and watched her, that faintest of smiles on his face, a look of gentle anticipation in his eyes, just as though he knew without a doubt what her answer was going to be.

Discussed in passing before, now it came down to it. Now there was a place for these scrubs. There was place for people like Jess and a value, to replace the payment the stakehold had gotten for turning over their problem children to Interforce.

"Oh yeah," Jess finally answered, into all that patiently waiting silence. "We're not gonna send anyone else outta here," she said. "Anyone who turns out to be scrapper, we got ya. Specially people like me, Duncan."

Duncan lifted his hand up to her, curled into a fist, and she reached over and bumped it with her own, as the room let out shouts and whistles.

Dev folded her hands in front of her and watched with pleasure at the reaction, seeing the looks of happiness and relief across the room, especially on the faces of the elders.

Dev picked up the next credential as the cheers wound down again.

It was, she thought, one of the best days ever.

****

Tonight, there would be no mixup. Jess stood outside the mess door and watched the scramble as scrubs scattered across the floor, heading for the back hallways, and for the upper levels, and on the fourth and fifth level where the bio alts lived, there were groups gathered in excited conversation.

She put her hands on her hips and watched all the swirling activity, including the groups of residents standing together in the big hall, still full of the energy of the night.

"Quite a day." Kurok came out of the hall and stood next to her.

"Yeah." Jess nodded.

"We ended up in a better place than I'd thought we would," Kurok said, frankly. "I thought they'd sign the contract. I wasn't sure about the rest. I thought they'd have tighter terms."

Jess folded her arms over her chest. "Get the feeling they know something we don't?" She suggested, giving him a sideways look.

Kurok gave a little sideways nod. "There was something there," he said wryly. "I was expecting at least a pushback on the cred amount. Were Interforce hammering them that much as all that? I checked all the records again here, by the way. Seems like the Bay never was a target."

"Tracks," Jess said. "Though if anyone woulda caved to them it'd have been my brother."

"Would he?" Kurok asked. "What he did try was quite audacious, you know. Making the deal with station and negotiating with the other side."

Jess was briefly silent. "Nah," she said. "He fell into that. He knew what was going to happen to him if that got out."

"I wonder," Kurok mused. "I think there were some here who supported him, Jess." He paused. "I'm guessing they didn't survive the attack. You have no visible opposition here."

Jess smiled darkly. "Bet they didn't," she said. "Yeah, I know there were plenty of people who thought Justin was an ass, but that this was an ace op for a cred grab. Someone unlocked the shuttle egress." She looked around at him. "They knew they were in trouble when I offed Jimmy."

"Yes, I think that's true," Kurok said. "They made a bad bet. Interestingly, I did a quick analysis on the before and after of the bio signature here. I doubt you'd be surprised at what I discovered."

Jess's eyes twinkled. "Crazier now than before?" She said. "We got sturdy spirals, we're maniacs."

Kurok smiled briefly. "I said you wouldn't be surprised," he said. "Now it seems they—if there are any they left—must adjust their perceptions and start considering that to be a good thing. Not something to be bred out of the place."

"Can't be."

"No, I know," he said. "But they didn't know that."

"Dad knew," Jess said, suddenly. "I think someone here skunked him." She half turned to regard Kurok. "Someone wanted an easier chump here to work with."

"Are they still here, I wonder," Kurok mused. "Twenty-two enemy agents died in that little fracas that took your father out, you know. Took a plasma bomb to finally end it." He looked over at Jess. "Your father was in every way a Drake. He dove in front of it to keep it from rebounding into a street in Quebec."

"Stupid brave." Jess smiled ruefully. "Yeah. Bred into us."

Kurok patted her on the arm. "Anyway, let's just enjoy ourselves tonight, shall we? I thought the kitchen did a good job, didn't you?" He indicated the entrance to the mess. "We should congratulate the staff."

"Lead on," Jess said. "Maybe they have some extra brownies."

"I think they sent those all up to your residence already. There are no fools in that kitchen."

****

Jess left the kitchen, a packet tucked under her arm and started across the hall toward the stairs up to her crib. The hall had quieted down, and the most significant sounds were coming from the upper levels of available housing, where she heard banging and thumping as the scrubs got settled.

Jess spotted Dustin come out of the house ops admin area, a large fully stuffed pack on his back. He held a small bit of plas in his hand and looked very confused. She suppressed a smile and altered direction to intercept him. "Yo."

He looked up in surprise. "Yo, cuz." He stopped walking and waited for her to arrive. "Sup?"

"That's what I'm gonna ask you. Sup?" Jess inquired. "You finally find a crib?"

Dustin sighed and frowned. "Had to go in the back," he said reluctantly. "Found me a spot in the corner near the mixup."

'Yeah." Jess nodded. "Figured everyone would swarm for seven. Saw you got held up in the mess."

He nodded. "Up for clean," he said. "They said I hadda."

"You don't like it in the back?" Jess said. "Those are new."

"Too far from all the stuff I do." Dustin tipped his head and lookcd around up at the top levels of the cavern, where the entry to the landing bays and all the mech shops were. "And other stuff."

"Yeah. So that your chit?"

Dustin looked at his hand. "Yeah, I got it from ops but it ain't right." He showed it to her. "That ain't the code for those new ones. I dunno where that is." He shrugged. "I can go bunk in my old spot for now, I guess."

Jess took the chit from him and glanced at it. "C'mon." She slapped him on the shoulder and gave him a shove. "That way." She went with him across the hall to where the closed doors to the family compound were and pointed at the entry pad. "Put your paw there."

Dustin stared at her, then at the pad. "Cuz I can't go in there. S'not reg."

Jess pointed again. "Who do you think makes the regs here now?"

Hesitatingly he reached out and touched the pad, jerking a little as the scan pulsed over his skin. But the pad turned a benign teal color, and the door opened. He drew his hand back in surprise. "Yo."

"That's where this chit is." Jess handed it to him. "First door on the left there." She gave him another shove. "That'll have to be close enough for ya."

Dustin walked slowly over to the door and stood there. Then he turned to Jess. "Yeah?" He put his hand on the access pad for the housing, and it slid open. "What'm I doin in here, cuz?"

With commendable patience, Jess walked over to him. She planted her hands on her hips and cocked her head at him. "What's your name?"

His brows creased. "Dustin," he said, after a pause. "You forget, cuz?"

"Your last name."

He finally got it. "Oh!" His eyes widened. "Yeah! Drake."

Jess nodded. "You have a slot and an allotment, and along with Max and Tayler you're my closest family. When you were coded it assigned you here. Okay with you?" She gave him a shove inside. "G'wan. I'll get Dev to send the kids over to kit you out."

Dustin looked around. It was a small housing, one of the smaller in the compound, with a living space, a bedroom, sanitary space, and a little nook for a drink dispenser. There were no windows. But he had come from the outer barracks, where it was scrubs and hammocks. "Yo!" He breathed the word. "S'awesome."

Jess winked at him. "Hope the co hab works out for ya." She backed off and let the door close, then, shook her head. "Scrub." She made her way out of the outer door and turned left, heading up the staircase to her own crib.

****

Dev sat quietly in their small nook, a steaming cup of hot tea on the table in front of her as she gazed out over the storm still raging outside. Below her she saw the long line of the docks, the ships tied up and darkened, the crews overnighting inside the Bay for what was probably the first time.

Even Uncle Max was in his assigned housing, sharing a nightcap with Kurok.

So much change in so little time. Dev lifted her cup and took a sip of tea. So much good change. Her entire life had altered in the last months, and yet... Dev stared out into the storm. And yet, she somehow had a sense that everything had happened the way it had because it was the way it was supposed to happen.

There was nothing that felt wrong to her.

The outer door opened, and Jess came rambling inside, detouring immediately to the small nook. "Hey, Devvie, do me a favor woudlja?"

"Of course." Dev looked up at her and waited.

Jess sat on the stool across from her. "They threw Dusty into one of the apartments downstairs. He's got no idea what to do with it."

"Oh!' Dev chuckled. "Yes, no problem." She triggered her comms set. "Dev to House ops."

"Abe here." Abe answered instantly, as though he'd been waiting for the hail. "Good evening, Dev. Do you need something in your housing?"

Dev explained and then shut comms down. "I am sure they will take good care." She reached over and took Jess's hand. "That was excellent you put him there."

Jess shook her head. "I didn't. System did."

Dev eyed her. "Is that what you told Dustin?"

"Uh huh." Jess eyed her. "Why do I get the feeling you don't buy that?"

Dev turned her scanner around and displayed the screen.

Jess scowled. "Don't you tell him." she said. "Let him think it was just reg."

"I won't, don't worry," Dev reassured her. "I think it was

an excellent idea and it will make him very happy. He was very concerned that if he did not get an attractive housing, he would not be able to ask someone to habitate with him." She squeezed Jess's fingers. "You really are so kind, Jess."

Jess made a face at her. "I'm not supposed to be kind, Dev. I'm supposed to be a homicidal maniac."

Dev smiled at her with deep affection. "I was just sitting here thinking about how amazing today was. I'm so glad I met you, Jess. I can't think of a better place to be than here, and a more wonderful person to be with than you." She squeezed Jess's fingers again, then lifted her hand and kissed it.

Jess sat there for a minute just looking at Dev. "Back atcha," she finally said, in a serious tone. "Here's to a new life, Devvie. Let's make the most of it." She lifted her mug of tea up and took a sip. "Who the hell knows where we'll go from here."

"I'm sure it will be excellent."

"I'm sure it's gonna be chaos." Jess leaned over and kissed her. "But at least I'll have company."

About the Author

Melissa Good is a full-time network engineer and part time writer who lives in Pembroke Pines, Florida with a handful of lizards and a dog. When not traveling for work or participating in the usual chores she ejects several sets of clamoring voices onto a variety of keyboards and tries to entertain others with them to the best of her ability.

You can contact Melissa by email at: merwolf01@gmail.com

Visit her website: http://www.merwolf.com

Bringing Stories Along the Queer Spectrum to Life

Flashpoint Publications welcomes submissions from writers of every color and books featuring characters of every color. In addition, Flashpoint Publications encourages job applicants of every color whenever a staff position becomes available. We believe that EVERYONE is entitled to a seat at our table.

Visit us at our website: www.flashpointpublications.com